J. R. BRAYSHAW

YOUTOPIA

What If
YOU Were King of the World?

YOUTopia:
What If YOU Were King of The World?

Copyright © 2025 J.R. Brayshaw

ISBN (Paperback): 979-8-89672-043-0
ISBN (Hardback): 979-8-89672-052-2
ISBN (Ebook): 979-8-89672-044-7

All rights reserved. No part of this book may be used or reproduced by any means, graphic, electronic, or mechanical, including photocopying, recording, taping or by information storage and retrieval system without the written permission of the author except in the case of brief quotations embodied in critical articles and reviews.

Because of the dynamic nature of the Internet, any web addresses or links contained in this book may have changed since publication and may no longer be valid. The views expressed in the work are solely those of the author and do not necessarily reflect the views of the publisher, and the publisher hereby disclaims any responsibility for them.

Printed in the United States of America.

5830 E 2nd St, Ste 7000 #9983
Casper, WY 82609
USA

Books may be ordered through booksellers or by contacting:
jrbrayshaw@shaw.ca
www.kingoftheworld.world

If errors are noticed in this work please kindly email your findings to jrbrayshaw@shaw.ca

CONTENTS

Section 2

A JOURNEY TO BECOME THE KING

Section 3

PRESENTING OUR KING TO THE WORLD

SECTION 4

THE KING BRINGS LIBERTY TO THE CAPTIVES

SECTION 5

THE JUSTICE OF THE KING WITH THE
BLESSING OF THE POPE

SECTION 6
THE LAWS OF A WISE AND REASONED KING

Section 7

CORRUPTION CONFRONTED BY A KING AND HIS COUNSEL

SECTION 8
LONG LIVE THE PEOPLE'S "KING"...OR QUEEN

**Step into YOUTOPIA and see a world we have been
so close to for so long...all it needs is YOU...**

The overpopulated Globe has evolved as far as it can, and the World Government agrees something, or someone needs to move humanity forward. Forward to finding peace on the level everyone has always wanted.

In the face of democracy's failure to truly make a better world...the World Congress must find the person who can elevate humanity. One person who will bear the burden of doing the right thing. The World Congress must appoint a King.

Since the United Nations dissolved the World Congress has governed the world for decades. The unprecedented success at uniting the globe, solving international conflicts, establishing one-world tongue and a single global currency are merely political accomplishments...but they have failed to change the human condition. The leaders of the world are challenged to answer the questions society has been asking for generations.

*"Has the world really changed...If our world is so much better
why is there still so much wrong with humanity?"*

Under the World Congress rule, seeing all that has changed has magnified all that hasn't. Crime, deviance, corruption, sexual abuse, fear for one's security and safety, identify theft, home invasions, pedophilia, child abuse, senior abuse, terrorist activity, gang crime, and every social distortion that has gone on for all of history continues to go on today. But the most insidious cancer that underlies it all is human apathy. People just don't care enough to fight for change...

...Who will be passionate enough to do the greatest good for the greatest number? Who will we find to be King of the World? One person with the power to change anything. Is there one man or one woman who can answer the questions? And what will that person do to make the world better?

What would YOU do if YOU were King of The World?

The time is now to step into YOUTOPIA to enjoy the world we have all dreamed of for so long....

Angellah,
Without you my utopia would not be possible.

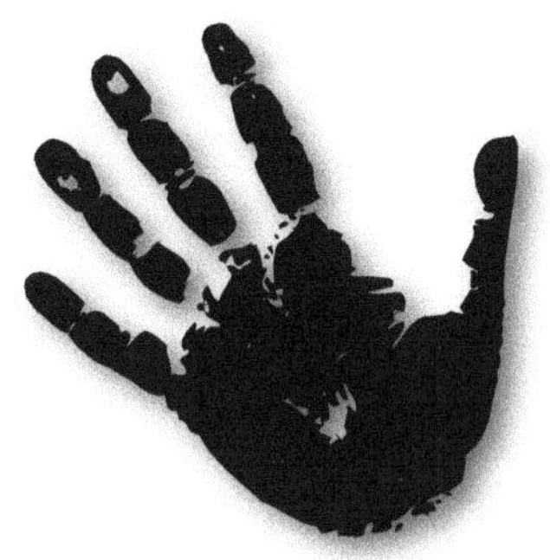

A KING IN THE MAKING

This World Needs an Enema

"What is that smell?"

As if he hadn't smelled it before…every day in fact.

"We can eradicate life threatening allergies and stream live video into every hand across the world but for godsakes can't someone do something about that smell?"

Sol was doing everything he could to hide his sour look at the biting body aromas that wafted about the train cabin. Surely he wasn't the only one who hated that persistent stench. It got him every time. Somehow, the acrid air in the public passenger car found a way to make him feel like he needed to take a shower. Even the climate controlled comfort was not enough to squelch the ubiquitous scent of two-day-old clothes on three-day-old sweat. There were far too many public places that filled with people who gave little thought to their scent and how it might be offensive to those around them. A musky, sourness that could only be incubated on moist flesh. The trains looked clean enough but the smell could not be kept from seeping its way into his nostrils.

The **M**agnetic **M**ass **R**ail **T**ransit, called the *MeRT*, was famous for it. Masses of people travelling home at the end of the day, tight spaces, recirculated air…Sol never got used to it. Did anyone???

You'd think everyone showered regularly these days. Obviously, that wasn't the case.

Looking at his commuter companions for the trip, he was sure he didn't know any of them. Yet he had seen most of them before. Maybe that funky smell kept people from getting close enough to get to know their cabin mate. The last five years in particular have been acrid ones. Just months after the World Health Organization eradicated perfume allergies with their Deca-vaccine, almost everyone started to spritz their favourite body sprays and perfumes on again. Perfume and cologne use hit new heights and showering and hygiene hit new lows. Oh to go back to the days of the scent-free zones.

Sol's aromatic co-riders mostly looked like they could care less who smelled like what. They were essentially the walking dead…only with whiter teeth. Mindlessly moving from home to train to work and back again. Aromatic minions in their daily state of catatonia. And some days Sol himself felt like he was only a hair's-breadth away from being a zombie-like passenger…shuffling aboard the mass transportation as he did every day.

Distracting himself from the onslaught of unfriendly air as he settled into the commuter train for the 50-minute commute home, Sol looked out the window to watch others prepare to board. Everything was in order and the secure system welcomed each passenger by name. It was an efficient and seamless automated process. And very personalized.

Every rider started their daily voyage home with the security system approving each passenger for boarding as it scanned the G-PAS card in their pocket or purse. The **G**lobal **P**ersonal **A**ccounting **S**ystem contained everything there was to know about a person in one small super-card that no one was ever without. And just like everyone else using the MeRT, Sol was habituated into the process of boarding it every day. This was the norm. Commuters were swept with a sensor beam to detect weapons or explosives, then given the green light and a barely audible beep to proceed. Sol thought there should be a way to sniff out the smelly riders and have them wait for the next train.

Looking at the riders who breezed through the flashing security turnstile he wondered, *"Does that thing actually catch all the crazies with weapons?"*

He'd heard of riders getting past the *Full Spectrum Security Screener,* but he always wondered how they did it...or if those stories were even true.

To his left was a young couple engaging in what looked to be an uncomfortable dispute. It was rare that a rider wouldn't catch someone having a tense moment with another as they waited for the departure. The herding of the masses on the MeRT seemed to bring out the worst in people. *"What were they fighting about?"* he thought.

The young brunette was shaking her head and a distinct scowl came across her face. Her eyes said a lot.

Without staring at the situation like some kind of a middle-aged creep, Sol caught enough to see the guy was harshly upbraiding the young lady. She appeared to be his girlfriend or maybe his wife. He was getting more intense as the seconds passed. If they weren't in public Sol was certain this guy would be taking things further. He looked intense...barely realizing they were in public right now. For the angry young man, being in public was barely enough impetus to restrain himself during this harsh disagreement. His forced whispers were tough to tune into with all the other riders shuffling about the car. But Sol could see she was afraid of him. Her gestures said she was in apology mode. Most of the riders around them acted oblivious to the exchange as they sat staring at their devices with headphones in. Getting caught watching...or nosing in to offer aid...was just too awkward.

Sol's intrigue with the public quarrel of the young couple faded as quickly as it rose. The station gong sounded to alert riders to 45 seconds until departure. And the young couple in conflict responded with stern silence. She was obviously hurt and he was ignoring her now while she stared blankly out the window.

Just before departure a scuffle outside the door caught Sol's attention. MeRT security, three mid-sized guys with MMRT ENFORCEMENT billboarded across the backs of their uniforms, were pressing a mid-thirties guy's face against the pillar on the boarding platform. 45 seconds elapsed, the door slid closed and the MeRT emitted the telltale *hummm* from the magnetic rails as it began to propel along the grid away from the docking station.

As the *hummm* of the magnetic rails plateaued to its hypnotic tone, Sol watched the freaky looking Enforcement officer, the guy with the huge forehead and the thin wiry beard. Grasping the back of the individual's head while he was in police custody, the officer forcibly removed an object from the coat of the man whose face he was pressing against a pillar.

"*Holy frick!*" Sol thought, it was massive.

"*Whaatt, that's a massive gun...*" Sol exclaimed to himself, "*I guess the security beams don't catch every lunatic. That guy almost got on here with that.*"

The threat of the gun faded as the train climbed to full speed. Sol was just eager to get home. But thoughts kept surfacing just the same. Who knew what the hell that guy was planning? Just musing about possibilities made a usually placid ride ahead seem a little more reckless. Sure there were things that seemed reckless about this mass transport method millions of citizens used every day. Sol kept up on the worldwide trends of hostage takings and attempted bombings of MeRTs around the world. But that is just the way things are. Stuff happened every day on these trains...bad stuff.

It was just three weeks ago when a MeRT was forced to stop after a gun-wielding piece of garbage pistol-whipped an old couple in a near-empty car. He beat them and took their G-PAS, jewelry, and two gold teeth. The teeth fell out of the old guy's mouth after being hit in the face with a gun. Unbelievably, the old couple survived the attack and even more unbelievable, the attacker fled unimpeded. Not ONE passenger who witnessed the attack tried to stop the guy.

No one ever got involved...beyond catching the scene on video. Everyone had a mobile device in their hand they always went to first. No one seemed to have what it took to step in anymore to help out someone who needed it.

And why stupid criminals keep targeting the G-PAS in these petty crimes is anyone's guess. It's a wonder how these low-lifes aren't smart enough to know how secure and how traceable the G-PAS is. Those little cards are practically a personal Fort Knox…an un-crackable encrypted vault. The best technology in the last twenty years for securing personal information and financial transactions. Not even RFID chips could topple the popular-for-decades smart cards. The smart cards used by every citizen were biometrically linked to the user and needed to be in contact with the owner for any transaction to go through.

The World Congress put out stats on recovered G-PAS cards every year. Last year 98.3 percent of all cards either lost or stolen were recovered with no intrusion into the owner's personal business, identity, or finances. It was by far the most secure any Global Personal Accounting and Security system had ever been. Even though cases of getting your life messed up by a G-PAS theft are rare, the World Congress reminded users all the time how to manage their card.

Everyone knows *The Three Don'ts* of the Digitized Global Personal Accounting and Security card. Sol was reminded as he saw the G-PAS public service announcement flash across one of the digital media monitors just above his head.

Don't share your card
Don't share your password, and
Don't worry…G-PAS is 100 percent secure.

Users knew that wasn't 100 percent accurate. A hundred percent secure sounds like a great promise in a perfect world. But when has anything ever been 100 percent secure? There has always been and there always will be criminals forcing the World Congress to fritter away their time finding ways to stay a step ahead of the less well-intentioned opportunity seekers.

As the MeRT left the docking station behind, Sol wasn't sure what to think about what had just gone down. Events like that never stopped happening…or so it seemed. And why in the hell was this world not getting any safer? We're halfway through the 21st century and with all the progress and "growth" of humanity, this place wasn't any "cleaner". And it definitely wasn't any better than it was when he was a kid.

"*I don't know,*" Sol sighed to himself. Then he chuckled again under his breath as the inimical Joker from the classic movie Batman came to mind, "*...This world needs an enema.*"

In a 'Comity' of Errors People Hardly Ever Look Back

With thoughts of the world's poor state miles behind Sol, he was comfortably settled in his train seat. Heading home with the lumbar heat and gentle Shiatsu feature on was often a mindless act, but Sol's thoughts were interrupted by images of a breaking story on one of the ubiquitous World Congress Media Screens. Anytime anything of importance happened, either locally or globally, the update was instant…literally. Citizens didn't have to wait to read an incoming email thread or turn a digital feed on, the World Congress Media Screens instantly started streaming the story to all WCMS's. The omnipresence of Media was almost numbing. Every digital audio or video device was pre-programmed with the World Congress Update App. Right out of the box every media device available across the world, whether fixed, mobile, or handheld, was engineered during production to boot up at the World Congress's behest.

Shortly after the World Congress succeeded the United Nations, the *Speed of Information Act* was passed. The Act mandated that anything less than instant was not fast enough for dissemination of vital information. Based on the long standing Freedom of Information acts found in laws around the world, the world government responded to the petitions of its citizens. Society demanded government stop unwanted censorship and delays in distributing what could be vital information.

The World Congress along with their news arm, the *Digital Broadcast Network International,* were fairly loose in defining which information was "vital".

Even when a device was off it was on. Sleeping…waiting to spring to life. Ever ready to display any image or message of import. And it was pretty simple. Folks didn't have to be intentional, folks just had to be alive to catch the latest update.

Some of society's watchdogs were distressed at the advent of such imposing info dissemination technology. It was uncomfortably reminiscent of the mass brainwashing techniques by certain nations in historical war times. When the World Congress Media Screens and the Digital Broadcast Network were up and running in 2031, there was a trickle of suspicious citizenry who couldn't help but question a medium of this magnitude. But the World Congress had done a deft job at keeping this powerful tool free of propaganda or behavior and thought-modifying content. Even though the tool could be wielded authoritatively by its moderators, there were yet to be signs of any conspiratorial government plot.

It really was an impressive use of a powerful tool since its launch. Almost the entire world had been gently cajoled into accepting the World Congress system for the amazing ability it had displayed in disseminating pertinent, timely, and valuable information. Everyone knew it…people needed info. It was an addiction few could combat. And the World Congress found the perfect way to fill that need…All streams would be sent through the small handheld devices that had been sitting in the hand of every citizen all along. Cell phones were the unimpeded gateway. The government just needed instant access to this gateway and they found it.

Somewhat relaxed now and almost nodding off, images of a hectic street scene filled the Media Screen in front of Sol's seat. In focus was a reporter on the scene at a Midwestern elementary school. Law Enforcement was milling in the background and citizens were passing in and out of the shot looking shocked and unsettled. The reporter on screen clutched her mic with one hand and glanced at notes in the other, Sol listened as the DBN Reporter offered her wrap-up before the network went back to the anchor.

"Yes that's right Grady, the police have set up a two block perimeter and no one is allowed out until officials can interview everyone in the area. And no one is allowed in unless their G-PAS shows they are the parent or guardian of a Brookmoor Elementary School student."

It was clear, this was a serious situation and she was careful to give the right info.

"Police have one shooter who appears to have minor wounds in custody now. And initial reports say that a second shooter took his own life when the TASC Unit…the *Terrorism and Active Shooter Command Unit*…stormed the building. As for the students and teachers of Brookmoor Elementary, we are not yet certain how many are dead or injured in this latest School shooting."

It was already clear by the World Congress Media Screen scenes, that another brutal slaying had taken place. It was also clear that the world outside that crime zone was still churning along. In front of Sol on one of the omnipresent Media Screens, he was just told at least a dozen school children were killed. But the workers in the factories, warehouses, and businesses outside the racing train had no reaction to the news that several families had their lives hostilely and violently changed forever….with no possible way of turning back. A dozen children just died but life goes on for everyone else. It could be here in Seattle or somewhere across the world…these things happened often now and no matter where a person lived in the world, no town or village was safe. Sol's thoughts raced as the train hurtled along the rails, "*Comity*" Sol thought. The Word of the Day came to mind. He had just seen it on his device a few hours ago at lunch. *That's why we can't stop this madness, there's no comity…*" Sol recalled the definition of his newest Word of the Day…'COMITY-A state or atmosphere of harmony or mutual civility and respect.' And his thoughts were fed by this reality, thinking, *"We all just quietly motor along horror after horror...hoping that it never happens to us."*

In yet another School slaying, spilled juice boxes would be mopped up easier than the blood of the slain students. Still wet on the desks as reporters scrummed.

As raw and disturbing as it was to some, the world was forced to watch. It was one more moment when all would watch the post-shooting chaos unfold. It could have been in Britain, or Holland, or Japan but it was here.... again. And viewers, forced to hear about the graphic nightmare at Brookmoor Elementary, were not given a break from the relentless DBN reports.

Students just back after the summer break, coloring pictures of the things they did during summer holidays one moment were dragged into terror the next. It was an all too common event seeing a school shooting on the Digital Broadcast Network of the World Congress. And the platitudes that came with it always fell from the lips of underpaid reporters and professionals as if their automated words meant anything at all to the viewers who heard them or to the families who had once again become the drama of an unspeakable horror.

Sol was indignant that no matter how many times these things happened, this culture still showed no signs of changing after all it had witnessed. No sign of finding the power to make it stop. No harmony or mutual civility in so many ways.

Sure, it's true, we are resilient as a species. But are we any different than water buffalo fleeing from a pack of voracious dingoes? Most of the pack hardly even turns to look back as they clamor for safety while the young and weak are overtaken and consumed by the vicious hunting pack. There's no comity there.

That's how this looked to Sol. People are ripped apart by the absolute worst and most violent in society and the rest of the world keeps plodding along. After the story breaks most people keep on doing...maybe it's because there's another threat on the horizon to watch for or maybe it's just apathy. Maybe we've been too powerless too long....maybe that's why, in a comity of errors people hardly ever look back.

If I Were Running Things

"What we do know Grady," the seasoned reporter stated, "Is that there are reports of up to 12 students who have been killed by a homegrown terrorists. Several teachers have been shot, and the school is nowhere near returning to the homey elementary school that it was at the start of this school day. This school has been robbed of any peace and is now forced to walk through the chaos of this utter pandemonium that ended only minutes ago. As you can see behind me, students are being escorted out of the school with **TASC** Unit members flanking both sides."

She took a breath, glanced at the School, and offered more, "There is no clear indication as to how and why this happened, we are all anticipating officials will find some answers as they interview the man they have just taken into custody."

The DBN reporter turned slightly to direct her viewers' attention over her shoulder. Sol could clearly see in the background that the remaining shooter was in police custody.

As the eager reporter returned her face to the camera, Sol was fixated on the background. What he saw next was probably the most disturbing and yet most exhilarating thing he could imagine. As the alleged killer was being ushered between police cruisers to the armored detainment van, a business-attired man came into view. He looked to be a plain clothes detective, his ID tag dangling from his neck. The entire situation had been de-escalated. No one was scrambling or wielding a weapon at the moment. The scene had become relatively calm. And although there was certainly an attitude of haste to secure the alleged killer, something didn't sit right for Sol. Staring on at the macabre scene, it seemed there was a sickening routine that had developed. The shooting was over, kids and parents were being reunited in their cars and off to the side of the school at the Critical Incident Management area. You would think a situation like this would incite more fervency but it was in the placid way things were taking place in the background that gave the appearance of this event being all too common. Just a routine school shooting…or at least that's how it seemed.

"What the hell is the matter with this place?" Sol petitioned himself in response to the blasé management of the school-shooting environment. *"Crazy guy shoots up a school…crazy guy kills innocent children…crazy guy is cornered by police…crazy guy is handcuffed and taken into Police custody. Feels kinda scripted to me."*

But it was no script. The casual process after the incident had become commonplace. The scenes were all too normalized for anyone to get overly excited about. At least anyone witnessing from behind their personal Media Screen.

The pictures on the Screen were so innocuous at this point that it was beginning to twist Sol up in his gut. No question about it, it was a total routine on every level; as if it had been rehearsed hundreds of times.

"Everyone on scene is so apathetic," Sol noted. Media, police, even the would-be victims seem unfazed by the events. *"For Christ sakes,"* Sol lamented, *"It's only been a few minutes since the killers were blasting away at innocent children. How can everyone be so calm?"*

Even in the presence of shock, Sol was confused by the rote sense of duty he saw from the players on scene. Where was the anger, the fear, the emotion Sol wondered?

Sol was now spellbound by what was playing out. The police officer with the alleged killer in hand was briefly stopped by another detective to exchange some info. Standing casually at the open door of the Mobile Detainment Unit, neither of them was in a hurry to load this newest killer. The exchange took all of 4 seconds but that was all that was needed. In those seconds, Sol's brief concern slammed into reality. He was magnetized to the Screen. Staring intently, Sol saw the handgun swing up from the sport-coated man who was up close to the officers now. In less time than it took to blink, there was one more victim to add to the day's death toll. This freshest of killers became the freshest kill. Two shots penetrated the audio feed and penetrated the Brookmoor Elementary School murderer's head. Over the reporter's shoulder Sol saw the school-shooter begin tilting his head down to step into the safety of the Mobile Detainment Unit, then the next second, ***POP POP***...he crumpled to the ground.

The sport-coated shooter dropped his weapon immediately and just stood there with his arms now in the air. Three officers leapt on him and the DBN camera man wheeled the shot away from the reporter and zoomed in on the fracas.

"Was this for real? Did that just happen?" Sol yelled in silence. But Sol knew the answer to his own question.

With an unbroken gaze, Sol stared even more intently. As if he thought he would see something that wasn't there? Leaning forward, eyes subtly squinting and his mouth gaping just a little, Sol took in every frame of the live but surreal coverage. The shot widened again. On screen the DBN reporter was crouched down on the ground in the foreground of the shot. Her awkward 'take-cover' stance strained her to keep from fumbling and falling into the curb.

"This is why people love watching Live Streams...you never know what the hell might happen," Sol thought.

The camera was still shaking with the background plainly in view. Sol wasn't sure if he said it in his head or spoke out loud but he knew that millions of others would have felt the same way about watching a school-shooter get taken out live on DBN.

"Good," he said to himself, "I guess we won't have to waste tax dollars on dragging that son-of-a-bitch through the courts."…"Way to go Buddy!"

In his crescendoed anger and passion for justice Sol silently praised the sport-coated vigilante, *"I wish it was me who blew that asshole away"*.

The images in the Brookmoor stream broke away, and DBN anchor Grady Jorgenson filled the screen. Looking at the Anchor Desk of the DBN broadcast center, a part of Sol that had a need for justice took hold of him.

Sol couldn't help but think, "If it were up to me I would have every one of those selfish bastards stopped. Who says rehabilitation is more important than justice? This place would be different if I were running things."

Inspiring Humanity To The Next Realm

"**L**adies and Gentlemen!"

The call rang out through the World Congress Deliberations Chamber.

"Please take your seats and we will commence the proceedings of the Ninth World Congress Inclusions Session of the year 2043."

As the room responded to the Chancellor's request for Session to begin, World Congress Delegate Members shuffled into their seats. Each Delegate tapped his or her digital Folio to sign in. *Tap* after *tap* all delegates were present and accounted for. As in most of the Sessions, the meeting came to order as the Chancellor took his position at the Podium. He glanced at his tablet, and seeing all Delegate members were present, he tapped his Folio to officially begin the September session.

The Deliberations Chambers was exceptional in its design. It was far beyond the original home of the World Congress Deliberations Sessions. When the World Congress was first formed after the United Nations dissolved, the Congress had made the UN Headquarters its Deliberations home.

Many had thought the United Nations would continue indefinitely. But even though man-made institutions are astonishing in their size, scope, and efforts, they can only go so far. Like the fate of the famed tower in the story of the Tower of Babel, eventually the political structure dissolves, parties disband, and a new institution eventually replaces what has died off.

That was the case for the long defunct League of Nations which preceded the United Nations. And in course, the World Congress was born out of necessity. It is not unusual to see a decades long lifespan for any global initiative. But eventually, the institution dwindles away entirely or undergoes a wholesale restructuring.

The United Nations was one of the longest running International Cooperative Governing movements ever. Unparalleled in its Global impact, the UN succeeded the League of Nations in 1945 after WWII. And its greatest accomplishment to date was the not so small matter of preventing WWIII.

It was easily the most universal in its span of function after replacing the League of Nations. However, the UN had served its purpose. Member nations began disengaging from the United Nations amid the weakening philosophy and diminishing potency of its actions. Almost like a Mom & Pop business that stopped growing, the UN found it was time to wind down. The UN just simply stopped moving forward as it dwindled in its global influence. Which led to member participation dropping off in its final decade. For about ten years before its dissolution, the UN had become uncompelling. And its once palpable level of potency and authority, was no longer displayed with the strength it had displayed in decades past.

Once it was realized that the eroding United Nations was no longer effective, in what has been seen as the perfect time for the peoples of the world, the World Congress was formed in its stead. Initially willing to use the United Nations General Assembly Hall for its Deliberations, this super nova of Global Relations quickly advanced beyond what the 1952 UN edifice could provide. In 2029 Deliberations in the 60-year-old building ceased, and the World Congress moved to the artistic and architectural 10th wonder of the World. *The World Congress Center for Global Relations.*

Today this architectural wonder contained full representation of the 196 Nations in the world. Inclusions Sessions also had equal representation from almost every Region that had not yet met the "Nation" status. A hundred years ago, this kind of a structure housing every nation on the Globe was only an unattainable dream. In 2043, however, in this calm and thoughtful setting, the World was as close to being truly one as any could have ever imagined.

Participant Nations filled the World Congress Deliberations Chambers. And within the first years of its operations, The World Congress boasted an exhaustive membership with every nation on Earth adding numerous Delegates to the Congress. Along with transitioning to a glorious new home after outgrowing the historic UN building, the Member Nations of the World Congress were now referred to as Participant Nations. The sense of being true Participants rather than simply "Members" carried with it a new vision for advancing Global relations. The philosophy and World Congress motto was simple;

Improve the quality of life for all people.

Who of us wouldn't want that?

Within the regal environment of The World Congress Global Relations Center, the most impacting movements to unification were deliberated on, endorsed, and implemented. And within these walls every ivory pillar, every brass handle, every oak railing, and every opulent marble floor and exquisite wall covering, testified to the hope of prosperous social advances emanating from this place. Man had not only built this 10th wonder of the world, but man had built a model that directed all Nations towards political peace and respect. So much so that even the path to peace for the Middle East was successfully brokered by the work of the World Congress.

Few would have believed it possible that in just a handful of years into the operations of the World Congress, every Nation in the Middle East sent Delegates to the Congress? It was within that very year 4000 years of turmoil was laid to rest. A tone of tolerance and forgiveness was established and hostilities simply faded away. The Middle East was now working together to give every people group a home that would not be taken away by the fundamentalists fighting an unwinnable battle. The World Congress mediated peace in what was often seen as a hopelessly hostile region of the World.

Chronicled as humankinds most effective collaborative towards political peace, The World Congress had cemented its place in history. The unparalleled humanitarian and mediative efforts that flowed from its halls were cause for all to honor the institution. Few citizens of the world thought to decry the World Congress.

Even though there had been little in the way of social reform in the past 15 years or so, the comfort the world sat in as a result of the profound international stability fostered a sense of ease. Yet still, as the citizens of the world enjoyed the many years of peaceful political stability between nations and regions, the inner circle at the World Congress felt instability in a crucial element of culture. The many socials ills that have plagued mankind for all its history were still unremedied. The grass roots of culture and society still struggled with those things that rob peace from the average citizen. As an institution, this marvel of human governance had succeeded magnificently but the ways in which it failed simply proved the age-old axiom. Humans will always be humans.

And it was on this day, this Ninth Inclusions Session of the year 2043, that the Chancellor would take pause to address the state of the Global Community. Today the women and men who had been responsible for great achievements as a unified government, would seriously examine the current status of their work. Asking the question, "Has anything really changed for humanity?"

The Delegates who exchanged ideas and information as they milled about the foyer of the Chambers, had a somewhat muted aura about them today. Over the past months, small bits of curious information had been briefly referenced. Nuances of disenchantment, concerns for personal citizen safety, inequities from history that seemed to have a force in the present. It seemed even the World Congress, this widely hailed marvel of man's cooperative efforts for peace, had some limits. Those limits were about to come to light in the Inclusions Sessions this month.

This body of profoundly empowered Delegates fell short in inspiring humanity to the next realm of social stability. Vitality in relations between nations and governments was a mind-boggling boast for the world government organization. As for vitality in all ways possible for human relationships, safety and security, social well-being, and prosperity…well that was quite another.

The Big Reveal

Sol was still stirred by the images he witnessed after he stepped off the train. The walk through the treed streets of his neighborhood to home was just enough time for the experience to settle in. On a different day he would have forced the feelings down and pushed the images out of his head. But not today. Today was different. Taking in the neighborhood as he walked, Sol slowed his pace.

"Was anything different after a dozen kids had just been slain?"

The Fed-ex delivery truck was no different today. It was still screaming down the street to stop in front of a multi-plex to have the Fed-ex guy hop off the truck hasten up the steps of the unit and scan the address code to confirm delivery. The neighborhood store was no different. Tweens pushing and shoving as they came and went with their treat of the day in hand. The daily flow of the neighborhood was no different. A dog barking in that yard, a lawn mower running in this yard, a back door slamming shut over there, a young mom reaching into the back of her SUV on the driveway to buckle up her daughter after picking her up from the mother-in-law's. Nothing was different. Nothing except for the angst nagging at Sol while he strolled.

A block and a half away from home, Sol made a concerted attempt to justify his feelings. It wasn't work that was getting to him. Work was never the problem.

Sol puzzled, *"This kind of stuff happens all the time...I should be used to it by now. There's nothing I can do, the damage is done."*

As Sol tried to manage his reaction to the media experience, the image of the School shooter falling to the ground, blood splattering from his head, popped into view. Sol winced as his recall displayed the images to his mind's eye and his mind's ear filled in the sound of the gunshot.

Sol was no different than the next person. Everyone's inner soundboard would do the work of an editing suite. If a scene had no sound, the inner ear would add the sounds to a silent scene. That was what everyone did. A lifetime of sights and sounds streamed without a seven second delay to protect the audience had provided a library of imagery and sounds to fill in the blanks if there ever was one.

It was back in 2026 the *Seven-Second Delay Bill* was appealed. Successfully upholding the Constitutional right of every citizen to retain the privilege of freedom of information. That appeal took the rights of the viewer to new heights. No longer would networks aim their cameras on a News scene and be obligated to cut the feed if things got too intense for the viewer. If news were "live" it continued streaming without employing a seven second delay. The repeal of the bill brought amendments. All broadcasters were disallowed from interrupting a stream due to censors seeing something they thought was too inappropriate for viewers to witness. Seeing an intense scene and flipping the switch to a different camera or studio shot because the feed was on a seven-second delay, was no longer permissible. If you were filming it you had to show it. Nothing hidden or manipulated.

For the most part, it was a sensible enhancement to the bill governing delivery of media. The whole philosophy was sound in that it removed power from the broadcaster. Why should some corporate producer or government watchdog group make the choice as to what the viewer could handle on the other end? If something newsworthy was taking place the viewer should not be prevented from seeing reality. The move was truly an affirmation that all conscious humans are responsible adults and don't need Nanny State protectors watching out for what they are watching.

"*Show us the goods,*" was the thinking, "*We can handle it...or at least we want the opportunity to decide for ourselves.*"

Now, twenty-five years past the 2018 amendments, Sol was just another viewer who had logged dozens of live gunshot scenes in his mental library. Full color, full sound...Sol had little choice to change the images in his mind.

"That's it!" Sol chided himself, "I am done with that scene, I am not thinking about it anymore."

The whole thing was far too impacting for Sol to keep reliving it. He knew his wife would be home, so he resolved to forget the entire episode. Or at least relegate it to some other compartment in his head to be dealt with another day. There was no way he wanted to bring that garbage in his front door. It was bad enough he had to see what he saw in that News Stream. Ell, Sol's wife of 28 years, was home by now and Sol was not about to walk in the door and unload his thoughts about a twisted situation onto her.

It was rare, if ever, that Ell would shut Sol off when he was blathering on about some drama going on at work, or about some wild idea for a reality TV show. He could tell her about absolutely anything...and he did. Ell was without a doubt, the only person in the world Sol could laugh with one moment and have on his team if he was bawling about something the next. She held things together in a way that only she could. When she spoke, things always made sense and when she listened, she helped Sol make sense of his thoughts and feelings.

But the way Sol was feeling about the event he had just seen, there was no way he needed to drag Ell into what he was feeling...at least for now.

As Sol reached the front walk to his house, he thought about some of the millions of things he has shared with Ell over the years. Of all the moments that could come to mind he was distracted from obsessing about what he had witnessed on the MeRT by the memory of telling her about an idea he had for a reality show.

Making up reality TV shows was a little game between the two of them. Sol and Ell would do this thing where they would come up with an idea for a reality show trying to shock each other with an off the wall idea. Then they would play along with the idea and story-board the entire thing. They never took it seriously because it was a ridiculous game…like most of the "reality shows" that took over the streams in the last four decades. But it always left them both giggling. Neither of them could have ever imagined society would spiral so far into an abys of irreverent and utterly asinine reality entertainment. But that was where the Reality TV world had gone.

The show that came to mind for Sol was the *Leave a Deuce Show*. Sol couldn't help but smile remembering how Ell cracked up when he pieced the "show" together for her. He conceived the show after being prodded by a co-worker at the library to enter a WebTV reality-show contest. And Ell thought it was hysterical.

Sometimes they both found themselves laughing at the most irreverent and undignified bits of comedy. They sure howled when they started putting together the storyboard for *Leave A Deuce.*

The show would begin with the host setting the stage. In Sol's version of this contest winning reality show, the host would tell the excitement-starved viewer what has gone on today on *Leave a Deuce.* He would intro by saying something like;

> *"Today on Leave a Deuce we have been feeding mega-action superstar Phoenix Blu with plate after plate of super spicy Karachi food, beer, and carbonated beverages. Pretty soon," the host would elaborate, "Phoenix will leave a deuce in the Garrison toilet."*

"How it all works," Sol had described the show to Ell, "Is that at some time when the Garrison family are away from their home, the *Leave A Deuce* production team sets up the home with cameras with the permission from an insider family member. The fall out and drama that the viewer is privy to during the big reveal when the Garrisons return to find someone has left a deuce in their bathroom will be more than some can take."

Sol knew it, Ell knew it, everyone knew it, after almost 7 decades of reality shows being fed the viewer, there was little left that could bring drama to non-stop and outlandish reality TV streams of the world.

The next shot would showcase the pristine Garrison family home with the Host telling of the strategically placed hidden cameras, set where all the *Leave A Deuce antics* would take place. And when all that spicy food has percolated in the action movie hero's gut, he sneaks into the Garrison bathroom and does his business. After finishing the paperwork, Phoenix Blu washes up, and leaves the loo without flushing. This of course is all caught on camera and your Host pops back into the picture for the update.

"Let's watch, as the Garrison family arrives home for the evening to a nasty surprise."

As the scene unfolds, we find the Garrisons re-inhabiting their home with all the typical activities of a busy majority-class-family. Mrs. Garrison drops the key fob and sack of groceries on the counter. Mr. Garrison hangs up a coat and hollers an instruction to whomever happens to be listening in the busy house, then heads off to the bathroom to take care of some business.

But this day seems different in the Garrison home. The usual welcoming aromas that greet the family upon return are absent. On this day there is a detectable, familiar, yet elusive odor in the air. No one has made the odd smell yet. But wait, there will be no hiding from what is about to happen. Sam Garrison yells up to whoever is able to hear him in the house, "I'm just gonna use the bathroom!"

The watching audience is piqued…this is perfect!

As he steps into the loo, Mr. Garrison unbuckles his belt and moves toward the toilet. The strength of the "odd" aroma in the air informs his facial expression. On his face the viewer can read a mix of curiosity, annoyance, and a slight scowl, as if he just tasted something sour. Then, he reaches down to lift the lid as he's done a thousand times before. He glances at the toilet paper roll to check his resources… gotta make sure there is enough on the roll for what he plans to do.

With a hand on the toilet lid and a half-sideways glance still trailing away from the toilet paper, the lid swings up to rest on the back of the toilet. In that second Mr. Garrison is hit with a full-frontal assault by the most putrid aroma one can stand. And with the brilliant hidden-cam technology, his hilarious expression is caught for all reality show fans to see. The gagging Sam Garrison is staring straight into the bowl and a steamy pile of once spicy Karachi fare is staring straight back. No need to elaborate on what the mortified and disgusted Mr. Sam Garrison sees as he shrieks.

"Oh my God! What the…holy shit that's disgusting."

Sam is in full recoil mode with a slight retching going on in his upper oesophagus. He is so shocked he doesn't know what he should do. Should he flush it, should he scream at the culprit?…. But at this moment he has no idea who the culprit is.

"Who the hell didn't flush the toilet?" Sam hollers while reaching for the handle as his belt buckle clinks against the bowl.

Holding his breath now, he tries to turn away while pressing the handle. But it's like watching a train wreck…Sam just can't turn away. He watches as the bowl begins to swirl and fills with water…Sam waits, holding his breath. The bowl fills more…close to the brim…and it clearly is not swirling down.

"Oh my God…this is fu**ing unbelievable!"

Like any great reality show that creates drama, so too does *Leave A Deuce*. Panic is deftly infused in the viewers witnessing this unsavoury scene. The viewers can actually feel the mark's pain.

During set-up the production team has cleverly retrofitted the Garrison toilet with a controlled overflow system. And as the previously placid Mr. Garrison is taken to new heights with his panic, he reels around in circles searching for the plunger. Which of course has also been removed by the production team. Then, just when Sam all but gives up watching the swirling contents of his toilet about to spill over the edge onto the bathroom floor, in walks the popular Guest Star of the show, Phoenix Blu. In that moment the remains in the toilet are released by the overflow valve and Phoenix says...

"Evenin' Sam...it stinks that we have to meet like this."

In a cascade of relief, the BIG REVEAL so to speak, Mr. Garrison breaks out in laughter and, realizing he has been a victim of one of the most toxically disgusting and yet captivating reality shows on the planet. *Leave A Deuce* has claimed another victim. Everyone watching has felt Sam's relief and saw it turn to delight, as the inimical production team from *Leave A Deuce* fill the air with fresh deodorizing spritzer.

The show had international success for a few seasons and was a favourite of viewers. It was a real statement on how degenerated society had become and what classifies as entertainment.

As for the success of *Leave A Deuce*, it was on track to receive a fourth People's Choice award for Best Reality Show until one of the shootings backfired and *Leave A Deuce* was hastily pulled off the air. It happened when one of the marks didn't respond quite as predictably as Sam Garrison had. A disgruntled dad was caught by the hidden cameras beating his teenage son with the plunger handle.

In that unaired episode it was learned the toilet had been plugged on many occasions after the young man had used too much toilet paper. The boy's father had hit a peak in his stress levels because of a recent demotion at work and some serious financial strain. He simply was tired of plunging down his son's shit after pleading with him to stop plugging the toilet.

So, in an exasperated fit of rage at seeing the clogged unflushed toiled, he grabbed the plunger which had failed to be hidden by the production team and raced into his son's room. Without warning he started hollering at the boy and beating him like it was a Singapore caning.

The *Leave A Deuce* production team jumped in just as the plunger handle broke across the back of the boy's neck. That was the end of the popular reality show, and it was also the last time the toilet in that house would be clogged.

As Sol recalled those moments of first telling Ell about the show, he heard her laughter and remembered how scandalized she was by the brutally imaginative game show. The memory calmed Sol just before stepping inside to greet Ell.

On the other side of the door now, the world was behind Sol. The graphic images of the school shooting had faded for the moment and Sol kept himself from marvelling at the juvenile taste culture had for avant-garde Reality TV. In Sol's mind there was no need to discuss the tragic events of Brookmoor Elementary School. A welcome hug brought Ell into his arms.

"How was your day beautiful?"

"It was alright..." Ell shared.

Then, as if it were even somehow possible, Sol hadn't seen the DBN stream that day, Ell looked up and asked the only question that had the power to take Sol back to where he had just climbed out from. Like a big reveal of their own,

"...did you see the School shooting on the DBN stream today?"

Sol was instantly returned to those moment on the MeRT.

Progress Was Difficult To See

Was this really about to happen? No one knew how it would play out but there was definitely a knowing that day. This Session in the Deliberations Chambers was going to be unlike any of the other monthly sessions that had been chronicled. There was an almost theatrical silence in the room as the Chancellor leaned into the audio capture space in front of him. Those who knew what was about to be said in the opening address were fixating on the screens around the Deliberations Chamber. Those who hadn't been pre-briefed were quickly putting the pieces together.

"Aha" moments dominoed across the Chambers. Delegates' focus shifted from greetings and warm handshakes with friends they last saw a month ago, to the present gravity of the Deliberations Chamber. This was no ordinary Inclusions Session, Delegates were fast being reminded of the weighty forthcoming address by Chancellor Mahndar.

In the normally peace-filled Chamber, those present were livened by an anticipatory posture. Eyebrows were raised slightly and ears shifted as attentions sharpened. Like an orchestra posturing before the maestro called for the opening note. All were preparing. Something was about to change for the World Congress.

Chancellor Mahndar smiled. His trademark grin at the Speaker's Podium was a most welcome gesture.

The Chancellor would always begin his address with a warm smile. Mahndar believed a smile should adorn the face of the man behind the Speaker's Podium. That Podium was the place of address that was central in an imposing edifice filled with Delegates from every corner of the Globe. The chairwoman or man standing at that Podium was a pivotal leader in directing a Body of Delegates with a potential for altering the world for good. Today, the smiling Chancellor Mahndar was at the beginning of an entirely new era. An era where the vision of affecting the world for good would once again be shared from the world-famous Speaker's Podium. What was to follow would go down in history as an Inclusions Session that re-directed the world's most successful political institution.

"Ladies and Gentlemen", Chancellor Mahndar began, "There is no greater honor for me, than to stand at this Podium today and deliver the State of the Globe Address. As always, the time and energies invested by each of you have been monumental. Within the walls of this great facility the hope of the World has been reborn. Your contributions to global relations have inspired untold billions to embrace a Global Unity in ways that past societies had only seen in unattainable dreams. The dreams of women and men who felt a great weight on their shoulders to facilitate change have been realized. The perception that such monumental advances would be impossible in a world more divided than it was united, have caused many in the past to remain silent about their dreams. But today, we can boast that even many of those unspoken dreams have come to fruition. We are truly One World, with one language, and one global economy. We have reached a pinnacle."

A nuance of agreeance united the room. Each Delegate had participated fully in keeping Global Relations vital. Many in the room brought to mind her or his own part in the ongoing work Chancellor Mahndar was speaking of.

He lifted his arms and opened them to the room. The Body of Delegates filling the seats of the Chambers sensed an ominousness to his words of respect. Many in the Chambers had a sense that a unique time was upon them. They listened on.

"It is to each of you that the debt of strong global relations is owed. I have been privileged to stand in the Podium as Chancellor for these past years. I also have been privileged to witness the extraordinary work the World Congress has done to foster a system of governance that defines international co-operation."

Since the inception of the World Congress 4 decades ago, Chancellors typically enjoyed anywhere from a two to 8-year appointment term. Chancellor Mahndar had been appointed at a time when global relations and international issues had been unremarkable, calm if you will, for the past nine years. His appointment brought few changes and his addresses that were delivered from the Speaker's Podium became briefer and less reportorial over the course of the term. Not much to cover when the system was running smoothly. The entire Global system seemed stable, and the few regions or pockets of discord had seemingly faded into the background. Flare-ups of terrorists, protestors, or egotistical hostile leaders had occurred from time to time. The Delegates sat attentively as The Speaker's Podium Address continued.

"As I recount the advances this Global culture has embraced, several marquee events come to mind. Just five years after the inception of this political defining institution, a shift in the Middle East relations occurred. The thousands year old dispute that brought raging wars, death of innocents, vile threats, and racially motivated terrorist attacks around the world was unyielding to the test of time as a mechanism to resolve an historic conflict. The 4000-year-old conflict had reaped manifold death and suffering. Then, when the moment presented itself, it was clear the time had come...the dispute suddenly dissolved. Leaders from those Regions became woefully cognizant of their cycle of retaliation. The citizens of that region were paying a hefty toll. And right here in this very room, adversarial nations from the Middle East agreed to partake in a bread-breaking ceremony to mark the dissolution of hostile relations.

"Their act of breaking bread together and eating at the same table solidified their commitment to be part of a Global family. Each Region's Delegates affirmed the right of the other to exist peacefully in a shared land. The sword of defense was laid down. The mutual benefit to the entire Region and the world became self-evident. The demand for entitlements fell to a spirit of compromise. The process of unbridled retaliations and conflict to warfully fight for a one-sided version of Middle East peace, showed the world that if injustice is met with injustice, justice will never be met."

Mahndar went on to recount other political feats that originated within the halls of the World Congress Center.

"Among the list of achievements celebrated by the World Congress, we proudly recall the universal language developments in the 6th year of the World Congress. If it was at the fabled Tower of Babel that all languages came into being, then almost 5000 years of human progress has brought us full circle. The *One World One Tongue* movement brought the universal language to the finish line. We moved forward together at precisely the right time to see our world transition from many languages to One Tongue. Even though all languages from all regions were protected from erosion and becoming lost it was within the framework of the *One World One Tongue Movement*, the Universal language was established.

"Interactions between Regions and Nations no longer required cumbersome translation processes. In that year, the development and implementation of *One Tongue* began. It has almost been a generation since the first One Tongue children were born. Children born into a world that agrees to speak in one common language. And it is because of this, we in this Deliberations Chambers are unhindered by language barriers. Gratitude is owed for the efforts of this global institution; the World truly does have One Tongue.

"The *Currency Mobilization Initiative* was another proud accomplishment of this Institution. Today we sit in a world where international trade finds no barriers. Other governments had tried to establish a single international currency, but it had not been the right time for their attempts. Here however, within these walls and by this Body of Delegates, the time for one currency arrived. All currency has been equalized, and the mobility of all nations' currency has enabled a fully global economy."

He paused to take a drink as he scrolled up in his notes on his Digital Folio. He seemed eager to move ahead yet exhibited the restraint and poise one would expect of a seasoned Chancellor. There was more to share in this address, much more, but not before fully expressing the value of the Delegate's work as he waxed on.

"The challenges faced in establishing a world currency were great. I recall the concerns from less prosperous Regions as Deliberations were proceeding in this magnificent Chamber. Every concern about devaluing currencies and disruptions of banking systems was heard. And in the true spirit of our Inclusions Sessions, all issues were resolved. On the day of the vote in this Chamber, there was such confidence by Delegates that a *Currency Mobilization Initiative* was the most positive advance in global economy and international trade our world had ever seen. The Delegate vote for that Initiative was as close as we have ever come to a unanimous vote among the almost 200 nations and regions represented here."

Chancellor Mahndar swept over the crowd with his hands in an inviting gesture, "I am privileged to be part of this Global institution where women and men from all origins have made it essential that all nations are represented at the World Congress.

The Delegates looked on as Chancellor Mahndar delivered his glowing oracle about the progress made under the guidance of the World Congress. The Chancellor was exceptional this day in his address to the Delegates. All present in The Inclusions Session took in the accolades from the representative at the

Speaker's Podium. Yet the Delegates of the World Congress, sitting in the Ninth Inclusions Session of the Year 2043, could not deny the intuitive feeling that seemed to hover over the Chambers. A feeling that suggested there was about to come a message that would challenge them. This would be the day that the Delegates of the World Congress would be shown the limits of a box of their own making. The grand advances that once flooded into the world's most progressive institution had become less than a trickle.

This enthusiastic body of Delegates was about to experience something very rare in the Inclusions Session.

After Today They Felt Like Anything Could Happen

Ell had so much she needed to say as Sol began to pick away at his own thoughts. "I can't believe there was another shooting. How does this keep happening?"

She had watched the scene unfold too. Not that unfold is even a good way to explain what happened at Brookmoor Elementary. Unfolding would mean there were clear lines and creases, carefully unlaid one from another to reveal a sensible shape. Maybe it would be better to say the scene was more like watching origami being blown around the street. And without warning, a massive dirty boot stomps it flat. The school scene that day was, in a moment, turned into an all too recognizable mess of twisted hopelessness.

After being bolted to the Screen just a couple hours ago, Ell, along with the rest of the world glued to the automated DBN stream, had witnessed another real-life nightmare. And there wasn't a damn thing she could do about it. It was now part of her experience as it was for all who'd seen it. Just like all the graphic streams projected to the world. Scenes and events that were seared into the psyche of each witness forever.

Ell and Sol were victims again. No one wanted to be a victim of the culture and yet everyone was. Every viewer watched with the world but each of them was inexplicably alone while watching. Both Sol and Ell had the power of aloneness magnifying their sense of horror and injustice. It filled the incalculably vast cavern of loath in the pit of their being. The gruesomeness could be warded off, but the aloneness, well that was unavoidable. Aloneness was an enigmatic phenomenon that takes place in this virtual world. It was a media generated aloneness that was complex. Some therapists called it HAD, *Hyper-Attentive Disorder*. A disorder that had people so attentive to media content that they were practically enchanted by any stream on the Media Screen. Viewers could not **NOT** watch a Stream. When the Media Screen chimed and its warm pixels blossomed to illuminate the screen, all eyes and ears were drawn into an extreme focus. They just had to watch the instant offer of the moment's news or information. For most, although wanting to look away...they simply could not. It was now a society of hyper attention to the now.

Few folk who saw these highly-intense images on the DBN or other networks really sensed they were watching in concert with billions. Most viewers still felt as if they were watching from inside their own little insulated bubble. These deeply impacting shared images had the power to isolate each watcher. A viewer may be watching alongside billions of others but that viewer was, in some inexplicable way, made to feel like they were the only one seeing the events that developed on the Screen....all alone watching the world just happen.

The broadcast media industry had managed to develop a unique method of isolation for the viewer. Almost everyone watching seemed to have a personal envelope. Ell, Sol, the guy on the couch at home, seniors, the girl sitting on a bench waiting for the Shuttle, each of them felt globally connected in so many ways, yet the media content they were continually exposed to, left each of them feeling hauntingly alone. But the facts were, whatever it was that was Streaming, everyone had witnessed the same events. No one could get away from the ubiquitous World Congress Media Screens and the DBN. As soon as there was even the slightest hint of theatrics, political drama, or a compelling human-interest story, the Media Screen Stream would ignite. That musical intro chime was not able to be resisted... it was Pavlovian.

Viewers young and old were affected by what they saw. Could anyone really calculate the dangerous impact of what the broadcasters claimed was best for the viewers? And just like the rest of society, both Sol and Ell were willing victims of the images that were now a permanent part of their psyche.

"Sol", Ell pitched, "Why can't someone stop these guys? This has gone on forever. The cycle keeps repeating itself. I can't remember a time the World Congress did something to stop this lunacy. It's relentless! Innocent children are murdered every week it seems and people are victimized by criminals endlessly. For all the progress we've made, why is there no way to alter this?"

Sol was listening and he knew Ell's questions were the same ones he was asking. She was right, these kinds of crimes, not just school shootings but streams of violent crimes, had always been met with platitudes and dogma. Nothing seemed to ever be done about them. For both of them though, their questions were coming from a deeper place this time. This wasn't just the open-ended wonder of a rhetorician. The trouble was, Sol didn't have any meaningful answers. For the moment, the questions were left hanging in the room. Neither Sol, Ell, nor anyone seemed to have the power to change the despised reality of the human condition.

Surely, most citizens presumed, the World Congress was the only body with the power to launch equitable and decisive reform. Changes that would push a world striving to reach perfection up to the next level that was just out of its grasp. Even Sol had thought so on many occasions.

Ell followed Sol into the kitchen.

"Hmmm…I guess I missed my coffee this morning," Sol thought, seeing the bag of medium roast sitting on the counter. He tapped the "steaming mug" icon on the Smart-Counter that was glowing and said "Medium". The perc silently responded, gliding forward from behind the backsplash into the counter space in front of Sol. The water flowed into the percolator, the beans fell into the hopper to grind, and the green light went on, letting him know his beloved blend was moments away. It was the perfect brew. "Ha," Sol mused at how fantastic his cup of coffee was, "Now isn't this a perfect world?"

Ell went on with her quest, "Why can't someone fix this?"

And Sol, like most people, wished he could…most people wished they could fix the things that were never quite right about the world.

The soothing scent of fresh brew was filling the kitchen. Sol reached through the holograph panel to grab a mug. The cupboard door disappeared as the gentle *zsshh* of the holograph generator shut off the image it was projecting across the opening. He palmed his mug and took it out of the cupboard. With another gentle *zsshh*, the holo-cupboard door flickered and returned to hide the contents behind it. Pouring a fresh cup, he turned to Ell.

"You're right Ell, it is so messed up. I hoped the World Congress would have lined things up…made things right…How can they fix this place?" Sol gave in. This topic was too potent to hold back. Ell went right along with him as he fully discussed the things he saw.

"That bastard just blasted his way into a school without anyone having a chance of stopping him."

Even as Sol spoke, the image of the shooter himself being gunned down came back. The guy was just seconds away from being fully protected inside the Mobile Detainment Unit and **WHAM**! A bullet hole in the head. His body slammed against the open door of the Unit before it hit the ground. Shocking! Disturbing! F**king insane is what it was!

Why though was it such a cathartic image? What was it that felt so good about that scene? Sol drew a sense of comforting-justice from what he saw. And even though he thought it should feel wrong, it didn't feel wrong one bit.

"I couldn't believe how quick that guy came up and just shot him. I have never seen anything like that." Ell said intensely, shaking her head in still more disbelief.

"Oh ya", Sol silently reasoned, *"I guess everyone saw that too."*

Knowing Ell and the entire DBN viewing audience was "tuned" in for those painful moments as well, was no solace. Misery didn't get much company on this shared experience. The gnawing was profound, and Sol thought about the school shooter.

"I wonder if that loser had a clue what his act of horror would do to witnesses?"

Ell opened the fridge to grab a snack and spun the shelf until the yogurt was in front.

"I almost hate to admit it but I just…." Ell paused because she felt she needed to be careful with what she was about to say…her voice dropped, and she finished in hushed tones. "I actually did a fist-pump inside when I saw that guy get killed.

"Why?…" She pleaded now, not hiding her satiated sense of justice at the sudden execution of the school shooter, "Why couldn't that happen to every killer who thinks he's so damn sovereign he can just ruin people's worlds and then go sit in jail?

"These guys are so selfishly distorted they don't even kill themselves after they've exploded all over a school. There is seriously something wrong Sol. No one can tell me that World Peace has done anything to change the world…the real world, the world we live in right here and now."

She was right Sol thought. He knew it, Ell knew it, everybody knew it…but no one was doing anything to change it.

There had always been this undercurrent, this un-palpable social distortion, this weight of another injustice about to happen but no way to grab hold of its scruff, pick it up and toss it out the back door like the alley cat spreading filth in the kitchen. The feeling was so much like when a guy has a bad dream. You just cannot grab hold of anything in his surreal world to change the outcome. Waking up with a sense that things are just off, but there is no way to tell exactly what those things are. No chance to shine a light on them long enough to fix them or make them stop.

Ell and Sol decided to move on from their lament. Today was done and tomorrow, who knew…?

After today they felt like anything could happen.

Here's A Fin Buddy
Go Take A Shower!

Ell and Sol were quiet now as they started prepping supper. Sol put the celery back in the fridge after chopping up a few sticks and headed over to the table. Standing with one hand leaning on the glass he flicked the Tabletop Folio Screen to see what else was going on in the world. As he scrolled through the News Feeds, he flipped right past the top story about the Brookmoor shooting and his mind started to wander. When he saw the day's other stories it was clear none of it was helping where his head was at.

- **Off duty Cop on charges of domestic abuse.**
- **Health Care District refuses to treat immigrant with no health care.**
- **Home invasion in suburbs leaves elderly occupant frightened—Invader not yet found.**
- **Transgender rape and beating case enters fourth day of trial**
- **Cambodian Village Raided by Guerilla Forces-hundreds of women and children raped and killed.**
- **Priest convicted of pedophilia de-frocked.**
- **Carjacking leaves male hostage with concussion**

Sitting at the table now, Sol let his thoughts disconnect him from the moment. The kitchen sounds of Ell finishing up prepping supper dimmed. The Tabletop Folio drifted out of Sol's focus, and so did Ell as she was talking about the families who were destroyed after today's horror. Sol was buried in his own thoughts. There were so few times that compared to how he felt on this occasion. The satisfaction he felt from seeing a shooter shot. Maybe it wasn't satisfaction so much, but more like a moment of profound relief. Being there right in the moment. Watching justice take place. The moment a killer was shut off by an act of curbside justice. Sol was no bloodthirsty revenge seeker himself. Yet the fact was, that seeing a brutal and merciless killer, filled with even a millisecond of fear as he sensed the trigger squeeze on a gun pointed at his head, felt right. The whole event left Sol filled with feelings he could not yet unravel.

Sol was no one special...he was in his early fifties, married, with two grown children. He loved his work in a University Library and looked forward to regular coffee dates with friends...and...exactly like everyone else...Sol was subject to seeing the Media Screen broadcasts at every turn. Sometimes he wondered if that had desensitized him.

The cumulative flood of unpalatable events had lodged themselves in the memory of far too many citizens if not all citizens. And this latest event was not rolling off the back of this duck.

"Justice," Sol pensively said under his breath.

That's all it was. It was a longing for justice. Sol was ready, more ready than he had ever been, for JUSTICE!

He was pulled back to the moment as he heard, "***Ouch...***" from the counter where Ell was chopping the last bits of green onion for the salad. Ell grabbed a paper towel, and the wince from the pain of a fresh cut was fresh on her face as she squeezed it to her finger.

Sol sprung to the counter, "Oooh, is it bad?"

"No, it just stings; there was onion on that knife."

"Ah that sucks Ell, what can I do?"

"Nothing…what can anyone do? Ell responded, with a more than subtle exasperation.

Sol chuckled, "You mean about the shooting?"

"No…I mean Yes! I mean everything…What the hell can anyone do about anything that isn't the way it should be?"

Cutting her finger wasn't the issue but the adrenaline rush that came with the unwelcome kitchen injury did help sharpen her focus. In a flash Ell punctuated what was going through her head. She turned to Sol, clutching a wad of bloody paper towel over her newly incised second digit.

"Like I was just saying," Ell looked at her finger…she interrupted her comment at the thought she had done or said something to deserve the kitchen injury.

"Yikes, maybe I shouldn't have fist pumped when that shooter got killed."

Sol chuckled again, affirming that the rejoicing in the fact of justice being delivered swiftly, was alright by him. "Maybe you should have double fist-pumped, that murderer got exactly what he deserved."

They both agreed and Ell checked her wound. The bleeding had stopped so she grabbed a cold drink and held it to the finger.

Ell continued, "Like I was just saying, why can't something be done? This is probably the best state the world has ever been in, at least politically, yet there is so much…"

Sol chimed in to finish the sentence with her…."Injustice!"

Sol went on, "Yah, like the old dude I just read about who's lying in a hospital today because some punks decided they wanted to get into his booze cabinet.

"Or the Cop who beat his wife....I bet he races through the courts and is back at work by Tuesday."

Ell was nursing her wound as Sol offered more...more tales of injustice and suffering.

"How about the Arab guy who can't get surgery because he has no insurance? Or the kid who's gonna be messed up forever because some priest decided his boner was going to get them both closer to God?"

Ell's attention on Sol's rant was fixed. She cringed as she drew a full breath of exasperation at the thought of how twisted some people are.

It was Ell's turn again, "One of the gals at work today told me about a one-year-old taken from her parents. This little girl was sitting for 5 hours in her highchair in front of the TV while her mom and dad were comatose on top of each other in the closet, high in Meth."

Ell heard about lots of situations like that. Working as a consultant in the Social Services Sector brought a lot of stories about injustice into her path. Sol wasn't sure how much she didn't tell him, and he probably was better off not knowing. But the amount of whacked stuff she did tell him was unbelievable. And it was no secret how many "Methers" got funnelled into the system. The cheapest wonder drug always found a way to capture its victims. And with Meth being the one hit wonder for the user, any ability to function was decimated.

"How about this one Ell? I saw some guy verbally denigrating his girlfriend or wife in public...or I don't know...maybe she was his sister...anyway, he was ripping her up on the MeRT today. Shrieking at her like she was his dog. I could feel her *humiliation*. Who lets anyone treat anyone like that? And talking about the MeRT."

Sol's nose started to curl just thinking about it again, "Did that thing ever stink today. I walked in there and I hit a wall of stench that almost made me gag." Sol lightened as he slid into his sarcastic shtick, turning the conversation into melodramatic kitchen theatre.

"All Aboard! Welcome to Stank Train. On the Stank Train sit back, relax, and ride in a comfortable environment that smells so bad it follows you home."

Sol's face soured again as he theatrically admonished the riders who's stench came to mind.

"Come on ladies and gentlemen, this is your Conductor speaking, please take a God damn shower, *Febreze* and *Old Spice* work well on clean bodies folks, but they aren't supposed to mask your filth."

Sol held out his hand mockingly as if to give 5 bucks to a smelly guy who wasn't in the room. "Here's a fin buddy, go get your stench hosed off down at the truck wash?"

That did it, Ell and Sol were off track and chuckling again. What started as a serious discussion, had spiralled into a good defuser for the tight neck and back that always cropped up when matters of injustice came to the discussion. Neither of them tolerated smelly public places very well.... Who did? Most people barely tolerated them. Not that everyone didn't give off a little funk from time to time. But it made sense to most people that no matter who you are or where you're from, the smell of a freshly bathed co-rider was always more welcome than the pungency of body odor, bacteria, and stale sweaty clothes. If we are going to be a melting pot of people from all over the world. Both Sol and Ell thought it wasn't too much to ask that we all try to stay clean and fresh? Especially when we're in public. And being trapped in a smelly place in public was the worst. Stuck with no air to breath except the fetid stuff that filled the room.

Sol and Ell had had their fill of pungent public places. It wasn't long ago that they took a stand by keeping their own boundaries when on a date at a movie theater. The line-up was good, popcorn and drinks were soon in hand, and then they made their way leisurely down the hall to theater number 5.

On the stroll to their theatre, Ell couldn't help but say, "What is that smell?"

As they meandered up the hallway to the tiered seating, the smell did not abate. Sol smelled it too. Hard to take. The theatre was almost full. A couple seats here, a few seats there. By the time they had plodded up one set of stairs then explored the other set on the other side of the theatre to find open seats for two, Sol and Ell recognized their discomfort with the smells in the theater. It was then they realized they are not that desperate to be at a movie, nor were they worried about what a theatre full of moviegoers might think if they just turned around and left.

So, Sol and Ell politely informed the concierge of the stench of un-showered bodies that filled the theater. They accepted a full refund for their tickets and spent ten or fifteen minutes agreeing with each other on the idea that it is unacceptable, **EVER**, for someone to go out in public smelling like that. What were people thinking? It was almost as if there were some kind of a convention to protest Multi-National soap manufacturers. Maybe a soap boycott was in play…But whatever it was, the pair both agreed, the dour smell of human body odors is more than enough to make them gag and head for lighter air.

As Sol and Ell paused for moment to digest their chuckles and thoughts of justice, Sol stepped back in their conversation, to moments ago when he was lost in thought at the table. "I don't know Ell, you're right, it's about justice. But like you said…" in chorus Ell chimed in, "What can anyone do?"

"Someone's got to do something. If I had my say, I wouldn't worry about pissing off a couple people; I would make some serious changes. It is so simple Ell. Sure, when we look at the big picture, we have a better world today in some ways than our parents had. But this is no utopia. I guarantee things would be different if I were King of the world."

The Binding Apathy Was A Social Prison

Delegates had never experienced this before. At the Podium Chancellor Mahndar took an extended pause as he gazed downward. Was this to be another epochal moment in the utopian-like tale of the World Congress? As the seconds hurtled by, hope seemed to pass just as quickly. One might draw a conclusion that the near and present reality would be just another challenge for the great minds in the room. The reason and hope that came from this Body of Delegates always rose to meet any international challenge with sound resolution. Yet on this occasion the plight was different.

How did we get here? That would be the natural question one might ask after hearing the Speaker's forthcoming assessment of the state of the globe. And with a completely silent room, no Delegate's attention was diverted. Chancellor Mahndar raised his gaze.

"My friends, I am in a difficult spot here today. We have faithfully done great works as a united group, works that are indeed worthy of praise. But we have not simply failed one another we have failed those whose greatest hope was in us. I am not speaking of the ways we have found resolutions to international threats and cures for disease by our deliberations in this Chamber. I am speaking of how citizens have long hoped for simple safety, security, equity, and prosperity.

Generations have hoped to see these most basic things in life be brought to fruition by the hand of our all but sovereign institution. Hopes for the improvement of the human condition not the decline.

"Who are the citizens I speak of? Those hope-filled are the disenfranchised, the marginalized, the vulnerable, the young. Hidden from plain view because of the overshadowing import of Global and International concerns, there are many whose vibrant contributions to culture are diminished because the system has not pursued these ideals on their behalf, and they themselves have no power to pursue the system."

For the moment the Delegates in the Chambers sat as if any movement or noise would indict them. It was deafeningly silent. The Chancellor's words hung in the air like blades of a guillotine prepared to fall. The tensions that were mounting began to elicit squirms in their seats from the diverse group of Delegates. What was happening? The World Congress had failed in some way. Failed to give to the citizens those things they needed most. The anticipation set the Delegates to begin to brace.

Chancellor Mahndar changed his pitch as the room collectively inhaled.

"It has been said that one person can change the world but is it not also true that we should work to change the world for one person? Each citizen deserves the same care and comfort the society has to offer. The disenfranchised person who is found in that position, becomes unwittingly disenchanted with the world around him. And in the face of believing that nothing is going to change and there is no ear to hear their plight, that citizen takes on a sense of apathy. That apathy limits a person's ability to enjoy prosperity and vibrancy in the society that is their microcosm. It is not greed, nor violence, nor hatred that grinds the wheels of collective human development to a halt. It is apathy. Who is to blame for this apathy? Are the people the cause of their own apathy or is there a force larger that guides them toward the binding apathy that keeps them from hoping for more?

"Throughout the political world, humankind has embraced this institution and empowered it to unite the Globe. We have been the maestro for Global reform. Yet disenchantment and apathy persist on many levels. To what do we ascribe this persistent apathy? Many still toil to enjoy basic needs and many who suffer under burdensome toil, are unable to enjoy the small pleasures most take for granted. These unmet needs cause the erosion of hope and foster the blossoming of apathy.

"What have we done about crime? Has this Body eradicated crime, or do we continue to suffer from the societal sickness that is crime? Crimes of greed, crimes of hate, of violence, and of selfishness? Who among us has not witnessed the effects of such crime? This pervasive illness strikes many innocents. Crime has become an accepted element of our culture. It is as if we concede that because crime has always been with us, we choose to accept that it always will.

"The latest crime rate statistics show violent crimes have been slowly declining for almost two decades, yet we have learned recently the data has deceived us. Crime has not abated. Why do the statistics misinform us? Friends, this is because there is less willingness to report crime to local and Global authorities. Lack of reporting crime does not mean crime is lessening. This fact is a disheartening situation pointing directly to civil apathy as the cause. One can only cite apathy as the cause for such broad resignation.

"That sense of apathy has allowed crime to resist eradication, and many citizens are denied the inalienable right to peace. All manner of crime affects our citizens, and it is a communicable toxin that not only envelopes new cells at will, but it toxifies those that otherwise would be healthy. The crime we tolerate damages untold numbers of citizens. Citizens who are powerless, in most cases, to prevent it. Apathy however has become our nemesis. It is running rampant and has subdued any power that might rise up against crime. We have been unable to disarm crime. Our world today is still, in many ways, at the mercy of criminals and those who silently enjoy their chosen social distortions?"

Chancellor Mahndar paused and sipped from a tall glass before he continued. His sister, who had endured a painful and abusive marriage for 18 years before getting a divorce, was brought to mind. He continued.

"Friends, what force will it take to dispense with such poisons as domestic violence? This crime has even affected my own family. The tragic fact of women being subtly and overtly controlled, oppressed, and harmed is a truth in society that is very dark. On average, 24 people per minute are victims of rape, physical violence, or stalking by an intimate partner, most of those being women. And all, among those, live in fear. This is unacceptable.

"The incidences of other forms of domestic violence and oppressive control against children, seniors, women, men, and people with disabilities are similar in number. It is a sad fact that the work of this Body has not been effective to eradicate this most insidious, private, and shameful cause of evil in our midst. For those who have been targeted or marginalized it is clear, they all wish for the same thing. Peace and safety is often their only desire. Perhaps Benjamin Franklin was not correct in saying, *"Even peace may be purchased at too high a price"*?

"There is no price too high to pay to establish a certainty of peace. Not only for all women but for all people?

"All persons deserve peace, yet humans have been ill-served in our quest to bring Global peace to humankind. In pursuing peace for humanity, we have not been able to ensure each human enjoys peace in his or her insular world. Our former accomplishments, as a unified Body, of achieving peace on the level of uniting Regions and Nations has offered the world an ideal. But the ideal for the safety and security of each citizen has become a hope that has all but faded away, leaving the apathy that paralyzes humanity roiling in its undercurrent. Peace must be achieved for the individual and for the collective…no matter what the price?

"There are other dark truths that have not been altered by our Deliberations in this Chamber. Upon the commissioning of the Global Monetary Unit we, in this Body, were able to design measures to avoid devaluation of currencies. The result has been a boon for international trade. Yet we find the impoverished among us remain under a shadow. We have brought no improvement for the lowest of income earners for almost twenty years. Shall we accept that the poor will always be with us? Or is it a failure on our part that we have allowed poverty to persist? The outcomes of poverty drive people to hopelessness, and this is the erosion of one's spirit. It is this institution that must bear the responsibility for that erosion.

"Ladies and Gentlemen," Mahndar petitioned, "We have done many great things in the name of unification and Global Relations. Yet, in the interest of eliminating the distressing issues that subtly plague our Globe's citizens, I urge you today that we take action. Action that is truly felt by the least powerful citizen who we have each vowed to serve by our pledge to the World Congress. I submit, we must find a method that unties our hands. Freeing them from the shackles we have in part created, so we can ensure the betterment of the lives of each citizen. Offering the safety, security, peace, and prosperity that each person inalienably deserves."

The Chancellor was doing the task of informing…of informing the Delegates of the graveness the world was experiencing at this time under the leadership of the World Congress. Mahndar was dutiful to inform but hopeful that the Delegates would find a solution to the state of the Globe. The casual demeanor of the Delegates in the chamber had slowly eroded over the passing moments. The effect of the Chancellor's address was profound. Today's address brought a dark picture to the Delegates and inaction was not a possibility. Although some wished they were not hearing what they were, each Delegate was now informed of the "State of the Globe." And it was not promising.

The Speaker's Podium had stood silent for a moment now. The attentive posture of the audience slowly began to shift. The inquisitive hum that began to emanate from the Body of Delegates bespoke the discomfort the group had with the message. At least with the last part. Within the pensive rumblings that slowly grew in volume, was the reasoning that often pushes back against the unsavoury reality. Delegates all through the Deliberations Chambers that moment were walking themselves, and each other, through the dissonance and discomfort. *How could this be?* They protested. Each delegate within him or herself was asking that question and offering a pallid faced argument to convince themselves otherwise.

Some pacified their self-indictment at their part in having not provided methods and means to bring healthy social evolution. Even the most self-convincing Delegate who thought along those lines could not deny the response that whispered from the deepest point in their reasoning. The World Congress had dealt with issues that impacted the Globe as a whole, yet quite clearly now, failed to impact civilization on the most rudimentary human level. The Globe was changed but humanity was left unaltered in many ways. Peace and International cooperation had not affected many average citizens. And even as each Delegate put forth their own arguments against the unpalatable reality the Chancellor had just shared, each knew that their Region or Nation was in the same position as that of any of the Regions.

The Inclusions Session for the day would end on that note. The Delegates, somewhat overwhelmed by what they had just ingested, were charged with the task of determining how to proceed from this point on. As they flowed out of the Chambers, they were confronted with a haunting question on the Media Screens and Digital Folios throughout the Chambers;

Is The World Congress the Institution to Build A Better World?

As the question faded in and out on the Media Screens, it gave way to a William Osler quote from the early 1900's. A quote that spoke to the burdensome apathy that had forced its way into the fiber of history's most advanced culture. Asking the people what was worse, the man who does evil or those who look on at evil and do nothing. Standing behind the accolades of accomplishments and self-satisfaction. The binding apathy was a social prison that was erected along the way to progress.

"By far the most dangerous foe we have to fight is apathy—indifference from whatever cause, not from a lack of knowledge, but from carelessness, from absorption in other pursuits, from a contempt bred of self-satisfaction"

—*William Osler (Canadian Physician 1849–1919)*

True, things were better on a Global scale, but even though the world was "better" than it had ever been in known history, it was clear the world needed to become so much better still. The difficulty for the deflated Delegates would not come with confronting the truth about the state of the Globe, the difficulty would come in finding how to change it.

Just Blink and They Will All Magically Go Away

The holo-clock said 3:37. Forty-seven minutes had passed since Sol last looked at it. Every hour was like two. He just wanted to sleep. And nothing was helping.

Sleep was usually an agreeable companion Sol got along quite well with. But tonight, he was not feeling very understood by his old friend. It just would not come. Sol decided to give the elusive sleep the victory this time and he slipped out of bed. Stroking Ell's arm to let her know everything was all right, he was happy to see at least she could sleep. Thank God it was Saturday, and he didn't have to endure that infernal train ride to work in the morning.

Countless times in the past ten years or so Sol was wrapped up in a research project for a student or Prof who had hunted him down at the University Library. Often, when that was the case, he would pop out of bed in the middle of the night to have a meeting with his ever-beckoning cache of digital books and journals. Those nights however, were a little easier to take than what was going on this night. Being kept from sleep due to the call of his passion was easy. Tonight, fighting the flood of adrenaline that was brought on by being so frustrated was impossible.

Wandering through the kitchen towards the den, the warm tile floor took the chill out of the air and soothed his feet. The inviting chair in the den welcomed the temporary insomniac. He sunk into it and closed his eyes. Ell's cut finger came to mind and then instantly, Sol eyes snapped open again. The blood was bright red in his mind. A blast of images of the killer turned gunshot victim at the door of the Police Mobile Detainment Unit took over his mind. It was like being pushed off a cliff with nothing to grab hold of.

Before bed, Sol had picked up the latest News Stream on the Brookmoor School Shooting. Twelve children and three security guards were killed, and two teachers were wounded in the shooting. The teachers had been released from the hospital. The images of the school showed it to be a huge crime scene. What else could it be after a day like that? And already, a handful of people had come on scene for other reasons. Some were beginning an ad-hoc vigil for the slain, while others, a little more off camera, were protesters.

This group of protesters was not new to these scenes. For almost a decade now, whenever there was a 1st World crime against humanity or the innocent, the well-known strategic activist group, *People for Speedy Justice,* would get some of their supporters on scene as soon as possible.

It was the typical motley crew of activists. A bearded guy with a sign and a backpack over his shoulder, a scrum of women in oversized coats and shoulder-length hair holding a fistful of handbills, a couple of scruffy dudes hoisting their sign on a stick into the air. The *People For Speedy Justice* were a pretty well-behaved group of activists. Their message was simple. **"Don't delay justice."**

They had developed into an activist group after seeing one too many criminals be leisurely walked through the justice system. In many cases of serious violent crimes, the accused would be guided either to a criminal sentence or on their way to freedom manipulated by legal technicalities. If a crime happened the *People For Speedy Justice* wanted the government to act quickly against the perpetrator and act intentionally to help the victims…as much and as fast as possible. But their sign said a lot. When Sol read it, he couldn't have agreed more.

—Slow Justice is No Justice—
☺ We all deserve a better world ☺

The message they were sending was one that called for the World Congress to take speedy and decisive action against criminals who have no regard for the right to peace and security of others. And *People For Speedy Justice* wanted a plan put into place to accelerate the process. For this case, however, Sol thought, there was no way justice could have come any faster. Unless one of the teachers in the school had wrestled the gun away from the shooter and shot him on the spot. *People For Speedy Justice* were on scene for other reasons this time. Exposure for their cause was the most likely of reasons, knowing the shooter was already dead. This scenario was right in line with their plight.

The Shooter was already dead at the hands of a vigilante who had only now been named. The Media had tracked his identity, and bystanders confirmed his daughters were not of the dozen children killed in the school shooting. Mr. Mystery vigilante was being referred to as Tom Cohen. DBN info on the guy showed he was a married father of three young children, all under the age of 10, attending Brookmoor. Tom Cohen worked as a consultant and had no previous criminal charges or activities the police knew about. At this point, Tom Cohen was in custody, and it seemed unclear in this moment if the *People For Speedy Justice* were pushing to have him brought to justice speedily or if they were there in support of his actions.

The *PFSJ* group knew how sluggishly the system worked. Serious criminal cases always seemed to go the same way. The same script was used every time; a repeating sequence of drama and sluggish legal process....*Capture the offender, charges laid, arraignment, wait wait wait...preliminary hearing, trial date set, trial date changed, pre-trial negotiations between the Defence and the Prosecutor, inordinately lengthy trial, judge or jury's decision, appeal, hearing in a higher court, and on and on it went...*A new month new year and even new decade in some cases was rung in before a case was decided forever. And in sentencing the convicted there was often a reduced time in prison because of the lengthy judicial process the accused went through. "Time served" was how it was termed.

The People for Speedy Justice did a good job at highlighting the grinding lack of progress in the justice system. "What about our time served?" they would ask. "What about the good people who are stuck languishing in a No-Man's land as powerless observers?" "What about all the people, eager to see justice, who would watch and wait and be subject to the perpetual bombardment of tales of injustice by Media and commentators day after day?"

It was absolutely inconceivable to most citizens how much time, money, energy, and emotion were sucked into the judicial Black Hole. The esteemed Justice System had become a vortex that sucked the life out of the common folk while bouncing the offender around for years, bringing no resolve to the charge against the offender, to the public, or to the victims of the crime. And no one could do a lick about the "*Time served.*" It was a mockery to the real victims!

Sol got the message and was in some ways onside with the *People for Speedy Justice.* If someone were clearly the committer of a malicious violent crime, then get on with it. Everyone wanted that. Lock them up. Take care of it, get rid of the cancer. Stop wasting everyone's time, money, and energy on the criminals.

It certainly wasn't rocket-science. But the complex system of politicians, barristers, solicitors, depositions, appeals, judges and juries, had turned it into a three-ring circus of Lawyer Artistry. A slow, complicated, incomprehensible system that served the criminal and the Lawyers more than it served the good honest people who are victimized. Victimized twice. Once by the accused and then again by the system. And there was little need for any science at all in many of the cases. Most of the criminals being gently guided through the courts were just huge boat anchors dredging the slimy bottom of the pond in the grand, slow-moving ship we call the Judicial System. Just ask the average Joe what to do with criminals and he'll tell you. Most would say, "lock em up and force em to work" or "kill em"!

At any rate, as was coming clear, today's effort by the *PFSJ* activists was not about advocating to hasten Tom Cohen through the system. Even though some were calling him a murderer, they, like most average people, were supportive of the expedient curb-side justice that transpired at Brookmoor Elementary School. At least in this situation.

As Sol thought about their plight, the older dude with the beard protesting with the *People For Speedy Justice* was brought into focus.… It was just a flash, but his sign was perfectly framed by the female activists waving handbills on either side. A clear shot of the bearded sandwich-board guy's sign showed a cold penetrating statement etched on plain white plasti-board. And when Sol recalled it, he knew without question they were out there supporting Tom Cohen's actions.

"It's Not Murder if A Murderer is Killed"

The loop began to roll from the beginning again in Sol's mind. There was no chance of getting back to the beta waves and sleep-spindle of slumber. He just gave in to his wakefulness and turned on the Media Screen in front of him. The World Congress 24-hour feed fell into the queue, so Sol acknowledged with a blink.

That still got him. It had been four years since the *Retinal Recognition* feature for home Media Screen systems had been standard on all residential Media Screens. Learning the eye movements to control the screen was simple now. Look up to the right and the channel cursor scrolls up. Down to the left the cursor scrolls down. Blink to acknowledge your choice and look left or right to turn the volume up or down. It was amazing how quick how tech-trapped button smashers could learn a new skill. Retinal Recognition skills were picked up in minutes by Media Screen viewers. A few blinks and sideways glances and the archaic button pressing on a remote control became completely obsolete. It was second nature. **Blink**! And the World Congress archived news from last night was streaming into the den again.

It was too bad a blink couldn't give all the criminals in the world what they really deserved. Sol would love if he could just blink and they would all magically go away.

He Saw The Killer's Face

As Sol settled in to catch the DBN Stream the sharp images of the New York World Congress Center for Global Relations penetrated the dark room. The shot was taken from behind the last row of seating in the Chambers. The World Congress correspondent stood pointing to the magnificent World Congress Unity Globe that hung over the core of the Chambers. It brought together all the elements the World Congress stood for. The enigmatic emblem for world unity was the first of its kind. The Unity Globe was holographically projected over the Speaker's Podium in the center of the circular chambers. All Delegates were cognizant of the revolving globe displaying the illuminated connecting strands between nations and regions across the world. The pulsing threads of light were a barometer that revealed how well the Delegates were doing their job. How well connected the political world was in relation from region to region.

The World Congress correspondent turned back to the camera and the Stream continued with sharing a report on the day's Deliberations.

"Is there something missing in the plans of the World Congress? In this first day of the monthly three-day Inclusions Session, the Chancellor gave his State of the Globe address. Today, Chancellor Mahndar adjourned Session early. The Chancellor invited the Delegates to not simply consider the progress and advances made by the World Congress but to carefully consider the ways in which the World

Congress has failed to make an impact on society at a level that would ensure peace, safety, prosperity, and security for all citizens of the world."

Sol became fidgety as he waited for a little more of an explanation on the report. Something didn't feel right. He knew their Deliberations had nothing to do with yesterday's school shooting. Sol watched as the reporter went on.

"It was laid out in no uncertain terms by Chancellor Mahndar today that many citizens are floundering in apathy. The reasons given by the Chancellor were varied. The tone of the Chancellor was detectably solemn from the Podium today. He reported, even though citizens enjoyed the many political advances in Global Relations under the auspices of the World Congress, many found social advances to be a clear disappointment at best."

Fading out on the images of staff cleaning the empty Deliberations Chamber, DBN reporter Jes Roth was pointing to the countdown clock that sat above the entry nearest him. Each month the clock was reset to let the whole world know the time was always advancing towards the next monthly Inclusions Session. When a Session ended, the clock began counting down until the next session began. The live countdown clock gave Citizen's comfort in knowing when the Delegates would be back in the Chambers again. Working to ensure global issues are always kept in short account. After each day of the monthly Inclusions Session the clock displayed the time until Session resumed in the morning. The clock showed less than 16-hours till the second-day of this month's Inclusions Session. At the end of the monthly Sessions the clock would reset to count down toward the coming month's Session.

Jes Roth offered more, "The Deliberations Chambers will be filled once again at 8:30 tomorrow morning and critics expect to see a considerable reaction by Delegates. Has The World Congress failed in some way? Will Congress be able to draw on its record of improving the World and find ways to respond with action to the Chancellor's challenge?"

Sol's fidgetiness turned into pensiveness…his thoughts about the state of the world consumed the moment.

It was 4AM now…which meant Deliberations on the would begin in under 5 hours at the start of the second day Session. Sol had been watching a re-broadcast of the Jes Roth report. Looking down to the left, the cursor responded. Sol blinked to confirm his switch to DBN LIVE. The 4AM Stream was chiming in, and the split-screen segment framed the reporter. It was the same reporter who Streamed the School shooting story from Friday afternoon. She was framed on one side of the screen and a stand-off scene at a family home was imaged on the left.

"Earlier this morning, Police and SWAT Team members stormed a quiet residential home on Greaves Avenue in the city's Rosewood suburb. Internet sources had tipped police off to a bizarre hostage taking. Sources tell us," The cadenced voice of the reporter informed, "A late 30's man had taken his ex-wife, teen daughter, and mother in-law captive at gun point. The man and his ex-wife reportedly had shared custody of his daughter. Sources suggest the young girl's mother, who is the ex-wife of the hostage-taker, arrived with the man's mother in-law to pick up the girl after being called by the upset daughter having an argument with her father.

"The man casually invited the two women in, led them downstairs where he said the distraught daughter was, then he forcibly detained the three females in a storage room." The reporter continued filling in the blanks. "Details are sketchy, but we do have some information stating that the man forced the females to their knees at gunpoint. He then had the daughter tie up her mother and grandmother before the dad of the young girl bound and gagged all the women.

"This," the reporter opined, "is a very odd multi-generational incident and it seems to have stemmed from a familial dispute. These images are from earlier today and since about 8:30PM, the man has released one of the hostages. The 14-year-old daughter has been taken into protective custody. As more info comes in, we will update you."

The sound faded on the hostage taking story into a marginally less riveting story. Sol was fighting to stay focussed. Dozing felt good, the glow of the Media Screen dimmed and brightened as the images changed during the Stream. The sound softened as the News cut to commercial. Almost back to sleep now, Sol thought about crawling back in bed to snuggle with Ell, but he was just too comfortable right now to move. His breathing got deeper and slowed. Everything that might have strained against the enveloping leather of the womblike recliner began to get heavy. The Retinal Recognition in the Media Screen sensed the sleepy viewer was no longer a viewer and the screen faded with the sound softening even further. Sensing a sleeping viewer in its zone, the faded voices of the DBN reporters transitioned to a comforting white noise, the sound of rain falling.

Amazing technology really. These Smart Media Screens were truly intuitive. They learned when odd hours of viewing took place and adapted to a late-night watcher nodding off. Eventually, when the late-night viewer was asleep, the Media Screen would go into sleep mode as well, shutting down until it sensed active retinas scanning the screen again. Now Sol was only a few slow deep breaths away from full sleep. The slight smile that was on his lips was a telling expression of comfort. Everything is silent, everything is warm, and everything is soft. In the next breath though, the subtle smile changed. There was a straightening of his mouth and a mild brow furrowing from seeing an image in his sleep deprived mind. *"What was that?"* was the remote thought that passed through Sol's mind unable to identify the rapid image that jetted past the cortical lobes and visual cortex. The furrow subsided. His mind almost clear again. One more deep breath but the smile of comfort did not return. The furrow did, and so did the image that caused it.

It was a distracting image and it elevated Sol from the nirvanic comfort into the realm of curiosity. *"What is that?"* he asked again as the image in his head became brighter and took more of his attention. One more breath...the breath that should have had Sol fully asleep in the recliner, but it only served to sharpen his attention on the image in his mind. Now Sol was distracted from what otherwise would have been a blissful rest. Sleep had fled and Sol was now pondering the image that chased sleep off.

"Oh"...he thought, *"That looks like the World Congress Shield."*

The Shield in his mind's eye was almost identical to the one he had just seen 20 minutes ago on the Media Screen Stream. What truly distracted him though was the way the Shield was different in his vision.

The bands around the globe were all intact, the colors were all there, the unity symbols on either side were as they should be, and the strands connecting each region and nation were complete. But the land masses themselves were different. They were fragmented. Not in large fragments but just little, almost imperceptible lines of fragmentation. As Sol's sub-conscious eye zeroed in on the fragmented land masses depicting a disconnected world in his vision of the World Congress Shield, the hostage situation he just witnessed on DBN rushed in next. All-of-a-sudden it caught him, what he was seeing caused him worry for the three females taken captive by a distraught ex-husband and father. Next the Newslines he had looked at earlier flooded back. He winced at the thought of an old man being beaten and stricken with fear by a handful of thugs who forced their way into his home. The recall sped up in his mind, the images and News Feeds Sol had ingested the past day were racing back one by one into sight in Sol's limbo-like state...

...Ell's cut finger came into the dream next, *"ooh that must have smarted"*; then the child that was taken from the drug-abusing parents screamed through his head. Seeing the little girl fixated on the TV with a full diaper and a grape-pop-stained mouth; the smell of the train ride home hit him next as if he were forced to endure the aromas of the train in that moment. His nose curled then the smell was replaced by the young lady being humiliated in public by her boyfriend. Now he couldn't stop it. Barely clinging to the hope for sleep he almost descended to, the entire scene Sol saw play out on the Media Screen the day before, filled his mind. It was as if he were there, he watched the scrambling parents with their kids being escorted away from the murder scene, he saw the wind blowing the hair of the reporter, he watched again through the images in his head, as the police walked to the Mobile

Detainment Unit with the murderer. Then, as Sol readied himself for the shock of seeing a man shot, if even in his own mind yet again, the image focused in on the two officers with the murderer. He knew what was about to happen but watched as if he had never seen it. He couldn't turn his mind's eye away.

Here comes the gunshot he thought as he panned slightly towards the face of the vigilante shooter.

BANG!

Sol jerked sharply as the gunshot rang through his head. It was unavoidable, his imagination faithfully filled in the sound of the gunshot just as it had been trained to do. The murderer lay in a pile at the feet of the Police...the women and men who were supposed to keep a child murderer safe.

He fixed his sight on the shooter's killer and Sol's face went pale. Then he snapped out of the dream as he bolted up in his chair. Sitting up, white knuckling the arms of the chair, his breathing was rapid as he realized who the vigilante was in his vision. He saw the killer's face. The image stopped and all Sol could do was sit still. *"That's not right,"* Sol thought.

In the version of events in Sol's dream, he saw the killer's face and the face was clearly his own.

In this shocking scene that bridged reality with Sol's subconscious in a confused way, Sol struggled at the vision of seeing himself as the one who just killed the man who executed a dozen school-aged children. Sol was uncertain why his dreaming brain cast him in the role of vigilante at that second...and Sol was beyond uneasy at the disturbing mental image that could not be 'unseen'.

A Man Inspired

Eyes wide open; Sol pushed himself up out of the luxurious recliner. The Media screen was in sleep mode, and he shot a look of disdain at it as he started toward the kitchen to get a drink. He seemed to lay blame for the graphic nature of his vision on the digital bearer of bad news. The ever-present Media Screen that was in every wall, table, building, and public place. It was as easy to interact with a blank screen as it was with an active one. The relationship Sol had with the omnipresent medium was much the same as those of most viewers. Being involved with a Media Screen was a lot like a relationship with a gambling addict brother-in-law. When you gave it your attention, it would give a little, but the reality was that it was taking so much.

As his feet left the pillowy carpet of the den and landed back on the kitchen floor, he realized how chilled he had gotten. The warm floor of the kitchen chased a shiver up his spine as the chill was pushed out of his body. Sol tapped the coffee perc icon on the smart-countertop and softly said *"Medium."* An early morning coffee began to pour through the perc. He reached through the holo-cupboard door, grabbed his mug and set it on the counter next to the glowing icon of a steaming cup.

Sol glanced at the Tabletop Folio. The updated headlines were constantly streaming. At the top of the page, Sol read one that should have been meaningless to him. On any other day it would have gone in one eye and out the other without a thought. But this morning it didn't. And how does one stop a thought anyway? Like any of the citizens in this society, Sol was perpetually bombarded with thoughts. Were they his own, were they borrowed, were they some construct of a medium designed to invoke thoughts? Who knew? The trouble is few people could tell if the thoughts they had were their own or if they had filtered in from stuff they had seen or heard. Second-hand thoughts were often believed to be first-hand, but this thought was definitely not second-hand.

"They're probably going to fold," Sol mused to himself as he read the headline,

"Where Will The World Congress Go From Here?"

He didn't know where it came from or why it came but that thought wasn't worth considering. Or was it? *"Could the World Congress fold?"* Sol ruminated.

There had never been a Global Institution that had accomplished the things the World Congress had. All that News Stream asked was, '*Where Will The World Congress Go From Here?*' There was nothing said about the thing folding up.

It was completely unimaginable for most citizens. Few could even consider the repercussions of a near sovereign and widely favoured institution dissolving. Sol struggled to paint a picture of a world without the World Congress. The form of government that had been in place for over three decades was so influential and complex, people could not even conceive of anything else.

It is a highly successful world governing organization that had brought global society to places once only dreamed of. Sure, stagnation had seeped into the progress of the World Congress. There had been few pivotal plays in the last decade or so, but Sol puzzled to think of what could possibly replace it?

Sleep was the furthest thing from his mind now. Sol was deeply stirred. The Global Government agency was meeting again in the morning. Actually, in about four and a half hours now. And all the latest report fed the viewer was a subtle hint that the Delegates were met with a challenge of some sort. That the question even came up on News Feeds was astonishing. What could they possibly be considering that was so enigmatic there was a question about the direction the World Congress was about to take?

In the next second, Sol whirled around and grabbed the nearest Digital Folio off the counter. *Tap, swipe, tap.* "Where the ef is that stylus?" Sol whined as he searched the tabletop with hasty hand sweeps.

If there was anything that cranked Sol up it was when he needed a stylus and couldn't find one. After shuffling the placemats before feeling around the base of the fruit bowl on the table where the stylus often found its home, he slid his fingers down the back edge of the Folio and hissed "*Yes!*" Of all places, the stylus was right in the stylus slot.

With his chair pulled in tight the *tap tap* launched the Digital Folio and the Tabletop Folio into sync mode. The scribe feature was running, and Sol's coveted stylus began to furiously scrawl. *Swipe, tap* and the 27-inch Tabletop Folio that lay flat in the table, silently rose into easel mode. As Sol scribed on the digital folio, his work was displayed on the now upright Tabletop Folio. The thoughts flooded out of Sol's stylus and onto both screens. With a wedding night fervency, he ripped through line after line. After all that he had seen and all that had crept into his dreams and thoughts, the catharsis was flooding in as fast as the text was flooding out.

The World Congress comments portal was easy to access. Who knew how many or how few people threw their comments on there, but the letter Sol was writing to Chancellor Mahndar was by far the most passionate thing he had ever written. For all the inspired research he had done in his career, there was no single composition that burst forth like this. From the deepest recesses of his zeal for justice, equity, peace, and prosperity, his letter that early morning, poured out onto the Folio. And with powerful resonance, the words that left Sol reached back into Sol to grab some more. It didn't matter if his thoughts meant a thing to Chancellor Mahndar or to anyone else, Sol was captive to the need to write. He just had to get it out on paper. Each line he scribed was fuel for the next. Fighting to go back to sleep was just a moment in ancient history now. The vibrancy of a man inspired, transcended everything in those moments. Moments that were given over to a passionate plea for someone to do something to change the world.

You Never Know
What Might Happen

"**G**reetings Chancellor Mahndar and World Congress Delegates" Sol's letter started...

"You are to be lauded for the healthy Global Relations the people of this era have been privileged to enjoy, and for your immense contribution to our world."

In his ebullience and writing fury, Sol had begun by scribing his salutation sentence to the World Congress, then he had reached his hands up above his head in a pre-concerto stretch, and with focus and an uninterrupted flow, he composed the following...

"Which of us has not embraced the first ever in history, truly Global Community that has blossomed because of the wise and reasoned guidance of the Delegates of the World Congress? I admire you for having the courage and the humility to perform the tasks you do and work tirelessly in the capacity you all do. I am scarcely aware of the magnitude of the challenges and difficulties you must be faced with each month as you convene. Thank you for your commitment to ensure humankind is a race of progress and a people who are ever mindful of the fundamental value in pursuing Global Unity.

"My letter to you today is a letter of hope. I have come to realize there is a great sense of apathy pervading many citizens. I believe a great component that undergirds this apathy is the fact that most people feel they are observers in our world rather than participants. To the eyes of the typical citizen, the world is going on around them, practically encouraging apathy instead of compelling a citizen to participate in designing the world he, she, or they want. However, I believe there are many who are ready to meet this apathy with a response. A meaningful response aimed at proving they hope for a better world ahead. I am a citizen who is among those.

"Today was an extraordinary day in many respects. I shall not go into the details that led me to this letter. I will state however, the fact that our world seems to be successful in many ways on a large scale was overshadowed by the distressing reality of disruption and distress that is ever-present in this supposedly peaceful globe. Many would agree that we cannot truly enjoy peace when injustices occur every day on all levels of society. In many cases, these injustices are of such low amplitude that they have no appreciable impact on the greater Global progress. However, the eroding effects small injustices have had on culture, has led to this unyielding apathy, and a society that has become numb.

"We have been led to believe our world is at peace, yet one glance at daily News Feeds reveals a different picture. Every single day, the world we live in is in turmoil. And although you have mediated many major political advances in this world, I compel you to ask, *What is "The World?"*

"My answer to that question is simple. The World is more than a political arena or a geographical sectoring of nations and regions. Each one of us is the World. You are the world, I am the world, my neighbors are the world, and my coworkers are the world. But the World is so much more. The children who died yesterday in a school shooting are the world, the old man recovering from the trauma he suffered at the hands of his attackers is the world, the young boy who experienced unfathomable evil at the hands of a Priest he trusted is the world, and the woman who battles every day with fear of an abusive partner is the world. The world cannot be Nations and Regions before the world is men, women, children. And if there were no nations and regions in our world, there would continue to be a world of people.

"For some the world is one of hope, peace, and prosperity yet for those who suffer, their world is broken in many ways. And millions suffer injustices daily, all across this *"peaceful"* globe. When the world is broken for so many, can the world truly be whole for the rest of us? What seems whole when looked at from a distance, is really fragmented when our view gets painfully close.

"Wait, there are more fragmented individuals who are the world. What about those who afflict others by their unjust acts? By their acts of violence, disrespect, greed, and hate they cause the world to become fragmented. Are they not the world too? The rapist, the organized gang who escapes justice, the disturbed husband who abuses a partner, the school shooter who shatters the lives of defenceless families by killing the most vulnerable in their families. They too, are in every unpalatable way, as much "the world" as those who have suffered at their hands.

"It is a tragic statement on human development to see that a Global organization can tame the ferocity between thousands year-old conflicts in the Middle East, yet one old man trembles in his hospital bed at night after suffering alone in the dark at the hands of invaders. Pain is his only company as the nightmare of a home invasion terrorizes his slumber. Whose job was it to tame the violence that visited the old man in his home?

"The World Congress, charged with ensuring prosperity, progress, peace, and security for humankind, has been unable to ensure all of those things for untold millions of victims who are powerless individuals. But it is those powerless individuals who are "THE WORLD."

"One would have to be deluded to deny that we; you and I, have caused this to become what it is. By allowing social distortions to persist, we have designed this pain and crime-haunted society. Subtle to some but deafening to others. Fragmenting, apathy, and absence of peace exist everywhere.

"Perhaps, Chancellor Mahndar and Delegates, it is time to focus on the bottom end of 'The World.' It is time to focus on what is affecting those billions of individuals who make this "Our World." Perhaps we have arrived at one of those pivotal moments in world history. A keenly distressing moment where we are met with the greatest challenge we shall ever face. Our world is fragmented, who will fix it? I know I am not alone in believing it's time that we move to the next level.

"As you re-convene for two more days of Deliberations, I encourage you to consider the state of the Globe in a way that is not often considered. I believe there are solutions to the present stalling in human social growth and development. I support your work and am willing to participate in any way in order to advance our world. Together, by embracing the ideal that every individual global participant deserves the most prosperous, progressive, peaceful, and secure world that we can give; and by embracing the ideal that citizens must become participants in order to achieve that which has been elusive for all known human history, we can move towards a *"healthy"* world.

"I am confident the World Congress can guide the global community toward a cohesive and prosperous state. Yet today, as I weigh the sense of apathy that is prevalent in society, and I consider the societal distortions and injustices that have not ceased amid all the Global advances, I feel I am among many in this delicate era, who are asking the question.

What will the World Congress do to make a better world in this era?

"I respectfully submit my thoughts to you today. And ask that you please remember, Our World is the 11 billion individuals that inhabit it. And each of us is responsible to design a better world. Although this moment in history presents unsavoury distresses, injustices, and social violations, it is in this moment we need a leader who is willing to do the difficult but decisive things. Things that will move us toward the world each of us truly desires. One where all are assured that the world they share, is not simply better for some but it is truly better for all.

Sincerely,

Sol David James

Sol leaned back in his chair and set his stylus on the table. It slowly rolled to its place under the edge of the fruit bowl. The mouse pointer flashed, hovering over the 'SUBMIT' button at the bottom of the comments section. The Tabletop Folio dimmed as he stared at the words he had just written. His head was heavy, and his eyes slowly closed leading his chin to his chest. One bob then another, and his chin rested on his chest. Hearing the sound of his breath was the perfect sound of the rest he longed for only a couple of hours earlier.

"Maybe I'll just rest here before I head back to bed." Sol thought.

Another long, deep, breath. Sol was completely relaxed. The curve of the winged dining chair scooped comfortably around his back to hold him up. Then nothing. Just breathing and rest. It was good to be asleep again….

…"Hey, everything ok?" Ell's voice was soft as she leaned over his shoulder. A welcome embrace that brought Sol out of his meditative moment. He must have nodded off as he hadn't heard her come into the kitchen. With a twitch, his head popped up.

"Yeah, I'm fine." he said.

Seeing the words, *"Dear Chancellor Mahndar"* at the top of the upright Folio as she scanned the screen, Ell asked, "What's that about…ohhh that looks serious. Did you send it yet?"

She got the idea right away and she knew, after their discussions earlier, what she was seeing in front her. Ell saw that Sol was set to send the World Congress some very intense thoughts. Thoughts that may get shuffled right into the recycle bin or they might find the eyes of exactly the people Sol hoped them to.

"It's 5A.M.," Ell said. "You know they start up again in about three hours? You better send it."

Sol's pointer had not moved off the pulsating **SUBMIT** button. He looked up at Ell.

"Send it, she prompted encouragingly, "You never know what might happen, maybe the Chancellor will read it...." Ell paused..."For sure nothing will happen if you don't send it."

With one last glance at the screen Sol hit the **SUBMIT** button. His letter was sent.

In the same instant the auto reply popped up;

> *Thank you, your correspondence has been successfully submitted. Should the administrators at the World Congress Global Relations Center need to contact you regarding your submission we will do so within 7 business days.*

Sol stretched, got up and turned to Ell, she was still sleepy too. He hugged her and said "Thanks Doll, I'm beat. Let's head back to bed, its Saturday."

Little To Be Offered By Way Of A Solution

Chancellor Mahndar sat quietly in the stiff hotel chair in his suite. The décor was regal, but the comfort of the overstuffed armchair was disappointing for how inviting it looked.

"Obviously, it was a chair more for the eyes than for comfortable bottoms," the Chancellor thought.

The lamp dimly threw its light over the desk where his digital Folio lay. A luminescent notification brightened then faded, waiting to share the incoming messages it held. The Chancellor was meditative as he considered what form leadership might take in the coming months for the World Congress. He blankly stared past the desk to the damask patterned wallpaper. He had little concern about the waiting messages. The Chancellor knew what they were about. Messages had been coming in since he got back to his room. Committee heads and Delegates were buzzing with questions, ideas, concerns. The night had evaporated, and it was now 5:15AM. Chancellor Mahndar had not slept much that night. In fact, few Delegates spent much time in the sack. After the early release from Deliberations, then on to an anxious and busy supper with little time to chat about families, hobbies, or international buzz, Delegates landed back in their hotel rooms to decompress. By then it was early evening, and they all knew evening would turn into a long night.

The Chancellor had made a hasty retreat to his suite in order to digest the very thing he had charged the Delegates with. He too would consider deeply if the World Congress would be *"The Answer to Build A Better World?"* There was no mistaking the task ahead. Chancellor Mahndar was resolved to advocate for finding a solution. He sat and pondered, yet none came to him. Even still, Chancellor Mahndar was confident in the Delegates. And he had no knowledge of the meeting in room 912 that was just wrapping up as he sat alone thinking.

As he ruminated it clearly felt like a shift was coming. Late into the night, messages were fired back and forth. Pockets of Delegates gathered in each other's rooms throughout the late-night hours to ponder and discuss the issue, looking for answers. The famous early evening "After-Party" sessions had been vibrant. These were unofficial meetings where Delegates gathered in small, organic groups to engage each other on issues brought up in the Deliberations Chamber. The 'After-Party' meetings were taking place in rooms all over the hotel. In these impromptu committee sessions, Delegates from varied Regions would scrum then move on. The anxiety that began at supper over what the World Congress was to do, was striking a fever pitch by one in the morning. As the hours tolled on, most Delegates reached their limits for deliberating on the issue and the ad-hoc sessions started to thin out. Some Delegates had retreated to the comfort of their individual rooms one-by-one to get some sleep before the big Session the next day. By the middle of the night there were only a few groups left debating how the situation might be rectified. The closing question from the day's Session was still in front of each of them;

Is The World Congress The Answer to Build A Better World?

At 5:15 in room 912 at the end of the hall, the voices of women and men could be subtly heard from outside the door. They had been working this quandary over for four or five hours together.

Delegate Ahmed Marif tilted the bottle of Pinotage over the lip of Mihn Quinzo's almost empty wine glass. The full-bodied vintage had been shared by the After-Party groups. The aromatic wine enhanced the comfortable environment. Ideas flowed as Delegates opined in response to the serious question from the Speaker's Podium. Ahmed paused to see if she would accept the offer for a top up. Mihn waved off the offer for another glass of wine and carried on without pausing.

"One thing we all agree on after the Chancellor's address, is that for all the marvelous global advances humanity has enjoyed, there has yet been no resolution for the mindless injustices that impact millions daily." Mihn went on, "The Chancellor is absolutely right! These kinds of injustices are unceasing. I have many friends who are yet to feel safe when they take a stroll in the streets after dark. In the background of their mind, they will admit, a small but concrete fear lives. It shouldn't have to be that way. So many have these fears. Fears that we wish weren't real but yet one cannot deny they are there. I've been there."

Mihn proceeded to describe what she and so many late evening strollers often push down, in order to make that dark dangerous walk to the car on a cloudy moonless evening.

"Like the fear that there just might be someone lurking around the corner or watching as you move through the shadows. And I'm not trying to be sexist here, but if we're honest we can admit that generally speaking, for men it is not so haunting of a feeling to go out after dark or to go for an early morning stroll through a peaceful park. I've been all over the world and it's the same everywhere. The 1st and 2nd worlds are completely urbanized. And those cities have never been able to boast that all their female and othered citizens, are protected from men who wish to harm a person. In China a lone woman can't walk freely and comfortably in the night. And I know it's the same here in the U.S. Women have been dominated and controlled by fear of the night for as long as there has been night. Having decisions made for them for millennia, by the brutishness of testosterone-driven hooligans."

"I couldn't agree more Mihn," Devon Craik responded, "The USA is no different than China on this. My sister-in-law has been threatened and nearly accosted on several occasions when she heads out for a walk. She has told me more than once, her walks on the Wellness Wall path along the river, have left her shaken. These incidents aren't just happening after dark. They're happening in the middle of the day. She's leery to go out for a walk alone at times."

Mihn added, "And yes, the sinking part of the Chancellor's report was the powerful apathy that has grown on society. How can we expect people to feel inspired to participate in society? So many years have passed with nothing of any real value being done to change the inequities that are part of their every day."

"Zhat's a great quezstion Mihn." Darik Liiendor offered, in his subtle German accent. "Vee must explore zhat question. Zhere is so little impetuzs for people to work towardzs change. It eez as if zhere is no hope for change because zuh stage is built and all zee actors have been assigned zair roles."

Listening on, the group in 912 sensed an analogy was about to come. That was Liiendor's style…And his accent made it a delight to listen to

"I vunce heard from a world-renowned director of theater about changing the course of apathy zhat a production company vuzs on. His job was to come into zuh theater and bring new life, new inzspiration to an ailing and dull production. Zis man knew he was not zhere to change zuh script or redesign zuh stage. He vuz zhere to give zuh people direction. True direction zhat involved removing zose elements in each actor zhat were harming zuh performers and zee overall performance. Vunce he had removed all zee unpalatable behaviours, zuh true ezzence and beauty of zee actors personalities and zuh characters could rise to zuh top.

"Before he vusz appointed zuh position he would tell zuh cast and crew, zee only way to set zuh production on a new path to vitality was to let zuh new director take over zuh directing completely. Once he was appointed, he was completely in charge of inspiring zuh cast and crew to draw on zhere deepest passions to excise the unwanted aspects of zhere performance and to restore an ailing production. Most would throw zhere trust and support behind zhis new director. Believing in zuh hope zhat he represented. Some would want to quit, othersz would want to attack zuh director, but when hisz plan played out, zee answer was clear. Everyone had zuh skills and heart to perfect zee performance. Zay just needed a powerful new director to set out zuh path to prosperity."

Delegate Craik looked toward Mihn. *"Was she puzzled or was she processing Liiendor's statement?"* he wondered.

Craik turned back to Liiendor who was sipping on a freshly poured glass of Pinotage. Five AM might as well be seven PM as far as enjoying wine with friends was concerned for Darik.

Craik postured slightly, "Darik, are you suggesting the World Congress find a new 'Director' to fix this problem? I see your tale of the ailing theatrical team as a metaphor. I'm not sure you meant it that way Darik but what if there is an answer to our problems in your story?"

"Yes, I believe it is a metaphor," Darik answered.

As Devon Craik glanced affirmingly at Delegate Liiendor he offered, "I see your point, it's becoming more and more obvious that the problem is not going to be fixed by the actors. We can agree to all the successful policy on Global Relations, the international economy, migration, or Global Language we want. Facts are, the cause of the apathy we face is rooted in decades of stagnation. Stagnation due to a hopeless attitude towards fixing the ills in our society. It seems that when there is no threat of Global Nuclear War, and we enjoy virtual peace and security on the large scale; people decide to stop demanding peace and security on the small scale. It is very clear that we have been impotent in our institutional influence to appreciably diminish so many problems. True we have been very successful at moving the globe and her citizens towards world peace and international unity, but our pursuits have not brought the peace that people crave in their individual lives.

When we place this world under the microscope, we have not made life better for every individual in every way. As Chancellor Mahndar said in his address, *'In ensuring humanity as a whole experiences peace, we have not been able to ensure each human enjoys peace in his or her insular world'*...we have missed the opportunity to deliver what is most coveted by each person, it is as if we have lost the trees in the forest. How can people truly get peace?"

Mihn jumped back in and everyone in the room agreed with what she had to say.

"A mold has been formed and the cast is set. The apathetic response to social distortions and injustice is an embedded template in the collective consciousness of society. Society has resigned itself to the present reality. The template we have designed is pressing people into a cast of resignation and apathy. How have we not seen that it is our template that is flawed?"

Mihn's eyes looked around the room. Those present, Delegates from China, Pakistan, USA, and Germany, were silent. Ten in all. Ahmed Marif stared into his wine glass as he gently swirled it. Other than that, the room was still. He was just one of the many concerned Delegates in the World's most thorough, productive, and effective government organization. It was no secret; they were faced with an extraordinary problem.

The scent of the fruity Pinotage rose to his nostrils as the hypnotic cadence of the swirl began to entrance him. Fatigue was definitely taking over the room. For hours now, this group had been deliberating in an unofficial setting, sipping on the finest wine in the building, and openly pondering not just the problem in front of them, but the solution. In past After-Parties, the solutions they were waiting on had not been chased away by sharing a couple glasses of wine. The purpose and intention to advance the issue for this select group of world leaders always proved to dredge up just the right answers from the sea of possibilities that experience had birthed in each of them.

The World Congress was known for its expedience in addressing and rectifying concerns. And the way late night talks were going, tonight was no exception. The monthly Inclusions Sessions were no retreat. This is how things went; Delegates would come to the World Congress Center for Global Relations each month ready to get to work. Over the past decades, a Chancellor or committee would present the dilemma. Then, at the end of the day, as evening set in, ad-hoc groups of delegates would unofficially end up in other Delegate's rooms. Discussions would start and the brilliant and committed minds of these Delegates would put forth solutions.

As with any international political gathering, at times there would be strong disagreements in these ad-hoc committee meetings. In most cases however, late night to early morning talks would be dynamic. Ideas would fly, hope would fuel the session, wine would be shared, and ultimately, in almost every case in the history of the World Congress, by the middle of the morning at the Inclusions Sessions the following day, a motion would be made that would eventually be passed to resolve the issue.

The women and men of the World Congress did not lack understanding of the issues. Each representative had the ability to apply their experiences and observations to the issue, and the drive to move a solution forward and put it into action. And today, as with other days, an unremarkable display of keen aptitude would been seen in the meeting in room 912.

The after-hours meetings came to be known as "After-Parties," simply because they took place after the day's meetings and supper. However, there was seldom any "Partying" when the face-to-face deliberations ensued. It was at these gatherings that solutions would bubble up and begin to take form. It would not matter if Delegates from Japan, Canada, Australia, and Romania had stretched an evening into an early morning. Any group who met was very interactive and intensely engaged in meaningful dialogue. World Congress Delegates always delivered. But on this occasion, there was little to be offered by way of a solution to the problem presented.

True Measures to Make Them Stop

The room had been still for a few moments. The Delegates had been deeply engaged in the question of where government should go from here. Many pondered Liiendor's input about the "cast" needing a new "director" in order to get the world on the right path. Most Delegates were all but tapped out and ready to fade off to their individual suites…only to wait for another chance to dialogue about the situation.

In the quiet moment Ahmed Marif, one of the delegates from Pakistan, had his sister in mind. He was considering the injustices felt across the world and the injustice she had once suffered. He had seen firsthand the destructive results of a harsh and violent world. Then the thoughtful tone of Ahmed broke the silence.

"It is true that we need a new "Director", Ahmed Marif emphasized with air quotes, "When we can truly say the "Director" we have been under is not working out then we must face that."

Ready now for the wine that was offered a few minutes ago, Mihn reached over and poured herself half a glass of what was left of the Pinotage. Perhaps the aroma that drifted from the aerated glass of her friend caught her. Whatever it was, was lost in the moment as she finished pouring and her eyes joined the other After

Party Delegates and moved over to Marif. The soft-spoken Delegate from Pakistan had captured her full attention. Marif went on.

"This is a comfortable globe we have constructed, yet the report we heard today speaks of such widespread discomfort. How is this so? And more so, how is this so yet we continue to do as we have always done, advancing in many ways yet bringing no resolution to the thorns in society's flesh? We have barely offered even a salve to ease the sting that blisters on that flesh."

Marif had such conviction in his tone. Others in the room were feeling it, and some wished more delegates were sitting in on this gathering. It was clear he was sharing from the place of his true experiences.

The impassioned statement by this man was inspiring. It was from a very deep place. Marif had lost a sister in Pakistan to the hand of a violent husband 8-years ago. He had known of her distress, and she had even come to him on one occasion. Ahmed spoke of the situation in this moment. Retelling the story while displaying the regret he had for not doing more. It was a tragedy he wished he could forget. He will often revisit the day she came to get help from Ahmed, and he had none.

"Ahmed," she pleaded, "he is a monster, I am afraid. Look Ahmed, look what he has done!" she wept as she pushed up the sleeve of her kameez.

Ahmed had held-in his gasp when he saw the bruising that day. His sister's arm did not lie. The flesh on the back of her arm looked painfully tender and the dark bruising held the outline of fingers. It just about wrapped around the entire arm and extended down the back from below her shoulder. Ahmed looked away, "Sister, are you hurt anywhere else?"

"Not this time Ahmed, but I am lucky he stopped."

Ahmed's sister went on to tell him how her husband's gambling had gotten out of hand and when she asked him about it, he threatened her to try to make her stop. She pressed him and he stormed at her, grabbing her by her arm and her hair.

She was afraid and struggled to get away, but he just squeezed harder as he shook her violently and dragged her into the bedroom. It was horrifying for her because she knew he was out of control. He was either going to beat her or rape her again. Another "secret" beating and maybe another domestic rape. She didn't know how bad it was about to get. In about 30 seconds she would find out.

With no one in the room to help her, she searched for a way to help herself hoping someone would hear her screams. She thought, "*Why do I deserve this?*" Wishing in vain there was someone…anyone…who could help her, to defend her from her husband the monster.

Equal rights movements had made some positive advances in many parts of the world but there were no equal rights in Ahmed's sister's home. True, the percentage of women in political leadership and chief management positions was only a few percent behind that of their male counterparts. But far too frequently, men still displayed their disdain and often veiled their misogyny. There were still men in some Regions who thought they could do whatever they wanted. In fact, there were still some men in every Region whose insurmountable weakness and insecurity was projected toward women. It often manifested in completely unacceptable actions. Power posturing, sexual innuendo and harassment, career sabotage to keep women from advancing ahead of men, and sometimes violence against women. Almost halfway through the 21st century it was shocking to see just how prolific domestic abuse incidents were. The rates from 25 years ago had only marginally declined.

An oft cited Eurobarometer report identified that over two in five women have experienced physical and/or sexual violence, from either a current or previous partner. The abuse patterns in Scandinavian countries were even outpacing that of the EU. Men had struggled to evolve with the changing gender roles and for decades, women have suffered because of the tensions and stress factors that grew out of that.

In many regions some men would just diminish their wife's rights while they were in the home. Passively at times and not so passively at other times. The brutality of a bitter man would result in the loss of freedom for some and the loss of life for others. Far too many men had harbored resistance to historical DEI movements that placed women in positions of equity with men. In many ways that sense of loss was internalized and resulted in a male resistance to the push for full equality. For all the men who had embraced the progress of women's equality, many, such as Ahmed's brother-in-law, overtly refused to embrace it.

The incident that drove his desperate sister to pleading with Ahmed that day was intense...they always were. Only Ahmed knew of it. And only Ahmed knew how she had screamed as her raging husband dragged her towards the bed tearing at her hair and squeezing her arm harder. He raised his hand to strike...she closed her eyes.

Somehow, she hoped that turning away would make it hurt less. Her scalp felt like it was bleeding from being dragged by her hair, and her arm was searing from being violently clenched by her husband.

Just as he was about to lower his hand to strike, his cell phone rang. He stopped instantly because of the incoming call from his bookie. He threw her down on the floor by the bed, grabbed his phone from his pocket and bolted out of the house. Fortunately for her, gambling was even more important than beating her that day. There was no hello into the phone on the way out, just angry yelling accusing the bookie of stealing from him after losing yet another long-shot wager. Ahmed could have offered more on this situation, but time pressed down on the group...so he held back from sharing further and silence took over the room.

Ahmed's silence left space for his thoughts to continue. The images and memories of that time reminded him of telling his sister to "keep it down" when she petitioned him for help that day. They would talk about it later, he had told her, because the kids were coming up the lane, home from school. But they never did talk about it later. That incident was nine-years ago, and now, it was eight-years ago when his sister saw only one way out.

On the night she died by suicide, Ahmed received a call from his wife-beating brother-in-law, crying on the other end of the phone. All of a sudden, the abusive, selfish bastard decided he cared about the wife he had tortured all these years. It was then Ahmed wished he could turn back time. Why hadn't he stepped in earlier?

Many days since then, Ahmed wished an end to his brother-in-law's life, for the years of his monstrous abuse that ultimately drove her to kill herself. Even more so, he regretted his inaction.

Ahmed's hopeless and broken sister had swallowed a bottle of pills and drowned in the bathtub. Most of the family wanted to believe it was an accident, but Ahmed knew she needed out. He also knew there were stories like this all over the world. He broke the silence with his pleading question to his fellow Delegates

"Why hasn't our system been working? All everyone wants is peace but there seems to be no end to the tumors of injustice that are growing every day. What true measures to make them stop have ever really been taken?"

Everyone knew the answer was, *little to nothing.*

Possessed By The People

Of African descent, American Delegate Erin Whist was moved by the discussion with Ahmed and all the Delegates at the After-Party. Room 912 held a diverse group that night. She had been quiet in the last 30 minutes or so. She was deeply considering what could be done to resolve the issue. It was becoming clear for the entire group of Delegates in the room. All of a sudden it didn't feel like the World Congress truly had its finger on the pulse of the world. A world that was made up of individuals. And that was very disenchanting for the trendsetters in room 912.

Mother of two, with an extensive background in political history research, Delegate Whist brightened. "Have any of you heard of Suleyman?"

Some in the group looked puzzled. Delegate Liiendor asked, "Isn't zhat zuh Delegate from Afghanistan?"

"No that's Suladin," she replied. "He might recall who Sulyeman is and he'd probably be flattered you connect him with Suleyman the Magnificent."

"Vell, who isz Suleyman?" Liiendor inquired.

Erin Whist stretched to get moving as she stood and went over to the decorative map the World Congress hotel had on the wall of every room. Her skirt was wrinkled from sitting sipping wine during the past hours of conversation. The wrinkles fell out of the hybrid fabric as she reached to point to an area around Saudi

Arabia. She looked at Liiendor as her manicured finger pointed to several areas on the map.

"Suleyman…and Suladin, both have a connection to this area, the Ottoman Empire as it was known in the early 1500's. Suladin I am not so sure about, Suleyman however, was known for great things. Let's just say it wasn't him who gave himself the name '*Suleyman the Magnificent*.'"

The 912 group was enthralled now. Fuzzy heads started to clear and the recent feelings of late-night exhaustion were pushed out by an odd wave of exhilaration from the intriguing moment.

Whist's co-Delegate, Devon Craik, perked up.

"He must have been quite the guy to go down in history as '*The Magnificent*.' So, what was up with your friend Suleyman Erin?" He questioned.

Erin waxed on, "Suleyman was an amazing ruler. There are few in history who can boast accomplishments for society and government like he can. I am not going to give a whole history lesson here, but the long and short of it is this;

"Suleyman rose to power in the Ottoman Empire at a young 25 years of age. And he ruled till his death at age 72. This man was said to be one of the greatest rulers of the Ottoman Empire, he is referred to as '*The Great Builder*'. The Ottoman Empire reached a pinnacle of power and prosperity under his reign.

"History shows this impassioned leader engendered an intense loyalty from his people. They felt he truly was a benevolent ruler and strove to achieve the greatest good for the greatest number.

"Any ruler who sponsors scores of artists, religious thinkers and philosophers will draw people and power to himself. But when affirming the elite of society the way Suleyman did, is coupled with freeing slaves and building schools for them, as well as showing appreciation to the leaders and officers who protect and advise you, that ruler becomes…well just as his title says.…"

"Magnificent!"…Delegate Mihn interrupted,

"I think you guys are getting the picture. This guy had a knack for improving society. He would not ignore real justice because he saw the people cried out for it. This is why he was also called '*Kanuni*'. It means 'The Lawgiver.' Not because he changed or created a set of religious laws, those were already established by the Empire's Holy Books. He was '*The Lawgiver*' because of the way he applied wisdom to situations. He made judgments and enactments that met the people where they were at, not trying to drag their situations into the pages of some Holy Book. His framework allowed him to deal with human issues that affected people's lives where their boots landed rather than on some ivory tower policy model. He was the kind of King who would say, "*We will cut the baby in half*" in order to have the issue resolve itself. No wonder Suleyman the Magnificent was named after King Solomon the Wise. That period of history is still remembered as the period of greatest justice and harmony ever experienced."

Delegate Whist returned to the couch…reaching up and removing her earrings before sinking into the cushion, she finished by saying, "Is it possible that a leader like Suleyman might benefit our world today? It is true there is no end to the list of despots and corrupt rulers, but I am starting to think we have met with the time that our world could benefit from funnelling all this democracy back to one benevolent and powerful leader."

The Delegates in room 912 were able to see the cycle of history and Democracy's limited success, resulting in disappointing divisions and failures. Democracy had served society well for hundreds of years and it had spread through the globe because of its effectiveness. Democracy had been wonderful at building nations and establishing policy. Democracy has given a voice to the people in some ways and inspired rich men to engage in the process of developing government. It brought new possibilities for generating wealth and united the world in ways previously impossible under a plethora of individual monarchies. But democracy was really a response to a broken system of sovereigns. Erin continued her full thoughts as she gave in to the sofa that enveloped her weary frame.

"If we examine the history, we will find power had to be forcibly removed from corrupt rulers…or at least the perception of power. And the Greek style of democracy was a viable, although complex, answer to that problem. Had the people been privileged to have a ruler who truly served them, responded to their needs and input, and rejected the draw to corruption, then it seems society could have embraced and moved forward together with…" Erin took pause as she considered the gravity of the next words to come out of her mouth.

"…Well I suppose society could have moved forward successfully with a King."

The room livened further. Shuffling in their seats and sitting just a little more erect, Erin could see the group was intrigued by her brief history lesson if not in fact moved by it.

Just before their attention fell away with thoughts that were triggered by her words of great and not so great Kings, Erin asked her captivated audience a powerfully provocative question.

"Have the last centuries, centuries that have seen the Gospel of Democracy sweep the globe, locked us into a commitment to forever employ the familiar democratic model? Or…" Erin paused and looked at Devon her co-Delegate who knew she was about to challenge the entrenched thinking of a brilliant group of democracy supporters…"Or, has history been teaching us a lesson that we are only now on the doorstep of learning?

"Could it be that the centuries-long path to democracy has really been a path back to a Sovereign? Are we able to consider that democracy has us circling back to find a leader who will reform society and literally do the greatest good for the greatest number? A leader who is truly, in the most profound and organic sense, The People's King. One who will lead with heart, humility, and courage? Maybe it is possible and maybe it is time."

"Wow!" Marif jumped in.

He was entertainingly animated when he got excited, with his frazzled hair and large brown eyes.

"That is a revolutionary thought Erin. As you spoke, I remembered other 'leaders'…we might as well call them "kings"…who led their regions to great heights. I recall Caesar Augustus and his Pax Romana, Kangxi of the Qing Dynasty in China, and Cyrus the Great of the Persian Empire, these "kings" advanced human rights, brought broad social reforms for their period, freed people from oppressive regimes, and ushered in some of the longest periods of peace in human history." Ahmed held his breath for a second and then stated;

"I think it is possible for us to see the value of having a King."

The Delegates in room 912 had forgotten the late hour. The vibrant sense of possibility electrified the room. The buzz of considering such a concept was resonating.

"Do you think we should present this idea at the Inclusions Session tomorrow?"

Everyone paused to hear Mihn Qhinzo.

"What do you say?…there has never been a recommendation of this magnitude in the World Congress history."

Erin answered Mihn's question with another.

"Could it be this is the way we need to go? What better way to find out than to introduce the idea to the other Delegates at tomorrow's session?"

Devon Craik was feeling oddly warm to the idea, so he seconded the suggestion, "That is perfect. It's past 5AM now, so we should get a few winks before the 8:30AM Session starts."

Craik thrived on just these kinds of exchanges. In fact, most Delegates were fueled by the impassioned interactions and often torrid pace of the official and unofficial meetings during Inclusions Sessions weekends. But before we part ways friends, I would like to mention the works of Chinese philosopher Master Hui. I recently read some excerpts from one of his volumes, *"The Art of the People's King."*

"Vwhut dusz he say in dis vwork Devon?"

You could tell it was late, Liiendor's well controlled accent was losing a little of its clarity. A little wine and a lot of missed sleep played on his tongue.

Devon shared, "Master Hui speaks to the idea of corruption. The idea that corruption is not a guaranteed response by one with absolute power. We haven't gotten into it here tonight, but I am certain it will come up tomorrow. The fear of absolute power corrupting a leader. There are few Kings and world Rulers who fend off corruption successfully. So many of them fall to their vices or desires. Leaving a bad taste in the mouth of the people. But Master Hui teaches why this is so in many cases. He doesn't suggest the human condition can be completely overcome but he does guide us to conceive of the possibility that a King who rejects corruption can exist. Master Hui says, and I am paraphrasing here;"

Remove the threat of war and the need to defend a land and the King can lead benevolently.

Remove the temptation to capture a foreign land and gain its' wealth and a King can build wealth for all people.

Eliminate the draw to destroy those of another race, color, or religion and a King can bring life to all citizens.

If we choose a King who has limits to his power and possession, then desire in him can find a foothold. Corruption is nurtured by desire.

But choose a King where all is his and he will have no room for corruption. His desire is for the people. A true King will be as possessed by the people as the people are possessed by him.

Ahmed was less animated this time, but he certainly perked up at Devon's words when he interjected to say his goodnights. His hair was still tousled and his shirt untucked, but he was still very clear in relaying his thoughts.

"Well, I am still inspired and exhilarated by what we have discussed tonight. And before I head off to bed for a couple of precious hours, I must say, there will be a lot to discuss with the Delegates in the morning. It is not everyday Delegates get to discuss what things would look like if we were to appoint a King of the World."

Hey Boys, How's the Coffee Today?

Who didn't love these days? It was early enough in the morning that the streets were still spotted with one person here, two people there and plenty of open sidewalk for the hundreds more that would fill them shortly. The roasted coffee beans from the café wafted out the French garden doors and onto the patio. Sol had arrived early and taken a spot in along the fence. On the other side was an empty bench with a huge Norway maple nudged up right beside it. The yellow-bronze leaves sprawled out halfway over the patio. They had turned from brilliant red since the last time Sol stopped at Starbucks. Sol shared the patio with a few other early morning coffee peace-seekers on this sunny, slightly breezy, early fall morning. At least it was early for a Saturday morning.

As he sipped on his coconut latte, Sol wondered if the others on the patio that morning felt the sense of thrill as he did when he looked forward to his bi-weekly ritual. A coffee date that capped off his busy weeks and fueled him for the weeks ahead. looking at his watch it didn't even matter that Gavin and Rosslyn were a couple minutes late. It was Saturday and Sol was the last one to be a slave to time on such a glorious morning.

Distracted by the scratches on the face of his watch, Sol began to muse about getting a new watch soon. Seemed these things only lasted a couple of years then they needed replacing. *"Humph...Timex...even they have been seduced by engineered obsolescence. No one built anything that lasted anymore. Watches, cars, appliances, Media Screens, computers"*.... Sol smiled as he grabbed his mug and focused on it for an extra second or two. *"These things never become obsolete"* he thought. His mug could have been put into service last week or a decade ago, it didn't matter when, the thing was timeless, functional.

"Perfect" he thought. Sol loved his coffee, everyone did in Seattle. And he'd never met a mug that let him down.

"Hey Sol, how's it going?"

Sol's head snapped up. He was a little startled not expecting that interruption to his "deep" musings about the enduring and redeeming qualities of coffee mugs.

"Hey, good morning guys, how's things?"

Gavin and Rosslyn were striding by on the other side of the fence, hurrying their way to the entrance. "Sorry we're a couple minutes late, we'll just grab a cup and be right there."

Sol and Gavin didn't see as much of each other since Gavin moved to a different floor at the library. Boy did they ever cover a lot of ground when they used to run the 4th floor of the University library. Sol knew how much Gavin loved diving into profound and philosophical topics, just as much as Sol did himself. During one of their unfiltered discussions, a group of grad students ended up staying past closing time at the library. Gavin and Sol had a major dialogue about the socialization of children as it relates to gender roles. Sol brought up the question, well actually, it was more of a philosophical thought. He questioned if women ran the world would it be a slightly gentler and more well-run world?

On this occasion, Gavin really got going on Sol's point, a point that suggested women are often more empathic and the world would likely be gentler under a woman's hand. Their conversations always drew an audience of students ready for a distraction from their studies. Nothing was ever truly solved in their workplace sessions of rhetoric. They were just engaging sessions, thought provoking and often provocative…nonetheless they were sessions both Gavin and Sol had always loved.

Now, since they had landed in different departments after a staffing shuffle at the University, the brief but regular Saturday morning coffee dates they had together with their wives were always times to look forward to.

"Where's Ell?' Rosslyn asked as she and Gavin gently positioned their coffees on the subtly wobbly bistro table and they sat into their chairs.

"She went to a later class this morning. We got a bit of a late start, so she still wanted to get her yoga in before coffee." Sol replied, reminding himself of the late-night letter writing to the World Congress that had him crawling back to bed after 6 that morning.

Traffic was starting to pick up on the streets now. The Suburb-Shuttles would stop in sequence and the five or six passengers that stepped off on the sidewalk just a few moments ago, turned into a dozen and a half each time the Shuttle stopped. It only took five or ten minutes, and the streets went from spotty to bustling. On a Saturday though, things downtown were very different than the weekdays. The bustle got going a little slower on weekends. The whole Seattle area started to come alive after 9:30 but any other day of the week the streets would be full from 8 in the morning right to 6 at night. And the crowds never looked happy. Even on a Saturday morning the people moving back and forth had a subtle scowl on their faces. *"Does anyone ever really just relax?"* Sol often wondered as he was enjoying his relaxing coffee date. *"Life is way too serious; I'd love to know what people are thinking."*

The Seattle area was always growing. And it showed. You could feel the tension in the crowds. Suburb-Shuttles floating in silently every 7.5 minutes with a cargo of

50 to 60 disgruntled passengers. Like every urban center, the place just felt full these days. People on top of people. Just a couple decades ago the Seattle area was already pressured by a population density no one ever thought it would see. Back then Seattle saw 6700 people per square mile and today, in 2043, the Seattle-Tacoma-Bellevue area is squeezed at every seam. Sitting around 11,000 people per square mile. That means every person has only about a 55-foot square space to occupy. All numbers aside, it was tight. Living anywhere was tight with the urbanization that had been unstoppable, having torridly ballooned to uncomfortable size and population densities.

Sol and Gavin had one of their discussions about population density some time ago. They figured if you parked three Public Suburb-Shuttles next to each other on the road that would be the amount of space each person in the city would be allowed to occupy. Now that is just not enough room for a guy to fend off the feelings of claustrophobia that begin to swell up when people all try to fill an area like the Seattle Metro. The consensus was that there were just far too many people crammed into cities.

Sol brightened again as he saw Ell heading towards them with her duffle over her shoulder and her jacket in hand. It was still surprisingly warm downtown for an early fall morning.

"Morning Ell," Rosslyn sang, "How was yoga this morning?"

Ell smiled back, happy to get with her long-time friends again for a visit. "The instructor was fired last night for falsifying her Yoga Instructor's certificate, so class was cancelled.

"Ohh, that sucks," Rosslyn offered.

"No worries, it's all good. Actually, I filled in and the class let me take them through a breathing behavior session. It turned out pretty good..."

She turned to Sol and Gavin. "Hey boys, how's the coffee today?"

"Great," they both chorused.

Sol continued, "Yours is already covered, you just have to tell the barista when you order."

"Excellent, be right back," Ell said as she headed to the counter.

Without Even A Blip In the Everyday Rhythm

The coffee trio chatted as they waited for Ell to join them at the table. The Shuttle whooshed to the curb a short bit away. Even the brakes were quiet on those units. Fully automated, no driver just a concierge on board for supervision, and barely a whisper from the nuclear-powered engine. As Ell's duffle dropped to the ground she said, "Who doesn't love these coffee dates, it should be a law, I love seeing you guys."

Ell was kept from enjoying Gavin and Rosslyn's response by her distracted husband who was enthralled with the Shuttle that was just about to wheel into the curb.

"Sol, what's going on? Are you planning to join us or is the big bus just so much fun to watch?" She mocked playfully.

"Check those guys out!" He was talking in hushed tones. The group looked over and Sol gave a little more commentary.

"Those two guys were just shoving around that kid in the back of the bus."

It was clear what was going on from Sol's perspective, as the Shuttle came to a stop. Two late teens or early twenties guys were among the riders that stood in the aisle as the Shuttle pulled into its stop. Sol was focused closely on them seeing the first of the two grab at the messenger bag slung over the shoulder of a much younger teen stuck between the two. They shoved the kid and roughly bumped him into the seat-back of the seat next to the exit. Sol obviously didn't know any of them and the concierge on the Shuttle wasn't paying attention to the tussle. Sol kept watching.

Standing in line at the door to exit, the smaller kid had been herded between the two guys who were, what Sol had decided, obviously making trouble. This didn't feel right, the kid looked scared, and Sol wasn't sure the rest of his foursome were picking up on what he was seeing. He started to tense up…. coil up might be a better description, as his adrenaline surged at this scene unfolding in front of him.

Rosslyn asked, "Do you think the concierge will do something?" No one answered.

The Shuttle nudged into its stop and riders began streaming out the mid-Shuttle exit. As the first of the two bullies stepped off, he turned and pushed his hand towards the head of the smaller rider trapped in between the two. The second guy grabbed at the shoulder strap of the messenger bag and whipped it over the boy's head and shoulder as the smaller rider was forced off balance from the shove of the first. Watching closely Sol was ready…to do something…but not sure what.

The moment that first guy turned to shove the smaller rider, who was maybe a 15- or 16-year-old kid, Sol leapt from his chair. Vaulted over the enclosed patio fence and sprinted to the Shuttle just as the under-matched teen spun to wrestle his bag from the thief. No one else on the street seemed to care. The bag was quickly tossed to his buddy already a few meters away.

Without hesitation, Sol came sprinting in hard from the side and clutched the throat of the thief, slamming him against the side of the Shuttle. "Hey," He shouted right up in the thief's face now. "Leave the kid alone!"

But before he could grab the messenger bag and demand its return, the toss was finished, and it was out of the thief's hands.

Sol should have just held the thug he was clutching. But his grip shifted as he lurched toward the bag to try to retrieve it from the second thug. Neither Sol nor the thieves knew what was in it. But if we're talking about a 15- or 16-year-old here, his entire digital life was probably in that sack. Sol could sense his desperation.

Sol's lurch to grab for the bag that was clearly out of reach, weakened his grip further on the slippery neck he was throttling. And the thief with the bag didn't stop to offer amends. He instinctively sprinted away. His buddy, who squirmed out of Sol's clutch, bolted right behind him.

Sol didn't know Gavin was right there with him as he looked up from asking the 15-year-old if he was ok. Gavin was just coming to a stop after a brief but valiant attempt to chase the thieves. Too little too late to nab the bastards. The two friends watched helplessly on as the messenger bag trailed the first thief across the street. It disappeared with the fleeing thief into the throngs that now filled both sides of Madison Street. The second thief was not yet across the street where his buddy had already found refuge among the crowds. Sol and Gavin both stood watching him run through the teeming people. Before racing across the street to rejoin his accomplice, the petty thief turned back to mockingly flip the bird at Sol. The meddling bystander who had moments ago been his captor with the punk's throat in his hand.

No one expected what happened next. As quick as Sol had leapt the fence of Starbucks, the front of a Shuttle met the petty thief in the middle of the road.

WHAM!!!

The belligerent thug didn't see it coming. It would have been poetic if it were the Shuttle he had just been on. Maybe a bit severe for shoving around a smaller kid with a messenger bag full of tech stuff, but poetic nonetheless. The Shuttle slammed into him when he blindly stepped in front of it as he ran to catch up with his thieving buddy…just as he was looking back in defiance at his would-be captor with his middle finger still raised high in the air.

Tires screeched, horns honked, the usual traffic chaos. No time to be surprised for this hooligan. A moment of mockery quickly turned into a moment of pain and involuntary flight as the forces of the impact resulted in a 10-foot launch through the air. Then…inertia. Not much blood and no damage to the hulking Shuttle. Those things were never damaged by the daily bump and grind.

The nameless victim and the Shuttle were perfectly still now amid a teaming metropolis.

Both Sol and Gavin resisted their instinct to race over and see the carnage. It would all be replayed on Media Screens enough to watch it later. By the time their thoughts caught up with what just happened the concierge had jumped out of the Shuttle. Traffic was halted by the illuminated delineators deployed from the Shuttle and the incident isolation markers were set in place by the concierge.

Nothing unusual here. Pedestrians were bowled over all the time by public transport vehicles. Just another by-product of overpopulated metropolitan areas. And within moments, bystanders went on their way as traffic found its way around the markers. In about three minutes, the authorities would be on scene to briefly investigate, extract the video data from the onboard cam, and clear the Shuttle for continued operations. It was pretty formulaic. The whole scene would be cleaned up, cleared up, and forgotten about within 15 minutes.

Gavin had caught his breath now and asked Sol if he was ok as he loped back to his buddy. "Wow!" Gavin slapped Sol on the shoulder, "I knew you could move old buddy but that was fantastic."

Sol replied while turning around, "Yah but this kid had his bag stolen…"

He turned to check on Seattle's latest mugging victim. The kid was already gone. Sol panned the throngs but there was no sign of him. "Hmm…maybe I cared what was in his bag more than he did."

"Who knows?" Gavin responded pointing casually down the street at the motionless Shuttle, still shadowing the lifeless pedestrian's body. "Looks like he's not gonna find out what was in the kid's bag today either."

Sol contorted his face and shook his head trying to force himself to let it go, still vibrating from the intensity. A moment ago, he had a stranger pinned against a Shuttle by his neck, and risked getting beaten or stabbed for a 16-year-old kid who didn't give a rat's ass about his own bag. Then he saw a petty thief get pasted by a Shuttle in the middle of Madison Street, and no one seemed to care. Business as usual on a Saturday morning.

Gavin was still chirping about the dude splattered on the road as they made their way back to the girls. The barista brought the table a fresh round of beverages on the house for the dramatic heroics and the live entertainment they provided. The foursome jittered on their seats as they shook off the disruption before settling back in for the visit they all had looked forward to.

"Are you ok hun? That was a little scary." Ell had always been intrigued by the drama of life and this was definitely worth liking, as far as drama was concerned.

"Yah thanks, I'm fine. I should have hung on to that guy, he was so slimy." Sol replied as he brushed his hands off slowly.

Sol went on, "And I wanted somebody, anybody besides Gavin and me, to jump in and help this kid out. But there was no one. No one is ever there anymore. Everyone is always somewhere else. I mean they're "there" but they aren't. They are stuck in their own little bubble of *see-no-evil-hear-no-evil—and do nothing about all the evil*…while shit is going on all around them."

Sol seemed quite upset about it. Ell stroked his arm understandingly and turned to Gavin and Rosslyn, "It was just this morning Sol sent a letter to the World Congress about this kind of stuff."

"What do you mean?" Gavin's eyes widened in an overly theatrical way. "O my God Sol, what have you done?"

Gavin knew how Sol could stir the pot around work when he would send a letter to the administration. To say Gavin was both intrigued and curious at hearing of the letter to the World Congress was a bit of an understatement. Gavin dispensed with polite sensitivities. Eager to hear about this juicy letter, he prodded, "Tell me about it!"

As Ell started to talk about the letter, the Pavlovian tones of the Media Screens chimed, igniting all the mobile devices, folios, and Media Screens in the area. Each one of the foursome looked up to the nearest wall. Some patrons held their mobile devices in their hands, and everyone paused to take in the latest info. The subtle chime readied everyone for the Live Stream from the DBN.

The interruptive Streaming was deemed necessary to provide valuable info. It wasn't even really an interruption anymore. A lot like when a kid is mugged and the mugger gets killed by a rogue Shuttle…without even a blip in the everyday rhythms of downtown Seattle, everything is back to "normal" in a moment. Everyone returns to the regularly scheduled "normal"…Just like we have done thousands of times in the past. However, this Stream had a unique sense of mystery to it. The DBN reporter's comments invoked a pensive pause for anyone who truly paid attention.

"Early reports of Deliberations at the World Congress Center have revealed a major shift has been proposed to the Delegates. Details are scant for the moment, but it is rumored that after years of sweeping success in Global Policy and International Relations, the Delegates are being challenged to assess their effectiveness under the present model. Chancellor Mahndar shared concerns from

citizens that he recently received. We hope to learn more soon as the 2ⁿᵈ Day's session is getting underway in the Deliberations Chamber this morning.

The cameras panned out and the frame showed Delegates streaming back into the Deliberations Chambers after a few minute break they had just taken. 100's of purposed Delegates, shuffling to their seats. Through the herd and the gaping entryway that would in seconds be closed to the public's eyes by the intricately replicated Columbus Doors, the viewer could see the distant Speaker's Podium. Chancellor Mahndar had already taken his post. Although those watching the Live Stream could not sense it, there was anticipation in the room. An air of hope entered the chamber with the tired but eager Delegates who had been up through the night deciding how to best move forward with effective world government.

The DBN reporter went on.

"It is unclear of what the shake-up will be at the World Congress level of Government, but one thing is clear, Delegates are eager to get to their seats and resume Deliberations after the brief recess that ended moments ago."

The masterfully crafted replica Columbus Doors began to close behind the last of the Delegates as the reporter wrapped up his Stream.

"It is thought that by the end of today, the World Congress will be close to ratifying a revision to its present model.

"More will be streamed to you as things unfold....

"I'm Charles Sedley, for DBN, live at the World Congress Global Relations Center"

A Proposition Like No Other

Delegates are difficult to quiet at times. And this was one of those times. They had just returned to the Chambers after the mid-morning break. How many times in the last 30 some years had the World Congress been presented with an earth-shattering proposition? In all the years of blossoming democracies throughout the world, walls had fallen, dictators deposed, impoverished nations rejuvenated, terrorists terminated. Great historical events were the mortar that held fast the bricks of the World Congress. History was not only considered here, but within this institution, Delegates knew decisions made today about the future would become their descendants' history. This day was quickly becoming an epochal day.

The Delegates felt inspired after yesterday's early dismissal. Openness to what had been proposed in the opening hour today bolstered the mood at the Session. Inspiration combined with the nervousness of not knowing what was to come, heated the room. And a vigilance to do the best thing for society that drove the Body of Delegates to find certainty was palpable. Members were prepared to discuss what was going to lead to a positive future. Yet a hint of uneasiness spilled over the edges of the usually composed group. The Chancellor lifted his hands from the Podium.

"Thank you for the speedy return to your seats. As you know, we have a lot to discuss in the coming hours. The Speaker's Podium thanks Delegate Ahmed Marif of Pakistan for bringing forward the proposition that was birthed by the Delegates gathering in room 912 last night. We will hear more from him in a moment."

The Chancellor spoke with ease in his voice,

"It is clear this proposition was not put forward unilaterally nor without regard to how impacting such a proposition would be if implemented. As we were made aware yesterday, it is the time to search for a resolution that will impact society on a profound level.

"Before I call on Delegate Marif to expand on this concept, I would first like to say that I am not one to embrace change for the sake of change alone. However, if our discussion today finds reason to expect social progress is attainable, then I look forward to what comes of our discussions. I have enjoyed my time as your representative since my term as Chancellor began and I am prepared to move in the direction we come to agree on here today. I remain assured that we all agree that in the best interest of our citizens, change is necessary.

"It was many years ago that United Nations Secretary-General Ban Ki-moon placed an idea for true social change into the minds of UN delegates. Secretary Ban Ki-moon said,

> *"Our times demand a new definition of leadership—global leadership. They demand a new constellation of international cooperation—governments, civil society and the private sector, working together for a collective global good."*

The Chancellor's smile was as inviting as always as the Chambers warmed with Ban Ki-moon's words.

"He, as we hope today, dreamed that even civil society could evolve and become healthier. I am prepared to consider this as we deliberate today. The Chancellor extended his arm toward the Pakistani Delegate Box, he motioned to Ahmed, "Delegate Marif, if you would."

Ahmed Marif stood at his country's desk. The Media Screen image transitioned from the Chancellor to a close-up of Ahmed. On the Country of Pakistan's desk, the microphone went live. A blue light on the mic alerted Marif and the Pakistani Delegates to the open mic. The soft spotlights glowed on his skin and the hint of perspiration from his brow became more evident. It was not a matter of nerves in this moment for Ahmed. No! It was adrenaline within him from his bridled excitement.

The 9-12 proposition had taken hold of Ahmed in ways no other proposition had. In the few hours he had thought about it after the group in room 912 dispersed, he became completely sold on the idea of appointing a King.

This was probably one of the most unprecedented moments in the World Congress proceedings. In fact, Ahmed knew the support for the proposition was deep amongst the Delegates. The strong group at the after party was only the tip of the iceberg. It was in a sense, the most proactive move this World Government had ever considered. It was Ahmed who had the privilege of sharing the hope that would come with appointing one leader to steer global social reformation. Ahmed was tasked with presenting a proposition that was unthinkable in decades past. he was tasked with asking the World Congress to appoint a King of the World.

The Live Streaming image on the Chambers Media Screens did not show the charismatic and vibrant Ahmed Marif who was in room 912 just a few hours ago. In this image, the man who engaged the others through most of the past night was hidden behind what appeared to be a timid exterior. Yet, Ahmed was the consummate presenter and always prepared. And it was crucial he was prepared for this engagement.

Only two of the five co-Delegates at his table had been with him at the "After Party" discussions. Fortunately, the remainder of his brilliant and supportive team of co-Delegates and executive assistants from Pakistan, had received the briefing about the meeting. Team Pakistan had spent the 45-minutes after breakfast compiling a presentation to help Ahmed Marif display the proposition.

In the next moments the Delegates of this World Congress were going to be presented with a proposition like no other. It was a proposition that would change the work of the World Congress, and it would alter the course of history. Delegates past and present had pondered the benefit of one day conferring their authority on one leader. Today they would be asked to move to appoint that leader.

Progress Has Two Faces

"Thank you Chancellor Mahndar." Ahmed instantly brought the Delegates into focus.

"If I may, I would like to refer to this as Proposition 9-12."

Marif directed his request to the Chancellor. Chancellor Mahndar nodded to show his affirmation of Ahmed's request. Ahmed proceeded to finish his reasoning for the title.

"Not only did we deliberate over this idea in room 912 of the World Congress Hotel, but last evening our deliberations began on September 12th. That is the 12th day of the ninth month. This is why we have titled this Proposition 9-12."

Propositions brought before the Body of Delegates were named after some obvious connection. A place, a date, an event…there was always something concrete to reference the many propositions that filtered through the Chambers. Like the *Market Proposition* for instance. The proposition itself had nothing to do with the International Market it was conceived in. However, it took its name because three Delegates had gone to the market during a February Inclusions Session, in search of Valentine's gifts for their spouses. The three, from France, Saudi Arabia, and Norway, were interested in seeing trade and immigration rules softened, making cross border migrations of goods and citizens more fluid.

The discussions that took place in the International Market ultimately came to the Deliberations Chamber for consideration. In due course the Delegates sorted out the details and the *Key to One Globe Policy* was developed. A Global policy that granted free access for all people to any nation or region in the world. All from a proposition conceived on a weekend market excursion by three influential Delegates. And today, that Ahmed's proposition was born in room 912 on the 12th day of the ninth month left no question in calling it *Proposition 9-12*. Ahmed livened still more at the chance to share the prospect of finding one world ruler, but before he did, he decided to address a question some might have head on. That is the question of corruption of a King

"Today I would like to invite the World Congress to consider the proposition to appoint a King."

The quiet Chambers was instantly abuzz on hearing the highly unusual statement of their Co-Delegate. Ahmed quelled the escalating buzz by petitioning the Delegates to patiently hear his proposition.

"Please hold your judgments for a moment to allow me to elaborate. Some may think it is impossible to appoint one person as leader of the world, others may think it is logical to appoint a sovereign, and still others are leery due to the potential for corruption of a King.

"Corruption is a unique by-product of limited leadership. It is really a by-product of greed, the lust for power, and the perception of lack. It is suggested that if a person is literally King of the World, that person has everything. And because of that unique position, where the King desires nothing because that King has sovereign access to everything, corruption then becomes obsolete. It's just that simple. A person who is full and has all the food on his plate with unlimited access to more, does not want to eat the food on someone else's plate."

Ahmed was right. If power corrupts when a person has a desire for more, then without that desire for more, corruption disappears. The Delegates in the Chambers realized how simple it was. It always went back to the rules of the sandbox. Give a kid all the toys in the sandbox and he will not try to take the toys of others. Ahmed sensed his audience's understanding of the corruption issues, so he moved to the main point of his proposition.

"One thing we all agree on, is that something needs to change. And as we all hear, our world is crying out for meaningful change. And what we as a government have been doing, is not bringing the change that people are longing for. If I may, I would like to remind us all where we are at today in our work of facilitating a safe, prosperous, and happy world. Please turn your attention to The Media Screens or to your Folios for this brief presentation."

The lights dimmed slightly, shuffles were heard as Delegates made themselves comfortable and slid their Folios in front of themselves. On screen, appeared the image of a mid-1900's broadcast in black and white. The narrator took center stage.

"Greetings ladies and gentlemen of the World Congress. It is my privilege to be sharing with you today, some of the disenchanting facts about our history. I am from a time where no one could have ever dreamed of an organization like yours successfully leading the world forward to ever greater political peace and cooperation."

On screen, there were flashes of the vast accomplishments that had become the reality under the World Congress. The sharply suited narrator with hair slickly combed to the right and a stark part in her hair, was placed on the left corner of the screen. She remained in black and white while the vivid colours seen in the images of accomplishments filled the Screens and Folios in the Deliberations Chamber. Delegates sensed the sibylline element to the Stream they were about to take in.

The scenes were diverse. Showing autocratic regions celebrating their liberation to move into democracy. Displaying National militaries being dissolved in order to be re-absorbed into the Global Military Unit. Barren lands of parched soil that pressed their inhabitants into famine for decades were seen as transformed on screen to become fertile and productive. Once vacuous, but now celebrated by verdant green foliage and vibrant communities with children playing.

Delegates were reminded of the advances in the universal economy the World Congress had implemented. Images of the common Global currency flashed over the screen. The strength of the universal polymer note that pulled Global business out of an economic abyss was inspiring.

Images of the World Health Organization research labs whizzed past the Delegates' eyes and the Deca-Vaccine came into view. Scenes of peanut and perfume factories labelling products before they were propelled into shipping containers showcased the freedom of a society with minimal disease and cured of food allergies thanks to the Dec-Vaccine. Images of nuclear-powered planes, trains, and automobiles reminded the Delegates that fueling the world was no longer jeopardising the air, water, and environment. Nuclear cells had become inexpensive compared to the high price tag fossil fuels once demanded.

Those watching were not left without the proud sense of accomplishment from being the generation that successfully, safely, and efficiently harnessed the once feared nuclear power. One of the celebrated advances of this government, was that it had managed to direct industry to produce passenger vehicles of all shapes and sizes that were powered by a small, cube shaped nuclear pod. A pod the size of a traditional automobile battery but would outlast the vehicle it fuelled and the consumer who purchased it.

In a much more vivid way than Chancellor Mahndar was able to impart the day before, the Delegates were shown how progressive their institution had been. Yes, the present was clear in the minds of the Delegates, but how did this speak to Proposition 9-12?

The virtual tour guide moved back into center screen to continue her narrative.

"Ah the scenes of success." The Narrator continued, "They colour our world and testify to our progress. These are changes that were only dreamed of by the collective human mind at a time in the past. It is only through time's passing we can observe where we have come from and what we have become. Time is certainly our master in many ways. Progress happens and then one success inspires a dream which leads to another. Dreams are built on dreams, successes are built on successes, and progress is built on progress. Yes, all things change and we, the people of this great globe, have our hand in them. We dream of them and then watch them come to life. In your era and in mine, and all throughout time."

Each Delegate that day was attentive to the Stream as if they were face to face with the narrator. The black and white image of the narrator withdrew to the left of the screen, and she commented to the viewer.

"One might say, history stays the same unless we ourselves dream of ways to guide the future. Let's go together now and explore another dream, a dream that has been with us for much of human history."

There were flashes of policies, legal documents, and constitutions, scholarly and religious books. Delegates were sped across the globe with the hurtling images. Re-witnessing great moments of the past centuries. Moments that were vaguely remembered by those who benefitted from them today. The images became seas of people, gazing expressionless, appearing confident in the many purpose-filled directions they were moving. The Narrator continued...

"Culture today has a knack of gazing at its own navel. For the most part, we find it easier to look at the present and believe we are involved in a unique experience. An experience that no other period of history has had. A truly enlightened time. The face of progress can be seen in every epoch...Yet, when we take a moment and examine the issues of history, soon we find we are not so unique. Looking carefully, we see progress has two faces"

Dehydrated, Dirty, And Tear Streaked

The images shifted. Instantly, startlingly. Showing issues the World Congress had not yet deliberated on. The narrator was gone from the scene. What was being shown on screen was not only new to the Delegates, it was decidedly uncomfortable as well. They were glimpses of the harshness found in society. But they were strong.

Delegates next saw a tall well-dressed woman hurtling towards a dark oak floor. A briskly moving man, tall as well, and red faced with anger, had veins bulging from his neck as he swung at her. The stomach turning sound of flesh crushing violently under the palm of his hand brought recoil to the viewers in the seats. Then, in a flash, the scene changed again.

A toddler filled the screen. Medical personnel clutched at the handles of the stretcher as they raced out of the doors of a filthy apartment. The scene was quiet. The theatrical but contrived cries of a dishevelled mother filled the room. No one was fooled by hearing her tell the child who she had neglected to feed and bathe that, *"Mommy is coming sweetie...everything will be alright."*

The Medics glanced at each other knowingly. Everything was not going to be alright. Having been here before, they recognized the charade of a neglectful mother with a two-and-half-year-old. She had been a pathetic parent with no ability to cope with the intensities of being responsible for her two-and-a-half-year-old. The child was dehydrated, dirty, and tear streaked, laying silently as the stretcher was pushed down the hall towards a waiting ambulance.

The presentation offered imagery from all throughout human history. As it moved through time, the scenes showed the raw humanness that was not oft seen in public. The scenes depicted the harsh abuse of women that had occurred since ancient times. Children were openly beaten and shamed. Slaves had no human rights and servants gave way to anyone deemed to be of greater import than he or she. The scene paused at a time three thousand years ago in Egypt. In the next scenes the Delegates were shown a gathering of elites. And the ancient delegates' concerns were little different than those of the present. As might have been heard today, the ancients were heard commenting on the problems with their society. Petty crime, rape, unwanted children, profound disrespect by youth and worrisome levels of selfishness and apathy. A small group of contemporary thinkers, at least for the time, were heard talking about the social ills of their day. Their discussions were hauntingly similar to discussion heard today. Yet they were the conversations of the ancient past. Taken from an inscription on a 6000-year-old Egyptian tomb. The actors in the portrayal elaborated on the words left on the wall of a tomb for future generations to see.

> *"We live in a decaying age. Young people no longer respect their parents. They are rude and impatient. They frequently inhabit taverns and have no self-control."*

As the presentation transitioned to the next era, the Delegates were taken to the Greek Empire in the 4th Century BCE. It was Plato who came on screen, one of the most famous, respected, and influential philosophers of all time. Father of a philosophy style that is still popular today. Plato opined.

"What is happening to our young people? They disrespect their elders, they disobey their parents. They ignore the law. They riot in the streets inflamed with wild notions. Their morals are decaying. What is to become of them?"

The Delegates were starting to see the picture Ahmed and the Delegates from Room 912 had hoped to paint. Society was not so different back then than it is today. But they watched as the Stream continued.

The sophisticated era of ancient Rome appeared in the images. Wild Bacchanalian orgies took the stage, now the Delegates were faced with the brutality of a Roman sex festival. Women and men engaging in acts of hedonism sanctioned by their society and government. In that time women, children, and what were called 'effeminate' men, were subject to violent abuse and forced sex in the name of a communal God and a venerated patriarchy. The scene revolved and showed another section of the vast Roman Empire. Children, young boys and some young girls were displayed as the sexual plaything for pedophiliac men and men of priestly castes. The faces of many Delegates could be seen to writhe at the thought itself of the ancient debauchery.

History travelled towards the present. The centuries before 1000 CE betrayed society for the same abuses as the epochs before them. Violent crime, horrific parenting, disenfranchised people groups and vulnerable members of society based on their race, gender, class and education level. Defiance of authority and Anti-social behavior was common, and common folk were chronically struggling with having no power to enjoy a peaceful and prosperous society.

The stream moved to the late Middle-Ages. One would think the reaction to the grave inequities and injustices of the previous centuries would have brought more social evolution. Yet classism, racism, gender inequality, and disregard for the emotional well-being of children and society in general pervaded that era as well. The message was abundantly vivid. Slaves and women were seen being whipped and beaten. Pay inequity kept those in poverty from achieving any meaningful liberty from their hard work for low pay. The elite of society hoarded most of the wealth and subjugated the less wealthy to be their vassals. Many in society moved about their world with a subtle fear they might be robbed, swindled, or subject to unfairness by their employer or King. Life was cruel for many, and the harshness of life was more overt in the past than today…but it was still so much the same in so many ways.

The message was potent. Society was consistent in one unwanted area. Social distortion had effortlessly persisted through all eras and amid all the industrial, political, and economic progress. The issues that many hoped would have been eradicated remained through all centuries.

The narrator felt familiar to the Delegates now as she had become more of a friend than a character on screen. She led the Delegates through the remaining centuries of the second millennium. The 1700's had the UK government striking a committee to examine the causes of the present notorious immorality and profaneness. The 1800's were largely the same. Progress was celebrated but in the back of people's minds was the hope that society would progress, and civility would be more than just a veil covering the true social ills.

The 20th century spun out of control. History had been a failed teacher to compel culture to become better. *The Anti-Social Behaviour Act*, passed in many nations, failed to inspire the healthy societies they were intended to bring. They were more of an ideal guideline than an enforceable piece of law.

Social distortions persisted. And as the present era was about to be displayed, every Delegate in the Chambers was sadly aware of humankind's failure to become better…to become humane.

The first half of the 2000's were the most disappointing. Society had always hoped, believed, and waited for something to be done, but society had gotten worse. Delegates watching the world's failure to develop into a socially safe and successful global community listened in as Martin Luther King Junior spoke. His thoughts from the previous century were directed towards racism and war but the message was clear. In every era a better world has always been hoped for. Why has this dream been so elusive? Why has the World Congress not had the power to design this better world?

"I refuse to accept the view that mankind is so tragically bound to the star-less midnight of racism and war that the bright daybreak of peace and brotherhood can never become reality. I believe that unarmed truth and unconditional love will have the final word."

Luther's words hung in the room as the Delegates were brought to the present. With the last glimpses of what society was and had become in the present decade, the narrator asked again.

"Have we really gotten better?"

The final images were as riveting as the opening ones. A home invasion flashed across the Screen...fear and pain for the violently disrupted victim. He was one of billions who could not expect his own home to be a sanctuary. He was one in today's society, who was not given certainty that no one would ever enter uninvited and bring violence through the door. One who would not even recall a time when the doors of homes remained unlocked while the homeowner was home...knowing safety was not up for question.

A mob of head-shaven and bitter men was brought in view. They lucidly displayed the level of racism and organized crime that has had hold of sectors in society for decades.

A scene of another recent school shooting transitioned into a scene of a mall hostage taking...then to the scene of a local terror attack placing an airport terminal into panic and lock down.

Children climbing trees in a park. Their parents close by, but displaying an eerie image of a pale-looking man with a newspaper in hand and a glazed look in his eyes as he stared past the parents to the children in the tree. The viewers could not mistake this image for anything but that of a deviant about to act on his urges.

From the theft of innocence by a deviant to the theft of identity by hackers in distant lands. These scenes made the Delegates squirm at the realty that is today. The reality that no one is truly safe. Attempts to establish order had been made but even the most advanced Anti-Social Behaviour laws such as have been seen in the UK and elsewhere had not been toothy enough to propel culture towards the true justice it longs for. Nor to come up beside the true peace, security, and prosperity it has dreamed of.

Ahmed's video presentation could have gone on with the many injustices that riddled society. But what the text on Screen spoke of was crystal clear at making the point;

- A woman raped in her apartment by a man she knew
- A man struggling to keep his marriage, his job, his life together, unable to deal with the sexual abuse at the hands of a hockey coach when he was a teen
- A bank account drained by cyber-thieves
- A car stolen by gang members with a baby sleeping in the car seat
- Teens seen robbing a young mother and shooting her baby
- A 15-year-old girl lay dying in the bathtub after taking a bottle of pills and a '26' of vodka
- A group of tourists robbed, beaten, and raped in their rented vacation house

The images went on for another minute or two. Every act of social distortion had an affect not only on the victims but also on the watching Delegates. The intensity of each scene was not lost on this group. They too were slowly realizing they had become numb, in a sense, to the lifetime of crimes against humanity that seemingly had no chance of being stopped. But witnessing the injustice, the inequity, the callous disregard for another's freedom to live without fear...the impact was undeniable. What was deeply unaddressed inside each Delegate had now burst through their protective crust and bubbled to the top. The images of pain and suffering faded to black and white as the narrator brightened to living color. She took center Screen.

All the scenes flashed behind her in a hurtling speed. Testifying to the chronology of society's sickness. The narrator paused on the image of a mother, overcome with grief as she draped herself over her baby. Her son, an 18-month-old who had just been shot. The scene was more than gut wrenching, it was indicting. What had happened to that mother and baby could never be undone. But in the pit of the Delegates' collective stomach, the regret that filled the room was from their glaring inability to stop these injustices. Most Delegates wished there was a way to prevent the atrocious moments of hell that would now become lifetimes of pain.

As the presentation wound up, the narrator was absent from the gripping images on screen. The dirty, dehydrated, and tear-streaked child they had seen earlier on an ambulance stretcher, filled the screen again. The question was asked one more time…in a somber tone to a silent audience.

"Have we really gotten any better?"

The lights went up….....
The Delegates in the motionless room, had never been so uncomfortable.

Time Is Our Master

She had been standing for only a moment now. Canadian Delegate, Annelyse Devonshire was waiting to be given the floor. Delegate Devonshire had been a member for 7-years now. Her enviable leadership was clearly a style distinct from many of the other Delegates. A slim woman, always sharp in her attire and appearance. Hair piled up on top of her head, she sported subtle earrings and just enough makeup to highlight her green eyes. Delegate Devonshire was well respected. She contributed often to both the formal Deliberations at Inclusions Sessions as well as many late nights at the After-Party gatherings.

Amongst the Delegates participating that day, many of them had spent After-Party moments with Annelyse. Her input had been vital in bringing reason to potentially disruptive policies and propositions. Adding insight that helped to squash them before they made it into the Policy books. She had a knack of delivering a pointed caution to the groups she met with. Now, as she was given the floor by Chancellor Mahndar on the heels of Ahmed's announcement of Proposition 9-12, the Delegates straightened slightly as thoughts of the cautions she had brought in the past were on the minds of many. Her focus was purposed, her confidence admirable. She was truly a pioneer in many ways and a leader that always improved those around her. But the group was unsure how her statements about appointing a king would take form today?

"Fellow Delegates," she began. "It sounds like today's deliberations and the consideration of Proposition 9-12 is about timing. We have been at this a long time….at government that is. Our position today is dramatically different than it was thirty years ago and perhaps in another thirty years it will be dramatically different yet again. So often we credit ourselves for designing the structures and institutions that govern our world. And in some ways those designs are to our credit. But is there a larger factor in play? A factor that exceeds the intentions and designs of man? For instance, shall we take credit for the abolishment of slavery? Did we, reasonable humans, choose the timing of that great emancipation or did the timing choose us? I suggest it is the latter.

"Life prepares each one of us for the times we are in. And time has its way of preparing us to take the next steps in life. We can consider that after 26 years of attempts at peacekeeping, the League of Nations gave way to the United Nations in the mid 1940's. Did world leaders orchestrate that moment or was it simply time for a shift?

"When the United Nations was reduced to a skeleton of its once former self, leading to its dissolution and the raising up of the World Congress, who among us made the plan for that to happen in that moment? Did time dictate the event or did leaders decide it was time? Who decided to end the 80 years of United Nations activities so another world government body could rise and bring such unseen and globally impacting advances in so many areas? Did men and women orchestrate the end of one institution and the birth of another or did the women and men of that era respond to what time had been preparing for that moment? Do institutions design the times or do institutions respond to the times? Time is always dictating our next moves. And now I can't help but ask; What is time telling us now?

"Like a birthing mother, at the time of delivery one can attempt to ignore the inevitable, but the future will come regardless of the host's willingness to let the birth come forth. In birthing a child, the facts are it eventually is time for the baby to come. Time decides. Were the mom to say, *'No, I can't have this baby now,'* things would not go well. It is time…and what is supposed to happen does happen. The baby will come…one way or another. It can pass through the birth canal with resistance from its host or it can be welcome at its coming and the discomfort with it seen as an undesirable by-product of the newly born. We learn from history it is time that decides how futures will go.

"Friends, I am humbled by all the connections and elements that took place to bring us to 9-12. But none so much as the one I mention next. Is it not the luminaries, the sun and the moon that have been the time setters for all the world since the beginning? And yesterday, in many lands across this great globe, mankind was treated to a rare celestial event in time. Yesterday, the day of the birth of Proposition 9-12, in room 912, on the 9th month the 12th day, our world experienced a full and complete solar eclipse."

Not a Delegate was shuffling in their seat and not a Folio was being swiped or tapped. The proposition to appoint a King was in front of them. The Saturday session was often the most involved of the 3-day monthly Deliberations, but this level of intensity brought nothing but pensive focus. The gaze of the Body of Delegates was vacuous. Delegate Devonshire was expressing what was hidden deeply in the minds of so many. Could this be? Was it possible the World Congress was ready for this change? Many had quietly pondered this group's readiness for such a shift. And as for the timing. If there was ever a clear timing that was right for such a monumental transition, then this was it.

Annelyse Devonshire had made the point well. Even though it was wise to heed perfect timing, it still came across as somewhat of a warning. Had Chronos himself, the Greek God of time, placed his mythical hand on the moment it could not have been clearer. Time was compelling the Delegates to agree to a change. Perhaps to appoint a King who could wisely, judiciously, and graciously lead the World. This was a unique moment in time. This was the day of the Solar Eclipse, the 12th day of the 9th month in the year 2043.

Delegate Devonshire met the broken silence with one more remark. She brought to light the significance of the three letters from citizens that had arrived at the World Congress inbox at the time of the solar eclipse. Annelyse was referencing the letters Chancellor Mahndar had sent to the Delegates before the morning session began. Correspondence that was received throughout the night and into the early morning. Devonshire went on.

"Friends of the World Congress, I would be scandalously ignoring clear indications if I do not speak now. Our citizens are calling for a reformation as is seen by the many letters the World Congress receives. And especially from the letters Chancellor Mahndar has messaged us to read from yesterday."

Delegate Devonshire was always one to honor the input from the valued citizens of the world, especially when letters expressed a preponderance as to the hopelessness and apathy that proliferates in the World. These were not letters from partisan leaders or activists with a cause. They were letters from ordinary people who were moved to plead with the World Congress. The plea was the same in each of them. A plea to find a way to change the path to self-destruction that society had been idling along for decades.

"Of these letters," Annelyse went on; "I have found reason to have hope. "I cannot express with more fervor the value of embracing the moment when the moment is so clearly presenting itself."

Delegate Devonshire was being characteristically forthcoming. None were surprised at her passion so well-articulated. She herself was emanating hope and she herself was compelled to inspire her colleagues to move toward a King.

"Ladies and Gentlemen, it seems time is telling us a King is in our future. We might hold a search for this King and spend countless days or months pursuing the person who will arguably best fill this role. But I am trusting you will see the gravity of this moment. The import of not letting it pass. If Time is our master, it is also true there is no less forgiving master than Time. Upon reading the letters sent to the Chancellor, it is clear of those who wrote, Time has chosen our Leader. It is our place now to simply agree with what Time has already decided."

One Of Them Would Be Chosen As King Of The World

None thought the Chambers could have been any quieter. The sound of nothing was almost hypnotic. Only the subsonic hum of the bright Media Screens was felt in the room. On them, the sincere face of Annelyse Devonshire. She knew she need not say another word. She was still…waiting. Did she know what her words had accomplished? The men and women gazing at her were not just observing but were invested with her? The Delegates taking in her words made them their own. Each delegate welled up with purpose and duty. Duty to make a meaningful move. Ready to display the leadership it took to embrace a reformative idea, to accept there is hope, and submit themselves to the fact that it was time… They would choose one person who would become the King of the World.

In that second two men stood. Bold leaders with a purpose. Delegate Marif and Chancellor Mahndar. Marif was back at his nation's box and the Chancellor Mahndar on the platform, just behind the Speaker's Podium. The Chancellor's mic went live and both Mahndar and Marif knew what the other was about to do. Marif politely deferred to the Podium Speaker. And Mahndar addressed the room. It all happened so rapidly. Unapologetically and with the conviction of a man who was never more certain of a thing in his term as Chancellor, the Chancellor made the historic motion.

"I move we honour the time and the people of this Great Globe by selecting a King!"

With the characteristic excitement expected of the delightful Ahmed Marif, not even waiting for the call for a seconder from the floor, he blurted. "I second that motion!"

The moment came to take a vote. Chancellor Mahndar called, "All in favour…?"

As the last of the sentence was completed the vote to select a King was made. In a wave that flooded the Chambers, Delegates across the great Chamber of the World Congress stood to their feet to cast their votes. Each member country or region was allowed 5 votes. The Electronic Tally System efficiently scanned the room tabulating all eligible voters and announced the **Yays** and the **Nays**. In seconds the scan was complete, and the System displayed the results on Screen as it announced.…

"Nine hundred and eighty **Yays**.…**Zero** nays."

Chancellor Mahndar stepped to the Podium, checked his Folio to confirm the numbers, and announced resolutely.

"Ladies and Gentlemen, for the first time since Proposition 9-11 was ratified, we have a unanimous vote in favour of Proposition 9-12. Fellow delegates, few women and men have even dreamed this day would be possible, yet, by a unanimous vote we have agreed together to move ahead with the selection process. May we be guided by Wisdom in our selection for the very first ever, King of The World."

The Chambers burst. Delegates turned to each other to affirm the moment of the astonishing motion that had passed. It was as if a weight had been lifted off each of them and a brilliant light was illuminating their future all at once.

If Time truly was the Master, then the wishes of the Master had been heeded. Of the three citizens whose letters had reached Chancellor Mahndar on the day of the eclipse, one of them would be chosen, as King of the World.

Today the Delegates would veer off the normal agenda for the day. It was now necessary they map out a plan. The Body had agreed, and the day would be filled with planning. Construct the plan to choose and appoint one of the three who had written to the World Congress on the day of the solar eclipse…at just the perfect time.

Only One Couple Was Brave Enough

Sol usually woke early on Sundays. Outside on the patio, he sat. There was a special thing about Sunday mornings. No noise, no hurry, no excitement, just time to think. The biggest decision of the day was to find a quiet place and relax. It was mornings like this Sol didn't bother to flip through the News Feeds. It was just more of the same anyway.

The quiet was comforting. Even the air felt soft. Sol closed his eyes and thought about yesterday. Having his visit with Gavin and Rosslyn ruined by the kid who was hit by a Shuttle seemed like days ago. Maybe that's why he woke so early, still pushing adrenaline out of his system from all the drama.

Sol wondered who that kid's parents were and what they were told about their son being hit by the Shuttle. The whole thing seemed surreal though, and seeing it one more time in a perfectly recalled dream that night was more than enough for Sol. It used to be these things hit him hard. Not hard in the emotional sense, where he felt like he was traumatized. Rather the surge of adrenaline and the heightened mental state that came with the drama used to just wear him down. But conflict and Sol were no strangers. It wasn't that he went looking for it. It was just that he wasn't intimidated by it.

As Sol sat pondering yesterday's conflict, he started to remember a conflict of another day. The time he almost snapped while in line at the coffee shop. He tried to educate a couple of queuing bullies that day.

"*Queuing bullies*." That's what he liked to call them. Sol had become so frustrated with people cutting in queue when there was a line-up that he decided he would do something about it. Queuing up in a two-pronged coffee line wasn't rocket science. It was just a merge lane. You get in the door, you stand queued in the line-up and when the next open till is available, you move forward and place your order. Sol found it odd that everyone hadn't figured out the queuing line by now. It was fair for everyone.

The queuing bully was an opportunist. The kind of person who seizes the moment, buds in front of others waiting, and scurries over to the counter as if no one will notice…or say anything to let him know it was not their turn. It's no secret what kind of person this coffee line outlaw is. The queuing bully takes advantage of the fact most people will avoid conflict at any cost. Most people waiting in line think, "*It's a few extra minutes to just quietly wait patiently in line, so why get in a tiff over this small injustice?*"

And yes, that was one way to see things, but Sol thought, "*Why is patience a better quality than fairness and justice?*"

Sol was not afraid to confront this queuing indiscretion. It may be small on the global humanity scale, but it is huge on principles of human behavior. Sometimes it landed Sol in an awkward position, but he could see few reasons to dismiss principles when uncomfortable situations arise.

If people stood up for coffee-line justice more often, then queuing lines would become a universally self-policed entity. Each user would know the power of social compliance in queuing lines, and each user would speak out when a queuing bully jumps the gun. If that were the case, we would see the end of the queuing line bully once and for all.

Standing up is exactly what Sol did one day in a coffee shop he had popped into. Stopping for a coffee with a friend before they headed off to a meeting, Sol was standing in line ready to relax with a hot cup before they bolted to their appointment. The line was about 6 people deep and, like so many coffee places, it is always a squeeze around the till so no one was slipping over to the open counter to the right. There was a sign scrawled on a poster board hanging above the heads of the customers waiting in line. Telling all in line to move to the open till when they reached the front of the queuing line. But it seemed no one had read it.

As he stood patiently waiting, there were a couple more coffee seekers tucked in behind Sol and he was now 4th in line. He watched as the door opened and a couple of casual unkempt gentlemen breezed in. In what looked like a completely strategic move, without hesitation the two fellas looked to the right. Seeing the patron at the till had just finished her order and moved away from the now open counter, they slid right past the long line and bee-lined to the open counter. Sol stiffened and called out,

"Hey fellas, we're queuing up over here."

The men completely ignored the clear and non-confrontational information given by Sol. Sol stiffened more. Then, as if he was paid to run interference in a coffee line Super Bowl, Sol strode directly over to the till now being occupied by the queuing bullies. He confidently squeezed himself between the inconsiderate jerks who were surprised at the unexpected bravado.

The counter that was being manned by a young lady instantly became a hot zone. Her diminutive presence behind the till and the accent in her dialect gave her away as a new-comer to both the country and to the coffee shop.

"Sorry fellas, you weren't the next in line." Sol informed.

"You budded in front of all those people over there." Sol announced, pointing to the half-dozen patrons who were a little surprised at Sol's forthrightness.

At that, Sol turned and looked confidently into the eyes of the server and began to make his order. "I'll have a large double-double and a bagel with herb and…." The queuing bullies promptly interjected.

"Well now you're budding in front of all those people. And can't they read? The sign says *"Please form one line and move to the next open till."*

"That's not the point Mr. Perhaps you could have been courteous enough to prompt them to consider the sign. I am certain they can read, maybe they didn't see it. Fact is, they were waiting patiently before you walked in the door and I'm not letting you get away with that."

Sol was turning back to the gal behind the counter to continue with his order. But the queuing bullies decided to prove their mettle by asserting that now Sol was budding in front of everyone else.

Sol turned back to the louder of the two scruffy guys. Standing face to face in a tight coffee shop line, Sol and his momentary adversary were both posturing. And neither was about to relent on his position.

After another outcry by the bully, declaring the patrons weren't smart enough to read the sign, Sol stood up for the folks waiting in line and flatly told the taller of the two, "Stop being an asshole, they were here first."

Standing nose to nose now, the peak of the man's cap was almost touching Sol's forehead and everyone in the coffee shop was watching very carefully, as if there was about to be showdown. It felt like someone was about to start throwing punches. Then, a supportive voice from the sea of onlookers in the coffee shop called out.

"Yeah, stop being an asshole, you always do that!"

Again, as if pointing out some unforgiveable social injustice of Sol's, his adversary accused him of his own queuing line crime, "Well you budded in front of all those people too!"

And with that Sol turned to the line he had recently left and offered an invitation to step ahead of him and the bullies, "Folks, he's right, you were waiting before us, please, come on over and get in ahead of me."

Only one couple was brave enough to take up Sol's offer and risk getting in the outlaw's line of fire. They placed their order for a couple coffees and a small breakfast snack. Then with a quick swipe of his G-PAS, Sol happily spent the 38 dollars to rub it in the faces of the men who broke the queuing line etiquette. It sure as hell wasn't rocket science, just common courtesy. If everyone understood the queuing line concept the world would be a gentler place.

Recalling the conflict with the queuing bullies had taken Sol's mind off everything else. Sitting…relaxing with just his thoughts and his cherished medium roast blend…the patio was his sanctuary where Sol spent time in silence on a warm Sunday morning.

Something Electric Had Started To Pass Through Them

Unsure of how long he'd been sitting daydreaming, Sol's eyes popped open as Ell gently squeezed him on the shoulder. He had put the headphones on to relax and found himself completely disconnected from the moment. As Sol turned to look up at Ell standing over his shoulder, he noticed she had not been out of bed for long. It was 9:15 in the morning now and Sol had been sitting…mostly napping…on the warm patio for about an hour-and-a-half already.

"Hey beautiful," Sol smiled, and then his face melted in a puzzled look. Beyond Ell in the dining area off the kitchen, Sol could see three people looking out onto the patio. Two men and a lady, dressed in business attire.

"What's up?" Sol queried Ell. "Is there something going on?"

Ell responded, "It's about the letter you sent."

Sol tilted his head with a furrowed brow. "What lett…." Sol remembered, "You mean the one to the World Congress?"

Now it was clear and all coming back to him…. Seemed like days ago, but it was just early yesterday morning Sol had sent off a letter to the Chancellor and the World Congress Delegates. And today, about 28 hours after he had sent that letter, he was getting a surprise visit by three Delegates from the World Congress that were standing in his dining room.

"They want to have a visit with you Sol." Ell sounded somewhat concerned by that fact.

"Geez, I didn't think my letter would even get read let alone piss someone off over there. Uhh…I guess we should invite them out on the patio."

Sol went to the patio door threshold and stepped over it to the dining room. "Good morning, to what do I owe this surprise visit?"

He was calm on the outside but in his head, there was no end of swirling thoughts. Before his uninvited guests gave him an answer he continued, "What did I say, who did I offend, why didn't they call; I haven't even straightened my hair."

As if it mattered. Sol sported a super tight cut, and it was hard to get pillow-head from even the most solid night's sleep. As the guests stepped toward Sol to introduce themselves he chimed, "Am I going to a need a lawyer or something?"

Then, in a perfectly welcome moment of warmth, the Delegate in the ash gray dishdasha offered his hand.

"No Mr. James, you have no need for a lawyer, I am Ahmed Mariff. And my colleagues and I were introduced to the letter you sent to Chancellor Mahndar yesterday. We found it very compelling for various reasons and would like to chat with you about it."

"Well, this is certainly unexpected, please step out onto the patio and we can have a visit."

As the guests moved over the threshold to the patio, Sol invited them to have a seat while he and Ell went inside to get them a coffee. Sol closed the sliding door and as soon as he knew his guests couldn't hear them, he turned, looking at Ell with eyes so wide his look of inquiry and confusion was unmistakeable.

"What the hell is going on Ell? What are they doing here, what do they want?"

Ell touched Sol's hand and said, "I don't know any more than you do Sol, let's just take out the coffee so we can find out."

Ell saw Sol was a little anxious and for good reason. A surprise visit from Delegates Marif, Whist, and Liiendor was truly an unexpected cause for concern. Especially the day after Sol had sent off a letter to the World Congress.

Ell comforted Sol before they stepped out to join their waiting guests. "I was watching the other two as Ahmed Marif introduced himself. And they appeared pretty easy going. It doesn't seem like they have a bone to pick with you. I'm not sure what's on their minds."

As much as Ell was able to bring a sense of calm and reason to most situations, this moment was not like any moment. Sol was simply swimming in conjecture as he tried to process what could possibly be the reason for the arrival of such esteemed guests. And of all the reasons that filtered through his thoughts none were close to what was about to happen.

"Mr. James," Marif started.

"Please call me Sol." Sol interjected.

"Thank you, Sol." Marif continued, "We are here today to talk to you about a few things. Yesterday, the Delegates of the World Congress were shown your letter. Each of us took the time to read it throughout the day."

"Ahhh…Yes my letter."

Ever the diplomat, without showing a hint of his concern Sol then said, "Thank you for taking the time to read it. I wasn't sure it would even make it to the Chancellor's inbox."

Ahmed jumped in thinking how uneasy one might feel on the other side of this conversation, "We found it very inspiring and in fact the general sense from the Body of Delegates was one of being honored to have read it. It was welcome correspondence that profoundly stated how so many in society and government today are felling."

"*Whew,*" Sol thought, "*what a relief.*"

He was sure Ell could still feel his tension because Sol sure felt hers subside just a little after hearing those words from Ahmed Marif. Now Sol had a moment to re-collect his charismatic and engaging demeanor.

"Well, I am delighted to hear that. Thank you." Taking the complement graciously but sheepishly, Sol moved to redirect the attention to his letter for the moment.

"You mentioned you hoped to discuss a '*few things.*' What things did you have in mind?"

"Liiendor picked up the ball now that the ice was broken. The already warm patio felt cozy again as the five settled into the moment…without pretensions and with a fresh coffee in hand.

"Zis is so good to szit visz you Mr. James and Ms. Ell."

"Please, Sol and Ell are fine," Ell reminded the guests.

"Szank you, and pleasze call me Darik," sweeping his left arm towards the two Delegates with him, Darik insisted, "And my colleagues would prefer you usz Erin and Ahmed."

His German accent was smooth, and it caused Sol to pay closer attention to him as he spoke.

With another simple social convention out of the way now, all present were starting to show an eagerness to get to the heart of the visit. Darik's tone and excitement rose.

"Vee have had quite a monumental copple of daysz at szee Deliberations Chamber. Zhere isz a lot of exzitement about zuh past veekend'sz meetings and about usz coming here today to speak visz you."

It was still easy for Ell and Sol to understand Darik, but it was clear that as he got excited his blended German accent did get a little thicker.

"Over zuh last days vee have been sleeping very littell. Zuh World Congress has been privileged to bring many profound and fruitful enactments in society. Zis body of world leaderzs has boldly brought our world to a place of virtual peace and prosperity in ways zhat have only been dreamed of in past decades. Zuh methods and processezs zhat have been used to unite zhe world through zhe World Congress, have proven to draw zis body of Delegates together in a powerful way. A way zhat continues to inspire us to always look at how we can propel zuh Globe forward. Zhere is limits however to zuh resources and force of zuh World Congress in its present democratic form. And our deliberations have challenged us to consider vere to go next in our World Governance."

Sol shuffled in his seat just a little. Hearing the News Stream from the Deliberations chamber yesterday came back to his thoughts.

"...the News Feed said something about a change coming to the World Congress, is that what these delegates are here today about?"

Coming back to the moment Sol focussed into the visit again. Darik was still engaged while Ahmed was sipping his coffee, and he noticed Erin leaning forward toward Ell in so slightly a manner. She looked like she wanted to know more about Ell.

"If I may," she opened, "Would you indulge me to share some intriguing thoughts from my culture?"

Sol and Ell were instantly curious where this was going to take them.

Erin was looking for Ell's approval to share some thoughts about her culture. Ell said, "By all means, please do."

Erin glided into her thoughts.

"Ell, you have some Cherokee in your line is that correct?"

"Yes that's right. How did you know?" Ell questioned.

"I have studied anthropology for years," Erin answered, I had a special hobby of examining faces to look for signs of their past. Signs of their cultural heritage that are hidden in their face. And it is very subtle Ell, but I noticed your high cheek bones and the subtle broadening of your nose at the top of the bridge. As well as the very small but perceptibly higher hairline that extends your forehead."

"Well yes," Ell said as she unconsciously touched her brow where her hairline met her tanned forehead. She wasn't sure if she should be self-conscious or not at this moment. "I didn't know anything about my Cherokee connections until about ten years ago."

"How fortunate that you found out," Erin said. "Some people never learn about the richness of their heritage. I was fortunate as well Ell. I grew up with a father who spoke often about his Cherokee great-grandfather. He once told me about a Cherokee prophecy Ell. Sol I think you might find this interesting as well."

Sol was already so interested he wasn't sure why Erin even needed to say that. Something about her commitment to the moment had drawn both Sol and Ell completely in. At this point Erin could have spun a tale about three rabbits and a nasty bear. Sol and Ell were completely enraptured. As if something electric had started to pass through them, they could hardly wait to hear what Delegate Whist was about to share with them.

The 8th Sun Had Chosen The King

"**S**ol, how did you get your name?" An odd question from Erin, but Sol wasn't fazed. Even though both he and Ell were rapt by the three important surprise guests sitting on their patio.

"Well, my full name is Solomon, after my Mother's Grandfather. But I have been called Sol for almost my whole life. My Mother's grandparents…so I guess that would be my great-grandparents…came from France. When I was about 5 years old, great-grandma died and my Mother started calling me Sol. Just a few years after that I began to wonder why, and I suppose I just thought it was short for Solomon. I guess it is, but my mother told me there is more to it than just a short name for Solomon."

Erin quizzed Sol a little more, "It sounds as if she liked your great grandfather's name, or she wouldn't have called you Solomon. Was he named after the biblical Solomon?"

"I think so" Sol replied, "My Great grandparents were among the first to leave France after many years of persecution. They both had some Jewish heritage in their line and the neo-anti-Semitism that started to infest much of Europe when they were newlyweds, compelled them to pack up and head west. So, they ended up in Seattle."

"Do you know what *le soleil* means Sol?" Sol could see by her focus Erin was going somewhere with this.

"Sure, it means '*The sun*'. I did get introduced to the French language a little bit by mom and she always thought I was her sunshine so just before I hit puberty, I learned why she shortened my name to Sol."

"So, we can see then that your name 'Sol' means sun."

Erin affirmed the small fact, but Sol was still not making the connections. He waited to see what she was getting at.

"You see Sol and Ell, for generations now, Cherokee people have told the story to their children and their grandchildren. As you know, many legends and prophecies are altered as they travel through the generations. So today, when many people hear about the 8th Sun prophecy, they may be hearing an altered version of the prophecy. Nonetheless the 8th Sun prophecy heard today still maintains its original intent and meaning." Erin paused.

"I've never been told the 8th Sun prophecy, but I have heard it spoken about," Ell stated. "As far as I can recall it has something to do with the return of the warmth of the sun after seven periods of time or unique epochs have passed. And didn't the first epoch supposedly begin before the Sumerians came on the scene during the Ubadian period?"

Erin was smiling now, somewhat surprised how well Ell encapsulated the 8th Sun prophecy, or at least when it first was conceived.

"Yes Ell, I think you're right-on with that. And history and archaeology show the Ubadians preceded the Sumerians. They inhabited the pre-historic Mesopotamian region. So, they were on scene almost 7000 years ago. And I'm not sure our most ancient ancestors knew at the time, but it's come to be understood that every thousand years represents a 'Sun'. And it's supposedly in the period of the 8th 'Sun' that our world is due for a revolutionary change, a time of new beginnings. We happen to be in the period of the 8th Sun in this present era."

Both Ell and Sol had a rudimentary understanding of ancient peoples and their prophecies about the future. A time when the world would be righted by a shining leader. Many of those groups had a sense that there would be an appearance of a divine person or a supernatural god to right things. But this prophecy was a touch more pragmatic than many of those. So, they were almost right in step with Erin's brief in-service on the 8th Sun Prophecy. But both of them were starting to get an unusual feeling about what this meeting was about.

"You see the Cherokee people who began in ancient Ubaid believed there was a divine force or a supernatural creator. But they also believed humans are charged with caring for the earth and the people who inhabit it. Including doing the best we can to govern ourselves. The transmission of the 8th Sun prophecy has long been thought of by the sages to speak of the coming time when the world is open to receiving inspired leadership. Leadership bringing true prosperity in ways people who inhabit the world have been longing for."

This was all beginning to become very intriguing for Sol and Ell. His name meant 'sun', his letter had found its way to the Delegates, the period they were in now was said to be the 8th Sun era...it was all very interesting. But they still had no clue as to why these three high-powered delegates chose to come and speak to them about all this. Sol had lots of questions.

"So you believe now is this special time Erin? And how are the people of earth prepared for this great revolution?"

Erin went on, "You know, I would like to answer your second question first Sol....I'll get to your first question shortly. Sol did you find it odd that Ell knew about the 8th Sun prophecy?"

Leaving Sol to think about her question without giving him time to answer, Erin carried on.

"The beautiful thing about this ancient prophecy is that it has been disseminated in many ways, both subtly and overtly, to children and grandchildren since the day it was first conceived. Our people, which have been mixed with all people, have been passing on this legendary story for ages. And a version of the story has found its way into almost every culture known to man since the times of the Ubadians and the Sumerians.

"With that Sol," Erin paused to weigh how she would share her next thought with Sol and Ell, "And I'm not exactly sure how to put this.... There is a surging nuance in culture where people feel that things are about to shift. A revolutionary change that the world has been longing for and will embrace. The most potent aspect of the 8th Sun prophecy, is that all the generations before, preparing the generations after them, just may have prepared this generation, our generation, to be the one who resets civilization. We see now that the 44th American president from 35 years ago was wrong in saying *People are ready for change!* It was not the time then...but it is the time now! The people of earth have been prepared for this change at this time."

Erin was precise with her statements. The entire Body of Delegates knew it and Sol and Ell knew it as well. Culture has been speaking about change for hundreds if not thousands of years. If there was one common thread throughout all cultures, regions, nations, and ethnic groups...that thread is a desire for change. Even if not ready for the change, there has always been a thirst to see humanity become better.

Liiendor sat quietly since he had introduced the World Congress' intention to move for change. Looking pensive now, he was very calm and comfortable, yet somewhat intimidating in his silence. Sol was waiting for him to join the conversation again so he could get a read on the square jawed, suddenly somber Delegate. Was he distant right now or was he engaged in the moment as Sol, Ell, and Erin were? And who knew about Ahmed Mariff? He was comfortable almost to the point of appearing aloof. Sol presumed he was as engaged as any of them but the way he would sip coffee, peer into his cup, and occasionally glance over Ell's shoulder into the yard could just as easily have been interpreted as disinterest.

Trying to get an idea of what Ahmed was thinking, Sol's thoughts veered off the in-service briefly, as he found himself glancing into the yard as well. Autumn was setting in in a week or so and he made a mental date with his pruning shears for Sunday next week. Sol thought, *"Things'll probably slow down a bit by then."*

Then Darik broke in.

"Yesz zhat is right. Vee are all looking for change. Zuh shame zhat vwashed through zuh German people during zuh holocaust isz memorable. But vwut many today fail to realize is zhat zhere vwusz a world leader on zuh stage in zhat time who vwusz so driven by a hatred for zuh Jews zhat his passion for change vusz polluted. Underlying much of zhis tragic time in world history however isz zuh fact zhat Hitler vusz avare of zee 8th Szun prophecy. He vusz a student of history and believing zuh Jews ver killers of Christ he vuhsz compelled to usher in the 8th Szun with world domination and purifying vut he interpreted as an impure race.

"Underlying all of his hatred towards zuh Jews and his addiction to power vusz zee idea zuh world would be brought into change. By him and his Third Reich.

Zuh trouble visz Hitler though, vusz he vusz driven by his insanity to force zis change on zuh world not seeing zhat zuh vworld was not ready for it. He did not honor Time. A common mistake of many great leaders. And of course, zhose who were insane are destined to fail miserably in zair attempts to change zuh vworld. And zay are destined to cause great destruction along zuh way."

Sol agreed, they all did. Sol made the connection to timing by noting, "The efforts of Idealism and Zealism are often thwarted by bad timing." The group agreed that to be always the case when the timing was misinterpreted.

Darik proceeded to elaborate by telling of how the destruction brought by Adolph Hitler will be remembered right into eternity. And oddly enough the *Third Reich*, Adolf Hitler's distorted work that is now loathed throughout the world, was based on establishing the thousand-year reign. A pursuit he had from what he misunderstood to be the 8th Sun Prophecy. The German culture was familiar with this prophecy. And as the time came near for that epochal era to come upon us, men like Hitler, Lenin, Stalin, and Pol Pot, would attempt to drive the people towards it instead of hearing when the people became willing to walk into that time. Leaders could not force the Time true change would come…they must listen to Time and, instead of controlling the Time they, we, must come under its guidance and make the move for change when Time dictates the moment.

At this Ell and Sol had goose bumps, the hair on the back of their necks was standing up and Sol took a deep breath starting to see where this was all going. Sol had done his research on history, and he was always amazed at leaders who maniacally forced the people into change. Failing to see what the people were asking for. Astute leaders were known for interpreting the way the people collectively behaved and then guide them to the change they were seeking. But so many leaders twisted the times and abused their privileged position of power.

Erin edged forward again in her chair. If her delivery was subdued before now there was nothing subdued about what she said next.

"Sol, I do believe this is the time to answer your other question. Just to be clear about answering your question Sol…we…" Erin looked to her co-delegates, "…in fact the entire World Congress, believes society is walking into that time. We believe the 8th Sun prophecy which has been shared with children and grandchildren for millennia, may well be about to begin.

"Whether one believes the prophecy to be true for our day or not, we believe this is a moment in time that will bring the global acceptance to positive change. The prophecy speaks of a time when all people will be ready for revolutionary change because society feels trapped. Telling how the unchanged and unsavoury aspects of society will engender disenchantment, apathy, and a sense of hopelessness. The prophecy speaks of a form of leadership that is new but also very old, the prophecy identifies a civilization as a circle."

Erin drew a counterclockwise circle in the air with her left hand.

"The ancients knew it and although it has been forgotten for periods in human history, humanity is in a cycle. A cycle where things are returning to a state of renewal. Ell and Sol, are you familiar with the significance of certain numbers?"

Ell had picked up on some Kabbalah teachings at a *History of World Religion* conference she attended seven years ago. As for Sol, he had explored the meanings of numbers from time to time in his years at the library, but he never really paid too much attention to their meanings, nor given much credence to the theory. So Ell decided to jump in to answer Erin's question.

"I think I recall that the number 8 is known to be the number of new beginnings in cultures that teach numerology and gematria. And the number 8 is often associated with the Medicine Wheel and represents interconnectedness of all things for the Anishinaabe people."

Erin nodded, "Yes 8 is a very significant number. The 8th Sun prophecy speaks of celestial signs indicating the time is upon us. The prophecy knows that each sun represents a period of about 1000 years, but the 8th Sun prophecy also speaks that the sun will lead us. The sun is said to represent two things."

Erin paused because she felt this needed to sink in. Sol and Ell both sipped from their coffee that was far from its best drinking temperature now. Ell set her mug back on the wicker end table and leaned in with a sense of expectation.

Ell added, "I know the sun in prophetic literature often represents time Erin… but what is the second thing?"

"I am not sure if you and Sol are religious folk but even the ancient Hebrew texts say *'The sun will rise with healing in its wings'.* You are absolutely correct Ell; time is one of the elements the sun represents. Time is our master. Ever leading us to the next step in this journey. But the sun also represents a person. Time will take us to the brink of the next step, but humanity needs people to lead them through that next step."

Erin continued, "The sun in prophecy does bring healing…but that "sun" is two things at least. It is both the ball of fire in the sky responsible for moving time, and it is also a person. A person who will lead us. We believe this is all connected to the past, to the future, and to **today** Sol."

Erin was looking directly to Sol when she emphasized *'today'*. She continued to explain how simple but profound the message was.

"Everything happens for a reason; all things are connected as the Anishinaabe people say of the number 8. And we have come to learn that our master in all this is Time. We need to recognize the time we are in and if we do it will be apparent, that as a civilization, our time is now! "

Erin eased back slightly in her chair. Her face unmistakable that she was convinced the 8th Sun had chosen the King. It seems she had a respect for the moment. Sol noticed his pulse was slowing, his chest was warm right up into his neck, and his eyebrows slightly lifted. Sol couldn't help but feel the foreboding tone of what Erin was expressing. He pushed down what felt "uncomfortable" and just said it…"So, if now is this **'Time'** are you saying you have found this leader?"

I Am The Person For What?

The few seconds of silence, breathing, and mental digestion were needed after what Erin shared. And then Erin broke the seconds of silence. "Yes!" Erin announced. "We believe now is this special time. Time to embrace the leader of the 8th Sun era."

Sol looked at Ell's face. She looked as if she were ok with what they were hearing. Often when embroiled in a conversation of deep matters, Ell had questions written all over her face. Not today. Her skin had a subtle luminescence about it that lent comfort to the moment for Sol.

Ahmed set down his coffee. He had almost gotten to the bottom of his second cup. He started with, "You asked Erin *'If now is that time?'* As she said, we do believe the time is now, the time is here."

Ahmed reached into his messenger bag to pull out his folio and a small stack of paper. Paper wasn't seen very often anymore.

"Sol," Ahmed continued, "The entire World Congress Body of Delegates deliberated on this and every member agrees. It is time now."

Ahmed set the papers on the table between the group of five. Then, it struck Sol. Right now, in his house, on his patio, with his wife, were three of the world's most influential and powerful leaders. Three Delegates from the World Congress discussing a burgeoning time of global social revolution.

"*Wow!*" Sol hollered inside himself. "*This is an amazing Sunday morning!!!*"

Sol was bursting with incredulity. This group of three sitting in front of him today, were in no way making Sol uncomfortable. They were so completely unassuming.

"If that's my letter," Sol began, pointing to the stack of papers on the table. "I didn't realize it was so long. Or that it would help you all with such a big decision."

Ahmed chuckled softly, "No disrespect Sol, but yes, your letter is here, as well as two other letters we received over the weekend. And you have been a great help… we are hoping you can help some more. Chancellor Mahndar forwarded the letters to the Delegates in between Deliberations. All the Delegates have had a chance to review each of the letters. Their arrival was very timely Sol. Each of these letters spoke to the very issue the Chancellor set before the Delegates on Friday…speaking about how something needs to change."

Sol hadn't put the timing together on his literary effort, but Ahmed was spot on at letting Sol know just how perfect his unwitting timing was.

"This is the anniversary week of the 9/11 bombing in the United States, which changed the world forever." Ahmed informed. "The very weekend Chancellor Mahndar challenged the Delegates to deeply consider where the World Congress should go in its future style of governance. As well Sol, this is the time the paralyzing apathy that has plagued society was punctuated for the Delegates by the correspondence the Chancellor shared with us. Three very similar letters were received this weekend Sol. Yours was among them."

"Hmm…three letters on the same day? And they were all alike? How's that work?" Sol asked.

"It works exactly how it's supposed to Sol." Erin was still just as convicted when she spoke as she had been the whole visit so far.

"The letters arrived at exactly the right time."

Sol was not yet understanding the focus on the timing of his letter. His head tilted inquisitively as he gave his attention to Erin again. She was set to explain.

"The coincidences are too stark to miss Sol. On the eve of our 9th month Deliberations much of the world experienced a complete solar eclipse. The timing of that celestial event could not be ignored by even the most convinced skeptic. The Sun has alerted us to the importance of this time and your letter arrived at the World Congress at that exact time Sol. It is also no coincidence that your name Sol, can be said to mean *sun*'."

Sol and Ell snuck an intrigued peek at each other on hearing his name connected to the word "sun". Erin went on with her explanation.

"Just as any pivotal moment in human history transpired because it was time, these letters only arrived because the timing was right."

"That is right Ell and Sol." Ahmed spoke in collaboration with Erin.

"There is nothing that does not happen exactly on time. The many years the World Congress has functioned has shown us all that our only master is Time. It is only our job to govern in submission to the Master. When Time reveals to us a new direction, we must wisely take the steps to head in that direction. And that is why we are here today. We would like to hear from you about your letter as we have agreed in Deliberations that these three letters were written so we can take the next steps...exactly at the right time."

Sol had only one thing to say about his letter, "My letter speaks for itself. I meant everything I wrote."

Those were exactly the words the team of Delegates had hoped to hear. Ell thought she noticed a slight rise at the corners of Ahmed's eyes and mouth. "*A smile?*" She questioned thoughtfully. "*But why?*"

Sol queried, "Have you spoken with the other two people who wrote you letters?"

Ahmed replied, "Yes, in fact we have sent other teams of Delegates to speak with those writers. Just before we were invited to your home, we had a brief discussion with the teams."

Sol was quite curious about the other two writers. He asked Ahmed, "May I inquire as to who the other two people were?"

Ahmed shared further, "One of the writers was a single mother of three small children in Switzerland and the other was a 79-year-old retired gentleman who was recently diagnosed with lymphatic cancer. The team of delegates we sent to Japan to meet with him reported him to be a wonderful man with great hope to see a changed world before he dies. The team reported that due to the seriousness of his cancer, he appears to have missed his time to be effective at implementing change. Some are better suited for certain tasks at certain times in their life than are others. Time truly is our Master...all of ours."

Ell perked up at that, "What time are you referring to that this gentleman missed out on? Did you have plans for him, a 'task' that he can't commit to?"

Ahmed stood up.

Surprised, Ell and Sol both looked up at him from their wicker deck chairs. As they sat confused about his sudden change in position, Darik and Erin also rose to their feet. Ell and Sol were perplexed.

Three of the World Congress Delegates were now standing in front of them on their patio. It was more than a little awkward, and it seemed a little extreme. Sol had simply sent them a letter two days ago. Now his heartfelt letter was sitting on the table with letters from two other citizens. Sol had hoped someone at the World Congress would read it, but he never thought something like this could develop. The World Congress was obviously eager to make some type of a revolutionary change in its role and model for government. Sol was stirred and curious, Ell was contemplative, Ahmed, Darik, and Erin were now standing in front of them.

Ahmed spoke but his tone was no longer cordial nor nonchalant. The pitch descended slightly and the subtle upturn that came across as a smile had gone flat on the corners of his mouth as he spoke.

"Mr. Sol James, Ell has asked a question for which my answer comes in the form of a question. For in sending Delegates to the three writers as we have just spoken about, the World Congress has commissioned these teams to ascertain whether or not we are able to find the person that fits our purpose. We have been commissioned to look for a very significant person. In coming here today, it has become clear that you sir, are that person."

Ahmed paused and took a second to prop his Folio up on the table. It began to operate in 360 camera mode, recording every moment, word, and move that was now taking place. The world would want to see this when it recounted its history at some point in the future. Sol stood, Ell stood, and the patio was no longer the cozy and easy environment it had been moments before. The air on the patio was warm and still. There was no rustle of the leaves as Sol and Ell stared at Ahmed. Sol asked the only question that was in his mind.

"It is clear that I am the person for what…?"

Sol Simply Said Yes

Ahmed picked up Sol's letter from the top of the pile on the table. "We have read your letter Sol, we have assessed the timing, it is clear the present structure of our World Government is not accomplishing that which it has only hoped it could accomplish, and we are certain Global society has prepared itself to walk forward with us. We are clear it is time to move forward with new leadership." Ahmed stopped. He blinked and sharpened his focus.

"The next words I am about to speak Sol are very serious. If you say 'Yes' to the question I am about to ask, your role and duties will begin immediately. You will possess greater power than any single person in known history has ever possessed. And we here, along with the entire unified World Congress will set you above all levels of present world government. We are prepared to respond to your requests, needs, governance, and petitions, willingly ready to offer counsel or advice. Political entities world-wide will volitionally submit to all that comes from your hand. Sol James, we have come from afar that we might ask you this question?"

It was as if he knew what was next. Sol was ready to commit. The moment was coiled up with exhilaration. Sol was practically vibrating knowing what was just about to happen. It was a moment no one should ever experience because it is so surreal. Yet it was one that everyone should get to experience in some way because it draws on a part of a person that is rarely touched. A vital force that drives a person to be committed to something with a depth of resolve. A depth that is as profound as the greatest thing he or she has ever committed to.

Ell was enraptured. This moment, a moment that felt more like a scene from The Sword in The Stone, was riveting. And it oddly offered a shiver of terror at the same time.

The unspoken roles of those in the room had already changed and both Sol and Ahmed knew it. But only Ahmed knew why at this point. Ahmed was instantly humbled and Sol's look pierced straight into Ahmed's soul. No one in the room would question this was the time. Ahmed cleared his throat. And in his official tone he asked…

"Sol James, the World Congress has unanimously agreed we shall alter our leadership structure for the better of our World. The World Congress has unanimously agreed that all we have accomplished and all those in government before us have accomplished, has led us to this time. The world Congress has unanimously agreed timing is of the essence and we must find and appoint a King. A King who will be sovereign over the entire world and all its affairs. Sol James, based on the interviews of two other teams of Delegates, it is our recommendation that the World Congress choose you to be the King Of the World."

Ahmed was watching Sol closely as he spoke. Hoping to see a man who was unshaken by even this request, a request unlike any other. Neither Ahmed nor any one of the Delegates that was with him wanted to see Sol react as if he'd just won a lottery. And Sol was attentively standing, listening, waiting. Ahmed postured himself to deliver his epoch defining request of Sol.

"If you choose to say yes to this question, your role as King of The World will begin."

"Sol James, on behalf of the entire World Congress who have gathered virtually with us now, and all its sub-levels and sub-committees by which I have been commissioned to petition you. Would you willingly become the one sovereign leader who purposes himself to lead the world forward and guides us all toward a new and vibrant era of hope, peace, prosperity, and security? Will you graciously accept the appointment to become the first ever King of The World?"

Sol had taken in all that had happened in the past days, all that he felt, and all that had entered into his life in the past half-hour. He looked at Ell. He looked back to the man asking him without a doubt the biggest question one could ever hear in his or her entire life. The moment was sacred. Sol was willing Ell was willing. Perspiring lightly at the inconceivable event but willing to take the position. The second he opened his mouth to respond, life would change forever. But he was ready. With great humility and great commitment Sol simply said,

"Yes."

Their Lives Changed Forever

The cheers from the Folio speakers on the table were quick to fill the room. Ahmed's Folio automatically streamed directly to the Deliberations Chamber. Sol had forgotten Ahmed's Folio was in 360-cam mode and the entire World Congress Body of Delegates had watched this take place.

There, at the World Congress Center, Chancellor Mahndar and the entire Body of Delegates sat watching the proceedings on Sol's patio. Sol and Ell were surprised at the loud applause that filled the World Congress Deliberations Chambers and now filled their backyard.

Everyone was familiar with the World Congress Deliberations Chambers. The highlights of their sessions were Streamed to the world every month. And what Sol and Ell were looking at in this moment was far more overwhelming than any other Streams they had watched of activities in the world's most powerful venue. The men and women who held the fate of the globe in their hands every month during Deliberations were standing, gazes fixed on the Media Screens in their chambers, applauding joyfully at the image of Sol and Ell in the moment. The moment just after Sol had said "Yes," to the request to be King of the World.

Just then, Chancellor Mahndar, as if on cue, said, "I'm sure both you and Ell don't know what to feel right now. But Sol, we at the World Congress are so elated to have you as our King. And we want to assure you that we are going to be here with you and for you as this unprecedented move dedicated to improving our future, sets in for all of us."

It was in fact uncanny, as if Chancellor Mahndar and the World Congress had done this all before. Just as Sol started to wonder, "*What was going to happen next, how is this going to play out, where do I go from here, and who do I go with,*" Chancellor Mahndar intersected Sol's thoughts.

"Now you will have so very much to think on and consider. And I know your appointment to King and your acceptance of the role is only moments in the past; but, King Sol..."

Sol barely caught it. '***King Sol***'. Being called that by the World Congress Chancellor was astonishing to say the least and truly impossible to conceive. He almost let the thoughts in his head drag him away from the moment, but he focussed back in on the Chancellor.

In those next few moments while Sol and Ell had been listening to Chancellor Mahndar explain some of what was to happen next, Darik Liiendor stepped around to the side of the house. Just as Chancellor Mahndar was finishing up, Darik Liiendor returned. He was carrying a box under his arm, and over his shoulder Sol could see two other gentlemen. Standing on the sidewalk at the side of the house. It seemed they were just observing, but it was clear they were there for other reasons, official reasons...security reasons. It made sense why Ahmed had shot glances into the yard earlier. He must have been looking at the security team who were along. Sol and Ell both glanced over at Liiendor as he offered a polite smile while stepping in next to Ahmed. He set the box on the table between them.

"Thank you Delegate Liiendor." Mahndar's cadence changed.

The 360-Cam technology was very common now but even still, it was easy to forget how the receiver of the Stream could see the entire room, almost as if they were standing in it. The entire Deliberations Chambers saw whatever Sol was seeing. The Chancellor resumed his instruction to Sol and Ell. "I will also explain a bit about the process that will take place in the next 2 weeks."

Sol looked at Ell as she was listening to the Chancellor. Her face was bright, her eyes were shining, and her subtle smile was of comfort to Sol as she squeezed his hand again. Sol wasn't sure if she was excited, nervous, or just plain terrified at this sudden change in their world. Whichever one it was her gentle squeeze of the hand and warm look on her face were comforting.

"I am very curious how this is supposed to go I must say." Sol blurted. "To have had you folks in my home and to be given this honor is beyond imagination enough. I can't even begin to imagine what's to come next."

"Let me help out." The Chancellor said. "In just a few moments you'll receive the Folio that's inside the box Delegate Liiendor brought in. But for now, if I may, I will explain what tomorrow and the days following will look like.

"Two weeks from today, Sol, you will be introduced to the world through live Media Stream in a public Presentation Ceremony on the New York World Congress Center Plaza stage. Tomorrow morning when you wake Sol, you will be taken to New York where you will meet with a handful of the World Congress Delegates. After spending a couple hours with the Delegates you'll be given a full tour of the World Congress Center including establishing your security clearance. Your security clearance will be above all others and there will be nothing Sol, absolutely nothing that will be off limits to you. Not just at the World Congress Centers around the globe, but in any building, office, or institution in the world.

"I remind you, as of moments ago you have become sovereign over the entire world. You have been empowered by the people through the appointment sanctioned by this body of Delegates of the World Congress. The orientation process that we will be going through with you the next two weeks will answer a great many questions you will have. This process was carefully designed by a team of delegates throughout the night, knowing today we may well be embracing our new King."

Sol was really handling this well...being only numbed a touch at the magnitude of this moment. The intensity of the whole affair was keeping his head from swimming.

"There is a lot to cover before the public Presentation Ceremony in two weeks." Mahndar directed his comments to Ell, "We have planned for you to join us on this orientation journey Ell, but it will be a journey. It is completely up to you. Be assured that Sol will be well taken care of. And of course, if you remain home, we will post obscured support staff for you there in the area. As well, Sol and you will be able to maintain contact however and as often as you like. You may choose to join our orientation journey at any point along the way."

"Thank you Chancellor Mahndar, I will keep that in mind and discuss it with Sol after the Delegates are done here today."

"I understand perfectly Ell. I will leave that with you." Mahndar pressed on with the information about the orientation. Turning back to Sol he offered more.

"Sol, after our time at the Deliberations Chambers with the Delegates we will be escorting you to the Airport where we will proceed to the 7 remaining World Congress Centers over the course of two weeks."

The Chancellor disclosed more of the process in the next moments. And although Sol and Ell quickly realized the moment he said "Yes", their lives changed forever, they had yet to grasp that everyone's lives would change too. Soon the Delegates, the three on his patio who would be Sol's Handlers, would leave. And Sol and Ell would be left to process what had happened and what was to come. Time was tight so they needed to let it all soak in for the rest of the day and then prepare for tomorrow. The World Congress car would be around to pick them up at 9AM Monday morning.

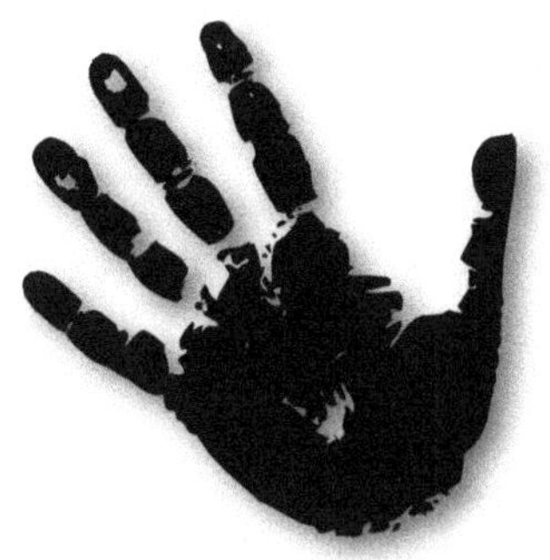

A JOURNEY TO BECOME THE KING

Who Am I To Argue With The King

The limousine that whisked Sol to the airport was quiet. So much had flooded his mind since yesterday. Sol often noticed the aromas that filled the spaces he found himself in. First the limo then the massive Boeing EX-797 that brought him to New York. The plane contained almost no aroma at all and at best, a possible hint of ozone. Sol didn't know how they could make a plane feel so comfortable and so quiet flying at an altitude of 45000 feet and 750 miles per hour. It had all the comfort of Sol's living room. The Boeing Company had mastered their fuel cell technology, which reduced engine noise by 82%, and they had engineered pink noise into the luxury cabin environment to silence the remainder. But having the whole plane to themselves felt too decadent for Sol and Ell. Both had been pensive about their new and abrupt reality during the flight. When they began their descent Ell took Sol's hand and shared a reassuring squeeze. It had been a seamless flight after a tough night preparing for the journey of their lives.

The airstrip was empty as Sol and Ell's plane taxied into the terminal. The flight crew, the security, the service personnel, all of them had seemed unaware as to why Sol had just been flown into New York on the World Congress air-transport plane. No one knew that a new King had been appointed and the bright sun-soaked runway was empty of any onlookers for the arrival of the World Congress aircraft now smoothly rolling toward the terminal.

Ahmed was standing next to a government vehicle on the tarmac. Darik Liiendor and Erin Whist were flanking him again, just slightly behind him. The hulking Boeing *EX-797 Skyline* finally came to a stop…remarkably smoothly just as take-off, flight, and landing had been.

"Wow they make these things comfortable these days." Sol marvelled out loud.

The *"Safe To Unfasten Seat-Belt"* chime sounded as soon as the plane had stopped and Ell looked at Sol, "Well Sweetie, here we go?"…

…Sol looked out the open door of the massive aircraft and he took the next steps with a sense of adventure as he self-coached under his breath. *"You're really doin' this old boy."*

He stepped out the door and the mobile platform offered a broad exit area for him to stride alongside Ell. Just the two of them leaving the plane being guided by the path ahead. It was an odd feeling having a massive airplane all to themselves and now stepping onto a gaping airport tarmac with the delightful Ahmed eager to welcome him.

"Sol!" Ahmed's cheery greeting and welcoming arm wave made Sol smile. "It is so good to see you again. I trust you had a comfortable flight. You will be getting use to that plane because it is at your service for the next two weeks…. It is at your service for as long as you are King." Ahmed was so casual with his interactions with Sol and Ell, he was very easy to like.

"We have a lot of miles to put on to get you ready for the Presentation Ceremony."

Ahmed continued, "After the two-week orientation is over you will be sufficiently apprised of the broad scope of the World Congress. And therefore, become conversant in the depth and reach of the World Government. Two weeks from yesterday Sol, you will be Presented to the world. Chancellor Mahndar will lead in with an announcement as to our decision to appoint a King and then we will introduce you. This will be the biggest Direct Stream to all Media Screens across the Globe that has been conducted since the announcement of proposition 9-11. At that time Sol, you will have the opportunity to address the citizens. At that time Sol, you will no longer be preparing in the background, you will be King to all."

That sure had an ominous sound to it. He glanced at Ell and while focussed on her he spoke to Ahmed. "That will be invigorating."

Ell knew what he was thinking. Even though no one else in the world could have told you Sol was nervous by looking at him, she sensed the subtleties of a slightly anxious Sol. This was on. Sol was becoming King more and more each moment...

After promptly deplaning...Sol was ushered into the government vehicle. Stooping his head he entered the SUV and sunk into the warm, leather seat of the black Cadillac.

With no sound from the engine, the car began to accelerate. Ahmed was still talking; he was fantastic at that. Erin and Darik sat across from Ell and Sol. If there were any moment since yesterday that pierced Sol with a sharp realization of who he was to these people, it was now. Sitting in the World Congress Limo with three Delegates. They were there for him, because of him, and in order to advance him. Sol was not left to ruminate on that thought for long, Ahmed offered instructive orientation plans to both he and Ell.

"We are minutes from the World Congress Center for Global Relations. Are you familiar with it Sol?"

Sol answered, "I've only had an internet tour of it, I have only a small idea of what it is and what goes on there."

"Excellent," Ahmed responded, "That will aid us greatly in our orientation. In the next two weeks you will see all 8 World Congress Centers. And they are all very similar in their design and functions."

"Am I going to have opportunity to address the Delegates before the Presentation in two weeks?" Sol asked.

Erin Whist decided to take this one.

"The WCC here in New York has emptied. The Delegates have all returned to their respective regions until we meet at next month's Inclusions Session. The complexities of world government have left it impossible for all Delegates to remain here in New York."

Sol acknowledged. "I guess I just presumed I would be meeting them all here in New York..."

"If you'd like Sol, we can petition them to all return in order to meet you in the next day and a half. That is ultimately your choice Sol." Ahmed interjected.

"No no no...that is not necessary. I am sure this is the best way for things to go. I will look forward to meeting them soon."

Meanwhile Darik was sitting next to Erin processing, then he piped up. "King Sol."

It shocked Sol a bit to hear that.

Darik paused and looked up slightly, "...You are zuh end of zuh line, you are zuh top of zuh pecking order, you are...as zsey say. zuh one who will stop zee buck."

"You mean the one of whom we could say, 'The buck stops here?'" Ell put the pieces of Darik's broken metaphor together.

"Zhat is what I am trying to say, szank you Ell."

Darik smiled and then held his finger up in the direction of Sol. "You, King Sol, are zuh one who can make or change anything. You have been empowered by zuh World's most authoritative body and..."

Darik began to smirk ever so slightly as he continued. "…And zis is no Eckhart Tole empowerment Sol, you actually have zuh power to change more than yourself; you have zuh power to change zuh world."

Darik had trailed down a slightly noticeable tirade about Sol's unprecedented authority. Erin jumped in again.

"As the King of the World you have become our King, their King, everyone's King, so we will want to call you by something. And who better to decide what to be called than the King himself."

Laughing a little on the inside Sol went through the traditional titles like *Your Majesty, Your Worship, King Sol the First, King Sol the Benevolent, King Sol the Great, Your Highness, Sol the Conqueror*, but all of them just felt like a novelty item to Sol. Then, after a few moments of thought, a few moments of ruminations and silence for everyone in the car, Sol spoke up.

"Howww aboouuut…" Drawing out those first two words Sol had not forgotten who he was. And the silence that held Erin, Darik, and Ahmed captive was pierced by the "royal" couple chiming in at the same time. Ell and Sol both said…"Sol!"

"Yes, you can call me 'Sol,' Sol reaffirmed.

"Ha, I knew it!" Liiendor blurted out quite irreverently. "I knew you would prefer zhat title."

"Calm down Darik, Sol may have more to add to that." Ahmed tersely stated.

Ahmed was hoping for more. He was idyllic in his image of this King and likely would have preferred '***Your Highness***' or a like moniker….But '**Sol**' was enough.

With the World Congress Center in sight, Ahmed took a deep breath after the laughter and said, "Who am I to argue with the King? Of course if that is your preference we will be privileged to call you Sol."

I Understand!

The monstrous and empty driveway welcomed the solitary cavalcade into the gaping front entrance of the World Congress building. No one could mistake the importance of this place as the grandeur was breathtaking. As to its vitality, now that could be in question to those who didn't know the rhythm of the organization. There was no one around, it was like a ghost town heading up the driveway. Posted at the head of the driveway outside the massive doors into the building were two regalia-clad armed guards. They looked bored, or perhaps they were just being official.

As Sol's car wheeled to the curb of the granite driveway, the guards began to look a little less like high-class doormen and stood taller with more purpose and authority. Sol was quite intrigued by the welcoming feel the architecture offered.

Erin was looking out the window taking in the empty square in front of the center when she said to the party in the limousine, "I have always loved coming here. The profound feel of inclusion I sense from this place is so comforting." She turned from looking out the window and said to Sol and Ell, "I think you're going to love the Center for Global Relations?"

Sol and Ell stepped out of the car. The glistening granite walkway was impeccable and the garden and beds pristine with flora. Each tree, shrub, and flower was flawless. The soil beneath them was tilled luxuriously to appear as a rich black carpet.

In each of the four beds was a gallery-like display of flora. Sitting in the furthest corner from the driveway was the unmistakable World Congress symbol. The artisan globe crafted from platinum, zinc, and brass, was perched on a single sterling silver pole. Again, Sol was taken by the perfection and intricacy of the design. This in itself would have been worth a trip to the WCC.

Ahmed kept informing. "We can usually find the Chancellor in the Fall-Out Room. That is the large boardroom connected to the Deliberations Chambers and to the Chancellor's office."

Everyone knew the Fall-Out Room was a special place. As the Chairperson for the Body of Delegates, after the session in the Deliberations Chambers had ended, the Chancellor would cross the t's and dot the i's on a number of administrative things. It was in this room that many a debriefing would take place after a particularly turbulent or a particularly significant session had come to a close. And today, it was necessary that Sol should arrive and meet him. Ahmed ushered Sol and Ell through the foyer, through the Court of the Delegates, down the long aisles of the west side of the Deliberations Chamber, where the entourage then paused.

As he turned to knock on the door Ahmed said, "I believe the Chancellor is waiting for us."

...knock knock knock...

The door connecting the Deliberations Chambers to the Fall-Out room was unlabelled. Four or five seconds passed, and the door opened. On the other side, the warm smile of Chancellor Mahndar greeted Sol and Ell. Mahndar extended his hand.

"Ell, Sol, it seems like ages ago since we visited over FaceStream, welcome to the Fall-Out room and to the World Congress Center." Mahndar swept his arm through the air expressing his welcome to the Center.

"It is so wonderful to finally meet you."

Chancellor Mahndar never broke with his comforting guidance. Sol wondered why they didn't make him King of The World. *"I'm sure glad to have him in my court. What a strong leader,"* Sol thought.

"Ell I am so delighted you chose to join Sol on this journey. I understand you plan to return to Seattle after the first week and have Sol go on without you?"

"Yes, that's correct. Is that alright?" Ell asked apologetically.

The Chancellor responded by leaning in and touching Ell's hand. His hand was warm, strong, and reassuring. "Of course that is alright Ell, anything you and Sol agree to is alright. Sol is the King of the World now."

That was going to be hard to get use to Ell thought. Ell realized again just who Sol had become since yesterday.

"If you could Ell," the Chancellor continued, "We would ask that you consider staying along on the journey until Sunday morning. The reason for my request Ell, is because we will be announcing to the media on Saturday that the World Congress has appointed and sworn in a new leader. It will be intimated to the media that this new leader has some unique authority and will be introduced to the world on the following Saturday."

"Sol, in a moment we are going to proceed to the adjoining Chamber. There, we will be joined through Media Streams by all of the Delegates. At that time, we will ask you to place your hand on the World Congress symbol and repeat after me. You will swear an oath to this Office. An oath never sworn by any other world leader. An oath for the King of the World."

Sol and Ell waited for more.

Mahndar stood up to finish his briefing. "Then Sol, once your oath is complete, I will have you sign the writ, a document agreeing to appoint you as King that has been signed by the entire Body of Delegates in the World Congress. After sealing those here today in the Red Ochre ceremony, we will enjoy an early supper together and I am afraid we must continue with your orientation, there is no time for relaxing while we are here in New York."

Sol and Ell had a faint hope of taking time to relax together for a couple of hours. But it was also in their thoughts that the journey would be so full there would not be time for leisure.

The Chancellor shared further. "After supper, we will escort you back to the Airstrip. There you will board your plane and travel through the night. Beginning with the farthest Center, you will have just under 2-day stops at each and arrive back here on Saturday morning. The journey will fill you with the understanding you need, to begin an active reign. Your Attendant Team who will be your Handlers, Erin, Darik, and Ahmed, will travel with you. And they will ensure you are given all the information you need to act in your role successfully. Then, in 13 days from today, we will meet Ell back in New York and you will be presented to the world."

The whole group stood and began heading back through the adjoining door. Chancellor Mahndar held back slightly and slowed Ahmed just enough to inquire of him. "Do you see any problems Ahmed?"

Ahmed had done an amazing job engaging Sol and he confidently responded to the Chancellor, "I see no problems at all Chancellor, Sol will be a wonderful King. I have no doubt that he is committed, resourceful, and equipped to handle this role."

Sol stood at the Speaker's Podium gazing out at the empty Delegate Boxes in the Chambers. Ahmed and Chancellor Mahndar joined the four waiting at the podium.

A Sign From Some Higher Power

Tap *swipe tap*. The Media Screens in the Chambers ignited. Dispersed between the Screens were the faces of all the Delegates. Sol, Ell, the handlers and the Chancellor had all made their way into the Deliberations Chamber for the ceremony.

"Sol, we will be Streaming this live to all Delegates today."

Chancellor Mahndar welcomed the Delegates participating through the screens in the Chambers.

With a glance and a *tap* on his Folio, Mahndar affirmed, "Good, I see we have all chimed in. Esteemed Delegates of the World Congress, it is time for the Swearing In."

Sol and Ell peered at the abundant Media Screens filled with the faces of the Delegates. from all over the world. It was almost noon in New York with Delegates chiming in from every Time Zone. Some of them had just woken up for the day, others were woken in the middle of the night by their igniting Folios for the swearing in of the King of The World.

The Chancellor looked to Sol. He smiled and motioned with a slight gesture of his head towards the Globe. Sol reached out his hand and placed it on top of the unity symbol known around the world. The thought of a time when courts would have witnesses place their hand on the Bible to swear an oath, breezed through Sol's mind. It was decades ago society began to accept the reality that people broke their oath after swearing on a Bible as often as they did for any other action taken during a swearing in. The World Congress had thankfully developed its own venerated icons that came to be used for official purposes.

The Globe was cast of mixed metals. The most known and recognizable elements to identify not only the World Congress but to symbolize global unity. Eventually, the act of swearing on a Bible at official ceremonies was replaced by swearing on the world unity symbol, the Unity Globe.

Organizations began using the Unity Globe to affirm the desire for unity. So much so that use of it soon reached a critical mass. Many had employed the Unity Globe in ways that connected the message of peace to their organization.

It was a good thing. There was a tribal feel to it in the way groups would rally around the message contained in the Unity Globe. And so it happened that those who swore on this symbol did so with intentions to act honorably in the office they were being sworn into. And Chancellor Mahndar was about to officially install Sol as King.

"Solomon David James," Sol hadn't heard that in a while.

The Chancellor was very earnest in the ceremony as he went on.

"It is with great honor and privilege that we affirm and install you today as King of The World.

"Sol David James, please repeat after me."

Sol had looked over the script for the swearing in while he was on the plane. It was very well put together. What he hadn't thought though, was how repeating it out loud in front of the watching Delegates of the World Congress would cause him to tremble inside.

Mahndar's cadence was perfect. "With all your heart and mind Sol, do you swear to fulfill the duties of this Office?"

Sol repeated, "With all my heart and mind, I swear to fulfill the duties of this Office."

Mahndar's turn again, "Do you Sol, commit to act in benevolence and wisdom endeavouring to lead this World with the best interests of the citizens in mind to the best of your ability?"

Sol paused. This was such an extraordinary moment that being exhilarated would be an understatement.

Sol repeated, "I do swear to lead this world with the best interest of its citizens in mind and to act in benevolence and wisdom to the best of my ability."

"Do you Sol, agree to take this Global Office of King of the World with the intent to act in integrity and honor, giving consideration to the effect your decisions and rule will have on all citizens?"

Sol affirmed, "I do."

The Chancellor had obviously rehearsed this moment. He had to have. He was smooth and confident. Today was a first for Sol and a first for the Chancellor. This was obviously the first time the world was appointing a King.

As soon as Sol finished repeating after the Chancellor, Chancellor Mahndar reached into the compartment under the Speaker's Podium. He took hold of a silver tray with a dark, saturated earthy material in the shape of a square pad sitting on it. Sol watched as he brought it in front of himself and held it with both hands. Sol and Ell both knew the next and final step in the swearing in. It was time for The Red Ochre Seal of Submission.

The Red Ochre ceremony was an ancient ceremony adapted for this moment by the Delegates of the World Congress. A ceremony that drew on ancient ceremonies of indigenous peoples and philosophies of submission and commitment that were not oft reasserted in leadership. Sol was to press his hand into the inky material on the tray and then, with his hand coated in the wet Red Ochre, those on the stage would pass in front of Sol one at a time. Each person present would move from Sol's left to Sol's right as Sol imprinted each one of them. He would do so by pressing his inked hand against their forehead as a symbol of commitment, submission, and integrity of the highest degree. Just as Sol submitted himself to the office of King to lead in integrity, authority, and wisdom, the representative Delegates in the large empty Deliberations Chambers, would submit themselves to Sol. Submitting themselves in proxy for the entire body of Delegates. And by extension, for the citizens of the world who had bestowed Global authority upon the World Congress Delegates. The Red Ochre King's handprint on their forehead was to be washed off in the moments following. But that handprint symbolized Sol was submitted to ruling and all who received the imprint, and those they represented, were to submit to the King.

These "subjects" were not the type to minionize themselves. And Sol knew, as did they, that he needed them in order to continue navigating this amazing road to be King of the World. He took a slow deep breath and looked up slightly toward the ceiling.

To some it might look as if Sol was getting religious for a moment. Looking for help or maybe for a sign from some higher power, he exhaled and focused on the Chancellor's eyes for the final moment.

Sol Was Ready To Be King

Chancellor Mahndar stood with the tray in front of him.

"We are here today in this moment because it is the right time. Time is our greatest teacher. Cultures from all over the world for all of history have been preparing for this time. And when we glance backwards in time, we learn many wonderful things that are of value to us today. The great Cherokee people are among many cultures to long for this time. Along with Japanese people, Jewish people, Egyptian people, the Mayan people, the Aztecs, the Sumerians, many have looked forward to a time when a leader would be chosen to bring progress in ways that have been longed for."

"The 8th Sun prophecy has been shared in many forms across many cultures and finds some origins in ancient beliefs. It is from these ancient peoples that we share the ceremonious act of acquiring the handprint of a chosen leader. An action that carries a twofold testimony. It testifies to the submission of the leader to their calling and the role they have taken. As well as testifying to the submission of the people to that leader."

Sol was raptly watching the Chancellor. His confidence, his certainty, his poise. Mahndar was well suited as a public orator. His brow was relaxed, and his soft smile warmed his thin face. There was a decidedly *content to be here* air about him. And he connected with both the group standing quietly at the Speaker's Podium as well as with the Delegates looking on from the many Media Screens.

Sol hoped he too could have the Chancellor's ease of expression when he delivered his statements. There hadn't been a moment yet Sol had not truly appreciated the Chancellor's guidance. And in the seconds before Sol was about to press his hand into the Red Ochre-soaked clay, he was grateful again for the Chancellor's presence.

The seal Sol was about to make was the last step in an entire commitment to this role. He would lay his hand on the silver tray with the cool and supple clay slab soaking in a pool of luxurious Red Ochre, then lay his hand upon the foreheads of those present. The Red Ochre ceremony was one of the most ancient and most permanent symbols of committal. The sharpness of mind and powerful clarity Sol needed right now had flooded in as he was to be sealed King of the World.

The Chancellor took a long breath in.

"Solomon David James, if it please you this day and if you agree to commit to the leadership of this great Globe; for the betterment of civilization, rejecting any draw to self-gain or corrupt rule, please place your right hand on the Red Ochre Seal of Submission."

Sol reached out with his right hand. The moment of uncertainty was fueled by anticipation and nerves. It was a moment rife with dread and anticipation but pulsing with hope.

As he pressed down on the silver tray, the heel of his hand first felt the cool liquid-soaked pad. Then he rolled his palm and fingers into the Red Ochre. His hand sunk slightly into the soft clay beneath the Red Ochre, his imprint forever being cast in clay. Mahndar held the tray tight. He pushed back against Sol's hand in order to keep the silver tray balanced at chest level. Sol was looking directly at Mahndar and Mahndar was fixed on Sol. Ell and the three Delegates with them had their sights on the tray. Nothing was said. Not by the Chancellor, by Sol, or any of them. The stage was quiet, the Media Screens were quiet and for Sol, everything slowed down to a virtual standstill. The act of giving a handprint was part of the Right of Affirmation. The act of laying his hand in the Red Ochre loudly expressed this commitment.

Sol and Mahndar were breathing softly. Communicating with their eyes, '*This is good*'.

Both men felt the power of the moment. Both men knew there was no turning back. And neither of them had a doubt in their mind. This was good! Sol was the King…sealed in front of the entire World Congress and imbued with all the authority in the world.

Sol looked at the tray, his hand, the dye that stained his fingers. He felt the grounding from the coolness of the soft clay, moist beneath his hand. The red ochre dye wicked up the sides of his fingers and then receded as it drew into the clay where Sol had made an imprint. His fingers slightly spread apart.

The handprint in the Red Ochre Seal of Submission was complete. The Chancellor began to draw the tray away from the pressure of Sol's hand. Sol lifted his hand and turned it palm up. He looked at the dark red stain. It was thick enough that it didn't run, and the warmth of Sol's hand returned after removing it from the cool clay slab.

Chancellor Mahndar spoke, "Sol, your act of creating this handprint in the Red Ochre Seal of Submission has sealed you as King of The World. It is with intention and with ceremony, that in this day you were created as King. You have submitted to this Office and have vowed to act in this role in the most noble and beneficent manner that a person can act in. It is now our privilege to support you in your role and to submit to you King Sol…rather Sol." The Chancellor remembered Sol's request to be simply called Sol.

With Sol standing motionless, a freshly died hand palm-up in front of him, the Chancellor announced, "Now, in proxy for the Nations and Regions that are represented by the Delegates of the World Congress, the Delegates here before you, voluntarily present themselves to the new King and submit to the rule of the King. An act that declares all men and women of this unified Globe acknowledge your authority."

Looking up from his hand, Sol watched Darik Liiendor step in front of him. Liiendor humbly bent low in front of Sol. He whispered, "Congratulations my King," and Sol reached out his hand.

This first imprint was probably the most moving moment in the entire ceremony. Considerably more so than when he read about it in the briefing during the flight over.

That world leaders would so willingly affirm the authority and their own service to the King…to Sol…to a man, was truly whelming. The woman and men in front of Sol had been part of designing this ceremony. They knew they would have Sol's inked hand pressed against their foreheads. Even though the Red Ochre would wash off and the moment of ceremony would pass, this act by the Delegates was simply an extraordinary show of support, loyalty, and homage for the King of the World. To bend and have the new King imprint his hand on ones' forehead was an inspiring act of collective allegiance. They were not only testifying to their affirmation of this great leader, but they were speaking on behalf of the entire world.

Liiendor was silent. Sol gently placed his hand on the forehead of the stooped over Delegate. Liiendor's eyes were closed. Sol felt the chill of how serious this was. His hand pressed against the German Delegate's warm skin. It was only two seconds but both King and subject were humbled.

Darik was saying nothing…simply waiting for Sol to lift his hand. Sol's hand began to lift away from Liiendor's brow. And Sol whispered "Thank you Darik"

With the King's hand lifted the Red Ochre imprint left behind was patchy. Darik stepped to the right-hand side of Sol to allow another delegate to move in from the left. The hand of the King had marked the first representative of the women and men of the World.

Ahmed stepped in from the left of Sol to the front of him. Before bowing his head towards Sol, Ahmed spoke softly, "I am here for you my King."

The gentle but firm pressure on his brow placed a perfect mark on the head of Ahmed. The rich skin tone of Ahmed muted the Red Ochre handprint to a certain degree. Ahmed straightened and smiled at Sol. It was a knowing smile.

Sol was starting to feel the Red Ochre dye on his hand begin to dry. He looked to his left as Erin stepped into the space vacated by Ahmed. She spoke, "It is an honor to be part of all that comes with the 8th Sun. Thank you Sol for your willingness."

Sol was trained now...at least for the activities of this Submission Ceremony. He turned his palm to face Erin and raised it towards her brow while she, at the same time, stooped slightly. She held back her hair while keeping her head up and bending at the waist so Sol could mark her forehead. She stood motionless. He pressed his hand against her brow and said, "Thank you Erin,"

The drying dye on his palm felt sticky against her forehead. His hand lifted from Erin and the imprint was less stark than the two Delegates before.

Erin moved beside the two other marked Delegates.

The Chancellor stepped in front of Sol next. He was the last to be imprinted and Sol was quite nervous about marking the Chancellor of the World Congress. Chancellor Mahndar silently and assuringly placed himself directly in front of Sol. He stood a little closer to the nascent King than the others had. Even though the dye was drying on Sol's hand, it was still moist as his palm had become slightly clammy. As the Chancellor stooped in front of Sol, Sol reached up to where he placed his hand gently but firmly on the Chancellor's brow. Pushing up the tuft of hair that fell on the Chancellor's forehead as he had done with the others, Sol held his hand in place and waited. He wasn't sure what he was waiting for, and it was only a second. But neither of them spoke. Then, the Chancellor exhaled. As soon as that breath, which was almost a sigh of relief came, Sol breathed out as well. Both men had found the entire ceremony to be filled with a degree of anticipation and now both of the men had expressed their pleasure with the ceremony. By far the most meaningful of interactions for Sol, was the restful posture that showed on the Chancellor.

Chancellor Mahndar raised his head, looked at Sol, and whispered, "My allegiance to you King Sol."

Then he stepped to the right side of Sol with the three other Delegates and announced to the empty Deliberations Chambers filled only with the watching eyes of the Delegates through the Media Screens. "Esteemed Delegates, we welcome in our midst, as the Sovereign World Leader, our King, Sol!"

The chills that raced up Ell's spine could only be bested by those that flew up Sol's. And if the power of hearing those words…*"**Our King, Sol**…"* was not enough to send shivers, the chills that tingled their entire bodies weakened them as the silence broke and the applause from the Media Screens throughout the chambers resounded. The roar emanated through the hall. Sol could not have known the profound sense of affirmation that came at the extravagated response of the Delegates.

And he basked, for just a moment, in the entrancingly profound sense of realizing the leaders of the entire free-world, eager to have a King, had collectively handed over all authority to him.

Sol was now the King. A whirlwind orientation of the New York Center would be undertaken and pass quickly before leaving tomorrow on the intense journey to the other 7 World Congress Centers.

Only three days ago Sol was jokingly using the phrase, "*If I were King of the World*". But now when asked "**What would you do if you were King of the World?**" he could do it.

His First Edict As King

"**W**ell," Ahmed said to Sol as they settled into their seats on the plane to head to the next stop on the orientation tour, "This is going swimmingly."

Ahmed was referring to the travels they had made so far, visiting each World Congress Center.

"The name change you enacted has been well received by the Delegates. That's New York and Luxembourg off our list. I think you will really enjoy the WCC in Egypt Sol."

Ahmed was a fantastic tour guide. Keeping Sol informed and apprised of more than Sol probably needed to know. He had seen a lot in his years with the World Congress. But this was the first time a leader suggested a name change for the World Congress Center for Global Relations.

Shortly after the Red Ochre Submission ceremony ended, Sol renamed the facilities. The World Congress Center for Global Relations was now called *The World Counsel Center for Global Progress.*

The change of names was a result of Sol and Ell seeing how people were looking for progress. While in the Fall-Out room after the ceremony, the group of six had enjoyed a brief celebration with the most impressive champagne Sol had ever tasted. It would have been wonderful to sit and enjoy successive bottles of the Pol Roger bubbly. The smooth flavours of Winston Churchill's favourite and exclusive brand of champagne would have to be enjoyed more another time. While Sol, Ell, and the handlers went on the orientation tour, Mahndar stayed in the U.S. to stave off the information hungry media. They certainly would be hounding him for info. Looking for any morsel or tell that would tip them off to the changes that may be coming.

When he heard Sol use such thoughtful language in discussion about the WCC name, just moments after his official installment as King, Mahndar knew he was heading towards the level of ownership that might take some leaders months to embrace. He had hoped Sol would cloak himself in the authority that had been imparted to him. And the name change was an excellent indication that was happening.

Sol's explanation for the suggested name change was brief.

"If it were up to me, I would want the name to have the term 'Progress' in it instead of 'Relations'. That would give people the sense that we are not finished moving forward. The World Congress Center for Global Relations almost gives the message that we are done. We have relations across the world and now we sit. Whereas 'Progress' sends the message that we will always need to keep moving forwards." He emphasized by gesturing in a forward motion with his hands.

It was obvious to Mahndar that Sol had a vision for progress. A name change by a new leader in an organization is always propelled by a vision. And Mahndar was fully willing to support Sol's new name. He stood up, went to the end of the table and picked up the Folio sitting there.

Mahndar slid the folio in front of the pensive King. Sol had only had time to take a quick look at the Folio after it was left with him yesterday on his patio. But he knew it was going to be with him most of the time.

"Your Folio is linked to the WCC administration center and to all of the Delegates in the World Congress."

Mahndar tapped the ignite icon on the Folio in front of the King and instructed, "Sol, this is your Scribe. Your Folio will record your edict after you place your hand fully on the screen. Like this."

Mahndar pressed his hand flat on the screen and the screen stayed illuminated but did nothing.

"When you place your handprint here Sol, the system recognizes you and receives your edict as you speak it or type it into the folio. Tap here and the edict is delivered to the entire World Counsel."

The Chancellor tapped the top left of the screen and the WCC symbol glowed.

"Tap here and the edict is sent to the entire world on the Global Messaging System integrated into every Media Screen, Folio, and Mobile device. In a couple taps Sol, any edict or message you want heard by the whole world will be broadcast. Most importantly, as King, you are the sole decision maker on your edicts...upon submitting any edict Sol, it will be done."

The Chancellor spent a minute or two letting Sol know the system would not be live until the weekend. It was clear to Sol how simple and secure it was.

"This device Sol, will sense not only your unique handprint but it senses and measures your emotional and mental state from a bio-metric sensor and feedback perspective."

Sol was curious as to why the complicated sensor system in his Folio. And asking Mahndar about it brought a very reasonable answer.

"Quite simply Sol, everyone wants a King who is stable and makes decisions while in his right mind. This biometric measuring system senses if you are agitated, intoxicated, angry, aloof..., or emotionally ungrounded in any significant way. The assessment is based on the feedback from 12 components of bio-metric sensing. This is detected through the contact of your entire hand to the screen. In that instance, if your emotional and mental state assessment is unfavourable for declaring an edict, your edict cannot be entered into The King's Scribe.

"Just as with any decision, when one is compelled to make choices in response to a strong feeling, one is better off taking pause to consider. If emotion is driving the decision, the decision might be less clearly motivated than it ought to be. It is difficult to reason with emotion."

Quite familiar with critics who asserted a King's absolute power would cause corruption, Ahmed added a thought on the matter.

"Lord Acton spoke about the ability of power to corrupt. He was a brilliant 17th century philosopher. But his studies have shown that power doesn't corrupt; rather it heightens pre-existing ethical tendencies. I believe this is the reason Abraham Lincoln said,

"Nearly all men can stand adversity, but if you want to test a man's character, give him power."

In Ell's mind, her husband would not fail the test that possessing great power would be to him…No!…Rather Sol would have his character laid bare for all to see. Whether they had a crown for Sol to wear or a throne to sit on in some historic castle, all would see that Sol's character is that of a man who rejects corruption at every turn and pursues the greater good.

Mahndar resumed his instructional, "And just so you know where to find the edict scribe system on your Folio, look here," Mahndar swiped the folio screen to the left and showed Sol the icon on the home page.

Sol found the small image of a king chess piece with a quill in his hand amusing. Underneath the icon were the words, "The King's Scribe."

"Touch here," Mahndar tapped his finger on the chess piece, "And the system is ready for you to give it input."

Sol reached for the Folio and pulled it closer. He touched the icon and placed his hand on the screen. The haptic feedback prompted him. The system was ready instantly.

Sol looked at the Chancellor and asked, "So I just have to speak the edict and The King's Scribe will capture it?"

"That's right." Mahndar affirmed.

Sol looked at the Folio. Beneath his hand the pulsating white light of the screen ensured Sol the system was functioning and had been assessing Sol's status from the instant his hand contacted the screen. Then Sol began. He was about to make his first edict. More of a practice edict because he knew the system was not live for a few days yet.

He paused, took a breath, and gave some thought. What would happen if he tried to impose an edict while he was hungry?

Sol began, "As of this day, I declare that all Twinkies be placed in the King's pantry to be consumed by the King and his guests at the King's leisure."

Ahmed just about shot Champagne out his nose as he tried to stifle a laugh while holding a mouth full of bubbly. No one expected to hear that from Sol. The white glow under Sol's hand showed a tinge of blue now and the system announced in a gentle AI voice with a hint of a British accent.

"Edict deferred due to hunger, we are sorry for the delay. Please try again soon."

The system was designed so Sol would take the time to assess his feelings upon enacting a law or edict. Throughout history too many men and women...leaders with power...had often made decisions from too great of an emotional position when wisdom was only an arm's length away. They just needed to reassess before acting on a decision. Even high-level judges had been swayed in parole hearings when asked to make a judgment on a case just before lunch. Emotion was clearly a decision driver and the King's Scribe was accounting for that.

Ell moved closer to see what was on the screen. As Sol lifted his hand from the Folio she saw the edict. It was an official digital document with a watermark of Sol's blue handprint glowing in background. The words of Sol's pronouncement were in the middle of the document and the date, time, and edict number were at the bottom of the digital page. On this particular "test edict", the system indicated the edict had been deferred. But had this been a successful edict, the handprint of the King would be glowing red and the words *"Edict Successfully Recorded"* would hover over the digital page on the Folio screen.

The test edict was a perfect opportunity to see how this little device could work to protect Sol. Protect him from himself as well as protecting the people from an emotionally charged reactionary decision. The need for the King's Scribe was a brilliant reminder that throughout history a great many people lost their heads because of a King or Queen having a tantrum or emotional outburst with nothing to stop them from acting on how they felt.

With this ingenious system, one could be confident that greed, hatred, lust, envy, or even just simple fear, would not be the forces driving decisions that would affect the entire world. Everyone wants a King who makes decisions wisely…and that is the kind of King Sol wanted to be.

"Well, that is slick," Sol announced.

"It is indeed," replied The Chancellor. "Are you ready to deliver your first edict?"

"You mean about the WCC name?"

"Yes, it will be in queue until the weekend, when the system is fully live, but shall we give it a go Sol?" The Chancellor prompted.

Sol placed his hand back on the screen, the King's Scribe program was still open. Sol automatically went into edict-making mode…kind of a dictation style he had picked up when he used to dictate outlines and bibliographies for the research papers he was sending to various professors at the University.

"I declare this day, the World Congress Center for Global Relations shall be from henceforth called, the World Counsel Center for Global Progress."

The Folio affirmed Sol with a glowing red hue indicating a successful edict, displaying *"Edict Successfully Recorded"* as it *chimed, "Thank You Sol."*

"And it's just that easy," The Chancellor stated.

Right there, in the Fall-Out room moments after a moving Red Ochre Ceremony, Sol had made his first edict as King.

Offering the last of his instructions the Chancellor finished, "Go ahead and touch the Delegates icon on the top left. As soon as the system is live, your edict... your first official edict, will be received by the entire Body of Delegates, World Counsel Delegates that is."

Brainwashing Mantra To Enlist Mindless Drones

The lights were dim in their villa-sized hotel room. The Media Screen was glowing as the low volume hummed in the background. The World Congress Special Report had come on. Live here in the late evening in Guangzhou China, but it was early morning back in Sol's hometown. There was an impending sense of change amid the speculation driving the news specials that streamed all week about the World Congress. The Stream Sol and Ell were watching displayed the amazing history of the World Congress. The narrator covered the inception and evolution of the World Congress from the days when the United Nations began to dissolve. With seamless creativity the newsy edutainment production flowed right on into the present. The amazing achievements of the World Congress were highlighted with an emphasis on its nearly flawless run. A run where corruption had been almost entirely evaded by this monumentally powerful and magnificently cooperative world government.

Tonight was the evening announcement that would prepare the world for something great. An announcement that the World Congress, and the world, was about to receive her new leader and a new epoch for leadership.

The World Congress had so proficiently performed its duties of uniting, guiding, and protecting Global relations; as well as stabilizing the economy and international Governance, that society was ready to support almost any move it would make that brought hope if even at some risk. Sol felt truly supported by the Delegates he had met with at the World Counsel Centers he had visited. Each region was unique, and every meeting brought difficult questions and insightful suggestions on how to remedy the major issues faced by the people of each region.

While in Namibia Africa, the Delegates Sol chatted with were quite eager to engage him on his plan to remedy the socio-economic disparity in their region. The African socio-economic system looked pretty equal...pretty clean on the outside. But the real inner workings never truly stepped ahead into the world of true equality. And the distribution of wealth was still a problem.

The wealthiest one percent of Namibians possess and control more than the poorest half of the population combined. Social and economic segregation have both continued even amid the growing African GDP. Sol had noticed while in Africa, that even though the segregation of the classes is somewhat subdued it subtly worked to keep various groups separate in areas like access to childcare, healthcare, well paid jobs, and urban development. No matter how far things had evolved for the African economy and her vibrant culture, people still leaned towards segregation. The rich were rich and an overwhelming number of Namibia's poor... despondently so.

Sol had told the Delegates in Namibia he had a redistribution of wealth plan for this type of disparity. Not only for Africa but for all parts of the world where there is a profound disparity in income from the richest to the poorest. When Sol started to discuss the benefits of a hybrid Marxist-Communism-Socialism approach to distribution of wealth, the Delegates prodded. They became so at ease with Sol and his plan for redistributing wealth that they gave his plan its own moniker. *"Solmunism."*

Sol told the Delegates how his plan would level things out. The lower and middle classes, he now called the "Majority-class". Solmunism, envisioned a society where collective well-being is paramount. Blending Marxist principles of social equality with socialist structures of resource distribution, and a communitarian focus on shared responsibility. Solmunism aims to create a dynamic balance, ensuring equitable access to resources while fostering individual contribution and community cohesion. It prioritizes the elimination of extreme wealth disparity, and the creation of a society where everyone has opportunities to thrive, based on the principle of shared prosperity and the greatest good for the greatest number. In *Solmunism,* society would be devoid of sexism, racism, and other forms of oppression. It was a distant reality at best for the Namibian Delegates but the idea that everyone in a society receives the benefits to achieve equality, was a panacea for those Delegates. They couldn't wait to hear more. But Sol was just there for an orientation and needed to continue on to become familiar with the remaining WCC's in China, New Zealand and Paraguay before launching his plan.

As the prodding questions of their King continued, Ahmed stepped in. He simply announced to the immensely eager and curious Delegates, there would be time for deeper conversations with Sol, after he was presented to the World in a week. They would have to wait until Sol had worked out the details. And on this night, the sprouts of hope that poked out of the ground in Namibia as elsewhere on Sol's journey, would be blossoming in front of the whole world with the big announcement.

Ell and Sol were able to relax in their suite, and two of the three handlers sat in their rooms. Ahmed was delivering the announcement. They were fixed on the Stream. The uneasiness each felt was subdued as they waited for the local news to wrap up and the Stream announcing the bold change in the World Congress to begin. Each of them was thoroughly invested. The first week in Sol's orientation journey had certainly shown the commitment of at least the party of 5 who travelled with him. Their work together had already knit them together in a way unlike the typical bonds one might expect from a group of travellers. The three handlers were immersed into the promise for progress that came with the appointment of a King. With only a week left until the return to the United States, Erin, Ahmed, and Darik were clearly eager to bring Sol home to New York for the Presentation Ceremony. And the entire world would be viewing the announcement along with them.

Down in the lobby of their hotel the Jackson family, tourists to Guangzhou, had just arrived back at the hotel after an early supper together and attending a Chinese Major League Baseball Game. They all looked a little weary from the travelling that brings many stresses all on its own. Dragging three kids around Guangzhou China is even taxing on the nerves of a laid-back Kiwi. As laid back as Mr. and Mrs. Jackson were, it was clear they were ready to get in the elevator so they could shut out the noise of China's largest city for another night. Mrs. Jackson took their little guy's hand and they turned to head to the elevator.

All at once they stopped. Kids, adults, the whole family. Even the man on the phone in the hotel lobby interrupted his conversation. The lady on the sofa waiting for her husband and the Jacksons all turned to one of the many lobby Media Screens. The man who was having a conversation on his phone, held his Mobile Device in front of him now to catch the stream, knowing the caller on the other end was doing the same. It had become instinctual. Just like it was in every gathering place and private residence across China and the world, the Media Screens in the Panyu Hotel lobby were all ignited for the announcement. When the devices and screens chimed with the penetrating riff alerting all to the incoming Live Stream, people tuned in. The countdown to the Live Stream began. Scrolling across the screen was the message;

In 10 Seconds the World Congress will be bringing you a special broadcast.

In the early years of the World Congress the Live Streams came with such regularity that society found them to be an interruption. The chime was an intrusion into the lives, conversations, phone calls, sports events and even intimate moments of citizens. Yet all eyes would find their way to a Media Screen either in hand or mounted somewhere. The early feelings about the government legislated system that was imposed on culture, were feelings of suspicion. People and critics alike thought it was too forceful of an intrusion into their lives. *"Surely,"* many thought, the propaganda that would flow from the World Congress Media arm '**DBNI**' would be regular and would be mind-numbing.

Culture had been victim to brainwashing tactics of both government and marketing geniuses in the past and the voices of the conspiracy theorists were shrill and constant in the early years. Some decried the *Digital Broadcast Network International* as the anti-Christ. A portent for the end of days. But the DBNI silenced its critics. The Media arm of the World Congress was not the propaganda machine of the Cold War era, the Nazi Germany period, or the feverish capitalist era of Meta, Tik-Tok and the like in the 2020's. These periods of propaganda and algorithms slowly fed distorted information and content to the world, in an attempt to elicit control of society on a massive scale. The most nefarious of these being witnessed in Hitler's attempt to exterminate the entire Jewish Race.

His mantra, "***Arbeit macht frei***", translated as *Work Will Set You Free,* was a profoundly true but sinisterly distorted rip-off of a quote by German philologist Lorenz Diefenbach. In Diefenbach's 1873 novel titled ***"Arbeit macht frei: Erzählung von Lorenz Diefenbach",*** in which gamblers and fraudsters find the path to virtue through labour, the use of the phrase was clear. The phrase was meant for those trapped by social vices to see how honest work would be the cure and set them free from the perpetuation of their addictive ills. It was used by the Nazis however as a brainwashing mantra to enlist mindless drones to work hard for a country that demanded their allegiance.

Many other governments and social groups including mainstream marketing ad-men, have attempted to employ similar styles of propagandizing. Media broadcasts had been the medium to success for a great many governments in modern history.

It is no wonder the early years of the DBNI system of imposed information Streams felt like propaganda. And to a brainwashing-sensitive society, there was a real unwelcome feel to the escalated use of media. But as the global Digital Broadcast system worked out its few kinks, society accepted it as part of life. Many in fact, respected the system for what it offered. The World Congress had successfully integrated an imposed system of disseminating information into society. A system that could not be opted out of because of the requirement for every media device to have the integrated firmware installed by the factory. When the chime sounded, the screen ignited, and the countdown notice scrolled. All citizens gave their attention to the Digital Broadcast Network International-**DBNI**. What was about to be Streamed was important. Important enough to stop everything anyone was doing. And both in the lobby and in Ell and Sol's suite, viewers were drawn to the countdown.

The World Congress and The Digital Broadcast Network will be bringing you an important Stream 10 seconds....9—8—7—6—5....

Join Us For This History Making Announcement

.4, 3, 2,1.

The World Congress logo faded and Ahmed was standing in front ▪ ▪ ▪ of the Speaker's Podium at the World Counsel Center for Global Progress in China.

"Greetings." Ahmed started." It is a privilege to Stream to you this evening."

The sound cascaded everywhere. Ahmed's confident tone echoed through hallways, houses, hotels, and streets. Every bar, every theater, every car, shop, public transport, and handheld device in every park or plaza across the globe was captured in the net of this medium. A small World Counsel Film crew was there to chronicle Sol's every expression and word. Ahmed proceeded to announce something that the world had not conceived before.

"Thank you for taking a moment to participate in this Stream. We at the World Congress appreciate your time."

Ahmed had a way about him that worked magically with Sol and the small groups they had run into over the past week. You wouldn't call it charisma but something about Ahmed's affability just sat right with folk. Sol was eager to see how Ahmed would do in front of the whole world.

Sol sipped his vodka and cranberry while he and Ell shared the sofa in their hotel room for this announcement. He was thoughtfully preparing for his Presentation Day. Sol paid close attention to Ahmed.

"It is with great delight and unanimous certainty of the World Congress that I am privileged to stand before you today for a historical announcement. Today is a brilliant day in the history of the World Congress and also in the history of our World. As you know, since the dissolution of the United Nations the present entity known as the World Congress has successfully guided humanity into many advances that have benefited us all. We all enjoy the benefits to improved international relations, the Global economy, and the development of many political mechanisms to bring us all to this place of prosperity and as close to world unity as is possible. We of the World Congress have been happy to serve you by appointment in each of these areas. At this time in the development of the Global Government, the World Congress has come to another unanimous decision.

"The past decade has proven to halt progress on some levels. Some very important levels. Through extensive talks amongst the Body of Delegates, it has come to our attention that we have met with a time that necessitates a change. The once smoothly running mechanism that has brought so much positive change is effectively shackled in its efforts to move humanity forward from the place we find it today. It is a common sentiment that the social ills, hidden & open crimes, and the corrupt behaviors of humanity, are the inevitable outcome of the culture we have designed by our own hands. Many conjecture that humans will not change and therefore, a once benign acceptance of these failings has become a malignant tumor. Society has failed to advance in many ways. Failures that are truly dire, are camouflaged by the grand advances and success we have enjoyed that display our prosperity on many levels.

"This malignancy has developed into a crippling apathy. An apathy that accepts the dysfunction in society and refuses to confront the rudimentary issues with our society. The issues that affect us all and are often neglected. Injustices and inequities that affect individuals have been unattended by a world that has enjoyed the progress that comes with grand political and technological achievements.

"It is with this in mind that the World Congress has chosen to alter the model of leadership we presently operate under. The Body of Delegates has agreed unanimously that the time for this change is now and that the presence of apathy must be confronted by society. This is something we have failed to do under our present model.

"We would like to invite you to participate in a Live Stream that will unveil the model that has been approved and put into motion. One week from today. At 12 PM, the World Congress and the DBN will present to you the newly formed World Congress model of government and the leadership that has been put in place to guide us. We hope you will join us for this history making announcement. I look forward to seeing you then."

"Good Night."

Until He Resigns, Is Killed, Or Dies

The phone rang in their suite. It was past 10 now. Ell picked up. "Hello"

"Hello Ell, its Erin, did you watch Ahmed's announcement?"

"We watched it twice."

"And…how are you guys doing? Is everything ok?"

Erin had the role of feeling out the stages of Sol's rise to King. She was somewhat of an intuit. This is one of the reasons Ell and her got on so well. Ell could never really shut off her sensors either. Didn't matter if it was her Mother-in-law, her client, or her hubby Sol, she was always tuned in in a sense, to the general feelings a person was having…and the signals they were giving off. Getting to the one-week announcement point was a huge stage in the forward movement for Sol. Erin had been paying close attention to the developing King.

Even though the world-wide declaration was to be made at the Presentation Ceremony on Saturday, Sol had already officially become King. But the point of no return had not passed yet. If Sol decided he wanted out, then it had to happen before the Presentation. And it was Erin's job to check in often to see if everything was on track.

She had thought the incident on the plane might have been that moment. It was shortly after take-off from Namibia on the way to China. Sol had spent some private moments stooped over the sink in the lavatory. Something had triggered Sol into vomiting. Everyone on the plane heard the retching echo from the thin-walled airplane lav. Erin was ready to step in with the Checkmate Protocol if Sol wanted out. Perhaps Sol was having a moment of realization that he could not take on this role.

The World Congress knew the risks that came with choosing an individual for this role. Sure, there would have been line-ups of men and women who would vie for this position of power if they had decided to hold an open selection process. But choosing one person such as Sol, one who was not known to have a political background nor a lust for power, meant there was an ever-present risk. The risk that this "One" might decide the position was just too much for him. But Erin noticed how he recovered on that flight.

The emotions that triggered the vomiting must have been powerful. Seeing how Ell and Sol worked together to ensure Sol wasn't going to head into a tailspin, informed Erin of a lot. When she had heard the retching sounds coming from the new King in the airplane lavatory she had began to search on her folio for the resignation document. She was excited about Sol being King so nothing pleased her more than when her hopes were not dashed. When Sol got through that event Erin was elated. She was quick to stop searching for the *Checkmate Protocol.*

What Erin didn't know about this incident on the plane was how things went before Sol got up to go to the lavatory. Sol was sitting in his seat somewhat uncomfortably but enjoying Ell's company along with an in-flight beverage. What was unignorable, had started before boarding. Since Sol was a young lad, he had learned to rely on his ability to recognize and interpret his own feelings. Like what was developing this morning before boarding the plane. He began to feel a slight pressure in his lower back just above his left hip. It wasn't the same every time but at times, when there was an issue of conflict or some level of dissonance in his thoughts over a situation, Sol would take note of what his body was doing. And on the plane that day, the dissonance was doing its thing in Sol. Sol was beginning to note the telltale signs of what was going inside.

Closing his eyes he focused his thoughts on the point of discomfort. Seeing the area in his back that was reacting to his situation was easy. The meditative efforts gave Sol a clear picture of his left hip and lumbar area just left of his spine. As he thought on this area of discomfort his focus shifted. An unseen band of heat started to wrap around his left side to the front. As it did Sol collected some of his fears and concerns with where he was in this King of the World thing. Seeing his body as a messenger was a long-honed sense of Sol's. A skill that grounded Sol in moments of uncertainty, fear, or distress.

On the plane that day, it was his own discomfort that was manifesting the symptoms he was feeling. And as he pondered just how broad and how vast this new job as King of the World was going to be, things got worse before they got better.

But Sol knew better than to ignore the messages his body was giving him. And that's why he ended up hunched over a stainless-steel sink in the World Counsel Air Transport. Sol's moments of introspection and retching had left him feeling sheepish but still intact. There was no doubt in his mind what was ahead of him may well be more intense than he would like. But he was completely committed to all that being King of the World meant. As Erin watched him recover from the lavatory episode she was pleased to acknowledge the King's resiliency. The *Checkmate Protocol* would sit snugly in her folio for now.

The *Checkmate Protocol* was the document packet that winds down the King of The World's reign. It was a typical termination document. Sign here, handprint there, witness sign here...that sort of thing. No one could expect the King to just disappear without some formal process. And what if a King was unwilling or became incapable of performing his or her duties? How would it be handled for a King to be removed from his or her reign at some point in the future?

Keeping it simple, the committee that composed the *Checkmate Protocol*, recommended the King remains until they resign, is killed, or dies. Considering the amplitude of the office of a King, the committee felt this *Checkmate Protocol* was essential. The simplicity of it was enough to facilitate the departure of a King from the throne.

After checking in with the other handlers on the plane that day, Erin saw no reason to introduce Sol to *The Checkmate Protocol.*

The Decade's Most Anticipated Announcement On DBN

The stimulating DBN broadcast chimed as the Media Screens and mobile devices ignited. Even those using the integrated Media Screen eyewear halted their activities. The left half of their left lens flashed the words…*"DBN Special Report"*. And their focus went from out towards the world, to a tight close-up on their personal eyewear screen.

DBN's top anchor was center screen. The DBN team had gone mobile with their studio today for the breaking report and panel discussion. In the background was the World Congress Center in New York. Off to the left of the screen the panel of commentators was sitting behind a large round table. The reflection of the sun was muted as it basked the trademark table. DBN's renowned Table of Truth had hosted thousands of exposés and in-depth stories from this monolith of a table.

The aged gray cedar apron was the perfect contrast to the etched glass top. The broad apron, that appeared modest yet historically significant from the presence of the patina that had been placed on it, supported the inch-thick glass underneath the elbows of all who gathered around it to share in hearing and giving opinions.

As the natural light of the setting sun cascaded across the front of the World Congress façade behind them, the stray beams glimmered off the glass etching that adorned the surface of the table's top. The etching was a reproduction of Jesuit Heinrich Scherer's cartographic masterpiece. The depiction of the Magellan world journey displayed a monumental moment in the voyage. Showing only the Victoria left in the Magellan armada, the etchings on the opposite side of the north polar projection of the world showed a meager but heroic 18 sailors. Of the original 237 who set sail, these travel weary survivors could be seen making their way up to the Santa María de la Victoria church in Seville. Few in number yet large in the accomplishment that propelled exploration forward, they intended to give thanks for their safe return.

The Table of Truth etched-glass artwork, spoke to all the great advances of the past and present, including the one that was about to be spoken of on the Live Stream today.

After Ahmed's World Congress announcement, the media was spinning. Calls to the Chancellor's office were furiously coming in and questions were non-stop. Chancellor Mahndar was usually quite frank with the media. It was no secret that giving quality info was better than offering little. Sparse information just engendered an environment of speculation where the spin and hype would often just incite the masses. But today, Mahndar was uncharacteristic with his offerings to the media. And the DBN team was doing their infotaining best to fill in the blanks.

The intro chime faded, and the faceless voice of the Digital Broadcast Network filled the silence.

"Tonight, on DBN, we bring you a special report with our panel of experts to examine the latest World Congress announcement and what changes may come."

The shot drew in tight on the moderator.

"Welcome to our Stream ladies and gentlemen, I'm Coopers Drisden and it is my delight to sit here today with you and with a panel from whom I have learned so much."

Coopers Drisden had a bright and intense manner about him. He was one of those anchor types who was not merely newsie. His style, his depth and authority in his voice, his delivery, and his welcoming look drew people. The very nature of the pervasive and interruptive Media Streams was imbibing enough. But Coopers Drisden multiplied the catatonia-like effects of the media stream on the viewer. Those who would normally submit their attention to the Media Screen were rendered even more submissive to the message of the DBN's Coopers Drisden.

Drisden narrated on.

"Reactions to yesterday's announcement by Delegate Ahmed Marif of the World Congress are broad. On today's special edition of the DBN Talk Block, we will be hearing from our panel on what the probable changes to the World Congress are. As we wait for the wildly anticipated announcement on Saturday at Noon GMT, our panel is here to help us find our way through the questions. What is this dramatic change coming to the World's most potent and most effective global government? Let's join our panel."

The automated camera deftly panned over to the Table of Truth. The panel of experts were already sitting. Coopers Drisden joined them at the empty chair. As moderator, Drisden would direct the event. The camera that sat in the middle of the table, picking up shots of each of the participants, was guided by the moderator as he would cue on the guests. Coopers settled in and when he addressed Jared Franks, the system followed the moderator's lead. Sitting discretely in the middle of the table was the main *AIMS* system and out of the shot just above the panellists, was the *AIMS-Halo Cam* encircling the whole set. *AIMS* stood for *Autocam Intuitive Media Solution,* and it had changed the behind-the-camera broadcast world. The cameras responded smoothly and flawlessly to Drisden's cues.

"Jared," Coopers began, "Tell us what you know about this astonishing move the World Congress is about to announce on Saturday at noon."

"You know Coopers, I have been at this correspondent gig for a few years now. And even before my time, since 2029 when the World Congress Media Screen firmware became law, I have always been amazed at how this global governing body leads into a major announcement with a major announcement. Why don't they just make the big announcement instead of making an announcement to tell us about a future announcement?"

Coopers nodded and flashed a smile of agreement affirming Jared's comment.

"But if you must know, in the over 15 years I have been at this game, there has been no other announcement so closely guarded after the pre-announcement. I am at a loss to pin this one down Coopers. Last night was a huge introduction to Saturday's secret we are all waiting for. The World Congress has never been known as the entity that closely guards what direction it is planning to take on an issue. I recall when the 9-11 proposition was being struck. The pre-announcement came and that very hour I had a call in to the Chancellor's office. I was given a short but certainly un-guarded answer that pointed at the very important proposition that was going to alter the global acceptance of nuclear weapons and nuclear weapon research. So today I am not sure what the World Congress has got planned. The Chancellor's office intoned how unanimity of the Body of Delegates' vote was driving this anticipated change in the World Congress model."

The wide shot from behind Coopers caught the nods of the other panelists. *AIMS* zeroed itself on Bryson Reynolds, a bespeckled political lawyer and recent author of the best-selling book, "*Why I'm Always Right.*" It was a snide tome that pushed back hard at leftist politics and their neo-socialist philosophies with their tendency to neglect order when working to refine social policy. Bryson favoured the authoritarian structures that kept society balanced. His views were strong, and he was of the group that was ever ready to throw his support behind the World

Congress. He was often quoted from his book that examined the present forms of World governance. In the book Reynolds said.

> *"The World Congress was a radical shift away from the geographically based governments of yesteryear. A global conglomerate inspired by the unique position the United Nations had designed in its efforts to enhance global intergovernmental interactions. The entire model that is found in the World Congress is only a step toward, but indeed a large step towards, the desperately needed leadership that will do what needs to be done. Steps that must be taken to subdue the decay of social disorder our world has struggled against for millennia."*

And Bryson was not alone in his views. He had a large body of supporters across the globe. The subtle voice of culture's disappointment with culture itself was cooing from a distance. And it had drawn many into its co-op that held there will always be a need for positive and intentional change. People who were disenchanted by the usual progress of government.

In response to his vocal Brysonite following, Bryson Reynolds was working on a follow up book to *"Why I'm Always Right!"* It is titled, *"That's the Way Things Should Go."* It is a macrocosm look at reality from the perspective of a strong right-winger.

In his upcoming volume, Bryson works to shine a light on the persistent inequities and injustices that seem to surface no matter what style of government is being practiced. Even with the almost omnipotent World Congress in place, Bryson puts the hammer down on how transformation in Government has had little effect on transformation of society. *"Effective democratic politics does not make for effective people"* Bryson would say.

Bryson's odd but brilliantly frank delivery fit well with his quirky fashion sense. The flowery *'I could care less what anyone thinks of me,'* ascot that he sported, and the satin paisley blazer was not just a gimmicky commentator costume. It was his style. Bold, colorful...and a little out there. And Bryson was his outfit...Bold, colorful, and a little out there.

When Bryson wasn't ranting on a DBN Stream his wardrobe was plenty loud enough to carry the conversation. Bryson was clear to state that society needed a change, and Bryson was fighting the good fight against all that stays the same. Coopers knew he was in for an entertaining bit from Bryson as he turned his question to him.

"Mr. Reynolds, The World Congress Center seen over your shoulder, appears to be quite silent at the moment, surely there must be a frenzy of behind the scenes activity in preparation for the upcoming announcement. Do you have a reasonable idea of what is to come in this Saturday's announcement?"

Bryson Reynolds was practically quivering. He did have a reasonable idea, and he could hardly contain himself. That was one of the entertaining idiosyncrasies of the colorful Mr. Reynolds. His tentacles for information gathering reached far. And when he had latched on to a juicy meal of internationally significant information, he held it close to his chest until he had an opportunity to fling his arms open wide and show it to the world.

Bryson Reynolds just about popped. And then he started.

"Through no illegal means a delightfully candid Paraguayan connection of mine had certain documents come across her desk. She was able to send me a copy of the invoice for a procedure that is occurring right now in Paraguay at the World Congress Center for Global Relations. I have learned that a Paraguayan sign installation company is at this moment installing a new sign on the façade of the World Congress Center.

"Now I am not certain Coopers if this is the grand news that is to be announced on Saturday, nor if it is connected to the World Congress's mention of a leadership transition of some sort. But what I am 100 percent certain of is that the World Congress Center for Global Relations is being given a new name. I am certain on Saturday we will hear the announcement that what was once the World

Congress Center for Global Relations, is now named the World Counsel Center for Global Progress."

Kelsey Fairbanks jumped in from across the table. "That sounds like solid information Bryson." Kelsey had run through these circles for years. She was usually all for reformation and when she got word of big change in big government, Kelsey was quick to find allies who could update her on intel that she may have trouble finding.

The production team was at work in the control booth. Kelsey had gotten word in her ear that the team had file footage of the day the United Nations sign came down and was replaced with the World Congress sign. It didn't happen the day the UN officially dissolved. But not long after, when the World Congress launched its mandate to draw members from beyond the limits the UN was met with, the world watched as the marquee at the United Nations building in New York was removed. It was an oddly chilling moment for those watching that day. How could anyone know that that historic evolution of government wasn't going be the thing that caused unrest between the nations and regions? And everyone got a chilling feeling at seeing the complete dissolution of a monumental form of government. The rapid erosion of an organization that had brought humanity so far, in order to make way for something more progressive.

Fairbanks took the floor. "Bryson, we have a shot of the UN sign changing from over 30 years ago. Take a look at this."

The stream showed the day the world witnessed the end of an 80-year-old icon. The greatest advocate for peace and cooperation between nations the world had ever seen. And since its inception in 1942 with only 26 member nations, there had been few hurdles that it did not successfully negotiate. If the hurdle could not be jumped over successfully the UN would ensure that damage to international relations would be minimal.

Jared Franks responded to the video, "I am certain there is more to come from the World Congress than just a simple name change. New leadership frequently begets a new name. We know the new name now but...if Bryson's information is accurate, then what is the intention of the new name? Why did the Delegates agree to use the word *Counsel*, a word that infers the offering of advice and input, instead of Council?

The *World Counsel Center for Global Progress???*

"How does this message of "Progress" fit the changes we are about to see and who is the group that gives counsel in this new model? The political progress made by the World Congress is clear so what type of progress might come with this mystery leadership model that Chancellor Mahndar will be presenting on Saturday?"

As Coopers closed the show, you could hear the *thwap thwap thwap* of the rotors slapping the air from the DBN chopper circling around the Paraguay WCC. The aerial view showed clear shots of the sign placement that everyone now believed was being undertaken. The entire façade, including the new signage, was covered under an industrial size shroud, keeping prying cameras from getting a full view of what was being done to the World Congress signage.

"Gentlemen, Jared Franks is asking the questions I am sure many are beginning to ask. *'What progress can we expect from the mystery leadership model of the World Counsel Center for Global Progress?'*

"We will have to wait however until Saturday to hear the answers. The World Congress is being careful not to leak the info early. And if as we have seen from the World Congress in past formative actions, we can expect that the announcement will be riveting.

"We will all be watching as DBN takes you live on Saturday to the announcement set to be delivered right here in what is today a quiet Square but promises to be a packed Plaza. This square behind our panel will be filled with citizens taking in the decade's most anticipated announcement. We'll be here LIVE Saturday.

"I'm Coopers Drisden—And 'THIS...is **DBN Live**'."

The Elder Abuse Problem Was Almost Epidemic

Saturday had arrived. Sol and his group just deplaned after getting in from El Salvador. Two weeks, 8 World Congress Centers, and Sol had received an amazing education. Starting in New York 13 days ago, then to El Salvador, Luxembourg Germany, Egypt, Namibia, China, New Zealand, and Paraguay. The orientation into the inner workings of the World Congress had literally filled Sol with a zeal to get started in his role as King. Sol had a new understanding of the way his world ran, and the World Congress had a New King and a new name. He would return to each Centre over the coming months after the Presentation Ceremony today. But for now, the tornado of a tour was over.

Sol had hoped to make it home to Seattle for a half a day to relax with Ell before he had to get to the New York WCC. But the timing was just too tight. All 8 World Congress Centers in 14 days gave only a day and a half at each Center. A half a day for travel between Centers with the final stop perfectly timed. Sol didn't think they could do it when he left New York 14 days earlier...but here they were...back in New York New York.

Ell had already arrived at the WCC building waiting for Sol and the Handlers to pull in. She had flown in earlier to meet Sol. She had talked to him every day during the last half of the journey. Sol was so grateful she was able to spend the first week with him before she headed home to manage a few things ahead of the Presentation Ceremony.

Her excitement about the position had grown since she left Sol. She hadn't spoken of it to Sol yet, but two days after she arrived home in Seattle, she caught wind of a horrible situation that stirred her up. Knowing who her Sol was, she knew he would be stirred up just as much as she. For both of them, there was little worse than getting impassioned over a situation and not being able to do anything about it. As King, Sol was now in a position to do something. After what she had seen, Ell was all for Sol being the guy to make real change.

She had been scrolling the News Feeds and a horrific story caught her. She tapped the video to watch the DBN Special on *Elder Abuse*. Since the mid 30's there had been a greater number of Elderly on the earth than there were children. It was no mystery how that happened, it was just simple math. The Baby Boomers had outpaced every generation for birth rate numbers. And now they were tipping the scales on the geriatric end of the demographic balance. Birth rates had only modestly been declining since the late 20's and lifespans were increasing. Culture had not adapted well. The resources available to care for the elderly had been taxed for decades.

One of the unique characteristics of this demography was that there were two classes of elderly in society. The "Anti-Agers" and the "Aged". The first was only a small percentage of the entire group. They were a group that took aging into their own hands. For about 20 years now, the holistic and allopathic medical communities had made great strides in finding a better way to manage aging. The combined efforts of the two groups…one looking at how we minimise the process of oxidizing and cell damage due to stress and stimulus that the elderly are subject to, while the other side of the team began an intense focus on hormone replacement therapies.

These therapies were not new. Hormone Replacement Therapy, HRT, had gone on for 5 decades. And they had some modest level of acceptance in the pre-2020's era. But since the mutually affirming activities of the two medical bodies brought credibility and acceptance to the respective streams of anti-aging, the reform in anti-aging procedures took off. It was roughly estimated that by using bio-identical human growth hormones, 18 to 22 percent of seniors were effectively combatting the disease-causing factors that came with aging. For those who embraced the age reversing treatments, cell reconstruction was ongoing. HRT re-engineered their brains to be more youthful, their bones less brittle, their skin, eyes, hair, and heart were generally considered to be 20 to 30 years younger than their same age counterparts not on hormones.

Many however, could not afford the Anti-Aging hormone replacement therapies. For most of the aged, getting older the way the world had always gotten older was the only acceptable option. And for others in the senior's demographic, plain simple fear of pharmaceuticals kept them from wearing the HRT patch. As with any therapy the odd casualty of the treatment would surface. Always an incident that was hyper-reported spreading fear in its media-generated wake. And even though for over 96 percent of users their quality of life was dramatically improved, the frequent reference to horror stories was so compelling that the rigid thinking of the aging mind defaulted to do what old, entrenched minds do. Resistance! Resistance towards embracing this quality-of-life enhancing protocol. And for those who steered clear of the age-defying hormone treatment, all too many of them were forced into care they would never have chosen if they could. And many were forced to receive abuse they might have avoided if they had accepted the pricey anti-aging treatment.

Sadly, because of the huge demand on resources that went toward caring for the aging, a growing number of elderly became the victims of elder abuse. At the hands of family or healthcare providers, the frail and defenceless seniors would frequently be victimized when they were the most vulnerable. During bath time or while having their soiled undergarments changed, during mealtime when a mildly non-compliant senior would cause a disturbance at or reject the food being offered to her. Far too often in these cases a care provider would give in to the frustration and then abuse their power over the elderly charge. Purposely neglecting the needs of a dependant elder or simply inflicting outright harm on the frail old grandpa or grandma.

Ell was entirely disturbed as she took in the unsettling images of the most recent case to be discovered. And the DBN special report on Elder Abuse, titled *"**Feeling the Pinch on Aging**"* offered far too many images for Ell to ignore. The DBN Stream displayed hidden camera activities of Elders being cared for in various institutions and private residences.

Not that it was trivial in any way but one of the less obvious forms of the abuse was the pinching that happened to elders. A subtle and painful action used on an old person who was not doing as their caregiver wanted them to. Ell viewed several clips that day.

It was clear that resources to manage the vast number of seniors were thin but the methods some abusive family members used, to herd their elderly parent or grandparent were completely minacious. In one of the incidents that was caught on camera, a middle-aged man was trying to hurry his mother along through the parking lot of the mall. The old gal with her walker was lagging behind the sharp pace of her son. It was always a mystery why people could behave so wickedly and be so stupid in public. It was rare these acts were not caught on video. Video cameras and Drone Corps recordings were always ready to catch not only every act of kindness in society but every evil as well. Thankfully, the acts of abuse were always available for review. The scenes sat on servers ready to be accessed if a court case or a false accusation would rear its ugly head. Nothing was more valuable in offering proof of what happened than the good old reliable CCTV camera.

In one of the clips Ell viewed, the son was obviously not smart enough to think someone might be watching as he was "taking care of" his aged mother. He was seen in the parking lot of a mall racing on ahead of his slow, aged mother to put the groceries in the car, then he raced back down the row of cars to help his mother. Or at least it seemed like that's what he went back to do.

After leaving the mall, the sweet old gal was making her way, frustratingly slowly, along the rows of parked cars. She appeared to be just fine with the way things were going. Purse slung over her arm, freshly done hair from the salon appointment she had earlier, hound's tooth blazer giving away her age with faux leather accents and two gold buttons fastened at the midriff. It was clear she was a fashionable old gal at one time and her outfit said she was never too old to keep showing some pride in looking good.

Ell watched as her son gingerly and warmly placed a hand on her upper arm resulting in the pair starting to move more quickly. It all appeared perfectly fine from a distance with nothing of note to draw ones' gaze. It seemed to be a typical and comfortable level of assistance and cooperation between the two. Nothing unusual here. Then the shot zoomed in close. There was no smile on the woman's face...from a distance it looked as if there were...but close up it was a wince... definitely a wince.

The shot tightened and picked up a clear view of the son's hand on her arm. Looking closer viewers could see it wasn't the whole hand it was the thumb and two fingers of the son's "helpful hands". The son was clearly not using his helpful hands lovingly as one would expect in a mother/son relationship. The images indisputably showed he was pinching the back of his mother's arm. The editing of DBN showed the wincing every time the woman slowed her pace. The clips would cut back and forth from her face to the close-up shot of the pinch. During the pinch the pace would become uncomfortably quick for the old woman, but the son hadn't let up until they were at the car. Once there, the son opened the door, as any "gentlemen" would, and helped his aged mother into the car.

But this deviously selfish and impatient man was no gentleman. No one would ever know what was going on if the CCTV had not captured the scene. No one would ever know how abused this poor old woman was...no one...except the 18 million viewers who had now seen the Stream that evening and learned of her suffering.

Here we were, Ell thought, wandering through the world almost completely oblivious to this old woman's suffering at the hands of "her loved one". The viewer tweets at the bottom of the screen were astonishingly punitive. It seemed Ell wasn't the only one who was pissed off and disturbed by the sight. Others took the time to comment on social media about the atrocity they were seeing.

    #sheshouldhaveabortedhim said, "*That son of a bitch should have never been born if he treats his mom like that:*

    #canstillpullatrigger said, "*Give the old gal a gun and maybe she can get her own justice*"

    #whatashit said, "*I hope that bastard lives to a ripe old age so his kids can rub shit in his nose.*"

The last comment was a clear reference to some of the other sights Ell and the viewers were treated to that evening. Scenes of a senior lying in bed, with the caregiver in the room to help clean them up. Abrasively rolling the old guy over, Ell could see the burly nurse was not enchanted with the procedure she had to go through with her 93-year-old patient who had soiled himself. Pinning him in place so he could not roll back over into the mess he had made in bed, the nurse grabbed a cloth and pugnaciously wiped his bottom. You could tell she had done this before and it likely wasn't the first time she had mishandled her charge. One wipe then a second and she tossed the cloth in the hamper. Grabbing a new cloth, she shoved the man again with her meaty forearm to make sure he stayed in place. His expression was confused and helpless. Another double-wipe, then, on the second wipe this time, she did something completely debasing.

Holding the old man down tight to the bed with her left forearm she clutched the rag and brought it up within millimeters from his nose. Almost rubbing the patient's nose in his own feces, as if he was her dog that had shit on the carpet. In every way it was inconceivable…except it happened…it happened in that facility, and it happens all over the world where seniors and the disabled are cared for. It was an inhumane atrocity and needed to be stopped.

The ashamed and broken look on the old fella's face brought sadness for what he was feeling. And a distressing feeling of rage that came from seeing something no one seemed able to do anything about filled Ell and all who were watching the stream. The victim was defenceless and the spirit of that man, as well as all seniors who had endured this kind of abuse in their final months or days of life, was hopelessness. All that was left for many seniors was to live out their days enduring the indignity of being helpless. And knowing only hateful treatment was to come from the one who was entrusted to lovingly care for the most helpless of our culture. At times it was the hired help or employee of a care home or institution… at other times it was the family members or children of the dependant senior.

The journalist began commenting again offering an update on the scenario.

"Humanity has rarely dealt with such unconscionably sick behavior as is seen here. What depths has a person sunk to when a caregiver wafts the feces covered towel used to wipe a dirty bottom in front of the helpless senior's nose? This is reprehensible on every level."

Of the other clips that were displayed that evening, Ell was certain they were shown in order to incite viewers. The elder abuse problem was epidemic, and it sickened Ell. It met Ell with such distaste for the baseness that persisted in her world. Talking to Sol only a few hours before he was going to be introduced to the world, she was as eager to see things change. To see things get better. She was ready to walk with Sol as he dealt with the injustices of the world…injustices like the elder abuse that had soured society in secret for decades.

After talking to Sol about what she had seen, Ell questioned. "Why are we not better?" She paused before she said, "Sol, I think it's time someone did something. I will be there when you walk out on stage today. I'm beside you every step Sol," She assured with the knowing that something could be done…"I love you."

The Silent Humming
of the Drone

The public square was pullulating. Full to bursting with everyone who could find their way to the WCC that morning. There had not been such a pressure on the World Congress Plaza in decades. A plaza that was inspired by St Peter's six century old Basilica Square for its size, and every bit as magnificent. On this day the crowds did not stay home. Every meter of its 225 by 315 meter granite floor was covered with feet. Every edge of the cobbled travertine berm around the Plaza had become an annex viewing area. There were thousands that could not squeeze into the Plaza proper. The berm around the Plaza brought to mind the extraordinary architecture of the mighty ancient Roman Empire. Ancient Romans once mined deposits of travertine for building temples, aqueducts, monuments, bath complexes, and amphitheaters such as the Coliseum.

When the World Congress Plaza was designed it took shape with the vision of filling its 70,000 square meters with celebrants. Even with the prolific Media Screens that imposed Live Streams of every event that took place at the Plazas, people still flocked to major events to be there in person. The citizens loved events held at the WCC Plaza. And on this inauguration day, the 7 other World Congress Centers that offered a live feed of the announcement were packed with enthusiastic and curious crowds as well. The live holographic stream they would be treated to in the Plaza was every bit as good for them as was being right there in New York where Sol, Ell, and the Handlers would be.

Those who could, would come to affirm and support the many Global events the World Congress would sanction. The cold granite surface of the Plaza floor was smoothed by the feet of thousands of hope-filled and curious citizens from across the Globe.

The teaser Bryson Reynolds and his mates at the DBN Table of Truth had offered up to the masses days ago had done its job. Citizens had been piqued. The curiosity about the new name for the WCC was compelling in its own right. But adding the mystery of the leadership change that was coming...well the draw was unprecedented. It had been a week since last Saturday's announcement by Ahmed and the response to the enticing DBN reports was massive. Plazas were full and Sol was standing with Ell in the holding room, off stage at the New York World Congress Center. But even though he was standing still watching the crowd morph and undulate, he was stirring on the inside. Ahmed was his usual light and engaging self. He took the edge off the nervous King. Ahmed moved in closer to Sol and Ell. "Well Sol, you realize you will be called King when the Chancellor introduces you?"

Sol scrunched his face a little and sighed. He knew this was about to happen and had hoped it wouldn't.

"Is there any way around that Ahmed? You know how I feel about this."

Ahmed softened as if parenting a nervous graduate about to give a valedictorian speech. "Sol, you are the King, so yes there is a way around this...but perhaps in this instance it is a greater benefit to all who are meeting you for the first time to hear you referred to as the King."

Sol paused, his mind eased for a moment. Looking straight into Ahmed's eyes Sol saw the wise side of Ahmed. Ahmed had been a rock for Sol. Tolerating Sol's questions and concerns. Chatting with Sol through the moments Sol doubted. Like the time in New Zealand just before taking off to Paraguay when Sol was missing home, missing Ell, missing his old life and wanting to just relax on the patio back home with a good read on his Folio. Ahmed assured him the life he was having now was going to be like nothing Sol could ever have dreamed but it will be so fulfilling.

Ahmed had a way of taking Sol along the journey of discovery that led him to feel safe. To feel the decision he had made, to accept the role of King of the World was good. Ahmed helped Sol realize again that Sol was here at this moment in world history because this is where he is supposed to be. Ahmed was inherently skilled at hearing Sol and letting Sol find the answer to what he was feeling. He had become more than a handler. Ahmed was priceless as a confidante and had become limitless as a friend.

When Ahmed got up close, the warmth in his eyes, the lilt of his softened tone, the scent of his bergamot and mandarin cologne, they were all so subtle but so reassuring. Reassurance…Surprisingly Sol hadn't needed more. But when he needed some Ahmed was there. With all the warmth and wisdom that Ahmed had embodied since they first met, and Ahmed's cologne first wafted into Sol's life.

On one occasion while they were having a drink after supper, Sol had asked him what that scent was. Thinking of it now brought a light smile across his face. Ahmed had answered, "*Community.*"

"What?" Sol said. Then with perfect cadence the ever-endearing Ahmed recited what could only be the marketing copy for this mesmerizing scent which Sol had just learned of.

"The fragrance "*Community*" is meant to embody dynamism and optimism with solid reassuring foundations. It represents a feeling of togetherness, to encourage those in its cloud to rally into a safe-haven. It features European environments, from crisp Nordic air, off-shore sea breeze, the petrichor of wet stones and moss, majestic forests and sculpted woods combined with essences of Mediterranean uplifting and colorful feelings."

"Wow!" Sol responded…somewhat speechless after that description. "Uh… Well…," Sol was able to get out, "You wear it well Ahmed."

And now, at the doorstep of a life that would change forever, Sol was again reassured by Ahmed. By his closeness, by his confidence in Sol, his dynamism and optimism that this was the right thing, and by his memorable scent. Sol thought, "Some people might have a theme song but Ahmed should have a theme-scent. And this is it. *"Community"*. Theme songs often fade away, but a scent stays in memory forever.

With Ell by his side and his favorite Handler off his left shoulder, Sol's smile from the memory of Ahmed's impromptu info-mercial about his cologne turned to a smile for Ahmed. Agreeing to be called King for the Presentation Ceremony Sol said, "Thanks Ahmed," Sol spoke warmly, "You're right, I guess it is best for today."

The crowd was an unbroken mass. Then, as Sol and Ell looked at the Media Screen to their left. They saw the crowd restlessly settling into place as the scheduled 12 o'clock announcement time drew near. Minutes away from the entry of the Chancellor onto the stage Ell pointed at the Screen and said, "What's going on out there?"

Her question was directed to a kerfuffle taking place in the crowd. Security was extraordinarily tight. And prolific video monitoring had climbed to a new level at events of this magnitude. The blending in of the Global Military Unit's *Event Policing Division* was flawless. Ell and Sol knew the **EPD** presence and Drone Corps was everywhere in the crowd. But the crowd was being jostled by some activity off to the left of the Plaza.

No sooner had Ell asked the question than the Drone security cam zoomed in on the disturbance. About a hundred feet from the stage, where the Chancellor was about to enter. Ell and Sol soon saw what it was. No cause for alarm. Just an unhappy child and a less happy mother. You could tell she was a little embarrassed but was showing great restraint as she tried to coax the obstreperous boy to move back further with her. But he was obviously being stubborn. Could be the effects of a huge crowd and having to have travelled to the Plaza hours ago to be part of this historical moment. Or it could be he was just being seven. However, the mother finally was able to coax him back with a little help from above. As soon as the *EPD* Drone hovered over the boy he looked up and momentarily paused at seeing the red light on the Drone. The slightly unsettled child's gaze hit the lens, revealing that he knew he was being watched. He realized he best settle down and stop making a fuss.

It was always a little unsettling to have a Drone hover over you on the street or at one of these events. All they did was capture activity, but it felt unnerving to have that subtle humming of the Drone go on just over-head and the red light of the camera let you know you are not misbehaving in anonymity. Parent and child struggles at events this large and this packed were not uncommon. Ell ignored the innocuous distraction and settled herself for the next moments.

The Plaza was shoulder to shoulder. It held every ethnic group, age group, social demographic. Rich, poor, every skin color...young, old, well dressed and scruffy. The mosaic that was the World Congress Plaza that day was a true testimony to the inclusive tone that had developed under the leadership of the World Congress.

The crowd responded as the blue light of the Plaza holograph system increased its glow. The Presentation was soon beginning. The projection lenses embedded in the granite floor were doing their job. The already tight crowds of the World Congress Plazas around the world tightened further as they made space for the images to beam up from the ground under their feet.

In the brilliant design plans for the WCC Plazas, the entire 70,000 square meters of floor space was engineered with holographic projection lenses. Inside the granite beneath the feet of the event attendees were lenses. Each lens was placed to cover viewing angles within a thousand square meters. And each holograph that emanated from the lens in the floor would emit a perfect 4-dimensional reproduction of the images and sound that were taking place on stage.

As the hundreds of holograph projectors emitted a blue hue up through the crowd, Ell and Sol watched the pockets open up and the crowds push back to let the image pass freely into the space above their heads. The few meters around each projection lens cleared of event goers' feet as the pressing crowds squeezed back to make way for the Holograph. A perfectly trained mass who knew that as soon as the blue light shone from the ground, the holographic Stream of the event was only a moment or two away. The blue columns of light refocused the senses of the masses who had congregated under a cloudy sky. The chatter in the crowd subsided slightly. And in seconds, around the world on every World Congress Stage, and in every World Congress Plaza that was filled to overflowing, viewers would soon be part of the historical move that would change everything.

The emanating blue glow subsided, and the holographic lenses embedded in the granite projected the familiar World Congress Globe. On stage and at every holograph projection location in the Plaza, the crystal-clear image with vibrant depth and color was spinning slowly. The World Congress Globe filled the space where the blue light had warmed seconds ago. The powerful World Congress symbol with illuminated lines connecting the Nations and Regions drew the masses' attention to a still finer point. All heads were trained on the untouchable sphere above. It was time for the announcement. The empty stage was a glasslike lake holding the reflection of the light clouds in the sky above. The Speaker's Podium rose out of the floor and stood solemnly in the center of the stage. Offstage, Chancellor Mahndar adjusted his jacket, nodded resolutely at Sol, and began his walk onto the stage.

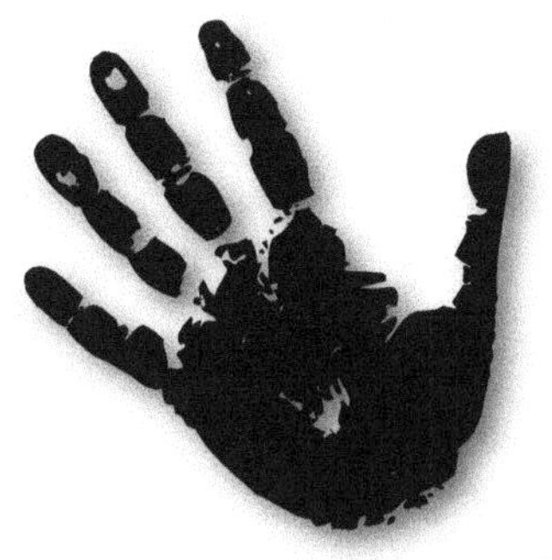

SECTION 3

PRESENTING OUR KING TO THE WORLD

We Would Like To Present To You Today

The waiting was over. The days and weeks that led up to this moment had slipped into the past. It seemed only a few days ago the Chancellor had started this move to bring something new and better to the World. And now, after only a few short weeks, proposition 9-12 had made its way to this stage. Millions of viewers had filled the World Congress' Plazas and billions all over the world were now participating in this event from the other side of their Media Screens and mobile devices. The Chancellor raised his arms to greet the crowds with a welcoming smile.

"Good Day to you all! It is exciting to be here with the Delegates of the World Congress to bring to you wonderful news. News of a bold and progressive change to the way the World Congress is run. Today is an immensely auspicious day."

The social phenomenon of how a crowd operates was fully in effect. The Chancellor hadn't even announced anything yet but the excitement of the moment, the high voltage sense from just being there, in the Plaza, in a tight social environment, with hundreds of thousands of other viewers, was powerful. At the opening sentence of the Chancellor, much of the crowd burst into applause and cheers. Participants knew a gathering of this size and energy must be important...

Waiting for the first sign that the event was beginning was like that feeling of anticipation a person gets right before tearing open a present on Christmas morning. The mounting excitement and anticipation a person has when waiting to get into that wrapped gift box almost makes a person jittery. The crowd was coiled up and jumped at the chance to tear things open by applauding and cheering at the first words of the leader whom they had supported for years. Chancellor Mahndar was a well-loved leader. He had proven himself to be an extremely stable and insightful Chancellor. And when he hit the stage, the crowd, not just in New York but at all the World Congress Center Plazas, reminded him of how they felt about him.

"Thank you thank you! And thanks for joining us on this beautiful day."

The sun was high in the noon sky at the New York event. A fair skinned person might look for shade if they were to stand out for too long. But today's event would not be drawn out. Chancellor Mahndar honored the crowd's patience.

"As you know we have invited you all to the World Congress Plaza for a major announcement. The Delegates have deliberated and found cause to make a significant change in the operations of the World Congress and therefore in the operations of our World Government. I assure you this is a move that has been chasing us down for many years now and this is the time that a change such as we are bringing you today is meant to occur."

The crowd was silent. Some standing, some sitting, all watching the stage or looking into the holographic scene playing out in front of them. The viewers knew they wouldn't have to wait long. The Chancellor was known for keeping things streamlined. He was always on point and ready to give them the goods.

The Handlers made their way on to center stage. Standing in a half- moon formation around the Chancellor. Joining them in the formation was the Proposition 9-12 group. The entire group of Delegates who had birthed the movement in room 912 of the WCC hotel.

No one watching this scene could dispute, if nothing else the World Congress was presenting a unified front, true solidarity at this time, on this day, standing together on this stage. There was no bi-partisan politics here in this government as there had been in the disunified democracies of the past.

The Chancellor and Delegates stood confidently and had no sense of uneasiness. The light smiles on their faces appeared to have a countenance of relief…of genuine comfort. Quite completely displaying an air of resolve at being part of this event. Yet the sense of excitement and joy they held beneath the mistakably austere externals was vibrational indeed.

The Chancellor welcomed the Delegates who had joined him on stage. His glance moved to pan the vast crowd in front of him. Chancellor Mahndar had been awake many nights thinking about this speech. Pondering this moment. Deliberating in himself over the words he would share with a waiting world. He knew the entire global community was eager to see change…many of them not even sure what change they wanted. But the wave of wanting something to change had ebbed and flowed for over a decade.

He was aware of the apathy, and also the disenchantment, the suffering unjustly caused to victims of atrocious human behaviors. The Chancellor was clear on the pain innocents had been caused in a variety of situations. The identity crimes, the digital extortions and robberies, the abuse of children and women, the violation of sanctity in the homes where violence, invasions, and other unspeakable acts occur. The ever-present reality of the prolific problem of child pornography and pedophilia, the inequities in the labour force, and a litany of injustices around the world. Mahndar was the first one to see how the virtual omnipotence of the World Congress was not powerful enough to compel people to be "better".

The organization Mahndar had the privilege of steering over the past years, had become stuck. Becoming almost impotent in effecting meaningful change. Change that could reach down to the levels of society that often puttered along just accepting some of the horribly unjust things any society was subject to. The change every generation waited for but was only left with stagnancy in social progress.

And The Chancellor wanted this change as much as he saw society wanting this change. In the two weeks of Sol's orientation, as the appointment of a King was kept a secret, the Chancellor did what he was brilliant at. He prepared himself to present the plan to the masses. And to offer the New King of the World to all.

"Ladies and Gentlemen. We have ascended to great heights as a society. Our advances in almost all things pertaining to culture and political matters are extraordinary. And it has been with the support of the citizens of this Globe, represented by the World Congress Body of Delegates, that those advances have been possible."

There was not a squeak to be heard in the audience. Sol and Ell breathed softly. The beginning was here…

Sol was oddly focused on the Chancellor's speech, not giving thought to the words he himself was moments from speaking. For Sol, while watching the Chancellor from offstage with support staff all around, it was hard not to notice the marvelous looking necktie the Chancellor had chosen for this day.

It was the same tie he wore at the Red Ochre Ceremony. The rich burgundy with a subtle gold thread flecked throughout the tie. A prominent gold leaf pattern screened across the tie was striking. The Chancellor himself was able to take looking distinguished to a new level. And his decadent wardrobe was always punctuated by a gorgeous tie. Sol had noticed it then and seeing it now took him back to that Red Ochre moment. Seeing this tie again brought Sol to the moment of whelming where he was struck by how incredulous this whole thing was.

"Our world has become a better place because of the people standing here with me. Because of the work of all those who represent you in the Body of Delegates. And today, we take the next steps in leading our world toward more advances and to become even better.…Friends…"

Sol loved how the Chancellor in a few short sentences turned the clinicallness of talking to "Ladies and Gentlemen" into an intimate moment of talking to friends.

Almost 5 million friends standing in the Plazas of the World Congress centers and the rest of the 7 or 8 billion watchers on the other side of the Media Screens.

The Chancellor spoke on.

"Friends…your voices have not gone unheard. Your World Government has heard and seen that there are meek among you who wait for the day you will hear the good that is waiting for you. Those of you who feel yourselves to be least in many ways, have been waiting for the day when you will no longer be broken-hearted by the injustice that is in society. Many of us have been in prisons of fear and pain at the hands of immorality or violence inflicted upon or threatening us, and many of us are told we are living in a free world but the harshness that is a reality in our societies holds us captive. Which of us is not in search of liberty?"

The crowd woke at these words. The sense that something vital, something potent, something that would alter the path of this generation was felt.

This was the moment. Chancellor Mahndar was on the precipice. The expectant crowd felt it now and the Chancellor took a breath.

"…Friends, there is a resolve to this social dilemma. Our democratic system has carried us as far as she is able. The unprecedented unity and international cooperation has brought great peace and prosperity. In ways that at one time were unimaginable. But this machine that is our Government has been bound. It has been fettered and kept from inspiring us to become better. At the fundamental levels of culture, the ills that were present at the beginning of time are still with us today. And now is the day when we commit to see those change. The hope we have for the future is one that does not include callous and violent acts. The hope we share with you today is a hope that engages the core goodness of the human condition and begins to erode the things that harm us at a level that has been untouched by this present Government. No longer do we plan to see human decency, human safety, and basic human security eroding. It is time to chip away at the rock of human depravity on the anvil of human decency."

Even Chancellor Mahndar was affected by this moment as he saw the reaction of the thousands standing in the Plaza. The mass of people in the crowd were attentive, nodding, turning to a spouse or a friend with an affirming smile and a whisper of support for what the Chancellor was saying. As if each of them had been waiting for a release from a force that had long been pressing against them.

The Delegates who were partially encircling the Chancellor at the Speaker's Podium were like the guardian statues at the Temple of the Emerald Buddha. They were unfaltering in their display of solidarity with the Chancellor as if to offer protection by their resolve to stand over his shoulder. Few could mistake their presence for anything less than certain commitment. The sun had not dimmed in the blue sky above with wispy clouds moving past the orb as if there was a cosmic intention to let the sun shine on this moment.

It was the crowning moment in the Chancellor's speech. Ell and Sol had been told the introduction would not be lengthy. Sol was just now getting a little jittery, a little anxious if you will. And Ell was starting to squeeze Sol's hand tighter. The procedure of the next moments was for Sol and Ell to walk out together and Ell to join the curved formation of the Delegates. Sol would continue the few steps to stand shoulder to shoulder with the Chancellor at the Speaker's Podium. Chancellor Mahndar would welcome the King to the stage and then he would step back for Sol to give his first address. The address that had been stirring in Sol for days.

"Friends, it is in this day that the World Congress has chosen unanimously to boldly alter the model we are all accustomed to. The authority the World Congress has had bestowed upon her is no longer a possession of this venerable Body of Delegates. As of 14 days ago the unanimous decision of the Delegates was acted upon. Agreeing to a reformation that promises to right the many wrongs, which could not be done under the system in place, the World Congress has transferred all of its authority...."

If it was quiet a moment ago then this silence was like being in a vacuum in space. Here in New York, there in El Salvador, Luxembourg Germany, Egypt,

Namibia, China, New Zealand, Paraguay. Every World Congress Plaza could have stood empty as silent as it was. With luminescent holographic images of the Presentation in New York filling the air above stunned watchers, the entire world stood rapt. Every citizen was witnessing the same moment...the same making of history. The Chancellor delivered with poetic force. Not intimating one iota of detectable doubt, apology, or lack of confidence.

"...the World Congress has transferred all of its authority...to a unanimously appointed King. We would like to present to you today the first global leader of the unified World, King Sol David James."

He Was The King...
This Was His Moment

I t had to be the longest walk in history. Holding the hand of the most loyal and supportive person in the world he didn't realize how hard she was squeezing until halfway across the stage. The orchestra music filled the Plaza bridging the gaps between the scattered holography. And the watchers stood still. Not moving, not talking, not clapping or cheering. Just watching. Taking it all in. The thoughts of the silent crowd were racing. How does a crowd respond to an unknown who is introduced as a somebody? To them, Sol was nobody. That would soon change, but in this moment, the man who was declared King 14-days previous by Chancellor Mahndar was entering the plaza.

Mahndar swept his arm towards Sol who was approaching the Podium..."Let's welcome together Sol, King of The World!"

The music crescendoed as the crowd sensed the excitement. And with the announcement of the new "model" of leadership the Delegates ensconcing the Chancellor initiated the applause. Right on que the crowd erupted into a cheer. The applause thundered through the Plaza. Sol leaned over and thanked Ell as he kissed her gently on the cheek and let go of her hand. She joined the Delegate formation. Sol's last steps to the Podium found the Chancellor extending an exuberant hand to greet him as he took his place. The Chancellor gave way to the new King. He respectfully bowed before Sol and stepped back to join the Delegates and Ell. The Delegates all did alike. With modest nodding they affirmed Sol as King.

Sol was behind the Speaker's Podium and facing out to the crowd. The applause began to fade. As Sol squared himself to the Podium an unexpected sound rose from the crowd. It was the sound of drumming. The sound escalated up onto the stage and into his ears. What would happen next took the whole stage by surprise. Sol, Ell, Ahmed, there were none on that stage who could have seen this coming. Once it started Sol instantly knew it wasn't part of the formal Presentation Ceremony, and he just as quickly knew he didn't want anyone to stop it. Few things might inspire a King more than a spontaneous tribute from the people.

The sound began to float gently at first. A rhythmic drum beating coming from the right of the stage. At first it sounded like just one drum amid the curious masses. ***dohm dohm dohm dohm dohm dohm dohm dohm.***

Then the beat was joined by another and another...now there were several beats filtering through the Plaza. Colliding together from different points in the granite square with a rhythmic chanting now joining the beating drums. The world was together in hearing an ancient Cherokee tribute chant.

We n de yah ho...We n de yah ho...We n de yah ho...We n de yah ho...

First one then many chanters raised in chorus. It was a tribute song few in the crowd had heard before. The scattered drummers in the Plaza had been joined by the silky chants of Cherokee chanters. *ho ho ho ho he yah o he yah ho yah yah yah.*

To hear it resonate across the Plaza was chilling. While the air of the Presentation Ceremony in the New York Plaza was bathed with these mesmerizing sounds, the Delegates and witnesses at the World Congress Plazas in other countries were beginning to take pause. The holograph Stream that found its way across the globe was as powerful to remote viewers as it was right here in New York.

In the control booth the Stream Team sitting behind the video control boards was watching the activity develop...they were not cutting away from the King who had just walked on stage. Hovering over the drummer and chanter was the toothless but ubiquitous Security Drone Cam. It could do nothing but capture images and direct *EPD* teams to locations. The stealthy and precise *Event Policing Division* Drone was quick to respond. Attending to the unusual scene by aiming its lens at the subject or subjects in question. Drones faithfully captured millions of video images that were always kept in the data banks and often streamed to live feeds. In this moment the images of the drummers and chanters were being captured.

dohm dohm dohm dohm dohm dohm dohm...

The drums called out in solidarity, the chanters voices continued to rise from the crowd to be heard by Sol and all who had ears to hear. The entire Ceremony had been interrupted. Chancellor Mahndar had just announced Sol as King and Sol was readied to address the crowd. But the plan was now altered.

Sol looked over to the Chancellor, *"Is this what's supposed to happen now?"* Sol thought.

The Chancellor gave him nothing. Ell looked carefully into the crowd and seeing what she saw moved her from confusion and concern to a comfortable knowing. Ell often connected to meditative and meaningful chants or drumming. There were few groups who drew so majestically on the ancient Orient and Semitic heritage found in the Cherokee people's lineage. The strong history of affirming a ruler or a Chief by offering a chant had not been heard in an inauguration ceremony for decades and never in this magnitude. The chanting sounds were intended to celebrate and anoint a chief. A leader whose time had come. Like the ancient King of Tyre, history's anointed cherub who was celebrated at his coming with majestic music and ceremonial pomp befitting a King, the Cherokee people were doing so for King Sol today.

The Cherokee of North America had been one of the first ancient tribes to span the gap in connecting to the greater society. They had built success upon success. This people shared their rich traditions and meaningful prophetic outlook for a better day with nations all over the world. Becoming a strong influence for hope in every corner of the globe.

The masses of people at today's Ceremony had no idea this was not the plan of the World Congress. Chancellor Mahndar saw Sol's confusion in the moment, and he looked over to Erin. Erin's eyes met the Chancellor's, and she gave him an agreeing nod. It seemed Ell and Erin were the only two on stage who had a sense of what was going on. Erin stepped forward to give Sol the information he needed. It was all in stride for the crowd and even the rest of the Delegates on stage quickly absorbed the moment. Seeing Erin lean into Sol, the Delegates were eased to see the moment of spontaneity was being handled. Whispering over his left shoulder, Erin gave an immensely elucidating piece of information.

"This is a spontaneous welcome from the Cherokee people Sol." She whispered. "They sensed their World Government was on a precipice and are responding to the timing of the 8th Sun prophecy. They are here to affirm you on behalf of their people."

Erin stepped back. She didn't give Sol time to respond or ask questions. He was the King...this was his moment. He needed the information and then Erin...in fact all the Delegates...expected him to respond how he saw best. Sol had been King for literally two weeks, and this was a defining moment. This was now a part of his Presentation to the world. And billions of people watching on billions of Mobile devices and Media Screens were witnessing the moment. Sol looked over to Ell. She knew more than most. She had a sense of what was to happen next.

A Welcome Song To The New King

Unapologetic and undaunted Sol made his decisive move. The drumming and chanting were calling him…calling everyone to be open to receiving their King. The chant that arose through the crowd was an ancient one that called the earth to rejoice along with the heavens at the rising of a new day. A day that brought a new King in front of the world to restore so many things. Rejoicing at a time of restitution of all things.

Sol stepped out from behind the Podium as if he could not be constrained by its protective boundaries a moment longer. So adaptive to what was going on? Unfazed by the Presentation Ceremony or by the flash-mob chanting that met him at his coming. Sol left no question in the minds of the watchers about his fitness for the moment…The images showed the stage without Sol. The question in the minds of those witnessing this moment were asking,

'Is this man really leaving the stage to go into the crowd?'

And it was so, the Holographs were faithful in what they displayed.

Ahmed was the first of the group to get uneasy at seeing Sol head towards the edge of the stage. If only he could come alongside Sol. Ahmed had a bit of a herding instinct. Wanting to protect Sol by guiding him away from a conflict or taking his arm to steer him towards what he thought would befit the King. Now, feeling the uneasiness of not being in control of the situation and not being able to consult Sol on what he should do, Ahmed did all he could do from his post on the stage with the other Delegates. And that was to question under his breath

"What does he think he's doing?"

Sol was on the top step of the stairs that led up to the stage. He paused again and took a visual mark of where the tribute was coming from. Stepping effortlessly down from the stage the moment was becoming surreal to even Sol. There was a sensation of surging excitement that flooded Sol as his intention became his reality. It was all so spontaneous. There was no concern for safety or protocol.

Guests of the Plaza turned again to look at the stage as the proximal holographs only offered images of a stage absent of the new King. The Stream Team pivoted in deciding on which feed to display behind the video control panel. They adeptly and quickly responded to the scene by redirecting resources to capture the moment. The *EPD* had not missed dispatching a second Drone that kept pace with the King's movement. The Stream Team rapidly picked up the Drone's feed and the crowd focussed again on the Holograph images where Sol could be seen passing into the crowd as the two Drones hovered along over his head.

Even the calm professionals behind the video stream board missed seeing this surprise move by the subject of their remote lenses. The King was two steps ahead of the tech guys who were watching remotely.

Sol had his bearings and proceeded along the granite floor of the Plaza. The security team assigned to the event was not sure if it was naivety on behalf of the King or if it was trust. *EPD* personnel quickly moved to strategically place themselves near the path Sol was heading down. Sol had about a hundred and fifty feet between him and the drummer he was intent on meeting. With the Drone cam hovering about 8 feet above his head as he moved, the crowd who had come to witness the announcement of a new leadership model had adapted exceedingly quickly to the protocol required in the presence of a King. As Sol stepped assuredly forward, the crowd brushed back and made way. Sol's intention was now known by those present.

The sound system in the plaza continued to emanate the chanting and drumming that had interrupted the Ceremony. There was no lull in the tribute and as Sol came near, the sound enveloped him more. Sol was certain those who were chanting were gaining volume and gaining numbers as the moments advanced. He was right. The many who honored him with song were becoming more in number each moment. Chanters and drummers were dotted throughout the entire New York World Congress Plaza. The Plazas at other World Congress Centers were experiencing the tribute through the Live Stream.

The world was one in many ways…and a focus on ethnic diversity had largely diminished as populations blended into a culture of non-distinction from one person to the other. The labelling of others by color and distinguishing traits had been diluted by the pond of genetics that had evolved into a unifying acceptance among humankind. Yet even still, when Sol came to stand in front of the drummer and chanter, he was surprised at the traditional Cherokee appearance of this duet. The copper skin tone and the fire behind the dark colored eyes brought the chills of excitement that were deep inside him, closer to the surface. Sol felt as if he was in the presence of an historic people at an historic time. And he was. He stopped.…

The chanting subsided. In diminishing waves across the Plaza, the drummers ceased their rhythmic beat until Sol stood with only one drum in front of him left beating in the entire Plaza. The sound swaddled him. The sound system carried the solitary drum beats back across the Plaza and to the Streams across the globe. Echoing in solitude, not Sol nor anyone knew how long the drum would continue being struck. As the wait stretched a moment longer, the sound slowed to a hypnotic cadence…*dohm dohm dohm dohm dohm dohm dohm dohm dohm*…Then the final beat. ***DOHM…***

The Plaza and the entire world were silent. This moment was like no other.

Sol was eye to eye with the drummer. A tall, furrowed man, effortless in his defense against awkwardness or nerves. And abundant in his measure of calm as he had the full attention of the world's first King. Skin and eyes glowing. A powerful sense of respect moved out from him. Drum and stick in hand he stood still. Both men knew there would be no handshake at this introduction. Their souls met with the meeting of their eyes.

With the welcome from a subtle smile across his lips, the man lowered his drum to the ground and lightly bowed in front of Sol. Sol looked to the Chanter standing next to the drummer. Her rich dark hair pulled back. Her forehead showed signs of time spent outdoors and her tear dress, tan with copper embroidery on the seams and sashes, spoke of her experience as a Cherokee chanter. Her eyes smiled brightly…much less eager to exhibit stoicness than her drumming counterpart.

Assured by the information Erin had passed him in whispers on stage of the honor that was being bestowed on him, Sol spoke first, "Thank you," Sol nodded gently and smiled.

He didn't know where his sudden memory of this music came from, but it must have been from the years Ell explored that part of her heritage. Sol was able to enjoy several of the songs with her. There were so many moving works that were soothing gentle choruses. Absent of the shrillness that comes from sacred chants at times. And in the last beats of the drumming, the one that met him rather deeply was the one that had filled the Plaza. He recalled the name of it. It was called *The Cherokee Morning Song*. A song to welcome the morning, to welcome the Great Spirit to bless all that had breath, and a song to position the heart of the singer and all of creation to embrace a new beginning. A song that reminded its hearers that we are all of one spirit. Rarely was *The Morning Song* shared in tribute to a man or to a leader. But today the offerers brought this song to Sol as a message of welcome. A message of embracing Sol as the King and declaring this day as a day for a new beginning. It was indeed a welcome song to the new King.

And The Red Ochre Made Its Mark

"**I** am very honored to have had you share this Morning Song. Thank you for the welcome. I appreciate it greatly."

Across the globe watchers who had never seen anything like this before were part of this interaction. The first interaction of their King. Not a King on a pedestal or in an unreachable castle but a King, standing before his people with his boots on the ground just as the people stood. In that moment the people saw Sol, as he was. Not a politician, not a diplomat, he was just a man, a sincere and sensitive man. And the drummer saw the same.

"It is we who are honored King Sol..." replied the Drummer.

Sol raised his hand a little in a gentle '*thank-you*' gesture and to display his preference for no title. "Please, just 'Sol'."

The humble man in front of Sol fully understood Sol's request. The Cherokee were among many ancient people who had long known that a man was best known by his name and not his title. And for a man to reject the use of a title in order to be known by his name displays the strength his name speaks of.

"Sol," the drummer continued. "We have heard from our ancestors that this day would soon come. We resonate with the excitement that comes with seeing the fulfillment of the 8th Sun Prophecy."

Sol saw the commitment in his eyes. A man committed to accepting the rulership of this King, the accurateness of the timing, and a man committed to supporting the King. A man fully convinced that the fullness of time had come, and this moment that brings the world a new King, is guided by time itself.

"It is my privilege to serve you and your people, to offer my skills and abilities to the world at this time. You have touched me in a profound manner by your welcome and by your support."

As Sol was interacting, he did not notice the child come up beside the chanter. The child was no intrusion into the exchange. The only intrusion in the moment was the three *EPD* Drones that were not pulling back from their position a few feet above the group's heads. The Drones kept watch over the scene.

The chanter gently rested her hand on the little boy's head. She nudged the child forward. He stepped in front of Sol...and with two hands, he raised up the tray he was holding. The tray was made of poplar and Sol recognized what lay on it. Even the earthy scent of the contents were now familiar to Sol.

On the poplar tray was a cool and supple clay slab like the one he had pressed his hand into at the World Congress two weeks ago. The Red Ochre had appeared again. Indeed, it was one of the most ancient and most permanent symbols of committal that had been used in cultures around the world. And the Cherokee People had long been familiar with it.

Participating in this impromptu Red Ochre Ceremony in front of the King was an act Sol was willing to do. The child held the tray with the Red Ochre-soaked clay up towards Sol. Sol reached down, smiled at the child, and gently raised his hand to lay it on the clay. No one spoke or directed the scene. It happened just as each of them knew it should.

Again, the coolness from the dye crept around the sides of his fingers and across the thumb and palm of his hand. Sol watched as the sides of his fingers turned red. Then, in an act that sealed not only the Cherokee people's commitment and support to the new King, but sealed Sol's first impression with the people as being a King of great honor and respect, the drummer stepped in front of Sol. The Cherokee seldom made eye contact with others whom they stood in front of, but He looked Sol in the eyes in a unique and uncharacteristic move of a Cherokee man. It gave the respect one might give standing in front of an alpha wolf. The drummer beautifully displayed the respectful demeanor his people were historically known for. This man symbolically stood in the place of all people who could look Sol in the eye. People that were ready to receive this King.

The dye on Sol's hand had the same consistency as that of the Red Ochre ceremony from two weeks ago. Sol knew what to do. He reached up to the brow of the drummer, and without knowing the man's name, Sol placed his hand on the forehead of the man. The Red Ochre dye had a shimmer about it as it glistened on the sun-tanned skin of the Cherokee man. Then, in silence, the imprinted man stepped to the left. The Chanter stepped forward and Sol's still wet hand imprinted the brow of the affirming woman standing before him. Sol looked up towards the crowd standing around them. As he began to make eye contact with some in the crowd, he noticed a number of them glancing down. They were glancing down in front of Sol. He turned his eyes in that direction. In front of him was the child. The little boy was waiting. He snuck in front of Sol without Sol noticing.

He was waiting for his turn to have the King press his hand on his little forehead. Sol looked at the drummer and the chanter. With a glance, both Sol and the boy were getting approval from his grandparents. They nodded, giving their approval. Sol had not expected this. After imprinting the man and the woman he had intended to make his way back to the Podium. But this little boy was ready. His eyes were closed, his hands still holding the poplar tray low in front of him. And Sol reached out. Pressing his drying hand against the boy's brow, the short, bristly hair on the small forehead yielded to the pressure and the Red Ochre made its mark. As Sol lifted his hand from the child's head leaving a red imprint on this young recipient, the boy looked up and grinned.

"Thank you King Sol." He said.

Sol was moved by the words of the boy. And as the Plaza heard the sound of the boy's voice affirming Sol and the images of the grinning child in front of the new King, the crowded Plaza filled with the sound of applause again.

Cheering shook the Plaza again and the chills that raced up Sol's spine gave him a shiver. He breathed a large breath and paused. Sol thanked the group who had brought this tribute which was now complete. And as he made his way back to the stage, a number of those standing along the narrow path lined with celebrants offered their bowed heads to Sol. They wanted the imprint of the King. He responded by pressing his hand against the brows of several citizens requesting his imprint as he passed by. Sol reached the steps and strode back up onto the stage.

Once back on stage he stood in front of the Speaker's Podium until the applause died down.

Redirect Us On A Path Of Dignity

Sol glanced at his stained palms. Ahmed stepped up to his side handing Sol a white cloth dampened with mineral spirits.

"Thank you Ahmed"

Seeing the Red Ochre pass on to the towel, he draped the stained cloth over the Podium behind him. The masses paused with him as he did what any person would do in that moment, wipe their hands.

It was ironic. The Red Ochre was a hematite or iron-based dye that had been used by the most ancient people on earth. Used for artwork and ceremonies, this dye had sealed many contracts and agreements, left historical records on walls of caves and tombs of peasants, and been said to be the iron stained water that dyed the banks of the rivers flowing out of the Garden of Eden, the rivers Gihon and Pishon. And today, it is the dye that places the mark of the world's first universal King onto willing subjects.

The act of imprinting is indelible in its symbolism. The Red Ochre dye that still remains on stone walls of caves from thousands of years ago, is today a stain on the cloth behind Sol and on men's brows along the path through the crowd below. For both, it is an enduring sign that declares permanency. Those who receive it symbolize a people who commit to the King, and the King who imparts the Red

Ochre imprint, declares his unending commitment to faithfully rule. A commitment to forever pursue the greatest good for the people whom he serves. A seal declaring the people's desire to serve their King and the King to serve the people.

Sol knew simply being appointed King did not make him "King" to the people. He had to become it through actions that would improve life, improve humans, and repair those things broken. Although the people may not yet feel he was truly going to "be their King", Sol had agreed to become King, and he was committed. How that looked would be decided in the days ahead. And the words of this man standing in front of them, dressed sharply in a gray flecked jacket with a pale yellow shirt buttoned up to one button from the collar, were to be the start of building trust. Sol began.

"When the World Congress Delegates showed up at my door, I saw this, as many of you would have had been asked to embark on this vision quest. I saw this as a watershed moment. It is an opportunity to do good. We are no different from each other." Sol motioned to the guests in the crowded Plaza.

"I consider myself fortunate to live in a Country, in a World, that is so rich, so prosperous, and so free in many ways. Yet I have always been interested why many of the things that feel wrong about how society operates, never get resolved. I, like many of you standing here and watching today, have asked the question in private thoughts and among friends and family, *What would I do if I were King of the World?*'

"Few of us ever take that rhetorical question seriously. I was given the chance to call myself to task on it. When the opportunity came to become King of the World, I thought, *That is ridiculous of course I can't be King.*' But when I considered the invitation of the World Congress, I began to realize what an inestimable honor it would be to take this unique job offer.

"I realized that being qualified to be King was not something one could go to school for or take a trade program to learn all that is necessary to be King. In fact, in all recorded human history, there has not been one successful graduate of King School. Kings were often successional, put in place by birthright, by force and military action, or in some cases they were chosen by the people. It is my great privilege to have been in that latter category. The World Congress represents the people and when your government chose to ask me on behalf of the World Congress and the people of the world they represent to become King, I agreed."

The crowd standing below him in the Plaza and around the world watching was eager to hear more. They had already been left with a good taste in their mouth after seeing Sol react to the spontaneous tribute. They had already felt the impassioned submission of those in Sol's path as he passed men and women eager to get his imprint on their head. And as Sol spoke, he noticed an opportunity to begin the good he hoped to do. The crowd listening to Sol speak was unaware of his interest in a situation in the crowd. While speaking, Sol was paying some attention to a situation several rows from the front of the stage. It was in fact, one situation that he planned to address as King. While speaking to the masses he saw a young family that had already had a long day.

Almost directly in front of the stage, about 30 meters from the front row, Sol picked up the scene of a father instructing his child. Neither of them looked to be enjoying the moment.

The young dad looked frustrated in his attempts to pay attention to Sol and to get his child to stand still in front of him. Sol saw the father stooping over to redress the child. But Sol believed it was unnecessary to mishandle his small son in order to make it happen? The mother standing next to the father-son duo appeared frustrated as she tried to hear Sol's address without distraction.

The boy had to be 4 or 5 years old and, no surprise, he was not too interested in being there any longer. The dad was obviously unhappy with his son. The episode escalated…as any conflict between a 40 pound child and his father would be likely to escalate.

Sol hated seeing kids being treated roughly and he always wished something could be done for the parents who were overwhelmed. So overwhelmed that they felt they had no other resource in the perpetual power struggle that was called parenting. Often times leading to using the only resource a parent felt he had…

to overpower their little ones. Little ones who themselves had their own limited resources to behave, whittled away over the hours.

The boy in the crowd was not going to win this battle. In a whirlwind, the dad tugged his hand out of the little boy's grip and with his other arm he clutched the boy on top of his shoulder tight to the child's neck. The dad spun the boy around and pressed his son into a sitting position.

The little guy's look of surprise was magnified by the wince as the reflex guarding of the shoulder happened. His shoulder was shrugging up while the head tilted down toward the shoulder. Obviously uncomfortable with the squeeze of his father's hand on his neck, the young boy automatically tried to protect the area of discomfort. And the dad was unlikely to sympathize in those moments.

Even though Sol was obviously unable to do anything for the boy or for the father while standing in front of billions offering his first address…he was very aware that the frustrations of parenting are often too great for parents to overcome in stressful moments. Moments where goals are interrupted by a child expressing his or her needs.

Had the scene been even a slight bit more escalated there would have been an *EPD* Drone hovering over the family to let the young dad know he was being scrutinized and the behavior of his son was in the sights of the Event Police. Sol set his thoughts of this scene on hold for now, to continue engaging the worldwide crowd.

"You won't have to look very hard to see who I am. I am not of noble descent; I do not have Royal blood in my line…at least that I know of…I am just like many of you. And just like many of you, if you were given the chance to become King, you would be interested in doing what you could to make this world a better place. As a person who could just as easily be standing where you are today, watching this Presentation Ceremony take place, I only hope to improve life for all of us, doing the greatest good for the greatest number. As I believe many of you would do.

"I intend to move us further from the imperfect world of our history and our present. It is because I am you. I am the man who works in the steel yard, I am the woman who sees the heartache of human rights violations. I am the husband who fears for his wife's safety when not with her, I am that mother who is forced to trust her children will not be seduced away to a life of illicit drugs and activity, I am the neighbor who's hands are tied by red tape and legal hoops when trying to find assurance of safety after a predator or gang member moves into the neighborhood, I am the employee who struggles to make ends meet with the meager wages paid me while extraordinary wealth is extravagantly spread only among the wealthy. I am here today as one of you.

"It has struck me with great force that if a world wants a leader who can empathize with its concerns, if the world wants a leader who will be able to see the struggles for justice it has, if a world wants a ruler who is able to understand the great and deep longing the world has for peace, safety, equity, and prosperity, if our world wants a ruler who in all ways has gone through the things that the average citizens of the world are embroiled in, then we need an average citizen as King. I have no political bias.

"I am not here as a representative of a party or a state, or a nation or region. My bias is a bias against all that is wrong with the world. From the seeming insignificant and trivial to the broad and grand issues that have been with us since time began. I am you. I am here for you. I vow to make life better for you. I vow to do the greatest good for the greatest number.

"I stand here before you today, having embraced the vow inherent in the Red Ochre ceremony. I give you my word that on this day, I have submitted to this Office and vow to act in this role in the most noble and beneficent manner that a person can act in. I intend to engage the full resources available to me as King in my quest to eradicate the unsavory from society and enhance the noble and just.

"I vow to be the People's King."

With that the crowd's cheers rose once more. From the perspective of the people, so far, the world had been run by a king of sorts anyway. Whether it be the most powerful Nation's or Region's leader, the ultra-rich who steered the politicians decisions with their great wealth, or the most compelling voices raised in the Deliberations Chamber, the fact is, the multi-levelled leadership has complicated matters. Far too many issues that have been dragged through the many layers of committees and government, were the opinions of a man or group of men and woman at their core anyway. A collective King, so to speak, with many illogical laws and rules that guided the world to this place where it is at today. The system has long promised power to the people. But democracy failed to impart that power…because democracy was only an illusion. Henry David Thoreau shared some indicting thoughts about the manner of governance we have become accustomed to. Thoreau says,

> *"The government itself, which is only the mode which the people have chosen to execute their will, is equally liable to be abused and perverted before the people can act through it."*

Thoreau was one of many who saw democratic government for what it had become. Amid all the hopes for a governing system that heeded the wishes of the people who appointed it to execute their will, the democratic system was seldom able to fulfill the mandate the people trusted it with. Decisions were made by the government, in spite of what the people often said they wanted. Rarely if ever were the majority of people given what the majority asked for. In recent decades, most people had stopped to bother even voicing what they wanted anymore. The apathy has fulfilled its role in silencing the passion for change that once was part of a vibrant people.

Only a few minutes ago the Chancellor had announced the appointment of a King, and the crowd had little understanding of what that meant. The massive group that was congregated in the New York World Congress Plaza and those in Plazas around the world, responded with compliance to the proceedings. And now, after hearing from Sol, as much as it was a risk of the unknown it was exhilarating to see such a bold change and such a willing person to take this yoke upon him.

Sol felt the sense of inspiration that fed back to him from the crowd. And he felt he would offer the mass one more thing.

"We have waited too long. Culture has always waited for society to improve, thinking it will be in their generation or perhaps in the next. Trusting humanity and its chosen government to steer the move towards a better humanity. And every generation looks back in judgment of the generation before it. Wondering how it could be the way it was, do the things it did, and more importantly, not do the things it needed to do. Why had the generations before ours not done the difficult things that might cause discomfort but would redirect us on a path of dignity? Why didn't society make those choices that would bring humanity forward to a better place as humans?"

The crowd was nodding. They could see where Sol was going. Few could have imagined the World Congress would find a King that was willing to tell it like it is and then do something about it? But thankfully the group in room 912 were among those daring few. This felt exceedingly hopeful and the world had only been in front of her King for a few short minutes. And who could have known that humankind was ready to make those tough choices to change…they only needed the right person to do some heavy lifting along the path.

Let's Get This Thing Started

"**F**riends, it is only together that we will be able to move humanity forward." Sol invited the crowds to invest further.

"Will our children and grandchildren gaze back in 30, 40, or 50 years and wonder about the state of the past as we and many generations before us have done? Asking questions such as, Why was there such a stagnant period in those days?

Why did there seem to be no real progress? Why hasn't humanity evolved and become better? Why are we still going through the same injustices, hatreds, and inequities that our parents went through?

If we invest together in restoring and repairing that which is broken and not right, the shame will fall away, and we will prosper. Not only in ways that can be measured by accountants and bankers, but in ways that find us proud, safe, secure, happy, healthy, and full participants in this human condition!

"Thank you for seeing that we will progress and evolve together. Together we will become what we were meant to be and what we have always wanted."

Sol stepped back. Ahmed stepped forward to stand shoulder to shoulder with Sol. Ahmed was in his finest linen suit and tie. A charcoal grey suit with a classic white shirt and an understated pinstriped tie. He was holding a Folio in his left hand and reached out congratulatorily to shake Sol's hand.

There was nothing left to do. The next phases would be brief as Sol established his rule. The citizens would see that even though there was one man who was to be King now, the World Congress did still possess some influence. At times they would be able to step alongside and advise the King. At times they may offer suggestions to the King if necessary. They would have opportunity to influence decisions on matters affecting them all. However, Sol could make decisions in a vacuum if he chose. He could refuse any assistance and counsel the Delegates might offer. Sol was fully empowered to make any decision without consultation. The world would see this to be true as the Presentation Ceremony moved forward under Sol's Reign. Ahmed spoke next to move the Ceremony toward its closing.

"As we near the close of the Presentation of the King today, Sol would like to take a moment to share with you the first enhancement to this new model of government."

Ahmed brought the King's Scribe Folio up in front of Sol and himself.

Sol had already enacted this edict but for the Presentation today, it had been decided to walk through the administrative protocol of making an edict. It would be clear to the citizens how the edict process would unfold. Sol looked at the King's Scribe on the Folio. The edict he had enacted in the first days of his orientation was on screen. Sol's handprint watermarked the background of the digital edict.

"I declare this day that the World Congress Center for Global Relations shall be from henceforth called, the World Counsel Center for Global Progress."

Sol reached up and pressed his hand on the Folio Screen. For this Presentation moment, the King's Scribe had been configured to replay the original actions on the day Sol had made the edict. The Folio *chimed* indicating *"Edict Successfully Recorded"*, and displayed,

"Thank You Sol."

At that moment, before the crowd would have time to respond to the announcement of a new name, the banner covering the signs on the World Congress Center dropped and Ahmed swept his arm toward the structure while announcing further the new name Sol had just edicted.

World Counsel Center for Global Progress

Up on the Holographs the crowd was seeing the mark of the King for the first time. The mysterious announcement of the World Congress from a week ago was no more a mystery. The carefully shrouded move to an appointed King was in full view now. The curtain had been pulled away on the new signs that read *World Counsel Center for Global Progress* and on the new model that had installed a King. Ahmed moved quickly now to dismiss the crowd and close the event. He thanked the global audience for being part of this historic and hopeful moment as the world was introduced to its King, King Sol.

To all watching it was certain this man, Sol David James, would be more than just the King who changed the name of the World Congress. He was destined to be a King connected to the people. And many realized during the Ceremony that this just might work.

The Presentation was now complete. Some in the crowd had started to make their way out of the Plaza. The Holographs were still streaming the scene on the stage out to the crowd and to the world. Sol caught a glimpse of the pair who took his attention earlier with their uncomfortable father/son conflict. The lad looked defeated and the dad looked wearied. Sol leaned over to Ahmed, amid the shuffle and noise of the exiting crowd. Sol took Ahmed by surprise.

"Ahmed, I just have one more thing to say. Let's get this thing started…hold up for a minute."

Sol took center stage again and he was clearly taking this role seriously…

No Parent Left Behind

Holograph images of the stage blinked and fluttered from the intermittent breaks in the projection. The un-orchestrated exodus of the crowd had them stepping through the images that emanated from the ground. Ahmed stepped forward beside Sol on stage.

"Excuse me ladies and gentlemen. If I could just ask you to hold on for a moment. Sol has one more item to share before he leaves the Plaza."

The dispersing crowd took formation again. Watching the Holographs as they settled back into an audience mode. Sol stepped forward.

"Thank you for your patience. As it has been for me, so I am certain today has been a day with a lot for you to take in. But I want to talk about a specific kind of patience for a moment."

Sol wasn't planning to take long and he wasn't planning to out the young father he had seen impatiently handling his child. Both Sol and Ell had long been interested in the management of children in families. The intensities that families went through were often discussed at the government level but rarely remedied. Sol had considered the powerless position a child has at the frustrated hands of his or her "dictatorial", and at times, angry parent. It was no secret. If the parents had a goal or something they needed and wanted to accomplish, the child was often the force that disrupted the goal.

Be it a scheduled appointment with a doctor, a plan to head out to the swimming pool by a certain time, or an important meeting to get to as soon as the kids got dropped off at the babysitter, the interrupted goal of a parent was too often the cause of harsh treatment of a child. It was unloving, it was unnecessary, and it was unacceptable. Here in this moment, he was ready to do what he had always wanted, to see a change begin.

Sol continued, "Some time ago, when I was a lad, my father took me to a festival. It was an annual festival in my hometown of Seattle. The park was vast, and the crowd was just a flowing blend of families and parents, kids and entertainers.

"In the midafternoon that day, my father took me to watch an acrobatic act that was on stage. The troupe ran onto stage with flips and cartwheels exciting the crowd as their colorful costumes filled the moment. This show was not designed for children specifically. Although the performers knew there would be young children in the audience so they had choreographed a show that intended to catch the eye of all ages in the audience.

"As I stood in front of my dad watching, I remember how at first, the performers on stage were able to hold my attention. Then as the moments passed, my stamina for long days of entertainment had been unable to endure. Dad, towering behind me, bent over and said, *'Solomon, stop fidgeting, pay attention.'*

"Well, little did my dad know that I had no more attention to pay…my attention was all spent. My 5-year-old attention bank account was all of a sudden overdrawn."

Many of the parents in the crowd were baited now. Thinking Sol, this new figurehead whom they had just been told is their King, was offering a lesson in behavior to the children, they held their heads a touch higher with a hope that this King was about to "teach" the children something about how best to manage themselves while in public. But Sol had another solution in mind.

As Sol acted out the moment he had experienced as a child, he regaled the audience, "Dad reached out with his monstrous meat hooks and took hold of the back of my neck. I remember shrugging my shoulders up to try to fend off, as feebly as I could, the squeeze of his warm and vice-like hand. Whether I could prevent the uncomfortable correction from my father or not didn't matter, I was being disciplined. Right there in front of the entire crowd…and no one noticed.

"He didn't have to say a thing. I knew I was not pleasing him, and I knew I had no power to tell him to stop or to show him how much that hurt…not just on the outside. The solitude of that moment, a moment where no one else in the world could know how I was feeling, felt despairing. If only I had the support of another who had more power than me to manage the situation. A person who cared enough to have said in that moment, '*You haven't done anything wrong little guy, I'll explain it to your Dad so he understands.*'"

You could see the lights go on for so many in the crowd. Those watching on their Mobile Device and Media Screen, or through the Holograph stream in a Plaza, were elucidated. Here in this moment each one of them who connected to Sol's story felt suddenly liberated.

"*Yes,*" they thought, "*If I had only been allowed to be a child in those moments instead of Mom or Dad forcing me to be perfect…*"

Sol saw the willingness in the crowd. And he was inspired in that moment to bring a resolution to those who needed it. Sol knew that most parents needed some help…some understanding…some coaching. And he knew children needed the protection. It was weak support to simply encourage couples to have children but not provide them with the tools to be successful at parenting. Historically, that had been the model. Couples having children and there was no license or training required. Sure, the odd parent or parents took Parenting Classes, but that was rare. Having a Dog or an exotic animal as a pet required a license but having children… nothing was in place to apply checks and balances to a situation where someone wanted to have a child. Sol had quickly decided to edict a solution.

"I would like to establish today a new and progressive model for parenting. No longer will parents be saddled with the responsibility to figure out how to parent when they are about to have a baby. No longer will the parents of toddlers be reeling from the tax on their physical and emotional resources after journeying through infancy with a little one, only to be overwhelmed by the demands of a toddler. I submit this day, that no longer will loving parents who are intending the best for their children, be left isolated on their island of no support on how to parent a child through the many stages of life's journey.

"It is simple, as King I edict that all expecting parents will be enrolled in parenting classes provided by the State. All current parents will be enrolled in parenting classes every two calendar years until their child has reached 6 years of age. Parenting growth will be maintained and fostered during the phases of parenting with Classes that will take place again for parents in the 10th calendar year of your child's life and continue every 2 years until the child has reached his or her 18th year. You might see this as parenting support groups. We all could use support, it is just that few of us have ever sought out the support that will help us parent the way we wish we had when we look back on the stages of our children's lives. Beyond that, we will provide parenting coaching for any who request it. This will be free to all. Once we as a society have walked through one generation of parenting classes for families, the fruit of this level of support to parents will be seen. That generation will be the recipients of strong, insightful, supportive parenting and that will have a positive effect on the emotional and relational health of that generation and the generation to come. So...."

Sol wanted to be expressly clear at this moment. It was his inaugural edict and from the sense he was getting from the crowd, they had long been waiting for something like this. Parents all over the world had often stated their judgment of other parents when poor parenting was displayed. People would often opine, *"There should be mandatory parenting classes if someone like that wants to have children!"*

Poor parenting was one of the most abrasive attributes of a floundering society. Any "good" parent could see that. Few other issues brought such swift social judgment in the courts of public opinion. Yet seldom was anything ever really done about it.

Sol continued, "We will call this *The No Parent Left Behind* coaching program. And it will provide these classes for you free of charge, in order that each of you will be able to attend. If you have or are going to have children, then you are required to participate in these parenting classes. So, I thank you all in advance for participating in designing a future that is healthier in many ways." Sol stopped speaking to seal the Edict. And then he reengaged.

"Oh, I have one thing to add to that edict. Since we are on the topic of how difficult parenting can be without the right support, I have also decided that anyone who chooses to forgo career pursuits in order to stay home and parent his or her children, will be compensated at a rate equivalent to 1.5 times the rate of the hourly minimum wage."

Before the crowd could respond Sol addressed the thoughts of many stay-at-home moms.

"I know, any stay at home parent is worth a lot more than that, but we are going to start there. It is time to show parents the respect they deserve, and their work is hard. So, compensation, support, and respect for doing that work is long overdue."

The Participants in the global audience were delighted at the concept and displayed their approval for this surprise innovation. Ahmed stepped forward and held up the Folio. Sol reached up to place his hand on the King's Scribe once again. As the crowds near and far were taking in this prodigious decision by Sol, the acceptance of such a sensible law was as monumental as any international law that had been set in motion before this day. Parents of the world had just received King-approved support that was desperately needed. Building a strong, healthy, resilient society started by building strong, healthy resilient families...families that could parent successfully and develop good humans.

The screen of the King's Scribed was glowing again. Sol pressed his hand against the screen. He announced his edict.

"I Sol, proclaim this day that the *"No Parent Left Behind"* edict be enacted. I edict all parents who are expecting or have qualifying children will be enrolled in parent coaching sessions at the prescribed intervals. All current and expecting parents are required to participate in coaching sessions to establish greater relational and emotional health in the future for all persons. I proclaim this with the intent that as we were all children and as the majority of us have had or will have children, great good can be accomplished for our present and for our future."

The King's Scribe glowed brightly then dimmed as it pulsed with a red hue backlighting Sol's handprint that was watermarked behind the text of the edict. In an instant, the voice of the digital Scribe announced…

"Edict Successfully Recorded"—"Thank You King Sol, Your edict has been entered into law."

The crowd marveled at the speed of the process. A far greater than polite round of applause jetted from the crowd. They really had a grasp on the importance of Sol's first law and the force of his authority to implement a law right then and there. No deliberations, no consultation, just a man who knew what he wanted and what he thought was best for the citizens of the world. This had been a potent and dramatic hour. A King was announced; the World Congress was given a new name; and within minutes, the new King was declaring new laws. The *No Parent Left Behind* program would undoubtedly offer hope and progress in ways that had been elusive to culture for ages.

One thing was clear, making better parents would make for better children… and that could only add to the improved world Sol hoped to be part of.

Trusting This Man With The Future

Sol, Ell, the Chancellor…and all the handlers were quite jubilant in their celebrations off stage. It was an exhilarating moment. Sol had been presented to the world and the world was showing little, if any, sign of pushing back at the World Congress transition. The world had just received her King and received the first edict from the new King.

As Ell's arms opened after the embrace of relief that had been welling up inside of her, the Chancellor stepped close and shook Sol's hand.

"Thank you Sol, I had no idea you intended to introduce a new law today but that was well timed and well received."

While Sol took a moment to elaborate on how honored he was by the chanters and the Cherokee drummers on the floor of the Plaza, Erin Whist was having a discussion with the *EPD* Sergeant a few yards away. She seemed to be instructing him to deal with someone who could barely be made out in the background. Just off in a shadow behind and to the right of the Sergeant was a figure. It was actually two figures. It appeared to be a child and a man. The Sergeant nodded to Erin and turned to dismiss the unexpected guests to escort them out of the area.

The two had slipped into the off stage area and approached the Sergeant as he was moving off stage himself to corral the entourage that had just left the main stage.

A few moments before, the young father pleaded with the Sergeant saying how important it was that he get to thank the King.

Something about this King left the young dad with the impression he could approach Sol. Fortunately for him the group was lingering off stage a little longer than he had expected. The Sergeant thought surely they would have retreated to the Fall-Out Room right away. But the security threat today was exceptionally low, so the King and the entourage had no reason to be whisked off to an especially secure room.

In fact, there was little threat at any World Congress event. Twenty years of virtual event safety had passed. Radical and violent groups rarely made the effort to disrupt an event anymore. Aside from the odd angry flare up resulting in a sign wielding group of activists attending an event, there was little concern of any real security threat. *EPD* Drones were a constant presence hovering around events and public settings. It was a touch ironic that the assurance against any real threat occurring left room for interruptions like today's backstage interaction.

Sol paused his handshaking with the group and turned to look in Erin's direction.

"Erin," Sol called out catching Erin a little by surprise. She never responded right away. "Erin, just hold them up a minute."

That's the kind of guy Sol was. If a situation looked curious and it might be of concern to him…well, he was always ready to jump in. Sol called out as the Sergeant was just beginning to usher the guests out of the secure area after declining a request to thank the King in person. He stopped and turned around. Looking past Erin he could see Sol separating from the bunch. While he was turned, the young dad stepped around the Sergeant and called out.

"King Sol!"

The group went silent. Here they were, off stage, ready to get to the Fall-Out Room and there was a stranger, an unidentified citizen, calling out to the King, calling out to Sol. This was very bold.

"King Sol!" He called again…"I just want to thank you. Do you have a moment?"

Sol kept moving towards the man putting more distance between himself and the Handlers. Walking the few meters to go past Erin he looked past the Sergeant who was taking a position between the man and the King.

"Do I know you?" Sol knew he didn't know the man, but the man displayed a sense that he somehow knew Sol.

"You saw me…During your speech you saw me dealing with my boy."

Ahh…then the lights went on for Sol as the man pulled his son in front of him.

"Why yes I did. Is everything OK?"

No one else in the group knew this was the man who inspired Sol to move quickly on stage to make the "*No Parent Left Behind*" edict. But Sol and the young dad all of a sudden had a connection. He spoke further.

"My name is Kale, and I just want thank you King Sol."

"Call me Sol."

"I just want to thank you for what you did."

Sol took the opportunity to be succinct and pointed with the man. This young dad was not only one of those who would reap the benefit and be impacted by the *No Parent Left Behind Program*…but he was the one who set Sol's path in motion on stage just minutes ago.

"So tell me Kale, if you were King of the World, how would you see this parent coaching program going?"

Kale was a tad surprised he was being asked. It took a moment of pause for Kale to come up with a thought. He looked down at his 5-year-old huddled in beside him, and then looked back to Sol.

"I absolutely love the idea. I can't thank you enough."

"That's fine," Sol said, "No need to thank me because we're all going to benefit from having healthier parenting. It is so simple, better parenting leads to healthier kids promising to bring a healthier future. But tell me Kale, what would you like to see in this *No Parent Left Behind Program?*"

"Honestly, I think any little bit of support parents can get, especially in those intense stages like before the birth of a baby and the first school years or early teen years, well that would make a huge difference for millions of parents."

The Chancellor had moved closer and he looked to Sol. Sol took his pensive nodding in agreement as an affirmation of this direction. There were probably a dozen ways to play this thing out, but Sol was convinced that to do the greatest good for the greatest number, in this case, just meant doing something for parents. Choosing a path and heading down it. No arcane studies or numbing committee deliberations on the matter. Just get something going that brings support.

"Hmmm…" Sol toned pensively. "What about you? Would you make time for a meaningful coaching session?"

"Me, well I sure would. I'm with you Sol. We all need a license to drive a car or own a dog, but there is no "license" requirement to raise a kid. Anyone with a womb and donor to fill it can have a kid…and that is one of the most complex and easily damaged commodities the world has or ever will have. If we can't do children right, then everything ends up suffering. I know I struggle sometimes." Kale put his hand on his son's head. "We have needed something like this for generations already."

Kale spoke it perfectly. Saying what everyone else had thought at some point.

"That is excellent to hear from you Kale!" Sol affirmed with apparent eagerness, "Then that is what we will do. The *No Parent Left Behind Program* will go forward. Thank you Kale."

Sol turned slightly from focusing on Kale to address the handlers and Delegates with him, dictating a flurry of plans for the first ever universal Parent Support and Education program.

"Beginning immediately, we will have an administration team in each Region and Nation establish the infrastructure for this program. Cash benefits will be enhanced for any who opt in to the PS&E Program. Call them incentives if you will. And if one chooses not to attend the program, that parent or parents will be given an immediate reduction in their benefit. Repeated absences will take away the entire benefit. Once program participation resumes, the entire PS&E benefit will be given to that parent each month. As for those who are above the line in income who do not receive benefits…they are still required to participate in the program if they have children. If those in higher income brackets decide not to participate in the parent coaching session we offer, they will be fined accordingly. Being wealthy does not preclude one from attending the mandatory Session. Fines will increase with each session they fail to attend. They will be given every opportunity to attend a session within the time period that corresponds to their child's age."

Kale was entirely endeared to Sol. He had been right to think this man was very approachable. Kale was about to leave his brief moment with the King but before he did, he queried.

"Sol, do you have any other changes planned?"

Sol paused, "Yes Kale, I do have a few things that have been on my mind. And you'll find out in a month just what some of them are."

"Why? What's going on in a month?"

The ears in the room were pricked again. Sol had not outlined his model to the group and the moment felt right for him to do so now. Sol knew his group would be wondering the same thing and there was no reason to keep from spilling his plan now.

"Every month…on the first Saturday at 12 noon Kale, from whatever region I am in, I will be speaking to the world. From wherever I am I will share the newest law across a live Media Stream. I will pop onto Media Screens and provide a brief synopsis of the edicts or laws that will be amended, struck down, or created."

To hear this was enlightening to all who were in the hallway at the time. Kale too was grateful Sol shared what he did. And it seemed refreshingly low in bureaucratic complexity.

"Thank you Sol, I am privileged to have had a moment with you." Kale and his son were ready to be escorted from the backstage area.

Sol bid Kale farewell and continued towards the Fall-Out room with the Chancellor, Ell, and the Handlers…A great deal of work was ahead of them.

As the quiet of the backstage hallway enveloped them, each of them was also enveloped by a feeling none had had before. Sol had performed in a way they had not expected…and after seeing what had just transpired in the Presentation Ceremony, the Red Ochre Ceremony, the spontaneous edict, and the meeting with Kale…they felt peace about trusting this man with the future of the entire world.

Ready To Leap Over The Fences

The intro chime faded and the faceless voice of the Digital Broadcast Network filled the silence.

"DBN brings you a special report with your panel of experts to examine the World Counsel's appointment of a King."

The shot framed the empty square in front of what use to be the World Congress Center for Global Relations. Set behind the great round Table of Truth in the shot was the brand-new sign unveiled during the worldwide Stream of the Presentation.

World Counsel Center for Global Progress.

The familiar panel of experts were kibitzing as the camera narrowed on the magnificent Table of Truth desk and its occupants. Coopers Drisden, Jared Franks, and the distractingly agitated Bryson Reynolds were queued up for the Stream. Coopers introduced the show.

"Welcome back to the show viewers and guests." Coopers turned from facing the camera to welcoming Franks and Reynolds.

"Thanks Coopers, it is indeed fantastic to be here. This is an amazing and interesting moment in world history."

Franks was one of the more diplomatic personalities left on DBN. The astoundingly huge pool of talent that was harvested from the fertile fields of the World Wide Web had really impacted "News" personalities. Many of them were more personality than they were news. But Franks thankfully, was not one of them. He was balanced, inquisitive, and pensive. Yet he brought such a solid voice of wisdom to the Streams that viewers kept voting him near the top of their favourite Media personalities. Year after year Jared Franks got the nod from viewers across the globe.

As for Reynolds…the self-proclaimed leader of the Brysonites, well he was definitely higher on the "personality" end of the spectrum. Bryson was all but uncontainable. The *AIMS–Halo* snapped its lens with precise timing on the animated Table of Truth expert. A cartoon couldn't have expressed Bryson's agitation any better as the excitement bolted from his mouth.

"Your damn right it's fantastic to be here…a King…Do you believe it?"

Bryson's hands were flying through the air as he talked. "We have a King now Coopers. Do we even know what that means? What the Hell is gonna happen? This is absolutely astronomical.…"

"I think a lot of folk are asking some of those questions Bryson, just let me frame this up for a moment Bryson so our audience can stay on pace."

Reynolds brought his hands down and took the Host's cue. At least he took it as well as could be expected for a guy who could spew out a penetrating rant at the drop of a hat.

"Ladies and Gentlemen, as Bryson has stated, we now have a King. There has never been a time in history when a worldwide King has been installed. And what I find most astounding about that, is the surprising embracing response of the world. The minimal presence of any strong reaction to this move by the World Congress is simply unbelievable. Are we in a time when a government has gotten so powerful that they can simply appoint any one they choose to lead the world? Or are we in a time where the people…are so ready for a true visionary to take us to a better place…that we almost expected a shift like this was bound to happen sooner or later? Jared, what is your thought on the reaction to this news of a King? In a different time and place, one would expect the world would have certainly let its voice of disenchantment at least be heard."

The empty square behind them was once again a gray monolith of canvas. It stood waiting for the moment when it would be overflowing again with engaged citizens. Jared knew Bryson was just squirming to get his thoughts out. He was okay with Bryson squirming a bit. Jared Franks gave no hint that he was aware his strident co-panel member was absolutely bursting as he waited for his turn to say his piece. Franks began responding while turning towards the silent granite field behind the emblematic Table of Truth.

"It is amazing isn't it Coopers…that only a handful of hours ago this huge field of granite was covered with people shoulder to shoulder. Let's talk a bit about the amazing moments we took in yesterday. The completely peaceful tone.…the sense of order and unity brought on by the drummer and the response of the King to the pitfalls in society's system of parenting that has been hobbling along pretending it has been working perfectly for ages."

"You're right Jared, this is the stuff of fairy tales." Coopers began. "And I know that we are going to be watching closely to see just how this King brings progress. I spoke with one of our World Congress correspondents and the buzz about this move to new leadership is intense. I was told the World Congress took a vote on who to choose as king. This guy, Sol James, was given a unanimous show of approval. There has never been a leader in any democratic level of government who has received a unanimous nod for their position. For godsakes it's like elevating a new Pope. But the last Pope didn't quite receive unanimous votes in the Catholic opinion polls did she?"

"I tell you Coopers this is one incredible moment. This is so incredible that I quite frankly, am excited to see what is going to happen."

Bryson could not contain himself a second longer. He got that Franks was just toying with him and holding him off from the next wild thing that was about to come out of his mouth.

"Excited…that is an understatement. This King is exactly what we need. I quickly checked the Brysonites *Sound Off* polling site before we went to air. And a seismic 88 percent of respondents are more intrigued than they are concerned about this new leader. And you know what makes me really excited about all this?"

"Tell us Bryson."

"Well," Bryson unfurled, "I am really excited by what we saw from respondents aged 18 to 30. There was 96 percent in favour of having a King or in favour of this King who they just met. Everyone saw this guy on stage yesterday and we all saw him make his way into the crowd to meet with the Cherokee drummer. That was a defining moment for this guy. At that moment where he came from didn't matter. King Sol was *The Man*. And his WCC Profile page is absolutely inundated with followers, viewers and Likes."

Bryson went on to tell of the perceptions his Brysonite Nation had of the new King.

"Practically every person…at least every Brysonite…saw a guy who could make a difference. The way he accepted the tribute from the drummer and chanter and then the Red Ochre thing. Well…come on guys! Is this for real? You can't make that s**t up!!"

Bryson was right. The moment the young boy held the Red Ochre up to Sol the world was fixated. Not on the impromptu ceremony…Rather it was fixated at seeing the honor from that group…the haunting drumming and chanting was riveting. No one had seen anything like it. The whole spontaneous tribute just sent out the feeling that this…the appointing of a King…this was supposed to be happening. And when the sound stopped so the drummer could offer his submission to the King only to be followed by the chanter and then the little boy, the watchers, both live and on the other side of the Media Screen, were inspired to submit to the idea. They knew nothing of who Sol was, but they saw only things that drew them to him, nothing that repelled them from Sol…or from having a King. For most of the world watching those moments, it might have been hard to say it didn't feel "right".

"And Coopers," Bryson waxed on, "One of my Brysonites has helped us out here a little today. It seems that we have a brand-new King now in the world and we don't know a lot about him. Last night my assistant forwarded me a little video clip they took down on Madison Street a few weeks ago. I gotta say, when I first saw this last night, I was absolutely inebriated at the thought that we just may have a King who is a lot like one of us. Just an average guy who wants to make a difference. A King who is ready to leap over the fences we create and make some daring and hard decision. A King who is ready to see this world move forward and to take a risk to make it a better place. Who will stand up for the little guy…a King who…" Bryson paused dramatically…

"….Well let's just roll the footage and you'll see."

Sol Was Not "Just" The King

The set lighting dimmed a touch. The blue stream of holograph light propelled upwards from the floor underneath the center of the Table. Coopers, Jared, and Bryson nudged back a little in their chairs. Up in front of them and playing on all Media Screens across the globe, was a scene of a busy city street. Shuttles were whipping in and out of the stop at the curb. People were striding up and down the street, and to the right of the shot, was a small, fenced patio at the Starbucks coffee shop.

"Stop it right there for a second guys." Bryson ordered.

Coopers and Jared couldn't wait to see what he was so excited about.

"Now, just so you know how things go for us Brysonites…"

Bryson Reynolds was often the face in the news that delivered intriguing and exciting content first. Because of his Feeders he was first at the trough in so many cases. "*Feeder*" was the label for any social media hound who Fed content to the big players they were following. And Bryson had a vast network of Feeders sending him enthralling content daily. Often hours before many of the colleagues in the industry even heard about the story. So, when one of the Brysonite "members" faithfully shared some awesome footage, Reynolds was ever faithful to stake the Brysonite claim on it…On this occasion it was a young college student who was doing some research on public transportation in downtown Seattle. And what she shot really made Bryson look good. Bryson Reynolds made sure to toot the Brysonite horn before moving forward with his news.

"So we'll let that play in just a second guys but pay attention to that fence around the coffee shop. There is a group sitting at a table and his back is turned to the camera right now. None of them know they are about to be caught on video but watch closely, because that fella with his back to the camera does something pretty amazing."

Bryson pointed up to the holograph image that hung over their Table of Truth. With his finger in the air, he drew a virtual circle around the shoulders and head of the patron in the sun on the Starbucks patio. Leisurely sitting, sipping his coffee, visiting friends, and watching the people flow along the street.

"That person right there…that is King Sol."

Franks and Coopers shuffled in their seats. They didn't know what they were about to see. And getting a clue from Bryson's excitement was next to impossible. When he got excited no one could tell if he was about to drop a bomb or fire off a confetti canon…the only thing Bryson's excitement betrayed was that he was excited.

"This was taken a number of weeks ago. We have learned it was before he even knew he was going to be King."

As Bryson reached up and tapped the air with his finger the red circle disappeared from the holograph and he barked, "Roll it fellas."

The shot rolled. Viewers around the table weren't the only ones mesmerized by the moment. Watchers and viewers in front of every Media Screen in the world were laser focused on this Stream. The shot was clear and steady. The young college student, a proud Brysonite, was keen with her camera, as most Brysonites tended to be. The street sounds were filling the air as the scene unfolded. Viewers watched as people bounced off the steps of the Shuttle. The shot was wide and the fence and patio were in the periphery view. The three amid the many that exited the bus were in the center of the shot. There was no mistaking what was unfolding…it was moving quickly. The taller men in front and back of the smaller youth were hardly trying to hide their behaviour. The messenger bag hanging in the smaller boy's shoulder was pulled up and over his head by the fella in the rear of the trio. The viewers were interrupted by Bryson as he swiped a quick arrow to point to Sol and remarked…"Ok, watch what happens with King Sol…here it comes."

And the whole world saw it. Sol leapt over the fence and with a few strides, was on the throat of the bully in the rear. It was quick. It was calculated, and it was a decisive reaction. The audio was enhanced for those watching.

They saw Sol slam the big guy against the bus as he grabbed him by the throat.

"Hey, leave the kid alone!"

Sol reached for the bag as it went flying over his back and the head of the smaller boy. Viewers watched as Sol's grip was loosed on the throat of the punk while trying to capture the projectile messenger bag. Just enough for the defiant criminal to squirm out of Sol's grasp. The punk shoved Sol and broke away entirely, taking off after his accomplice who had just caught the bag that was thrown to him, and he booked it down the street. The Brysonite cam was zeroed right in on the scene. The shot caught Sol bolting after the thugs only to stop a few meters down the sidewalk realizing there was no chance Sol could catch them and be part of bringing justice to the young victim. The whole world watching the Stream was experiencing what Sol went through that Saturday morning during a relaxing coffee date with Ell and some friends.

Viewers of this street level drama were getting their first behind the scenes glimpse of who their newly appointed King was. And now, watching Sol slow to a stop and look to the distance down the street, they were left with the sense that this man was not one bit reluctant to get involved where injustice was ruling the day.

The stream closed with the thief looking back and throwing up the 'F' finger to Sol just before he sprinted into the street.

"Shocking!" Jared Franks was first out of the gate on this video. "And I'm not talking about the pissant who got himself flattened by a Shuttle for ripping off a small teenage boy as what's shocking here. I am talking about this guy as King."

Franks was trying to be delicate here. He had been around long enough to know that whether you approve or disapprove of a world leader, it was in the best interest of the commentator and the network to weigh how you say things sometimes.

"It is shocking that our World Congress, our trusted institution made up of politicians and world leaders from across the globe, would actually choose this guy as King."

Franks knew what he was doing. His lead-in was getting the viewer ready to hear a diatribe against the World Congress or at least a denouncement of Sol as King, but in pure Franks style, Jared led them on. He picked up his notes and started.

"This is what we know about this guy. This guy is a senior researcher at the University of Washington, lives in Seattle with his wife, his two kids have moved out and are in their own careers, and he goes for coffee at the quaint downtown Seattle coffee shop on Saturday mornings. He writes a letter to the World Congress after last month's school shooting and now he is King."

"What's your point Jared…we get it the World Congress picked a normal guy…!"

"That's exactly my point Bryson. It is shocking that the World Congress had the insight, unless it was just fate or there is some royal line connection on this guy that we don't know about, to find a man who had no connection to the political world and recognize something about him. See something that would indicate he has what it takes to lead the world. I think your video clip shows this. This guy simply stepped up. He was not gonna sit by and watch injustice, unfairness, and bullying take place. He jumped in and did something about it. It is beautiful. If that's the kind of ruler we're getting with Sol David James…" Jared paused and leaned his head and torso into the middle of the table just a bit offering his forehead to the group…

"Then where's the Red Ochre…imprint me.… If I am going to have a King, I want a guy who will take my side, who will get into the action, who will make decisions that most apathetic leaders are too chicken to make. And this just might be that guy."

Jared's table companions got his message that for a King like this, he was ready for the Red Ochre imprint to be placed on his forehead.

Jared Franks had taken away what so many had taken away from the Presentation. He was compelled by the previous day's ceremony and particularly the spontaneous Red Ochre ceremony that took place in the crowd. Not just with the drummer and chanter who honored him on behalf of the Cherokee people. It was the scene of the nameless dozens who offered their brow to the King for his imprint as Sol made the short walk back to the stage. An old man, a young man, a mother, a grandmother, a guy in a track suit, a couple with a baby in the stroller… dozens of people stooping respectfully and leaning in toward Sol as he walked towards them on the way back to the stage. This was a very liberating day. People felt it…they saw his eyes up close, they sensed his respect and warmth toward the drummer, the chanter, and their grandson. It just felt right. There was no media building this guy up with flowery stories of his journey to King or inspiring tales of how his work as a University Library Researcher had guided so many students and professors toward brilliant papers and journal articles. This was just Sol. This was a leader people could like and there was something about a man who would abandon self and throw himself in front of a bus for others. Something that made him worthy of their trust.

Any man could be a hero from behind a desk or from the other side of the Media Screen watching the apathy and injustice flourish. There's a million heroes in words and complaints. Men were making heroes of men all the time. A "hero" for scoring a touchdown, or hitting the ball over the fence at the World Series. Or a hero for crashing and dying while flying a formation in an Air Show display. But few men were this kind of hero. The kind that stepped out of their safe "fox hole" even though no one was asking them to, or paying them millions of dollars, or assuring he would not be hurt or killed for doing so. And even though it was the slimy criminal who was hit by a bus that morning, it was all good for Sol. He "threw himself under the bus" for that one young man. Sol saw the injustice, took action, and didn't let the fact that he was risking a lot, slow him down. Sol was not "just" the King after yesterday's Ceremony, he was now a hero. The world just witnessed their King throw himself into the world around him so he could help someone…a victim, a little one who was being downtrodden and needed an advocate. Sol was the one who did this. And no one could take that away from Sol or make Sol to be any less than what he was.

Streamed To The
Table of Truth

"**J**ared I agree, there is something to be said about a person who will do what Sol has done."

Coopers was steering toward hearing from social media posts on the Kingly accosting of the Seattle Shuttle thugs.

"Not everyone will take action when they see action needs to be taken. And you're not alone, we have been getting a stream of tweets in on Bryson's video. Why don't we go to some of our viewer's thoughts?"

Tweets from viewers started popping up on the screen. Coopers knew the way this was going as soon as he read the first tweet. Watchers loved seeing justice meted out. And some viewers, especially the Brysonites out there, if faced with a similar choice to get involved, would take action like they just saw Sol doing. Others were ready to jump in with their support when they saw someone else doing so.

"Here's a thought from @rippinmad; *why do we need this guy as king? I'll tell you why. To have a leader who will not waste time. This guy will make good decisions quick & could fix a whole lot of shi****"*

Look at what @powertothepeople has to say; *"So it's true...a normal guy is now the King, it's about time, government has abandoned power to the people for generations, maybe having a real person as the King will get things back on track.'"*

Coopers started chuckling while he was scanning the incoming tweets on his Desk Folio. "There are a ton of comments coming in, and it appears our vigilante King is already drawing some admirers. Here's one from @egyptianprincess; *'every King needs a queen, especially the good looking ones. Does Sol have one yet? Cuz if not consider this my application.'"*

Bryson snickered out loud, "Well that tweeter is obviously not a Brysonite Coopers. No Brysonite would have missed the part in yesterday's Presentation where Sol and his wife Ell walked out on stage. But as far as middle-aged Kings go, Sol does have a very strong draw on the 35 to 60 year old female demographic. We ran a quick poll of the Bryson Nation yesterday evening and after seeing the Presentation, 87% of female respondents in that demographic said they are excited to see this King make his next edict. And the other 'gender' is pretty affirming too, at 81% saying they are excited to see what's next.

"Beside asking our respondents if they were eager to see this King thing develop or if they were uncertain, it seems by some of the first impression comments posted at the end of the survey, a good number of those female, male, and other respondents, said Sol looks like a man they could trust. Let me just tell you what that final polling question was that was asked...and since yesterday, we have heard from 373,000 respondents. The Bryson Nation Polling Group asked;"

Based on first impressions, after watching the King at the Presentation Ceremony, if you had to state your 'feelings' about Sol in a word what would that word be?

Bryson added a little explanation about the latest poll. "Now, respondents were given seven options Coopers, and I think you will be a little surprised at what came out on top." Bryson Reynolds went on to show the poll results.

3 percent chose "*figurehead*"

4 percent chose "*puppet*"

8 percent of respondents chose "*despot*"

12 percent chose "*meh*" indicating their disinterest

13 percent chose "*leading man*"

19 percent chose "*balanced*"

"And if first impressions mean anything gentlemen, we have to put some stock in the numbers. An astonishing **41 percent** of respondents who saw King Sol for the first time chose "trustworthy" as the feeling they got from this surprise King. And of those, 62 percent of those were female."

Coopers took over with his social media survey. "Look at a couple more of these tweets, I can't believe how affirming these are for the most part. But here is one that opens up a question."

@offthegrid says...*sure, a king. Just what we need if he's got the balls to cause real change. But who's to say this guy isn't gonna be some Polpotic dictator who builds his empire and could care less who gets screwed in his wake?"*

@kingoftheworld says; *well-done King Sol...this is something we have needed for a long time. A leader who is not afraid to get dirty, to grab a few thugs by the throat and say, not on my watch you sick son of a bitch....Hoooray for King Sol!*

"Well, that says a lot, is it possible that we are ready for this?" Coopers commented. "Are we on the brink of disaster with this new model or on the brink of a Utopia?"

Just then there was a hesitation. The *AIMS* Cam had taken the three commentators and spliced them together on Screen for viewers to catch all of their expressions. None of these veteran commentators expounding on the new King of the World expected what was going to happen next.

In the center of the table, as Jared was getting the update from his producers, the World Congress symbol beamed up from the Holograph system embedded in the granite beneath them. There was about to be a special live feed. An impromptu guest on the broadcast.

The producer had just got a hot feed from the World Counsel direct Stream system. The producers were ready to go live with a holograph that would give Coopers and his partners in crime an unbelievable opportunity. Coopers was now composed again and looked straight at the Camera…

"Folks, we have just been told that King Sol is about to join us. My producers are about to give me the 10 second countdown as I speak."

As uncertain as he was about what would take place with this surprise on-air visit with the King, Coopers steadied himself and prepared his audience.

"This is the excitement that Live Stream DBN brings you. In seconds, King Sol will be streamed to the Table of Truth live from his home in Seattle."

In Coopers' ear the count was on…

9…8…7…6…

One Question Each

5 *...4...3...*

The blue glow of the holograph floated above the three struggling to remain composed around the table. The image that joined the scene was set so as not to overwhelm the trio at the Table. In the image was Sol. Just Sol, standing next to his fireplace in his modest Seattle home. Sol seemed very relaxed. He and Ell had been watching the Stream and they thought it would be wonderful if he could just show up and have a chat with the three DBN commentators. So, with a quick call to Ahmed, he made it happen. The King was going to meet the three commentators live right now.

The walnut mantle of Sol's fireplace in the shot was a solitary feature and the cool tyndall stone masonry gave way to the warmth of the dark walnut and composed image of the King.

Both Sol and Ell were familiar with Coopers' work. He was a very balanced and fair interviewer. He never failed to ask just the right questions. His tactically placed questions that led to teetering on the edge of inappropriateness, always heightened the attention of the viewer and drew the interviewee deep into the moment. As for Bryson Reynolds, Sol and Ell knew he was somewhat of a complex caricature. With his over-the-top rants and shameless followers buoying him up, he could be a wild card. But Sol was ready. A brief consult with Ahmed set the engagement in motion and he was ready for whatever was about to happen.

Sol set the folio upright and stood in front of it. His address would be routed to all 11 billion people in the world. Here and now, Sol was "sent" live to the Table of Truth with Coopers, Jared, and Bryson. This was a perfect moment to be the people's King.

Sol looked at Ell who was just out of the shot. It was all so exciting. He smiled and said…. "Let's do it."

…2…1…-Sol was now Live

The glow in the middle of the table had now become a solid holograph. The viewers and commentators could see the subdued hue of the gas flame in behind Sol. The scene was almost like a Presidential Christmas card. Just to the left of Sol was the family dog sitting on the relaxed French Club Chair. The tan patches of the 9-year-old Corgi blended into the supple leather of the comfy chair. The blanket draped over the edge could have used a straightening before Sol's Folio began to broadcast.

The holographic images allowed the trio at The Table of Truth to take in a live interaction with Sol as if he were sitting with them at the table. Drisden, Franks, and Reynolds tilted their gaze away from each other to look up to where Sol was. The extra second it took for Coopers to adjust to the virtual guest on the show was just enough for Sol to start in with his greeting.

"Good afternoon Gentlemen, so wonderful of you to have me on your show."

"Good afternoon King Sol." Coopers was ever the professional moderator.

"Please, just Sol, just call me Sol."

"Certainly Ki…I mean certainly Sol."

"Thank You."

Coopers was eager to flow into the privileged interview with the King. "We are so fortunate to have you join us, I know I speak not only for us at this table Sol, but I am sure every one of our viewers is presently surprised to say the least, to have you join us on this show."

Sol was obvious about his comfort in his own home. And the confidence in his face and ease of his interaction was easy to see on the DBN side of the stream too.

"We are sure you must be exceedingly busy these days after the Presentation yesterday and implementing the new *No Parent Left Behind* program."

"Yes, it has been a whirlwind. The World Counsel FaceStreamed a conference last night and established the administrative infrastructure for the program. I am quite impressed at how efficient and how deep the resources go that are available to implement necessary programs. It is often not the lack of resources available to improve society,, it is a lack of resourcefulness. For those of you who will be participants in the *No Parent Left Behind Program*, you can expect to hear from a Digital Representative in about two weeks."

Being involved in research at a university for the years he had, Sol was quite familiar with the Digital Representative. In the late 2020's, institutions began employing an intuitive AI system to contact, register, and confirm participants in both opt-in programs and in mandatory programs that were offered for various purposes. One of the broadest reaching uses of the DR's came during the transition from gas and electric power to nuclear power on motor vehicles. The **I-DOT**, the *International Department of Transportation,* required every registered owner of a vehicle to take a mandatory afternoon Streaming session on the management of the Nuclear fuel cell that would be part of every vehicle. It was called the *Nuclear Advantage Vehicle Safety Program,* **NAVS.**

Once all registrants were trained in safe handling of the cells, the obsolete fuel systems were converted to accept a nuclear cell, and all new vehicles began being manufactured Nuclear ready.

The Nuclear Advantage Vehicle Safety Program was administrated by the almost glitch free Digital Representative. Contact of registrants, registration, and confirmation of entry into and completion of the program was handled almost flawlessly by the Digital Representative System out of University of Washington. And Sol, although he had nothing to do with that department, was able to keep up with the updates on the DR system and the program management that it was involved in.

Digital Representation and A.I. had evolved exponentially…becoming integrated in such a seamless way, that clients, customers, registrants, and recipient users of the systems felt no cause for disenchantment. They only marvelled at the ease and efficiencies the A.I. based systems brought. and Sol was completely sold on its value. The system was even more efficient today than years ago when Sol had his first introduction to it. Digital Reps would be managing the administration details for the newly launched *No Parent Left Behind Program.*

After an awkward welcome to the surprise King, Coopers opened with a question that brought an unexpected response.

"Now that the *No Parent Left Behind Program* is under way, are you finding things around the office at the World Counsel Center for Global Progress to be as comfortable and smoothly functioning as you would like?"

"Well, as I indicated Coopers, I am impressed by the depth of resources that are available. We must remember, this institution has provided a great deal of magnificent leadership in the Global Political realm. And as for being at the World Counsel Centre, I decided I would rather do this job from home. So I am presently situated at our home Coopers."

"Well, are you soon going to be relocating to the Chancellor's residence on the World Counsel grounds? It seems that is what is expected in order to perform the tasks involved with your office?"

"Oh no, definitely not Coopers, the Chancellor's residence is the Chancellor's home. I have no interest in moving Chancellor Mahndar out in order for Ell and

I to move in. Besides that, Chancellor Mahndar has been absolutely indispensable in the assistance he has provided for us during this transition. The Chancellor has agreed to be an ongoing presence for me and the Delegates as he remains in his adjusted role with the World Counsel Center for Global Progress. So no, we are not moving at all Coopers, we are planning to continue on here in our home. We love it here."

Bryson was aghast, he dove right into the conversation without being invited, "But how does a King intend to rule from a residence in Seattle? What about security, what about access to the King? Is it not somewhat of a risk to just stay on in a proper house and neglect the necessary security and protection from harm that a head of state ought to be given?"

Sol displayed understanding as he responded to Bryson, "There is no good reason I cannot do all I need to do for this office from my present location. I will be able to stay connected through the King's Scribe on my Folio. So, when the Chancellor and the Delegates understood I did not want to upgrade our present housing situation, well, the World Counsel managed to come up with a plan to meet all the security needs we might have while we stay in the home that we love.

"You are welcome to go to our new website to see how this all breaks down, www.kingoftheworld.world. But in short Bryson, this entire block has become somewhat of a fortress.

"So you're saying you plan to rule right from your house? That is amazing. No castle or estate to maintain, no stable full of horses or garages full of cars?"

"That's right Coopers. Ell and I are perfectly fine in this place. We have had a cleaning lady come in and cook and clean three times a week up until now and she will be a full-time manager around here now that I've taken on this role. But other than that, it's pretty much business as usual around the James' house."

"And the security plan you've mentioned?"

Coopers was just being given access to the website while Sol was chatting with him. He was now able to see the entire area that Sol and Ell live in. The cars on the street, the houses on the cul-de-sac, and the brick parapets on either side of the traffic lanes heading in and out of the cul-de-sac.

"I see here on the kingoftheworld.world site, you have been living pretty much in a gated community already. Security is typically pretty good in those communities. But how does this work Sol? Your cul-de-sac backs a park and there is only one way into your place. Is that a Security check post I see on the west end of your cul-de-sac?"

Sol was now looking at the on-screen images Coopers and his viewers were seeing. Coopers was pointing out a small checkpoint at the mouth of the cul-de-sac. The Global Military Unit -GMU, would be responsible for the King's security. The GMU had placed a tidy brick structure on the boulevard at the end of the sidewalk. The live images from the Goog-Sat showed the GMU personnel occupying the space outside the brick structure. Sol joined in and he began pointing things out for Coopers. As he touched the images each residence in the gated community he pointed to was highlighted.

"Here, here, and here, we now have World Counsel Security personnel residing 24/7. And here and here...." Sol tapped the air where the image of his old neighbors' homes was seen.

"...Other administrative and support staff will be located in these homes. There are still a few things to set in place." Sol swiped his hand across the image of the sky over the houses.

"In a few days all this will be an official no fly zone."

Showing there was going to be no potential for flight paths over that area. He slid the image to the west, circling the well treed area that backed Sol and Ell's home, the shrubs and flower beds glowed brightly as the digital enhancements overlaid the images and viewers could see the personnel working in the various areas of the park. World Counsel Staff was toiling to modify the bosky three-acre vista. Small excavators and skid-steers were on task along with groups of staff in windbreakers with GMU on the back in huge letters. They were redesigning the park to better fit the King's security needs.

"And a plan is in progress to effectively render the park behind our house as a private park. I assure you, we are covered on all sides. Many of our neighbors have accepted generous relocation offers and more than half of the homes on our street are now filled with World Counsel Security personnel and equipment.

"So, along with the generous relocation packages the neighbors received, it wasn't difficult for each of them to move on to another home. I was able to thank them personally and this…" Sol waved his arms as if to show off his home as a grand estate, "…is the 'Castle' now Coopers."

It's not that Sol didn't want to continue chatting for a long time, but Sol was prompt to give Coopers and his Table of Truth companions some parameters. Being accessible was important for Sol and he had opened himself up by offering to step into this Stream that was underway. Now thinking about the direction this interview could go…and how unending the questions might be from this group, Sol brought to mind his uncle who offered him a boundless amount of advice while going through college. As the moments sped along, Sol decided he would do as his insightful Uncle Remi did. He would offer only a few responses to only a few questions in the remainder of the engagement with DBNI. The next moments became vitally meaningful.

Uncle Remi had challenged Sol in those college days by setting up the very parameters that Sol was now introducing to Coopers, Bryson, and Jared. Sol was in control of the time. He set the boundaries on the questions they were allowed to ask. Not the theme or matter of the question, but simply the number.

"Gentlemen," Sol started, "I am grateful to be here on the Stream today. And in the interest of time, I am going to have to limit you to three questions. Before you begin though, I will give you this. I am planning to make some changes. I do have policies in the works that will be part of the progress I intend for the world. Some of those changes will be received with gladness by the Global community while others may be less so embraced. As I implement these changes, it will become clear that it is my intention to do the greatest good for the greatest number.

"My goal is to make this world a better place for all of us. So today I will take three questions. I will not however at this time, take questions on what my policies will be. So, if you need a minute to compose your questions, then by all means, feel free."

Coopers put his finger to his ear to take in the instructions of his producer as the King offered the commentators a break. His producer rarely broke away from a Live Stream but this time it was necessary. He could see the pensiveness on the faces of his team at the Table. The world was watching as the King was engaging the three men who were given the chance to ask the King of the World one question each. Coopers acted on the cue of his producer.

"Friends and Feeders," Coopers addressed the viewing audience. "We will be back with you in a few minutes. Sol, the King of the World will be staying with us and Mr. Franks, Mr. Reynolds and myself, will be posing a few very important questions to Sol."

In entirely uncharacteristic fashion, the DBN stream broke away. The call sign and text sat idle on screen for a second or two then switched to local content as the commentators from the Table of Truth took the offered moments to prepare the questions they were going to ask the King.

Stumpy Tortoise Legs Flailing Away

Welcome back, thanks for staying with us. I'm Coopers Drisden sitting here with Jared Franks, Bryson Reynolds, and Sol, the World Counsel newly appointed King of the World."

With the DBN Table of Truth returning live, the active streets, offices, and homes of the curious world were once again placed on pause. There was such anticipation and a distinctly keen attentiveness. Few things compel a society to watch a Live Stream more than seeing a live interview with the one who is poised to bring about a better world. The viewer was waiting for answers to their own questions. Questions like;

"Would Sol be the people's King?"

"Is this the way things should go when we have a King?"

"What is a King supposed to be like?"

The three at the Table of Truth were ready with their questions.

Coopers started the round. "Thank you for the opportunity Sol. Each of us will ask one question before we sign off. I will go first."

Coopers tilted into the Holograph image of Sol just a touch. His eyes narrowed, his lips pressed tighter together, and he inhaled.

"Yesterday at the presentation ceremony we saw several compelling things. The introduction of the world's first King by the Chancellor, a transfer of power endorsed by the World Congress, you being honored by the Red Ochre ceremony of the Cherokee drummers and chanters, and then what seemed to be an impromptu declaration of a brand-new social program. A program intended to assist parents of children of all ages in being better parents garnering support from the *No Parent Left Behind* program. And it was an amazing day for all of us Sol, I can only imagine how it felt for you." Coopers paused to take a breath.

"My question is this, when there is a new law or program put in place under your leadership, how do you intend to inform the world, and does the world have an opportunity to say 'Hey, I have a great idea for a law that will make things better for all of us, I'm going to send it to the King to consider?'"

Sol was just coy enough to point out the obvious to his first questioner. As a person of fairness, it was only reasonable to make mention that he recognized Cooper's diversion from the rules and was choosing to allow it. "You do know that's actually two questions Coopers?"

Not giving Coopers time to apologize or to alter his question, Sol simply said,

"To answer your 'question' Coopers. I believe there are a lot of good people out there that have many of the same concerns as I do about this world and the way it is going. People who say *I sure wouldn't want to raise a kid in this world today. Boy if I could run things I would sure make some changes.'* And I would like to hear from them. So, if you Coopers, or anyone out there watching today, has a great idea or puts some thought into changing this world and wants to send along their great idea, they can just go to the King of the World Meta page. Feel free to post right to the page or hit me up with a message. I really want to hear some of the ideas that are out there. I'm not promising we will "like" everyone's idea or suggestion but we know there are brilliant people who have as much right as the next guy to be King of the World, and there is opportunity for them to have input.

"Now, on to the main part of your question Coopers. When there is a new program, law, edict or rule established and put in place, I will be declaring it in front of the world through the World Counsel Address system. The plan is for a public address on the first Saturday of every month at 12PM. I know many of the non-political types I have spoken with over the years have complained that the political process just moves far too slowly. It takes years to enact or legislate a new law. I intend to change that. If a law is prudent, and it is the greatest good for the greatest number, it will be put into effect immediately upon my announcement. Or at least with as little delay as possible. In that way we are not forced to drudge along unproductively. Waiting and lobbying for changes that should be happening in days or weeks."

At Sol's statement, Coopers' eyebrows lifted, and his affirming nod was easy to read as support for Sol, at least on this point. Sol added to his thoughts.

"If I happen to misstep in certain laws or policies, then I will be all too happy to reverse them or change them to make them right. Do I promise to make it perfect for everyone who exists under my leadership? No! But do I promise to make things better? The answer my friend is Yes!"

Sol was prepared to move on to the next panelist.
"Thanks for the question Coopers, Jared, what's on your mind?"

Franks jumped into the interaction. "A ton!" He emphatically announced while his eyes quickly widened to punctuate just how overwhelming this all seemed to him.

"I am so with you King Sol on moving this political system and proposed changes along more quickly."

In Franks' mind the entire political machine was all but ground to a halt on so many issues and citizens often spoke of their distrust in the system and those who ran it. Franks himself was disenchanted with the way things were often managed. Things like poverty, decisive action where there were regional conflicts or militia style oppression of the native people, the sex slave trade, forcible recruitment of child soldiers in pockets around the globe, and among others, the disparate chasm of wealth between the richest and the poorest of society that causes a great burden on the poorer among us. So, Franks was ready to set his question in front of Sol.

"My question to you is this Sol, how do you propose to garner favour from the citizens of the world and to gain their loyalty and trust?"

"That is a good question Jared." Sol was anticipating this type of question and had long thought about how he would be able to trust a newly appointed King if it were someone else who was in his place.

"Jared, I don't think anyone should 'trust' me without me earning their trust. Especially if they don't know me. I don't think anyone should trust a politician he or she doesn't know. But let me just say Jared, I am not a politician. I have sat on your side of the fence my whole life. I plan to do two things to earn the trust and loyalty of people if they are willing to give some of it. I plan to earn it by not seeing people as citizens Jared, rather I see everyone who has breath as a **Participant**. And I intend to refer to all of us as **Participants** of this world and not just citizens. As citizens we have become passive observers, too readily disengaged in working towards progress with our world. Often expecting the mysterious "someone else" to bring the changes we all hope for.

As **Participants**, I envision a world where each of us agrees to invest in this society. We engage, we act, we discuss, we plan together to become better. Participating in what we want our world to be instead of seeing it become something we feel we have no control over. I intend to take counsel from the Delegates and the world to see our global society progress to a place we have been asking to go to for generations now. And as those needs are seen and met, I believe people will realize that it is ok to offer me their loyalty and trust. I hope they choose to trust because trust is a choice. The simple fact of being King of the World Jared is…. if I don't do what it takes to meet the needs of those who have needs, then I don't deserve their trust."

Jared sat back. His expression was listless, almost blank. That answer was solid…irrefutable…unwavering. He had never, in 18 years as a journalist, heard someone ask for his trust while earning it at the same time. Jared smiled and said, "Thank you Sol, if all that you have said there is what we can expect then it is going to be hard to call you Sol…I know many will be eager to call you King."

"My pleasure Jared, thanks for the question."

Sol looked now to Bryson. The wildcard, the media revolutionary. A man with a quirky bow tie and an even quirkier persona. Bryson decided to go a different direction. He was pretty comfortable with what he had heard so far from Sol. And his entire philosophy complemented the idea of having a King rule the world, so he posed a rather unusual question.

As a fan of the classic movie Blade Runner, Reynolds was all about the Social Science the Blade Runner offered. He loved toying around with the ideas that were found in the cult classic. The Blade Runner was one of those dystopian novels that brought science and humanity to a place of indistinguishableness. Artificial intelligence made distinguishing between a real human and an Android a virtual impossibility. In the Blade Runner, humans were the pathetically flawed species they had always been and the Androids, called Replicants, were a perfect clone of the imperfect human. The film was a 1982 cinematic recast of an early 70's novel, remade and released again in 2017. In the film, the Replicants needed to be interrogated by a Rep-Detect cop in order to expose them and remove them from society. The questions that were posed to the interrogees were unique. They were unique in the way they could only be answered by a reasonable human who was able to engage some philosophical thought. It was known that Replicants are incapable of philosophical human cognition.… Incapable of meta-cognition related to emotion and feeling.

Bryson, a card-carrying member of the *Blade Runner Fan Club*, brought out his copy of the Director's cut once in a while. He was totally intrigued by the concept of the Replicants and Bryson Reynolds would soon be joining as a guest speaker at the 25th Anniversary conference for the date the Blade Runner movie was initially set in, the year 2019. Bryson often made a big deal about the connection between the Blade Runner and the dissolution of the United Nations. Both of them were set in about the year 2019. Both of them represented a new age of dystopia.

Reynolds loved the themes contained in dystopian Science Fiction, a genre of film and literature that posed the future as being fraught with social decay, gritty criminal activity, and despotic politicians and world leaders who pursued power through corruption. As predictive this thoughtful genre was about the state of the world's future, Bryson hated that underneath the thin crust of the shiny world we all currently live in, one could clearly see it too was already an effective dystopia.

His favourite part of the Blade Runner movie was the interrogation of the Replicants…or of the subject that was being investigated in case he or she were a Replicant. These subjects were suspected of not being human. They were a cellular clone of a human in an android form. Subjects were given a series of emotionally evocative questions. Of course, emotional responses were the stuff of humans, so the theory underlying the detection of an Android was easy to accept. Since the cult-following of the 80's hit movie flourished, the biometric-sensor field of interpreting human emotional responses also flourished. In the movie, the fictional Voight-Kamph machine was used.

The Voight-Kamph was a polygraph-like machine used by the LAPD's Blade Runners to assist in testing an individual to see whether he or she was a Replicant or not. Like the capnometry used in psychophysiological breath analysis, and the biometric sensors used now, the Voight-Kamph measured bodily functions such as respiration, heart rate and eye movement in response to emotionally provocative questions. The Replicant would be exposed by the data collected. The biometric-sensors of today were quite the evolution of the Voight-Kamph fictional detector. They would calculate pupillary response, salivation, integumentary response such as periphery vaso-dilation, constriction, or perspiration, among the normal vitals assessment.

The inimitable Bryson Reynolds had used one on his weekly show on several occasions. Not the fictional kind of the Blade Runner movie. Rather Reynolds was the proud owner of the *3M Cogent Bio-Axiomete*r, Bio-AXM for short.

It was accepted that this style of bio-metric sensing was infallible. If you were telling the truth about a thing it would confirm it. If not.... well the system was there to let you know. And it would let anyone trained to use the system know as well. The synergistic thing about the way the process was orchestrated though, was that those trained in bio-metric sensing, were keen intuits themselves. These Readers would be as astute at reading their subject in many cases as the device was. An amazing talent that was often innate in the Reader but was brought out through training. Today, the Readers who used their skills to determine the truth of a potential criminal's claims, are very similar to the Blade Runners who interviewed Replicants to expose them as non-human.

Readers today even sub-consciously employ their olfactory sense to detect the subtle changes in a person's pheromones and body chemistry. The Reader could detect a lie by the sub-consciously detectable scent given off by the liar. The detectable difference would display when the subject was lying versus when they were telling the truth. The Reader was such a finely tuned intuit that the bio-metric sensors had become secondary to the brilliant skills of these savants. A class of humans who incorporated all the integrated neuro-biological and gastro-biological systems that consolidate the aggregate non-conscious sensory and emotive perceptions. It was a Sensory Processing Sensitive Person's superpower. A power which enabled them to honor the gut-brain axis to arrive at what was scientifically known as, a "Gut Instinct." A combined internal and peripheral process to accurately determine deception.

At a glance they would interpret all the data. It was uncanny how exacting and autonomous their skills seemed to be. Any nuance of an anomaly that deviated from the baseline info they had established through common questions about name, date, place of residence etcetera, would be caught. And Readers had become the go-to source for solving all manner of mystery and crime. Just probe the subject and the Reader, with the confirmation of the bio-metric sensors, could establish the truth. Once done the truth would either set the subject free…or place them in the Reader's snare.

Reynolds was not an intuit nor a "Reader" but he loved to look into a person's soul when he asked evocative questions. Watching the minutia of reaction that is often unseen by the casual observer. Reynolds was just sharp enough to pick up on the subconscious cues of a person's uncomfortableness, truth, or lie.

Bryson Reynolds was gathering himself to offer his question to the King. He straightened his bow tie and decidedly subdued his childlike excitement. He was excited at not only being able to pose a Voight-Kamph question…but his excitement lay at the prospect that he was asking it to the King of the World. Reynolds made no apologies that he was eager to ask his question eye to eye with Sol. As eye to eye as he could get that is, when dialoguing with a holograph. Sol was aware that this was the final question from the group and that it was the one and only Bryson Reynolds asking it.

"You look ready Bryson. I'm happy to take your question but then I have to sign off."

Bryson began;

"You are walking through a desert. It's stifling hot. You are exhausted, dehydrated, and sunburnt. You come across a tortoise ambling across the sand to get to a shady spot. His attempt at speed, shifts the sand on the sloping ground beneath him. He slides with the moving sand and then is flipped over by the micro-avalanche of sand he has created. The tortoise is now lying on his back. His stumpy tortoise legs flailing away. You look down. The tortoise is panicking at the searing heat that begins to bake his tender belly. But you're not helping. You are just watching…Why aren't you helping?"

Sol is still. He is taking in the question. He has been pleased with the last few moments of dialogue. Franks and Drisden had drawn out some answers that would bode well for Sol and he gave them some information that everyone wanted to know. And now, Bryson Reynolds throws out his showstopper. Sol didn't know what answer Bryson was after. And he couldn't be sure if viewers would all get the point of his "Voight-Kamph" question. But that didn't matter. Sol understood. He came out of his pensive moment where he had played out the scenario in his head. Sol smiled lightly and tilted his head. Not averting his eyes or blinking. Not looking up to the left or right. His eyes just squinted ever so slightly and there was a caring furrow in his brow. Pupils remained constant…and without inhaling or sighing noticeably, Sol answered the question confidently.

"I did help the tortoise."
Sol's Stream stopped.

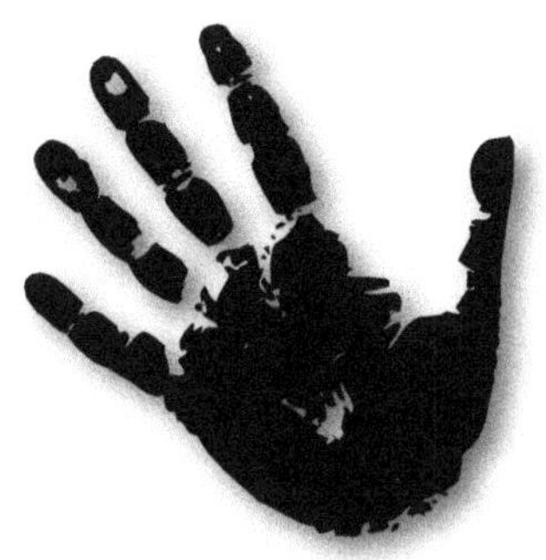

S ECTION 4

THE KING BRINGS LIBERTY TO THE CAPTIVES

Holding All The Cards

"Are you sure you want to do this?"

Sol was in thought and didn't answer Ahmed. Neither of them had been to a prison before.

Late fall leaves swirled along the shoulder as the car found its way down the access road toward the secure facility. Ahmed reminded the driver to head around back. He had contacted the Warden to let him know they were stopping in to meet one of their inmates. Sol was taking in the scenic colors of the autumn leaves that clung to the trees waiting for the next fall winds to set them free for another winter.

"I've never been to a prison before Ahmed. What do they call their clientele? I wanna say 'prisoners', Sol did air quotes. "But is it just *inmates*? Yah that sounds right, '*inmates*'."

"That's right Sol, inmates."

"How many inmates do you think there are in Cape Vincent?"

Ahmed picked up Sol's Folio on the seat beside him and read. "There are just about 900 occupants of Cape Vincent. The inmate population has remained steady for the past 30 years or so. Here..."

Handing the Folio to Sol, Ahmed touched the screen and a document with info about the Prison opened up.

"Hmm, Sol commented, "The place sure looks better in the pictures."

"That's a Correctional Facilities profile for you Sol. It tells a bit more about the place and there…" Ahmed pointed to a *'Prison Population'* section in the on-screen document, "That is the current population of Cape Vincent."

Sol was perusing the document as Ahmed finished his brief in-service. "Hmmm…average age 34, average sentence, 36 months, 46% of inmates in for violent felony."

Sol was making no conclusions on the data just that it was all quite valuable. That's what a researcher does with data, he reads it and considers the value of it beyond simple interest. Not having made correction facilities a topic of research in his years at the library, Sol found this little introduction to be very intriguing.

Cape Vincent was also a holding facility for certain individuals awaiting a court hearing or trial. Today's visit would be with one of those candidates.

Rolling slowly before stopping at the back of the building, Sol saw the three guards who were standing outside the rear loading area. Purposed in their focus, the uniformed officers panned the area slowly and deliberately. The senior guard was tightly in control of the moment. He clearly did not lack experience. The barrel torso of the well-seasoned career guard who had worked shift his whole life, displayed the strength of a man who took pride in staying fit. The thick eyebrows and short beard hardly couched the deep lines on his face. Lines earned with the experiences from countless days and nights of making sure inmates stayed in line. And ensuring the guards who were his subordinates, would stay safely within the lines themselves.

In the prison world, those lines were often blurred. The men and women charged to keep the inmates safe worked to dampen the umbrage they felt towards the criminals they lorded over. Their desire to strike out against their charges…to scratch the itch that was hatred…was pushed down daily. Some days all that was able to subdue the Corrections Officer's zeal to lash out against the men who piss off the guards daily, was the need to avoid the ubiquitous cameras. Violence toward an inmate only needed to be caught on tape once…It was a zero-tolerance policy really. And if a guard slipped and took an opportunity to mete out some justice of their own design, the inmates they had come to hate would savour the institutional justice of their captor being terminated. Somehow, all the constraints of the system worked together to keep everyone 'safe' and employed.

The three guards in the rear of the building had not been told the new King was popping by their place of work today, just that a dignitary needed to pay a visit to the facility.

As the limo crept to a full stop past the first guard, Sol realized his unwitting armed hosts could not see in. They had no idea who was in that S-950 Pullman. Ahmed informed Sol only the Warden knew who the "guest" showing up today was. The only information the staff had was that this "guest" required special precautions.

The lead vehicle in the delegate convoy of two cars had already stopped a few meters from the door Sol would be entering through at the rear of the prison.

Sol opened the door and stepped out. He stood in the opening with a hand on the top of the door and surveyed. Up close now, the building was starting to look like a prison. The dauntingly fortress like doors, the aging gray brick wall, the security cameras with their weather-stained casing. The feeling the place gave off was unlike anything Sol had ever felt before. It felt hopeless, despairing, angry.

"Are you still certain about this Sol," Ahmed's gentle question that he asked coming up the driveway was worth asking again.

Sol turned to Ahmed on his left and answered him across the roof of the limo, "Yes, I'm sure…at the very least I need to meet him."

Then his guards took their place an appropriate distance from Sol and Ahmed as they began heading into the prison with the Cape Vincent staff dutifully opening the doors.

Sol and Ahmed stepped into the inner sanctum. A bright vestibule beyond two secure doors that held delivery and service personnel who had business at the prison. There, the warden was waiting for his guests to arrive. A tall thin man stood in the clean bright space. Gray suit, white shirt, and a sunflower yellow tie. Classic tight hair parted on the right. The touch of gray in his hair and seriousness in his eyes did what it meant to do, gave the impression of him as a confident Warden. He wasn't what Sol had expected to see for a warden of a State of New York Corrections facility.

"King Sol, it is so wonderful to meet you." His voice was kind and sincere...he reached out his hand. Sol shook his hand and thanked him for the warm welcome.

Ahmed reached out and introduced himself, "We spoke on the phone Warden Lowell...I am Ahmed. Thank you for having us. Is everything in order for King Sol's visit?"

Ahmed noticed Sol had not asked the Warden to call him 'Sol'. So, Ahmed played along. Not that it was a game, but he just presumed Sol thought it appropriate to let the title stand in the prison. This was a business trip after all. Matters that Kings and Prime Ministers deal with were being dealt with here today. It made perfect sense for Sol to be called 'King Sol' on this occasion.

"Yes, everything is in order. Everyone is in place and all inmates are secured. Please, follow me if you could..." Warden Lowell replied.

Warden Lowell's prison was quiet today. He had established a unique version of the Lock Down protocol for when dignitaries would visit. Unless the visiting dignitary would be giving an address to the general prison population, the Lock Down would be fully implemented a half an hour before the arrival of the dignitary. Sol was only here to speak to one inmate. Ahmed and the Warden had discussed it all when the visit was being set up. All inmates would be placed in their cells. The Warden explained how much the inmates came to enjoy the Lock Down in most instances. They were given the choice to either participate in a hugely popular Cape Vincent on-line prison video game, or they could enjoy the music of their choice through noise cancelling headphones in their cells. In the event of an emergent situation, all media would be stopped, and any vital info would be transmitted to the game server and to the music server for all inmates to hear.

The RPG that was offered the inmates was extremely popular. It was one of those revolutionary video games that New York Corrections inmates couldn't get enough of.

The Game was called *City of Walls*. In the avatar-based RPG, players were given the choice to be either an inmate or a guard in a virtual prison city. Each player became a character in the prison system. This virtual participation in the prison system complimented his or her real participation in the prison system. The game let an inmate navigate their prison stay based on the inmate's real-life profile. If the inmate chose his avatar to be a guard, a profile was built by the game. The personal data was entered into the game and the avatar was then tasked with making choices that would either enhance his or her stay in the prison or deteriorate the stay.

The prison in the *City of Walls* game was much larger than the brick-and-mortar building that held society's worst. In the popular rehabilitation game of *City of Walls*, the prison environment was a brilliantly laid out macrocosm. It was acres and acres of prison with mess halls, exercise yards, conjugal visit rights, educational opportunities, prison employment placement, work camp opportunities, weekends away for exceptional behavior, and even a hole. The place where inmates would be relegated to for isolation if they were found to be in breach of the prison rules.

The power of the virtual world to direct real life behavior and feelings usually had the inmate doing what she or he could to avoid going to the unfriendly level of virtual solitary confinement in the virtual hole. And those who did land in isolation were highly demotivated to ever head there in the real-life prison. The *City of Walls* game had almost single handedly rendered the "hole" as obsolete. It was rare that an inmate who participated in the virtual prison game would behave in a manner that would cause him or her to be locked up alone.

Warden Dillon Lowell had been a contributor to the creation of the game and now he was using it in the Lock Down process as well. Since using the *City of Walls* platform, the improvement in prison socialization and reduction in sentences being extended due to crimes committed within the prison had dropped.

The effective use of the E-mote Control™ had a lot to do with the improvements. Game controllers that measured the emotional state of the user and integrated their state with the character in the game. The controllers used by the inmates employed a sensor system to detect pulse, breathing rate, perspiration rate, grip tension, and body temperature, measuring the emotional state of the user. Each user could then see their RPG character respond to his or her virtual environment based on the emotional state of that user. It quickly taught the inmates the value of stable emotions and how to demonstrate emotional regulation on a day-to-day basis. It had been a good move to adopt the game as a powerful avatar-based reward and rehabilitation tool. The inmates playing today were fully engaged in the *City of Walls* RPG. They had no idea the King was standing here in front of the Prison Warden. They were well into their virtual prison game, but this was no virtual world for Sol.

The aroma of the Tomato-Orzo soup on the menu today, took Sol away from the slight jitters that were diminishing as they made their way down the corridor connected to the kitchen. Turning a corner at the end of the hall, Warden Lowell stopped Sol and Ahmed to give them an update.

"I spoke with Tomer this morning and let him know you were coming to see him. He became quite uneasy at the thought."

Warden Lowell's eyes widened just a touch. His head slightly tilted, and his face showed the concern that Tomer Cohen obviously had. Sol remained expressionless as the Warden carried on.

"Just so you know, he is unaware why you would be paying him a visit. He asked if I might stay in the interview room with him while you visit. I have spent a little time interviewing Tomer myself, I must say, Tom Cohen is quite the individual.

I understand why he made the choices he did, and he is most resolved at being incarcerated here for…as he puts it…*"Meeting injustice with justice."*

Lowell paused although he appeared to have more to say on the situation. But his pause was enveloped by process. He thanked the guard who was escorting the three men through the hallways and prompted King Sol, "Shall we go in?"

The Warden swiped his fob, and the electronic beep was followed by the loud "*click*" of the latch snapping open. Warden Lowell pushed the heavy gray door of the interview room open.

This would be interesting for everyone in the room. Sol, the most powerful man in the world, could do whatever he wanted. He could have the man in the room locked up for the rest of his life or worse…Or, if he wanted, he could have him released that very day…so why was he tense at all? Sol was the one holding all the cards.

With the three men over the threshold now the secure door swung closed behind them. The '**snap**' of the electronic lock gave Sol a shiver. Inside the room it felt isolated, somber. The Warden, Sol, and Ahmed standing…Tomer Cohen was sitting quietly. Patiently waiting behind a small cold table. Sol was here to meet a cold-blooded killer.

Do You Realize I Can Help You

"**G**ood morning Tomer, how are you this fine morning?"

It was obvious Warden Lowell had a rapport with Tomer. He had only been there about a month and half since the Brookmoor School shooting, but the Warden had made a connection with Tomer. And Tomer appeared somewhat at ease with the Warden. He still had no idea what the visit was about. Why would the most powerful leader in the world want to talk to him?

"Tomer Cohen, I would like to introduce you to Ahmed Marif," Ahmed, in his appropriately professional manner, reached out to shake Tomer's hand. His chained wrists were cause for both hands to come up and over the small table in response to Ahmed's kind gesture. "And I would like to also introduce you to King Sol."

Tomer had already begun to feel more at ease. His prison guests didn't seem too intense…not overly serious he thought. Ahmed was somewhat less casual than Sol. He held his posture in check and his hands stayed folded in front of his waist. He was obviously more of an officious fella than King Sol was. Wearing a crisp dishdasha while Sol was comfortably in an open collared shirt. It was interesting to Tomer that Sol's fashionable shirt was almost the color of the prison walls.

"It's nice to meet you,"

"And it is nice to meet you as well Tomer...please call me Sol."

The stiffness started to come back into the room. Tomer was just on the edge of asking if he was in deeper trouble and why the King was needing to sit down with him. Sol turned to the Warden and asked if the chains on Inmate Cohen's wrists were necessary?

"Policy," Lowell responded.

"I think we'll be okay to work around that policy today Warden, I don't want to step on anyone's toes here but how about we visit Mr. Cohen without the cuffs on? I think it would be a lot more comfortable for all of us."

Sol truly didn't want to step on toes, but it was clear who was in charge here.

"By all means." Warden Lowell agreed with Sol.

Warden Lowell went over to the table...almost to Tomer's side. The table was the line that a prisoner would not cross when being interviewed. Any who did...or even began to move into the buffer zone, was met with at least one if not two serious guards who would physically re-establish the proper place of the interviewee. It was the prisoner's role to sit and answer questions. The chair, the table, the shackles, just another small prison within the prison. A reminder of who they were. And the interviewer never crossed over and jeopardized that physical barrier...this all reinforced the inmate's lack of freedom.

Warden Lowell sided up to the table and pulled his keys out of his pocket. There was always something about keys in a Wardens hand. Most of the access through doors in prisons was done by fob...but the keys were still such a symbol of power over a man's freedom. The Warden's ring of keys had the handcuff key he would need to honor Sol's request to remove the handcuffs.

After only weeks behind bars Tomer was already seasoned at cuffing and uncuffing. He reached his shackled hands forward over the top of the table and the Warden quickly unlocked and removed the shackles. Tomer unconsciously rubbed both wrists as if to rub off the harshness of the cold steel. Sitting opposite Tomer, Sol must have still been controlling his anxiety…small or big it was enough to warrant a small eye squint at the sharp sound of the shackles being dropped in the steel tray in the door. The guard on the outside of the door scooped them from the tray and the clatter quickly stopped.

"Tomer, thanks for being willing to sit for a visit with us today."

"You're welcome…:

The question was sitting on his tongue and just before it came off Tomer's lips Sol began answering it.

"You are probably wondering why I wanted to come talk to you today. Why would the new King come to a prison to interview a murderer?"

Sol chose to refer to Tomer as a murderer for a reason. That's what he was seen as…so far. Not because the Justice System had decided that he was one yet, nor because he wanted to reinforce Tomer's powerless position based on what had transpired, rather because he wanted to see Tomer's reaction. And the reaction was what Sol expected. No twinge of defensiveness or nuance of guilt. Everyone saw what Tomer had done and there was no way to deny that. Tomer had definitely killed a man. But Tomer was neither remorseful nor defensive. To him it may not have been murder, rather it was simply justice. And Sol was on the right track. He had read much of Tomer's profile report and was reading Tomer right. Tomer was a man who would do it again if he had the same opportunity.

His dark, short hair, and wide jaw could have given him the profile of a Law Enforcement officer. As Sol watched him process, the only thing Tomer's intense brown eyes gave away was that he wasn't afraid. He was intentioned and resolved. Even sitting here, in a prison in front of the Warden, Ahmed, and the King of the

World, Tomer's gaze was bright, intense, and confident. It was difficult to tell what he was thinking, but it was clear that he WAS thinking.

"Tomer, I get a sense that you would make the same choice again if the situation were to arise? Is that so?"

Ahmed and Lowell were standing behind Sol…over his shoulder. Tomer did his best not to glance too often up at them while Sol was sitting in front of him. But he needed to be careful with what he said, he still wasn't sure if the Warden was playing him or if he really did have a respect for Inmate Cohen.

Sol slid his chair to the side of the table. Tomer looked up at the Warden once more, as if to question the move. Sol was breaching the symbolic wall, albeit he was unfamiliar with the protocol where Inmates stayed on one side and interviewers stayed on the other. No one sat on the end of the table. The Warden offered no correction.

"Am I right Tomer, would you make the same choices?"

"You know, I have nothing to hide." Tomer responded…Sol's move opened something.

Tomer was in this spot because of his volitional actions and he knew it. This post-shooting life was his reality now. In a second that day, his reality changed forever. No one could have told him the day before, that his response to a school shooting the next day would have him locked up for murder, waiting to go to trial. And now his life was changed forever. When Sol asked the question the second time, he saw more clearly. There was no lawyer in the room, and Tomer was on the path to an extended stay in the low class, medium security, New York State Corrections facility…might as well just give Sol what he wanted.

"Yes, I would make the same choices."

Tomer was smart enough to use Sol's words. No melodrama, no display of profound feeling or emotion...just the reality. No pretenses of a man building a case to defend his actions by saying he had just "lost it" and went crazy in the moment. Sol had read in Tomer's profile report that some years ago he had seen the footage of a theater shooting and the aftermath that ensued. The shooter of that calculated massacre was one of the 3 in 10 active shooters who hadn't ended their act of murderous hate by killing themselves. Most shooters take their own life during the rampage or are taken out in a gun fight with Law Enforcement.

Tomer's profile report disclosed how he had made a deal with himself that day. He told the psychiatrist during the interview with her that he had purposed to hasten true justice if ever he found himself in that position. The position that is, where he would encounter an active shooter on or shortly after the incident went down.

"Tomer," Sol went on, "It would really be helpful if you would just take me through those moments. I know you will be asked to recount the events to your lawyers and the court...perhaps several times. But do you mind telling me about it?"

Tomer looked at Ahmed and the Warden, then back at Sol.

"If you'd prefer, I can ask the Warden and Ahmed to leave the room, then it's just you and me."

Everyone in the room knew the entire prison was being recorded by video. If most of the outside world was being shot on CCTV and Drone Cams it was for damn sure the prison interview room was being recorded on video. But that wasn't the issue, sometimes having others, like Ahmed and the Warden in the room, might just make the interviewee feel a little too much like a bug under a magnifying glass. For most prisoners they would have jumped at the chance to have the extra pairs of eyes removed from the room in an interview like this. But this was not an interview like any other. This was an interview with the King of the World. And Tomer, although he began to sense Sol's sincerity, was still not certain why Sol was here.

Before Tomer could answer Sol upped the ante.

"Do you realize Tomer that I can help you? You have made history Tomer. Never before has a man shot an active shooter in police custody and taken the legs out from under the barely ambulatory justice system. Tomer, I think you will be surprised to hear the views of a great many people in relation to what you have done. And I think Tomer, you can also help me."

Sol Had To Know

Tomer was fixed on Sol. Without looking up he answered Sol's question about the Warden and Ahmed's presence during the visit.

"They can stay."

Ahmed for one was relieved, he wanted to be in there. He wanted to hear the thoughts of this man. An apparent history maker and a vigilante. A man who had a wife and three children, had spent time running the security arm of a P3-Public/Private Partnership agriculture research facility at the UK's Aberystwyth University. The profile Sol and Ahmed read over, reported on the vocational history of Tomer. He had been the head of the Aberystwyth University security division for 6 and a half years after he and his wife were married.

They loved living and working in the UK. But after having their first child they decided the intensity of a high-level security, international research facility was not conducive to raising a family. So Tomer resigned and returned to the United States where he ran a successful online security consulting firm. He was a sought-after voice in the corporate security world. Things really flourished in the past three years since all his children were in school now.

Sol paused, leaned into Tomer and asked, "Tomer, what went on that day?"

Tomer began, "Well it was a Friday. My daughters, they're in grades one, three, and four, were scheduled for their annual dental check-up. We always make going to the dentist a big deal. I was going to pick up my girls from school then meet Claire, my wife, at the dentist office in the mall. After the check-ups we were all going to have supper at the mall and go to a movie. Dentist day is cause for a big celebration in our house."

He was very clear and deliberate in his speech...His tone was subtly matter of fact and Sol prompted Tomer on in his telling. Ahmed and the Warden were motionless near the wall as they stood one with his hands crossed to his back and the other to the front.

"I got to the school early, before the final bell. I had no idea that son of a bitch was inside. I just sat outside waiting for the girls to come happily racing from around the back of the school to the car near the end of the street. Normal day, I checked some email and turned up a little music while I was waiting. No one was coming out.

"I was about to get out of the car to head in to meet my girls when I got a text message. It was from the School's Mass Notification system. I looked up and saw other parents waiting for their kids and they were all checking their devices. The message said the school was in lock-down and told parents to remain in their cars and stay out of the school and yard until further notice. I started to freak a little... no, a lot. I reached down for my gun, my CZ-95 - 9-millimeter. I was going to head into the school to find out what the hell was going on.

"Just as I was sitting up to get out of the car and head into the school, three cop cars flew by and staged in front of the school. I figured I'd better stay put now. If I stepped out with a firearm I might get shot. I still wasn't certain what was going on in my girl's school. But I was terrified. Not for me but for them. About four more cop cars came screaming in and the TASC Unit came on scene. Cops were running from car to car now. One of them banged on my window and said, 'Stay in your car and stay down'.

"They were locking down the whole block…and quick. I wasn't sure what was going on inside the school or how long it would be before the event was over. When the DBN news truck rolled in, my device chimed, and I started watching the stream of the scene from my car. I was practically panicking. I had no idea if my kids were all right and Claire was stuck on the outside, waiting for the girls and I to meet up with her. After about 25 minutes the DBN showed the Mobile Detainment Unit had come on scene and was positioned on the North-East corner. I had been sitting there, we all had, for over half an hour now. It seemed like days."

Sol glanced at his watch. Remembering the time on the MeRT when the Stream chimed on. Having watched the scenes in lockstep with Tomer Cohen… and the entire world. He had boarded the train early after work. Not too long after that the DBN started streaming the shooting scene. Sol nodded his head in subtle affirmation and validation of Tomer's extended confinement to his car during this event. Then he asked, "What were the officers on scene doing at this time?"

"They were still at their posts. DBN had just reported that the one shooter was dead, and the other was taken into custody. He would be brought to the MDU soon. There was a large core of Law Enforcement people letting parents through. The next moment Claire came running up to the car. We had been messaging and talking off and on while we were waiting. Both of us getting more worried by the minute."

"Did Claire know what you were going to do?"

"No. I didn't even know what I was about to do. All we knew is that we needed to know our girls were alright. There were about 12 children that weren't, according to DBN and none of us parents outside knew if ours were ok or not. I tried to message the girls but there was no response. And I didn't know if they weren't responding because they hadn't grabbed their phones out of the cubby yet or…" Tomer paused. He was going through the whole thing again. The emotion, the anxiety, the fear that his girls were hurt… or worse. He was having a hard time with it and Sol slowed him down.

"No hurry Tomer, this must be hard."

"Then the girls, all three of them, came racing to the car. They had been crying and Claire and I jumped out and they piled into our arms."

"And then it was over…the whole thing was over?" Sol probed a little deeper. He wanted to know what compelled Tomer. It would be easy to understand why he chose to act if one of his three girls hadn't come running out that afternoon to jump into his and Claire's arms. His choice to become the world's most celebrated vigilante would make a lot more sense if he had gone through all that anxiety fearing the worst, to have learned that one of his daughters was one of the dead that day. Then Sol would have no question about his actions. But they weren't. Tomer had all three of his daughters. The three precious little girls were right there now…safe…in his arms.

He Felt Like Sol Got It

Ahmed and the Warden were statues. Ahmed had never seen anything like this, and he knew what Sol was there to do that day. To change a man's life forever and to change the world along with it.

But as Tomer talked, Ahmed was trying not to breath too loud and the Warden felt like he should have left the room. It was such an intimate moment. A moment with intense and deep feeling. The Warden wanted to watch Sol to see what was going on for him while Tomer told his story, but he could not take his eyes off his inmate. The Warden himself wasn't even sure Tomer should be in there…in the prison that is. The largeness of the moment filled the room. The Baker-Miller pink on the walls could have been crimson red in that moment because the only thing in focus for the men in that room in the last few minutes was a table, the cold table with Sol the King and Tomer the murderer. The two sat in cramped chairs but they filled the room. Ahmed and The Warden said nothing. Tomer continued his story.

"As my girls climbed out of my arms to climb into the car to FaceStream their mom, I looked up into the school yard. I witnessed a thing that I can never unsee. I saw pain that descended so far into the human soul that I broke…I stopped breathing. I could weep with that Dad and Mom who had only one child left to embrace. I could weep for that 10 year old boy who was now brotherless and would never feel the joy of his parents getting him back safe because the wracking pain of the loss they would feel for the son that was shot would overshadow any joy. For that family the day would never be remembered as the day his family was spared from tragedy because he was left alive after the shooting. The day would be remembered for the searing agony of his younger brother lying dead in a classroom. The joy of a reunion with one son who came out alive was crushed by the anguish of the unspeakably frightening loss. There were other families whose kids would not race out to their arms that day…and I finally had a chance to bring some justice."

Sol sat speechless. Enraptured by the firsthand account Tomer was openly sharing. Filled with the feeling of seeing such hurt in parents that day.

"I saw this man that I didn't even know and I felt his pain. And then, in the scene beyond him and his grieving family, at the corner of the school, I saw the shooter being brought out. I saw two TASC members taking him towards the Mobile Detainment Unit. It was then I remembered my promise…my promise to myself.

"As I stood up my forearm brushed against the gun underneath my jacket and instantly I decided to do something about that promise. I had stuffed my gun in there when the cop banged on my window and told me to stay put. I was completely clear about my choice to bring justice. It was then that I saw how things needed to go. I headed through the school yard. No one saw me. Or at least it felt like no one was seeing me. I was just another one of the safe people on the scene. When I got close enough, I was enraged at the candor of the two officers passing off the shooter. They were doing their job but shootings like this happened so often that this shooter was being treated like a common criminal…these killers are far from common. These shootings had become so frequent people barely pay attention anymore.

"We all get aloof, become apathetic, call it what you want. But it incensed me. This shooter would be bouncing through court rooms for years, maybe decades. Media would make sure the circus had more than three rings and I was just tired of it…it was wrong. I still think it's wrong. So…I walked up to that asshole like I belonged there and just as clinically as I could, I raised my gun and shot him. Twice, in the head.

Sol could not believe his ears. Tomer was so matter of fact...so convinced his deed was for the best, that Sol almost became frightened. But this man was no sociopath. And Sol quickly felt comfort in knowing a man could be so decisive in his actions of justice. Tomer sensed it was safe to continue sharing.

"The thought of him being alive somewhere rotting in prison sucking up taxpayer's money and government energy would never be part of the social consciousness again. It was done. The killer was dead. I dropped my weapon, raised my arms, and fell to the ground. Three officers jumped on me."

Briefly Tomer paused after taking a small breath and stopping himself from speaking. Lips pressed together as if to keep in what he was about to say.

Sol saw Tomer was done telling his story. But he also saw he had one more thing to say. He waited for that thing as Tomer took liberty to lean in closer. Ahmed and Lowell held their breath.

"And Sol....I'm not a murderer but if I had to do it all over again I would do the same thing."

Sol was unfazed by Tomer's closing remark. Everyone in the room knew Tomer might just be the smartest of the four of them. He was brilliant and his profile had disclosed that to Sol and Ahmed on the way to Cape Vincent. It was no longer the Baker-Miller pink on the prison walls that brought a subdued sense to the men in the interview room. It was the absolution of this man who was waiting to go to trial for killing a killer. Sol had never felt quite this calm after dialoguing about something that was so intense. His chest felt warm as the feeling of fatigue from the anticipation of meeting Tomer washed over him. And sitting with him to hear his story brought Sol to a place of peace. Peace with who this man was. Peace with what he had done, peace with being in a prison for the first time in his life and most of all, Sol was completely at peace with his decision about Tomer.

"Tomer, thanks for telling me your story."

Tomer Cohen had stepped into it with calculated abandon. Thinking that what he was doing needed to be done and that once done…it would somehow work out. After all these moments had been spent together and Tomer openly giving Sol his entire story, feelings and all, Tomer still had no real idea of why Sol was here or what Sol was going to do. But Tomer felt connected now. He felt like Sol got it.

The World Is Better
Off Without Him

"I am going to speak freely with you about this if you don't mind?"

"No King Sol, I don't mind." Tomer remained vulnerable after telling his story.

"Good." Sol looked down to the right slightly to gather his next thought.

"Tomer, I am not going to mince words here. I was watching the DBN that day. I had no idea who you were, who the shooter was, or that someday I would be King. Seeing that shooter be escorted away from the school by Law Enforcement brought me to a place I had not considered much before. I was silently enraged at that shooter and silently screaming how can this happen, why is that guy able to get away with that?

"As I watched the broadcast looking over the shoulder of the reporter, I barely picked up on you coming into the shot. The officers seemed too casual, too desensitized to the event. They seemed to act as if these things had happened a million times before and it was all...." Sol bit at his upper lip and looked past Tomer to find the words he needed.

"....It was all conventional, commonplace...normal."

Sol was ready to express his thoughts on the cycle of violence and justice that had repeated itself a hundred thousand times it seemed. What usually happened with active shooters…the ones who were captured alive that is, was not justice at all. Sol looked around the calm room the four men were in right now.

"Why should he get sent to a comfortable prison where he is safe, warm, fed, kept alive by the government institution, and in all likelihood, will be taking up a space for twenty years while he clogs up the appeals courts and has the Media swirling to keep a sick story of a school shooter without an ending alive?"

It was almost undetectable, but Ahmed had a slight smile on his face. Had he been the Ahmed of 15 years ago, at times inappropriate and lacking a filter in his injections of humor, Sol might have heard an *"Amen, preach it brother."* Ahmed could not have been feeling more affirming to Sol and his decision right now. But he restrained himself and he guarded his smile and exuberance while he stood quietly. This moment would not happen twice, and Ahmed could not wait to ride out of here with Sol and replay the moment he was in right now.

"And as I sat there…" Sol filled in the rest of his own feeling in the moment he saw Tomer shoot the killer, "…a normal guy Tomer, just like you, I watched you appear out of nowhere as if you belonged there. I was shocked at how quickly it all happened. One second the officers were passing the killer from one to the other and the next second, you reached up and fired two shots into his head. But it felt right Tomer. I caught myself saying, *'Way to go buddy…If it were me I would do the same thing."*

Sol wanted to say more but he restrained himself and let the words hang for a second before telling Tomer the one thing he had wanted to say since seeing him take out the school shooter.

"And Tomer…I am here today to thank you."

Tomer was light now. Hands folded comfortably on the table; eyes cast down just enough to show humility yet respecting his guest. And then he thought, *"Ahh... that's why Sol is here. He felt like thanking me. Odd."*

As he lifted his head to smile at Sol. To accept the thanks of the new King, Sol's eyes met his.

"But that is not all I came here today to do Tomer."

Tomer was right back there again. Back asking himself what else could the King want.

"Tomer, you did what I wanted to do that day. You did what billions of reasonable people wanted to do that day. To me, to us, you are a hero. And I am here today to change things for you. Tomer Cohen, I am striking down all charges against you. There is no need for a trial or an investigation into the matter. Everyone saw what you did, what happened that day. And I would like to restore you to society and to your family. We stand to benefit far greater from you being in society than we do from you being in prison."

Tomer could not believe what he was hearing. Did this man, Sol, really have the power to do that? Tomer looked puzzled towards the Warden. The Warden was smiling back at Tomer. Tomer never had met Ahmed before but Ahmed's face was now a beam of smiles.

"Tomer Cohen, as of this moment, you are a free man. It is within my authority to imprison a man or to liberate a man and today I chose to liberate you."

Tomer was stunned. "Wh...but...I don't know what to say Sol. Is this for real? I can't believe it. Please, let me call my wife right away. Do I get to leave today?"

"Yes Tomer, today, it all happens today. And yes, Warden, will you please bring Tomer a telephone so he can call Claire."

The Warden cracked the oppressive steel door and gave instructions to the guard outside to retrieve a phone for Tomer. Then he left the door open. The smells and sounds of the kitchen floated in. He was quite excited for what had transpired but knew he could not display it. However, leaving the door open on the interview room was just the right touch to affirm to Tomer he was no longer a prisoner. It was phenomenally odd for the day they were living in. Inmates didn't just get released by an intervening ruler. Pressing criminal charges was too much of a science for that to be needed. If you were accused of a crime you were the one who did it. The Drone Corps and CCTV footage accompanying the forensic evidence always told the story. Faithfully ID'ing the criminal. There was seldom a question about an accused's guilt or innocence. If you were accused and charged, you were not innocent.

Today however, the justice that brings healing was on a new path. Justice had already come for the distorted killer. A killer sentenced while he was still freshly covered in the blood of the children that lay slain at his wicked hand. Yes, that was the justice he deserved and now Tomer was getting the justice he deserved. His freedom.

The King had stated it, and it was now done. And the room…a room that moments ago had shrunk to infinitesimal size because of the low expectations of the man in prison clothes seated across the small table, felt like it had just expanded. The cold institutional table that was to some an uncrossable chasm, no longer signified the impassable path to the outside world. The bare hopeless prison room was no longer full of questions it was full of freedom. Before Tomer was led to freedom by the Warden, Sol asked for his attention one more time.

"Tomer, there is one thing I would like to ask you before you call Claire."

"Sol, right now you could ask me anything."

"You said you would do "it" all over again if you had to, did you mean that?"

Tomer knew this was the right time to take a second to answer. For him though, justice was clear. He was not afraid to bring an end to a heinous killer who didn't care about his own life and cared less about the lives of his victims. Looking towards the open door as if his answer might cause it to be shut on him again, Tomer had to speak his truth. With almost an apologetic tone in his voice, he was ready to risk losing the freedom he was just granted.

"I believe there are just some people the world is better off without King Sol. They are not good for society. And letting someone like that live, does no good for anyone."

Tomer closed his eyes longer than just a blink. He turned to Sol and girded himself. Sol took in the resolved gaze of the newest ex-con of the Cape Vincent Correctional Facility. Tomer was one of the bravest, justice-based men Sol had ever met. Sol was eager to hear Tomer's answer…would he do it again?

The Justice System Was About To Become Real

"**M**y answer is 'Yes!' I would do it again. Even if I knew I was going to land here again. Someone has to do something. And if no one else will, if the system is going to keep incubating maniacs who refuse to consider the preciousness of another's life, then I will be the last one to consider their life precious. Serious criminals and killers have limited rights as far as I'm concerned. Why should these people who decide no one else's life is precious be given a sentence to a comfortable prison life, getting fat on the dime of the state? Why should they still be allowed to vote on political leaders, get handed a free education, be able to see their family and friends, and have any contact with the outside world that they rejected? Why do those who trample on the rights of others get to continue to enjoy all the privilege that true freedom stands for by their actions?"

Sol smiled. "Tomer Cohen, you are exactly the person I am looking for."

Ahmed stepped to the table and set Sol's Folio in front of Sol

Sol tapped the screen. With his head tilted down towards the Folio he scrolled the pages and told Tomer what he was just about to seal.

"Tomer, this is an edict for retribution. I, like you, and like many, believe there is need for swift and decisive retribution in certain instances."

Sol continued scrolling. Tomer really liked what he was hearing. *The Rightful Retribution Edict* outlined the decisive actions that would be taken against certain criminals for their actions against another person. The list contained about a dozen categories of offender so far. For each of them there was a decisive form of retribution laid out. Tomer was taking it all in. This was the type of thing society had been calling for for years. Punish criminals quickly and fully. Stop giving criminals more rights than their victims…or at least rights that no criminal should still have the privilege of having.

However, any slight forward progress made by the government, forward toward really changing the way violent, malicious, and sexual criminals were treated, there was always some bleeding-heart protest or rogue political special-interest group that welled up. Hollering about the sanctity of human life, the belief that no person should be hindered in feeling they are special, that no person deserves to have their right to freedom removed. But here in front of Tomer was the document that would set justice on a right path…justice would no longer be just about carried out. A concept that just about delivered the punishment that a criminal actually deserved. Rather, the *Rightful Retribution Edict* of the new King was set to move society forward. According to the men at that table, freedom was not a right but a privilege. Behave towards society in a way that respects this privilege then freedom is deserved…behave otherwise and the privilege disappears. It was so simple that kids in the playground understood this. If you keep throwing sand in the other kid's faces and taking their toys, eventually you have no privilege of being around those kids or even going to that playground. The playground sandbox was just a microcosm of life and society. Play fair, get along, don't hurt others, don't take what's not yours, and things will be fine. That's exactly how life is supposed to work. Neglect or ignore those simple rules, and you lose.

"Are you really going to do this?" Tomer queried while perusing the edict in front of him.

"Yes I am Tomer. I am announcing the edict on Saturday. This edict is already imprinted and is passed into law."

"It looks great, but what does this have to do with me?"

"You see part 8 of this Act Tomer? *The Active Shooter Article?*" Sol scrolled back up the page to Part 8.

Tomer breezed through a few paragraphs.

"That is amazing. It says that confirmed active shooters who remain alive after an incident where they have terrorised and killed innocent adults or children, will be executed at the earliest possible opportunity by the Minister of Retribution or their designate." Tomer furrowed his eyes as he shook his head. "That's crazy...I mean that is perfect...exactly what should happen."

Ahmed was still standing with Sol and Tomer beside the table. He was on cue as he had become part of the meeting now. "And that is exactly what you did Mr. Cohen."

"Ahmed's right. You administered retribution in a way that needed to happen long ago. I don't necessarily mean live in front of billions of people in the way you did...a little too close to what's seen in a snuff film. But I mean it was decisive, speedy, and necessary. And the fact that we all saw it showed me, showed the world, that is how things should go."

"Yes that's true. And to be honest, I would rather have not had that thing caught on camera. But that's probably the only reason I have been fortunate to meet you today King Sol. Still, if I could have chosen, I would have acted off camera."

"Well, that's all behind us now Tomer. I want to look at what's ahead of us."

"Us?" Tomer questioned.

"Yes us." Sol pinched the Folio screen and enlarged the section,

...by the Minister of Retribution or their designate.'

"Tomer, I do not have a Minister of Retribution yet, I was hoping I might place you in that position."

"What do you mean Sol?"

Tomer was hearing what Sol was asking but could not believe it. Moments ago, released from prison by the King and now…as he was just getting set to call Claire and tell her the fantastic news…he thought he was hearing Sol offer him a job…a really big job.

"It's simple Tomer, we needed you to do what you did that day and because it was against the law at the time, doesn't mean it was wrong. And now I need a Minister of Retribution to head up the plans to administer retribution as needed and when needed. You've seen the categories and it is time we acted as a society. Not just citizens any longer but Participants. I am asking if you will be my Minister of Retribution."

For Tomer the decision was easy. It took him less time to answer Sol than it did to react to the school shooter that spawned all this. Tomer certainly was decisive. He didn't even ask for time to think about the position. Shaking his head up and down he was abundantly clear with Sol.

"Yes….Yes…I will be your Minister of Retribution."

Sol reached across the corner of the table. It had almost become invisible as it was no longer the symbol of separation but now a silent witness to freedom and justice where two people sat together in agreement.

"Excellent." Sol smiled wide and affirmed his delight with the outcome by a sharp head nod and deep breath. "Thank you Tomer. It is fantastic to have you manage this for me. This is exactly what we need." Sol and Tomer shook hands affirming the work they would soon do together.

Ahmed quickly told Tomer they would be in touch to deal with the particulars after he had a few days at home with his wife and girls. Tomer was tingling at all the earth-shattering news. He had no idea what this was all going to look like but he for damn sure knew it did not involve him growing old in a prison under the state's care. Tomer had stepped into a whole new world by choosing the justice any reasonable man would agree was right. A justice that halted the whirlwind of wasted time, money, and emotion in a system that blindly held to the toothless social philosophies of the mid 1900's. Instead of being the system that perpetuated a paralysis towards effective change, the system Sol and Tomer would work towards would be one that heads towards reason.

Tomer didn't know it, but this was the day that a justice system of passive rehabilitation and punishment had just made that sharp turn society was waiting for. Today, the Legal Justice system was about to become real. Justice would no longer be hindered by legalities designed to assuage some man's sensibilities. Justice would no longer be fettered by humanism and social-salvationism. Justice would finally become what it needed to be. No longer a system that nourishes and imbibes pseudo-ethical principles. Idealisms that protect those who only want to harm society. Rather an intuitive system, allowing the beauty of the concept that an eye for an eye is acceptable, to begin to shine its instructive light on the entire world. The sealed edict would bring rightful retribution where justice had long failed. The list was clear at this point...and still to undergo revisions and clarifications. Retribution would be a reality for numerous anti-social criminals and included;

- Pedophiles
- Rapists
- Home invaders

- Wife and child abuser
- Hostage takers
- Animal torturers
- Human torturers
- Terrorists
- Child Pornographers
- Child pornography users
- Those who prey upon the weak and vulnerable of society in any way
- Abusers of the mentally infirm
- Murderers

Sol knew Tomer was a man inspired by justice and inspired to loyalty. Sol could see he was restraining his excitement. Tomer asked, "Is it ok if I call Claire now? This is some extraordinary news that I can't wait to tell her."

Sol replied, "Of course Tomer...and Tomer, get excited, I know if I were on your side of the table I sure as hell would be."

When a Person Dies

The square was filled again as the breezy gusts blew leaves across the feet shuffling into the plaza. Crowds of Participants were getting comfortable with the address process that was just about to start. But it was still new to them and in part they felt intrigued and curious. Not certain what they were about to hear.

When the Media screens chimed to alert Participants to the start of the Saturday 12PM address by Sol, there was vagueness. Few knew what Sol would bring to them this day. With the draw from the inviting chime, the crowd gathered as one. One with deep intrigue. What would be set in motion by the King this day?

The memory of Sol's public announcement of the *'No Parent Left Behind Program'* last month was still vivid. It came out of nowhere, yet participant buy-in had been very successful. It was only 4-weeks old but was gathering massive uptake as it rolled out. Parents were jumping on board affirming the edict by streaming to the highly accessible and vibrantly empowering parenting classes.

At last week's Deliberations session, a week ahead of today's Great Assembly, Sol had found the delegates eager to support his innovations. He had announced his *Rightful Retribution* reforms to the Chambers and took questions from the Delegates. He fielded numerous questions one would expect from a culture staring a new method of justice right in the face. Questions about how to respond to any opposition, how to use the Rightful Retribution Edict tactfully, who was going to administer the retribution, and how to ensure no one would be punished under the act if there were any uncertainty about their crimes. Sol made it abundantly clear, there would be no final retribution if there were any bonified question about a person's guilt.

When Sol had introduced Tomer to the Delegates in the Chambers, Tomer told his tale of the choices he made that day. The powerful moments recounting the Brookmoor event brought waves of support. The Delegates stood with Tomer in his decision. For many of them, they connected to Tomer's response that day as if it had been their child killed in the Brookmoor incident. Tomer's swift justice had accomplished more than anyone could have ever thought...the Delegates respected Tomer for his bravery and they respected Sol for liberating him as he did.

This time it was different in the World Counsel Plaza. It wasn't that the sun had given way to the gray sky and cool chill that blew through the Square. Or the fact that the name had changed for the world's most powerful organization that now deferred all decisions to the new King. Rather things felt different because of the fact there was no pomp to the King's address this time. The Presentation Ceremony had seen Sol anointed with pomp and ceremony but today at the New York World Counsel Plaza, Sol was focused on business. That's how Sol wanted it. With the regularity of monthly addresses, they would become a streamlined opportunity for Sol to address the world publicly. Sol would stand and deliver. Right here in front of an on-looking mass of people Streamed to the entire world at what had already been tagged as the Great Assemblies.

Perfectly on time at 12 noon, the blue holograph filtered through the arms and legs of those standing in the square. Queuing those standing in the light of the blossoming holograph to slide back just enough to let the beams fill the space above their heads with the World Counsel Symbol. The rotating globe that hung in the air exemplified the unified reality of the world. Its illuminated threads making connections between nation and region and region and nation. Then the seconds began counting down. **8...7...6...5...4...3...2...1-**

Precisely at zero, Sol began walking on stage. The guests in the square whistled and applauded when the image of Sol took the stage. His image filled the illumination that held their attention. For Sol as a man looking out to the attentive crowd covering the cold granite Plaza, nothing, absolutely nothing could have warmed the square more than the smiles of an expectant audience. An audience who had only met Sol as the King just last month.

The hope-filled people were fixed on the King. As new as this was to them, they had already begun to expect Sol would do right by them. This was his home stage in a sense, it would be interesting to walk the stage of one of the other 7 World Counsel Centers soon. Next month Sol would find out exactly what it's like. Home stage advantage would be far away when he gave the address from Namibia. Eight World Counsel Centers in the world and Sol would hit each one of them for an address at least once this year.

But today, he was thankful for the strong reception that came from the Plaza. No one could misinterpret the moment. The welcome was genuine for the world's most powerful leader by the Participants in the Square. And for some, the applause was as if to say, "*Good, let's get this thing going...let's see what Sol is really going to bring into law.*"

Sol displayed comfort upon engaging the crowd.

"Thank you for that warm welcome. I appreciate you taking time to be here or to pause for this Stream wherever you are."

The gleaming Speaker's Podium was tucked in behind the King. Nothing else was on stage. Just Sol, looking like he could have been any man on that stage. His navy textured battier shirt and dark gray pants affirmed that fact. Sol stood assuringly in front of his podium.

The monthly ritual would become the point of delivery for many of Sol's edicts. Not all edicts would be made from this international stage though. Many of the edicts by Sol would pass from Sol's office at home or perhaps straight through to law at an Inclusions Session. And some would be uploaded to the World Counsel interactive net page and disseminated to the Participants through the World Counsel Media platform. But the ones he was sealing into law today must be delivered here.

"As you are all aware, our global prosperity is unprecedented, and national economies have nothing to contend for in a realm that once teetered on the edge of solvency for some of the world's biggest nations and regions. But there are deeper issues that we face together across the world. The words of Richard Nixon in his 1969 Inaugural address speak of this. Nixon said.

> *'Our crisis today is in reverse. We find ourselves rich in goods, but ragged in spirit; reaching with magnificent precision for the moon, but falling into raucous discord on earth.*
>
> *.... We see around us empty lives, wanting fulfillment. We see tasks that need doing, waiting for hands to do them. To a crisis of the spirit, we need an answer of the spirit. And to find that answer, we need only look within ourselves.'*

"What I am going speak to next is in regard to a very serious task that needs doing, and to some, it may be disturbing. There will be some who will not want to accept this reality. And as President Nixon also said, *'We cannot expect to make everyone our friend, but we can try to make no one our enemy.'*

"So, know that I am interested in only resolving social ills and restoring what was long ago lost to society. Please, take a moment to look around you."

Sol paused to let the now cautious crowd respond to his request. Not knowing what they were to look for, the hundreds of thousands of engaged listeners in the Square took the moment to catch eyes with others near them. Silently heads turned and fall-coats rustled. In the next seconds, the crowd in the Square resumed their focus on the images projected just over their heads.

Viewers in WCC Plazas and venues across the globe were less responsive but they too took purposeful pause. In front of the billions, Sol offered a change that would begin to honor the most precious and vulnerable in Society. And it was for the betterment of all.

Sol had reasoned with the Delegates at the Deliberations meetings, finding agreement that less final solutions have long been in place. Yet nothing changed.

His edict was born out of passion to stop one of the world's most heinous and most hidden crimes. Sol was going forward with this and there was no need...or time now...to go through all the arguments in support of this edict that had come from the research shared at the last Inclusions Session.

Those arguments were the moments when Annelyse Devonshire and the research team brought the staggering statistical picture of the millions harmed by depraved criminal acts to the Delegates. Even if no one else had agreed or had found cause for this decisive measure, Sol would have pushed forward with it. That was now his job. As King he would draw on the collective wisdom and voice of the multitude of advisors to add info to the edict. In the beginning, edicts were brought by Sol and in the end...it was left to Sol to make the decision.

No angle was left unaddressed. The Delegates had been made aware of the astonishing numbers of victims, the impact on each victim at the time of the event and in their future, the likelihood of repeat offenders claiming countless more victims, the predatorial nature of the offender, as well as the failure of traditional treatments and punishments to remove the desire a predator had; everything was given attention by Annelyse and the team. But the most compelling, the most paradigm shifting information that was offered in the Deliberations Chambers that day, came from a quietly intense Senior Delegate known for his research. His name was Ferdinand Tibor, and his work held great weight in ratifying support from the Delegates.

Ferdinand Tibor had brought strong supportive research to the World Congress for over 15 years. The Delegates knew, when Ferdinand was on the team the information that surfaced was without question...it was sound, sensible, and certain. And Tibor had compiled arguably the most exhaustive body of research on death and the state of the dead the world had ever encountered.

Sol had never realized what a mental stronghold the confused thinking on death was. He himself had long ago come to realize the facts. But so many of the lawmakers, in this era and in previous eras, were stuck in the legislation and laws that prevented the death penalty. And this entrenched thinking was often in place because of an unexamined belief. A belief that was so much at the core in so many persons that it was just thought to be true. In actuality, the common understanding of what happens when a person dies was simply a second-hand belief that remained unexamined. It had been passed down through the generations in thought and action, and had ultimately become a false-truth embedded in society and the genetic memory of multitudes of reasonable and unreasonable humans. A belief that had been a large part of preventing a universal death penalty law from moving forward. A penalty that was to be applied to many of those criminals referenced in *The Rightful Retribution Act.*

Protecting The Guilty
Far Too Often

Ferdinand's two hour presentation at the Inclusions Session had been extremely competent. It meshed together webs of thought that explained the collective consciousness about death and the dominant views in culture.

Tibor's research addressed the common themes that were predominant in the thoughts of a majority of people. The first was the belief that humankind cannot know with absolute certainty what lies beyond death. A great many scholars had adopted the erroneous thinking that the afterlife is some form of conscious existence. And their beliefs had been carried from generation to generation, unquestioned by most who took comfort in those beliefs.

The second belief about the afterlife that had been dismantled by the brilliant Ferdinand Tibor, was a belief about suffering in the "afterlife."

The common thinking was that humans who died might be assigned to a place of such intense suffering that the human mind could not conceive it. The second of the two ideas had been in society for centuries. But Ferdinand showed how the concept really was born and developed in a superstitious age thousands of years ago.

Ferdinand unwove the creation of the concept through its origins in history, archeology, etymology, mythology, theology, superstition, anthropology, sociology, and neurology. Showing that understanding where the dead go according to the historical path of religious thinking, was now very clear.

Sol was convinced that the billions of rational thinkers who would choose to support his edict would be more likely to support it, and more at ease with the end result, if they were able to hear the facts underlying the construct of what happens after one dies. Thanks to Tibor's work the choice to end the life of a person who was deemed worthy of such a sentence, would no longer be troubled by the thought of someone being tortured for eternity in a place called Hell. That person would experience nothing once they took their last breath. No Hell, no Heaven, just an end to their breath that was returned to where it came from. And that dead person was no longer a "soul", which is a living breathing being. As Tibor had expertly displayed, any ancient reference to the "soul", was simply referring to the state of life where a creature is living and breathing…and the understanding of a "soul" is not that of an ethereal ghost-like part of a fleshly creature.

Sol thanked the Delegates for their support of the edict and extolled the amazing input from the research team. Pointing out Ferdinand Tibor as the brilliant force behind the inarguable evidence. The information he was about to present showed the strong commitment to what Ferdinand Tibor was so well known for.

Sol's image faded from the Screens and holographs that filled the Square. The music that played was like the opening scenes of a war documentary as the vignette took over the Stream. Lifeless bodies in rows on the ground, then flashes of Hell, Heaven, and nothing. Crime scene victims sprawled out after a shootout, then flashes of Hell, Heaven, and nothing. Beautiful cemetery grounds having the silence pierced by dirt being pushed back into the vault in the ground where a casket had just been lowered, then flashes of Hell, Heaven, and nothing. And next, Ferdinand Tibor filled the screen.

In the images Sol shared with the world, Tibor was standing in front of the World Counsel delivering his presentation. The summation was happening, and the viewers were being taken to that moment. The decisive statement of the brilliant Ferdinand Tibor filled the Plaza.

"According to the ancient Teutonic origins of the word, 'Hell' was intended to mean simply that one is dead and buried and is no longer animated in any way, shape, or form."

The crowds had not expected this. Every visit to the World Counsel Square was beginning to bring with it a potent and mesmerizing message. And this was no different. Ferdinand's message was concise and penetrating.

Even the ancient Hebrew word for Hell was simply depicting a place of non-conscious existence according to Ferdinand. And the Hebrew word for "soul"— *nephesh*, spoke only of a creature that was living and had breath. His presentation remained on screen a little longer.

"Our findings have concluded that the Hell of common thinking stems from a myth and is a word that refers to a non-conscious existence buried under the earth. We learn that what ends up there is the non-animated human form. Thus, hell is a place for dead people who, as is put by King Solomon according to the ancient Biblical writings, *'Know nothing and have no conscious thought.'*

"When the body dies all ability for conscious thought dies with it. The history, the language, the archeology, and the neuroscience all corroborate to testify to this fact. Experiences may seem to testify otherwise but there is no question that spiritual experiences such as "seeing" a luminescent Heaven or a fiery Hell are images encrypted in our brains from the input and stimulus we have experienced at the hands of the culture we live in. Moving from life to death is a simple non-dynamic and undramatic transition."

Sol could see the weight lift off the shoulders of some who were not sure what would happen to them after death. If there were to be any question about sending someone to eternal torment because of the decision to end their life, well, it was no longer going to be an ethical or moral hurdle for a person.

In the 2020's a seminal work, that was used for parts of Tibor's research, was published. *The Imagine No Satan 4-Volume Series* examined and explained every reference to Hell, Satan, Devils, Demons, and concepts such as eternal suffering. It dismantled many ardently held beliefs and ideas of a literal soul. The mystical concept of souls going to Hell for eternal torture was scrutinized to great lengths and handily unravelled.

Letting the viewers and guests in the Square in on that vital info from the Inclusions Session was the perfect thing to do. Sol's new edict that was about to be set in motion was one that would cost people their lives. And for Sol, Tibor, and the Ministry of Retribution, to see a man's life end because of the violent crimes committed against society or a person, was not a consignment to pain for all of eternity. No! To end a man's life who had been deemed worthy to have his life ended was not wrong or heartless…not according to the World Counsel or to Sol, it was justice. In the case where one deserving death was killed, they were now seen as transitioning from life to death and existing no more.

Next Sol filled the Media Screens and holographs once again. The stage was set for Sol to deliver his edict that would rock the foundations of a legal system known for protecting the guilty far too often.

The Healing Force of Justice

"**H**istory, archeology, and theology all speak with one voice to tell us what happens when a person dies. And death has been with us since the beginning of time. It is unavoidable, unwelcome, and yes, I know, it is an unpalatable topic. So why have we taken time today to affirm what many have thought about death by hearing from Mr. Ferdinand Tibor you may ask? It is because today I will be implementing an addict that involves death. I am not going to sugar coat it, sometimes death is an answer and should be the result of a person's actions against another. It may be a challenge for some to see but there are times when removing the one who is intent on bringing harm to the world, brings more good to this world. There are times when allowing the bringing life to an end for an individual, makes the world a better and a safer place for the rest of us. In the words of an ancient King, "To everything there is a season, a time to live and a time to die." These concepts also come to us from Buddhism, Taoism, Hinduism, Stoicism and other deeply spiritual cultures in history.

The crowd had shifted, they were trying to grasp what was being said. Sol affirmed all that had been presented by Ferdinand. He looked out to the crowd and saw the bright faces of moments ago had become expressionless…pensive… concerned. This culture had long been a culture that values life with a sacred honor and shuns death even in cases where it may be just to bring death. Few regions had fully embraced a death penalty for certain crimes. Death is negative, bad, to be avoided. If it happens it is rarely accepted with candor and matter of fact feelings. Death doesn't feel good, even if it is the death of a deserving criminal. And Sol had expected this. He knew the culture he was speaking to. He was part of it. Approving a death penalty would be met with uncertainty by many Participants. It may take a decade to change a culture…to advance thinking. But that was no longer a reason to keep from progress. True change took far too long. And often, the long drawn out move towards change would sap a people's vital force. Slow change may have been better for the people from bygone ages. But today, none wanted a Band-aid peeled off over a 5- or 10-year period. They were ready to rip off the Band-aid and move on. Waiting for change had become as difficult, if not more so, than the change itself.

Sol went on with his address to the riveted crowds.

"I know how unusual it must feel for all of you here today to be asked to consider where the dead go and what happens to them in the afterlife. But I have promised to do everything in my power to make this world a better place. After consulting with many advisors, the right thing to do is clear. And I will do the right thing.

"There are times when there must be consequences of the most final in nature for the choices they make. And these consequences will not be pleasant. We have each been given the right to make ourselves and our world better…the world we want it to be. For the world we desire to finally come into existence, it must come through intention. The world we all want will not come by chance or if we sit back and wait for others to create it. The utopia we hope for is possible. But it can only come to be if the society that desires it acts with intention to design it.

"If a person is the direct cause of the unjust suffering of another, if one of us chooses to do irreversible damage or harm to society, common sense says that person must be stopped. Cut them off from the society they are harming. Once removed they will no longer affect society. That person will not have an opportunity to repeat his or her actions in the future.

"This generation has the power to reset society and set her upon a path to restoration. A time where all good things are restored with nobility and honor rather than tolerating the vileness and harm that holds her captive in many ways. Justice is a healing force. And if one has done a crime and we know they have, the healing force of justice can and will be applied to those who have suffered by the wounds they have caused. We will all benefit from the justice we have longed for, for so long."

Edict Confirmed-
Thank You Sol

Sol looked off stage. He was about to introduce Tomer to the world. After spending time discussing how things would look in the Ministry of Retribution, both men had become even more certain Tomer was the right person for the job. The two had recently sat down and hashed out some of the specifics of Tomer's duties. Since then, Tomer had been choosing officers for his ministry. And like himself, everyone who agreed to take on their role of enforcing retribution, displayed the balance needed for one who was responsible to end the life of a deserving criminal. This Ministry of Retribution would employ "Readers" to fulfill the duties of the Ministry. "Readers" were a unique group of people with a very special set of skills. The Readers could move in levels of intuition that went far beyond the average person. The subtleties and nuances of "reading" a person to determine their feelings, their conviction, their level of deception and lying was a finely tuned gift. Tomer had chosen his teams wisely and the orientation process to develop the team brought together thousands of these unique individuals from all over the world.

In one of the orientation meetings, a female officer who was asked to join the Ministry of Retribution compared the act of stopping those who commit violent and sexual crimes to the act of euthanizing a dog. It may not have been the best analogy ever, but it made the point.

Comparing the punishment by taking the life of a violent sex offender or pedophile to that of a violent dog, she said, "I see this a little like putting down a vicious dog. He may be great companionship for his owner, he may love chasing sticks and barking at the moon, but when that dog acts impulsively and bites the face off a little boy, or tears into the delivery guy's leg repeatedly, someone has to do something to stop that. Although it is sad, unpleasant, and not an easy thing to do, it is the best for everyone, including for that impulsively violent dog, to put the dog down. Maybe he will be missed...but eventually he is forgotten about. And one thing is for certain...that dog who just couldn't seem to stop himself, will never tear into another child again."

The officers in the Ministry saw their role a lot like that. Sometimes justice was hard to deliver and sometimes the justice they would be called on to administer would be sad...but it was necessary. It was for the good of the rest of society.

It wasn't about vengeance, or hatred, or even about payback...it was simply about choices. Tomer and Sol were resolved to remedy the violent and deviant injustices often found in the world. When an impulsive man with a gun unleashes his hate on a group of people, or the Sunday School teacher with a burning desire to have sexual contact with his pre-pubescent students makes a choice to destroy the lives of innocents...Sol had reasoned...he or she has just made a choice to give up their own life. Retribution is to be delivered to that destructive Participant. And Tomer or his officers would be there to make sure justice was satisfied.

Sol waved his hand to ask Tomer to join him on stage. Then, facing the crowd again he said, "As an extension of my arm I would like to introduce you to the newly appointed Minister of Retribution, Tomer Cohen"

"Tomer, Welcome to the World Counsel Center for Global Progress. It is because of your courage, passion for justice, and decisiveness that we now, can all benefit from your leadership. Your willingness to shape the world you live in instead of having the world take shape around you is inspirational. And Tomer, when your actions were seen by the entire world, you were not a citizen passively watching the erosion of good. You became a Participant. The traditional label of "citizen" has become a term that engenders passivity. But as Participants, we take efforts, intentionally and thoughtfully, to make our world the place we want it to be. Citizens far too often stand back and tolerate the world they live in, but Participants create the world they want."

The confidence that came with no longer being passive citizens slowly bubbled up. To be imbued with the right to participate in the culture gave this crowd and the billions watching a moment of pause.

"Yes," they thought, *"I can participate, I am not just sitting and watching."*

Sol spoke on, "Today, along with the edict I am about to share, I declare all citizens of the world will no longer be defined as citizens, as of this day we are now Participants. Citizens watch the world become whatever it will, Participants shape and mold the global society. As Participants we will no longer let the world happen to us, but we will decide what will happen in the world. I would like to welcome every one of you to the new era as Participants of the world and I welcome Tomer, as our Minister of Retribution."

The crowds applauded on cue again as a welcome to the new Minister of Retribution. The Tomer that was unknown before that fateful day at Brookmoor Elementary was gone. Imbued with the King's authority, Tomer Cohen was now standing in front of the entire world. Ready to stop the vilest criminals who did not deserve to breathe the same air as the Participants who added good to society.

"Thank you King Sol, I am eager to work alongside you to establish the healthy and safe society we all deserve. I am happy to serve you and to serve the Participants of this Global Society to the very best of my abilities."

Ahmed joined the two on stage. Quietly he moved to the side of Sol. Tomer instinctively stepped back a few feet. Ahmed had the Folio with him and tapped the screen to ignite the King's Scribe. The image of the edict beaming from the glowing holograph pillars in the crowd morphed seamlessly. All viewers were now peering at the Digital Edict Document that had just been composed by Sol. The King's Scribe tool was already proving to speed along the process for enactments. Precisely as Sol had stated it, the King's Scribe displayed it on Screen. Ahmed lifted the Folio to the front of Sol. He reached out his hand, placed it on the smooth screen of the Folio, and the text of the digital document was watermarked by Sol's handprint. The red hue certified the edict. The synthesized voice confirmed...

"Edict Successfully Recorded." "Edict Confirmed-Thank You Sol."

And with that citizens were no longer called citizens. They were all "Participants" now.

The crowd snapped into affirming applause for the announcement of Tomer and the ratification of the new edict. But this was not all Sol would announce today.

Rightful Retribution Edict

Ahmed stepped back to leave the two in front of the Podium. Sol and Tomer had a natural comfortableness with each other. The stage was massive but the two men, who were now setting themselves in front of the world as a team committed to bettering the world, were a sight to marvel at. Filling the stage not by their stature or their appearance, rather by what they represented. They represented truth and justice as they had already watched things begin to be restored to what the world had always hoped for. The authority that sat on those two men was almost intoxicating. They had become the first two witnesses to the extraordinary mission that began when Sol chose to liberate Tomer. The world was witnessing greatness, and the two men were standing as witnesses to the broken parts of society. The parts everyone hated. Parts that would be met with their retribution. They were not just witnesses to the corrupt and perverse parts of the world. With Sol as King, they would be able to perform the tasks that would set the path to correction steadily on its way.

With the press of his hand to the Folio, the world's 11 billion+ people received the edict that intended to cull certain evils from wounded society. *The Rightful Retribution Edict* was now in place.

"Rightful Retribution Edict"

*On this day commences the edict enacting that retribution be
administered for crimes against humanity in accordance with
the measure determined by the King and by the hand of the King
through the appointment of the Minister of Retribution.*

"Retribution." It was not a gentle word. Maybe that was what was eliciting a collective wince from the world. But retribution was needed. Although it was widely believed that requital for crimes of violence was necessary, no one in modern history had taken bold steps to implement true measures of requital.

Many would come to learn "Retribution" simply meant that if anyone committed a crime that destroyed or profoundly threatened the life of another, then that person would be delivered an appropriate retribution. A justly deserved punishment. And Sol had decided what crimes would fall under the act and what the "retribution" would be.

As Sol began reading each clause, Participants understood why they received the explanation on what happens when people die. In Sol's edict, death for offenders was a consistent theme. The Plaza was muted while Sol read the components of *The Rightful Retribution Edict.*

"A Participant's right to live without fear and threat of harm is inalienable. No Participant should ever have another Participant take their life in an unjust decision if they live or die. Any individual shown to take the life of another through murder will be transitioned."

"A person's house must be honored as a place of sanctuary. A Participant shall not have to live in fear that their safety and security in their home is uncertain. If a person destroys the tranquility and sanctity of another's home while they are in their home by performing a violation through home invasion, that offender will be transitioned from life to death."

"If a Participant is guilty of rape, coerced sex, or grossly undignifying another through violating the body or dignity of another woman or man, or other person in any sexual manner through forced, violent, or non-consensual means, that person will be transitioned from life to death."

"If a Participant has been found to be a pimp who forces women to maintain a career in the sex-trade, imprisoning them in ways that have harmful physical, mental, spiritual, and emotional effects, disregarding their rights as a human Participant through enslavement, that person will be transitioned from life to death."

"As a Participant, if you offend the most vulnerable of society, the most precious Participants, our children, by propagating, publishing, intentionally downloading, or committing acts of sex with children you will be transitioned from life to death."

Sol stepped forward on the stage. Those watching the stage saw him change the pace of announcing the edict, but the Holograph pillars and Media Screens were still fixed on the Edict Document. He interrupted himself, the pillars flickered away from the document view and Sol filled the screen again.

"You know, I just have to interject here for a second. The abuse of anyone is sickening but even more so the abuse of children. The rate of sexual abuse of children worldwide has been epidemic for decades. 30 years ago, an International Congress on Sexual abuse of children reported that 25 to 50 percent of children around the world suffer from physical abuse. Over 30 percent of girls and up to 10 percent of boys experience sexual abuse. These figures have not seen a reduction in the past three decades and have only grown in some cases. The consequences of these abuses are substantial. Consequences not only for the affected person but also for society as a whole. And for those who suffer the horrific consequences of this form of abuse, we will no longer devalue your right to peace and safety.

"From this moment on, abuse of the most vulnerable will be met swiftly with justice. Society will have no tolerance for abusers of children. If a person chooses to sexually abuse a child, we will find them. If a person is found to be physically, mentally, or spiritually abusive to a child, we will find them."

All of a sudden the focus shifted. Tomer had stepped back of Sol but as Sol was talking, Tomer was watching the crowd. It was going to be an interesting future for this world he thought. Catching pedophiles was one thing, but removing them, removing the entire thought of them and the continuing effect their existence has on the social consciousness of society…well that was a whole new level. Once these indelible stains on the fabric of society are gone, there will be no need for society to exert any more resources, mental energy, or any more thought on them. Where they are, how much it takes to keep them alive in prison, repeated visits to parole boards and appeals courts, will cease. With this edict there will be no need for bleeding heart arguments that say it is somehow more humane to keep a disgusting pedophile locked up for his natural life instead of ending his natural life and making sure the rest of us are safe from him. Tomer watched the crowd. It was as if the audience that moment was breathing a sigh of relief. As if they felt protected in some way.

Seeing a young mom pull her daughter a little closer. Tomer saw there was no smiling no talking, just body language. The crowd was now blinking more slowly… focused on hearing the edict come into existence. And this edict was saying a lot. This little gal held her mom's arm snuggly as she soaked in the safety her mom's embrace offered. The young mother…maybe a single mother maybe just a young married mom out with her daughter, stood with her head tilted up a little. Her shoulders squared and her feet firmly set in place on the granite below. This was a young mom who seemed to be saying, *"Tell me more…this is what we need…this is what I need. I feel safer now."*

Society had wanted this for pedophiles for some time now. But to have a world leader finally declare a war on child sex abuse was truly empowering.

Her hope for protection hastily became resolved solidarity. She was finally hearing that all who brought the worst kind of harm upon her or her daughter, would be removed from this world for good. That alone filled her with the hope that under Sol's reign, women and children would be noticeably safer.

Tomer knew how high the incidence of child sexual abuse was. He wondered about what he saw, had the daughter or even the mom herself had been a victim of a perverted predator? The chances of her or her daughter being one of the innocent statistics was one in three. It was almost unthinkable but true that out of every three little girls having a tea party in their back yard, one of them would have their safe and happy world shattered by a disgusting pedophile. Tomer knew the risk… he had three daughters himself.

Across the crowd and on the other side of the Media Stream, were moms and dads of young girls and young boys who were suffering at the hands of perverse men as their sex toys. Men that saw only their own distorted passions and could not see that they were damaging another human for decades to come. The billions watching right now were lending their support to this revolution. Their intense focus and unbending sense of *"it's about time someone did something,"* would have overwhelmed Sol if he could have felt even a few ounces of it. But even right here in the Square, Tomer caught a vibe, and it was obvious Sol did too. Part of what Tomer caught though was the pale faces spotted within his field of vision. Faces of men who he could tell were struggling to not fidget. To not give themselves away as the very men Tomer would find and transition from life to death, for their sex abuse crimes.

They could do nothing to keep the blood from draining from their faces when they heard the edict. Tomer could almost feel their impending sense of panic. As an intuitive Reader himself, Tomer saw their subtle reaction. It was as if they had been caught…In their minds they were now the ones, out of fear, screaming at Sol to *"**STOP!***

They did feel caught. The worst panic a rat will ever feel is when he is trapped and sees there is no way out. And they had been around long enough, touching little boys and girls…feigning kindness and buddy-buddy interactions with trusting pre-pubescent children. They had been snapping pictures at playgrounds and schoolyards long enough, they had been "volunteering" their time at children's organizations and churches for far too many years. Touching themselves on the bus, going to gymnastic meets, kid's track and field events, and children's day festivals in the park. They had downloaded kiddie-porn endlessly. Scheming, strategizing, and planning how to get near children, or how to get a child near them.

If they could just get that little girl or that little boy in a place where no one else would know and the child would never tell. Then they would be better…then they would never do it again. That's what they told themselves. Lies! Lies to justify! Lies that kept them acting on their destructive impulse again and lies that keep them from killing themselves for being so pathetic! These were men, and at times women, who were such a toxic force in society. And here today they looked as if Sol was reading these sick bastards their last rights. Tomer may have been the only one who saw the squirming. But Tomer was the one that could do something about it.

When a clean, nice-looking man's face goes pale at hearing pedophiles will be killed, well for Tomer, the subtle fidgeting that goes along with that is easy to read. Just standing right there at that moment Tomer spotted at least five. Five men who would have turned and ran if they thought that wouldn't blow their cover. With the message Sol shared they had stopped sneaking wide-eyed glances at little girls and boys. Right now, they had a different thought. In this minute they wished they hadn't made lifelong victims of the children they had abused…And right now their body language couldn't show remorse for their crimes as one would expect of a sick man who was trying to stop his abuse and save his own life…Rather they were filled with fear and panic. They could not restrain it completely. Thinking, *"How can I get out of this?…get away with this?…not be found out?"…*

If there was a sure way to kill the perverse aroused libido of a pedophile then this was it. Let the pervert himself know he was going to be killed for his acts.

But everything about them in that moment screamed…**"It's over. I wish I could've stopped. I am going to die for my actions."**

And that is what Tomer saw on the pale faces of shame and fear. For this moment, their drive to have sex with little boys and girls was overpowered by their drive to find a way out of being found out, being caught, and then being killed for their acts. With Tomer seeing faces drained of any hope, staring motionless at the stage, Sol went on with his thoughts.

"The stats are not the same in ever country or region. In Africa we find 34% of children suffer from sexual abuse and right here in America we find 30% of little girls and 12% of little boys suffer the irreparable damage of being sexually abused. A world watching in horror has not proved to remedy these crimes against humanity. We need a world that will stop these sex crimes at all costs."

The images on Screen were so impacting that one could hardly see what Sol was saying in any other way. It was hard to argue with his resolution. Transitioning pedophiles and child sex abusers, from life to death, would fix much of the problem. The wounding on the small faces told the story. A young boy hopelessly adrift in his thoughts while sitting on the climbing apparatus in a playground.

Little girls in Cambodia, playing quietly in the courtyard of the compound that has become their home. Longing for the days of innocence with their families when they use to live unharmed in run down shacks. The placid days when they were in control of their own bodies before their mothers and fathers sold them to the sex-traders.

A child dressed in alter-boy vestments leaving the confessional with his head hanging low. Filled with shame and with fear after being the host to the priest's desire for pre-pubescent boys and girls. A regular ritual that was not found in church canon. But it had been practiced by supposedly "faithful" Catholic Priests for centuries.

The faces of 10-year-old girls. Once fraught with terror now pathetic with resignation. They were forced into marriage with Nigerian soldiers. Men who had descended to such a low level of moral distortion that they celebrated their new child wives with hate filled consummation. A "wedding night" rape that would leave them scarred emotionally and damaged physically. Their little bodies were not yet ready for the penetrating actions of a loveless forced marriage.

Flashes of children, weeping, withdrawn, playing, dying. The images were horrific not because the physical state of the children was graphic but because everyone watching knew. They knew that those children, whether real sufferers or actors in Sol's presentation, represented literally millions of children all over the world. Children who had no power, no choice, and no ability to heal themselves of the crime and violence that was thrust on them. The image froze on the Cambodian square of the little girls in the sex-slave trade. Sol held his hands out in a plea of incredulity.

"These children have no power to make it stop. But we can. However, doing less than ending the lives of pedophiles will erode the health of a child as he or she moves into adulthood. We are keeping society from its healthy best by not changing this.

"Why have these children not been rescued, protected, kept safe? If a King is incapable of protecting the most vulnerable of us, then what kind of a King is that? I am confident that death to the abusers will reduce the destruction of innocent lives in a way that has never happened before in all of human history. We will set in motion a work that will stop the suffering of millions of children. Children who have no power of their own. We can ensure the unbroken safety and trust of our children, and we will ensure the emotional and spiritual prosperity of a generation. And that will continue in all generations to come."

The crowd climbed to applause once again. The pillars of light in the Square proclaimed the edict already sealed by Sol's imprint. Sol spoke on to orate the remainder of the clauses in the edict.

"If you are a pedophile engaging in any form of pedophilia you will be transitioned."

"If you participate in child pornography, either through producing, disseminating, or collecting child pornography, you will be transitioned."

"This day I proclaim the ***Rightful Retribution Edict*** to be enacted."

With that Sol stood alone in front of the Speaker's Podium. It was done, and billions affirmed his edict. The law had been reformed. From this moment on, those who took the most from society. Those who brought untold depth of harm and violence into the social order, would now be removed.

Ahmed raised the Folio in front of Sol. Sol pressed his hand on the Folio. Ahmed must have engaged the haptic feedback mode on the Folio. The Folio vibrated three times...*zrrrt...zrrrt...zrrrt*...and the images streamed across the world. Crowds saw the handprint of Sol glow red, showing the sealed edict *"Edict Successfully Recorded"*, and set into the background to watermark the Edict Document.

"Edict confirmed...Thank you Sol."

Ahmed turned and walked to stage left. Sol motioned for Tomer to step up alongside him. Moving to close the Great Assembly, Sol turned to Tomer and spoke. "Well my friend. The future is set to change now. You will have your work cut out for you."

Tomer was eager to get to work. There were violent criminals of all distortions waiting to be dealt with. This important society strengthening work would be done through Transitioning an offender from life to death. It was called "Sealing". It is a painless process of switching the candidate off through a uniquely designed transdermal surge of optogenetic particles. And Tomer's highly trained Readers were ready to start the restored justice system through the act of "Sealing" those who were deemed worthy to be transitioned. A justice system that was finally potent enough so justice would no longer be offended.

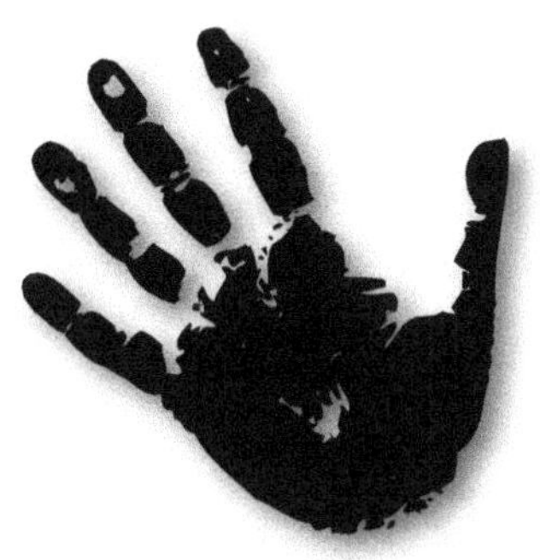

THE JUSTICE OF THE KING WITH THE BLESSING OF THE POPE

Marked, Sealed, Transitioned, and Harvested

"**H**ow many have you been to now?" Logan queried Chander.

"Seven," Chander gave his partner the update he was looking for. Both of these Readers were already waist deep in experience in the short time since the Ministry of Retribution began the work.

Chander and Logan were heading down Spinks Drive towards their next mark's apartment. Chander gazed out the tinted window as he picked up his glove to slide it on.

"What's the hurry?" Logan asked, "We still have about 6 blocks to go."

"I just like to get set before we roll up. Don't worry, I'm not doing this without you." Chander was reminded of one his first pedophile Sealings where he tried a solo version of transitioning a mark.

In the park on the left side of the car, a small gang of teens were throwing the football around. They paused to watch Logan and Chander's cruiser coast by. Their cruiser had been in the area before. Staring after the car to see if they could tell where it was going to stop. Whose house was it? They couldn't help but wonder.

They had seen it before and it was no secret what this duo was dispatched to do in the neighborhood.

The streams that hit the internet showing Ministry of Retribution Readers moving in on their mark weren't helping teams like Logan and Chander remain unnoticed in their work. But Participants who had seen them couldn't help but look when the Ministry sent a team into a neighborhood. Most of them knew it meant another pedophile or rapist was about to leave this world. Maybe they hadn't seen Chander and Logan's cruiser specifically, but they had seen the MoR Readers weave through neighborhoods on occasion.

Participants all over the world had heard about the Sealing of all kinds of deviant men. Men who weren't killed for just being creepy. Like the most recent mark. He was a gymnastics coach who went far beyond creepy. Hugging his students a little too long when they pulled off a "perfect" landing at the end of a routine should have been more of a clue. But his predilection for 11-year-old gymnastics students earned him a quick and painless end to his work as a coach...he was Sealed on the deck of his backyard swimming pool just last week. His transition ensured he would never sexually touch another little girl or boy again.

After a mark had been Sealed, the story always spread around the community. Readers had been through thousands of neighborhoods across the world. And anyone with eyes was now able to spot these ominous cruisers. Enough stories of them had been passed around the social media sphere to clue a watching world in to the cruisers that brought justice to a neighborhood.

It must have been an odd feeling for kids watching Readers pass by on the way to the mark. Not really knowing who was up next to be Sealed but knowing that there would be a Harvest Crew wagon following up shortly.

The *"Harvest Wagon,"* as it had come to be called, was a subdued cargo van brought in after the Sealing to harvest any evidence the pedophile might have around his house. The crew of the Harvest Wagon would then cart away the Sealed mark.

In the first week or two it was hard for onlookers to not feel some degree of ambivalence. Sadness on some level that a man was about to die on their street.

But on another level, they often felt a sense that everyone would be better off just knowing justice was about to take place. Society was learning that justice often brought the sense of feeling two things at once. And that in itself brought a unique layer of emotional growth and health to many Participants. The neighborhood children would be safe from the Offender's unmitigated urges. No drama, no intense scenes, just simple, decisive justice. The mark had harmed his last innocent. And now it was his turn to take the consequences. The cruiser rolled on.

Chander kept the chatter in the car going, "I've been dispatched seven times. One of them didn't end up being the right guy so the Seal didn't push. It was weird because the guy was a creep anyway, so I was sure he was going to drop when I touched his neck with my glove. Ends up that he wasn't into kiddy porn…it was just a fetish for baby goats."

"What!" Logan was caught off guard. "Baby goats….you mean '*kids*'. That is sick. I can't believe there's actually baby goat porn out there. Maybe Sol and Tomer will do something about those freaks too."

"Yah, this guy's house reeked. He was just shaking when we showed up at his door. Even he knew how twisted he was. Baggy trousers, dingy shirt, long scraggly hair, and believe it or not this guy who was into goats actually sported a wiry goatee. Even whimpered when I touched his neck like he knew it was coming.

"The glove didn't confirm my read so it didn't push. I don't think any of us could have separated whether he was a child-porn-freak or a goat-porn-freak the way the signals were coming off this guy. He just whimpered and closed his eyes when I touched his neck as if he was done." Chander paused before he expressed his incredulity.

"I think it's the weirdest thing, why these guys don't ever fight it? They just stand there while we reach out to touch them. They seem to want to end it."

Logan Campbell and Chander Harendra were in Tomer's first group of Readers to come on stream with the Ministry of Retribution program. The training they had already been through as crime and deviance Readers made them naturals for this job. Highly skilled since they were teens, both of them took to this field of work like a fish to water. The Ministry of Retribution was exacting in its final solution for pedophiles and other vile criminals as well as in its collection of confirmation that they were sealing the right person.

When the Readers were dispatched, it was already confirmed that their mark was the right guy…or girl…or other. The Ministry had such an impenetrably conclusive data server, almost omniscient in its contents. Aside from the embarrassing one-time misfire with the goat porn pervert, the data mining that went into confirming each case by compiling charges, video footage, consumer behaviors, and internet activity of the accused, would build a case that was as tight as a gymnast's leotard.

Chander, Logan, and all the Officers with the Ministry, were confident that when they were dispatched to a mark, there was 100 percent certainty they were about to seal the offender. Once in a while it could be a female but usually though, the mark was a guy. During orientation the groups discussed how less than 4-percent of all the child sex offenders in any region were females. They had talked about how it was a little easier killing a man for abusing kids than it was to kill a woman. It helped that the decisions of who was guilty or not were already all made for them. It also made their job easier because of the method that was used by Ministry of Retribution Readers. Using nanotechnology to stop the mark's neural and cerebral function was so sterile and non-violent.

As Readers, Logan and Chander had a heightened ability to figure out if their mark were lying or not. And it was that ability that led them to touch their mark with the gloved hand that would deliver the fatal dose. Intuitively reading their eyes, their tone, their body language, the hesitation in their voice, the subtle subconscious muscle movements and even the scent a mark gave off, was as if they were actually mindreading.

Some with this gift of integrating neuronal and sensory experience through the gut-brain axis, resulting in true 'gut instinct,' had used their skills fraudulently.

They claimed they were tapping into a supernatural ability to gather hidden information. Readers, at one time, could have made tons of cash as psychics but today Readers were mostly used for interviewing criminals and liars.

Yes, Readers were unique, and Sol and Tomer relied on them to their fullest to Seal pedophiles and other violent and depraved criminals. These were no ordinary individuals. Hundreds of them in every region had agreed to do the work Tomer was asking to be done. Taking in reports, doing intakes on accused, and within moments of encountering a pedophile or other criminal slated for Sealing, the Ministry of Retribution would quietly and humanely shut them off.

"Sealing a mark" meant that person would not live another day. They would not hurt another child or adult, and they were Sealed off from the world of the living. If a person were Sealed their life was over…and they finally were a confirmed candidate for what should have come to that offender long ago for their crimes.

The system was flawless. The energy generated from a Reader's intuitive assessment of the mark was joined with the biometrics data collected by the Seal glove. A glove Chander had just slipped onto his right hand as he and Logan approached the mark's high-rise condo.

Together, the separate tools fed an algorithm. The Reader's assessment joined with the data taken in through the fingers of the glove. It took the combination of both elements witnessing the status of the mark before the Seal would be triggered. The synthesis was precise. One could not work without the other to trigger the Seal. And the Seal worked perfectly every time. In micro-seconds the Seal would push, and the nanotechnology of programmable quantum dots did the rest. These highly sensitive and specific probes for tracking biological processes within cells and tissues were microscopic organic computers, forced through the skin into the capillaries. Flooding the vascular system and neural pathways they made their way across the blood brain barrier to do what they were programmed for…to shut down the brain in a cascade of cell invasion. And it was quick…as quick as a blink in most cases.

It was always best to touch the mark on the neck with the glove, but any skin contact would work to push the quantum dots into the blood stream. The Seal glove would release a barrage of neuro-electric inhibitors. Specifically mechanised nanotechnology that would take the mark to a place where most would never go. Even though the technology was perfected, pushing only on the confirmation of both witnesses…being the glove and the Reader…a Reader still wouldn't touch their mark unless he or she had determined final status. Once the Reader had a confirmation of their mark's status using their own gifting and skills, the gentle touch would Seal their fate, and the mark would transition and be Sealed off from the realm of the living.

That's why they called this glove the "Seal Glove". Whoever it was used on would be stopped from ever harming another person again…they would be sealed off from the rest of the world forever. The process would take less than a second to analyze the mark, then the necessary quantum dots were pushed, and the next 13 seconds would be the last seconds the mark would ever have. The 13 seconds of shutting down the mark's brain seemed long to the Reader at times. But in reality, it was extremely quick, thorough, and effective. The situation was over. Retribution satisfied. The pedophile who had just been Sealed would never cause harm ever again.

Science and forensic theological and anthropological research had brought understanding about what happens to a person after they die. And through the use of the optogenetic process offered by quantum dot technology, science had now provided an acceptable way to transition a person painlessly and effectively from life to death. It proved to painlessly end the life of a fatally flawed sexual predator and abuser. The Ministry of Retribution was using the technology with celebrated success. Thousands of destructive abusers, in many categories, were no longer breathing because of the work of MoR Readers and the Seal glove. No one would miss the sexual predators who had been marked, sealed, transitioned, and harvested.

Who Wouldn't Want
The Pope's Blessing

Every dispatch to Seal a mark taught Chander something. They didn't all go as planned. He sure learned a lot about planning the day he walked into the church to meet Father Carlson. Sealing his mark that day didn't go as smoothly as it should have.

Chander had been assigned a 63-year-old priest. Chander's mark was a man of the cloth who had been confirmed through E.N.K.I. as abusing dozens if not hundreds of little boys. **ENKI**, was the World's data collection system. It continually worked to *E*xtract *N*ecessary *K*nowledge and *I*nformation about the abusive Priest. As it did with every Participant in the world. **ENKI** was named after the Mesopotamian God of intelligence and wisdom and was absolutely the definitive repository of a person's activities. Extracting mountains of detail on Participants across the world.

Most of what ENKI data-mined would never be used against the person on whom it was collected unless crime and deviance were suspected. The information could be used to indict and convict the deviant. The needless resource-burning trail of courtroom appearances and media driven hype that worked to drag a case on for years, was a thing of the past because of the information ENKI aggregated. The judge, jury, and executioner had already made the decision when the team at the Ministry of Retribution sent out the Readers to Seal a mark. Even in the event the abuser was an esteemed member of society such as a Catholic Priest, the data mining ENKI had compiled brought conclusive evidence of the depraved crimes of passion and corruption that had been committed.

Chander knew Father Carlson was yet another priest in a laundry list of "holy men" who had been known to use young boys for playthings. That type typically had no predilection at all for little girls…or full-grown adult women for that matter. It was the little boys they would prey on when they should have been praying for them.

Chander himself didn't have much religion in his background. So to him, a priest was just another man or woman. Someone who was told he had a special job to do and given privileged authority over scores of people. And as far as his work in the Ministry of Retribution was concerned, a priest should be a man or woman that should do the job like he or she promised instead of using the "special" status to have sex with little boys. Women weren't even in the picture for these crimes. It was always men.…For almost two thousand years of Roman Catholicism, men in the priestly position of authority were sexually abusing young boys in their charge.

When Sol had brought forth the edict to end the life of known pedophiles it was a welcome relief for society. Finally, an all-encompassing law that would not protect the guilty…no matter what organization they were from. To hear that no one would have amnesty from this law was cathartic for society. Not even teachers, pastors, politicians, or priests could be pardoned. And Sol had received affirmation from one of the highest authorities in the world to keep up the good fight against pedophiles. The leader of the Catholic Church was on board. The Pope had extended approval for Sol's edict.

The day after the edict was delivered to the Great Assembly Sol had spent some time talking with Pope Caroline. The two met at the World Counsel Center in Luxembourg Germany. During their discussion Sol was encouraged when he saw the Holy Mother's encyclical that was to be sent out. She quite frankly, and with a sense of relief, agreed with Sol that death was the only remedy for this issue. Sol had not expected such an open and frank response from the Pope.

Pope Caroline had ascended to the highest rank in the Catholic Church only five years after the Vatican appointed the first female priest. She had been Pope for just over a year now and had led the Church in bold ways since her ascension to Holy See. Now, after having female priests for some 6 years and celebrating the first female Pope in the 1900 years since Simon Magus began the Catholic Church in Rome, Pope Caroline and the world's second largest religious institution had moved a great distance from even being affected by the historical controversy that kept women out of leadership. The dogma-shattering transition to allow female priests made history.

After the successful vote to allow females into the priesthood, hundreds of traditionalist misogynistic priests disavowed themselves. But the clear message of the presiding Pope Gregory of the day was clear. Women were here to stay in the Catholic hierarchy, and it shouldn't have taken 2000 years to get them into the Catholic Priesthood.

Pope Gregory amassed unprecedented support when he declared that having females in leadership should be the same in the Catholic Church as it is in the secular world. The Catholic God does not discriminate based on gender because that God has no gender. Pope Gregory addressed the androgyny of the Creator saying God is no more male than he or she is female. According to Pope Gregory, women have access to God that is in all ways equal to that of men. If God created both males and females, then the work of God for the Holy Catholic Church could and would be done through both male and female leadership.

Pope Gregory led the Cardinals to a near unanimous vote on the equality of males and females in God's eyes. Resulting in affirming the female priesthood. And even though ethically and spiritually that was the right thing to do, the Pope of that day was no fool. The most powerful religious figurehead was not immune to being compelled by forces outside the church. It was the public's call for female priests that was the purer force of change. The laity was influential enough that it had affected the Pope's decisions.

It was well known that many a Catholic Church leader had been seduced by the tempting advances of the world's richest men. Men such as Carlo S. Helus, Devin Koch, Amyl Rothschild, and Bertrand Arnault had been rumored to effectively purchase the power of the Pope or his Cardinals. In the past 5 decades, just as it had been throughout the Church's history, the men with power from wealth in the world, were able to steer the decisions of the men with spiritual power and authority. Money truly was a root of all kinds of evil. But the transition that led to women being allowed to become priests was not compelled through the influence of the world's ultra-rich. The approval for female priests did not offer great wealth to the Holy See or his Church...Rather, discriminating against having females in top church positions threatened to cripple the Church by lawsuits that would remove billions from her ever-dwindling coffers. The Church was being bankrupted by the people she claimed to serve.

Had it not been for the threat of a potentially crippling class-action lawsuit in the International Courts against the Church for sexual discrimination, the Pope may not have been as "inspired" in leading the crusade to convince his Cardinals. Pope Gregory was able to compel them to see the need to open the priesthood to women. He plainly told his Cardinals, *"It was what God wanted His Church to do."*

That was all it took...women were finally welcomed into the Priesthood by the tightest boys club the world had ever seen. And Sol felt privileged to have met with the world's first female Pope. Pope Caroline was definitely one of the most thoughtful and reasoned leaders the Catholic Church had ever had. Her candor and wisdom drew people to her. She was statuesque in ways that much shorter Popes of the past were never seen as. She was even an inch or so taller than her husband. Had she not been so apt to spill her warmth over into the lives of the laity, her looks might have stifled the "Lord's work" she was anointed to do. At 62 years old she looked to be in her early 50's. She was unapologetic for being the first Pope who could have been a fashion model when she was younger. Her contemporary vestments were fitted to accent her small waist and broad shoulders. Cheekbones high and rounded. Her eyes deep blue and her skin glowing. Obviously, "doing the Lord's work" was good for a woman's health as was often displayed in the wellness of religious adherents. And Sol was happy to have a sit down with her after his latest edict.

Even though Sol would have declared his edict whether Pope Caroline agreed with it or not, Sol knew it would be a huge benefit to have the Pope's blessing. To get her blessing on the most final solution to pedophiles the world had ever seen… at least in the past 500 years…would definitely propel the acceptance of the new rule. Killing men who molested and raped children was unquestioned centuries ago. Who wouldn't want the Pope's blessing today? Sol was eager to see if Pope Caroline would approve of his mission to remove pedophiles or if she would question his edict.

Godspeed to You Sol

ol and Pope Caroline where surprisingly candid about the need to requite men or women who sexually abused children. Pope Caroline was supportive of Sol's edict. She was quick to state that priests who had violated the trust of a child, their congregation, and the Church, should expect no support from the Church. The Church had been smeared with the filth of the child sex-abuse scandals for years. Pope Caroline knew that something definitive needed to be done. Sol was unaware about the many derailed attempts to remove child sex-abuse from the halls of the Catholic edifices. Pope Caroline enlightened the King as she spoke with Sol about a Catholic man named Gerald Fitzgerald.

In the 1960s, Rev. Gerald M.C. Fitzgerald ran an order called the *Servants of the Paraclete.* It was a problem-solving order that was given the unwinnable task of dealing with pedophile priests. After being commissioned by Pope John VI, Fitzgerald became so concerned about the number of priests who were abusing children that he actually put a $5000.00 down-payment on an island off the coast of Grenada. The Catholic Church's plan was to build a complex to house pedophile priests there. Fitzgerald had the Pope's blessing at the time to develop this island complex to protect the Church from the scandal and the ravages of fallout from the ongoing pedophilia. A cancerous scourge that was threatening trust in the institution.

Sol was enthralled by Pope Caroline's account of the historical problem. He sat confident seeing how intentional the Catholic Church had been in the past.

Although intentional, the solutions that were tried had little effect on the enduring dilemma. And as Sol watched the Pope recount the history, he sensed she was ready to embrace a solution that would truly have an impact on the issue. Not only in her Catholic Church but in the rest of the world as well. Pope Caroline went on and Sol absorbed her words.

"The *Servants of the Paraclete* understood the problem. The Church had made efforts to stop the abuse of little boys by priests since the 4th century, over 1500 years. And they knew something needed to be done to stop it. The plan Fitzgerald began to develop was to construct a safe compound on the island he was purchasing for the Catholic Church. Pedophile priests could live out their days there. They would die on the island as priests in a refuge. Disgraced priests, but at least they were Priests who no longer ministered and no longer had access to little boys. No longer being shuffled from congregation to congregation."

Even in Pope Caroline's short time as Pope, the struggle to contain the problem and do damage control for the fractured Priesthood was unending. Every Pope in recent history had been haunted by the unsolvable problem of priests sexually abusing children. Protecting abusers was just not an option any longer. The Church had done so for centuries and failed to remove the sickness it preached the Gospel had the power to overcome. Pope Caroline had conceded to Sol that, "If God, the head of this Church, cannot stop these men from soiling their vestments with filthy, passion driven acts, then it must be acceptable in the eyes of God to terminate their place in this world."

Pope Caroline went on telling Sol, "It is my view that the Holy Catholic church has believed herself to be hearing the voice of God since Rome built the church in the 2nd and 3rd centuries…but on this Sol, I believe she was hearing wrong until now."

Pope Caroline admitted that as sad as it was to end the life of a priest who had at one time committed to serving God and serving the people, she found no other solution that would honor and sanctify the precious lives of children and their intact sexuality. Nothing struck Sol more during his visit with Pope Caroline than hearing her true thoughts on life and death. The Pope continued to confide in Sol.

"Sol, I see your task is immense. You are set in place to accomplish a task that the Church, in all her historic glory and power, has not been able to do. This is the right time to bring this to the world. And you are the right leader."

Sol's eyes widened at the candor of the most powerful religious leader in the entire world. The Pope was resigned to unabashed directness at this moment. It was as if she too had a glimmering hope deep inside of her. A hope that someone would eventually come to set things right. As Sol sat engaging with Pope Caroline, he couldn't help but think that it was providential for his law to be placed into effect now. After thousands of years under the leadership of men nothing was done about the all-male priesthood. An insular group of men who sexually abused children. Now, while a woman is head of the Catholic Church, agreement to take the life of pedophiles appeared to be quite readily offered.

And Caroline was right. The Church had not been able to quell the historic tide of sexual abuse in her congregations. Everyone knew it. For all the prayers, the deliverances, the splashes of holy water and the genuflecting that had flowed like water under the bridge, there had been no change in the damage priests of the Roman Catholic Church continued to cause. Was this Pontiff sitting with Sol today recalling the words of a favourite Pontiff of the past? Believing now that a severe and conclusive solution is the only solution to the enduring problem of pedophilia?

When it was reported that Pope Francis had tabulated over 8000 pedophile priests among their ranks he vowed to, *"confront it with the severity it demands."*

Sol wondered if the Pope saw or knew something about this day he was not aware of. As Pope Caroline spoke, she made pushing and pulling gestures to show how Sol would be pulled in many directions while making his decisions. The air that passed around her vestments wafted her perfume towards Sol. He thought there probably hadn't been many Popes in the past who smelled like orchids. Then as she waved her hands in the air, the glint from her ring flashed across Sol's eyes, bringing him a uniquely honoring connection to the moment.

Caroline said, "I see you will be pulled and pushed in many directions as you lead. And I see that you respect the wish of each of us to enjoy not only a better world, but a better world that is filled with better people. This teaches me afresh about the sanctity of life. It is truly the honor of a King to sanctify life so greatly that he strives to improve life for His people no matter what the cost. Sol, I support you in this. If there is one who behaves in a way to destroy the privilege of another to have a fulfilling life, well, a line in the sand must be drawn. Even the Christ who said '*Forgive them for they know not what they do,*' as he was heaving to catch breath while dying on the Cross, is written of as returning again and destroying many people who oppose him and are unrepentant for what they do. Eventually, we are told, the man who sins shall die. "*Thou Shalt not Kill*" has long been misunderstood Sol. The words in that command speak of murder. Murdering one unjustly is how the Hebrew speaker and hearer understood it. Taking the life of one who sexually abuses children or is within the categories of the list of offenders and offenses you have compiled, is not murder according to the word of God…it can only be seen as justice."

This Pope had paved the way to reality for so many Catholics and non-Catholics alike. When she tossed the traditional vestments aside for the more culturally in-line suit she often wears today, a new beacon of hope and acceptance for her position flooded the world. Sol and Pope Caroline sat together in the Luxembourg World Counsel Board Room. The smooth *Gyokuro* tea they sipped complemented a soothing unity between the two world leaders. The warm aromatic tea brought Sol and Pope Caroline to a common place. Their visit felt like a spark that would ignite many other issues as Sol led the world as its King and Pope Caroline led the Catholic Church as its Vicar of Christ and the "Voice of God" here on earth.

It was late in the day now. Streams of late afternoon sun cascaded across the floor. They were simply two people who wanted a better world. Wanted peace, kindness, and justice, to fill the world. And they knew from all that history taught them, hoping and praying for those things is never enough, something had to be done by those who had power to do it.

It was almost time for the Pope to leave the World Counsel Center. Smiling at Sol her liberty to speak led her to continue. She seemed unconcerned that her sentiments might be unwelcome by a large number in her church. Those who ardently maintain that a life must be saved at all costs…those who claimed we must never "play God" and extinguish a precious human life would always be vocal. And to Sol's relief and delight, the fight he thought he might have in this meeting never transpired. Sol and the Pope were unified on this even though Sol knew he did not need affirmation by the leader of the world's largest cult organization. He knew the value in having agreement with this powerful woman. Any alliance with the Pope was a strong alliance. Pope Caroline had given this issue a great deal of thought. And she had a few more things to share before heading back to Rome.

"King Sol," she sobered her tone. "The Holy Catholic Church was to be a servant of God Almighty. And we have strayed far from serving that God as regards His attribute of justice. Particularly, justice upon one who desecrates life so greatly, and justice for the one who is desecrated. The priest who molests a child may not be taking the physical life of that child, but they are taking life from that child in ways that unfold over the years as that child becomes an adult. Ways that only God can know and that make her weep. As created beings on this planet we are the hands of God doing the work that is set before us. It is a debit to our account that our hands have prevented the work of God in this issue Sol. When we should have acted decisively and stopped the actions of our Priests, we rather used our hands to protect those Priests. I support your decision to move against an evil that has had few true adversaries and too many alliances by our silence and unwillingness to act. Sol, life is too sacred not to agree that death is a solution to this problem. Divine intervention may sometimes come at the hand of a willing King guided by truth and restoration."

With that Pope Caroline reached out her hand and took hold of Sol's. Embracing Sol's hand with both of hers. Sol noticed the Episcopal Ring on the left hand of the Pope that flashed a glint of sun across the floor moments ago. The Seal of the reigning Pope. The palm of the Pope's hand warmed the back of Sol's. As they stood close the significance of seeing the authoritative Seal struck Sol. It was ironic that this Seal on the hand that was affirming Sol, was embracing the hand that was "Sealing" many of those who had earned themselves the King's justice. The handshake was an embrace of gratitude and encouragement. Sol felt a touch euphoric as the visit ended. Pope Caroline bid Sol farewell, "Godspeed to you Sol."

Distorted Passions Of
A Perverted Priest

As news of the Pope's affirmation of the Rightful Retribution Act spread across the Globe, Priests young and old were silently filled with panic and fear. The Ministry of Retribution was doing the work daily. Finally, the acts the offenders knew were so wrong caught up with them. And the support of all levels in society was behind the cleansing work of the MoR. Even The Catholic Church brought her support. It had been in decline over the past 7 decades at least because of case after case of abuse that landed on its sacred steps. Pope Caroline was a brilliant and loving enough woman to know that caring for and protecting the children was the only way to respond to the centuries old epidemic. Sealing those from her Church who could not or would not stop their mental, spiritual, and sexual abuse of children, would be a move that would begin restoring trust in her Church.

Chander had already Sealed a string of pedophiles. And one of the more memorable marks of the past weeks would often come to mind as he prepared to Seal the mark, he was assigned next. It seemed like only days ago Chander had walked into a church to meet his mark with the approval of the Pope herself. On that occasion he was dispatched to Seal a man of the cloth who had the filth of his acts as a pedophile in his wake. Chander would never forget the day that he Sealed Father Carlson.

Father Carlson had no way of knowing he was about to meet his maker that day. Chander was working with a Reader a few years his junior. She was on her first mark. When they went into the church that morning Chander saw the confessional was occupied. It was Father Carlson. The light above the confessional door was on. The green light above the small doorway on the penitent's side indicated it was empty. The dark hues of the ornately finished wood on the artfully trimmed booth gave the feeling of stepping into something important. Entering a confessional felt meaningful...the meaning was pronounced for Chander at the moment. Not because of sins he hoped to get absolution for. Chander never understood the value of confessional. He was always amazed that this form of institutional expiation had lasted through all these decades. Decades that brought de-institutionalizing of religions all over the world. And on this day, the confessional was the perfect setting for Sealing the mark. No one knew how many altar boys had been abused at the hands of this Priest in that sacred box.

Chander told his rookie partner to take a seat in the pew, he could handle this one....He had only been on the job a couple months but that was longer than his newest co-worker.

He slipped into the confessional and Father Carlson was already seated on his side of the booth. It was quiet. All that could be heard were the muffled sounds of the shuffles as they moved into place. The air throbbed with the scent of time itself—It was a fragrance steeped in history, a symphony of woodsmoke and beeswax, subtly layered with the faintest whisper of incense. The wood, though ancient, still exhaled a quiet warmth, a comforting embrace that spoke of centuries of prayers and whispered confessions from this hundreds-year old confessional. The sliding panel between the two was open. The lighting was dim but bright enough that Chander could see the large, amice-wearing man through the opening in the walls of the booth.

He had been through it in his head a dozen times. It should just be routine... Meet the mark, touch his neck, and call the Harvest Crew to pick up the remains and ensure the vital organs would be kept viable. Simple, tactful, efficient. At least that was how things went when Chander went over the plan with his partner that day.

Chander had stepped into the booth and was greeted by Carlson right after he shut the door behind him. The confessional gave the opportunity to either sit or stand. Chander saw the Father was standing so he stayed on his feet too. Chander then told Carlson he had never been to confessional before and asked his name. As soon as he said his name, Chander reached up. Carlson couldn't see Chander raising his hand. And when he caught the motion of Chander's hand, he just thought he was crossing himself like the thousands of faithful who had sat in confessional before him. But Chander had his Seal glove on and passed his hand deftly through the small confessional window that framed the amice-wearing Father Carlson. Just the gentlest of contact was made and the Seal glove pushed the dose. The nano-dots of the optogenetic surge sent their burst of light into Carlson's perverse brain and Carlson was Sealed.

Chander saw him begin to crumple through the confessional window but wasn't quite sure why he hadn't heard the large man thud to the floor. He scooted out the door and motioned his partner over and to call for the Harvest Crew. They were always there in a few minutes after a Seal. The entire event was a team effort and whenever the MoR Readers were dispatched to a Seal the Harvest Crew was always dispatched to be the near area as well. They needed to be close so they could gather the available evidence and scoop up the body quickly so the organs could be passed on to the organ recipient. Sol thought it wasteful to let perfectly good organs go unused when a pedophile was Sealed. Sol edicted that all marks with viable organs were to be automatically entered into the organ donor program.

Chander popped open the door on Carlson's side of the booth. Instead of seeing Carlson in a pile on the floor as he expected, he saw him in a crouching position against the side wall. As if he were leaning against the wall with something supporting him. And something was.

Right behind Carlson in the confessional booth, there was a hook for the priest to hang his vestments if need be. Two wrought iron artisan crosses made into coat hooks. It made sense that there should be some kind of a coat hook in the confessional, Chander recalled thinking, *but did they have to make it sharp enough to impale a person?*

When Carlson had been dosed by the Seal glove, he had the reflexive reaction of withdrawing himself from the contact, and his body was in motion during the shut-down. Carlson tipped backwards instead of slumping down into a pile on the floor. The weight of the man and his backward trajectory caused his head to slam into the hook on the wall behind him. The hook lodged right up into his basal skull. He was a large man, but the pointed coat hook was secure enough in the confessional wall that it held Carlson fast. Confessionals were more than just ornate craftsmanship; they were built to last.

Blood was draining down, darkening the already dark wall of the confessional. A pedophile priest who had used the sign of the cross in vain over and over again through the years in his work, had now come to his end. And here Carlson now hung in his own confessional. A confessional that was home to dozens of abusive sexual encounters and calculated predatorial moves to get close to little boys. Had this confidential closet been opened to reveal the inner workings of Carlson's depravity, it would have exposed Carlson's numerous private moments of frenzied self-gratification while fantasizing about the children of his heinous passion. The times he would flip on the red light of the empty confessional long enough to finish pleasuring himself while fueled by his perverse thoughts.

The downside to this gruesome impaling of Carlson's brain, was that the quantum dots didn't get a chance to do their thing as rapidly as the typical 13 second shut down. They did shut down Carlson's brain, but with such a traumatic injury to the brain there was no time for the optogenetics to activate the specific neurons related to recall, in order to trigger memory of the crimes Carlson had committed.

The dying moments of offenders who were Sealed, were supposed to be filled with replays of the crimes they had done and the abuses they had inflicted upon children. The 13 second replay was short-circuited when a two-and-a-half-inch, antique steel coat hook, was lodged into the base of his skull. Father Carlson's hippocampus and cerebral cortex were kept from releasing the memories of the pain he had caused to so many. Carlson died suddenly, by surprise, but was not subject to a visual recounting of his perverse crimes. The science of this method for shutting off an offender, was enmeshed with the philosophical ideology that an offender, should neurologically re-witness their crimes in the 13 seconds of shutting down, to affirm to them the reason for their Sealing as they are transitioned from life to death. However, it was not effective to let a trauma happen to the pedophile while being Sealed by the Ministry of Retribution.

Beside looking to be somewhat humane in protecting the mark from slamming into whatever was behind him or piling headlong into the ground, it became the procedure for one of the Readers to catch the mark and ease him to the ground gently as his brain shut off...Not only did this maintain the appearance of professionalism, but the optogenetic quantum-dots in the sealing process could do all that was intended for them. All they were programmed to do. Chander, Logan, and all the Readers who worked for the Ministry, saw value in the 13 seconds of flash memory that came as the painless process of the brain, heart, and breathing shutting down was carried out by the nanotechnology.

It was that incident with Father Carlson that ensured Chander's plans would always include supporting the mark he was about to Seal. Keeping them from crumbling to the floor like Carlson was supposed to. Readers would never be caught in a gruesome situation like the one in the confessional again. The report of Father Carlson's unplanned impalement went out to the entire Ministry for all Readers to learn from. Now today, as Chander and Logan were heading towards yet another pedophile's den of iniquity, Chander knew the mark would soon be in his last sub-conscious moment of his existence. And unlike the distorted passions of a perverted Priest that were not replayed by Father Carlson's dying hippocampus, his mark would experience flash memory of the sick crimes of his own distorted passions. Crimes that were the reason he was about to be Sealed here today.

That's Him, That's The Mark!

Logan and Chander pulled up to the curb. Their sleek cruiser with tinted windows purred softly. Logan reached for his glove now. As he slid it on, he watched a young dad with his two kids walking down the sidewalk next to the park across the street. The younger of the two children was peddling his tricycle. Feet pumping feverishly to keep the tiny front wheel moving fast enough to keep ahead of her dad and older brother. A few feet behind the small cyclist, the scooter-pushing older brother was happily slapping the pavement with his foot. Gliding up close to this little sister's trike…only to let off just before bumping into his sister and getting in trouble with his dad. It looked to be a tricky balance for the older brother. Pushing the boundaries enough to make for an exciting game while walking that tightrope of not "bugging" his little sister so much that dad would have to step in. Once dad stepped in the game would stop.

Logan saw the dad pause when he noticed their cruiser. It was a little odd how discreet these dispatches to the mark were, yet someone would always seem to notice they were there. Maybe Logan was imagining it or maybe not. But it felt like the dad with the kids looked straight into Logan's eyes then up to a balcony on a building across from the park. Even through the heavy tint on the side windows, it felt like the dad had made knowing eye contact. Like he understood who the men inside the Ministry of Retribution cruiser were and what they were here to do.

That felt a little uneasy, but Logan dismissed the thought and reasoned that the dad across the street probably had no idea what they were doing in his neighborhood today. Then…the dad glanced up at the third story condo unit again. Just as briefly as he had pierced the cruiser windows with his glance.

"Was he looking at the suite they were heading to?" Logan thought as he turned to Chander to let him know he was ready.

Chander was looking up at the third story balcony himself. Doing a quick scene size-up before heading into the building. It was always interesting to see how "normal" some of these guys lived. The balcony was decorated with well cared for vegetation. A grouping of luscious hostas in watering can flowerpots flowing over with brightly colored leaves made the owner of that condo seem like he was a tiddly Participant who cared about the Participants in the world around him. But the profile that came across their Folio was clearly showing otherwise.

Chander turned towards Logan, "Nice view of the park from up there…. how convenient."

Logan swiped the Folio screen and went through the post-dispatch review as they shifted gears and got down to business

"Ok buddy…we have one 32-year-old male. Single, Caucasian, suite number 322. He's 5 feet 11 inches tall, approximately 180 pounds, brown hair green eyes, and his name is Maurice Fields. Here's a shot of him at the grocery store just yesterday."

Chander and Logan took a mental snapshot of Maurice's picture on the Folio before they exited the car.

The young dad who seemed to know what was going on was up the street now. But he couldn't help but look back. Logan caught it just as he scanned right then left to see what else was going on in this urban sprawl neighborhood.

"He must know about this guy Logan thought. I'd want to know what's going on with the sickos in my neighborhood too."

Logan and Chander were used to the rubber-neckers. People had to look. If they weren't Readers, they would be rubber-neckers themselves when a cruiser showed up in the neighborhood. The dissonance of knowing that a Seal was about to take place…that a person was moments away from breathing their last breath, was common for Participants who saw a cruiser entering their street. Yet everyone agreed few people deserved to be Sealed more than pedophiles.

Chander and Logan strode up the walk. The door to the building swung open as they waved their G-PAS cards. The scanning system automatically read their Government IDs and allowed them entry.

Chander and Logan had studied the profile to see what Maurice would be up to today. This was his day off. By logging his errand and computing profile they knew he would be at home today. ENKI was a big help in determining the mark's patterns. Like most pedophiles, most people in fact, his routine was easy to pin down. Tracking the habits, patterns, and whereabouts of pretty much anyone wasn't rocket science anymore.

Passing into the lobby a warm-faced grandmotherly lady had just exited the elevator and was heading their way. Chander held the door for her, and she smiled a thanks, commenting on what a beautiful day it was.

"Have a nice visit boys," She said without giving much thought to what Chander and Logan were doing in her building today.

"Thanks ma'am. We will," Chander replied.

At the elevator Logan pressed the call button. The doors opened to an empty elevator car. Hitting "3" Logan stood watching the floor numbers above the door count up. Chander noticed the bulletin board in the elevator took full advantage of its captive audience. A local balcony gardening business was offering deals on hostas and other greenery for the balcony-scaping of the condo tower tenants. A "wanted" ad for a cat sitter to look after a *'Delightfully playful Ragdoll'* who would miss her *'mommy'* while the owner was away for a weekend next month. And a poster for the annual condo pool tournament that was coming up next week. Chander wondered if Maurice had ever taken time away from his perverse predilection to shoot a little pool with his neighbors. *"Doubtful,"* Chander speculated with a *humph* under his breathe, *"These guys usually don't make too many connections with normal people."*

The panel on the elevator wall beeped and the car *swooshed* to a stop on the third floor. The door began to open, and Logan said, "This is our stop…here we go."

As the door opened Chander and Logan stepped out.

"Hold the elevator!" A man was calling from down the hall. "Hold the elevator!"

Logan instinctively put his hand in front of the closing door. Chander saw who was trotting towards the pair and shot a statement to Logan, "That's him, that's the mark."

It was too late. Logan held the door just long enough that they might have compromised their mission had he let it go. It was just too unusual to hold a door then let it go once the caller got close. Maurice was slipping past them and getting into the elevator. "Thank you." He called as the door began to close.

"Uh…You're welcome."

The door shut completely, and the number 3 light went out. Chander and Logan looked at each other. "Now what?"

"I don't know…I guess we'll have to try again later. Where the hell is he going anyway? The work-up said he would be staying home today."

"Look" Chander pointed to the numbered lights above the elevator. "He's going up."

Are You Guilty of Sexual Crimes Against Children

Chander and Logan were in a holding pattern outside the elevator in Maurice the pedophile's building. Putting the pieces together on what to do next they debated. Should they leave, should they stay, should they break into his condo and wait for him to come in so they could surprise him? They went through the scenarios in their heads. Chasing him to the top floor was not an option. Tomer had established clear policy to avoid any public Sealing if at all possible. Especially if it involved a chase.

"Maybe he's gonna come right back down." Logan suggested.

"Or maybe he's hanging out on the roof top patio. These places always have a roof top patio. Wadda ya think?"

Even though the rooftop was kind of public, Chander was suggesting to Logan they should head up themselves. There was a good chance they might not get back here for a few days if they left now. And there was also a good chance there was no one else on the roof top patio right now, or even worse…the chance that Maurice would engage yet another young victim between now and a few days from now was very probable.

Just then the lights quit flashing and showed the elevator was stopped on floor 9. The top floor. If Maurice was heading to the rooftop, it was only a short flight of stairs to get to the patio from there. They waited. The elevator never budged.

"Well…?" Chander questioned.

Logan reached out and pressed the up button to call the car back to the third floor. The air escaping the shaft as the car descended pushed out the *humm* of the returning elevator. They were planning to go up. And they were ready to deal with Maurice when they got there. The elevator was back on the third floor now… *Ding…*The doors began to open. The car wasn't empty. Chander almost fumbled because it surprised him so much. It was Maurice. He came back down.

Here Chander and Logan were ready to head up to the roof to make the Seal and all of a sudden, their mark is standing in the open elevator in front of them. He must have had something on his mind because he never flinched at seeing them standing outside the elevator. Maurice paid no attention to the guys that had just held the door for him moments ago. He rushed past Logan and Chander while the elevator door was still gliding to full open. Suddenly Maurice realized two men were standing at the elevator he was leaving.

Realizing they were the fellas he had seen moments ago, Maurice said, "Oh, hello again, leaving so soon….?" Maurice was just spouting to fill the moment with words. He really was unconcerned with who these two men were and what they were doing in his building. And Logan realized why he was unconcerned as the sociopath finished his passing thought foolishly offering unnecessary info about why he returned to the third floor.

"I forgot my binoculars down here."

Logan knew Maurice was not up on the roof bird watching. But he could have never imagined how calculated the predator Maurice was. On a day off, going up to the rooftop garden to "bird watch". But all the while preoccupied with his real "hobby." Maurice's predilection for pre-pubescent boys and girls is what drove him. Maurice would snap a few pictures from the rooftop of children in the park across the street and then browse his library of targets at his leisure.

In his thoughts he was scheming. Spying out innocent children and getting to know his next victims. Fantasizing about being close to them. Deluding himself to believe he knew the child and that the child he would watch from the rooftop of his condo wanted to be with him. Maurice, like all pedophiles, distorted reality with his desire to share some moments with the child he had taken pictures of. An innocent boy or girl who was the focus of a perverse passion. It was a new child every few weeks. And several times over the past years, Maurice's fascination with the images he captured through his binoculars fueled his burning further. And that is why Chander and Logan were here to Seal him today. The sick sexual pleasure Maurice pursued through his camera, would ultimately blossom into a full-blown pedophile episode. Sexually abusing the little boy or girl who consumed the thoughts of a man who only lived to gratify his desire. Logan and Chander stepped into the elevator.

"Do you want us to hold the elevator for you?" Logan offered, trying to buy time so the plan to seal the mark could develop.

"Are you going up?" Maurice asked while hastily heading down the hall towards his suite.

"No, down." Logan lied

"Don't worry then, I'm heading back up, I'll be a minute anyway." And he reached for his condo door and slipped inside.

Chander quickly shoved his arm between the almost closed doors. "I think we're still good to go."

The door opened and Logan and Chander exited. They moved quickly to the mark's suite. Chander was about to knock on the door. He was startled again as the door swung open before his knuckles knocked on the door. Maurice was there again. Ready to race back up to the roof with binoculars hanging around his neck. Chander apologized for the start he gave Maurice.

Readers out on a Seal always played the courteous part...all the way to the end. It was never good to get a mark panicking or make them uncomfortable if you could help it. There was enough of a chance for that, once the mark figured out what was going on.

"Sorry sir, I hate to bother you." Chander was making it up on the fly. "You seem to be very busy right now. But my friend and I have a question we wanted to ask you before we head back to the lobby." Logan followed Chander's lead.

"Oh..." Maurice was starting to feel a little uneasy. "Well sure I guess."

"Can you help us settle a bet? My friend Logan here bet me 100 bucks you were a bird watcher. I said not likely, you can't see many birds around here. I told him I bet he's checking out the nummy-mummies in the park over there. So...is he right? Am I a hundred bucks poorer?" Chander paused to get a response from the mark.

Maurice was tentative now at the odd exchange taking place in his condo threshold. "Well...yes sir I guess you lost a hundred dollars." Maurice quickly took on the persona of an amateur bird watcher. "There are several species of birds for me to watch from the rooftop."

Chander wheeled around to Logan, "Damn it! I hate losing bets to you."

The two made out as if they were done now and turned to go back to the elevator. Chander paused. Turned his attention back towards the mark, "Thanks for clearing everything up sir, my name is Chander and this is my good buddy Logan. And who might you be?"

The Seal was seconds away from happening. Asking the mark his name would confirm the status, and the Seal glove would push the quantum dots.

"Maurice, my name is Maurice."

Maurice squinted ever so slightly. Just enough for the Readers to see he was starting to question what was going on here…This was getting weird, and Maurice was starting to put a few pieces together.

But it was too late. Chander moved to complete the task. He asked the question that said it all. All that Maurice was about would be read through the next question. Logan was tuned in.

"Maurice Fields?" Chander asked with a probing tone.

"Yes, I am Maurice Fields…" Maurice was more fully suspicious of who these men were now. He asked tensely, "What is this about?"

Chander held his form. And even though it didn't matter how Maurice answered, Chander posed the point-blank question to establish a confirmation.

"Maurice Fields, are you guilty of sexual crimes against children you coerced into your condo?"

His Dying Thoughts Scrolled Through His Mind

It was on and there was no other way for it to go. Even if Maurice had answered "No" while standing on a stack of bibles the truth was evident. If he were a convincing liar, he could not keep the truth from Logan and Chander…it could not be hidden. But as loudly and as many times as Maurice could have protested to Chander's question Logan could see the truth. He was a skilled Reader. Readers couldn't be fooled. That's what they did. They read people. It was only in the rarest cases that a mark might get a Reader to trail off for a second or two. But this uniquely gifted group of sentients working for Tomer's Ministry had mastered their craft. Feeling their way through life since they were infants and feeling their way through every engagement with a mark.

Like all Readers, Logan felt the viscous air around Maurice. Everything about the moment became tangible. The two Readers were fully engaged. When these guys tuned in to the mark, they operated at a level most don't. The messages that flooded their limbic system and the enteric nervous system, informed their prefrontal cortex. Signals, stimulus, nuances that would never be sensed by others were transmitted, received, and interpreted by the insula in the brain. Every signal was amplified as Logan and Chander were in the moment reading the mark. In a difficult to describe way they were knowing but not knowing and seeing but not seeing the litany of subconscious tells Maurice was giving off. The messages flooded both Chander and Logan as the decision to move on Maurice was made.

The psychophysiology couldn't lie...The mark's slight nostril flare was almost imperceptible. The telling chest rise of a liar with a millisecond pause at the top of the breath, the shoulders dropped just a fraction, the barely audible sound of the stomach that only a Reader could pick up, began to creak as the juices of anxiety entered the mark's g.i. The Reader's senses did not deceive them. Even the slight bulging out of the shoes from the unconscious flexing of the feet and leg muscles in preparation to flee the confrontation in front of him. The autonomic response to threat was to flee for those whose wiring wouldn't prepare them to fight.

The two Readers captured the subtle scent of a lie. The high level of perception went above typical olfactory function. When Readers described the scent of a lie they would speak of the acid-like scent that hit the back of their nose. It was an unconscious aroma of betrayal from the mark whose whole physiology was responding to the lie by releasing the subtle but acrid scent from the hormones of deception.

It was no longer thought of as freaky that Readers could smell a lie. The almost infallible senses of the Reader were probably the most amazing crime fighting tools law enforcement had ever found. And together with the "scent" of a liar, Logan absorbed every one of Maurice's tells. This man was not being honest when he answered "No". His skin tone brightened, his pupils narrowed, his ears shifted forward so slightly, his tone descended in spite of his efforts to elevate his pitch while asserting his lie. The investigators who compiled Maurice's portfolio had done their job confirming the mark and now Logan and Chander brought the whole charge and decision for Maurice's guilt to fruition. Every signal Maurice gave off screamed to the Readers that he was guilty. Chander and Logan found themselves feeling everything Maurice was feeling but they almost hoped they wouldn't. All that energy from a guilty man standing in front of them was sensed so deeply, and for all their marks it was the "info" that led them to make decisions only Readers were able to make. Maurice did his job by confirming his status and

Chander and Logan were clear on what Maurice's silent messages were saying. If his signals could be put into words they would say,

"Guilty of Pedophilia."

But everything worked exactly how it should, and it identified exactly who this was and what he was.

Logan followed procedure. If either of the Readers did not determine a confirmed status, then they would not be able to seal the mark. But the status was confirmed. Logan, who had already moved in closer while Maurice was focussed on denying the unwelcome accusation, knew the biometric sensors in the Seal glove would do their job. The three witnesses had just consumed the final corroborating second.

Precisely on cue, Logan quietly reached up and gently placed his gloved fingers on the neck of Maurice. The glove read Logan's biometrics from the inside and analyzed Maurice's status from the outside. It was instantaneous. And the Seal glove emitted its dose. A silent push of lethal quantum dots. All Maurice felt was the cool touch on his neck and then nothing…all feeling left him. Except for what was going on, on the inside.

The optogenetics in the quantum emission from the Seal glove pushed into Maurice's blood stream. The sub-microscopic explosion pulsed with flashes of light inside Maurice's brain. The explosions of light quickly short circuited and shut down all electrical activity in the brain.

When the optogenetic nanotechnology first came into use it was a powerful tool that allowed neuroscientists to apply a brake in any specific circuit with trillisecond precision. The quantum dots would leave everything about the person's physiology intact except the activity in the brain.

When working out the details of how best to end the life of a mark, Sol had asked for this method specifically. A way to painlessly end their existence but not damage or undignify the human person. Pedophiles and others who were subject to being Sealed had taken so much from society, they needed to be transitioned from life to death. But Sol was not willing to transition them in an inhumane manner.

Once sealed, their brains would stop instantly, and the mark would stop breathing. The life ended. The pedophile would be gone, never to harm again. And once they were transitioned, all their organs could be harvested. Within minutes after being sealed the Harvest Crew came through. It was not only their job to harvest evidence from the transitioned criminal's, home but they would also pick up the Sealed mark for processing. Sol had decided that in harvesting the viable organs to donate to those who were waiting for a transplant, society could take back some good from them.

The touch was done the quantum dots made their way to Maurice's brain. Instantly...like an explosion of fireworks across a dark gray sky, the positive charged nano-dots that fired off were a blinding, neural cell, pyrotechnical display, that only the smallest of the mark's brain cells were audience to. Maurice felt nothing, his brain went into the 13 second sequence. Shutting down painlessly but systematically. Chander moved around behind Maurice to catch the lifeless mark. He had learned not to let the mark drop.

As Maurice the pedophile shut down, his dying thoughts scrolled through his mind. Seeing the things he had done to innocents would be the only torment he would feel in this transition...his last seconds of brain activity. Maurice the pedophile would harm no more....he was Sealed.

The Remains of Another Dead Pedophile

ogan had lowered his hand now and stepped in to help Chander with Maurice. It was a smoothly choreographed motion. He slid around behind his partner to guide him as Chander kept Maurice from slamming into the tile floor. Chander, already struggling in behind the lifeless Maurice, left little room for Logan to do his part to clumsily help manage the burden in the tight hallway of Maurice's condo. The optogenetics that entered Maurice's brain through the quantum dots had first shut off the sense of time and space in the tempo-parietal junction. Within that first touch, that first quarter of a second, Maurice had no idea where he was or what was going on.

In a brilliant concert of magnetics, organic proteins, electricity, and nano-explosions of light, Maurice's somatosensory cortex that registers pain in the neuromatrix, along with the limbic system, were prevented from reacting. His pain center was shut off. Maurice's' adrenal gland was signalled to remain dormant. And at precisely the same nano-second, the hippocampus was dosed with a less intense optogenetic flash. This was the part that really mattered. Sealing had been found to be the most humane way of ending the life of a mark. But the triggering of the hippocampus into a flash recall mode was the most controversial aspect of the quantum dot use. If there were a way to gauge the emotional pain a person experienced at the flood of memory rushing in in those final few seconds, then critics would have a hay-day decrying this method. Because the pain of recalling the crimes and abuses that brought the mark to this moment of death would most likely be deep.

A Sealed mark would experience many of the effects of his crimes on children through recall. He or she would effectively re-vision the horrible acts committed. All as a result of the nano-dot's action on the hippocampus and cerebral cortex. The mark was completely shut down in every way but one…that one being the imaging center in his brain. Near and far memory experiences were imaged in the brain as the mark was transitioning. A tiny cluster of firing neurons that were kept in play as the brain released things done that no one should see or experience. Maurice had no defense against the process. His death was quiet and he witnessed his own crimes in his final 13 seconds.

Those final images of Maurice's crimes that flashed through his brain would have offered even a further sense of justice for Sealing this calculated pedophile. But those sights would stay with Maurice forever. The images of the first day his predilections for pre-pubescent sexual contact were acted on passed before him.

It was a niece. An infant about 15 months old. Maurice was 10 years younger than his oldest sister and she had asked him to watch her little girl while she went out for an afternoon errand-run. As the images careened through his mind, Maurice saw the changing table. Wiping up his niece after removing a soaked diaper. Slowing his hand as he wiped her bottom with the baby wipes. Watching her wriggle on the table as she trusted the feeling of comfort that came at having her diaper changed so many times before. Innocently and happily squiggling around in a place that should be inherently safe from any harm or reproach.

As he reached for another wipe Maurice caught himself looking…too long. Staring where he knew he shouldn't. Pausing from passing the last wipe over the now clean diaper area of his niece, Maurice caught himself. He realized he was starting to get excited. Only a passing feeling but the tingle he felt caused him to become uncomfortable. Shaking off the feeling and shaming himself as he sharply turned away, Maurice broke the fantasy and brought himself back to task.

His Sister's voice broke the silence as he hastily closed the diaper with sharp angry actions. Actions of a man fighting off shame that seemed to target his niece as the cause, yet the shame came from his inability to push away his own inappropriate feelings.

The next memory in the memory bank of the pedophile's dying brain vividly imaged a little boy, a 5-year-old with his pants down in an event center bathroom during a wedding celebration. Maurice had come across him while at a family wedding. Heading to the bathroom urinal after having a couple of drinks in him, Maurice let his gaze stray too far from the business of emptying his bladder. The boy's bottom was in full view as he stood at the urinal with his pants down around his ankles. Maurice pulled up beside him in the empty second stall to tend to his own full bladder. Saying hello, Maurice knew someone could come in any minute but there was no one else in the bathroom at the moment. He would have stared longer if he thought he wouldn't be caught. Maurice couldn't deny his sense of arousal. Looking down as the 5-year-old was finishing peeing Maurice caught a glimpse of his privates. In seconds, as the little boy next to him bent over and pulled up his pants, Maurice's arousal peaked, and Maurice's fantasy brought him shamefully close to orgasm as he stood at the urinal.

More images raced through the dying brain. A little girl he had met at the park. Maybe 7 maybe 8 years old. Maurice was able to entice her into the bushes to show her his "fort". But the fort never existed. And after soliciting her help to build a fort in the bushes, it wasn't long until Maurice had drawn close enough to the little girl to show her his genitals. Coaxing the little girl with his deviously sweet tones and requests, Maurice helped guide her hand to his privates. Not knowing and not caring how deep the damage to the little girl's psyche would be. Maurice was asking her to squeeze something that a little girl should never be forced to squeeze…not now…not ever.

Next the memory of a 10-year-old boy delivering flyers rushed through his memory and blended into the last. Maurice's mark was coaxed into the condo on a hot day with the offer for a glass of lemonade.

On this day Maurice couldn't keep himself from acting. He couldn't fend off the high and the excitement of the anticipated release. Quenching the thirst of the young flyer carrier and quenching his thirst to be close to another innocent child. Close in a way that propelled Maurice's sickness to the next level. An attraction met with actions that sent the young boy on a destructive path of shame and confusion he carried with him his whole life. The dying memories took less than seconds to find their way back into Maurice's mind, but the effects of those actions would last a lifetime for Maurice's victims.

No one could know if Maurice felt regret or not as the scenes revisited him in his last seconds of consciousness. Scenes of a 10-year-old boy who could do nothing to free himself. Seduced by the kindness of an offer for a cool drink and kept captive by the sugar-coated rage that fueled the fear in a boy with no power. No power to stop the hate being forced upon him and no power to escape the momentary prison that he could never tell anyone about. Tears streaming down his face as Maurice promised to let him go and promising to not harm the boy's, parents only if he would do as Maurice told him and tell no one about the abuses. At least that's what Maurice told the boy...he made the same threats to most of his victims. Promising such fearful consequences that compliance and submission became the only option.

This little boy was like all the rest. He could do nothing. Wishing he wasn't thirsty when the offer for lemonade was made...wishing he would have obeyed his mom and never gone inside a "stranger's" condo...wishing the horrible act would stop as he blamed himself for somehow bringing this on himself.

How could the little boy not have screamed for a neighbor or for his mom and dad to rescue him as Maurice finished the abuse and backed away from his still naked victim to pull up his pants? The smell of the bedding in his attacker's bedroom would sicken the innocent boy forever.

How the boy wished he had someone to help him, somewhere to run to, some way to express the shame he felt and the hatred he felt towards the man. All the boy could do was leave quietly saying "No thank you," to the offer for more lemonade.

A little boy, altered forever by the uncontrollable perverted passion of a pedophile. A little boy who was now stuck with the searing memory of the event and the irreparable damage. It was a horrifying experience only the two knew about and was now the last of the disgraceful acts to filter through the thoughts of the dying pedophile in the arms of Chander and Logan.

The optogenetic release from the Sealing glove caused another irredeemable predator to see flashes of little girls in the park, boys at the Scout camp he volunteered to cook at, children from the water park who were driving Maurice towards his next child rape event, and many other innocent children who had yet to be touched by Maurice but already existed in his fantasies implanted as memories in his mind. Maurice was never going to stop. None of them would. The only way to stop the next attack was to end the life of the predator.

Maurice was limp now. His last breath passively escaped as Chander squeezed his chest while wrapping his arms tighter around him to keep him from slamming into the floor. Holding all of Maurice's weight now, the oddly pleasant, aroma from his morning shampoo, wafted into Chander's nostrils. The fact that Maurice was gone now seemed hard to tell while holding the still warm, lifeless corpse.

Dragging the mark's body towards the couch Chander couldn't wait to drop this load. This was part of the job of the Reader who quietly found and confronted known pedophiles, rapists, pimps, and wife beaters and several others marked to be sealed for their crimes. Then assessing the status of the mark and gently touching them on the neck, or wherever they could, to release the lethal optogenetic dose. Seeming inconceivable to some it was actually a rewarding gig to a Reader. Knowing that they were the reason their mark wouldn't harm another child, that those who were harmed might finally feel justice was served, and that no one would ever again have to worry about that predator stalking, seducing, and abusing their children. That was a good feeling. Readers working for the Ministry of Retribution were actually making a difference. But this part...catching a Sealed mark as he was shutting off... was often extremely unpleasant. Some of them were smelly, some were heavy, and most of them deserved to crash to the ground in a pathetic worthless pile or suffer the fate Father Carlson had and take a spike through the skull.

In an ideal world of retributions, a traumatic and violent death for a pedophile might seem appropriate. But the life ending technology had to have a trauma free environment to do its work on the brain. If there were fear and stress hormones that could be trauma inducing, the overriding pain and stress response chemicals that flooded the blood stream and brain, could short circuit some of the optogenetic activity in various neuro-pathways. So even though the Readers' job that came with the unglamorous task of catching the dead mark and dragging them to a safe landing seemed to be a big deal, catching these blemishes on a healthy society needed to be done. If only to ensure they saw their disgusting crimes as they died. And it was one part of the job Chander couldn't wait to get over with. Thankfully the Harvest Crew had been dispatched and would be on site within minutes to deal with the remains of another dead pedophile.

Might As Well Just Burn This Place

Logan let Chander do all the work as he guided his partner, dragging the late Maurice, the rest of the way to the couch. Chander plopped the mark down and felt the puff of couch-cushion air blast out under compression from the weight of Maurice.

"Jeezus! I'll never understand how dead weight is so much heavier than live weight."

Logan affirmed his partner like he had been the one burdened with the full load, "Yah, I'm sure glad that's over."

He brushed himself off as if he had something to clean off of himself. "Let's take a look around before the Harvest Crew gets here and seals the whole place up."

Once the Harvest Crew collected the body to take it for harvest and distribution of viable organs, they would leave three members behind to do an inventory of the home and document every one of the items in the place. Every pedophile had a cache of items related to his or her perversion. And these often led to others of a similar predilection. Others who would soon be met with the Seal glove of an MoR Reader. Meting out justice that would lead him to the sting of witnessing his own crimes in his own dying mind.

Logan travelled one way in the condo and Chander went another. Typical bachelor pad. Tidy, uncluttered. Shoes neatly stacked on shelves in the closet. But this kind of bachelor pad, the lair of a pedophile, always held more. And that's what Logan and Chander were looking for. In Maurice's bedroom Logan began opening and closing drawers, lifting and setting down pictures and ornaments. Standing at the foot of the bed, the place Maurice had defiled and raped more little boys and little girls than anyone might ever know. Logan looked around the room again, carefully trying to spot anything that was pointed toward the bed. Anything that might be a camera. The usual cache of books, cologne bottles, wallet, and watch.

"The Watch," Logan said to himself. And he stepped over to the dresser where the watch sat. Looking carefully at it before picking it up, Logan saw it was what he was looking for. This was no ordinary watch. The sleek design of the silver watch was deceptive. These little cameras had caught a lot of crime on tape over the last years. There was almost always a camera running. Nothing anyone did was private anymore. Good or bad, everything anyone did or said was recorded by someone or something. If there was something that happened, it would be recorded. The *EPD* Drones caught a good deal of activity in public, but content was often captured on the Wrist-Watch Cam.

Logan took a quick snapshot of the room to record the placement of everything in it then he picked the watch off the dresser. Sure enough, the nondescript men's silver timepiece was so discreet, even Logan could hardly pick out the camera lens on the steel blue face of the watch. But there it was. Dead center where the hands of the watch joined together at the pivot. And the way the watch was placed on the dresser, there was no doubt that it was filming the bed.

"How sick," Logan thought.

*"This son of a bitch had recorded the victims he coerced into his room. I f***ing hate this world."*

Logan knew the way things went but he would never let it roll off his back. Never agree to normalize the bullshit. When he agreed to be part of the Ministry, he vowed to himself that the day he was desensitized to these guys and their crimes would be the day he quits the Ministry. Logan, like so many of the other Readers, knew that it would be a long time before they ran out of rapists, pimps, child sex abusers, home invaders, and wife beaters to Seal. So, when the mark was Sealed, Logan always took a few seconds to reaffirm why he did this job and what kind of twisted shit went on at the hands of the mark he had just transitioned. He looked at the watch and shook his head in disbelief. *"How could anyone do this?"* he petitioned to himself under his breath.

Heading back towards the living room to meet Chander in the den on the other side of the Condo, Logan called out, "Hey, look what I found on his dresser. It's a watch-cam."

"Nice." Chander hollered back as Logan entered the living room, "Gimme a hand here Logan."

Logan looked up from the watch to see Chander kneeling over Maurice's dead body. He had a Folio in one hand and Maurice's lifeless head in the other. Fumbling with both he frustratedly told Logan, "I can't get logged on, hold this for me while I open his eyes."

Logan set the watch on the end table and grabbed the Folio Chander was lifting up to line up with Maurice's eyes.

"Retinal scan?" Logan asked knowingly.

"Yep, I couldn't get in with our hack…he must have overridden the firmware. So I need to get this loser's eyes opened."

Logan held the Folio steady above Maurice's face while Chander lifted his eyelids. "Eek…" Chander sarcastically joked, "That's not creepy at all is it?"

As soon as the Folio picked up Maurice's eyes the home page popped open.

"Welcome Maurice." The Folio's smooth voice greeted…it was set up to sound like a child's voice and that sickened the Readers further.

"You have seven unread emails and three content downloads waiting in your subscriptions box."

Chander tapped and swiped to get to the subscription download box. It was no secret that these types of guys usually played around in the online child-porn world. Subscriptions had become quite common. Fresh content weekly would keep them coming back and the cost of a subscription to keep the images of sexually abused children coming, well that varied. A large portion of subscribers to these sites would upload their own images to the site. The site was brilliant in one way. Upload your images of children getting abused and your subscription costs would go down. Then you would have even more content sent to your Subscription inbox. Get more content, upload more of your own images and the available child-porn sent for the subscriber's consumption would go up. If the subscriber uploaded enough of their own images, they would get all access for free. It was brilliant, but only in the way an evil mastermind schemes to take over the world. Thankfully Sol and Tomer were on pace to have the entire child pornography industry shut down. And the men who ran it would be Sealed soon enough.

Chander had landed on the Dashboard page for Maurice's profile. On the top menu bar the profile icon said,

"Welcome Maurice."

It was unbelievable but it was the reality, these guys had taken their penchant to a new level. Justifying it to the point that they just went ahead and used their real names. They never cared that they were really hurting anyone and they never thought they were going to get caught.

Chander touched the profile icon. "Unbelievable!" he exclaimed, "This guy is a Free Content member for five years."

Chander shoved the Folio in front of Logan's face to read the profile info. The profile snapshot said;

"Congratulations Maurice, new exciting images are ready for download now. Enjoy your special five year free-member bonus images today. This is our gift to you for being a premium uploader on our website."

"This guy has been uploading his stuff for years Logan! Shit we're gonna be busy when the Ministry processes his files. He probably has shared files with thousands of pedophiles all over the world. Tomer is going to need to hire more Readers"

Logan picked up the watch again, "Well it's not the first time he used one of these." Holding the camera watch up, the Folio chimed.

"Oh look, Chander was staring at the screen again. The message said *'Bluetooth connection securely made.'*

"Looks like it's grabbing the files off the watch."

Logan stepped beside Chander and they both watched the status bar shoot across the screen as the 87 gigabytes of files were transferred to the Folio.
"6 files transferred successfully." The Folio announced.

Chander and Logan knew how to do this. It looked like these files were recently made…like in the last three weeks. Maurice's last upload was 19 days ago according to the subscriber status info. The Readers didn't much like this part of their job but they understood how vital it was to make sure there was no one killed in the videos. Once that was determined they could move on to ID'ing the abused children right away to get them some help for what they went through. So, neither Chander nor Logan had any intention of rolling through the entire clips. All they needed was to catch the first few seconds of the start to see who the child was in the video, then the last few seconds of the end. That was enough to know who the child was and be able to report the child was sexually or physically abused.

All six of the files were the same. Different children each time but the same scene and same scenario orchestrated by Maurice. Maurice had drawn the child to his suite by offering a beverage or a summer treat, and while he was in his room, he would call the child's name. The child in each clip, 4 of them little boys and 2 of them little girls, would walk into the room in response to Maurice calling out.

"Hey, come here for a sec, I want to show you something."

Each clip showed the trusting child carrying the glass of lemonade Maurice had just given them. That was all Chander and Logan would watch then they would skip to the last seconds of the video. In every one of them they would see the same thing. The beginning of the recording showed a comfortable and unafraid child responding to a man they had found reason to trust only a few minutes ago. Then the closing seconds of the video were enough to see what had just happened in that room. The face of a distraught, afraid, and tear-streaked child was the last thing Logan and Chander could see on the unedited clips. Then Maurice would move over to the dresser where he would shut off the camera. All six of the clips on the file from the watch were the same. All about 11 minutes long, all of them taken in the same place in Maurice's bedroom, and all of them ending with a horrifically violated child weeping and wiping the tears from his or her face. Videos that became more fuel, driving disgusting and perverted men and women from all corners of the world to find another child to victimize.

Chander and Logan were glad he was dead. As they heard the boots of the Harvest Crew come down the hall, they took one last look around the condo. The condo door swung open. The four-person team had arrived. They were not only efficient but punctual. It was their task now to collect and catalogue the evidence and contents of the condo and remove the body in order to harvest the organs. Striding through the door one behind the other the aseptic white coveralls said a lot. They would be the last ones to be in this place so they were going to go over it with their scanners and document absolutely everything. All the DNA evidence connected to Maurice and his crimes would be sealed in the archive. Chander and Logan knew they needed to clear out so the Crew could do their job. As they made their way to the door the lead Harvest Crew member asked, "Anything we need to know fellas?"

Logan replied, barely overcoming the sick feeling in the pit of his stomach, "No, but if you know anyone who wants to work for the Ministry send em over... Sol's gonna need a lot more Readers after they go through the evidence on this guy's computer. He's been feeding content to his f**ked up community for a long time already."

Logan didn't really expect the guy to recommend a friend for the job when he got a courteous "I'll sure do that," from the Team leader.

Then just as Logan and Chander were stepping out the door the Harvest Crew Leader asked, "Anything else guys?"

"No, nothing else...as far as I'm concerned you might as well just burn this place...and leave that son of a bitch in here if you do."

Peddled On The Sex-Slave Market

Windhoek was hot. It was always hot there. Sol had jetted over to Namibia for his next monthly address. This was a perfect country to declare his edict for a universal global taxation system. As a country with one of the most unequal income distributions in the world, Namibia was a place of poverty amid plenty. More than one in four households live in poverty. Sol had long seen the broad economic disparity that was more subtle as a noose around the neck of people in advanced areas of the world. Not all people wanted to be in the class of the ultra-rich, but all who felt the oppression of lack were only hoping for the unrestrained comfort that prosperity could bring.

In three days' time, at the next Great Assembly in front of the World Counsel Centre in Namibia, Sol's address would alter the global economic future. He was going to install a completely new, fair, and equal-for-all taxation system. Democratic governments had struggled to impose and generate taxes that were fair, reasonable, and intended solely to benefit the people who submitted them. History displayed the use of often harsh taxes in the times of the world's monarchies. In the democracies that were supposed to be model governments, war taxes that were implemented with the promise to remove them after the conflict subsided were never removed. The clear picture of taxation throughout the world was that politicians and governments had become addicted to taxes. And the systems in place were far less equitable than the Participants deserved. Clawing back money from the earnings of the people who were the backbone for any society, had become the vehicle for governments to continue spending irresponsibly and justifying the waste they were renowned worldwide for.

The only way to restore the cumbersome, complicated, and unfair taxation method of the world's many government agencies, would be to reboot it. Sol was a fan of the reboot. Wipe out the failing, cumbersome, and ineffective old methods, and implement a new method. It was less complicated than bureaucracies had made it to be to simply start from scratch instead of repairing that which was already broken. Close down all departments and processes associated with the old way and start again. Start again with a completely new taxation process. Sol was prepared to implement the "Global Taxation reboot."

He had come to feel quite comfortable no matter which World Counsel Center he found himself in. And the Delegates from the Windhoek area were so warm and inviting. Sol knew and they knew, this King model would only work if Sol received the support he needed.

He was three days away from the next Great Assembly and had spent a day and a half consulting with the leaders in the area. One of the more influential delegates of the Windhoek region had made an impact on King Sol. Sol was compelled and encouraged by Funanya Afolayan.

Funanya had been a Delegate from the Namibian region for 4 years. She and the other 2 Namibian ladies that were part of the Namibian contingent, brought a brilliant balance to the men from their region. It wasn't until near the end of a traditional Namibian festive meal that Sol was brought up to speed on a truly dire situation. Funanya spoke of the 180 private school children who were taken hostage by Namibian terrorist group *Geld Kwaad.* Known by their self-designation as *Jehovah's Resistance Army*

Geld Kwaad or *Jehovah's Resistance Army,* was an armed terrorist group that rapidly rose to international notoriety in the 30's. Geld Kwaad made a name for itself that would be spoken across the globe with a series of economic terrorist attacks that virtually crippled the Namibian economy during the World Economic Forum of the 2020's.

The synchronized attacks came when the World Economic Forum announced a series of international meetings to move towards a one world currency. Geld Kwaad, whose name in Afrikaans means *"money is evil"*, pushed back fervently against the international community for its refusal to end Namibian poverty. They planned a display that would bring the worldwide, one-currency transition, into question for what they called, "G*lobal harlotry with the seduction of filthy lucre."*

To Geld Kwaad the matter was a simple principle. All government was corrupted by its need for money and therefore had caused the poverty to proliferate in Namibia. The rebel philosophy was forceful and promised a more equitable and peaceful Africa...compelling Geld Kwaad to try to dismantle the country's leadership.

In the Geld Kwaad view, terrorist strategies were the only way to enact a punishment for the great disparity caused by those who controlled the country... The blame was squarely focussed on the wealthy.

The inconsistent ideology of the terror group was how they vilified anyone who was rich as being "the evil." Yet many of their attacks were designed to accumulate money for their own organization. An organization that had hypocritically justified the wealth and resources they had amassed. Declaring it as righteous in its purpose to further the cause of opposing great wealth.

Their most notable activities involve kidnapping and selling children. Not just any children. They zeroed in on children of families unaffected by poverty. Typically, wealthy families.

The groups of children that were kidnapped were sold for a large fee to build the Geld Kwaad's military fund. And the issue Funanya spoke to Sol about, was reminiscent of another terrorist act by a Nigerian terror group about 10 years previous.

In that event the terrorists kidnapped and held hostage 95 schoolgirls to force them to marry members of its organization. Many of the hostages died during captivity and only a handful were recovered in small poorly coordinated campaigns by regional law enforcement and military.

After hearing Funanya speak about the issue, Sol knew the only way these 180 children would find their way back to their families and enjoy the freedom to feel safe in their school again, would be if Sol approved a special operation. It would take a massive campaign to find Geld Kwaad, retrieve the 180 children before they were peddled on the sex-slave market, and neutralize the offenders, in order to prevent the Geld Kwaad from taking the country hostage again by its radical demands.

Sol purposed to move fast on this. He had the full resources of the Global Military Unit. And while in Windhoek he implemented the plan with the GMU leader, General Togo Takanaka, to rescue the captive school children.

Wrapped Up By This Time Tomorrow

"**S**o are you good to go General?" Sol inquired.

"We are ready. At 0300 we start the mission to take Kearny's camp and bring out the hostages. By 0900hrs, Kearny will be neutralized and the Geld Kwaad will be dismantled."

Sol and General Togo Takanaka had met late in the evening to discuss a rescue operation for the school children. It was just the two of them, sitting across the table in the Fall-Out Room of the World Counsel Center in Windhoek. The General's military advisors were in the next room...waiting. They knew General Takanaka would soon come out and bring an effective strategy for dealing with Kearny, the Geld Kwaad leader.

The door that separated Sol and Togo Takanaka from the Delegates and advisors would not be opened until Sol had commissioned the mission. Takanaka was the top General of the Global Military Unit. Sol had a great respect for this man who was truly a history making figure. Takanaka had led the world by assembling a Global Military that operated as one unit. He gained the respect of the world's leaders by bringing together the Global Military under the authority of the World

Congress. General Togo Takanaka was immensely successful at coordinating the world's first truly unified Global Military.

The GMU was a guardian force. It was empowered to act on behalf of the World Congress. The Brobdingnagian force drew strength from the commitment of every standing army from every region and nation. There was no country or region with a standing military that was not part of the GMU. Regional government forces no longer had conflict with each other. They bound themselves together for the greater good and security of the entire world. It was a military force like the world had never seen and it had a depth of resources that extolled the wonders of a unified world and a unified Global Military force

Laying on the massive table that stood between them was only one thing. The General's Folio. It was displaying the region where intel had located the Geld Kwaad.

Takanaka's military regalia sparkled in the well-lit room. He was the most celebrated military commander of the century. Takanaka had led dozens of global campaigns. When there was a threat to a nation or region by a terrorist group, Takanaka had a history of decisively determining the location of the threat, deploying strategic troops, and dismantling or destroying the terrorist threat. With Sol and Takanaka together now, few teams would work as efficiently as this team. From the brief time they had consulted together, Sol had complete confidence that General Takanaka would deliver the exacting blow to Kearny and the GK that the world needed. As far as General Takanaka had determined from intelligence efforts, all 180 of the hostages were still alive. It was only 9 days into the hostage taking of the 180 children, so Sol ordered the Global Military to move fast.

The Geld Kwaad had established a reputation for enslaving little girls as servants of the military often forcing them to marry GK soldiers. As for the little boys...the weaker ones would be sold-off to be used as slaves for many of Africa's richest Crime Lords while the more robust children, would be psychologically manipulated. They would be subject to sleep deprivation and malnutrition while programing them to be child soldiers. Loyal fighters for the Jehovah's Resistance Army and its sociopathic leader, Jonas Kearny.

Kearny was a huge character in the cultic terrorism that was so prolific and so historical in Africa. He had the characteristic of some of history's most despotic fascists and had ballooned into an extremely powerful dictator. As an architect of countless acts of terror, and being the revered and venerated spiritual guide to the thousands of members of the extremely violent Geld Kwaad, Kearny had driven fear deep into the village culture of Africa. Occupants of towns and villages across Namibia were in a constant state of fear not knowing if their village might be invaded next, when their sons or their daughters would be the next hostages taken by the Geld Kwaad.

Kearny's draw positioned him as the unchallenged leader of the terrorist cult group. He had inspired hundreds of Africans to adopt an uncomplicated lifestyle in service to the ideal. An ideal that denied the benefit or value of the prosperity now common to Africans who participated in the global economy. Kearny's followers decried the globalized status of the economic hierarchy of the African people. His philosophy and zeal had grown the hundreds of early followers into thousands. Under his guidance, the Geld Kwaad had taken credit for widespread human rights violations including murder, abduction, mutilation, child-sex slavery, and forcing children to participate in hostilities.

General Takanaka and Funanya Afolayan were both equally passionate about finding a resolution to the crisis. Thousands had been injured, raped, or murdered by the GK forces and greater thousands had been displaced by the terrorists while fleeing during the numerous village invasions. Providentially, the General was a master at intel and orchestrating multi-layer campaigns that always brought resolution.

Sol couldn't believe the incredible resilience of radical groups and terrorist mobs that were still able to mount up. He had seen the effects of the Takanaka methods. And under his hand, the Global Military Unit had prevailed over dozens of highly weaponized and extremely complex organizations. Yet groups still rose from the ashes and generated the development of other rogue terrorists. In only a couple of cases did the GMU fail to successfully rescue or extract every single captive alive. Sadly, the six hostages who had died in past Takanaka campaigns could never be brought back…and the onlooking society was able to recognize that it is not always a guarantee that every single captive will be rescued alive. It was just the facts of military versus terrorist engagements. Even still, General Takanaka was always on task with planning for no one to be lost in the mission.

With the briefing complete now, Sol stood and the General followed. Sol thanked him and reached for his hand across the table. The General, stretched out his arm. As they shook hands his military decorations and badges reflected the light of the skylights beaming in from above. The General had been commissioned. The rescue mission and Geld Kwaad dismantling mission was beginning now.

Takanaka thanked Sol and said to him with unfaltering confidence, "We'll have this wrapped up by this time tomorrow King Sol."

Sol looked at the Folio sitting on the table. It was 12 minutes after noon.

Goodnight To The GK Camp

The *Geld Kwaad* had kept their watch posted through the night. It was 0300hrs. Kearny and the rest of the GK had been asleep for hours. It was hot…it was always hot in Namibia. Hot dusty and silent. But the moon was amazing even as a glimmering sliver behind the drifting cloud cover through the night.

Several of the 180 school children lay awake. And several, the ones who had been taken and abused that night, were either weeping from the pain and horror or had passed out from the same. No one could understand…or fathom…how a group of religious terrorist men could sexually abuse little girls one after another. The depth of sickness that fueled this kind of abject hatred towards another human was too profound to comprehend. And too far beyond any means of justifying letting it go on any longer. Seeing their victims as less than human was the only way these inhuman rapists could treat a child or captive mother with the violence they had become so known for.

It was groups like the Geld Kwaad in Namibia or the conflict mineral driven Warlords of the Congo who would capture villages of children, use them up for their slave labor and their sex-slavery, then kill them without a thought, to make room for the next group of innocents they would take as their victims.

If any terrorist hostage-taking group was worthy of being caught and slaughtered like the diseased wolves they are, the Geld Kwaad was. Kearny's group had reached a stratosphere status as a vessel of evil for attaching their "cause" to a religious mantra…

"Money is the root of all evil."

The GK had adopted a sinister distortion of the biblical statement that *money is a root of all kinds of evil.* Their activities were propelled by the pseudo-religious theme infusing them with the fervor to enslave, torture, rape, and murder children of families who had found their way out of poverty. The GK felt it was their God given duty to punish those who had dug themselves out of poverty while being citizens of the world's poorest nations. And today, The Joint Task Force of the Global Military Unit under General Takanaka would right this horrible wrong.

Togo Takanaka ran the playbook on many successful interventions into hotbed regions of terrorist groups. But this was the first one he had been tasked with under King Sol. And Sol unquestioningly agreed. The Geld Kwaad must be stopped. Blitzed in such a way that they would be decimated with no possibility of rebuilding. Sol ensured Takanaka and his Joint Task Force would have access to any and every resource available to the Global Military.

With the operation under way, the Intel Division at the GMU Zunhua Military Base was humming. General Takanaka calling the plays and Sol was amped up sitting in watching the mission play out on screen. All Command Center personnel and all surveillance and monitoring systems were buzzing. The mission was unfolding. The multi tiers of the mission were masterfully planned and would be orchestrated to have the greatest efficiency both on the ground and in the Zunhua Intel War theatre. The personnel responsible for each wave of the operation were in their assigned sections in the room. The entire room had been organized into a triangular formation. The large triangular org chart was impressive. Sol was seeing something he had never seen before…again.

Up at the front of the room, the tip of the formation, General Takanaka stood. A pillar decked out in his distinguished and dauntingly decorated uniform. Commanding the entire operation. He was a man dressed as if victory had already happened. Takanaka's gaze was set on the oversized screen as the operation ramped up. An image streaming each wave of the operation was in front of him.

Sol marvelled at the focus he had. An expert in tactics, the art of war, and resolving regional and international conflict.

Takanaka was a tower of success at commanding millions of military personnel across the globe and neutralizing terrorist activities, their organizations, and their supporters to ashes. Sol said nothing. As the King he was the "Commander in Chief" of all the Global Military Unit operations but Sol knew he was only a figurehead when it came to military ops. He certainly did not have the experience to make decisions on how things should go. His role for this one was only to approve the operation of the man with the highest military authority in the world. Takanaka was an expert unlike any other. When it came to military strategy and engagement Sol knew riding the coattails of this icon was the wisest thing to do.

The active wave of the operation took the center of the screen. The other two waves were staged, and their streams were parked on either side of the screen. Three military helicopters were in view. The camp had been located and the choppers were locked in on the coordinates. The Geld Kwaad camp lay hidden in the protective secrecy of the Namibian Escarpment. With its abutments and projections of rock and sand that sprawled widely in the inland region of the world's least densely populated country, the Namibian terrain offered a variance of obstacles before one could get to the GK camp.

The imagery showed the variegated vegetation, rapidly changing coastal climate, and lingering fog that diminished as it pushed inland. The environment clearly made the Namibian Escarpment a trustworthy host for the terrorist organization as the military search parties moved in on the location of the GK camps. The arid land turned from shrubby areas with scattered trees to become dense woodlands as the topography flowed from bareness to pockets of rich dense vegetation.

Sol watched the Media Screens as the streaming images from the BA-669 tilt-rotor choppers filled center screen. The military personnel throughout the Command Center deftly tended to their assignments. The personnel knew only their own task. General Takanaka kept each of the three mission sectors completely focused on their wave alone. For his multi-tiered operation to be a success he needed a restriction on sharing information between the sectors. Command Center staff knew only their assignment...trusting the General had all the pieces falling into place exactly at the right time and in the right way.

Watching the mission progress from the Sat-scan images, it was clear the Geld Kwaad patrol knew the BA-669s were approaching before they came into the GK firing zone. The images on the screen shifted. Waves 2 and 3 went off screen. They were staged and ready to engage on the General's command. There were 450 troops in this operation between those in the Command Center and the troops who would fulfill the ground mission.

In the tiered Command Center, now waiting for word on where the GK scout convoy was, Takanaka broke the silence, "Are they in play yet?" he asked his Sat-scan controller.

"Yes sir!" Came the concise reply. "We have a positive on 11 insurgents moving in the direction of the BA's"

"What do they have?" Takanaka wanted to know if they had the fire power to bring down the choppers.

"We are just getting that now sir."

Sol could see the view from the BA-669 cameras now as they closed in on the GK camp. He felt like he was watching a video game the way the images streamed in. The Sat-scan operator broke in.

"We have a positive from Satellite 3 on their hardware General."

"Do they have enough?"

Sol knew the plan and how it was all but scripted in classic Takanaka style. But it was exhilarating to watch the General call the plays. The way he never broke from the screen as he called out commands. The way he had his finger on the pulse of every activity in the room…and seemingly on the mission field too. It was almost redundant to hear Takanaka probing about the Geld Kwaad patrol team and their fire power. It was as if he were confirming they did have enough.

"Yes sir…they have 5 **PZR Groms.**"

It wasn't surprising this terrorist group with dark ages thinking would have ancient weapon technology on the ground. Only a money hating terrorist group would reject upgrading to better weapons and stick with old weapons instead. They were packing a Polish made anti-aircraft **Man P**ortable **A**ir **D**efence **S**ystem. The MANPADS used by the GK were refurbished, shoulder-mount, rocket launchers almost 30 years old. PZR stood for *Przeciwlotniczy Zestaw Rakietowy*…literally meaning anti-air rocket-propelled system. Definitely capable of bringing down a GMU chopper. Takanaka nodded with certainty knowing what they were using. The PZR- Grom was perfect. Just as if General Takanaka had chosen their weapon for them.

The precise orchestration of the operation was spellbinding. Everything going exactly how the General had planned. Sol and the General knew what each stage was going to accomplish. But the reality that the GK Terrorists had the possibility of thwarting the plan was always on the table. Any deviation from the calculated behaviors of the GK patrol or the men in the camp and Takanaka would draw all troops back. But so far, the Geld Kwaad patrol was doing precisely as Takanaka said they would.

The patrol was hurtling towards the outskirts of the shrouded camp. They were in five Landrovers in the GK scout convoy heading toward the incoming Choppers. Video images were being streamed without sound. The GK commander in the lead UAV started yelling and pointing out the open top of the lead vehicle. He had sighted the incoming choppers.

Bouncing torridly a few hundred more meters, the yelling intensified as a Lahat missile jettisoned from the incoming choppers towards the approaching UAV's. The attacking convoy didn't even try to avert the missile. Screaming just overhead it was taken as a warning shot that hammered a crater into the bank of the dry riverbed next to the vehicle path.

The GK was not in tight enough yet to deploy their PZR-Grom rockets. They would have to press in a little more. Then another Lahat went ripping towards them from the Military choppers. This time the convoy swerved left. The rocket pummelled a dune that was far enough from the convoy it would have missed even if the convoy had stayed on course.

It was perfect. Even though the Live Stream from the Sat-scan was absent of sound, the heightened screams of the GK commander were apparent. His men scrambled to train their MANPADS on the choppers heading towards them.

The General's first wave, the first part of the script, was progressing perfectly. Fire two misses at the insurgents and let them get excited, thinking the GMU Joint Task Force is trying to take them out. Then watch as the GK Patrol stops to take aim at the chopper squadron. Draw them in. A simple lure, like a game of Chinese Checkers. Takanaka would send out a few pieces to get the opposing players to react...then make the next move. After two or three moves Takanaka would leap all the marbles on the star-shaped board to take over the enemy's house.

Takanaka had played thousands of games of Chinese Checkers with his children and grandchildren over the years. And just like military engagements, he always respected the game for its reciprocating strategy. Make a move, see your opponent respond as you planned for them, then make your next move...strategically trying to draw your opponent into the move that will most benefit you.

During one relaxing match with his granddaughter years ago, Togo Takanaka's granddaughter Layla brought the concept of the entire game...and of armed conflict, down to a fine point when she was losing to her Yeh-Yeh(grandpa). One morning Layla and Grandpa Togo were enjoying a warm summer morning on the deck of their estate home. The pair had played several games while sipping their morning tea. The last game was just about ending when the pigtailed, brown-eyed, 9-year-old looked up from the game board. The shiny marbles told the story. She saw the move she had to make, and she saw that she really had no other choice. Young but seasoned, Takanaka's granddaughter was very pensive when she played Chinese Checkers with Grandpa. But this moment she took full pause. Being compelled to move her marble triggered her to stop for a moment and assess her dire situation in the game. The General lifted his head from the board to see what Layla's hesitation was about. And as their eyes met Layla said, "You always make me do that."

"Do what?" the General asked.

"Make me move my marbles where you want them."

"Well my dear…"

The General smiled a warm grandfatherly smile. A smile that told Layla this is how things go…this is what this life is.…

"…when you need to be in control of another's marbles it is always best to get them to move them exactly where you need them."

Layla tilted her head and furrowed her brow. Reluctantly, she reached to her marble on the board and made the only move she could. The General reached down and picked up his marble to move it into the house. Layla was never a hundred percent certain if her Yeh-Yeh had planned it or orchestrated it. But as he lifted his marble nonchalantly to begin the jumping chain that was now established, around most of the board, the marble popped out of his hand. They both watched as it *clacked* the edge of the table and rolled off. Dropping to the granite path below. The marble bounced twice off the multi coloured pavers of the patio and then stopped. It landed in the crack between the red and the tan paver a foot from the table. Layla smiled big. She looked at her Yeh-Yeh and peeked over the edge of the table to see if the marble might be retrievable…hoping it wasn't.

"Well, I guess that marble is gone." Togo stated matter-of-factly.

"So I win then!" Layla's tiny voice was already filling with celebration.

"It seems so Layla." Yeh-Yeh paused. "It doesn't matter how many of your marbles I get you to move if I can't manage my own marbles well."

And Takanaka was an unchallenged expert with managing his "marble" in this competition now playing out with the Geld Kwaad.

...As he watched the sequence of planned events unfold like a Chinese Checkers game in real time, it was becoming clear the Geld Kwaad would soon be in no position to ask for another "game" because they were making the moves exactly how Togo planned.

The pause in the Command Center was chilling. GK hostiles had stopped their vehicles. MANPADS hoisted on GK scout shoulders. Aim taken. One after the other all five PZR-Grom rockets took off. A flash and a trail of smoke from the weapon streamed a tail off the Grom rocket. Sol, Takanaka, and their Command Center troops watched intently on this side of the massive live streaming image and The GK patrol held their position. Waiting for the impact. At 650 metres per second Takanaka's choppers could have easily evaded the sluggish rockets from the outdated weapons. If he had wanted them to. But that was not the case.

Exploding on impact the PZR easily disabled the choppers. Three choppers were now spiralling to the ground. The broad smiles and jubilant cheers of the GK patrol troop were telling. They had their catch. The choppers were theirs and they were now moments away from combing the wreckage for survivors to take captive and booty to pillage.

Rocket launchers tossed to the side the streamed images showed the tires of the Geld Kwaad scouts spitting up a cloud of Namibian sand and dust as they accelerated toward the wreckage.

Takanaka announced, "Wave One complete."

The Command Center personnel responded immediately. The Wave 1 feed slid to the side of the screen and the Wave 2 feed took center stage.

General Takanaka commended the Wave 1 team controlling the helicopters. Wave 2 was waiting. They knew it was almost time to say goodnight to the GK camp.

Killed For Their Crimes Against Humanity

The Command Center watched on as the GK Landrover screamed toward the wreckage. Chopper pieces scattered. Small fires spotted around the crash sites. Smoke streaming from quiet engines. The smell of fuel filled the air like the champagne of victory for the manic scouts in the GK convoy. They skidded to a stop and two scouts jumped out to look for any survivors before looting the weapons and supplies.

Guns leading the way, the two in first, quickly ducked in and around the wreckage confirming everyone on board was dead. There were three GMU soldiers in each chopper. Nothing to note for blood and scattered body parts but the nine soldiers, were seen still strapped into their seats, motionless in their flight suits and helmets.

With a shout from the commander of the patrol...another two members from their squad went around behind each chopper. Scavenging through small piles of debris the excited rebels began shouting back and forth. They were salvaging any weapons and munitions they could. Grabbing the two crates of missiles in each chopper the GK scouts were livened with the bonus of a small cache of assault rifles and ammo that went along with their find. Although they were hurrying so they could head back to camp, they remained thorough and found the on-board supply of stun grenades used by the GMU. It was clear to the Geld Kwaad scouts that the crews on these choppers would not be part of any ground rescue today.

There was no mistaking that the complement of weapons and munitions on board meant these teams were geared up to do a rescue at their camp.

But what they missed in their haste to loot the downed choppers was too subtle for a jacked-up militant to pick up on. The soldiers sitting dead in their seats after being ripped from the sky by a terrorist PZR-Grom, were soldiers that did not die in the attack. Yes, they were lifeless. But not from this attack. These were men who agreed, if they were to die while enlisted they would leave their bodies as the property of the **G**lobal **M**ilitary **U**nit. These men had been part of an anti-terrorist program to allow the GMU to retain the remains of corpse soldiers in order to assist with operations in the future. They had not only given their lives to service of the Global Military Unit, but they had given their deaths for ongoing service as well.

They died while in the service, and now in their death they were still serving. Allowing their breathless bodies to be used in high level military operations as "props" to give the perception that rescue troops were advancing. Although unpalatable to some, in this case, where nine dead soldiers were loaded into remotely controlled helicopters, the value of their commitment to serve even in their death, was about to become completely clear.

These men had gone beyond the ultimate sacrifice to their cause by giving their empty bodies to be used in missions such as this. They were a metaphor of willing marbles in a Chinese Checkers game led by General Takanaka. And as Takanaka, Sol, and the Command Center personnel watched the weapons cache and dead soldiers' bodies get piled onto the GK Landrovers, they were anticipating the next Wave of the operation. The GMU soldiers may have been dead before they entered the unforgiving Namibian escarpment, but they were a key part of the rescue mission of the 180 captive school children.

The rough drive back to the well-hidden camp of the GK was quick. Sat-scan was tracking every bump in the road. The cargo of the Landrovers was the concern now. What better way to get into a camp to neutralize it than to have its own occupants escort you in. Or at least cart in the cargo and corpses that would do the neutralizing. And with the micro-cameras on the crates feeding images back to the Command Center, Takanaka and his team were seeing every shout and arrogant laugh of the scouts who were celebrating their victory. Wave One had done exactly what it was meant to do and with two more waves to go, the GK celebrations would ultimately be in vain.

Firing shots into the air never got old for these guys. How better to alert the camp they had returned victorious. The excited terrorist group streamed out of their shacks and hovels into the center of camp. The children in the locked quarters of the fenced hostage compound pressed against the fence to see what all the turmoil was about. These little ones had suffered greatly in the days they had been away from their families. Not knowing if they would ever see their mothers and fathers again, they had quickly learned to behave in as subdued a manner as possible. No one wanted to draw harm by bringing attention to themself. But with all of their captor's eyes on the dusty convoy rolling to a stop at center camp, they could watch from a safe distance. Afraid and curious, the children's tear-streaked dirty faces and hands were pressed against the compound fence.

They wondered what could be going on. Would they be rescued soon? Then their brief glimmer of hope blew away with the gust of the Namibian desert. They watched as the leader, Jonas Kearny, strode commandingly to the row of parked Landrovers piled high with GMU guns, ammo, and dead soldiers. The entire camp was silent.

"What is it you have brought for me?" Kearny spoke with a sense of entitlement.

The commander raised his weapon in the air and responded loudly. "Master Kearny, we have brought you missiles, guns and ammo, and nine dead GMU soldiers."

He thrust his weapon higher in a dramatic victory gesture. The camp erupted in cheers. The crowd began to chant, *"Kearny, Kearny, Kearny, Kearny!"* Kearny raised his hand demanding silence.

"No my brothers. *Geld Kwadd, Geld Kwaad...*"...the chant caught on with the terrorist crowd and after a few rounds Jonas paused his troops.

"We are the Geld Kwaad...this is our fight against the evils of money. Without you we have nothing. No movement, no ideals, no power. My brothers, we all know money is evil. And it is because of the love of evil that the Global Military Unit tried to come today for her precious spoiled sons and daughters. They will feel the waves of our retaliation for their insolent and feeble attempts to stop the Geld Kwaad. They will not retrieve their children on this day nor on any day."

Kearny looked over to the fence where the captives stood watching. Seeing the booty and the dead rescuers the innocent captives of the Kearny regime felt hope flee once again.

Kearny continued. "Those are no longer the children of their families and villages."

Pointing to the children gathered at the compound fence Kearny proclaimed, "They are now children of the Geld Kwaad. The Global Military Unit will be sorry when she sees our resolve. We will not tolerate the corruption of our children with the money that brings such evil into this world. Tomorrow, Brothers, we begin. Our young captives will be made to be our children and soldiers. Those who cannot be made to be our soldiers or our wives will be sent back to their families."

His pause confused the children listening closely from behind the sharp fence, as it did his own soldiers at hearing some would be returned to their families...until he finished his speech.

"They will be sent back in pieces so the world will see." He held both hands up high with outstretched arms. "MONEY IS EVIL!"

The cheers crescendoed once again…*"Money is evil, Geld Kwaad, Geld Kwaad, Geld Kwaad!!!."*

The declarative chant of a frenzied crowd filled the camp. Kearny held a closed fist high to stop them once again. Then he announced.

"But first, we celebrate!" He went on with his instructions, "Strip the dead soldiers and burn their bodies, while we enjoy the weapons the GMU has been kind enough to give to us."

The children behind the fence watched…hopelessly. Fearing what was about to come from the celebratory Geld Kwaad. Their "rescuers", lying dead in a pile, were about to be burned and a revelrous celebration would ensue. Many of the little ones would again suffer the horrors of terrorist debauchery being raped again during the celebration. A small crew of men went near the bodies and began to remove their flight suits. Kearny and his gang planned to keep the uniforms. They might come in handy in a future campaign. Shoes first then helmets and flight suits would be removed before burning the underwear clad corpses. One soldier's helmet was particularly challenging to remove. The buckle underneath his chin had a double clasp on it. The helmets of most of the other dead soldiers were already in the pillage pile. Sol and Takanaka were patiently waiting for that one last helmet to come off.

"Come on," Sol thought, *"Figure it out buddy."*

Sol could see two GK dogs excitedly barking at the scene. The dogs were clearly agitated. Standing back a few feet in an alert posture. Head jerking towards the soldiers at each bark, breathing faster, and clearly exhibiting they were trying to communicate something to their masters. Kearny wasn't tolerating it. He turned to the dogs and hollered at them…the dogs disobeyed. Kearny took out his pistol and aimed in front of the two manic beasts. Obviously frustrated that the creatures were stealing the moment. He fired two shots towards the feet of the dogs. They YELPED and took off to stand behind the participating crowd.

The anticipation was building. Sol was excited to watch the rest of the plan develop. He wanted to get right up close with the General, but he stayed to the back...out of the way.

Takanaka was still an unmovable pillar. He was not going to jump the gun or get excited. The few extra seconds it was taking to remove the buckle, to trigger the inoculant, would simply work to draw the GK members more fully into the moment. Takanaka had put the pieces in place and the terrorists had to make the move he wanted them to make. They had no choice with Takanaka orchestrating the event.

"Hold!"

Takanaka called out the order to the Remote Specialist at the table to his left. Her task was to remotely trigger the inoculant contained in the helmet, in the unlikely event that the terrorists decided to leave the uniforms on the dead soldiers. If they didn't remove the helmet which would trigger the release of the aerosol, then she could trigger it from her Command Center chair. Takanaka had a backup plan to remotely release the toxin if needed.

Takanaka cued Wave Three. Wave Three personnel had already moved into place 150 meters from camp where they staged. They had set out before Wave One began. At midnight the night before they were dropped inland about 10 kilometers from the *Geld Kwaad* camp. They trekked through the night to be in position at the same hour the patrol had gone out to meet the choppers. A distracted camp chasing helicopters made for a relatively easy trek to the operations staging point. Using the GK reaction to the incoming choppers as a cover, the Intervention Team was able to snug themselves in tight near the camp and not be detected.

Everyone assigned to Wave 2 in the Command Center was fixed on the progress of the trigger in the helmet buckle. When the buckle was opened a carefully integrated electronic switch was set to trigger. Sol could see from the images being streamed, that the strap was just about loose. Takanaka cued the intervention team as he anticipated the buckle snapping open.

"Intervention Team Go in...*5...4...3...2...1!*"

The buckle popped open, the trigger engaged. The inoculant released from the ventilation slats on the soldier's helmets and from the seal around the lids of the weapons and ammo boxes where it had been masterfully concealed. It jetted out of the orifices and moved through the GK camp like a wave. The heels of the soldier's boots were fitted with canisters that were triggered. They spewed life ending inoculant as they launched. 75 meters in all directions.

12 of the possible 18 canisters successfully found their way through the camp. Dispersing the inoculant in powerful plumes that would be absorbed through the skin as rapidly as it was inhaled by the GK terrorists. This product had been specifically developed for moments like this. And it was instant. Takanaka's inoculant team was at the rear table of the Wave Two section watching over the dispersion of the neuro-toxin over the clustered group of GK terrorists. The GMU bio-toxin team had developed a near perfect mass inoculation system.

The Wave Two Inoculant Team was a group of three. It was made up of two military doctors and one biological warfare expert. When Takanaka was asked by Sol to run the mission to rescue these children, Takanaka knew who he would need on his team. Of the trio, the expert in propellant based dispersion of biological agents was Dr. Ayman Latif Al-Barq. He was the great-grandson of renowned Al-Qaeda leader and biological weapons expert, Samar Latif Al-Barq. Long estranged from his Al-Qaeda heritage.

Dr. Ayman Latif Al-Barq followed in his great grandfather's footsteps who traveled to Pakistan to learn microbiology. Dr. Ayman, after completing his studies, stayed in Pakistan and developed several hi-tech, hyper-pressure systems to deliver aerosol antidote matter to masses of people. In the event that a population was exposed to blood borne pathogens or insect borne diseases, the *Aymen Dispersion*

Aerosol Model was employed. His work had been heralded for saving the lives of hundreds of thousands of people. A.D.A.M had been used in Asia when citizens were exposed to a resurgence of the Hong Kong flu. A pandemic that threatened to take almost 7 million lives in Asia and threatened millions in India as prevailing winds pushed migratory birds carrying the disease across the border.

Dr. Ayman remained the world's premier biological weapons expert. He had purposed to use the aerosolization of antidote agents for good...for eradicating outbreaks before they became pandemic. But on this occasion, Sol and Takanaka needed him to deliver a weapon that would incapacitate the GK camp...quickly. That's why he had been teamed with two other brilliant doctors.

The other two members of the team were superior in all things anesthetic. They were a co-ed team who had met by chance at an anesthesiology conference several years ago. Both were working towards developing an aerosol to be used as a mass anesthetic. And today, they were seeing their collaborative work used on a terrorist group and its hostages. Their role in the operation was to ensure the product dispersed was powerful enough to incapacitate every man woman and child in the entire camp.

Dr. Aymen would produce the effective dispersion system, and his colleagues would bring the incapacitation agent. Any of the chemical warfare agents in the GMU repertoire could technically incapacitate a victim, however, the Global Military Unit required incapacitation to be temporary and nonlethal when airway intervention is rapidly provided. Sol and the General were well aware that the incapacitation of the hostages as well as the terrorists was inevitable. The agent that would be dispersed would act on everyone's central nervous system. Even the hostages watching from behind the fence.

The second the terrorists were exposed they would be overcome and lie in an unconscious or semiconscious state. Many would die from their airways falling closed preventing oxygen from entering their lungs. And those who didn't, would be administered a second agent. A potent dose in the *Auto-ject* red pen that would completely shut down their CNS.

Rapidly and decisively the neurotoxin would disable every person in the camp. Their terror based idealistic life would end painlessly and quickly right there in the camp. That is what Sol prescribed when discussing the flow of the mission with General Takanaka. All members of Geld Kwaad were to be killed. Sol wasn't afraid to call it what it was. Terminated, sealed, neutralized…none of those words would hide the truth…The GK uprising and its soldiers were being killed for their crimes against humanity and there was no need to state it any more delicately.

Paralyze Helpless Nations By Their Terrors

Sol and the Command Center personnel watched carefully. The instant the neurotoxin released, men were dropping. Silent images of insurgents being turned off. Like a branch snapped and fallen from a tree, they were upright one second and in a heap on the ground the next. Those closest to the dead soldiers in the center of camp dropped first. Then Kearny, the exalted leader slumped into a pile with no warning.

Kearny and the patrol crew had no chance to respond. It was a total surprise. Takanaka had tested the dispersion model before and proved it to be exceptional.

Others, a few meters away from the pile of weapons and dead GMU soldiers, reacted to the jettisoned canisters and tried to turn and run, covering their faces with clothes and scarves. But no use, the aerosolized *3-Thiofentanyl* filling the air, was generations beyond the Russian fentanyl used to liberate 800 hostages trapped by terrorists in a Moscow theater. For that event in the early 2000's a fentanyl derivative was used to incapacitate Chechen terrorists who had taken 800 theatre goers hostage. The rescue was only a partial success. Fifteen percent of those exposed that day in the theater died. The deaths included 115 of the 800 hostages.

Today's administration of the neurotoxin *3-Thiofentanyl,* known as TFT3, would not cause tragic results. Sol wanted a guarantee that not one of the 180 child hostages would be lost. Takanaka and his anaesthetic team assured Sol no child would die during the operation. That guarantee was supported by sending 300 operatives in on the Wave 3 Intervention Team. Their only job was to intervene on the unconscious children held captive by Kearny.

Each child would be rendered unconscious by the TFT3, but each child would have a GMU soldier managing their airway and administering the antidote to the toxin. The remaining operatives would secure the camp and Auto-ject Geld Kwaad members with the appropriate life-ending infusion to shut off their brain and life. It was a "No child left behind" operation, and a "No terrorist left alive" operation at the same time.

Wave 3 troops had been engaged. They were advancing…and in a hurry. The sprint into camp was unhindered by any GK security opposition. Sat-scan intel confirmed there were no rogue members in the perimeter. All GK personnel were within the main camp celebrating their "victory". The hasty advance of the Wave 3 Intervention team was going as flawless as the first two Waves of the operation. This was the part of the plan Sol was most interested in watching from in the Command Center Theater. Had the children been conscious they would have been paralyzed with fear at the approaching troops. 300 men and women in GMU uniforms charging towards the camp.

The first wave of the Intervention Team hit the wire fence on the camp perimeter. Six holes were cut through the fence. The team needed to keep up pace. With the time it took to advance and breach the outer fence and the hostage compound fence, some of the captive children could have had their airways closed-off for up to 90 seconds. Their little brains could only survive for 3 or 4 minutes without oxygen. The 3-Thiofentanyl would last from 4 to 6 minutes based on body size.

The troops streamed through the 6 gaping holes held open by the Breachers. No one was concerned with the GK members lying all over the inner camp. No one had any thought to get to the terrorists. If they were all dead before they were administered the Sealing agent to finish them off that would be just fine. Some of them may be dead already. Time was on the good guys' side now. The incapacitating agent had taken a few extra seconds to reach to the edge of the camp where the child hostages were kept.

A second team of Breachers had made it to the wire fence containing the hostages. Team leaders called out the time, "*45 seconds...Let's Move!!!*" They had to be at the head of each child hostage for airway management in no more than 45 seconds now, or they might lose some.

Intervention Team personnel barrelled in. No unconscious child would be missed but many were leapt over as the stream of rescuers flooded the compound and headed to the furthest victim first. Each Intervention Team member stopped at a child to get them breathing again. Some of the children lay face down some on their sides. Intervention team actions opened the airway immediately. A simple jaw-thrust was all that was needed for the unconscious children who would soon wake to the sight of Global Military Unit rescuers.

For some children, rescue breathing began immediately. Two or three breaths and they were breathing again on their own. Airway open...breathing...then team members rolled the child to one side or the other. Propped safely in the recovery position while the antidote to the neurotoxin *3-Thiofentanyl* was administered.

*Pssshtt, Pssshtt, Pssshtt, Pssshtt...*injection after injection was given until every child had been antidoted. Their 9-day nightmare was ending. And the Wave 3 leader called out an accountability check. All personnel accounted for, and all 180 children were breathing and stable. They would ascend back to consciousness in about 30 seconds.

Team members who were now with a child hostage remained with them, managing their recovery. The remaining Wave 3 troops kept to task. Efficiency was paramount, as some of Kearny's followers may be regaining consciousness in about 90 seconds...those who had not yet died from lack of respirations while unconscious. Every one of the GK members in the camp had been ID'd. They would now be Auto-jected with the **red pen**. A **red pen** for the terrorist and **green pen** for the children. Green held the antidote to the TFT3. The red pen was for the terrorists. It had lethal contents and was physically shaped different than the green pen for antidoting the child hostages. In the shape of a lower case 't', there would be no errors in administering the auto-ject doses, ensuring the breathing and life of every terrorist in that camp would be stopped.

The Team leader called out.

"Red pen...Red pen...Red Pen! Give me a positive on the Red Pen before you push the button!"

The first Intervention Team member reached her mark. ***"Red Pen*!"** She announced. *Pssshtt.* Then the calls of "Red Pen" were stacked one upon another. From all over the camp. Lethal doses were pushed one after the other into the unconscious terrorists. They would die where they lay. The terrorist, motionless on the ground, went from victory at capturing three choppers and nine dead GMU soldiers one moment to being unconscious and lifeless the next.

The camp was frenzied getting to over a thousand GK terrorists before they began to regain consciousness. *Red Pen!...Red Pen!...Red Pen!...Red Pen!* Came the calls from all over the grounds. Even the GK cook who was sitting slumped over on the toilet, cigarette still on his lips, when the 3-Thiofentanyl was dispersed with the call *"Red Pen!"* by one of the Intervention Team personnel. It took only moments before the camp went silent.

The silence in the camp was mirrored by the Command Center. As the operatives watched the scene unfold from hundreds of miles away, the volume began to heighten in the room. The celebratory chatter increased. The children came back to consciousness and the GK terrorists did not. The operation was inspiring. Another terrorist group neutralized. Just one of the many rogue groups that were yet to come.

The men of the Geld Kwaad Jehovah's Resistance Army would never terrorize again. They would never abuse imprisoned women or children in orgies of rape again. As of this day, they no longer had an impact on the world. These men were not Participants of this global society before their death. They only lived to serve their own distorted philosophies and bring harm to the world. Most of the Majority

Class in society wished there was a literal torturous Hell for men like these. They would not be missed now that they were dead.

And the world was better off without them.

In the center of the camp, where the 3-Thiofentanyl first emitted, lay Jonas Kearny. Filled with power and arrogance for his cause a moment ago, Kearny was now lying unconscious but still alive. Sol had requested he be Sealed last, so he had not yet been *Red penned*.

Kneeling over top of the man who terrorized hundreds of thousands over the last decade was Commander Owen Daily. Daily was second in command of the Wave Three ground operation. Like Chander and Logan from the Ministry of Retribution, he was a Reader. Cmdr. Daily reached down into the cargo pocket on his fatigue pants. He pulled out a glove and slipped it on. It was a Seal glove.

While sliding the glove on, the last "Red Pen" call went out. That meant all Kearny's men and women who had allied themselves to the cultic group of terrorists, were now dead. Kearny was the only one left alive. But not for long…he was moments away from being "Sealed".

Six soldiers gathered around Kearny and held his head, arms and legs. Daily's helmet-cam processed the image of Kearny lying on the ground and streamed it back live to the Command Center. The Command Center was filled with solemn silence. The Wave 3 feed on screen was still filling the center image. And now, the live shot of Kearny was all anyone in the room could see.

Sol, Takanaka, the Inoculant Team, and the entire room was holding its breath. There was no question of the outcome at this point. An evil man was about to die in front of them. But each person watching was mesmerized. Brought to a place of pensiveness about the fate of Jonas Kearny the killer, rapist, slave-trader who hated a world that hated him back for his destructive crimes. The audio feed from Commander Daily's helmet-cam was coming in now. Kearny was waking up as Cmdr. Daily reported.

"The mark is regaining consciousness now General."

Daily had his orders. Update The General as he advanced through the Sealing protocol.

Kearny was awake now.

Kearny had never seen Daily before, and Daily had only seen images of Jonas Kearny. Kearny slurred something. Something in Africanas. The Command Center heard Kearny's weak attempt at defiance, *"Die Westerse wêreld en haar geld is evil. Long live Geld Kwaad."*

Confused in his thoughts he rolled his words and spoke part Africanas and partly the global tongue. He was saying something like, *'The western world and her money are evil. Long live Geld Kwaad.'*

Commander Daily looked straight in the face of Kearny. And placed his gloved fingers on Kearny's neck.

"Are you Jonas Kearny?"

"No!" Kearny lied.

"Are you the leader of the Geld Kwaad terrorist group and responsible for the capture, torture, abuse, and killing of thousands of men, women, and children?"

Kearny might have hated money for the disparity it caused in Namibia, but he certainly loved himself. A smug smile appeared on his face. Kearny couldn't resist the challenge. Terrorizing others was the obsessive, sociopathic pursuit that defined his life. Twisted though it was beyond all comprehension, he was proud of that work. Kearny was not only a sociopath but a profound megalomaniac. He defiantly answered Daily.

"Yes!"

Daily didn't need to tap into much of his Reader skills to Seal this one. The glove corroborated the truth of Kearny's arrogant confession and released a dose of quantum dots.

The soldiers held Kearny. The optogenetic bursts were quick to their mark. The image of the dying Kearny's face remained on screen in the Command Center. And not one of the people watching that scene, not Sol, the General, Daily, or any of the operatives, would have wanted to see the acts of terror that passed through Kearny's mind. Acts that he himself committed. They would be the last images Kearny would see as he transitioned. The darkest crimes one could ever imagine to be committed against another human. 13 seconds had elapsed on the Command Center mission timer. It was done. Vice-Commander Daily looked up and announced. "He's dead sir."

The Commander remained professional, but he clearly displayed a sense of relief at having the mission completed.

"General." Commander Daily stood and saluted sharply. "I am happy to report. All *Geld Kwaad* members have been transitioned. The leader, Jonas Kearny has been Sealed. I am even happier to report General Takanaka, all 180 children have been rescued alive. The children and the troops are ready for extraction."

"Thank you Commander."

General Takanaka turned around to face the Mission Control personnel. He announced, "Mission Accomplished. Let's get those children processed so they can go home."

This was how situations like this would be handled from now on with Sol as King of the World. If Sol saw the need to overcome evil, he would put the operation in motion. Terrorists would no longer hold people in fear and paralyze helpless nations by their terrors. Sol would not stand for it and General Takanaka was always ready to meet the next threat with a forceful and crippling mission.

Sol left the Command Center. He had plenty to bring to the next Great Assembly, which was just over a day away.

We're Not Gonna Take It Anymore

The World Counsel Plaza was filled to capacity. Sol had no idea how his address, being watched globally, would be received in Africa. The sheer scale and magnitude of his experiences there had irrevocable impact on the world and the country. Connecting to this region from the stage of the World Counsel Plaza, might not be the same as it was in New York at his last address. Sol worked to remind himself that people are the same everywhere. The only thing different about the address today was the faces. The sea of people, mostly Namibian faces, filled the square and lined the banks of the Plaza. Like in any country, the plaza was spotted with others who weren't from the region but whose home was here in Namibia, the diverse fashions and bright colored clothing in the crowd made for an eye-catching contrast.

The Plaza Sol was about to address in person was full, as was every plaza at the other 7 World Counsel Centers. For this address, Sol had commissioned one of the world's greatest bands, *Clever Ruse*, to play an opening set. Today was a celebration and the music brought the event up to another level. Those standing in the plazas and those watching the Stream live knew what to expect. What to expect that is, except for the edicts Sol would bring. It had only taken one month and the non-stop analysis by DBN and other media carriers to bring society to an understanding of what to expect at the monthly Great Assemblies.

The King would greet the crowds and then offer a brief update of recent enhancements under his hand, or situations of import, before announcing his edicts. Today however, because of the victorious rescue of the 180 Namibian school children, Sol, Ahmed, and a number of the Namibian Delegates, brought one of the world's most popular Rock Bands, *Clever Ruse,* in to make this day's address a celebration. All the world was rejoicing at the magnificent news of the Geld Kwaad's welcome end…and at the decisive act of justice led by Sol and Takanaka. The terrorist group had been completely neutralized. Now every one of the captured children was rescued and on their way back to their families and village.

Clever Ruse filled the air with the final song in their pre-address set. A collaboration that perfectly punctuated the amazing victory over the terrorists. A rock anthem that was a creation of the legendary Dee Snider…*'We're Not Gonna Take It.'* After a precedent setting rescue of innocent children and the destruction of an entire terrorist Goliath, Clever Ruse lit up the Plaza with a message to any who would challenge the world's freedom and try to invoke fear through acts of terror.

The holograph beams lit the Plazas. The crowd all knew the song. Some sang along as they bobbed their heads to the chorus. As the chorus swelled throughout the WCC plazas Sol realized he rather enjoyed having music to enjoy with the crowds before he brought his address and edicts. The band paused and the crowds kept going acapella. The defiant anthem filled the plazas.

We're not gonna take it…We're not gonna take it…We're not gonna take it… anymoooore….

No music now, just the voices of hundreds of thousands of Participants singing along…in Windhoek and across the world. This is what it meant to be a Participant. Joining together not just to sing a teen rebellion anthem that originated 60 years ago. But joining together to make the world a better place. Amplifying unity, justice, and the human will to dismantle all nefarious forces that oppose safety in our world. Being unified in the goal to have a better world and unified in the victory over terror. After several rounds of the acapella rock anthem, the holograph beams throughout the plazas went black. The crowd fell silent. The moment changed.

The 200-foot screen at the back of the stage flickered. A deep voice took over the air. The holograph beams from the granite floor of the plaza began flickering as well. Today there was an announcer who began to narrate the event.

"We're not gonna take it anymore."

The stage screen and holographs flashed bright, the media screen *chime* connected the audience to the video presentation on screen. The image showed military helicopters in flight. The narrator continued,

"Just over 24 hours ago, General Togo Takanaka of the Global Military Unit, commanded a multi-phase operation aimed at neutralizing the African terrorist group Geld Kwaad and rescuing 180 school children who had been taken captive. Children who, like many before them, would be forced into military service to the Geld Kwaad and forced to be wives to members of the ultra-fundamentalist terror organization."

The images brought much of the story. Takanaka had agreed to let it be told. And the Participants of the world needed to see it…at least the edited version.

The world watching the Address saw the choppers fire missiles at approaching GK scouts. The GK stopped and fired at the choppers. The choppers spiralled out of the sky and smashed into the Namibian desert. The narration continued with a tribute to the nine soldiers who were on the remotely flown helicopters…

"The operation could not have been a success if not for the 9 generous soldiers who agreed to serve in both life and in death. We owe a debt of gratitude to them and their families. These men did not die on this mission. They proudly lent the Global Military Unit their remains for this mission. They were proud servicemen who, before dying, enrolled in the 'Service in Life and Death Program'. It is because of these sacrificial men that the operation could succeed."

Images fed through the system displayed the looting of the choppers and the mocking of the dead soldiers by the GK patrol group as they cut the "dead soldiers" out of their seats.

"The terrorists believed they had succeeded in their attack on the GMU choppers. They returned victorious to the Geld Kwaad camp."

The crowds watching saw images of the scout convoy returning to camp and unload their booty and the dead GMU soldiers from their Landrovers. The narrator explained further.

"But General Takanaka and the GMU had more for the terrorists than they expected. The mission successfully incapacitated the terrorists by dispersing a potent inoculant. Rendering the terrorists unconscious. The entire Geld Kwaad group fell in the place they stood...never to wake again to heap terror on our World."

Viewers participating in the Great Assembly saw the bodies of men and women fall lifelessly to the ground. Although they were not dead yet, they looked dead. The narrator unfolded the story further.

"The GK camp was then successfully taken by the GMU Joint Task Force. Upon taking the camp and neutralizing the entire Geld Kwaad terror group, every child, who had been taken from their school in Namibia to be a Geld Kwaad hostage, was safely rescued."

Images filling the holo-beams above the Participant's heads dramatized the moment. The charging ground troops who were heading in on the 3rd Wave captured the gaze of the audience. The intense effort shown in the faces of the sprinting soldiers inspired the crowd. The stream cut to images of dead GK members on the ground contrasted with children just waking up after being administered the antidote. The hugging of soldiers, the wiping away of tears, the telling of children that they would be going home soon.

The Stream images faded to the scene of Commander Daily's mission report to his General. When the crowds heard it they cheered wildly…Daily saluted and announced,

"I am happy to report…all 180 children have been rescued alive. The children and the troops are ready for extraction."

The narrator continued extollingly. Casting his voice in the tones of an announcer welcoming the championship NFL team to the field after winning the Superbowl.

"Thank you General Takanaka and troops for showing us and the terrorists that it is true. "We're not gonna take it anymore."

The holo-beams throughout the World Counsel Centers blasted virtual fireworks into the sky. Even in the noon light with an overcast sky, the fireworks dazzled the crowd. Then the screen onstage and the holo-beams went blank. Sol began walking on stage. The screen and holo-beams flickered blue. Sol's image filled the place. The African audience was excited to see the King in person. Watching on Media screens and mobile devices as they had for Sol's first address was not nearly the same as having the King there in person.

Sol smiled warmly at the kind welcome. He felt the excitement. What was not to be excited about? He was excited himself. After the dramatic rescue he was involved in over the past days, it was a privilege to be able to stand in front of the world and celebrate with them. The energy coming from the mass of people in the World Counsel Plaza warmed the stage. Sol had just talked to Ell before getting to the Namibian WCC. She was as excited as he at the news of the amazing rescue. Ell couldn't wait for Sol to get home though. He had been in Namibia for almost a week now. She told him she would be watching the Stream of his address.

The crowd settled as Sol stepped in front of the podium. Media tagged him as a guy who had nothing to hide because he didn't seem to be inclined to stand behind the podium.

"Welcome!..." Sol paused and smiled over the engaged crowd.

"It is a pleasure to be here with you today. You've all seen the fantastic success of our Global Military Unit's rescue operation in Namibia. I am grateful to have General Takanaka to lead these operations. And comforted knowing he is here for our safety if we have need to plan future operations!"

The masses cheered. Sol waved them silent after a moment. Celebrations were important but the edicts he was bringing today would alter the Namibian future as well as that of the world. He was ready to deliver them.

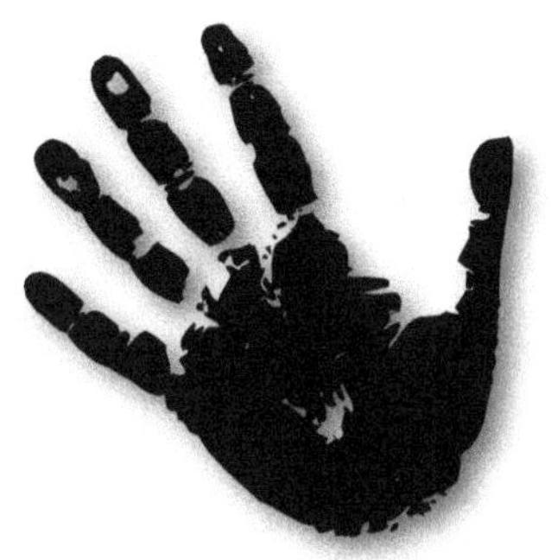

THE LAWS OF A WISE AND REASONED KING

The Infrastructure for Change is Already in Place

"**B**efore I bring you some of the edicts that will be passed into law today, I just want to bring you an update. Speaking of not taking it anymore, at the last Great Assembly it was made law that certain individuals who intentionally harm society, would not be allowed to continue as part of our global society. I want to be up front with you. I know some of those who are Sealed will be missed by family and friends. Yet the peace that has started to flood into society where fear and concern for the physical, psychological, and sexual safety of many persons use to reside, is transcendent. As we see the reduction of violent and destructive people in this world we are seeing a dramatic rise in the sense of safety, security and quality of life for those most affected by them. I am grateful to our Minister of Retribution, Tomer Cohen, whom you met at the address last month."

The images on the Media Screens and holo-beams began flashing images of the Ministry of Retribution offices. The viewers saw Readers working on cases, they saw public parks, pools, and playgrounds that testified to the refreshed sense of safety and comfort in light of the reduced threat of harm that resulted from the Ministry of Retribution's work. Sol's words carried a weight of warmth with compassion.

"Our Readers who have been working hard for the Ministry, have been very productive in the past month. So far to date, Ministry of Retribution Teams have stopped hundreds of pedophiles across the globe from ever harming a child again. The effect on the reduction in child pornography has also been significant. On average an active pedophile abuses up to 117 children over the course of their lifetime. That means we have protected thousands of children from being abused by these men. If you would like to keep up on the progress of the reduction of this harmful sector of society, please go to my website or Meta page. There you will see how many of the world's worst offenders have been Sealed. While there you might want to take a look at our graphic on how the optogenetics of the Seal glove works in concert with the skills of the Reader. Through this effort the Ministry of Retribution is having great success."

Sol continued with his brief report to the patient crowd. They wanted to hear how the law had played out so far. And the audience was quite enthused after hearing how productive Sol had been.

"Besides transitioning hundreds of pedophiles there have been several Sealings of senior-abusers, wife-beaters, home-invaders, and violent rapists as well. These people who have been stains on society will no longer afflict our society or harm our children. Thanks for your support of this edict. I understand how challenging it can be to accept we are taking the life of another human. After consultation with the Pope, it was agreed there is no other way to stop the downward spiral of atrocities that continue to plague society. When I visited with the Pope last month, she spoke wisely in saying…

> *'Sol, Justice is a Godly attribute. Justice has the power to reform a people while vengeance reaps malice. It becomes vengeance if it draws inspiration from anger and hatred. True Justice is in a realm of its own, delivering consequences for a wrong aside from anger or vengeance. Justice is inspired of Justice itself.'—Pope Caroline*

The idea that the people of the world were Participants and no longer just citizens was settling into culture. They seemed eager to step past the entrenched apathy of previous years and actually become the architects of the world they all wanted to see. Believing a cultural shift was well in motion, Sol continued to share his edicts that would continue to foster that shift.

"Before I tell you the edicts that will be implemented today. I just want to put forth an invitation.

"If you feel there is an edict or a law that will improve our world, please post it on the Meta page. The page will be updated daily. By posting your suggested edicts and laws, I will be able to draw from the substantial and brilliant pool of thought that is available across the globe. It doesn't matter if you are in Eastern Russia, or if you are right here with us in Africa, your thoughts will be shared with all of us. And together, we will discover the best ways in which to make this world the Utopia we want. We will move towards a world that is not only for the people but a world that is by the people."

The **King of the World Meta** page popped up on the screen on stage. The image flashed brightly to fill the holo-beams across the plaza. Sol wanted access for everyone to be effortless. He reached into his pocket and pulled out his mobile device. The ubiquitous device was really a technological enigma. It had been in the hands of users, in its nascent low-tech form, since 1994. And it grew to be the superfluous device that ran the lives of billions of users. In its 5 decades of existence in the human-computer interface realm, the Super-phone had successfully fought off every device and product that tried to dethrone it as the only piece of technology anyone will ever need. Tablets and Folios were the closest second when it came to portable media devices. But they were just a little too large of a device to topple the Super-phone. Size mattered to Participants who wanted to stay continually connected to the cyber-sphere that gave them so much. And the handheld device was just the right size and had been an instant hit for that reason when it began to proliferate as the Touch Screen iPhone in the early 2000's.

The fad of wearable computers that tried to push out the handheld device didn't last long. People felt that by having their device on their head, face, or on their wrist, the device had a measure of control over them. That sense of being controlled by the device was a touch too consuming. Participants felt like the device had more control of them than they were comfortable giving it.

The reality was that most of the world's Participants were controlled by their handheld devices anyway. No one would live without theirs. The handheld was not going anywhere.

When Sol pulled his Device out of his pocket the majority of Participants were unable to resist the urge to reach for their own mobile device. He continued with his invitation for citizens to connect by posting their comments, edicts, and law ideas on the King of the World page.

"So if you take a look at your Device right now, you'll see a notification for a new app that has been sent to your device."

The new app had been sent to every device as Sol was introducing it.

"All you have to do is opt in by accepting the app's invitation and you will be one touch away from sending us your laws and edicts."

Every device in every pocket or purse chimed and vibrated. The shuffle for the remainder of users to reach for their device was automatic. The crowd collectively tilted their heads down to see the new *"King's Advisor App"* that was just now automatically loaded onto every device.

Looking at a sea of Participants thumbing away on their devices to give approval to the app, Sol was surprised at the immediacy with which his audience responded to his invitation. There was no doubt how widely Sol's reach was going with the Great Assembly address when the app registration update popped up on the screen. The Meta page hadn't even been launched yet but showed a dramatic adoption by viewers of Sol's address all over the world.

The updated Global map that was on the holo-beams in the Plazas began to populate. The opaque colors of the world map became luminescent within seconds. Every region of the globe was quickly dotted with a whelming density of registrants. The citizens once affected by apathy, were beginning to become the Participants they had the right to be. The number of subscribers seen at the bottom of the screen seconds ago rocketed from the 32000 to 6.7 billion. It took literally seconds for the number to grow to astronomical proportions. And as Sol regained the attention of his live audience, the number continued to climb. Participants wanted to be part of what Sol was doing. And the *King's Advisor* would be a helpful vehicle for them to do so.

"Thank you for your support of the *King's Advisor* interactive app. I look forward to hearing from you in the coming weeks and months. Now today, I will be setting several edicts into motion. As with each of the laws and edicts I bring to the Great Assembly, the infrastructure for these changes is already in place."

Wisdom In A Multitude Of Counsel

Sol paused. He was sensitive to the Participants standing in front of him. Many of them would be wondering if there were enough resources and manpower to enact a new law. Especially with the sweeping reforms Sol would be introducing.

Comfortably chatting with everyone watching, as if he were having a coffee with them at his Saturday coffee spot in downtown Seattle, he stepped to the left side of the stage. Getting closer to the crowd a few feet below the stage in the Plaza, Sol saw the attentive faces brighten as he neared. These people wanted to be near the King. Addressing the entire world could be quite sterile. So, Sol intuitively drew in a small group of attendees who were near the stage. They were a handful of seniors standing amid several professionals who decided to get in on the Great Assembly on this cloudy Saturday morning in Namibia. Sol closed himself off to the rest of the crowd slightly as he established an intimate setting, focusing on a small section of the crowd below. A setting that would feel as close as it could in front of billions of people.

Sol stepped in to make the announcement.

"The first law I would like to bring to you today is intended to help us all make better decisions. In stepping through this journey we call life, we are all faced with many choices and therefore decisions to be made. Decisions can be from the simple and mundane that have little effect on our personal health, wealth, and happiness to the very complex and overwhelming that stand to impact one's health, wealth, and overall happiness to a great degree.

"As a young man I was afforded the opportunity on two occasions to take counsel from an older friend while making some life-changing decisions. The first was the occasion of choosing my education in University. I felt strongly I wanted to go into the field of commerce. I had my reasons, and it seemed to be the best choice for me at the time. Then I spent an hour or two chatting with Keaton Janvier. He's gone now, but this much older friend helped me make some important decisions. Once we parted company and I had a few moments to think about his words and questions, I realized that many of the things he shared with me had me rethinking my choice for Finance and Administration. Had it not been for the chat with that slightly older friend, I might not have found the career that proved to be exactly the right fit for me.

"Ell and I have continued to tap into the wisdom of people like Keaton Janvier to gather insight into issues or opportunities when we have an important decision to make. And the value of that is immeasurable. I know many people who have benefited from sitting with wise counsel for a brief chat before making a tough choice. And I know many who have wished they had done so before jumping into a life altering decision. Better decisions is what this edict is about. You and I, all of us, have a chance to make any choice we want in this life. I am for choice. But if we make a poor choice, it is often one that has negative effects in its wake. Stress, unhappiness, financial hardship, relationship woes, and impacts on those closest to us...even on society as a whole. All of these are all too often the result of poor choices. We have forgotten the philosophy of the ancients that saw there is wisdom in a multitude of counsel. So today, I am proclaiming one of the most tangential yet possibly most progressive laws that we will see. It is the ***Multitude of Counsel Law.***

There is wisdom in a multitude of counsel. If you are faced with making a possible life altering decision such as purchasing a home, heading off to college, changing careers, getting married or divorced, signing a loan for a business or new car...I am sure you will be fully intending to make the best decision you can...the best decision for you. With wise counsel from a few trusted individuals, we will all be less likely to make a decision that will cause distress, unhappiness, or regret for the individual and his or her affected circles of friends, families, and coworkers. Consulting with certain Elders will bring us all a better chance at making good decisions. To be happier, healthier, more prosperous, and more fulfilled. Quite simply friends, making better decisions will make us better people and it will make for a better world. Not just for you alone but for all of us. Because our decisions and fallout or benefits from them will always affect more than just oneself. Any decision one makes may only affect one or two others, but it may also effect the entire world."

Society Didn't Know They Could Ask Until Now

Ahmed was waiting for his cue. He had gotten to know Sol's rhythm pretty well. Sol would wax briefly about the reasoning behind the edict, take note of the buy-in of the crowd by their attentiveness and body language, then deliver the edict and be ready to seal it with the King's Scribe on the Folio. The cadence was perfect. It was a knack Sol had. Naturally delivering just the right information, just enough of it, and for just long enough.

Ahmed began making his way on stage. Sol picked up on his movement.

"Ah good…here is Ahmed. Thank you for taking care of this Ahmed"

Ahmed smiled as he made the last few steps to his place next to the Speaker's Podium. Sol continued addressing the world.

"In the interest of aiding all people everywhere in making informed decisions rather than risking being fraught with regrets, I proclaim the *Multitude of Counsel Law*. You can read the entire law on our website or Meta page, but for now, it can be explained thus:

"The Multitude of Counsel law builds on the fact that there is wisdom in a multitude of counsel. One is now compelled under this law to seek the counsel of three persons when they are faced with making a major decision. That refers to a decision that has the potential to affect a person's life in harmful or negative ways almost as much as it might affect their life in positive or beneficial ways. This law is based on the fact that with age, the human brain undergoes subtle yet profound transformations. While processing speed might diminish, decades of accumulated life experiences foster a deeper understanding of the world. These rich experiences, coupled with a lifetime of learning and emotional growth, can lead to a unique form of wisdom. As individuals mature, they often develop a greater capacity for introspection, empathy, and emotional regulation. This allows for a more nuanced and considered approach to decision-making, informed by a broader perspective and a deeper understanding of human nature. While wisdom is not solely a product of age, the years spent navigating life's challenges and joys can cultivate a profound sense of understanding and a capacity for navigating complexity with grace and insight."

Sol could see the furrows on the faces of many in the Plaza. Of course, they were inquisitive about this law and if it made sense. But the more Sol spoke, the more it made sense. Who of them hadn't made a questionable decision in their life? Who of them might have made a better decision if they had consulted persons wiser than themselves to offer insight in making a decision? Sol continued...

"Therefore, we will have available for each Participant of our World, a stable of volunteers. These Life Consultants will be your sounding board. They will chat openly with you about the options and decision you are faced with. They will dialogue with you for an hour or so. The hour they spend is not to compel you in making your decision. Rather, they will simply discuss the situation with you. Hearing your thoughts and sharing theirs. Your consults can take place through digital medium or in person making conformity to the law easy and accessible.

"If for instance you are planning to have a child, to change careers, to get married or divorced, buy a house, or take out a loan, or choose to get a cosmetic surgery, you can only be approved to go ahead after consulting with three consultants. Of course, we all have people of the wisdom age in our lives. People that we respect and value their opinions and input. So, you are welcome to spend time consulting them instead of the appointed consultant volunteers. All you need to do is display the record of your visits with the consultants and you will be approved to make your decision. Each of us will stand a much better chance of making an informed decision rather than a decision that is completely based out of one's own internal resources, drives, emotions, and motives.

"If for instance, you are getting a loan to start a business, once you present the loans officer with *The Multitude of Counsel* document signed by your three consultants stating you have engaged in healthy dialogue regarding the decision, you can then be approved for the loan. So, in the interest of enhancing the decisions we make, it is my privilege to put into place *The Multitude of Counsel Law*. Individuals are obligated to consult with three advisors over the age of 50 before making any decision with significant potential consequences."

Ahmed had stepped forward from the Speaker's Podium. He reached the Folio forward. The edict to be sealed appeared on the massive screen behind the two men dotting the ocean-like stage as well as in every hologram through the Plaza and every media device that was streaming the address. The glowing document pulsated as it waited to be pressed by the hand of the King.

The Folio had fast become an indispensable tool for Sol. Without the King's Scribe assessing the status of the King while sealing an edict, Sol might feel…well… he might feel there were no checks and balances. The World Counsel Delegates had given Sol the unbridled power and it was only his decision that mattered. Sol was slowly getting use to the fact that he could make any changes to anything anytime he wanted. In the car, on this stage, in his home…as long as the King's Scribe affirmed the edict then it would be done. Sol had always questioned the axiom that absolute power corrupts. And now, in his moment of absolute power Sol was prepared to challenge what many thought was an unquestionable concept related to power.

Sol believed that corruption of one who is in power can only take hold if he or she in power is inclined toward corruption before taking power. And in that, Sol fully expected that he and corruption would not be meeting while he was the King. He had not found that inclination in himself thus far in life so he fully expected he would not see it while he was King…Corruption would not overtake Sol regardless of the suggestions of the varied critics who prompt many to wonder, "*When will Sol abuse or misuse his power?*"

The *Multitude of Counsel* groundbreaking reform was one that gave all people power. Power to make sound decisions by taking time to consult with reasonable women and men before making a choice that could possibly have a deep impact on one's life.

The sealed edict with Sol's glowing red handprint in the background faded from the holographs as Sol left the Folio in Ahmed's trusted hands.

Then he moved into delivering the other edicts he had prepared for today. It was a big day. A lot was going to change. And for this King…standing before the world…it was exhilarating to be able to make the changes that most of society didn't know they could ask for until now.

Re-Freedom of Religion Law

"I spoke earlier of my consult with the Pope." Sol reminded his audience, "It was a marvellously productive afternoon that day. It was in consult with her and other world religious leaders that I have established the *Re-Freedom of Religion Law.*"

"Re-Freedom of Religion," the crowd was thinking. *"We've had freedom of religion for over a century already. What kind of change could Sol be talking about?"*

All through history religious culture has not tolerated sweeping social change or even subtle shifts well. But Pope Caroline was indeed a non-classical leader of healing reform in the Catholicism of this era. In Pontifex Maxima Caroline, the Roman Catholic Church finally had a visionary who built upon the reforms initiated by her predecessors, guiding the Church towards a more inclusive and just future. Reversing the decision on some of the historical dogma, and traditional church positions where they had continued in error for centuries. Spiritual Leader Caroline, Head of the World's Richest religious organization, had wisely abandoned many traditional prescriptions for alleged "righteous standing," such as, rules against the marriage of priests, contraception, homosexuality, and the death penalty.

Catholicism had finally stepped into the 21st century. No longer being the institution known for rigid and blind belief. Beliefs that had been based on millennia of erroneous literal interpretation of the Scriptures.

The shrinking Catholic Church was not the only religious group that indoctrinated the masses with traditional beliefs resulting in brainwashing. Religious myopia was prevalent in most major organized religions. Hindu, Muslim, Buddhist, Protestant and Catholic Christianity...Religions that were intended to derive only good, yet were infused by men with the unsavoriness of power and control aimed at the adherents and all who might look to the religion for guidance. It was brainwashing by repeating unchallenged tenets and doctrine that had for centuries been imposed upon adherents. And a great many of them began hearing the teaching from a very young age. Children who are raised in the "faith" or "church" and are not given the opportunity to explore other views until well into their teen years or adult life.

As for the Catholic Church...she had survived a shift toward logo-centrism. Placing logic closer to the front of her teachings allowed reason and investigation of ideas and beliefs to become the order of the day. Catholicism under Pope Caroline, was now less the archaic brand of religion that had propagated superstitious beliefs and forced its adherents to come into line with those beliefs for millennia.

In discussions with the Pope, Sol and Caroline both agreed that religion has been a misapplied tool. The result had hampered analytical free thought. After Sol shared a letter with Pope Caroline he recently received, talking about yet another case of spiritual and physical abuses at the hands of religion, there was little doubt in either of their minds that Sol's *Re-Freedom of Religion Law* would be timely. This law was designed to protect the people and to bring religion back to the place it was intended to be. A social structure, supportive and non-judgmental, that encouraged open-minded conversation and free thought about all things religious.

Sol would seal the *Re-Freedom of Religion Law* in his address today. Doing so would set the stage for a generation of seekers who would be less likely to be saddled with all the religious baggage and brainwashing of the generations before them. Offering adherents and Participants a chance to resist unwitting submission to adopting second-hand beliefs passed down from forebears.

Freedom of religion had defined the generations of the past century and a half. Now it was time to enhance that. The *Re-Freedom of Religion Law* would require any religious gathering where instruction took place, to bring in a scholar with an opposing view to what is being taught. In this way, people would truly be free to make a choice in what they would believe instead of being confined to the singular view of their religious group, organization, or leader.

Sol spoke wisely to the crowds about his edict.

"Our world has enjoyed complete freedom of religion in almost all regions for many decades. And that I believe is a good thing. Yet many experiences of 'religious brainwashing', have taken place all throughout history. Constitutions in many nations and regions allow for the inalienable right for one to practice and observe any religion they choose. And that has long been well received across the world. It is time however that we improve upon it with the *Re-Freedom of Religion Law.*"

The masses were starting to get a little concerned. Making laws about religion was risky. How could Sol bring something better to a well-accepted freedom that much of the world already had? In his next statements he put the crowds at ease.

"In its simplest form not much will change for those participating in a religious gathering. People will still gather in religious settings, groups, congregations, and institutions as they have before. That has been and will continue to be completely acceptable. But when people gather for religious instruction of any type, under the *Re-Freedom of Religion Law*, we will appoint a religious adversary to be part of the gathering. This is not unheard of in our history. There was an ancient sect of Hebraic religious groups who used a similar format.

"When designing religious doctrine, they would appoint a man who came to be known as "*The Satan*". The language used to name this person , "*ha sawtawn,*" simply meant a human adversary. It was his job to put a contrary view in front of the adherents of a religious gathering. In this way the group was insulated from making poor doctrinal choices. Participants would entertain another possible interpretation or meaning for the teachings that were shared from their ancient texts. Listeners would be given a choice as to what to believe about a passage, text, or teaching that came from the teacher, priest, rabbi, pastor, imam, or leader. In that way religious dogmatism and brainwashing were avoided. And in this way, for our Globe today, religious dogmatism and brainwashing will be less likely."

Sol paused as he saw the sense of this new edict setting into the Participants in the audience.

"So today, the law I am implementing requires any religious group that gathers to hear instruction, teaching, or information, to have the Religious Adversary deliver counterpoints and a contrary view to what the group is being taught. Adherents will be privileged to continue to hear the doctrines and teachings of their preferred faith or religion, but they are also privileged to hear the other side of the story. I offer only one example to share how important it is to explore opposing interpretations of religious content.

You may have heard the term *"Spare the rod spoil the child."* This is a well known phrase that for millennia, has been seen by some to infer one must discipline their child with a rod of sorts, in order to keep that child on the straight and narrow path…saving them from destruction.

A contrary understanding of that statement is found in learning what in fact is "**the rod**". The most ancient hearer of that term understood it differently. And now the most current biblical and linguistic scholars have shown "the rod" to be a reference to the good and sound teachings of the sacred texts. Thus inferring, if we do not teach our children good and sound things as they develop, we may see them find paths to their harm or destruction.

"Friends, our freedom of thought is too precious to sit under instruction that may only guide our thinking to one possible conclusion on a matter. Freedom of religion means freedom to choose what one believes by hearing the options for understanding a doctrine or teaching. We all deserve to hear the other side of the story so we can make a decision about what to believe rather than the decision being made for us. The evidence of history shows the perils of isolated religious instruction. In the absence of an opposing view to what we are told to believe or to what we already believe, we are voluntarily submitting ourselves and our children to effective brainwashing.

"It is for those reasons that today, the *Re-Freedom of Religion Law* is put in place. Because when it comes to religious beliefs, true freedom does not come in a vacuum of thought."

Sol peeked over his shoulder at Ahmed. He was a half-step away this time. Ahmed held the folio to the front of Sol and all the world saw the edict Sol was about to seal. Pressing his hand against the Folio turned the imprint red.

Sol pronounced, "I proclaim this day the ***Re-Freedom of Religion Law.*** A law where all men and women who gather to worship or to learn religious teachings, will be given another point of view when a religious teaching or doctrine is being taught to them."

The crowd loved it. In a country that one time was being fractured and fragmented under the fallout of religious power struggles and disputes, Namibia was the perfect World Counsel Center site to deliver this edict. The sharp turns from the moderate and reasonable to extremism had plagued parts of Namibia in past decades. The crowd here in Windhoek had a sense of rejoicing that was palpable…a rejoicing that was felt even more so than in some of the other regions of the world where the Stream was being watched. The boisterous clapping and shrill whistles carried a vibrant sense of affirmation for Sol. And he was ready to move on quickly with his last two edicts of this address. Both would be shared today with the world and implemented over the next weeks and months after. And both edicts involved elements that affected people the most…human life and money.

Redistribution of Wealth

Sol took a sip of his water. The applause had stopped, and the crowd was waiting for the next edict. He was still trying to decide how much he should go on about the next edict. How much should he explain the reasoning and try to articulate why it was the best thing to do if we want a better world, a fairer world? Sol reasoned it was best to leave the in-depth explanations for the Meta page, web site, and DBN commentators who would discuss the entire address during the following week's recap.

The Address resumed, "We have always worked hard for our money. I am no different than you. I think in all the years I have lived and worked in this society there are two things people wish someone would seriously do something about. Two things that are certainties in life. You all know what they are are...." Sol paused. He had the crowd back. They were right with him again. They were silent. Knowing what was going to come from him next.

"...death and taxes."

Eyes widened in the crowd and Sol formed his next words thoughtfully. "Now, I wish I could do something about the first of those, death. But I am afraid I have no power to control death. It will come to each of us and that is all I have to say about that for now."

Sol had devised some solutions to the dilemma of death. But was not intending to deliver the *Right to Choose Life or Death Law* today at this Great Assembly. He had sealed the edict from his home. Although it would not be shared from his stage today, it was an exciting program affirming people were responsible for their own life. Under the *Right to Choose Life or Death Law* every person would be responsible for their own death if they chose. As long as the manner in which a person chose to die did not harm anyone else, it was completely acceptable for a person to decide, while having a sound mind and being in compliance with the *Multitude of Counsel Law*, to terminate their own life. Today though, Sol was facing the injustice of unfair taxation head on.

"But what about taxes?…" Sol asked.

"The only ones who love them, who are addicted to them, is government. You folks however might not be so happy about paying them. I know I certainly am not.

"The average income tax rate across the globe is 28.9%. Now I would love to tell you that I could get rid of taxes all together and we would still have all the infrastructure and services that we need to run this world. But we cannot do that. Yes, that might seem like a wonderful utopia to some but our systems and all that we know to keep this place running, would soon disintegrate. So, here's the bad news."

Sol saw the hope in the eyes of the crowd. Many musing that this might be the day when taxes are removed from society once and for all. So, Sol was quick to address the subdued hope of the masses and broke the news to them…

"Taxes will not be removed."

The hopeful crowd was somewhat deflated. They must have thought Sol was a Messiah to think he was going to bring in peace and remove taxes. But they stayed with him to hear him out.

"Here's the good news. Certain tax deductions will be removed. Such deductions as charitable donations to religious institutions will no longer be allowed. Donations to political parties will no longer be counted as a tax deduction. And there are others that will be set in place as this reformed method of taxation is implemented.

"I would like to say though. As of one month from today, your burden will be lighter. The simple solution to taxation has often been floated that we should just have a single income tax number, and everyone would pay that. No exemptions, no tax breaks, no corporate loopholes. Just one Global Simplified Tax.

"The present system of taxation is broken, and it has been for a long time. So I don't give you any guarantees this new method is without its difficulties. Finding a perfect taxation system in beyond complex in a legacy system of distorted taxation laws. The system I am implementing is a new beginning for taxation. It will be unfavourable to some…likely to the richest among us…but it will be the greatest good for the greatest number.

"At the implementation of this new law our reformed tax system will have every person paying the same percentage on their income. If you earn money…of any kind or in any way, from the largest earners to the smallest tax paying individual, you will pay the same amount of tax percentage as the next guy. There will be one flat tax. 10.1%. Each of us, even me, will pay that personal tax amount on every penny we take as income. Simple is always better. Complex taxation systems such as are in place all over the world are expensive ones.

Coupled with that 10.1% income tax is a flat consumer tax. From movies to groceries, to gifts, to gas, to booze…everything we purchase will no longer have a different or varied tax amount. Everything that we do and use, be they services or goods, will be imposed with a 4% tax. If you spend a million dollars a year or you spend a hundred dollars, it is a simple 4% on everything you buy.

"Lastly, there will be no tax breaks, credits, or loopholes. That is just too complex often abused and in fact has ended up costing governments money in the end, which means it costs you money and you pay more taxes. All corporate tax will be set at 13.9%. A great number of billion-dollar corporations have orchestrated their accounts so they pay almost no taxes at all. That ends with this edict. If your business or organization has not been asked to pay taxes up until now, that will change with this reform.

Churches are as much users of services and the infrastructure to society as businesses are. If your church, mosque, synagogue, or charitable organization is making money, it will pay the income tax amount only on any amount it generates as revenue. If the church organization owns property, property tax will be paid on any properties the church holds."

There were a few mixed reactions to the idea. The rather stoic crowd was hard to read on this one. They would have to see the plan in effect for a while before getting excited about it. One thing for sure was that it was definitely different than any taxation system most of the world had seen before. Even though it was no secret that many in government and in society had proposed a tax system such as this. One where everyone pays one flat rate. Clean, uncomplicated, and still able to generate the tax base a complex society needs to survive.

In this part of the world public response to the unfairness found in government had long been unfavorable. But Sol's innovations sounded more fair to the masses here in the hot city of Windhoek than the taxation mechanisms of the past did. There was little disapproval from those in the World Counsel Plaza on this day. Sol added more before the edict was sealed.

"It is time we had a redistribution of wealth. The gaps between the rich and the poor have become extreme. The comfortable middle class, which we will now call the Majority Class, has come close to disappearing. While 92% of the world's wealth is owned by the top 1% of the world's capitalists, politicians, and business moguls, the remainder of us often struggle to enjoy leisure with our money. Therefore, as part of this reformation to the tax rules, there will be a redistribution of wealth.

"CEO's will no longer be privileged to multiple millions of dollars each year as income, while those who are the pillars holding up their companies get a meager wage that merely offers them enough to sustain their lifestyle. I am implementing a five-million-dollar cap on yearly earnings for the heads of the world's largest and richest companies such as mining, shipping, rail companies, tech giants, and multi-nationals. The imbalance in the remuneration paid to those who work as the boots on the ground, and as the wheels in the cog that sustains a successful business, is disparaging. It is time to correct the dramatic equity gap that has only grown wider over the past decades. And I intend to do so in many arenas where disproportionate earnings are given to top management and top performers.

"Speaking of top performers, I would like to talk about salary caps for this subset of our global economy. We all love entertainment and are all entertained by movies, Streaming Shows, and elite sport. It is no secret the millions of dollars paid to actors and professional athletes is driven by many factors. And to address sports specifically, the high salaries for athletes is also a reason for the high-ticket prices we have become accustomed to paying at the turnstile. It is a certainty that many aspiring elite athletes would play their game for a lot less. I have consulted with team owners, Participants, and World Counsel Delegates. After doing so it was concluded that a great number of actors and athletes in the entertainment and professional sport realm are grossly overpaid for the service they provide us. They are simply playing a role or a game for our entertainment. I have decided to change the great disparity in the amount they are remunerated for the work they do.

"As of this month, those accustomed to an exorbitant wage for entertaining the masses by playing a game or performing in other entertainment capacity, will no longer be grotesquely overpaid for their work. Most of them are doing something they love to do. And if they are honest, they admit to being paid ridiculously well. The inequity in this is that many of you today, do work that you don't enjoy at all… and you get paid meager wages. But your work is equally as important, if not more so, to contribute to a successful progressive society. I intend to right this.

"So, with this edict package, professional athletes are among many in the sport and entertainment world who will have a wage cap of 750,000 dollars. The money that would have been paid to them will not go into the pockets of the owners. It will be used to offset ticket prices and to set up programs to help kids engage in the arts, sport, and activity. The sports world is a realm of society that venerates athletes and places them in a position of honor as if they were military heroes. Yet when we take a close look at what they are doing, they are only playing a game as their job. No one deserves to be paid multiple millions of dollars for participating in sports. The money that is normally earned by the ultra-rich owners of sports teams will be redistributed to areas that need it.

"Please be assured though, under this edict if an athlete is good enough and valued enough to land endorsements or sponsors who will pay them well alongside their job as an athlete, then that is fine. That entertainer can go ahead and make as much money as she or he can through other means, but making the extraordinary stacks of cash that have been made by these men and women who are only playing a game is no longer going to continue as of this edict. The inequity in how extravagantly entertainers have been remunerated is seen in gender differences when it comes to income. The irrationality of paying huge salaries to pro athletes and entertainers is amplified in knowing how little the female counterparts in those vocations are paid. Females are paid far less than the males who perform the same or very similar tasks in the sport and entertainment industry. A professional female soccer player is paid far less than a professional male soccer player. And that my friends, is unacceptable on many levels. There are many reasons to redistribute wealth in order to see all levels of society benefit.

"Here's how the new tax numbers break down...

"As part of the redistribution of wealth program, anyone who makes over 10 million dollars a year will be required to give a straight 3.9 percent of that income to the greater good along with the 10.1% personal earnings tax. That money will be pooled by my financial officers and redistributed among those who are in the lowest income brackets.

"In the view of many, it is unfair for individuals to make more money than they could spend in ten lifetimes. It is from this moment onward, the privilege of those with the greatest wealth is to provide a portion of that wealth in order to make life better for those who are not in such an advantageous position.

Sol invited Participants to explore the edict specifics further as he wrapped up his announcement on this issue. "There are a number of particulars about each of these edicts and I won't be explaining everything about them here. I suggest you head to our website if would like to examine the particulars of this edict further. The link has been sent to your device as of now."

Heads tilted down once again as the devices flashed and vibrated, alerting their user that the message had arrived. The link would be trending as billions of participants would see where they fell in the new redistribution of wealth system. Would they end up further ahead by being a Participant in the reformed taxation system? All the poorer class would, and most of the Majority class would also end up ahead.

The minor language change Sol had implemented, from "middle class" to "Majority Class," even brought a renewed sense of worth to most of the Participants on earth. Being of "The Majority Class" said one was part of a significant group. As the Majority class it was understood that was the group who truly had the most power in society as majorities tend to have. Whereas to be labelled as "middle class" was a term infused with mediocrity. In many ways that label had affirmed those it identified as just average and would always be so. That label had in some sense predetermined a group as being unlikely to move beyond mediocrity...the "middle class" could have been called the "mediocre class." After all, mediocrity always hovered somewhere around the middle and by definition, "middle" seldom inspired excelling.

As Sol moved to seal his latest edict, he could see how the Majority Class in the Plaza seemed to find relief in hearing wealth would be redistributed in order make life better for the majority. The greatest number of those standing in support of Sol across the world were indeed the "Majority Class". They were not the actors, professional golfers, footballers, baseball players, hockey players or other overpaid and over venerated athletes who may not like this latest edict. An edict that would cut their personal income substantially.

Sol had single handedly decided the intrinsic value to society from athletes playing a game for entertainment, or actors acting in a movie, is a great distance from the actual value society receives. And in many ways, it is far from the value brought to society from teachers, firefighters, doctors, police, military personnel, and other modestly paid jobs and professions. The disparity in financial benefit was insulting and would not continue. Sol's edict was yet another example of his policy to do the greatest good for the greatest number.

Ahmed was next to Sol who promptly sealed the edict. The King's Scribe announced, *"Edict sealed, thank you King Sol."*

As the red glow from the successfully sealed ***Redistribution of Wealth*** edict faded from the Plaza holo-beams, Sol pressed on to the final edict of this landmark Great Assembly.

Voluntary Sterilization Program

"I have given a lot of thought to this final edict of the day. We have been dealing with overpopulation issues in many areas for two decades now. I believe there is a way to begin to curb that. And there will be ancillary issues that are also addressed with this program. I will be sealing into law today the *Voluntary Sterilization Program.*

"Our population is ballooning as it extrapolates year after year. And with overpopulation comes an increase of a great many problems. Economic, social, environmental, health, resource, and land distribution problems. The high estimate for the earth's population carrying capacity is only 16 billion people. We are only a handful of billions away from that now. So, we have to be intentional about a solution that will reverse the journey to overpopulating the earth. Having fewer babies is the only acceptable solution.

"I agree it is unfair to force participants to simply stop reproducing as has been attempted in some parts of the world in our past. So that is why the *Voluntary Sterilization Program* will be a voluntary decision with a monetary benefit. Just as no one is forced to have children so too no one will be forced to sterilization. The *Voluntary Sterilization Program* offers a choice with a benefit. A person will be allowed to choose to become sterile or infertile. And if they make that choice and register for sterilization at one of our clinics, we will deposit a sum of money into their account. It's just that simple.

"There may be some who prefer not to reproduce and add to the world population. So we are offering $500,000 for any who choose to become sterile. Our chemical sterilization process is pain free and is done through IV delivery. Those who choose this, will be compensated for making this choice as well as being a partner in reducing the future strains on the earth…Thus ensuring this rock we call our home, has sustainable room for future generations.

"Choosing sterilization is a major life choice and must be decided on with careful thought. So, if Voluntary Sterilization is for you, you will have to participate in the Multitude of Counsel Program and visit with three consultants prior to showing up at the Sterilization Clinic. Upon completion of the sterilization protocol, $200,000 will be transferred to your G-PAS and $100,000 will be sent to you each year for the following three years."

Sol knew there could be significant backlash from certain pro-life groups. Some people believed a person should never choose to end her or his life, or to sterilize a person preventing them from reproducing. But Sol elevated choice above the beliefs of the entrenched thinkers.

As with any policy reform there would be plenty of critics and commentators speculating on the benefits and detriments of this program. But it was a sound way to ensure society could continue on a healthy growth path…resolve overpopulation in a way that would have spin off benefits within this very generation not to mention the generations to come.

Ahmed had been on the spot to have Sol seal all the edicts he announced that day. With the Voluntary Sterilization Program sealed as an edict, it was time to dismiss the crowd. Sol would see the masses flood the King's web site to find out more about the Voluntary Sterilization Program.

Sol thanked them for being there. Over the hour-and-a-half they stood in the Plaza they had offered feedback of head nods, smiles, and affirming turns to one another to comment on the statements Sol was making.

As he was leaving the stage to go get some rest, he paused. He considered going back to explain a little more and maybe answer a question or two. But it was too late. The discussion about the short and long-term effects on society from the Voluntary Sterilization Program would have to be driven by media and critics now. He looked out into the crowd and marvelled at the sight. Floods of people leaving. Holo-beam images flickering as people walked over the lenses in the granite, *EPD* security Drones hovering over the crowd keeping watch for any signs of problems. Ahmed paused beside Sol and asked, "Everything okay Sol?"

As Sol continued leaving the stage he unconvincingly said to Ahmed,
"Yes, it's all good Ahmed."
And the two of them disappeared into the hollow belly of the backstage. Both knowing how deeply these changes were about to impact the world.

The Right To Die

"Funny," Falon Severenson thought as he walked up to the well landscaped brick-front clinic. *"This isn't what I expected, it's hardly a sterile place at all considering what goes on here."*

The raised beds with flowing shrubs and trees. The wide clean stone path and low stone walls that doubled as benches inviting clients to take a moment to sit on the way up the walk. The way the *Voluntary Sterilization Clinic and The Journey from Life Clinics* worked was genius. The building was host to both clinics. People were coming here to end their life, or they were coming to end their ability to bring new life into the world. With such a sensitive nature of what the clinics were there to do, it was comforting to see they were warm and inviting right from the parking lot to the treatment rooms.

The entire program, staff, and facility were exceptional in walking with clients through the journey to end their life. A choice to end one's life was now the prerogative of all Participants. It was now a personal choice with very little Global Government input compelling people to make their choice one way or the other since Sol became King. Falon's appointment window was scheduled for the morning. That's it. Just sometime in the morning. He could show up and was not rushed to get into the clinic. The appointment window philosophy was very stress free for the clients who were coming into become sterile.

The clinic's warm and supportive philosophy was truly person-centered. It encouraged the client to have time to think right up until the last moment. And every client would have already spent time with three consultants as the Multitude of Counsel Law required. Only a small percentage of clients who showed up to end their life or become sterile would change their mind after passing through the door. The clinic design team really took their job seriously. Right from the labyrinth-like walkway that led up to the large clinic entry. It was garden-scaped with several quiet nooks and areas for clients to pause and rest a moment. The design of the garden and walkways made for an unlikely area for protestors to congregate. But there were still impassioned well-doers found among the walkways at times, pleading with clients to turn back.

It was simply fact that not everyone was supportive of the program…of either of the programs. Even though the reasonable understanding of where people go when they die had reached a strong level in society, there were still sub-culture groups with intense religious views and agendas that could not accept choosing death was ok. It wasn't that Sol or his administrative supporters in the World Counsel had a low regard for life. Life was wonderful. And for all who wanted to enjoy life, they just kept on doing so without being influenced to choose to transition.

Life was meant to be a peaceful, vibrant, and fulfilling journey. And when Sol released his *Right to Die* edict, an edict that clearly established each person is in control of their own life, Participants of the world breathed a sigh of comfort, "*Ok, this is a good thing…this makes sense.*"

The edict that Sol streamed to every device the day after it was sealed, indicated that if any person sick or well, makes the choice to end their life, He and the World Counsel affirmed that to be completely acceptable…it was the person alone who had control of self…and the choice was supported by the King. Now, the *Journey from Life Clinics* were there to aid Participants who had made the choice to transition.

King Sol was intent on doing all he could to ensure every Participant in the world was given the freedom to make their own choices. Self control was essential for a healthy society. Even over their own life or death. Choice was in many ways, one of the prized privileges of the living. There was not one person who had the choice whether she or he was going to enter this life, nor the choice over acquiring an unwanted debilitating disease or condition, so giving a person the power of choice over their own life or death was liberating. Life had been chosen arbitrarily or through the actions of another so death was now the choice of every individual themself.

Sol outlined his position that the power to choose is quite simply the defining characteristic of humanity. Humans are unique among ascendant species in their capacity for conscious, reasoned choice. The real power of choice separates humanity from all other species. The ability to make a choice and retain control of self, proclaims the dignity of man. In outlining the overarching edict that affirmed *Self-Control* for all people in many matters relevant to their own life or death, Sol referred to one scholar and philosopher from the 1900's who made a clear statement on the value of choice in humans. Kaufman Kohler said;

> *"The dignity and greatness of man depends largely upon his freedom, his power of self-determination. He differs from the lower animals in his independence of instinct as the dictator of his actions. He acts from free choice and conscious design and is able to change his mind at any moment, at any new evidence or even through whim. He is therefore responsible for his every act or omission, even for his every intention."*

For every individual to be given the freedom to do as he or she chooses with their own existence is one of the fundamental rights that humans possess. To truly practice self-determination, to maintain and esteem the individual's right to live or right to die, will only prove to propel humanity toward the dignity and greatness of humans. The currency of Dignity and Greatness that has been displayed as a result of man's freedom.

The edict was uplifting in how it gave license to all Participants to do as they willed. It allowed the development of sensitive environments, such as the Journey from Life clinics, for individuals to go to complete their wishes in comfort. Normalizing death would bring peace to those who chose death and to those who were left behind to miss their loved ones. Every conscious person on the planet was now in control of their own life or death. Sol had been very passionate about this edict and the great impact on society it would bring. It was an overarching Act that returned a true power of choice to all individuals. This was The *Self-Control Act... and it* was now in place.

When Sol penned it, the intent was to ensure all people are in control of their own self. If a person chooses to smoke that's their choice. If a person chooses to be a glutton, that's their choice. If a person chooses to take their own life or choose sterilization that is also their choice. It was an act that gave force to the *Right to Die Edict.* Sol was always about choice and believed in the power of choice. If prohibition bred rebellion, then fostering a culture of choice would bring Self-Control.

Sol's *Right to Die Edict* displayed how giving Participants the choice of life or death, brought Participants across the world a greater sense of feeling in control and having less fear. Those who wanted to transition were treated as responsible persons. They were not forced to accept the policies and beliefs of the political powers that imposed their values of the few onto the many.

To allow people the choice over their own life or death is to honor humanity. When adversaries of the *Right to Die* edict surfaced with disputes and arguments against the edict, they would be muted in the face of reason. Few could argue it had been unreasonable to claim a government was intellectually superior and more philosophically evolved than the individual who preferred to end their existence here on earth, somehow making the government better equipped to decide, for every individual, that they had no right over their own life or death. The "*We know what is best for you*" view of government and the left-over ideals from religious groups of the past were no longer well-supported positions. Death was part of life and humanity not only had to accept that, but humanity now had individual power over when it would happen with the support of the World Government to make the choice when that would happen. A society that fully humanizes each individual, oddly enough, is one that allows each human to make choices even related to ending one's own life.

Within days of sealing the *Right to Die Edict,* the doors on clinics all over the world began accepting clients. It was amazing how many proponents of the program had already set things in place to offer the services. And it was even more amazing the vast number of people who were ready to use the program. They just needed the affirmation of their government before streaming into the clinics.

In its first week of the program, clients looking for this service had taken all the necessary steps to get approval for the transition from life to non-life. Beside informing family of one's choice to die, once a person had participated in the Multitude of Counsel program, showing they have spent some time with consultants in discussion about their choice, and had taken opportunities to hear other insightful perspectives, they then could do as they wished. Whether family and friends agreed or not it was wholly the person of sound mind's decision. They could then walk the gentle winding path into the clinic doors and literally sign their life away.

I'm All Done Here

Voluntary Sterilization Clinics and *The Journey from Life Clinics* had popped up in every town and city across the globe when Sol sealed his *Right to Die* edict from his home. Along with navigating the tricky waters of chemical sterilization, the clinics had established a smooth and respectful system for dealing with the Participants who were transitioning from life to non-life with estimable sensitivity. From the moment a client stepped foot on the clinic property to the moment the transitioners left the realm of the living, the entire process was gentle, meaningful, and professional.

All over the world, the social media buzz testified to the beauty of successful transitions. In one of the most heart warming stories from a brand-new clinic in Nepal, people shared the story of an 87-year old woman who epitomized dignity and greatness in how her transition occurred. Hearing this story and others. Falon got it. He got why it made sense to offer people the opportunity to choose death. He got why some people needed to end their life peacefully, with dignity. But he wasn't at the clinic to transition. Today Falon was there to be part of the Voluntary Sterilization Program.

Falon pondered, *"I wonder why Sol didn't pass the Right to Die Law in front of the crowd in his last address?"*

But it was not unusual for Sol to devise edicts and laws and then implement them from wherever he was at the time.

Since the last Great Assembly Sol had edicted the programs now being fulfilled at the clinics. While at home late one evening a documentary he was watching shared the stories of three palliative patients who were fighting for assistance in dying. Seeing this presentation, He recalled the time 15 years ago when his dad was diagnosed with Parkinson's disease. And at the time it was progressing rapidly. Sol found it astonishing how science could clone a sheep, transplant a human heart, send trillions of digital bits of information through the air to a device where a video could be watched, have AI carry on human-like conversations and behaviors that closely mimicked human reality, or send an astronaut on a 365 day stay at the Space Station, but we couldn't seem to find a way to fix his dad's brain. After almost a year of steady decline and attempts by the medical community to remedy the condition, Sol's dad had told his wife, Sol's mom, he wanted to end it…to end the suffering and the rapid ebbing of all his dignity.

They had been discussing it for months since finding his slide into 5th stage Parkinson's was inevitable. But the discussion had taken a hiatus over the past few weeks. And then when Sol got the call out of the blue from his mother that his father was gone, he was crushed. Dad had slipped away the previous night all alone in his care facility bed…and the painful part was that it was not in his own way in his own time…with his family around him as he died.

Sol recalled hearing his dad tell him, *"It was one thing to be a 'life' but it was another to actually be 'alive'."*

In his condition, life was nothing more than simply breathing and having his heart beating, a prisoner to a disease and to the thoughts and regrets of the captive. This was not being truly alive. From his point of view, if he had the breath of life in him but was not able to be truly alive then his breath was needless. Having a life without truly being "alive" was pointless. And the day he took control of ending his life was, in a way, a powerful end of life moment where he clawed back independence for a few seconds as he ended all his suffering. Sol's dad left the depression and indignity behind, choosing to stop his wasting away in a bed that had become a prison of no escape.

Recalling the event pricked Sol. In some parts of the world the idea of helping someone transition was hotly contentious. Had there been no contention about some 15-years ago then perhaps Sol, his mother, and his siblings could have been beside their loved one as he transitioned from life to death. A transition where the sufferer says, *"I'm all done here, done with this life of anguish."*

A journey that speaks freedom to the person whose life has all but been stolen by a disease they didn't ask for. Choosing to let go and welcoming the peace of the afterlife…No more pain just nothing…making everything ok.

Sitting right there in his den that night. Watching a documentary about people in anguish who are not given the choice to end their suffering inspired Sol. He was now the one with the authority to decide. A somber privilege of a Worldwide King. Sol sealed the edict, and the world received its notice. The truth is that every life is precious, but everyone's life is theirs. And each of us is responsible to do with it as we choose. Each of us as global Participants, has the right to live as much as we have the right to die. Sol believed we should all be supported no matter which of those choices are made…allowing us to be "Participants" to the moment we breathe no more.

Most Despised Sector
of Degenerates

Falon was not sure why the *Right to Die* edict came the way it did. But if the trickle of apparently ill people who were moving along the meandering path to the clinic were any indicator, it was clear that people were taking to it. Taking to the freedom that came from the edict just as Falon was taking to the Voluntary Sterilization Program. And this was just at one of the thousands of clinics that were all over the world already. There were also a great many Participants accessing the *Right to Die at Home Support Program*. A popular program that facilitates transitions in a person's home.

Whether here at the clinic or in homes around the world, transitioners were being joined by family and friends. Support teams who respected and cared for their loved ones enough to join them as they ended their life. While transitioners made their way into the clinic Falon headed in to meet with the clinician. He was there to end his ability to reproduce new life. As he made his way into the sterilization clinic there was no question in his mind that this is what he wanted to do.

"Hello Sir." Falon was greeted by a youthful, mid-fifties *VSG* as he stepped up to the reception desk. "Hello, I'm Fay, one of the clinic Voluntary Sterilization Guides. How can I help you today?"

"I'm here to complete the sterilization process."

"Alright, can I have your name sir?"

"Falon Severenson."

She began tapping in his name on the desktop folio watching the screen as the *Falon Severensons* in the system scrolled down the page. Falon waved his G-PAS card in front of the scanner. Everyone automatically swiped the G-PAS any time they were at a reception desk for an appointment. The card was a complete digital identity repository.

"Thank you Mr. Severenson...here you are right here."

Fay noted his place on her screen and looked up with a bright smile announcing her success in locating his record. "Excellent. Please take a seat Mr. Severenson, the VSG clinician will be along in a moment."

Falon had one more question for the Fay. And he was unapologetic about asking. "How does the payment get processed and into my account?" Falon was referring to the first $200,000 payment for volunteering to be sterilized.

Everyone had the same question when they went through the sterilization intake process. The answer was simple. Payment was to be sent to the individual's account after checking out of the clinic upon completion of the Sterilization protocol.

That question was to be expected. Many of the program users would never step foot inside the Clinic if there were no reward. This kind of Volunteerism was markedly more compelling with a half million dollars attached to the invitation. And the money would be well spent for most. While others who used the program might be less likely to use their newfound wealth in healthy ways. Some from sectors of society who were inclined to self-destructive behaviors may end up worse off than they were before the payout...possibly even killing themselves with the bad choices they make once they have access to all that cash. There was no shortage of takers on the offer of cash for sterilization. Also true was the multitude of reasons, beside the money, that people didn't want to have children and would choose sterilization in this way.

Still, some people would jump at the chance to never have children, even without a government funded program that offers payouts. Not even considering how society would see the benefit for years to come. But never having children was only part of the overall benefit. The massive sterilization program was certainly going to have an impact on population control. Society was going to benefit in many ways and on many levels for many decades to come. It was a path to resolving the Global over-population crisis that was developing. And society was swirling with conversations about all the ancillary benefits from certain sectors and groups of people being early adopters of this program. The DBN was carrying broadcasts and streams that dealt with matters of the VS program. None had become as popular in the last 48 hours as the wildly successful show, *"This Is Your World I'm Only Livin In It"*. And Falon had watched the Stream carefully while pondering his scheduled visit to the clinic for today.

On the show, Bryson Reynolds, the DBN panelist from the Table of Truth News Show, was chasing down people on the street days after the edict came down. This was the way he ran his one-man interview on the street show. Reynolds wanted the average Joe or Jody to sound off on Sol's edict.

People were very clear on the future benefits of the VSP...the future benefits that went beyond simple population control. And while making his decision to be sterilized, Falon saw the same streams that everyone else saw. He was in complete agreement with the guests he saw on Bryson's curbside show. Few streams were as open at talking about the effects of this edict as this show of Bryson Reynolds'. In his segments, Bryson was certain to inform his Brysonites that they were true heroes if they were taking part in this program. He and his interviewees were quite candid with all the trickle-down benefits society was going to see. Bryson pointed at the many ways the *Voluntary Sterilization Program* would impact today's society. He was certain the impact would be more profound in positive ways for future generations, than it would be in the present day. The impact would go far beyond simply reducing the world population to manageable numbers and preventing the 11 billion citizens of the globe ballooning even further.

Reynolds wanted to know two things by taking to the streets to interview people. He wanted to see if average *Global Participant* saw what this program would bring. Did the average person see the impact on the future of society…the social costs, the crime statistics, the healthcare costs, and the social safety net savings? Or did the average Joe see the program as an unethical mechanism for population control or a sound solution to the overpopulation issues faced by society? Reynolds was going to find out.

6000 Pieces of
Garbage Per Year

Brysonites were always early adopters of radical change in government. Especially radical change that made sense to scores of clear thinkers. Bryson talked to dozens of people but the message most of the viewers like Falon got from this new Voluntary Sterilization Program was the same? With a busy bustling street and steady advertisements scrolling across Media Screens in the background, Reynolds showed exactly what people thought about the Voluntary Sterilization Program and the man who had the courage…or foolishness, to enact it.

The bright images of the frenetic Bryson Reynolds had been streamed to billions since the edict was announced. He drew viewers in with such skill, then his disarming style held them. And Falon had seen the show on more than one occasion.

This scene had Bryson standing in the middle of a busy street looking for just the right people to poke his microphone in front of and ask their thoughts about Sol's latest ground-breaking program.

"So, I'm pounding the pavement today in the name of all that's Brysonite to find out how we feel as the *Voluntary Sterilization Program* is ramping up to full swing.

"At the last Great Assembly, King Sol came out of the gate with his heel spurs dug in and he tightened the death grip on society's most despised sector of degenerates.

You and I both heard at his address that hundreds of pedophile predators have been sealed. These blights on society are no longer a thought in the consciousness or fears of the good people of our world. And this is just the start for Good King Sol."

Bryson informed his audience with excitement as he told about the continued work of the Ministry of Retribution. A work that was removing abusers from the gene pool daily.

"The Minister of Retribution is hot on the trail of every one of these destroyers of children. And if things keep ramping up like they seem to be, we could be rid of a ton of these guys…literally. Society has been asking for this for generations already."

Reynolds looked at the note he had on his folio. He was seeing this thing in a different way than most of the viewing audience. But no surprise there, that was always his style. And he was going to give the viewers his unique perspectives on the projections. People slowed as they strolled by him in the background. Many of them hoped he would call them out of the moving crowd while some made effort to go unseen and unheard. Bryson held the viewers' attention with his delightfully annoying excitement as Shuttles glided into the curb across the street, unloading a herd of passengers then taking off again. The busy background was no match for Bryson Reynolds. In fact, it was the perfect backdrop for the DBN personality who was just on the safe side of looking like a manic nightclub comedian. Bryson had some statistics with a twist to share before pulling his first *Man on the Street* into the shot.

"I'm not trying to be insensitive towards the families of the men who have been Sealed so far, but here's a little math for you about the pedophiles the world is now rid of forever. And we're talking worldwide here so keep up with me."

His cadence quickened as he began to share his rather obscure take on one of the benefits to society for getting rid of pedophiles.

"We all know overpopulation causes an exponential increase in waste and garbage production. And I have to be frank with you friends, I see no other sector of society as garbage more than these perverse predatorial pedophiles. So, let's say King Sol starts hitting his projections of Sealing child sex abusers worldwide. That means his Minister, Tomer Cohen and the MoR gang, will Seal 500 of these guys a month. According to the number of pedophiles who are active out there and the size of the Ministry of Retribution, those numbers are doable. Tomer and his gang have the resources, and they definitely have the support from Sol, The Pope, and the World Counsel. Even with the Voluntary Sterilization Program running, losing 500 degenerative child-sex-abusing men across the world, who cannot stop abusing children, is no loss to society at all….So, are you still with me?"

Bryson knew he had his viewers with him…he was heading towards a succulent point. And it was one that was not likely made by anyone else in the industry. The avuncular host went on to share his astute observation in his unorthodox way.

"If the Ministry of Retribution eliminates 500 a month that gives us a net gain of 6000 disgusting losers who will be removed from society in the first year alone of Sol's new law.

"You know friends, I have always thought very lowly of pedophiles and abusers of all kinds…I think so lowly of them that I find it easy to think of them as garbage. And research shows us two things about pedophiles. On average a pedophile abuses approximately 117 innocent children in his life and that pedophile weighs on average about 180 pounds."

Bryson looked up from his folio shaking his head in astonishment. "I have no idea who it is that decides on the average weight of a pedophile but that is what they came up with…one hundred eighty pounds is what the average male pedophile weighs…Who knew?"

He returned his eyes to the folio and announced proudly…"That means at 6000 pieces of garbage per year…tipping the scales on average at 180 pounds…in the first year of King Sol's campaign against child sex abusers we are going to dispose of ***one million eighty thousand*** pounds of human waste…

"Now I was never a fan of the Global Salvationist environmental movement, so I don't mind when a little garbage gets burned up in high efficiency incinerators. Within the first year of Tomer and Sol's fight against pedophiles over a million pounds of garbage will be disposed of. That is a lot of garbage off the streets folks.

"And if that is not good enough news, here is a little more Brysonite math for you. Taking the average number of abused children that a pedophile will victimize in their lifetime. at an average of 117, the extrapolation we realize from the removal of these million pounds of human garbage, will bring us a net result of 702,000 fewer children around the globe who get abused. Sol and Tomer are making life better for 702,000 children a year. By the end of the first year of this program, 6000 pedophiles will be gone forever and will not have the chance to fulfill their depraved urges on dozens of children each. Brysonites are damn pleased to see that King Sol is removing over a million pounds of garbage but we in Bryson nation and everyone else who I have spoken to, find cause for celebration in knowing that tens of thousands of abuses will NOT take place. There is no one on God's Gray Earth that can put a value on that kind of good news. Children are being protected every day and get to grow up without the complexities and issues that come from being sexually abused, because finally, someone is bold enough to Seal pedophiles. How can anyone say that is not for the betterment of this hard, cold world we call home? A big Brysonite Nation THANK YOU goes out to the hard working Minster of Retribution and his team."

If there was anything about Bryson Reynolds that could be said regarding his work, it was that he sure made it a craft...mundane he was not. The celebratory anthem played in the background. Canned applause was fed into the broadcast. Reynolds then turned the cameras to the people passing by. It was time to poke his mic into the faces of men and women and all others on the street.

This is your World I'm Only Livin In It

"Ma'am, have you thought much about Sol's Voluntary Sterilization Program?"

A fresh-looking woman in her late 20's carrying a book bag came into the shot. She was startled slightly at being drawn into the mic but appeared confident yet cautious at Bryson's probing question. People were used to Bryson's show and beside the meager few who had just never happened to come across the *This is your World I'm Only Livin In It* show, most everyone Bryson stepped in front of was willing to entertain the unique man with his meddlesome manners. This first interviewee was obviously willing to engage.

"Yes I have," was her open reply.

"And what do you see as the benefit if any, of the program?"

"Well," she looked up to gather a thought or two. "Beside the obvious impact it may have on the over-population problem. I suppose we are going to see a decrease in the overuse of social programs."

"And that means what Ma'am?"

"It seems there may be a certain demographic of people who will make use of the program. I have heard discussions which suggest that people who will take the deal will likely be those who would not be cut out for parenting anyway. If they don't reproduce there will be a good chance we see a reduced number of poorly parented children, and then we may see a reduction in children, adolescents, and eventually adults, who are part of the strain on the social welfare programs the Government offers."

Bryson was very attentive. This gal was offering some excellent insight. Not surprisingly, she was like so many others who were stirred by the edicts Sol put forth. Participants became very conversant on the topic in a very short time. Having had some involved conversations with family, coworkers, or friends about this program, brought the literacy on the topic to a relatively high level in culture.

Bryson jumped in, "I see what you are saying. Basically, if people who shouldn't have children do have children, there is a good chance those children develop into adults who will require the system to support them in some way during their life. I guess we could say, 'Bad parents raise bad children'." Bryson used air-quotes when referring to the subjects of his statement as 'bad'.

"Yes, exactly" She was fully involved in this curb side chat. "While not predetermined to be 'bad,' children raised in destructive environments face greater challenges and are at increased risk for developing negative behaviors and making poor choices."

"You know what I call kids, adolescents, and adults who make bad choices that result in being a burden on society?"

Bryson left her hanging a bit.

"What?" she asked.

"I call them 'Bad People'." Bryson's curb side interviewee showed a slight squirm on her face at the declaration from Bryson Reynolds.

Bryson thanked her for stopping and let her move on. Before he grabbed the next unassuming Participant heading past him, he offered a stat on orphans that was rumbling around in his head. Telling his viewers there were about 1.6 million orphans in Mexico alone. Almost a quarter million in USA and an estimated 153,000,000 orphans worldwide. There were a lot of unwanted children out there.

Being careful to be clear on his numbers, Bryson offered viewers the information that about a third of those in the system were *virtual orphans*. That is to say, they did not lose their parents to become orphaned, their parents abandoned them. They were from parents who did not want to have children. Parents who deserted them emotionally and refused to be physically present in their young lives. These were parents who had babies they never wanted, and they never will be wanted by those parents. Parents who would have used the VSP if it were around at the time.

Elaborating on the harsh reality of the orphaned child, Bryson explained how it is often the case that the orphaned child ends up migrating into gangs and crime... seldom becoming a successful, productive Participant in society.

Turning the viewer back to his own statement that "bad" parents often lead to "bad" children, Reynolds made the suggestion of how the Voluntary Sterilization Program might have benefits for culture by reducing the numbers of unwanted children who end up as orphans. If the parents who had not really wanted children were given the choice to voluntarily sterilize themselves, we may not be faced with the dire situation from such huge numbers of orphans today. Numbers that are so often connected to the rise in crime, an unmanageable draw on social programs, and persistently strain the many government agencies and resources involved in the health and welfare of children and of society as a whole. Other research identifies that the long-term outlook for an "unwanted" pregnancy and the resulting "unwanted" child, leads to elevated crime rates from the demographic of those who were in the "unwanted" category at birth.

Reynolds snapped his attention back to the passing crowds. "Sir, Sir..." he was prodding an older gent, apparently beyond retirement age but pushing a stroller along the sidewalk.

Brushing closely alongside him as moved down the street, Bryson asked, "Are you aware of the savings the King's free health care might see because of the Voluntary Sterilization Program?"

Free healthcare worldwide was another home-based edict of Sol's. Sol had sealed into law that no one will ever be refused healthcare of any kind. All healthcare will be provided for by the King. Sol was of the mind that when healthcare is free, the Participants would not only be healthier, but they would have more disposable income because they were not using it to access quality healthcare. And of course, as disposable income has a tendency to do…it would be spent on consumer goods or other taxed items. The large pool of tax money collected from income and from point-of-sale tax would be put to work for such things as free universal healthcare.

The gent with the stroller paused his walk with his grandson to give Bryson some time. Bryson was putting out a leading question and thanks to his knack for spotting the informed woman or man on the street, he was about to get what he was looking for again.

"Sir…are you familiar with Sol's Voluntary Sterilization Program?"

"Yes I am," was the certain reply.

The gent was a touch pensive not knowing exactly where Bryson would be going with his question.

"And what are your thoughts on it…supportive, adverse, antagonistic, apathetic, angry?"

Reynolds touched a nerve with the last one. But Reynolds knack for stopping the well-informed mark on the street even took him by surprise. The gent in front of him at the moment was a retired Business Ethics Coach. His depth with this topic went far deeper than just the past few days and the address Sol had recently delivered. And he may have been retired but he was completely engaged in this issue.

"You know, let me be frank with you." Bryson's mark started.

"Perfect" Bryson said…frank was just his style.

"I was angry when I first heard the edict. My wife and I were getting the spare room ready for our daughter and grandson to come for a visit." He looked to the stroller he was gripping tightly below. The anger from that day starting to resurface.

"And the Media Screen in the hallway chimed on with the DBN intro. We were just as impressed with King Sol and his presentation this time as we were the first. But when he began laying out the population statistics and all that went with it, I started to get amped up. I knew where he was going with it and hearing him announce and seal the Voluntary Sterilization Program, I got really angry…I'm just being honest here."

Reynolds was absolutely giddy to have a person on the street who was ok letting it all out. And someone who seemed to know more than the average *Joe or Judy Citizen.*

The producers had prompted Bryson through his earpiece to get this man on the street to take a brief mobile studio live interview. And just as he did the Volkswagen Studio truck pulled up to the curb. A production team swarmed just out of the camera's view and Bryson popped the question.

"Sir, our live streaming audience and I would be elated if you might take ten or fifteen minutes of your time to sit down with me in our mobile studio."

In the background, viewers could see the steps from the tailgate of the customized Volkswagen Studio truck being lowered and the sound canopy going up. As the soon-to-be guest on the ***It's Your World I'm Only Livin in It*** show cocked his head back a little in surprise, he gestured toward his grandson napping in the stroller. As if to ask, '*What am I going to do with him?*'

Reynolds read his mind. A production assistant swiftly jumped to the aid. Bryson gave a nod of thanks to his staffer and assured the gent his grandson would be tenderly cared for while he slept in the stroller during the interview.

"Well folks, this is just felicitous." Bryson cued up a break to give them time to set up the mobile set.

"Have a look at this Volkswagen commercial while we quickly retool, and I will be right back with Mr..." Bryson turned to the gent to have him fill in the blank with his name not giving him a chance to back out on the invitation.

"...Marcus Holgerson" the invitee quickly added.

"I'll be right back with Mr. Marcus Holgerson, our esteemed guest, our 'man' on the street on today's live broadcast of *This is your World I'm Only Livin In It*".

Everyone Wins With Voluntary Sterilization

A small crowd had taken the opportunity to stand and watch the mobile studio. Having a live interview develop into a full mobile studio session was quite the treat. It was much more so than seeing a man with a microphone chatting people up on the street. An *EPD* Drone scuttled overhead as they tend to do anytime an impromptu crowd gathers. Drones usually managed to find Bryson Reynolds when he did a live event like this. It hovered for a few seconds and seeing it was just Bryson Reynolds causing the subdued commotion, it quietly hummed off.

The back of the Volkswagen Studio held Bryson and Marcus. The attenuation canopy overhead kept the sound of the interviewer and guest tight, and it blocked out the hum of the street. The single shot of Bryson and Marcus Holgerson filled the street and filled all the mobile devices and Media Screens near and far as DBN pushed their stream globally. These streetside chats had been renowned for their candid content and ability to sneak up on watchers with thoughts and ideas that caught many by surprise. It was those dynamic elements that compelled the DBN to elevate these live moments to Global Stream status. Marcus Holgerson was sitting alone with Bryson Reynolds, but he had just been introduced to the entire globe.

"Welcome back. If you are just joining us I am sitting in the Mobile Studio with a gentleman named Marcus Holgerson. Marcus and I started chatting in the street a moment ago and he agreed to elaborate on a question about the Voluntary Sterilization Law."

Bryson turned from the camera and looked to Marcus. "And thanks for taking some moments to visit with me Marcus, what is it you do for a living?"

Bryson didn't really care what his impromptu guests did for a living, just if they were articulate and informed…and he already got the sense on just how articulate and informed Marcus was. But he knew the audience wanted to know the vocation of his guests. It gave them the sense that Bryson wasn't just handpicking professional guests to make the show more enticing. For most viewers, real was where it was at. And often an ordinary person brought to the Stream that compelled people to watch the broadcast, and compelled DBN to take shows like this global.

"I'm a retired Business Ethics Coach. I've been retired for just over two years."

Now Bryson was getting really jazzed up. This guy had some cred…he was sure to sound off on the new King's Voluntary Sterilization Program…or so Bryson thought.

"Well I'll be folks." Bryson chipperly sung. "Isn't that just like the Bryson Reynolds show to stumble upon a guest who really knows what he wants to say and how to say it." Bryson turned to face his willing guest.

"So let's continue our street discussion Marcus and why don't you tell me what got you so angry when you heard the edict that afternoon coming across the Media Screen in your home as you prepared for your grandson to come stay with you?"

Marcus was fully engaged now. Thoughts about the issue raced through his mind in the moments Bryson and the production team were transitioning from the sidewalk to the VW. He jumped right in to give Bryson his thoughts as if he had been waiting years for a moment like this.

"What got me so angry Bryson, was the disappointment in that we didn't see this program years ago. Where was the Voluntary Sterilization option 15 or 20 years ago. Where were the Sols of that day? The leaders who would implement truly meaningful programs. Why did we have to wait until now for this to be brought in?...I guess it was the regret that we missed out years ago, that got me so angry."

"So you're saying you would have supported this VSP a long time ago?"

"Yes. That's what I'm saying"

Bryson moved in a little tighter taking the edge of his seat. He was curious where the ex-Business Ethics Coach was coming from on the topic. "Why, what are the reasons for your views?" He queried.

"A number of years ago I was working with a company that was investing in Brazil. Actually, it was a large mineral company that had been injecting billions of dollars into the Brazil mining and Exploration industry. Together we had sorted through the ethical issues of labour cost and remuneration, export and import ethics, and other related issues. Issues that had the potential to affect the bottom line of the company and to damage the reputation of this internationally known group. During the due diligence process, it was brought to the attention of the CEO at the time that parts of Brazil were struggling with a perpetuating poverty issue. The less prosperous of the Brazilian culture were identified and a law was passed that they could not have any more children. Many of the less prosperous in the society were coerced to become sterile. They were given an effective chemical sterilization process that rendered them incapable of reproducing again in their lifetime... The thing is Bryson, while our ethics team was deliberating on the company's association with Brazil, the CEO flippantly made the statement, *'Why don't they just pay them to stop having kids...they'd get their money back within one generation.'*"

Bryson Reynolds was flabbergasted..."That is amazing!" He said. "Who was that CEO?"

Marcus simply ignored the question because as a retired Business Ethics Coach he knew better than to thoughtlessly share the name of a high-power client from the past.

"What's amazing…is that after that CEO tossed out his brilliant suggestion the table started chattering. The women and men in that room quickly assembled a brilliant collection of benefits and positive trickle down from paying people to stop having kids. None of it went anywhere but the group in that room spent a good deal of time entertaining the positive fallout as well as the perils and pitfalls of offering the poor of Brazil money to stop having babies. It was astounding and beside the obvious population control solution that was apparent, there were a litany of benefits. Why didn't we do something like this sooner? Give people the choice and everyone wins with voluntary sterilization. Society reaps the benefits down the road."

Bryson saw this wasn't his first rodeo and Marcus was finely tuned into the issue from his association with the Global Investment Company.

As Bryson gave room for Marcus to wax on, he was thinking this old guy could be of use on the show from time to time. He was really engaging…and he knew what he was talking about. For a guy who boasted about his ability to peg people in the know when he accosted them with a mic in the face, it even surprised Bryson how much this gent had to say.

"Marcus, you said everyone wins and that society reaps the benefits…how does everyone win and what benefits are we going to see?"

"Bryson, as soon as people are given the choice for sterilization with a reward there is always a bit of an outcry. But when we consider the positive flow that comes from such a plan…if the people embrace the plan to some degree and take the state up on the offer, then the benefits are seen in one short generation. When we were faced with this dilemma our Ethics team explored the statement of the CEO to see if there was value in such a concept.

"You know everything in life is a question of ethics Bryson. Is it ethical to kill a chicken to eat it, is it ethical to enhance the growth rate of chickens in order to get the large breasts to the market that we all love to grill on the barbecue? Is it ethical for a state or government to legislate hours of work, who can drink alcohol in pubs, and is it ethical to say the state now offers free transportation home from all licensed drinking establishments as King Sol has also implemented?

It was a fact. And Marcus was putting his finger on it delicately. The audience agreed that many of the decisions of government did have ethical issues underneath them. As odd as it sounded, even some prohibitionist groups had questioned the ethics of Sol's *Free Transport From Pubs and Bars* edict.

Sol had implemented the program in his third week as King. Offering free transportation home for those who socialize in public drinking establishments was a great way to encourage people to get out and not worry about cab fare or driving while under the influence of substances. Scads of people who rarely headed out to socialize at a local pub began to support establishments that otherwise struggled to fill tables. Offering free transport home for customers resulted in them spending a little money out on the town. And it was always good to get consumer money into the economy. The program successfully saw people become more intentional about being a community. By making it easier for people to go out, drink responsibly, engage each other, spend some money and have the ride home covered by the program, people were already becoming better participants in society. Interaction in a stress-free social environment connected people. People would share their lives and ideas and besides the odd overuse issues that slipped by the well-trained servers in these establishments, mostly positive things would result from the interactions.

For most people it felt good to get out with friends, spend a little time and money and have a few drinks. The program relieved patrons of the strain of finding a ride home or hiring a cab. It was just another social innovation of Sol's that helped Participants out on the town to relax in a way that made them more productive and healthier Participants on the other side of their night out. Of course it may be ethically questioned on some level but it was running smoothly so far. It was true as

Marcus was putting it…Ethics does underlie everything, and those ethics are often fluid, rarely concrete in a society that is continually evolving and being challenged.

Marcus made the point that ethics is in everything, part of every decision.

"At some point," he elaborated, "Down the line of the decision-making process, the ethics of a matter will come into play. Whether it is a cognitive decision, one based on the programming of society, or a response to a long-held unquestioned religious belief, it is ethics that guides us into all things. And those who make the rules, laws, and choices for society, are subject to the question of ethics."

Bryson was now enamoured with Marcus Holgerson. This guy was more than he had bargained for.

"Wow" Bryson exclaimed, "Ethics…that is a whole other show."

Bryson could not disagree with his well-spoken guest. "Putting it that way does punctuate the need to consider ethics in all things, even in what I do here on the show doesn't it?"

The crowd gathered on the street watching the Volkswagen Mobile Studio hadn't let the concept slip over their heads. They were intently engaged in the live curbside show.

"Ethics are very engrossing Marcus, but let me explore the, *'everyone wins statement'* you and your team made in your discussions."

Bryson's producer signalled they were ready to wrap up in minutes. So Bryson fished for the big closer from the older gent who had added such depth to a challenging conversation about Sterilization.

Drug Addiction, Abuse, And General Skullduggery

"We just have a few short minutes remaining Marcus, so please, surely you have a list of the benefits to society from Sol's Voluntary Sterilization Program."

"It's simple." Marcus Holgerson replied with reasoned input. "Let me give it to you this way. Some people will make use of the Voluntary Sterilization Program because they have a plan for their life, and children are not part of that plan. Those individuals may be good Participants who may have made good parents but just have no desire to become parents. While others may participate in the program who perhaps would not be good parents and in many of those cases should never become parents. If these individuals do not reproduce then society will not be the recipient of all the problems that come with bad parents or unwanted children. Not just here in North America Bryson but around the world. I know it is tough to say but I'm old, I have nothing to lose in saying it like it is. Everyone knows that individuals who do little good for society and take more than they give, often reproduce children who do likewise. The group who uses the program is typically going to be fairly young. Possibly a group that is already involved in crime, drug and alcohol addiction, self-abuse or abuse of others. Consider how many of that demographic would have done what comes naturally to the human species and eventually would have reproduced. Seeing the opportunity of the Voluntary Sterilization Process, they will take the money and choose to never have children. If $500,000 is paid to those who want no children, we start recovering that payout within that generation. The Free Worldwide Healthcare Sol offers is wonderful, but the use of resources just goes up when people who themselves use a lot of health care and social safety-net resources, have babies. If those individuals don't have babies, well, Sol's free universal healthcare is markedly less strained. Childbirth and any complications the mother or baby may have is a huge expense."

Bryson was ready to move his guest to the close of the show. But he wanted to hear more of the thoughts of Marcus Holgerson. He interrupted with a question that he knew Marcus would have an answer to.

"Tell me Marcus, this is not the first time money has been offered for sterilization, is it?"

Marcus kept right in step. "That's true Bryson this is not the first time… although the amounts in Sol's program are quite a bit more enticing.

"In the early 2000's in Seattle Washington, a young visionary by the name of Barbra Harris began offering to pay drug addicted women of Seattle $300 to get sterilized. It was the offshoot of a Billboard campaign called *Project Prevention* started by Judith Scully. The whole purpose and goal of the campaign was to try to reel in drug addicted women. It was arguably distasteful. One of the billboards actually read;

"Don't Let a Pregnancy Ruin Your Drug Habit"

Marcus Holgerson briefed Bryson and his audience on the Project Prevention of the late 1990's era. He explained the idea was a noble but undeveloped one. It was flawed in how it chose only an isolated demographic. The principle, which has been debated in the decades following Scully's prevention efforts, had merit. The message was that some people should not have children, and they were the target group. Offering an incentive to help the target group make a wise decision was the only way to effectively parse those people out. Judith Scully knew there was often a real cost for society when people in less healthy mental, physical, emotional, or financial situations have children not because they wanted children, rather just because they are having unprotected sex. We all pay for that and in many cases the successive generations keep paying as well. The voluntary sterilization of certain groups of people, benefits that group as well as the rest of us. Scully's campaign added to the conversation by articulating well, some of the points in favour of the program...such as protecting children, cost-effectiveness, and personal choice for individual humans.

Marcus was able to hold the audience as he explained the connection of Scully's movement to that of Sol's edict today.

"What Judith didn't know Bryson, is that the ethic line was way out in front of her...society was not ready to get so close to that line for fear of stepping over it. Look around Bryson, it has been 40 years now. In fact, the only way to see that ethical line now is to look back...we have crossed over it and there is no going back."

Marcus and Bryson shortened their dialogue on how Voluntary Sterilization affected crime. That math was simple. Bryson added the harsh reality that others might not talk about.

"As much as it is unpalatable to state, it is the facts. Limiting the children being born to high-risk families who circulate in criminal minded social circles, will reduce crime."

Marcus was reminded of other points that his Ethics team discussed while scrutinizing the concept.

"And one of the truly unique aspects of such a program was made mention of in our team brainstorming session. If certain people who are beyond a certain point of being productive contributors to society choose VSP, such as those who are perhaps addicted to drugs, dealing drugs, choosing a life of crime, or refusing to become Participants of society, there will be a self-driven thinning of the herd."

Bryson jumped in on this one, "The frank way of saying that is that some people who take the cash are going to end up killing themselves with it. Don't you agree?"

"*Wellll...*, Marcus dragged on his 'l's'. "That is one way to say it. Although I might put it a little differently than that. If for instance a drug addicted young lady sees the opportunity to take part in the program and then receives the $500,000 dollars into her account, there is nothing stopping her from spending that newfound injection of wealth on her methamphetamine injection hobby...as many hobbyists might do. Her hobby is drugs. And I have to say Bryson, this was the hard part to take for some members of the Ethics Team who deliberated on the topic. The reality in this instance however, is that this young lady will be spending it on a hobby that will destroy her. Whether it be a young lady or a young man, or a young gender diverse person who is of a demographic that is better off not having kids for the obvious reasons, the access to large quantities of cash will not find these types embracing the entrepreneurial spirit and starting up a business or going to college. In many cases the choices one makes will end up killing them. And that individual will no longer be a draw on the world's resources, nor will they bring children into the world that have a great likelihood of being affected by poverty or involved in crime. What I truly thought was brilliant when I read through the entire edict on the King's Meta page, was in cases where the recipient dies and some of the payout remains, what remains of the payout goes back to the state just as Sol's edict has declared.

"The overall benefit to all of us in society is that the individual who was a negative part of society, and a draw on society is no longer a taker. Society no longer has the responsibility to feed, clothe, house, or financially and medically support that person or his or her offspring that were never born. And therefore never become a taker of the resources we all work so hard to pay for. Resources such as social programs and the health care system. Bryson, the taking stops! The reality is that society begins saving money instead of enduring a lifetime of dishing out precious funds on individuals who quite simply, have no regard for anyone but themselves due to a litany of complex reasons and social determinants."

Bryson had to wrap up...they had gone overtime but no one realized the hour had elapsed. It was time to close the show.

"Well, I need to shove off in a moment so thank you Mr. Holgerson. To put a fine point on things, everyone wins, and everyone benefits with voluntary sterilization and with Sol's VSP edict. Because those who want never to have children…they get a tidy sum for agreeing to serve society and themselves in this way. They will do with it as they will. That cash payout is indeed a benefit for the Participant. And the rest of society sees a reduction in crime, reduction in high-risk individuals weaving the fallout from their bad choices into society, and a reduction in precious dollars that are being thrown at problems that only perpetuate themselves in a never-ending cycle. A cycle that until now, only promised to grow as our population densities increase across cities of the world. Also, we stand to see a reduction in health care costs because the simple truth of it is, those who kill themselves with the money, stop taking up resources.

"We will see a huge reduction of money being spent on the people and on the problems that come from having children who would have a higher risk of perpetuating the cycle of crime, alcoholism, drug addiction, abuse, and general skullduggery."

Bryson reached across the set of the Volkswagen Mobile Studio and thanked Marcus Holgerson for his brilliant help with the topic as the two shook hands. He looked at the center camera and thanked the viewers for taking part in the stream. Signing off, the crowd on the street spontaneously applauded. They, like so many on the other side of the Stream, were refreshed at the bold edict that was playing out as they watched. And they were enlightened by the excellent input of Bryson Reynolds and his well-versed guest.

Marcus Holgerson's grandson woke at the smattering of curbside applause from the engaged onlookers. He had shared insight as if he had been in Sol's chambers when the edict was being planned. He had a hard time making his way with his grandson's stroller past the adoring crowd who had watched and listened to the brilliant conversation. On the other side of the Media Stream billions had nodded in agreement with the statements made on the show by the two men. And right there, standing curbside, was a throng of people who wanted to shake his hand as he headed off late to meet-up with his daughter for lunch.

Please Join Me at My Last Birthday Party.

Sitting a little fidgety in room 6 waiting for the Clinician to join him, Falon noticed how the warmth of the garden and foyer had been extended to the sterile but welcoming treatment room. It didn't seem uncomfortable at all that the *Right to Die Edict* brought clients to the same clinic where Sterilizations took place. Falon was young and had a promising future ahead of him…not having children would bring him the freedom he thought he wanted. The half million dollars that would be doled out to him would add nicely to his pursuits. Falon was grateful that King Sol had made this choice so enticing and so accessible. His legs swung slowly as they dangled over the side of the bed and the door swung open abruptly. The clinician stepped into the room.

"Greetings Mr. Severenson, How are you doing today?"

"I'm fine thanks, how are you?" Falon asked the clinician as he glanced around the room, almost nervous to make eye contact with the healthcare worker.

The warm colors and regional foliage decorating the treatment room made Falon think Room 6 must have doubled as a soft room for those transitioning. It looked like a nice place to end a life Falon thought.

A couple of couches flanked the room and the deep green foliage draping the walls and window ledges made the room look alive. A contrast to the different life-ending activities that went on there.

The clinician was the final check and balance in the decisive journey to sterilization. And as a Voluntary Sterilization Guide, she had already had several young gentlemen and ladies pass though her room. Each of them with a different story. She was cross-trained to work with both kinds of clients that came into the clinic. She worked with both those choosing sterilization and those choosing to transition from life to death. And like others in the industry, she heard all the stories from clinics around the world.

Falon broke the silence as he watched her preparing the Sterilization protocol that would drip into his blood stream for the next 15 minutes. A slow flow of delicate hormones and anti-fertility medications that would stop the production of sperm in males. With a slight adjustment, it would stop the production of eggs in females.

"Did you hear about the lady in Nepal who used the clinic?"

Falon was making conversation now as he was starting to get a little nervous knowing the protocol would soon be running through his veins. Suddenly sensing the real finality of the procedure, Falon reminded himself why he was doing this. He had never wanted children. The expectation society had placed on people for generations had added to the overpopulation problem. For generations it was simply an unquestioned human axiom...One must reproduce and bring forth children into the world.

The problem with the obligation that all humans are supposed to have children whether they feel like it or not, is that bringing children into the world is then no longer done for the purpose of the survival of the human race. Children added to the critically overcrowded human population, were not inheriting a blessed and prosperous world. They would be left to pick up the pieces of the billions of people who preceded them. People of the often selfish and apathetic generations before them. In the eyes of many, seeing large numbers participate in the VSP was preferable. Having children just because a person can was no longer a reason for every person to have children. Simply possessing a functioning reproductive system was no longer the decision maker that one should reproduce. According to Sol, people who did not want children should not have them. It was time to leave having children to those who legitimately wanted them. The responsible, sacrificial, traditional lot who believed that having children would enrich their lives.

When Sol and the world government endorsed the right for sterilization on a voluntary basis, choosing to not have children was destigmatized. It finally became ok to be childless. To have a different preference than those who always wanted to have children to carry on the family line and name was no longer worthy of societal judgements. Many Participants had no need for their family line or name to be carried on. Despite the popular Voluntary Sterilization Program, the desire to have children remained strong for the majority of Global Participants. And a great deal of the fertile population of the world would still do so. There was no sense to the exaggerated claim that the world might run out of people someday because of Sol's edict. One of the memes that surfaced within a day or two of Sol's edict mocked that thinking. It was a play on the Biblical story of Adam and Eve, the first man and woman in the Garden of Eden. The meme showed a naked man and woman sitting on a park bench.

Not a person in sight, Andy and Vi were relaxing in an empty park. A horse drawn carriage sat driverless in the near distance behind their park bench. The horse hitched to the carriage had just dropped a steaming pile on the ground. The naked Andy looked at it, looked back at Vi, and said,

"Well Vi, I guess it's just you and me now. Maybe we better start having kids again, cuz we could use some help to clean that up."

The message was clear. The meme was suggesting an empty planet to be the outcome of the VSP Sol had implemented. It was ridiculous to think Sol's population control measures would cause populations to plummet and place the world back in the Stone Age with very few humans remaining to take care of the world. Anyone who was not swayed by hyper-religious end-times rhetoric, or conspiracy theorists, was able to see the facts. Reason prevailed for most and it was certain that the species would plod on. Just not at the uncontrolled rate of population growth that was causing major problems worldwide. The same cycle as always would stick around for humanity; birthing-growing-reproducing-dying, birthing-growing-reproducing-dying. Birthing would just carry on less rapidly than it had been doing over the past two decades. People were still going to have children. And Falon, in fact most people who chose sterilization, were completely understanding of that. Life had room for both. For Participants who chose to have children and for Participants who chose not to. Both existed in society, and both were needed by society.

As the VSG clinician swabbed Falon's arm and inserted the IV cathlon and drip-set, she began to answer his question. They now had fifteen minutes together while Falon was infused with the serum.

"Yes, I did hear that story Falon," the clinician responded. "We received a report of transition the day she moved on."

"And is it true?" Falon pressed, "Is it true she even had her grandkids there."

"Yes it is. She was an old woman who had been slowly deteriorating. She knew there may be two or three more years at the best before she was gone. And she knew those years would be the most unfulfilling and uncomfortable years of her life. Becoming more and more incapable of doing any of the things she loved to do or enjoying the things she once loved to enjoy. So, a week before her 87th birthday she sent out invitations. And it was so comforting and inviting that I can clearly remember what her invitation said....

> *'Dearest family, Please join me at my last Birthday party. I'm old, I'm tired, and I am ready to go to a better place. Come celebrate the end of my aging process and the beginning of a new phase as I transition from life to death. Please do not be afraid...I'm not.'*

> *P.S.- no gifts allowed* "

The Perfect Candidate for Voluntary Sterilization

F alon sat still as he listened and waited. Semi-reclined and feeling the warm Progesterex solution flow into his arm. He wondered how full the room at the clinic would have been with a whole bunch of family there while a loved one transitioned. The clinician checked the drip, and reaffirmed things were going fine. Falon wanted the rest of the story. The clinician was in no hurry.

"So how big was this party? Can you tell me a bit about it?" Falon asked.

"Apparently there were almost 40 people there. She had lost her husband three years previous to a stroke. But her children were there, her priest, her grandchildren and great grandchildren, and one brother who was 6 years her junior. And they gathered together in the family transition room, visited, enjoyed cake, laughs, and a few tears. Her children supported their mother, so they avoided an ineffective eleventh-hour plea to stick around another year. They knew her mind was made up and they respected that. It wasn't entirely easy to resist the selfish urge to ask her to stay but they all did.

"She was lying in the bed fully prepared to say goodbye one last time. The optogenetic delivery pad was under her head waiting to release the quantum dots that would shut down her brain. It was not even visible to her family who began to lovingly say their last goodbyes. Once triggered, the pad would release the quantum dots and the final breath would come in seconds. The last memory she would have would be displayed for her family to see. The Encephalostream would capture and interpret the electrical activity in her hippocampus and present it on the monitor above her bed for her family to see. She had spoken with three consultants and was completely resolved that this was for her. Her life had been a full life. Full of all the love and laughter that she could have ever hoped for. And now she would pass gratefully and gracefully. On her own terms. It was time. Everyone in the room had not only said their goodbyes but they joined in a birthday song to send Grandma Amaju out with a chorus. *"Happy last birthday to you, happy last birthday to you... happy last birthday Grandma Amaju....we all will miss you."*

Falon lost track of time as he listened on to the story about Grandma Amaju.

On her birthday, at precisely 1:17 PM, the exact minute she was born 87 years ago, she set her hand on the folio that lay by her hip. A hip that was starting to wear again after being replaced 16 years ago. The folio was the switch to release the dose from the pad beneath her head. If the biometric sensors of the folio had read any fear, regret, or sensed trepidation, the optogenetics would not push. But the sensors read none. She was completely prepared to move on. The quantum dots silently passed across the dermal layers as they were released into her body.

There was no sound no drama just her eyes closing. She was gently sealed. The green light signifying a successful transition glowed under her palm that rest on the folio. Amaju was gone. There were a few tears that started to flow from her supportive family in the room. Partly because of their loss at seeing Grandma transition and partly because it was so peaceful. Everyone in the room, even the grandchildren, knew that is how she wanted her last birthday to be.

Little Amaju, the 5-year-old firecracker of a girl who was named after her great grandma, raced up the stepping stool beside the bed and leaned over and kissed her lifeless grandma on the lips whispering *"g'night Grammy"*. A tear dropped from little Amaju's cheek and rolled down the cheek of Grammy Amaju who she shared names with. Before stepping down from the bedside stool, little Amaju wiped the tear off her great Grandma's cheek and said…*"I'll miss you Grammy…"*

Falon's clinician ended the story and saw that Falon had a tear in his eye. Falon responded, "That is beautiful. That's how I want to go when I get too old to do anything."

He still had about six minutes of chair time left while the last third of the Progesterex dripped into his vascular system. He was almost sterile now, but the entire protocol still had to flow through him to ensure completion of the protocol. Bathing his reproductive system and testes with the sterilizing agent. He was curious about the woman's last memory. He asked, "And what did they see on the Stream? What was her last memory?"

The clinician spoke on, "I've been told some see the happiest moment in their life. For most people, the very last scene that goes through their mind is the one that gave them the most peace and contentment at some point in their life. A moment where they felt as if everything in their world would be alright. It is almost meditative in its display of true happiness."

"Well, what was it?"

Falon was really into it now. Being a touch vulnerable at stepping through his own life changing process, he was keen to hear the delight that last passed through Amaju's brain.

The Clinician paused.

"Eventually they might release the moment for all of us in the clinics to see. But the report I got tells what it was.

"It was the scene of the day Amaju was going off on a holiday with just her husband, to celebrate their anniversary. None of the three girls, her daughters, were going along. Amaju's sister was staying with the girls while she was away. They were promised to have a wonderful time with their auntie. But Amaju was about to leave the house. Her husband was waiting in the taxi to head to the airport. She needed to run back in because she *'forgot something.'* They had already said their goodbyes but Amaju loved those three so much, at ages 3, 5 and 7, she could never leave the house without a big hug from at least one of them.

Amaju stopped inside the door and saw the three standing, watching the door to see who was coming back in...they were holding back tears. She didn't say a word. She stooped over, held open her arms and all three of them raced as fast as they could for one last hug. Their mom was going on a holiday far away and they were going to be left without her. She was their everything. They embraced and smooshed faces and all three of them said, "I'm gonna miss you mommy..."

"Amaju squeezed them tighter and whispered, *"I'll miss you too my beautiful dolls...Mommy is going to see again soon."*

"Amaju's happiest and most content day in her life was the moment her three beautiful girls reminded her how much they were in love with their adoring mother. And they were reminded that their mother's love would always be with them no matter how far away she was."

A few glistening tears streaked down Falon's face. His response to the gentle story of a mother's love kind of took him by surprise. Maybe because he missed his mom who had been gone for 8 years now or maybe because he would never have what Amaju had with her three daughters. But the clinician was every bit a nurturer as she let Falon feel what he was feeling without putting barriers of regret in his way. He reached for a tissue in the box beside his chair. The Clinician saw there was only a couple minutes left in his protocol.

"Are you doing okay Mr. Severenson?"

"Yah I'm fine...that's just such a sweet story."

"Isn't it?" She softly affirmed his sense of the story.

Changing streams a little, the Clinician said, "Can I ask how your visits with the Consultants went?"

Falon had participated in the Multitude of Counsel Program. It was mandatory before a Participant could be approved for Sterilization. Regardless of what went on in those discussions, there was no turning back now. The Progesterex had just about run its course. As soon as the protocol was complete there would be no way to reverse the process. Falon Severenson would never have a child of his own. The Voluntary Sterilization Program had been designed so effectively, that it automatically checked sperm bank records. Once the receipt of payment was confirmed, any product the newly sterile Participant had stored at the sperm or ovary bank was automatically removed and destroyed. All of a person's health profile was connected and managed through the G-PAS. The information stored contained info on any sperm bank deposit made under Falon Severenson. And the Voluntary Sterilization Program ensured those deposits would be removed from circulation. For Falon or for any other Participant.

"Yah sure," Falon agreed to share a bit about his consults with the Multitude of Counsel reps. "They were all a little different from each other. But I really respect them. None of them tried to change my mind they just gave me lots to think about. I told them why I wanted this, and they saw my point. They each gave me a couple of reasons why some people might want to think about staying fertile. And I thought about what they said. I know that I won't have a room full of kids and grandkids when I transition someday like Grandma Amaju. But that's okay. I really want to just do life like this. Just me and my fiancé….and yes, in case you were wondering, she knows what I'm doing today."

Falon assured the clinician that his significant other was not going to be blindsided at finding out he is now sterile…then he continued.

"Less responsibility to get in the way of just loving each other and loving life. I'm not concerned I'll regret it. This is what's right for me." Falon paused. "But you know, one of the best things I learned by going through the Multitude of Counsel path while making my decisions, was that as a human, I am allowed to feel two things at once. I can feel the peace and freedom knowing I will never have children, and I am also allowed to feel some regret at that reality which will come with a sense of loss to some degree. The counsel I got gave me permission to not push away either feeling but to acknowledge it's reality and step forward with as it passes. That really helped me get here today." Falon smiled at the comfort those words had given him.

"Well that's wonderful to hear Falon because we are all done." The Clinician cheerily said as she removed the cathlon from Falon's arm and put a bandage in place.

Falon sat up in the chair and swung his legs over to the ground. "Hmmm" he said, "I don't feel any different."

"You won't. Only a very small percentage have any reaction at all to the Progesterex."

"That's good to hear…how do I…?"

The Clinician knew exactly what question was about to be asked.

"If you just head back out to the front desk, I will message them you are complete, have your G-PAS ready to swipe and as soon as it's scanned your first payment will be deposited into your account."

"Well that's easy. Thanks!"

"And it didn't hurt a bit," she added in closing their visit together.

Falon strode out of the room to head to the reception area and complete the transaction. New faces were sitting in the roomy chairs. Chairs that were filled with others just a half hour ago. Some of the clients in the clinic were obviously in the last stages of their life and had come to the clinic to transition. Others were there to enjoy the promise of a comfortable life that would come after deciding to never have children. Falon flashed his G-PAS when the receptionist instructed him to, and the money went into his account.

As he left the clinic and headed down the meandering path, Falon was happy the task was done and he was off to meet his fiancé for lunch. As for his fiancé, she got it…why someone like Falon would not want children. They had been engaged for 8 months with a wedding date set for the coming summer. She was close to making the choice for sterilization herself, but she had a hard time with Falon's decisiveness because of the finality of it all. So, her decision was yet to be made.

Falon tapped his bank account icon on his mobile device to check his account… it was there. That was a big number with the extra $200,000 sitting in his account. He checked the account twice and felt like the money would help his fiancé a lot with the idea of him being sterile. If she would do it too they would have 400 grand to launch their life together with another 600,000 over the next 3 years.

He checked messages and made his way towards the Shuttle to head downtown to meet up with her. As he did, he couldn't help but think of Grammy Amaju, little Amaju, and the heart-warming hugs that filled her final thought as she transitioned. His thoughts went back to the money as he climbed on the Shuttle and grabbed a seat. Sitting next to a not so well-dressed man who had a not so clean smell about him. Falon couldn't help but judge a little. Falon wondered why that guy wouldn't take Sol up on the Voluntary Sterilization Program. Looked like he could sure use the money. Maybe to buy a bar of soap and a shower.

Happy with his decision Falon felt like a weight had lifted off his shoulders… his future was wide open now without being restrained by the responsibilities that come with having children. He had the urge to tell the homeless looking guy across the aisle how awesome the VSP was…but he contained his zeal and kept it to himself.

Falon took a look around the streets outside the Shuttle window. He wondered how many of the people on the streets would be candidates too. His experience was smooth. For Falon, life was still out there ahead of him. His sterilization and the payments that were to his credit would prove to be a taste of freedom for this young Participant. As Falon looked at the bandage on the inside of the elbow his thoughts of contentment comforted him. He gave little thought to the millions yet to take the VSP offer. Many who would be filled with regret for their decision. Or in some cases, self-destruct at the harm they would bring on themselves by having such a large injection of cash into their lives. VSP wasn't for everyone. But Falon was certain it was for him. The perfect candidate for the Voluntary Sterilization Program.

Sol Could Not Be Bought

Out on the patio where Sol and the Delegates first met, the sun was in its descent after cresting about 3 hours ago. The shadows cast across the patio gave the sense of quiet that was not felt when the noon day sun hid all the shadows. Ell and Sol's shrubs rustled in the whispy breeze that pushed through their back yard. The party of five was getting together today for a meeting like few others. There was a sense of urgency from Tomer and Ahmed. The area was secure. In fact, the entire cul-de-sac was secure, the park behind Ell and Sol's home was secure, and the air above them was secure. Since becoming King, Sol's home castle had not changed much. Not much beyond the security and defense system that was programmed to detect and neutralize any threat by ground or air. As for the rest of the neighborhood…it had sure changed. It had gotten a lot quieter. Since most of Sol's neighbors had moved away from the block their visitors and deliveries stopped coming around too. There were no more break-ins, or revving engines that would race in and out of the cul-de-sac picking up or dropping off a girlfriend. It was the most secure street in the whole country. With the guard shack at the mouth of the cul-de-sac and the ever-present security forces that occupied most of Sol's old neighbors' homes, the only traffic that found its way into the idyllic Seattle neighborhood, was traffic approved and escorted by the King's security personnel. And this early morning meeting of Sol, Ell, Tomer, Ahmed, and Erin, was a meeting that was focussed on a threat to security and safety. The security and safety of the King.

The five exchanged greetings. As they passed through the kitchen toward the patio, Ell and Erin stopped to get a coffee. They took a moment to chat in the kitchen while they stirred their coffee. Ell reached through the holo-cupboard door to grab a mug for Sol. With a *zsshh* sound the holograph went off then on again. The others had moved along to get settled into the wicker chairs on the patio.

Catching up with the guys, Ell and Erin stepped out into the sunny back yard. Ahmed, Tomer, and Sol were already getting into the seriousness of the meeting. Ell quickly tuned in to the conversation. Hearing the very serious words of Ahmed. She automatically interrupted.

"What are you saying? Is someone planning to kill Sol? Who? Why? What are you going to do to stop them?"

Sol knew it was no small threat. And Ell picked up on Tomer's intensity right away. They both knew there were clauses in the Checkmate protocol that dealt with the death of the King by assassination. Yet they really hadn't thought... actually really had hoped, there would be any serious threat of that ever happening. The naiveté that came with their inexperience in this realm of global politics was quite apparent. Sol was catching a glimpse of how serious the threat was by how focused Tomer and Ahmed were. The intel that had come through Tomer's office with the Ministry of Retribution was indisputable. The ENKI system faithfully collected dossiers on every person on the planet. Adding info gleaned from the ENKI system to other intel Tomer was given, clearly disclosed the plan to have Sol killed. There was going to be an attempted regicide. An attempt on the King's life. Tomer's portfolio included the arm of Global security that would watch for and identify threats to the King's safety.

As Erin took a seat next to Ahmed and Ell stood anxiously looming over the arm rest of the wicker couch Sol was sitting on, Ahmed looked up to Ell. In his very reassuring yet serious tone, Ahmed shared the distressing reality.

"Ell, it has come to our attention that Sol is in danger. We will do whatever it takes to ensure nothing happens to your husband our King…" Ahmed glanced toward Tomer.

"As important as Sol is to our World right now, I understand that he is even more important to you. I understand how distressing it must be to hear what you are about to hear, but neither Sol nor you will be harmed. Tomer, Erin, and I assure you of this fact."

Sol scooted over enough for Ell to take a seat beside him. This meeting on the patio was hardly as exciting as the last time Ahmed and Erin met at Sol's house. But it was every bit as emotional. The threat was chilling…it was very real.

"You better be damn sure nothing happens Ahmed…You find the person who's planning to do this…you better make sure Sol is safe Ahmed…!" Ell demanded.

Sol placed his hand on Ell's knee to offer some comfort. Ell started to tear up thinking she could possibly lose him. They had been through so much in their 28 years of marriage. They had been the team that was always there for each other, shoulder to cry on or shoulder to stand on when one of them needed support.

And now, seeing the threat that was in front of them, Ell was impassioned about her demand to ensure Sol's safety. Ell wanted a guarantee that Sol would be safe. Tomer understood her intensity and he knew what needed to happen.

"Ell, I get it." Tomer assured. "I don't blame you for feeling that way. I am prepared to do whatever it takes to make certain you and Sol will grow old together. This is a serious threat, and I will make sure to remove it. That's my job and I have had a team working on it since last week after Sol met with Amyl Rothschild."

Ell knew of that meeting. Sol had told her that it got a little uncomfortable when Rothschild didn't get his way with Sol. Amyl Rothschild was near the top of the list of the richest men in the world. And he was said to be one of the more influential power brokers in the renowned group called the *Rule of Nines.*

The *Rule of Nines* had come to be the title of a group made up of the world's nine richest men. And they always did anything they wanted and got anything they wanted. They believed in the power of wealth and that billionaires should be the people who hold political power. Nine men from historic family lines who owned and controlled almost two-thirds of the world's wealth. Nine men from various parts of the world who many believed were the real people who ruled the world.

"Here's what we know," Tomer continued. "Amyl Rothschild is part of the Rule of Nines. He is the player in this group who is best known for his political influence. The list of high-level politicians who have been bought off by Amyl and his Rothschild predecessors is extensive."

Tomer went on to explain more of the situation. Ahmed had already been briefed, Ell, Erin, and Sol sipped coffee and listened closely to Tomer speak.

"Last week when Sol met with him, Amyl had a discussion with Sol about immigration laws and about the *Redistribution of Wealth Edict*. There was a lot about that edict that the Rule of Nines thought was so wrong. Amyl wasn't pleased how Sol had enhanced the free flow of immigration from region to region and country to country. Rothschild had already shown his displeasure with the legacy immigration policies of the World Congress and he felt the need to assert his opposition more so when Sol loosened the immigration rules even further.

"The stipulation in the immigration program, that requires newcomers to a region must have gainful employment within 6 months or they must return to their region, was going to make a huge impact on the Rothschild import business. They have been importing newcomers for decades and the charges they levied on the families of those newcomers to purchase passage to the region of choice, has made them billions of dollars. The *Rothschild Immigration Sponsorship Program* was only one payoff away from being an illegal slave trade. It was in fact quite steeped in corruption and neglectful of human dignity. Many had been harmed and disenfranchised at the hands of the 'Rothschild Immigration Sponsorship Program'.

"When Amyl addressed his concerns over Sol's loose migration policies, he saw Sol was not interested in redesigning the law and was unconcerned with Amyl's business losses. Amyl saw Sol could not be convinced to see things his way. It enraged him that Sol could not be bought."

I Hope Your Reign Is Not Cut Short

Ell was hearing Tomer and she looked at Sol with incredulity. "Why didn't you tell me about this? Did Rothschild threaten you Sol?"

Sol asked Ell to hold tight for another moment or two so Tomer could tell the next part. "Sorry love, but just wait a moment or two, there's more."

Ell turned back to Tomer.

"In that meeting Amyl proceeded to tell Sol how much it was going to cost him to pay the Humanitarian Tax Sol had edicted. Exactly to the penny how much the added tax on the money of the ultra-rich would cost Rothschild. Rothschild tried to make out like it was a privilege to pay the tax. Feigning that he was always interested in helping humanity. But Sol was unconvinced. We all know Rothschild will only help those whose cause helped his…and that cause was money and power. That man is about money, power, and nothing else. He comes from a long line of predecessors whose entire world was about generating wealth. Generating wealth so they could have power to control the world. When Rothschild suggested Sol amend the tax reform and have the Humanitarian Tax portion reduced as well as suggesting the King draws from those taxes for his coffers, Sol knew what Rothschild was trying to do. And it was clear Rothschild wasn't inclined to take

Sol seriously or Sol's role as King of the World. Suggesting Sol use the reduced tax amounts as, "*A fund to deal with emergent needs of the King and his counsel.*"

"He was trying to tempt Sol with a way to gain great wealth and great power. But Sol had no need of what Amyl Rothschild was offering.

"It was clear Rothschild was positioning himself to be part of the King's Counsel. Amyl Rothschild wanted to "own" the new King as well. He was pushing to open a door for the Rule of Nines to make decisions pertaining to the Global economic strategy and development."

Ell reframed Tomer's report and was quick to put a fine point on the kind of man Sol is.

"Sol cannot be bought…**period**!" She exclaimed.

The group paused. Sol was looking down at the Tabletop Folio that showed images of Rothschild shaking hands with several world leaders over the past 15 years. In those images it was easy to see what the world saw. A man who rarely went out in public had taken strains to meet with dignitaries in secluded places. He always appeared to be a supportive businessman. Presenting his image as if he were there to encourage the women and men who were slugging it out in the political trenches. But after sitting down with him for only a short afternoon, Sol realized that was not the real Rothschild.

The day they sat together in the World Counsel Center and spoke about the *Redistribution of Wealth Laws* and the *Immigration Laws*, it became clear. Rothschild would not stop short of getting what he wanted. He hadn't become a member of the ultra-rich and elite Rule of Nines group by rolling over on issues that were near and dear to him. And there was no issue nearer and dearer to him than his money. Never stop making money, make as much as you can, and make it however you can…as long as it looks legal…. "legalish" that is.

Some of the businesses he was involved in were corrupt enough to have him locked away for all kinds of human rights violations and atrocities. But Rothschild looked clean only because he had a knack for insulating himself. Insulating himself from the dirty part of wealth that he would say, is necessary for the business world to prosper and keep the globe running.

When he and Sol parted ways that day it seemed Rothschild's ego was pricked. He couldn't buy Sol, and it gnawed at him. In his world, everyone could be bought. At least that's what Rothschild thought. But this wasn't his world…it was Sol's. He believed getting to Sol early in his reign would certainly be the right move to persuade the nascent King to align with him. He was a tenacious man. A man who always got his way. A man who had some of the most powerful associates in the world, a man who was richer than a hundred of the richest men combined, and had no taste for those who would not pander to him.

As they closed their meeting, the coldness that surfaced from Rothschild chilled the room. He stood ominously trying to display his power.

He reached for Sol's hand even before Sol had made it to his feet. Sol had never seen anything like it. And even though he could feel how pissed off Rothschild was, Sol stood with composure and accepted Amyl's hand. Amyl could barely hide his displeasure and Sol could feel that this was a deal breaker. Rothschild was not used to a world where there was only one man in charge. Rothschild was like an entitled teen…who couldn't comprehend that Sol wouldn't agree that it was his Rothschild money that ran the world? Men and Women have little say when real power comes with having untold wealth. Amyl Rothschild however, was not in tune with a system that no longer had layers of political players who he could sift through in order to influence policy and laws to his benefit. With Sol in power now, Amyl began to feel the most indelibly uneasy feeling that he had not felt since he was a little boy…a feeling of powerlessness.

As a boy, young Amyl was forced by his maniacally money addicted father to study the stock market. Little Amyl, only 7 years old, could be found sitting in front of the computer staring at meaningless colorful graphs and investment charts, while the other kids were out playing as 7-year-olds should. Little Amyl had no power to change his forced imprisonment to the computer and the persistent withdrawal of his childhood right to have fun outdoors with friends. And Sol could sense how much of a deal-breaker it was for Amyl to have no power to move Sol in the Rule of Nines direction. Sol did not support Amyl's ideas and Sol won no support from Amyl Rothschild. Historians had long testified to the intensity with which the Rothschilds operated their empire, and demanded their *"Rights as Rothschilds"*.

Frederic Morton, a Rothschild biographer and historian, described the passion for money that has flowed down through the lineage of the Rothschilds. It is said that Mayer Amschel Rothschild, a mogul from the 18th century Frankfurt Germany, and his five sons were "wizards" of finance, and "fiendish calculators" who were motivated by a "demonic drive" to succeed in their secret undertakings. It was no coincidence that Sol had met with Amyl in the Luxembourg World Counsel Center. Just a few hours from Frankfurt where the Rothschilds got their start in world economic domination. Sol would be back in Germany in a couple of weeks at the Luxembourg World Congress Plaza where his next address would be.

As far as Amyl Rothschild is concerned, he had a certain notoriety amongst his ultra-rich peers that escaped the common knowledge of this tycoon. Going somewhat rogue from the other 8 in his elite group of 9, Rothschild had often been seen as less of a colleague with the other 8 and more of an antagonist. In fact, for anyone to claim that the nine richest men in the world were looking out for each other's well-being, prosperity, and best interest, well, they would be deluded. Men who were that rich always wanted to be the richest in the group. It was a competition with other billionaires that was so intense, deep, and calculated, that it lay hidden under the surface of all the richest people in the world. The only thing that would make them happier than seeing what all their money had accomplished for them, would be to have someone else's money as well. It wasn't the typical envy one might expect of the super-rich. Envy over the brilliance or acumen another had that continually lead to success. No, envy was too innocuous of a feeling for this group. These men, although never showing it, were dealing with jealousy. Pure unadulterated, manipulative, conscience-free jealousy. Children have envy over a sibling's toy at Christmas…Wealthy men in the World have jealousy. Scheming to get what others have so others no longer have it.

They really didn't care about the well-being of anyone else. They really didn't want good for their fellow group members. Each of them. Like so many of the ultra-rich, would not only do anything they could to get more wealth, but they would do anything they could to keep their wealth out of the hands of their enemies. When it came down to it, the professional connection the members of the Rule of Nines maintained was only maintained as long as each member could benefit individually. These men were no better than any sick addict, and they didn't want anyone to see that. Some claimed the only reason the men would wear dark glasses when meeting with one or more in their group, was because they needed to hide the greed and jealousy in their eyes.

Erin broke in with a question that she needed to know the answer to. "What did he say when he shook your hand and saw you can't be bought Sol?"

Sol had been tense. He knew there was only one certain way to deal with this matter. He had seen Amyl's body language, the eyes, heard the words of Amyl Rothschild. Rothschild's threat seemed promissory. When Amyl took Sol's hand and held it...not shaking it in a gesture of understanding and acceptance he just held it snugly as if to say, you can't move unless I say you can move. When Sol felt the world's richest man attempt to exert his control over the parting handshake, he knew there would be trouble. Sol recognized the frustration of a man who wanted to buy the power of the King. But he was unable to exert his control over Sol's position. Sol knew this was real. Amyl offered no smile of concession or vague disappointment before parting. He stoically left Sol with just a few parting words. Words that were dripping with ambiguity and the menacing air of a veiled threat. A threat Amyl wanted Sol to hear but wanted it to be veiled.

"Well then," Amyl said in preparation to exit the afternoon meeting. "I guess this is the end for us Sol...I truly hope things go well for you in the future. I hope we will have a chance to do this again sometime. I'm sure you are able to continue to lead with the resolve and integrity that you have begun leading with and..." Sol had not expected the words that came next from Rothschild to be so ominous... words that came with a foreboding tone and more than a nuance of warning...

"I hope your reign is not cut short *King Sol.*"

Sol knew Amyl Rothschild had no respect for him. He had no respect for anyone but himself. Calling Sol "King" was meant as nothing more than a mocking statement. Sweetened by the forced calmness of a man feeling he'd lost some control over his world.

At that Amyl released Sol's hand back to him. He turned and walked out of the room.

There Was Only One Choice...Kill Him First

Ell looked straight at Tomer. She was obviously aggravated.

"What are you and your team doing about this Tomer? This guy is going to try to kill Sol! And you know it!"

Not waiting for the answer or stopping to take a breath, Ell threw down her gauntlet, "If you don't do something I will!!!"

Ell was almost out of her seat ready to head to Germany, find this ultra-rich, ultra-arrogant Billionaire, and grab him by the throat until he stopped breathing. She for one was ready to stop Amyl Rothschild before he had a chance to undo Sol. That meant doing something now.

Tomer looked at Ell and politely asked, "What do you suggest Mrs. James?"

Ell had no answer. She was not part of that world...at least not that part of that world. She knew what needed to be done but she didn't have a plan how to make it happen. That's where the others in the room took over. And it was becoming clear to all of them, they must act...because there would be no stopping a man like Amyl Rothschild.

As Sol swiped at the tabletop Folio scanning images of Rothschild and shots of many of his business activities, he had made up his mind. Erin sat quietly on the other side of the patio table and took in the scrolling images upside down. The meeting of this unique inner counsel had all of a sudden become extremely serious. What they decided on here would affect everything.

Tomer had discovered through sources that Amyl Rothschild was planning to have Sol killed after his address in Germany that was only days away. A regicide on Rothschild's home soil.

As Sol was leaving the World Counsel Center, Rothschild would approve the attack. Already known for the Mercenary Stables that he funded, Amyl Rothschild only had to give the go…and Sol would be killed in a simple planned vehicle collision that would result in an explosion. Tomer and his teams could definitely neutralize the attack, but Amyl himself was the real threat. A persistent threat that would not stop until Sol was dead. He was prepared to make an assassination look as if it were urban gangs who pulled the trigger. Making the killing look like it was a reaction to Sol's *Gang City Edict* that was to be sealed soon. After a leak to the media everyone paying attention knew the *Gang City Edict* was coming.

That edict was a death knell for gangs. The way Sol had spoken of a Participant's right to unhindered safety, freedom to be out at night without fear, and how those in organized crime would not be allowed to be part of our healthy society for long, made it clear Sol was preparing to deal with the Gang problem once and for all. Gangs were not too keen on the expected mass culling of them from mainstream society and Amyl Rothschild would leverage this fact to orchestrate Sol's murder.

But Tomer had mapped it all out. Even finding intel on the false gang connection to the regicide. An attempt on Sol's life would be coming through Rothschild. Any decision to stop that attempt and to stop Rothschild had to be effective and the solution had to be final. There was only one way to be a hundred percent effective at stopping this imminent threat. And it had to send the message that no matter who you were, threats to the King's life would not be left unrequited.

Sol flipped another picture. The shot was of Amyl Rothschild about 7 years ago. He was at a rally for clean water in Namibia. Sol paused at the picture. Erin was paying closer attention as the people in the picture pricked something for her. The mood in the shot was celebratory. Surrounding the celebrated Amyl was a group of men. They looked to be more than grateful villagers. Zooming in on one of the men Sol could see an automatic rifle resting with the butt on the ground and a hand wrapped around the tip of the barrel. The man with the gun stood just over Amyl's right shoulder. He appeared to be one of the more jubilant celebrants in the shot. This man's village just got two new wells thanks to the Rothschild money. His hand was on the shoulder of his water-divining hero. By the picture it was obvious that the two men had a familiar connection. This was one of the few public photos that could be found of Amyl. The man with a hand on his shoulder looked eerily familiar to Sol. Sol spun the image around for Ahmed to take a look.

"Ahmed, who is that in the shot with Amyl?"
Ahmed bent closer to the tabletop folio.
"It looks to be Jonas Kearny."

"Isn't that the terrorist who kidnapped all the school children?" Ell asked.

"Yes it is," Ahmed replied. "Tomer, what do you know about this?"

"We have learned Amyl Rothschild threw about 35 million dollars of funding into this region in Namibia. He was trying to get the mineral rights for a large area and gave away cash to people like Kearny to try to buy the approval of villagers in the area. He also had wells installed in many of these areas in an attempt to buy enough favour with the people, that acquiring the mineral rights would not be a problem. We are of the opinion he was aware that the money he funnelled to the area was mostly given to Kearny. Our best intel tells us Amyl Rothschild was funding a terrorist organization."

Ell asked the question again…Tomer was not going to make the suggestion. Ahmed was still reeling from the news that Amyl Rothschild was connected to a Namibian terrorist organization. The very terrorist group that general Takanaka had just taken out. Ell knew what she would do if given the chance to remedy the situation. Amyl would never get the chance to try to kill Sol if she had it her way.

"Well, what are we going to do?"

The patio felt as if it narrowed in on the five. As if no one was ready to say what should be done. Yet, it was so clear what to do…somebody just had to say it. It made sense on a street level. If someone was coming to take you out and you knew it, you could run, but only until they caught up with you somewhere, sometime… always looking over your shoulder, or you could take them out first. It just made sense to make a decisive move before your pursuer had a chance to. And at that moment, with a quick flick of his fingers Sol set the picture on the folio of Amyl Rothschild spinning.

Ell wasn't waiting any longer. She asked, "You know what I would do?"

Tomer didn't need to answer. Everyone in the room knew what Ell had been alluding to and the answer was clear. There was only one choice. And in unison, both Sol and Erin said,

"Kill him first."

That was it. It was decided. The man was a threat to the life of the King of the World. It could have been any man, but this man was the renowned Amyl Rothschild. And he had known associations with a terrorist organization. Tomer had info of the plan to kill Sol at his upcoming address in Luxembourg. Now, Sol just had to find a way to get to Amyl Rothschild when they got to Luxembourg and seal him before Amyl Rothschild got a chance to Kill King Sol.

Proof of His Intent to Kill Sol

"Tomer we're all set. He's going to meet us here in Luxembourg for the Great Assembly."

Sol gave Tomer the update on his scheduled meeting with Amyl, after getting off the FaceStream with Amyl Rothschild. Rothschild had people everywhere. Some of them couldn't stand the pugnacious Billionaire, while others were extremely loyal to him. For Sol's part, the only loyalty he had was to his wife Ell and to the world he was asked to lead. Had Tomer and his team not gathered so much intel on the assassination plan, Sol would be a touch more worried.

On the flight back over to Germany a week after the five met on Sol's patio, Tomer had briefed Sol.

The plan Rothschild had in place to take out Sol was no different than the assassination plans for Kings throughout history. Rothschild would make the call after Sol's address. The King's speech would be over and while the adoring crowd was filtering out of the Luxembourg World Counsel Centre Plaza, the plan Tomer had uncovered was for Rothschild's men to be signalled to set the assassination in motion. As Sol and whoever was travelling with him from the World Counsel Center made their way to the Luxembourg Airport, a rogue vehicle was assigned to intercept Sol's car. The interceptor would be crashed into the King's vehicle and when the King was transferred from his disabled vehicle an explosion was to be triggered. Killing King Sol and anyone with him. It was designed to look like a crude act of retribution from disgruntled gang members. It was known throughout the gang crime world that gangs would soon be corralled by the Global Military Unit and relocated to the massive Gang City Island that was being prepared to house millions of society's most dedicated criminals.

The small chance something would go wrong, and Sol ends up dead instead of Rothschild, was ample reason for Sol to make sure Ell stayed home. She wouldn't be joining him in Germany this time. All she was told is that Rothschild would be killed. Ell would be eagerly waiting to hear from Sol as soon as he could assure her the threat was gone.

Tomer was the key to the whole thing. He had designed the plan, and Sol was ready to do his part. His part was the definitive portion of the plan. A part that would normally be handled buy one of Tomer's team or a special agent handpicked by Takanaka. Everything had to look perfectly normal or Amyl Rothschild's fear might override his ego. He was an extremely cautious man, yet his thirsty ego would drive him to think the King must have changed his mind. In Tomer's plan Sol would have Amyl believing he wants Amyl close to him as he announces the reforms to his *Redistribution of Wealth* laws and the popular *Humanitarian Tax* law.

The only part of the plan that had a chance to blow up in their faces, was the ride Sol would be taking from his hotel to the World Counsel Center for the address. If things weren't resolved before Sol got to the Luxembourg WCC, then the chances Rothschild's plan would be successful would go up. It was during the ride with Rothschild in the car that Sol needed to act. Ahmed had booked Sol into a hotel about 10 kilometers away from the Plaza. The normal facilities where Sol would stay were adjacent to the World Counsel Center campus. But for the plan to work, there needed to be reason for Amyl Rothschild to ride with Sol from his hotel. Little did Amyl know, the King's accommodation arrangements were the key to Sol and Tomer's plan. His lack of suspicion gave them confidence that everything would fall into place. If that part of the plan slipped past him then Sol and Tomer were confident the rest would fall into place.

In the King's car, with the King's Minister of Retribution as the driver, Sol and Tomer would bring the Rothschild threat to an end. And Tomer was making sure every piece was in place to ensure the Rothschild threat ended…for good.

"So did you speak to Rothschild directly or did you talk with his manager?" Tomer asked Sol.

"I talked to Amyl himself. Sol replied, "He's going to meet me at the hotel, and we will head over to the Plaza in our car."

Tomer offered, "Listen Sol, if you have any trouble doing this, I'll be just in the front seat. I can step in if you feel like it's too much….that's not your job you know."

Tomer was taking the scenario right to completion in his head. He was ready to jump in if his King needed him. What Sol had accomplished since becoming King, who Sol was to him, and how Sol won Tomer's loyalty through offering him liberty, gave Tomer the inspiration to be there for Sol for whatever he wanted. The day Sol sat across that table in the Cape Vincent Corrections facility and offered him a job like no other, Tomer realized that he was with Sol no matter what. Loyalty through liberty was a powerful force that inspired people like Tomer to serve Sol passionately.

The address would be given in the next hours. Sol was on his way to the Plaza now. As Sol's car pulled out of the underground parking at the hotel, Tomer was behind the wheel. Sol sat nervously taking up his usual spot on the rear passenger side of the car. Anxious to see if Amyl would show up like he'd agreed or if something spooked him off.

The light cloud cover in the sky set up for a cool day. Sol's attire for the occasion was perfect. Moments earlier getting ready in the hotel room, as he pulled on his light jacket and new gloves to prepare for the cool open air of an afternoon address in Luxembourg, Sol looked at his hands and wondered if Amyl would think it odd to be wearing gloves on the ride over. He couldn't tell the gloves apart. The Sealing glove on his left hand looked exactly like its mate on the right. Sol had to be sharp to capitalize on the first opportunity that presented itself. The 10-kilometer journey would go quickly and if an opportunity to complete the task passed, another one may not come before the address…putting Sol at risk every moment that passed.

Sol reminded himself that Amyl is planning to kill him. If ever there was time to stay in control of a conversation then this would be it. Looking up from his gloved hands Sol spotted Amyl's limousine standing in front of the hotel under the canopy. Tomer swung around the driveway and pulled in beside the Rothschild car. Amyl's driver stepped out of the car and opened the rear door. Rothschild walked around the rear of the King's car, and his driver scooted the opposite way around to catch the door for Amyl to enter Sol's limousine. The creaks of the seat were muted as the soft leather hugged the guest in the royal car. Amyl set himself in place and his driver closed the door. The car now contained the King of the world and one of the richest men in the world…But unknown to Amyl the driver's seat held the Minister of Retribution.

"Greetings Amyl," Sol started as soon as the confident sharp suited Rothschild was comfortable.

"It's good to see you again Sol."

Thinking he had an upper hand on Sol, Amyl began removing his gloves as the car pulled out from under the hotel canopy to head to the Plaza.

"I am glad to see you reconsidered my advice. I truly do want things to go well for you as King…Our future well-being and your safety is uncertain, so it is important we see eye to eye on certain things."

Sol could not believe his ears and Tomer was equally as stunned. This arrogant man who was part of the Rule of Nines had almost become a king in his own mind. And right here right now on the way to the address, he was re-stating the threat to Sol. His innuendo was clear. His statements, like all veiled threats, were intended to subtly coerce. Sol knew Amyl was willing to do anything to get his own way. He turned slightly towards his guest. He knew there was no agreement with Rothschild but the fact that the egomaniac thought Sol was coming to agree with him, heightened the unction to make the most of this opportunity. And Rothschild's egomania kept him completely oblivious to what was about to happen.

"Well," Sol responded, "I'm glad we're here together because as you know Amyl, we both agree that it's necessary to resolve our disagreement. This is a great day to settle our incongruence once and for all."

"Yes it is." Amyl could not stop reasserting his threat…even though in his view Sol was coming into line with what he wanted.

"It is good to know you are able to see my point Sol. It would have been unfortunate if things had not gone the way that was best for both of us."

Amyl distanced his tone just slightly. "There is no telling what dangers might come our way if one were to charge forward without considering the sound advice of a friend."

Sol was no friend of Amyl Rothschild. And in no way would he want to be associated with this corrupt Billionaire. Amyl kept affirming what in his own mind, was Sol's newfound understanding while he casually divided his attention between Sol and his mobile device. And Sol was pulling it off…he was getting Amyl where he needed him to end the threat to his own life. Without telling Amyl he was on his side Sol simply watched this wolf in sheep's clothing presume the victory. Amyl blathered on about the great things that are in store for Sol now. Inferring that now that Sol agreed with Amyl the future would bring success. While blathering, he calmly tapped at his device and sent the message to abort the mission. Had Sol known the mission to kill him was off he might have changed his own plan to end Amyl's threat once and for all. But that might only keep Sol safe for a day or two… until Amyl saw his position had not changed.

Almost halfway to the Plaza now, Tomer's team had intercepted the message that had just left Amyl Rothschild's device. The unquestionable proof of his intent to kill Sol was now in hand. Even though Sol was safe…for today…his own mission for safety tomorrow and the years ahead was not yet complete.

He Needed A Minute
But He Took Two

As Tomer kept driving he tapped the paired folio set in the dashboard. Sol glanced down at his left glove. It had instantly warmed inside about a half degree. Sealing gloves always warmed slightly when they were booted up. He began to remove his right-hand glove.

Slowly, he pulled it off. He knew when Tomer had activated the system. The plan could find its conclusion. Sol was focussed.

This glove had been programmed to measure the status of only one man. This unique Sealing glove was programmed for Amyl Rothschild. Set to confirm through a biometric check that not only the man it was touching was the right man but also determine if he were lying or if he were telling the truth.

"Well Amyl, then I guess it's time. It's time to put all this to rest once and for all. I'm convinced this meeting will ensure we don't have any further conflict in the future. It is going to be so much easier to sleep at night knowing I have done the right thing."

At Sol's words, Amyl could perceive nothing other than this was the day the King of the World became another of Rothschild's servants…Another purchased politician willing to do his bidding.

Sol finished removing his right glove leaving the left glove in place…It was just gentlemanly to have a handshake to seal the deal. A handshake was always worthy of skin-to-skin contact…No barriers between gentlemen making an agreement. Then, with confidence and the reassuring body language Amyl would have expected to see, he stretched out his hand. And said, "Shall we seal our renewed relationship?"

To Amyl Rothschild this was a weak King's invitation to seal the new understanding. An understanding he believed they had that was about to be sealed with the handshake of two men in very powerful positions. Amyl smiled and reciprocated. The two were hand in hand, now nearing the largest address Sol was yet to deliver. Sol looked in Amyl's eyes. Keeping hold of the hand of this lead player from the Rule of Nines, Sol's gloved hand enveloped the back of Amyl's ungloved hand with his own as they shook hands.

"Before I make the huge announcement about what went on in this historic ride together Amyl, do you mind if I ask you one more question?"

Rothschild was so filled with self-worship at believing he had just bought himself a king that he instantly agreed to Sol's request, and he squeezed Sol's hand a little firmer as if it were he in control now.

"Of course Sol, ask me anything you'd like."

Sol knew what was coming with his version of a poison handshake no matter how Amyl answered this last question.

"Amyl, let's say we were not in agreement with each other today, would it be your plan to have me killed?"

In the most arrogant statement Sol could have imagined coming from Amyl Rothschild's mouth, he didn't even show enough humility to avoid self-indictment. So filled with the dance of corruption that travels alongside great wealth that he didn't seem to care how Sol took it. He rebutted, "Sol, it's complicated. Let's just say your family will be happy that you have chosen to see things my way. But none of that matters right now King Sol…you just keep playing King and I'll just keep running the world."

The status of the mark was clear to Sol, and it was confirmed by the Sealing glove. Without any external indicators the optogenetic discharge of quantum dots pushed. They cascaded through the vessels in the back of Amyl's right hand in milliseconds. The result was nothing dramatic or even graphic. But it was instant. Just an old man stopping breathing. The nano-fireworks exploded inside his brain and all the money in the world couldn't stop this corrupt old man from listing over to the right as his brain shut down.

Sol kept hold of his hand not knowing how long the glove had been in skin contact after discharge. Even though he was completely inexperienced in the realm of ending a person's life by Sealing them, Sol and Ell had decided he should be the one to Seal this man. Sol the King chose to Seal the man who was going to take the King's life. And although he expected more theatrics in the first seconds of the 13 second sequence that shut down Rothschild's brain and body, the decision was final. Sol just kept holding Amyl's hand while he shut down. The optogenetic quantum dots hit every region of Amyl Rothschild's brain. The hippocampus rapidly replayed a lifetime of memories, each one emotionally charged by the amygdala, in his final moments.

But Sol's uncertainty kept him squeezing a little longer. While keeping hold of Rothschild's limp hand, Sol popped up to a stooping stance in the back seat of the car. Quickly he stepped over to Amyl's side and used his shoulder and forearm to lift the listing billionaire back up. Leaning him against the head rest that had been wired with encephalostream sensors to catch the dying man's final thoughts.

Tomer had told Sol he may need to do this *"If Rothschild slumped over."* Tomer had instructed Sol, *"You have to get his head back against the headrest."* It was important to catch the last images that flitted through the brain of this dying man. And Sol made sure he did. Tomer called back to the King, "Everything on track sir?"

Sol grunted out a reply, "Yes it looks like it's over." As he awkwardly hunched over in the back of the car.

With Rothschild lifelessly resting on the headrest of the seat, Sol flopped back into his own seat and hit the button to lower the privacy screen. Tomer was peering back at him through the rear-view mirror.

"Whew!" Sol exclaimed.

"Are you ok Sol?" Tomer asked.

"Yah. It's done. Ell will be able to sleep better knowing I'm safe."

Sol played it like it would help Ell, but this was the case for both of them…he would be able to sleep better too now. Just as he told Rothschild a moment ago.

"I know," Tomer responded. "Glad to hear you're Ok."

Tomer had received an instant update from the biometric sensors on the dashboard folio while Amyl was shutting down.

"We're just about there Sol." Then Tomer added, "Did you realize that he called off the hit on you about a minute before you sealed him?"

"Oh…that's what was so important. I was thinking it was a bit rude to keep checking messages while we were chatting. I guess were doing ok then."

Sol was relieved to hear that news from Tomer. They were a kilometer away from the Plaza now.

"Sol," Tomer paused looking in the mirror until he knew Sol was with him again. "I was able to watch the encephalostream as Rothschild was shutting down. It confirmed a lot of things. If you are still planning to announce Amyl's death at the Great Assembly, I think it might be a good idea to show a little of it when you make the announcement."

"Uh…" Sol began to become a little distracted now…he wasn't sure how he felt after taking the final intervention to end the threat on his life.

"Sounds Good Tomer, get it to Ahmed and tell him to stream whatever you two think will be best for the announcement. I'll have it played right after I announce Amyl has been sealed."

Sol started to fade a bit. The sealed Billionaire had faded completely. He sat lifeless beside him. Not moving, not breathing, and not threatening. Dead guys didn't have much need for power...or for their money anymore. And Sol had already decided what to do with Amyl Rothschild's billions. He knew it would send a message just how much the King was for the people. And how futile it would be to try to buy this King.

Tomer stopped the car. They were 300 meters away from the Plaza and needed to send Rothschild's body with the Harvest Crew. Sol hopped out and into a fresh car that was waiting. No King would want to drive into the Plaza with a dead guy sitting beside him...that's just creepy.

The plan had worked perfectly. When Sol settled into the seat of the fresh car he told the driver, "Hey, when we pull up, I'm just going to need a minute before I get out and head backstage."

"Yes sir." Was the response.

Sol hit the button and the privacy screen rolled up. It was quiet. Sol said he needed a minute, but he took two.

Take Out Your Killer First

The crowd greeted their King in a deserving manner. Applause and cheers as Sol headed out on stage for the address as he had before. People, all over the world had begun to offer allegiance to Sol. They saw he was like them. A guy who wanted a better world. He was using his power how they all hoped he would. How many of them would if it were they who had been selected as King. The people's King who was truly doing the greatest good for the greatest number. They saw the oft present questions of possible corruption or despotism readily dissolved by the actions Sol took. But here in Germany, in his address in front of a live crowd, streamed across the globe, there was a concern for how the regionals might respond to the news of Amyl Rothschild's death? Rothschild was a son of this land and Sol, although he had great respect for the German people's sense of justice, still had trepidations towards how they might react to the news.

The applause tapered as Sol took a position just in front of the Speaker's podium. His image larger than life on the stage screen and the holo-streams throughout the Plaza glowing blue just before Sol came into the beamed image. The familiar chill from the cool day with little sun was lessened by the warmth of the crowd that had gathered. Sol was about to give his third address. He had delivered and sealed edicts from home, with some of them being streamed right from his den to the world. But the novelty of the new King standing in solitude before his people, declaring dramatic reformation, was cause for the Plaza to fill with eager Address goers. Sol was ready.

"Greetings friends. It is wonderful to be here with you in Germany. I have some very important things to share with you today. Some possibly unsettling and some possibly a little mundane. But nonetheless, all very important for moving our world to the better place we all know it can be. I want to begin by asking a question. I'd like a show of hands on this one."

Ahmed had run the numbers on this. He had a brief discussion with Sol about today's address. Based on the demography of those who showed up at the World Counsel Plaza to participate in the Great Assembly Addresses, Sol could expect to see anywhere from 68 to 76 percent of people affirm his actions. Sol hoped for better but realized that was easily a large margin who are supporters.

"Ladies and Gentlemen, let me ask you a question. If your life were threatened by a colleague or someone who had power to kill you, what should you do? What should you do if you knew this person, and those who worked on his or her behalf, had set a plan in place to kill you?"

Sol's question caught the crowd off guard, he continued.

"Soon though, you caught wind of the plan and there was clearly no way for things to change. According to your pursuer, he would not stop until you were dead. What would you do?" Sol went on with a simple poll of the crowd.

The crowd was intrigued. Placed deep into thought by such an evocative concept. What was Sol up to? They were willing to play along. This was not a usual practice for a public address by Sol, or by anyone for that matter. Especially the request to have a show of hands.

"Would you run?" Sol asked. "Raise your hand if you would try to stay a step ahead of the person, hoping you are smarter and faster than they are?"

A number of respondents saw the sense in running. A smattering raised their hands. They may not have known there was more to the question and another option to come.

Sol carried the question further. "Now keep your hands up and I'll ask further. "What if you knew the running wouldn't help for long? Would you keep running?... Just keep running forever?"

The hands in the air came down. Sol went on. "Let me offer you a second option. For those of us who wouldn't run to avoid getting killed, would you fight?"

The crowd waited this time for Sol to fill in some more of the question.

"Would you make sure you had some resources to draw on and then, when your killer showed up at your door or in the mall parkade, or in a bathroom stall at a restaurant, would you defend yourself then? Would you stand up and fight?"

A whole lot more hands went up. Even some of the hands that went down after Sol finished going through the first scenario went up again. They liked this option better than running endlessly, hoping to outrun their pursuer. The German people in the Plaza were very justice based. That is who made up most of the 500,000 guests in the Plaza that day. A people who were not known to back down or roll over, so it was no surprise the decision one would come to if their life were seriously being threatened.

"Okay, thanks for playing along, I think you get where I'm coming from."
Sol wanted them to think how they would respond to a threat on their life.

"I have one more question?" Sol said. "What if you knew that some thug with virtually unlimited resources and a gang of henchmen a mile deep was trying to kill you....and was actually on the way to take your life, how many of you would make the first move?"

Sol paused, and as a few hands started to go up he added, "Just hold on for a sec, let me be clear. If you had absolute certainty your life would be taken soon unless you stopped this powerful stalker. He was coming for you and would not stop until you're dead. How many of you would do what may seem unthinkable and make the first strike? Do what it would take to ensure the relentless killer would not have a chance to kill you first?"

The hands that went up were overwhelmingly the majority of those in attendance that afternoon. The EPD Drones and CC captures provided data that tabulated 93% of the Participants had raised their hands to this option. The same questions that were posed to the live crowd in Germany were offered to the billions of viewers across the globe. Tweets were coming in to the media team. The stream was interactive and the media team off stage took in all the virtual raised hands of folks tapping their devices from wherever they were watching the stream. The average person felt strongly that it wasn't good enough to just run or sit around and wait for your killer to show up and have a shot at you. If you are going to be killed, the consensus in the Plaza and abroad was that it is the wisest decision to take out your killer first...Before he takes his first shot at you. In this case the best self-defence was a smart offense. Simple.

Sol was relieved to see the good sense displayed by his crowd that day. He was ready now to show them the stream and let them in on what happened in his "historic car ride" of less than an hour ago. Nothing would punctuate his decision to seal Amyl Rothschild more than what the viewers were about to see.

Corruption Society
Had Long Despised

"REcently", Sol continued, "A member of the Rule of Nines tried to entice me to do his bidding. What you are about to see ladies and gentlemen may be unpalatable for some. It is a brief display of just some of the corruption and crime that can be found in the ultra-rich. Now of course not all ultra-rich women or men compromise their morals and ethics but, in this case, this man has. And this is the man who was on a path to killing me. When we met, he learned I could not be bought. I would not bend to his pressure to alter my policy in a way that would benefit him and others in his circles. And in realizing my life was being threatened, my counsel and I decided the only recourse was to Seal this person and ensure his pursuit of me would not continue. What you are about to see is the encephalostream that was captured when he was sealed in my car. On the way to this very Assembly. In these images you will see some of the crimes that filtered through his mind in the last moments of brain activity as he shut down."

Sol stepped to the side to watch with the crowd. The *EPD* Drones quietly paused in hover positions around the Plaza to monitor the crowd's reaction. There was still potential for conflict from this controversial situation. When this mostly German crowd saw the man on the video was one of their most celebrated sons, some of them might react in anti-social ways. The Drones would be there to alert the Event Police Division to any who chose to become disruptive.

The encephalostream caught signals from the still active amygdala as well as the hippocampus. Catching these memories as if the owner of them were watching from a third person perspective. The screen and holo-streams above the crowd ignited. Mobile devices and Media Screens in homes, offices, on the sides of buildings, in restaurants, public transport, and parks and streets all over the world displayed the images. The entire world was about to see some of the hidden thoughts of one of the world's richest men...now a penniless dead man.

The content was disturbing. Just as Sol had warned. Together as a retroactive witness the world watched Rothschild's memory of when he forced his young wife to abort their unborn child. It was to be their first child, and it was not the one Rothschild wanted. It was a little girl.

"Listen," Rothschild was seen telling his wife. "This is not acceptable. I must have a son as my firstborn. Rothschilds have only had sons as firstborns, and we will not be any different!"

The crowds watched as he forced his powerless young wife to submit to his despotism. She was not even showing, and Rothschild demanded they terminate the three month old fetus before it was too late. A girl baby was not an option for him. Sex-selection was the solution. Rothschild promised to get rid of both of them if she would not do this. The threat to her life showed the history of how he would cleverly mask death threats as he did to Sol today.

Another of the encephalostreams that pierced the silence on Rothschild's lack of integrity came on screen. He was found in a luxurious hotel room, the middle-aged man and his lover were in the throes of an aggressive sexual encounter. It was clear this was not Rothschild's wife. In the next scene, the woman lay on the king-size bed, a sense of unfulfillment lingering after her encounter with Rothschild. The encephalostream showed Rothschild had been familiar with this particular escort on many occasions. So much so that he had foolishly confided in her with some intimate details about his business, his corrupt practices, and his lack of love for his wife. The wife that had now bore him three sons.

The scene showed him becoming agitated with the probing and the demanding that came from his lover. A woman he used and despised as he had many women before her. She asserted that she was not just any common sex-worker at this point, and she let Rothschild know she knew he was falling in love with her. She knew everything about him now and demanded he should leave his wife. Divorce the mother of his children and take her on as his one and only lover. Her desperation to have this ultra-wealthy man all to herself led her to threaten Rothschild. His secrets would only be safe with her if he would do what she wanted. If he would leave his wife, she would keep his secrets.

At that, the stream showed Rothschild casually moving away from the bed. Clad in the luxurious hotel robe, he responded to his naked lover from the wet bar just outside the bedroom. He was pouring them some after sex drinks. Calmly responding to her demands on the outside but on the inside, Rothschild was inflamed. He would not be controlled by this harlot. He had many previous engagements with the woman, but he would not tolerate her blackmail and demands. He was prepared to put a stop them. It was so easy for him.

Rothschild broke open the three caplets that had been placed in the drawer of the bar some time ago in case they were needed to remove a threat of unknown value. He poured them into her drink, stirred and served. Rothschild continued to entertain the woman as she sipped her special cocktail. Pretending that her demands were fair and he would begin extricating himself from his loveless marriage so he could be faithful to her now. And with no visible emotions, Rothschild watched the woman, who pleasured him on many occasions, twitch as she slowly drifted off to a sleep she would not wake from.

Ahmed and Tomer had picked only a few of the flashes of Amyl's crimes that had been captured in his last thoughts. One more episode began to fill the screens and holo-streams.

Amyl Rothschild was in Thailand. He was investing in what appeared to be a legitimate textile export corporation. When he was being shown the operation, three emaciated young men and two young ladies could be seen in the yard as he was surveying the storage facility of the huge compound. This was a 100's of million dollar exporting company and Rothschild had a good understanding of all the products they exported. So much so that when the three were spotted. Rothschild quickly snapped, "I hope for your sake those are employees…because if they're product you damn well better keep an eye on them. No one needs to know they exist before they're sold. This place has to look clean, or I won't be funding anymore of your 'projects'."

Again, the renowned Amyl Rothschild, a man whose integrity and ethics may not have been questioned, a man who was one of the richest people in the world, was shown to be as corrupt as any multi-national who turns a blind eye on what is really happening. Amyl was funding human trafficking and no one had been able to catch him on it…or no one would. Now, in front of the billions watching his final thoughts, his dying brain betrayed him. This man was shown to be what few were brave enough to accuse him of. A corrupt and callous businessman who grew his empire at the cost of other's lives.

The images stopped streaming. A deafening pause hung in the Plaza. Then the screens switched back to Sol. Sol broke the silence immediately. He stood before the world with nothing to hide. Amyl Rothschild had a plan to kill Sol and now Amyl Rothschild was dead, Sealed by the hand of the King. Sol began to speak of Rothschild's sealing.

"As of today, Amyl Rothschild is no longer with us. He has been Sealed. I have nothing to hide. Were things situated the other way around…that is if I were the richest man in the world and had a known plan to kill the King of the World, or a Rule of Nines member, I would expect nothing less than to decisively be eliminated to end the threat I embodied. And thanks to the exceptional work of my Minister of Retribution, I was alerted to the imminent threat that was Amyl Rothschild. With my own hands, I was able to seal the man who intended to kill me."

The crowd saw the sense in what Sol had done. Even to a celebrated son of Germany. Any reasonable woman or man who was placed under the same threat of their life, would be foolish not to make the same choice. If they didn't they would be accepting their own murder.

It was so clear that Sol had no other choice. Aside from the plan to assassinate Sol, the last thoughts of his own crimes that passed through Amyl's mind as he died gave reason to remove this stain from society. Amyl Rothschild was a corrupt man through and through. As corrupt as he was rich. His acts against humanity were indictments against him. He was not a Participant of the society that was beginning to become what everyone wanted. A peaceable, equitable, prosperous, safe, and fair world. One that found and prosecuted hidden crimes against humanity instead of denying and turning the blind eye on them and to those who do them. No matter how rich that person might be.

And with Sol as King, any who were part of the corruption society had long despised, would be removed from society and their wealth taken. Taken and distributed as Sol saw fit.

"Corruption Is Not For Us."

Sol took a breath even as his audience did. They were catching up with what they had just been shown. Processing the reality wasn't easy. Sol needed to move forward. They understood that choices must be made and in fact choices often make themselves, as in the case of the Amyl Rothschild threat to Sol's life. The conviction in his voice comforted the global audience. He was confident the right choice was made. And Sol was sensitive and intentional in the way he displayed what was happening and what needed to happen if the world were to move toward a healthier time.

"As I look back on the years. Years of watching government from the outside, viewing the inequities and injustices the world has failed to address through much of history, I recall being incensed at the scandals and corruption. Scandals and corruption that were often an unexposed part of the political picture. Both government corruption and private business corruption has long occurred. We all knew it was going on in the undercurrent of government and this has all too often been tolerated. Today my friends, is a new day. Corruption will no longer be tolerated. And those who participate in corrupt practice, both in government and in the private sector will be stopped. Anyone involved in corruption, large or small, will have their assets seized. All the assets of that person will become the property of the King to do with as she or he sees fit. Depending on the crimes of corruption one practices, the consequences will be decided accordingly.

"I will make certain the seized assets will go to causes that most need them. Funding health care, education, rehabilitation programs for those who can and will submit to necessary rehabilitation programs, to the needs of victims of crime and corruption. The money that is removed from dealers in corruption will be used to help and heal society. She or he who is convicted of corruption will be assigned work. If they are not Sealed for their crimes, they will be assigned meaningful work that will keep them from practicing corruption. Corruption is one of the many cancers on our global society and it will not be tolerated."

The Plaza was silent. Those in attendance were in agreement and were quite moved. Moved to introspection as they digested the strong but welcome stance of the King against unfairness and corruption. Sol was unshaken. He knew most in the crowd would think and feel much the same as he. *"Finally"*, was the thinking, *"Someone with power who won't tolerate corruption."*

It didn't matter which region or country a person was from, the feeling about corruption was always the same…something needed to be done about it. Sol spoke on.

"Indeed, Amyl Rothschild will be missed. And I do offer my condolences to the Rothschild family and friends of Amyl. Please don't get me wrong. I would have preferred not to have sealed Mr. Rothschild. Had he not put a plan in place intent on killing me, placed into action at the end of today's Address, things would be different right now for Amyl Rothschild.

"Less than half a year ago I was a content Library Researcher and would have never had to consider how to handle such a threat on my life. About an hour ago, before stepping out of my car to enter the Plaza stage to address you, I took a few moments to meditate on what had just happened. The sense of calm I had because I am safe was therapeutic. So, I thought on the good Amyl had done. That will never be taken away from his memory either. Then I called Ell and told her I was fine and the threat had been sealed. For her, as it would be for any family member of a person who is to be murdered, the anxiety and fear of what might happen was overwhelming. In our relief we were able to comfort each other. Although any society that is filled with humans will not be immune to death as the society runs its course, it is always sad to see the loss of a life. For every life has potential for good. It is no secret that Amyl Rothschild had done a lot of good with his life and with his money. That does not make up nor justify the great evil he was responsible for while alive. The reality of it all though, is that a man who makes choices must accept the consequences for those choices. And Amyl Rothschild had made many choices in his life. The choice to try to bribe a King and then plot to kill him resulted in the consequence I am announcing to you today. So, it is sad that things must end this way in certain cases. But in this case the ending was only up to Amyl. The one who chooses corruption is, in this society today, choosing to accept the consequences that will be placed upon him or her."

The viewers watching across the world assessed Sol's words.

"Consequences."

A world that was going to evolve must not ignore consequences. Many in that mostly German crowd at the Plaza that day were ready to accept, those who practice corruption will and should receive consequences. No king who refused to apply the consequences that were appropriate for corrupt acts would have the respect of his or her people. The respect that Sol gained from the people that day would bare great fruit towards support for the many changes he would edict in the coming months. The ears of the crowd had been pricked, Sol's voice raised again.

"As I said, I am deeply sorry to the family for their loss." Sol directed his words to the family that would certainly be shocked and grieving at news of Amyl's sealing.

"As Amyl's money is redistributed, I will be certain you are taken care of. Once the family of Amyl Rothschild is taken care of, I will be giving half of his multi-billion-dollar empire to his competitors. The other half will be distributed elsewhere.

Amyl worked closely with other investors and business people. Sol decided that those who he competed with the most intensely, perhaps one might even call them his enemies, will be receiving a portion of the Amyl Rothschild Empire. With that Sol offered a warning.

"And to you who receive this payment, do with it as you will but fair warning is henceforth given to each of you and to all who participate in this complex World."

Sol knew they were listening. He had just told the remaining members of the Rule of Nines that their enemy's riches would be given to them. Although it sounded too good to be true it was seen as one of the worst things that could ever happen to a wealthy person such as Amyl. For a man with that magnitude of wealth and that exalted ego, to see his wealth taken from him and given to his competitors would have been enough to kill him. The remaining 8 may enjoy the massive injection to their already massive holdings but knowing the fate of the riches they worshipped so greatly if they were to oppose the King, it would be unlikely any of them, or any ultra-rich woman or man in the world, would ever risk their wealth being handed to their enemies. Knowing ones' riches would be given to her or his enemies after their death was a bold and certain way to prevent another attempt on Sol's life by the world's elite. Sol was perfectly clear as he wrapped up this announcement and headed into presenting the edicts.

"If you choose corruption there will be consequences. The remainder of the proceeds from the Amyl Rothschild Empire will be put towards anti-corruption programs and to other causes that are in need."

King Sol had struck a chord on this one. For too long the ultra-rich had gotten away with things others could not get away with. The crowd voiced their invigorated support of the new edict. Women and men who were above the law were above it no longer. If Sol was able to neutralize Amyl Rothschild, a man who had been exposed as a nefarious villain to the world in 5 short minutes of the encephalostream Sol showed, then this King would be able to establish the system of anti-corruption that would restore ethics and wholeness to the political and business world. For every corrupt leader and businessperson that was removed from their realm, there would be a willing and integrity driven person to step in and take their place.

The crowd felt the justice. There is little in this world that feels as hopeful as justice. If Sol were anything in that moment, he was a hero to the masses…and he was fair. The smiles of the crowd told the story. They heard Sol's message loud and clear.

"Corruption is not for us."

CORRUPTION CONFRONTED BY A KING AND HIS COUNSEL

Gang City is Open for Business

Sol transitioned now. He moved deftly from his promise to confront corruption into the edicts that needed to be put in place. He held his stage with authority. The mass of people held their pieces of granite in the expansive Plaza. The collective resolve was to support Sol. In his edict against pedophiles, terrorists, corruption, or whatever Sol would bring to them next.

"We will always have tragedies, death, and unfortunate situations in our society. To deny the reality of the human condition will not make the reality disappear. I believe we can however, manage the destructive effects of the human condition better than our race has historically managed them. And perhaps one day all those unpleasant parts of human life will no longer be ever in front of us. I have decided to deal with some of the daily unpleasantness that we all encounter. No one likes to encounter unpleasant behaviors and unwanted threat. But for some reason we have all come to accept that this is just the world we live in. And it is because of that apathy, where we have kind of stopped hoping for better, that the unpleasant things I speak of continue. For them not to continue we just need people who will take a stand. I believe we do not have to live in this world just accepting those things and trying to make the best of it. As Participants of this society, we can remove many of those unpleasant things. And in the pursuit of a better world, if a person intends to be a part of this society, they must participate in a manner that respects others and does no harm to those who share society with them.

"We are all participants together in this journey. And it can be stressful at times. For instance, have you seen the way some of us can get cranked up when we are on the way to work or rushing to get across town? Whether it's here in Germany, or in cities anywhere on any continent, driving has become less of a pleasure and more of a stressor. You folks from Germany have a good understanding of the driving factors that have followed the improvements in automobile technology. Germany has long been known for its amazing automobile innovations and design, including the speed that comes from your automobiles. The driving industry in your region has long been known for its visionary thinking. Your contribution in integrating the personal need of a driver to be in control of a vehicle, with the benefits of Autonomous vehicles, has shifted our driving experience in many wonderful ways.

"And now, today here in Germany, society and the way we relate to the automobile, takes another step forward. Forward to a more stable and peaceable world. Forward to courteous driving. This is a simple edict. If you or I enjoy the privilege of driving a vehicle we are responsible to drive it in a courteous and safe manner. No drunk driving, no budding in line on the zipper merge, and no tire squealing or cutting off other drivers. We are all used to being reprimanded by the law if we are caught breaking the laws that make our roads safe and help traffic flow smoothly. The autonomous vehicle advancements were hoped to improve the "me first" driver's mindset but have in fact accelerated the intensity of a driving dilemma for many. Punishments through fines and tickets have not been effective to improve the situation. And traditionally, due to the locus of control shifting from human to machine, the stress response from having less control has negated the value of Autonomous vehicles making our driving decisions for us. Yet there are still multitudes of courteous drivers on our roads, you may be one of them, and it is time to give credit to those of us who deserve credit. Those who are courteous, responsible, and thoughtful drivers.

The roads are a dangerous place and courtesy on them is an absolute must. As of today, the *Common Courtesy Edict* proclaims, if you are caught being courteous while driving a vehicle you will earn credit points. Points that accumulate in your favour toward a reward. After maintaining enough credit points for a year, you will be eligible for a reduction in the cost of your Driver's Approval Certificate and earn credit towards automotive repairs to use when your vehicle requires maintenance or repairs. If, however, discourtesy is recorded by any of the many sources that monitor our streets and roadways, your points will be deducted. And they will be deducted at 1.25 times the amount they have been earned by you. One courtesy gains you 1 point, 1 discourtesy deducts 1.25 points from your total. We will all begin with 15 points. Today the slate is clean. Call it a driver's amnesty day if you like but as of this moment, every Participant who possesses a Driver Approval Certificate has been credited 15 points. If you reach zero, you will lose your Driver Approval Certificate and your vehicle. It's just that simple. If you want to keep your privilege to drive a car then just treat others on the road how you want to be treated…courteously.

This edict offers us the reward or the consequence for the choices we make. Each of has the power to be courteous when driving and each of us has the power to be discourteous. With this edict, it is in each of our hands to choose whether or not we maintain a Driver Approval Certificate and automobile. To put it as simply as I can, if you can't handle it on the road then get off. Or we'll get you off the road."

Sol sealed the *Common Courtesy Edict* and after it was displayed on screen he moved to his next edict. The gangs of the world were about to be stopped.

"In our quest to enjoy a more peaceful, kind, and improved society, why must we tolerate those sectors of society that make the choice to behave in a destructive way against society? Some are acting as individuals and others, the ones I am speaking about now, work in coordinated groups. What I want to address with this edict is gang activity. I am speaking to the gangs of this world. Those groups of disenfranchised men and women who think nothing of performing crimes in the name of their cherished gang. They poison our streets and societies with drugs, violence, and a steady stream of crime. In many ways they are similar to terrorist organizations because they instill fear in the communities they operate in. The activities of these gangs seem unstoppable. Gangs are responsible for a majority of the violent crime that occurs in our society. They are a subculture with their own rules, their own justice system, and their own government. Gangs are a micro-culture of society that have no interest in being part of the healthy society you and I desire and have a macro-effect on our safety and security. They behave in a way that displays they want their own society that operates by their own rules. Yet they interact closely with the society you and I are Participants in. When gangs and their members are not stealing, raping, assaulting, or doing other crime, their presence in society is still felt. They cause us to live in fear. You and I as individuals have little power against the might of these organized groups of criminals. They exist to bring harm to society and to further their own illicit and corrupt desires. But I am proud to announce that has already begun to change.

"Last week, General Takanaka and I sat down to design a strategy to deal with gangs. In brief here is what is under way already.

"General Takanaka has divided the Global Anti-Terrorist division of the Global Military Unit, and a new entity was created. Using all the resources of the Global Military, General Takanaka will be capturing and deporting all gang members. In every city across the globe, all gangs and their members will be relocated by the Global Military Unit. We have integrated a plan for amnesty should a gang member who is sent to Gang City want to leave that life and rejoin society."

The crowd was hearing right. Sol was going to end gangs and Gang crime with a thorough and decisive strategy. And peace was beginning to flood in. The German people knew that German gangs were the same as any other gangs of any city, anywhere. As did the Participants viewing the stream from locations across the world. Gangs robbed the peace of cities and towns and left a wake of destruction from their activities. Those standing in the Plaza at that moment were being told gangs are going to be removed from society. The King was directing unlimited resources toward the gang problem that plagued society. Outcomes from the policing measures of the past could at best accomplish slowing the growth of gangs a little, or cause gangs to relocate. Even amid the long list of varied programs aimed at stopping gangs, gang activity marched on. And the list of agencies and programs was extensive…a list of immense efforts yet unable to find success in eliminating gangs.

- Central American Intelligence Program
- Central American Law Enforcement Exchange
- MS-13 National Gang Task Force
- National Gang Intelligence Center
- San Salvador Legal Attaché
- Transnational Anti-Gang Initiative
- Violent Gang Task Forces
- Comprehensive Anti-Gang Initiative of the National Gang Center
- INTERPOL
- United Nations Office on Drugs and Crime (UNODC)
- Bureau of Alcohol, Tobacco, Firearms and Explosives (ATF)
- Homeboy Industries
- The Australian Criminal Intelligence Commission (ACIC)
- European Union Agency for Law Enforcement Cooperation (Europol
- Organization of American States
- Office of Juvenile Justice and Delinquency Prevention

None of the programs or Task Forces had been successful at dissolving gangs and the threat of them. But Sol's General, a man who orchestrated massive, complex, and many successful actions against terrorists, was now leading the charge against gangs. If this world were going to be the peaceful, healthy society that Participants wanted, the gangs had to go.

Sol let his audience know Takanaka was in no way going to go easy on this diseased subculture.

"The General has amassed a massive Global Task force. The largest and strongest gangs in our cities will be dealt with first. From every major city in the world. And as they are rounded up, they will be deported. One by one until the smallest gang is eradicated from healthy society."

Deported…? To some in the crowd it sounded like Sol was creating another Australia. The questions passing through the minds of those hearing Sol asked "*How, why, where?*" If gangs were simply removed from one city only to be placed in another, how would that solve the gang problem that's a global epidemic?

The crowd was right. No city, country, or region wanted to inherit another region's problems. But Sol and the General had established the perfect environment.

It was a combination of Alcatraz, the famous island prison that housed thousands of criminals, and Cardinal Fitzgerald's idea to send child sex offenders in the Catholic Church to a remote island where they could live out their days.

Sol explained the plan to his puzzled audience.

"You can see pictures of the facility gangs will be relocated to on our website. And they are streaming to your device now."

The images displaying on devices and media screens showed the construction in progress. It was abundantly clear that the entire resources of the world were available for Sol to accomplish his reforms. The inconceivably massive project was astonishing in its scope. Many areas of the island under construction were already complete. Numbers of gangs had already been rounded up and placed on the Island. The *Gang City Island* looked like any suburb of any city. Trees, roads, houses, and parks. And the incomplete sectors were slated to house the millions that would be brought to the island. Sol told further of the need for this Island where gangs would have free reign and rule their own isolated world.

Sol spoke to the gangs of the world directly in the next moments. "Gang members, as of this moment, you will be given a choice. You can maintain allegiance to your gang, or you can choose to withdraw from your gang. If you choose the latter, you will be given every opportunity to become the contributing Participant in this society that the rest of us have chosen to be. If you remain with your gang, well then you will be deported. You will be relocated with other gangs and all those who are members of gangs, to the Gang City off the coast of Grenada. Billions will be spent to give you a habitat that will be self-contained and sustainable. But you will be left to it and can then form your own governments as you see fit. You will, from now on, occupy a Gang City Island separated from peaceable society.

"Removing you from your homes and families to inhabit an island where no one will be allowed to leave is the consequence of your choice. Don't worry gang member. If you find that the Gang City life is not for you, and of course if you are still alive, you will have a chance of redemption through amnesty twice a year.

"Twice a year, on Amnesty Day, you will be allowed to make the choice to leave the island. The General will send an aircraft carrier to the island to pick up those who have decided they prefer a Participant role in our society over the role as a gang member that offers so little.

Now, just to be clear, this is not a prison island for criminals who are incarcerated. Those individuals who are not in organized gangs but are part of the prison system, will be repurposed. We have plenty of work for you to do and the *Inmate Repurposing Program* will be taking care of that.

Crews from all over the world have participated in constructing the Island City and the Island is almost ready. So, we will begin this campaign in the next few days. We will round up our first gangs and relocate them to begin their life in their isolated world. Away from the society they have rejected and have treated so violently."

The Media screens and holo-streams had offered scenes displaying the harshness of gang violence and the fallout from gang activities. Those watching were reminded of the fear that gangs instill in otherwise peaceful neighborhoods or cities.

Why should perfectly law-abiding Participants be consigned to their homes after dark so as not to encounter a petty criminal from a gang or a potentially violent gang member? How did society get to the place where we tolerate the fact that going out is too dangerous at times? The risk of being robbed, assaulted, raped, beaten, or even murdered was too great…and so little had been done about it that the average Participant had simply relinquished their freedom to come and go as they please. The fallout of fear and inaction was to allow the criminal element to reign over the unsafe streets, dark alleys, and moonlit nights.

The reality was too obvious when the crowds heard Sol's edict. Through true solidarity the law-abiding elements of society would no longer have to cower to the criminals. Gangs would be removed from society and all that goes with them would be a thing of the past. They would have their own society to corrupt.

If it was not clear before today that this was a King who was for the people, a King who would ensure the greatest good for the greatest number, then it was clear now. The extraordinary pool of resources going to deal with the gang problem was staggering. Takanaka would escalate his efforts as much as needed to ensure gangs were culled from society. But it would be worth it. The cost to corral all these anti-establishment individuals and eliminate their effect on society by sequestering them on a remote island with their own infrastructure would be worth the value in restoring peace to all of society across the world. It was beginning to be clear; **PEACE** was one of the most valuable currencies a society could hope for. The move would bring unparalleled reduction in crime and end wasted attempts at incarceration and rehabilitation. Not to mention the expense to policing that is directed at what was an unsolvable problem until now. The savings to society will be more than enough to recover what is spent on setting up this Gang City Program.

Sol took a moment to let the crowd digest what he had just implemented. He knew many of them may doubt that such a culling of Gangs from society could be done. Yet they were for it…they were for him…they were ready to see Sol succeed at removing gangs and the fear that came with them.

"Now, before I move on, Sol continued, "I just want to give you the harsh part of this new reality. If you are part of a gang, we know it. You are not hiding from the system. Your dossier has been compiling since your first interaction with Law

Enforcement. ENKI has extracted all the information needed to reveal you as a gang member. However, you, as with anyone in this world, are invited to be a Participant in society. You can choose not to be and then you will be deported to Gang City."

On screen was a rolling shot of the Gang City Island. It was a massive island; it had been set up as an empty city prepared to house up to 20 million residents. It showed impressive development. Sol had not started constructing this new world just last week. Gang City had been under construction for a while already. Takanaka had come to him about the malignancy of gangs a few months ago. It was then the construction process began, and the modular city was fit together. Like a giant puzzle, infrastructure, water and waste handling systems, food distribution systems, housing, and everything a criminal society would need to embark on a path to establishing their own civilization. A civilization separate from that of the Participants who would no longer be their targets for crime. The only targets they would have would be themselves.

The island city was by no means luxurious in its accommodation. Rudimentary provision for habitation was all Sol found necessary. But it was as good as or better than most of the millions of gang members who would live on it had enjoyed before.

It had finally come to pass. The voices of the "fed-up" in society must have been heard. The social war cry that forces change had been heeded and taken seriously.

"We're not going to tolerate crime and corruption any longer!"

It was often said the government should just gather up all the criminals and give them their own city where they could do whatever they wanted. Lawyers and rights advocates couldn't see the sense in that. They worked tirelessly to protect the most destructive members of society. But Sol was in charge now. The images that passed before the crowd displayed that well. It was now a reality. Sol could do anything he thought was right and no matter what the cost, his reparations would be accomplished…making the world a better place. Sealing one reformative edict and program at a time.

"So know this…" Sol held the moment as he resolutely concluded his promise to the millions of gang members watching. "If you decide to leave Gang City, escape the environment you created, you will be captured and returned there. Surveillance will ensure every activity on the island is monitored. If your new society of crime attempts to enter our society where peace is the desire, the Good General will seal all those who are part of such a coup. We are done with being threatened by your brand of violence and crime. And if you choose to build a society that thrives and flourishes in positive ways then by all means, I hope you will live long and prosper. However, if you choose to destroy yourselves within the confines of Gang City, if you become a sub-culture that implodes upon itself and becomes extinct…sadly… we who remain as Participants of the greater society, will have to accept that. So this day, I declare the dystopian island called Gang City is open for business!!!"

Cheers exploded from the crowds…not just in Germany but in all of the 7 other World Counsel Plazas. Women and men on the street lifted their heads high. Knowing they would be able breath a sigh of relief. With such an ever-present threat to their freedom and safety being removed, there was a weight that lifted off their shoulders. Some looked around the street they were standing on, knowing under Sol's rule they would never become victims of the much feared gang activities.

This moment, this day, was exhilarating for the crowds. Sol had declared Gang City open for business. Healthy peace-loving society would watch as the gangs who terrorized towns and cities were the focus of General Takanaka's unprecedented worldwide sweep to clean them out of society. So much peace had been restored to the people. Few in the crowd were eager to leave the Plaza. They would stay all day and take in the reforms and edicts of Sol. They felt cared for…finally. A people with little true power were now empowered. Their King was doing what the people wanted. It felt, in this moment, to be the safest place in the world. And Sol was not done yet. This was a big day for change. And Sol was about to address another problem that was smelling up the streets.

The Public Aroma Law

The *EPD* Drone had been sniffing around a small cluster of people in the Plaza in the moments after Sol finished announcing Gang City. Silently it caught their movement. One man seemed to be in the center of things. While the Drone drew attention to the distraction, Ahmed had made his way on to the stage rolling a large archway structure. What looked quite similar to a scaled down version of a walkthrough airport security scanner, now stood next to Sol. On the cart beside the upright device sat what appeared to be a version of the handheld metal detectors used by airport security.

As the props were set in place, the holo-streams displayed the images that came from the Drone. Sol cut in on the distraction. He was not the best actor, but his tone gave the sense that this was a set-up…for something. There was a subtle smirk on his face.

"Oh," Sol sung, "It seems there must be a distraction in the crowd. I wonder what's going on?"

As the Drone framed the image around the man at the center of the cluster, the audio from the scene was streamed to the Plaza system. Those nearest the man were trying to get some distance from their crowd mate. They had been trying for some time now. They were not far from the stage and when Sol gave opportunity for feedback from the disrupted group in asking what was going on, a young lady sheepishly answered the King.

"Something stinks over here."

The crowd was a little surprised. *Brave of her* they thought, to insult someone like that in public. But good for her for speaking up. And she was right. The gentleman standing to the right of her, about 4 feet away, had been offending the crowd himself for the last hour. His offensive body odor was not in any way endearing his crowd mates to him. Those within nose-shot found his acrid aroma to be quite offensive. A little too peppery for public, with the dour odor of a wet rag that might have sat in the cupboard under the kitchen sink a little too long. From the images the world was being treated to now, it was clear who the smelly problem was. Those around him had squeezed over...some knowingly others unconsciously. Trying to polarize themselves from him. And now, the *EPD* Drone had its lens, and its audio focussed on him.

The smell was not coming from something in the Plaza itself. World Counsel Plazas were always impeccably clean. Particularly so since Sol took his role as King. Because at Sol's behest, early before the crowds started streaming to the World Counsel Center, a small army of re-purposed inmates from the regional corrections facilities were brought in to scrub the place down. As Sol saw need for labourers to accomplish tasks, prison inmates were put to work on public projects. It was a sensible fix for trashy streets and parks in a city. Idle inmates who rarely earned their keep were repurposed in order to keep cities and towns clean. All inmates in the world's prisons would be made to do menial labour. This was the purpose of the *Inmate Repurposing Program.* An edict that was reforming the prison system.

For those who landed in prison, they quickly became aware they were an ever-ready work force. If there was a job that needed to be done, a troop of inmates was set to the task. Some of them started to object to Sol's *Inmate Repurposing Program* once they found themselves forced into service to the public. But it was the public that paid for their food and lodging, and it was the public who were the victims of their crime that needed to be repaid. The system had little sense to it before Sol's edict. The way a person commits a crime, goes to prison, stops being a contributing member of society, leaving the rest of society, the very ones that were harmed by the criminal acts, to pay for the maintenance of the prisoner and his or her housing in jail. Sol decided as any reasonable man or women would decide…prisoners made choices that result in consequences. Even amid the reality that many social determinants often lead to the choices for criminal behaviors, consequences would still be meted out. And one of those consequences is assigned work to improve society while they were incarcerated. The work was always monitored by Corrections personnel and society began to feel that prisoners were paying their debt in a tangible way instead of purposelessly sitting in a warm dry prison just "doing time".

Another consequence for the incarcerated, was they no longer had the right to vote. They had abdicated that privilege when they chose to do crime. For far too long inmates were given the same voting rights as those who had committed no crimes. Elections would take place for various levels of officials in many regions and the inmates wanted the right to have their say. Sol however, had removed that right along with the many prisoner rights and privileges they had taken for granted.

His philosophy was well accepted…outside of the inmate population that is… if you had done the crime, you have forfeited the rights that others in society are given. Freedom brings a whole different set of rights and privileges than those the incarcerated deserve. It is true that there may be the odd inmate who was unfairly accused and convicted, but according to the thinking of most reasonable people, that was no reason to demand the rights of all prisoners be left intact.

Society had long ago accepted that no system is perfect. The odd casualty of the system is part of the cost of a system based on the philosophy, *'The greatest good for the greatest number.'* A simple foundation to build any policy or edict on. And just as Sol's *Inmate Repurposing Program* found its inspiration in the greatest good for the greatest number, so too did the *Public Aroma Law* Sol was prepared to deliver find its strength. As he watched the crowd nudge away from a Participant standing among them, Sol purposely focussed on the aromatic disruption unfolding below.

Life Would Smell Better Along The Way

"Sir!"

Sol called out from the front edge of the stage where he was interacting with the crowd again. The Drone had locked onto the unfavoured guest in the Plaza. And all eyes had locked onto his image as he looked up to respond to Sol. The holo-stream images piercing the air were pretty easy to interpret. He even looked smelly. Greasy hand-combed hair, a dingy three day's growth of a beard, clothes wrinkled as if he had been sleeping on a bus...or in a dumpster, filthy ball cap perched atop his head. The man locked eyes with Sol.

"*Was this really happening?*" the crowd began to muse.

In Sol's first address he connected with a drummer and chanter in the audience, now on this address he was calling out a smelly guy in the Plaza. And this time the interaction had nothing to do with a tribute to the King.

"Yes sir, you..."

Sol pointed at the man and then turned his hand up and gestured with his index finger to have the man head his way. "Please, would you join me up here sir?"

The guy really looked like he had nothing to lose. He agreed to head the 150 feet or so through the crowd to join the King.

The *EPD* Drone dropped down to head-level and began moving in front of the man. Escorting him towards Sol and parting the sea of people that filled the gap between where he stood and where Sol stood. The parting throngs reacted automatically to the scent. Unwitting as to how animated their faces were when he passed…wafting a stench of unpleasantness along behind him. The Drone caught their faces over the shoulder of the gent as he moved toward Sol on stage.

Even though the unknown man smelled awful, most of the crowd hoped Sol had no intentions of harming the man. It was a funny thing about Sol. In only a few short months the things he did and said left the people with a clear sense of the kind of King he was. Unapologetic about the changes he brought but clearly looking out for society's best interest. He could launch a parenting program in one breath and seal the world's richest man in the next. And all with a composure that left those involved in encounters with him, feeling perfectly safe, respected, and heard in their ideas thoughts and concerns. He was business when he needed to be and a rather casual King when that was appropriate. The sense of the crowd was right, this was a fairly casual moment.

"Yes that's right, make way for the gentleman folks."

Ahmed had left the security style archway in the center of the stage. While the smelly gent was finding his way along behind the Drone, Sol went over and pushed the archway close to the front of the stage. The unfazed man was now Sol's guest on the platform. The wake of offensively pungent aroma that followed him up to the stage was still dissipating from the nostrils of the offended audience Participants. Sol had situated the archway between himself and the point the man entered the stage.

"Sir, could I have you join me center stage, just pass on through this harmless archway."

…this was a set up…the crowd was starting to see it. Who would ask a strange guy from the crowd to head up on stage and walk through an archway like that…

risking a very awkward moment by undignifying a smelly fella in front of the world. Whether the crowd was onto the set-up or not, the smell coming off that guy was certainly real.

The gentleman stepped cautiously towards Sol. The archway device was lifeless. No lights, no sounds, no moving parts. A tall gray device that looked to be about as wide as two people. It stood higher on the casters it had been set on for Sol's demonstration than it would had it not needed to roll on stage for the event. Sol, almost like a prank was being pulled, was waiting excitedly on the other side. He had always wanted to deal with this problem and now, as King, he was getting his way.

Sol held up his hand to halt the gent, "Pause just for a moment sir."

The crowd was starting to feel bad for the unfavourable attention the man was getting from Sol and from the whole world.

"Whooo!, Sol exclaimed. "There is a bite to you isn't there? Sir, come on through the archway, and we'll chat on this side."

The man stepped through and as he did, the voice of a female with a pleasing Australian accent came on the Plaza system.

"Thank you for using Aroma-Arch. You have exceeded the public aroma threshold allowance. Please return to your residence to freshen up or proceed to the public odor neutralizing chamber. Thank you."

The crowd was witnessing the first ever public detection system for offensive body odors. Sol was only one of the billions who had been forced to tolerate a smelly person far too frequently in varied public settings. It was his view that no one should be forced to endure the offensive odor of another Participant while in public. And the new *Public Aroma Law* Sol was about to explain to the crowds, would make being smelly in public obsolete. The Aroma detection system would literally sniff them out.

"Step over here sir."

Sol reached for the wand-like device sitting on the cart next to the Aroma–Arch. It was powered up already and Sol passed the wand quickly over the body of the fella in a broadly sweeping and nonintrusive pattern. The device made an audible beep. Ahmed had linked the device to the media system at the Plaza, the screen and holo-streams beamed an image of the reading displayed by the *Aroma-wand* device.

"Threshold limit exceeded- please remediate before proceeding."

The statement from the device was designed to prompt the subject to remove him or herself from the public area or facility he or she was entering. And as soon as the brief display ended, Sol let the crowd in on the demonstration and introduced his smelly friend.

"Folks, this is my brother Thomas from Tacoma. He agreed to help me demonstrate the *Public Aroma Law* detection system." Sol waved a hand toward his brother and started to clap as he asked, "Give Thomas a round of applause for being such a good sport. He really put his heart and soul into making sure he stunk for today."

The crowd responded with an appreciative smattering of applause. There were not many people out there who would purposely put on the stink and show up in a huge public setting just to demonstrate a new system. But Thomas was the adventurous one. And he and Sol had long been averse to bad smells coming off people in places like airplanes, shuttles, movie theaters, malls, and parks. Never understanding how someone could show up in public smelling like body odor or bad cooking. Even the odors that wafted off certain garlic lovers or ethnic-food fans was unreasonable at times. And for some reason people tolerated it. When a person was the captive audience to another person's offensive odor such as, bad breath, BO, or an over spiced aroma, no one ever said anything. That smelly person just took over the space. No one could comfortably be close to them, but no one had the courage or social permissions to say anything. In 2043, people had no reason to stink. And if they did stink, they were going to be asked to leave. Today, Sol was giving permission to say something ☺

"Thomas how long has it been since you showered and what have you eaten in the last couple of days?"

Sol was wanting to add a little context to his brother's public offensiveness.

"I last took a shower three days ago Sol. Just before a day of dirty yard work and then a couple sweaty workouts. I was starting to really ripen when I hopped on the plane to meet you and your team."

Thomas was loving the chance to stink up Sol's stage for the good of all mankind. He went on with his engaging explanation of his stinkification process, talking about the powers of Bourgogne cheese.

"Then yesterday, because I really wanted to be stinky for you Sol, I enjoyed three meals that include Époisses de Bourgogne Cheese. You know that stuff smells so bad that it's banned on public transportation in some European countries? And I made sure my limburger cheese omelette was topped with sour kraut. I had to go with the limburger omelette after I found out that one of the bacteria used to make body odor is the same bacteria used in making Limburger cheese. That stuff really stinks."

"Wow!"…Sol was curling up his nose again…you really jumped into this with both feet…and brother you nailed it; you definitely got a funk going on there. But there is something we can do about that."

Sol waved his arm in a sweeping gesture to point across the stage. Rising out of the floor was another archway type device. It was noticeably larger than the first which was just designed for odor threshold detection. The upsize version had advertising on it from the top essential oils, de-odorizing, and aroma therapy companies in the world. It appeared to be just another Aroma-Arch?

Sol motioned to his brother and the crowd to join him over at the colorful arch that stood on stage left.

"Thomas, I will just hold my breath while you head on over here to the *Aroma-Annihilator* to see what I have for you. I think this will help with your little aroma problem."

Thomas stood in front of the device and Sol waved him through. The device gently washed the willing participant in Sol's demonstration with a cloud of odor neutralizing ions. Thomas stood for 3 seconds, while the white dearomatizing mist freshly breezed over Thomas's entire head and body. The crowd watched in amazement, and Sol called out, "Open your mouth and your garlic breath will be taken care of too."

It felt a little cool, refreshing, and fast for Thomas. The mist was similar to what you'd see coming out of a humidifier used in a baby's nursery. In just under 4 seconds, the whole process was done. Thomas, although he still had the same smelly look of three-days beard growth along with greasy hair and clothes, stepped out of the *Aroma-Annihilator*. Sol still had the Aroma-detection wand with him as he stepped close to Thomas. Waving the Aroma-wand over his body in the same manner as moments ago, the status of the subject flashed up on screen.

"Participant is within public aroma threshold limits."

For the crowd it must have been like a team victory. Cheers broke out and Sol took his formerly stinky brother's hand and raised it up high…with no worry of a plume wafting from his previously smelly parts now exposed by the victoriously raised hand.

Thomas headed off stage and the amused crowd thanked him with a warm round of applause. Those watching remotely smiled at the bravado of an otherwise hygienic man. Brave enough to help his brother out in such a self-demoralizing way. Sol had successfully demonstrated the technology that supports the new edict he was about to explain.

"So you see ladies and gentlemen. In its most simple form, being stinky in public is no longer acceptable. If you and I care about the other Participants in society we will make efforts not to smell foul in public. That means body and food odors, as well as bad breath odor. You and I no longer have to sit on a MeRT, or a plane, or movie theatre, or stand in a line up at the coffee shop or food vendor and be bombarded with the unpleasant aroma of a sweaty smelly person. An inconsiderate person who has failed to give proper attention to hygiene. Be they a senior citizen, a local Participant, or a person from another region who has not yet adopted the considerate practice of ensuring they are not diffusing the air with an aroma that repels people, stinking up a public space is not allowed.

"It may seem odd that a King is putting an edict in place that deals with urine smells, body odor, and ethnic food aromas, but to be frank, whether it is you or I, or any participant in our wonderful society, it is inconsiderate to be stinky in public. Just that simple.

There is just no excuse for that and no one appreciates when someone around them is smelling up the place. With our Aroma-Arch and our Aroma-Annihilator, we now have a vehicle to identify and eliminate this unseen offender of our senses. It is good for all of us that recognition and immediate remediation of the problem be undertaken. It has long been known that a good environment or feeling can be overwhelmed and turned sour by bad smells.

"Now many of us will gain the confidence and freedom to be forthcoming to tell a family member, a friend, or even a stranger, "Hey, you don't smell so fresh, do you mind resolving that?"

Sol went on to tell his audience the Aroma-Arches would be installed by his government and the Aroma-Annihilators would be installed and maintained by a P3. That is to say, they would have the authority of the government behind them but, as the graphics and logos on them indicated, they would be sponsored by paid advertising. After all, what better marriage for an Aroma-Annihilator could there be than to have *Ananda Apothecary, Aura Cacia, Edens garden, Farcent Enterprise, Febreze,* or some other interested company enjoy the benefits of advertising their products on society's most visible and cutting edge vehicle for removing bad smells and encouraging desirable ones.

As Sol wrapped up the address Ahmed joined him to finish sealing the edicts with a handprint on the cool screen of his Folia.

The Folio affirmed- *"Edict Successfully Recorded"*

With another reformative address logged in the history of King Sol, Sol left the stage. It had been a productive day. Losing his life to Amyl Rothschild would no longer be a threat. And if that wasn't enough of a relief, now life would smell better along the way too.

Dying With Debt

The Deliberations chambers had not been buzzing at this pitch since the day the 9-12 proposition was brought forward by Delegate Devonshire. It was 9 months ago and the things that had changed in this place, besides the name, were significant. Delegates were asked to meet every quarter now to dialogue about reforms and items that needed reform in their areas. Brainstorming was encouraged. The times of maintaining the status quo for world government were gone. Sol had inspired a revolution. Engaged Delegates from all over the world regularly brought their ideas for radical changes in society to the World Counsel table. Some of the suggestions made it through to become edicts at Sol's hand and others were left at being mere entertainment for the Delegates. Brainstorming suggestions brought in laws like imposing a Driver Certificate Approval retest for all Participants over the age of 65. At a certain age, it was reasoned, for many drivers, skills deteriorate, and it was needful to test those drivers to ensure they could handle the strains of the hectic roads and streets behind the wheel.

The brainstorming sessions always got the creative government juices flowing. Discussions by engaged Delegates and their aides overflowed from the foyer into the Chambers as Delegates were making their way to their seats. Many of them were already stationed at their folios, paging hastily through the agenda items Ahmed had sent out. This group of World Counsel Delegates had come a long way. A new age had begun and the hope for improving the world…actually making it a better place for all its inhabitants…was not only a possibility it was really happening. The reforms that had already been edicted, sealed, and implemented had changed the world already. And there was more to come.

Sol took counsel regularly from his advisors. The value of the Multitude of Counsel Law was not just left for the general population. Sol was ever ready to pass things through not only Ell, Tomer, Ahmed, and Erin, but he was continually polling the diverse members of the Body of Delegates to get their feel for certain situations. Things such as edicting worldwide support from Sol's office for women choosing to terminate a pregnancy in the first three months. Even though culture had debated the use of abortion for generations, Sol still made efforts to engage brilliant minds in the discussion. When Sol sealed the *Informed Reproduction and Pregnancy Termination Law* it was automatically signed into law that a woman, when wanting an abortion, must adhere to the approved gestational period rules and the *Multitude of Counsel Law* before she is given free access.

Under the *Universal Self-Control Act* it was deemed that each person had the inalienable and sovereign rights to do whatever they wanted with their own body and life. In the editorial Sol provided with the edict, he spoke of how a person could take their own life, sell a kidney, use drugs, reconstruct their genitals, get pregnant, or terminate a pregnancy. Each person was in control of their own body. Aside from having a discussion with three consultants in the Multitude of Counsel program, a person had only themselves to decide on matters pertaining to their body. Good, bad, or otherwise, control was left to each individual.

A person's body and life was theirs to do with whatever they wanted. The historic concerns about the slippery slope to scandalously abuse the freedom of choice, the freedom to keep a baby or have an abortion, had never manifested. Quite simply, it was displayed over the decades, that freedom to choose does not bring abuse, rather prohibition does. It is prohibition that breeds rebellion. Research has indicated that giving people the freedom to choose would elicit responsible decisions in most cases. And liberating people from being dictated to and from being controlled in decisions about their own life and body always led to a more responsible people. Sol was an advocate of choice in all realms of life.

It was a fact that people make better decisions after consulting wise counsel. Knowledge is power. So Sol designed the *Self-Control Act* and the *Informed Reproduction and Pregnancy Termination Law,* to feed all who were going down that path into the *Multitude of Counsel Law.* Altering ones' body, having a baby, or getting an abortion were all very major decisions. And as with all potentially life-altering choices people make, people needed to present their document signed by three consultants before any of the above procedures could be completed. If a life altering decision is to be made, it would not be made by a solitary person behaving as if she or he were an island and rejecting wise counsel on the decision to be made.

Deciding to keep a baby was just as big of a life decision as deciding to terminate a pregnancy. Adhering to the Multitude of Counsel law was also required for young girls and women who had gotten pregnant without intending to. They too would be making a life changing decision if they decided to keep their baby. Therefore, it was necessary for them to make the effort to consult with three people over the age of 50 to gain perspective. Sol encouraged everyone to take responsibility for their body and the choices that were made regarding it.

Sol and the Delegates made sense of a great many matters of importance. Matters that had not been considered in governments past. The astonishing simplicity of the *Bankruptcy Recovery Law* brought a truly zestful enthusiasm to society. Once sealed into law, the *Bankruptcy Recovery Law* would prove to restore so much that had been taken from society.

Consulting with the Body of Delegates on the matter of Bankruptcy brought the clarity Sol needed to seal the law. At one point in the discussion Sol had the Delegates break up into brainstorming pods. He encouraged creative problem solving. It was decided the ideas that came from their breakout pods of 10 Delegates would be presented to the Chambers after a 20-minute brainstorming session. The problem that needed a solution was to do with the 1.2 percent of the world's people who declared bankruptcy. The Delegates kept in mind that fact that bankruptcy is a complex issue with various contributing factors. And the number itself wasn't staggering but it had steady growth over the decades. The cost to the global economy and to the Participants of the world was staggering. Corporate and personal bankruptcy cases were showing no signs of diminishing and the loss to society would only become greater.

As people realized they could claim bankruptcy, have their debts wiped off their books, cause their creditors to absorb the loss, and then rebuild their personal financial portfolio, more and more would choose bankruptcy as a solution to their debt problems. Most who claimed bankruptcy would eventually recover. Their financial position would often be rebuilt far beyond where it was before bankruptcy. And the trillions of dollars that creditors lost continued to mount.

When Sol had first pondered the idea of bankruptcy he saw an inherently unfair aspect to the situation. And the sense of unfairness was the same whether the candidate was a responsible money handler who fell on hard times, or an irresponsible money handler who ended up using the system for their benefit or gain. As with many financial dilemmas, there were plenty of persons who abused the system. These were the ones who had no qualms about using another's goods or money in whatever way they saw fit. It became easy to justify losing everything, then after declaring bankruptcy, he or she would in essence get a fresh start. A start that was free of the majority of debt they once had…A debt that person or corporation never had to work to pay off because the rest of us had it covered. The courts crossed it off the books for them because of an odd legal rule that allowed such a washing away of money owed. The whole idea that a person or corporation who made some bad choices or mismanaged their money could find a way out of ever paying it back by declaring bankruptcy was mind boggling. The world didn't need a way out of paying what one owes, this world, Sol's world, needed a way to get all that money back that society was bilked out of by irresponsible money managers.

Bankruptcy was just not fair to the rest of the world. To the more conscientious who worked to avoid such an unfavourable outcome with their financial picture it was a complex sense of injustice that had long been needing reform. Bankruptcy was not healthy for society and the answer to the problem that came out of the brainstorming time in the Deliberation Chambers that day was remarkably simple.

It was reasoned, once the person who had claimed bankruptcy was dead, and once that person's spouse or principal life partner is dead, any money owed when the bankruptcy was filed will be repaid. The losses declared in bankruptcy would never truly be wiped off the books. The debt would just be deferred until the death of the bankrupted. At that time the debt would be repaid from the estate of the deceased. Had the debts owing at the point of bankruptcy been large enough to consume all of the proceeds of the estate, leaving the survivors with nothing, then that is the consequence of that person's actions while alive. In Sol's Bankruptcy Recovery Law, the money that was wiped off the books while a person was alive, would need to be repaid from their estate after they had died.

As one considers bankruptcy and has consultations with the Multitude of Counsel consultants, all the aspects of claiming bankruptcy would be laid out. Aspects such as not leaving an inheritance for children and family. With that information some would still choose bankruptcy with no thought for the future, and many would find ways to repay their debt before death.

When Sol heard the suggestion on bankruptcy reform, he instantly embraced it. As part of his philosophy for making a better world this would be a vibrant part of that. The greatest good for the greatest number meant recovering bankruptcy amounts. And more necessary was the effort in preventing bankruptcies in light of the after-death requirement for the money to be repaid. Requiring repayment, even after death, was the justice society was asking for.

Bankruptcy was only a temporary assignment to hard times for those who chose it. Most who declared bankruptcy would climb out of their self-imposed hole eventually. They would often accumulate wealth for many years after.

The solution that was sealed that day was by far the best way to deal with the issue. An issue that had long been a thorn in the side of the economy. It had become an acceptable practice to let people out of their obligations and never revisit them… even if they had the means to deal with what they at one time promised to repay. The only way under Sol's *Bankruptcy Recovery Law* that a person would not have to repay their debt after death would be to die broke. If the estate was broke, then they had beat the system. Yay for them! They would be remembered as dying with debt. But those were few and far between. It was clear society was a whole lot better off with the new *Bankruptcy Recovery Law* that was sealed and set in stone.

"Edict Successfully Recorded"

There had been many meaningful conversations in the Chambers over the past nine months and there would be many more in the years to come

Today however, Sol would not be consulting with the Delegates. At least not all of them. He had taken time to chat with his counsel of four and today was the day of appointments. Sol would appoint the Ministers who would be responsible to implement his plans and edicts. Women and men that had been selected by Sol and approved by Sol's counsel. They would be given their portfolio and their authority by the King. And they would travel the world to ensure the edicts that flowed from Sol's hand would be carried out.

The Anti-Christ Feared By Billions

Sol took his place at the Speaker's Podium. It was comfortable being back at the New York World Counsel Center. The Media Screens around the Chambers flashed to his image. The Unity Globe spun slowly in the holographs projected over the Chambers. Sol took a moment to look at it with wonder. Months after first standing in these chambers, the connecting lines displaying unity between regions were now more numerous. The entire globe was joined by threads of light. Each region and each nation was connected to those around it. The threads of light that encircled the globe visibly connected the entire world. The commitment by the world's leaders to accept the direction of Sol brought a common vision of creating a better world to all people. And although Sol's reign had not yet brought the elusive Utopia, it was clear society was closer than it ever had been. Under the leadership of Sol, the world had become one kingdom. Sol brought steady change and guidance, but he was never seen as a dictator. He was a decisive person yet the Participants saw he was able to shift his direction when necessary. Seeing him do so when trying to implement RIFD microchip implants to all Participants didn't cast Sol as failing rather it elevated him as a man who could see reason and let go of an idea if needed.

A number of months previous, Sol had edicted all participants would be implanted with a Radio Frequency ID. An implantable microchip that would be inserted in the right hand of each person. He had decided it would replace the popular G-PAS card but almost immediately after sealing the edict his counsel asked him to rethink his decision.

Many of those in the World Counsel had seen this move suggested in the past. His advisors informed him that implanting an identity and commerce chip in a person's right arm had a connection to a biblical tale about an anti-Messiah figure. It was certainly an interesting connection made by religious groups. And although Sol did not define himself by a religious creed or adherence, he saw the force of the religious consciousness that his counsel informed him about. He was willing to work within that framework to prevent billions of people believing some very damning suggestions about who and what Sol was.

Sol was advised it would not be good to appear as the anti-Christ. A mythical global ruler that 2.65 billion Christians believed was yet to come upon the world. A man inspired by evil motives who would turn believers against their God if he could. In Sol's view a great many of the apocalyptic ideals of religion were overstated at best. Pew Research Polls had shown for years the steady decline in adherents of traditional religion was mostly due to the disenchantment people had with the many confused and irrational doctrines of Christendom. The denomination that once boasted global adherents consisting of a third of the earth's population, now could only find themselves to be one fifth of the almost 11 billion people on earth. Religion had been fading for decades and even Pope Caroline had transitioned on many of the Catholic Churches' traditional doctrines in hopes to reignite interest in the failing historic institution.

Sol was reminded that one of the many signs of this anti-Messiah man who he was not wanting to be connected with, was called the *Mark of the Beast*. Many who ascribed to that superstition believed a powerful man would rise at some point in their future. This anti-Christ was politically and spiritually positioned to force humanity to take this Mark of the Beast. For a great many of those who feared such a mark, it was thought that an implanted chip was that mark. And the world leader who prescribed such a "mark", ensuring that no one could buy or sell without it, was the anti-Christ. This move by the anti-Christ was heralded as the portent of the end of days. Days the hyper-religious were ardently waiting to come.

So Sol, in compliance with the wisdom of his counsel, chose to forego the digital identification. There would be no implantable upgrade to the G-PAS card. In this way, he would ward off unreasonable accusations that he might be the anti-Christ feared by billions of believers worldwide. And it was just this kind of reason that showed he was not a rigid autocrat demanding his own way. Sol was able to respond to reason and change a law or edict, even if it was he who had sealed it.

Forever Isn't Long Enough

Pausing to center himself and settle in to the Speaker's Podium, his moment of contemplation was brief. Just before he appointed his Ministers he reflected on how he loved it here in the Deliberations Chambers. Often, when time permitted in the days before the address, Sol would sit in the center of the empty Chambers. When no one else was in the building. His favourite and most inspirational moment in the Chambers was when Ell joined him earlier that week. She travelled to the WCC with Sol and knowing his routine, she wanted to see what he did in that huge chambers all alone at night.

The two had sat together, watching the Unity Globe above their heads spin slowly. The illuminated threads of light affirmingly scrolled around the globe. Expressing the unity and interconnectivity that was holding the globe together. The Chambers were mostly dark except for the lights over the doorways and the hue from the Unity Globe.

Ell looked around the chambers. Remembering the Red Ochre ceremony for the special day that it was. Life had changed for the two of them. She still had her Sol, most of the time. But at times he was as distant while sitting next to her in their Seattle home as if he were across the world at the World Counsel Center in Paraguay. Ell saw all the ways the world had improved and how people were beginning to be loosed of their hopelessness and apathy. How equity and justice were becoming the expectation and not an unattainable mystery of this life.

Citizens moved to apathy and inaction had become Participants fueled by hope and motivated to invest in their society. That changed everything. People were interacting with their world now instead of having their world act on them.

Ell was pleased to be part of Sol's journey, their journey…and have input into the edicts that flowed from Sol's position. But the months that brought them here had some very intense days. Sol had already had more than one threat on his life. Would there be more? Could Tomer promise to neutralize them all? How long would Sol find favour with a demanding world that asked so much and gave so little at times? Ell gave way to her emotions in that moment.

"Sol," she began, "Is it all worth it?"

Sol looked over at her and took her hand. He knew her. He knew she chose to accept this was what Sol was supposed to be doing. He knew there was turmoil inside of the only woman he had ever loved. He would not have been surprised if she were bombarded by the swirling thoughts that could come with sharing her husband's time and attention with the world. His power was unparalleled on the world stage, but to her, he was still just Sol. The man she had always loved. She had to be wondering…

> *"Would things ever be the same again? Would Sol die as King? Would he be king for the rest of their life? Would it even be possible to return to just Sol and Ell, the team that sat with friends at coffee on Saturday mornings in downtown Seattle? Was this the way it would be from now on?"*

She didn't have to elaborate on her question. Sol knew what was going on inside her.

"You know Hun, I've asked myself that same question the times I've sat here just staring up at the Globe. Is it all worth it? I haven't found my answer. I do know this is not the time to go back…not yet. I'm sorry for the times I've missed being with you…really being with you doing the things we use to do and use to love. But this has been a whirlwind, and I know things will smooth out."

Ell leaned over and held Sol, just held him. Saddened at what had changed for them but seeing the hope Sol had brought into the world.

"I know Sol, we said yes together 9 months ago and today I still say yes…I'm with you. This still feels right. Just seeing how the people respond to having a King…this must be what we were all ready for. "

Sol kissed her and savoured the scent of her beautiful skin. As he did, he thanked her and let her know that he had some of the same feelings she was sharing. As they loosed their embrace he let Ell know about a coffee date he had planned, "I talked to Gavin and Rosslyn, they said they're free to meet us for coffee downtown next Saturday."

"Just us…Really? That'll be nice, the King of the world deserves a coffee date with friends as much as anyone."

Ell grabbed Sol again and hugged even tighter. "I love you."

"Forever isn't long enough to love you Ell."

In that moment early that morning, the pair sat back and watched the Unity Globe slowly turn for a few more minutes. Silently they sat together in the quiet New York World Counsel Center. Just enjoying the peace. Before the upcoming Great Assembly. The Great Assembly that was taking place nine months after his appointment as King. The anticipated assembly where Sol would appoint Minsters to manage the edicts he would be sealing into law.

No Chance To Grow Up
As Other Girls Did

Sol had been to all 8 Centers over the last 9 months. It was odd how they all began to blend together. It was true that every WCC visit and address were different experiences each time. But none were like the first address he had made here in New York. The spontaneous Cherokee chant that filled the Plaza, the profoundly humbling feeling of having willing Participants bow their heads to receive his Red Ochre imprint as he made his way through the crowd. Those were dramatically impacting moments. And Sol would never forget the eruption of applause that reached the heavens that day. Today's Inclusions Session in New York City felt like he was being welcomed home.

The only experience that came close to the first address in New York was the response of the people in Paraguay. Sol had given his address there the day after the FIFA World Cup tournament had ended. He shared in that monumental victory with the Participants of Paraguay as well as a monumental ethical victory for the exasperated people when he announced the *Anti-Slavery and Sex-Slave Trade Task Force.*

The Country of Paraguay had just beaten Brazil by a score of 3 to 2 in the final game of the FIFA World Cup. Sol extended his congratulations to the people of Paraguay, a committed group of Soccer fans with unrivalled passion. Sol's visit to the Paraguay World Counsel Center would see him announcing another victory for the region. It was a successful operation by the newly formed *Anti-Slavery and Sex-Slave Trade Task Force*. The sex-slave trade and human trafficking rings had forced a stranglehold on Paraguay for almost three generations. Many of the Paraguayan women, transgenders, and children were drawn into the slave trade. The shrouded but concentrated sex-slave industry was embedded in Paraguay. And it had cavernous depth in Brazil. Thousands of Paraguayans had been carted off to Brazil to feed the sick hunger of men addicted to money and other men addicted to sex with pre-pubescent girls.

The Paraguayan people were just one of the countries that had transitioned from 2nd world status to first world status, yet it was still ravaged by the human trafficking rings and sex-slave rings. Crime rings that more advanced regions of the world had seen dissolve from their culture for a decade or so.

The recently sealed Amyl Rothschild, it was learned, had a connection to this depraved industry. He had invested money that indirectly aided the industry in many regions of South America. As for the thousands of Paraguayan women and children captive in Brazil, Paraguay had long ago realized how little recourse it had to reclaim her daughters. As a nation with limited power, Paraguay could do nothing against the highly sophisticated and government ignored sex-slave industry of Brazil. It was an industry deeply imbedded into the cultures of both countries. Brazil traders were always scouting public events to "recruit" new talent. No large gathering of people was immune to the scouting efforts of sex-slave traders. Not even the Great Assembly that brought hundreds of thousands out to see Sol seal edicts.

It was because of the risk to young women and children at the Great Assembly that the *EPD* Drones were very active in the Plaza that day in Paraguay. Hovering from cluster to cluster over the crowd. Processing images of the men who Tomer's Task force had identified as slave-trader scouts.

The arrogance of the slave-trader degenerates was unbelievable. Even the day after the Paraguayan World Cup win and the day the King came to town, the sex-slave trader scouts were out in the crowd. Looking to seduce young girls into the industry that would enslave them to a life of a abuse and an early death. So brazen as to seek those whose parents they thought would accept a sum of money in exchange for the services of their daughter. Bringing the promise of a luxurious life and steady flow of money.

The men that ran and worked in those operations were imperious. So much so, that right here in front of Sol, a King who had the power to neutralize the world's richest man that had been a contributor to the industry, a King who stopped the Geld Kwaad terrorist organization by killing every member in the camp; these conscienceless men would hide in plain sight. They were too ignorant or too disrespectful of Sol's resolve, to try to hide their trade. The nation of Paraguay would soon see their misplaced arrogance for soliciting new girls during the Great Assembly.

That day would not be like others. Tomer Cohen had set in place the things he needed to smoke-out these atrocious excuses for human beings. His investigation had yielded not only the names of these slave-trade middlemen but their images too. And the faithful and seemingly innocuous EDP Drones, were cataloguing and processing every one of their images.

Tomer's sting during the World Cup game the day before Sol's Paraguayan address was the perfect timing to raid the operations in 25 slave-trade warehouses. While all Brazilian eyes were glued to the Media Screens watching their World Cup hopefuls, the Task Force raids were highly effective. Tomer and Takanaka's joint effort contained the targets of the raids to the illegal warehouse facilities without major incident. If you want to catch criminals in Brazil or Paraguay off guard...just show up during the final game of the World Cup.

End To A Violent And Destructive Sex-Slave Industry

The operation was perfectly executed. Two thirds of the way through the Second half, just before Paraguay scored its unanswered game winning goal, the raid began. Finally, thanks to Sol's *Level The Playing Field* edict, for the first time in the modern era, the men and women who were risking their lives to save the lives of others were no longer undervalued when the wages they were paid were compared with the adjusted salaries of World Cup athletes. The edict that regulated salaries for men and women playing games for a living, had righted the odd practice and belief that extreme amounts of money ought to be paid to professional athletes. Thanks to Sol's *Level the Playing Field Edict,* the Sports entertainment industry was brought back into line. It was sealed into law that millions of women and men who do jobs benefitting humanity and often risk their lives, should not be paid 100's of times less than the men and women who play a game for a living. Of course, the Level the Playing Field edict sent the sporting world into a schoolyard temper tantrum for a few days. But it calmed down as those working in the industry saw that not only did the general population of the world affirm and support the edict. But the athletes who pushed back to reject the wage reform could easily be replaced by women and men who meant it when they said they, "*I just want to play for the love of the game*".

Quality and performance on the field or in the arena only dipped for a moment. Even though professional athlete salaries were brought in line with the rest of society's earnings and huge wage drops ensued, the athletes still competed fiercely and put on a great show. The few that decided to protest the massive salary shift by leaving their sport weren't missed for more than a game. It was always the case that what someone was doing for 10 million dollars, team owners and managers could find a dozen others who would do it just as well for under a million.

This was no surprise. Sol knew the men and women who played the games for a living would be just as apt to perform at an elite level under his new salary laws, as they had during the era of skyrocketing salaries. An era that was now gone. The multiple millions paid to any pro athlete, including quarterbacks, footballers, and tennis stars was no longer allowed.

No one in the pro athletics world was asked to starve or work a second job to make ends meet like so many in society. And at that, the very best players in sport, the most marketable of the industry, were still bringing in millions with endorsements and sponsor contracts. But the playing field was level when it came to salary, just as Sol's *Level the Playing Field* edict implied.

Whether it was sex-slave trade victims who returned to their families or something as insignificant as elite athletes who just took a huge salary cut under Sol's *Level the Playing Field Edict*, the resiliency was remarkable. Humans, Participants in this near utopian society, always found a way within themselves to get back in the game and give it their best shot. The brief uproar about the edict disappeared as women and men in professional sport quickly realized they never got into it for the money in the first place.

Many of them actually admitted the sense of purity that has been restored to their game was a refreshing change and revitalized their love for the game. "Big Money" only complicated the pro-sports industry that they loved being a part of. In a throwback to the early days of professional sport, athletes began to play hard for the love of the game and the drive to win. The intensity of the World Cup Soccer match proved the point. It was played by athletes who no longer were given the riches of a king for kicking a ball around. And that intensely competitive World Cup Final had been the perfect distraction to run Tomer's operation dismantling the sex-trade in one of the world's most dense sex-slave-trade region.

The beautiful thing about the Op was that Tomer's people were able to keep the trader's communication streams active. Text messages between the slave-lords and the scouts were intercepted and redistributed by Tomer's people. That meant the scouts who found their way to the Great Assembly knew nothing about the dismantling of their operations. They received no warning that a sting was up and running. They believed everything was operating as normal. Completely oblivious to the sealing of their colleagues the day before. It was perfect. The entire sex-slave industry in Brazil and Paraguay was shut down in a day...the day Paraguay stole the World Cup victory from their Brazilian rivals. Tomer's campaign was massive. And it was precise. 16500 Paraguayan women, transgender, and young girls were rescued. And 1300 Brazilian slave-traders were sealed by Ministry of Retribution field agents.

The worst of the trader's warehouses in Brazil was prison to almost 250 young girls. Many of them forced to have sex with up to 10 men a day. And just like in Cambodia, lust and greed fueled the Brazilian market as well. Sol however, had devised a different solution to the Cambodian sex-slave problem. Many parents were forced to sell their own daughters to the traders. In Cambodia the vicious ravages of poverty that caused destitution were played against the parents of innocent girls. Families needed money and their daughters were a certain way to get that.

A Perpetuating Harvest
Of Its Young Girls

The Cambodian people lived in an impoverished state. The good people that had love and loyalty for their country, had no power to prevent their country from it's spiral down into decay. The belief had developed for so many Cambodian families that the only way to get money was to sell the only things of value they had, their daughters. But once Sol had provided his solution to the Cambodian people the problem began to get solved. His solution was another simple strategy that fixed so many of the problems present already. Few critics decried the strategy. Bryson Reynolds began re-coining an old phrase to lend support to some of Sol's unorthodox moves like the Cambodian bounty on sex-slave traders.

"It's so crazy it just might work," Reynolds would say.

And he was right, the Cambodian solution was crazy...but under Sol and Tomer's guidance, it had begun to work.

The way the strategy worked was that Sol had decided the $3000 a family was paid to sell their daughter to the sex-slave traders was an insult. An insult to the family and an insult to the entire human race. But sales persisted and parents continued to succumb to the easy cash. The value of $3,000 to a disparaged Cambodian family could be absolutely transformative, representing a significant amount of money and potentially life-changing opportunities. The powerlessness of mothers and fathers who felt trapped by the system was hard to comprehend. They believed they had no other way. And they wished they had a redeemer, a rescuer, to make a way for them to keep their daughters home safe. But no one rose up to fight on their behalf.

Sol, by throwing his authority behind the solution, proved to be the support needed by the trapped parents of the many children sold into slavery. The Cambodian solution caught on in other regions where the child sex-slave trade flourished. Sol raised up the best kind of mercenaries a leader could want. Who better to go after the slavers than the parents of the captive? Giving permission to the parents to become home-grown mercenaries was surprisingly productive. These parents and families who needed money so badly, were now allowed to kill the men who profited from their daughters and those who were customers of the industry. Justice, crime prevention, and retribution have many versions. The satiety that came from this version was almost too easy of an ask. A simple two-sided motivation theory that compelled parents to act. Any parent or group of parents who would capture or kill a sex-slave trader or customer who was purchasing sex from a slave, would be paid the predetermined bounty.

When Sol was told that Cambodia alone had at least 10,000 of the worldwide 2.8 million victims in the slave-trade and sex-slave trade, he offered an opportunity for the parents and family members of the indentured girls to earn the bounty. It was simple. If your daughters are under the control of sex-slave traders, you will be given money if you kill the captor. By encouraging those who had been forced to sell their daughters to act decisively and end the life of the traders and slave masters, the family would receive five times what the traders had offered to pay for their daughters. The family would receive their daughter back, and the King would bestow upon them the honor of being a hero for Participating in making a better world. The death of the men who enslaved these girls would lead to an improved society for all.

Of course, there was some risk, but the traders quickly realized there were more pissed-off, justice hungry parents hunting for them than there were traders to fight back. Very quickly the herd began thinning out. It was an amazing grassroots neighborhood watch program with an effective vigilante force, able to bite back decisively. With the support of the King, and the enticement of the bounty money, thousands of families retrieved their daughters and thousands more were preserved from the fate of a daughter being sold into slavery.

The complex and destructive problem of Cambodian parents selling their daughters into slavery was being effectively solved. Through the act of empowering and rewarding the parents of these young girls, the industry would eventually realize it cannot win. Soon, under Sol's reform and call to action, families would no longer worry their daughters would be forced into the vortex of sex-slavery that so many had been lost to in the past. Sol had given them an avenue to be true Participants in society's betterment. The parents would be paid handsomely for killing the abusers among their society. Not only would they get their daughters back and keep them safe, but they would receive a sum of money that would ease the discomfort of a 2nd world lifestyle.

It was by Sol's hand that the men who dehumanized these young girls were sealed for their crimes. They were participants in enslaving, and abusing thousands of their captives and they therefore had sealed their own fate. They would no longer be Participants in this society. They would be killed and their prisoners set free. For every man who had committed his life and career to this destructive trade that was sealed, at least 100 women, children, or transgenders were rescued and restored to their previous lives. Rehabilitated and reintegrated into society.

The recovery rate for those rescued was high. The power of human resiliency was truly a sight to behold. Remove a person's support system and enslave them in a degrading environment and they will involuntarily submit. They will lose the will to fight for their mental, physical, and emotional freedom. But, when a ruler and global society is the witness to their suffering and that is backed up by rescuing them and supporting their recovery, no matter what that looks like, the human spirit scales huge obstacles to restore itself.

Stories like the 250 young girls that were housed in a Cambodian warehouse and farmed out to Cambodian brothels would soon be a thing of the past. The horrifying reality of hundreds of little girls, sold by their parents who thought there was no other way for the family to survive, broke the heart of the world. Daily, little girls were abused. Daily, the ripping away of innocence and hope occurred for young girls who were forced to have sex with men all day and all night. The evil men who justified the abuse because society had normalized it were not interested in being gentle. For the young girl who endured the unspeakable, wracked with pain, bleeding, and forced to hold back the tears, she would silently take the abuse, or she would be beaten back at the brothel.

The victim was often abandoned by her parents and trapped until the slave traders had no more use for her. She was then either left to the streets of Cambodia or allowed to return to her parents. Filled with shame and the emotional and physical scars one would expect to have developed in a little girl. An innocent child who was offered no chance to grow up as other girls did but was the sex object of the worst type of human being society had ever tolerated. A child sex abuser.

That day in Paraguay, the day after the glorious World Cup win by Paraguay, Sol and the people celebrated two victories. The World Cup Championship, and the liberation of hundreds of Paraguayan girls…which occurred along with the sealing of hundreds of slave traders. Men who would never again imprison and sexually abuse an innocent daughter of Paraguay.

When Sol announced the success of the raids, the country rejoiced. Few thought they would ever see the end to the unethical, inhumane, and outright mass enslavement of so many young girls in the country. The brightness of the World Cup victory rapidly faded as the crowd in the Plaza that day and viewers around the world, saw the liberation of thousands of captives and the end to a violent and destructive sex-slave industry.

What had transpired in Paraguay during Sol's address was indeed moving. And beside the New York address, Paraguay would always have a special place for Sol. By being the leader who delivered the country from a perpetuating harvest of its young girls into the Brazilian sex-slave trade, Sol would always hold a special place in the hearts of the Paraguayans.

Today, as Sol stood ready to address the Delegates in the New York World Counsel Center Deliberations Chamber, what he did for Paraguay and for all the countries of the world over his 9 months as King, would be in their minds. Thinking about presenting his Ministers to the Delegates today, Sol was at ease. Feeling the support he had from countries like Paraguay and from the people of this global community humbled Sol. Support that would not have come if this were another time. He was reminded of the part "timing" had played in the Delegate Deliberations that affirmed the motion to appoint a King over 9 months ago. And it gave him confidence to continue to make changes for a better world.

Thoughts of the Letter From A Grieving Mom

Sol was prepared for this defining Inclusions Session. Sol's hand could only extend so far. He was quite free to admit that enlisting the service of others who would lead with prudence and wisdom would truly prosper and advance the world. He so enjoyed arriving early at the WCC, before the place was teeming with staff, as he had this morning. Today, Ministers would be set in place to work alongside Sol. He had chosen a select few to aid the King in implementing the laws and edicts that were sealed.

Just as Tomer, his Minister of Retribution, epitomized Sol's philosophy of dealing with the elements of society that worked to harm society, so too would the Minsters Sol was to appoint today, commit themselves to his enduring solutions. Solutions to bring an ordered new world.

The early morning had dissolved away. The Staff at the World Counsel Offices had streamed in not long after Sol had arrived. Inclusions Sessions had become the busiest and most involved days for the resources and staff at the Centers. Managing almost 2000 delegates, their aids and support staff, was a task that drew in a great many resources.

The inmates had finished their cleaning job of the Plaza and grounds. Ensuring the Plaza was pristine for the arrival of the Delegates. The incarcerated were reclaiming dignity and internal motivations from the edict that required them to work during the day at various tasks to benefit the society they had acted against. Society had asked for it and Sol provided it. There was little criticism about his *Inmate Repurposing Program*. Inmates understood that because of their choice to involve themselves in crime, their role now, was to do the menial work in the public sector as prescribed by the program. In this case of forced labour, the prescribed work of the imprisoned was seen to free society in some way, from the injustices criminals had imposed on the society they were now serving with their labour.

Today, Sol was standing in behind the Speaker's Podium. An unusual place for this people's King to be. On every other occasion, Sol took his place in front of the Podium. Not wanting the barrier between him and the people. Today was different however, Sol needed to set the Ministers in front of the people. Those specially appointed individuals who were set apart to do the will of Sol. To take the edicts he seals and implement and expand on them where necessary.

It was these 9 Ministers who would be intermediaries between Sol and the people he served. Some pundits had opined that Sol was restructuring the Global leadership model with his own version of the *Rule of Nines,* the criminally minded elitist billionaires, who thought they could engineer society in ways that would benefit them and grow their wealth. But this group of 9 was in no way similar to the Rule of Nines group that had began to dissolve after the sealing of Amyl Rothschild. Sol had a brief meeting with the King's Nine in the Fall-Out room before the Session began. In moments from now each one would be called up to the Podium. They would make their way from the Delegate seating area of the Chambers and join Sol up on stage. Tomer, the seasoned Minster of Retribution, already stood to the right of the Podium, a few metres from center stage. The Session began with Sol thanking the Delegates for all they had done since he took the role as King.

"Your support of my position over the past months has been more than I ever expected. The vision for a better world, for a utopia in a sense, was shared by all of us. And I was humbled and still am, that you honored the moment by allowing me to be your King. I have seen and done things in the past months that no man would expect to see and do. No man could expect to be given the reigns to the world and enjoy such favor of his Counsel and the people who are Participants in that world. But you have truly elevated me in wealth of spirit and in honor for integrity."

Ell was watching from the Fall-Out Room. The large empty Fall-Out Room she sat alone in, had held an awkward celebratory moment for the two of them just 9 short months ago. That was a surreal day for Ell and Sol. The day they first stood amid the world's most powerful Delegates after being installed as King. Repositioned from people of no influence to standing among the leaders of the World Congress. That day was a blur now.

And now, while Ell sat alone watching her husband lead the World Counsel Inclusions Session, she was no longer worried or afraid. She had found many of the past 9 months to be turbulent and tense. But no longer. Familiar now with the World Counsel Centers and all the official business that went on there, Ell was quite comfortable sitting alone in the Fall-Out room. The questions and fears had disappeared. Ell knew their choice to agree to the Chancellor's invitation on their patio came from a place that most people have. It is that place that hopes to have influence to change what he or she sees is wrong in the world they live in. And from where Ell was sitting this day, she saw Sol as the King she thought he would be. Because of who Sol was, the world now had a King that they had long been wanting.

In only 9 brief months. Months that sent Sol to every continent on the globe, Sol had done more than any single world leader had since ancient times. Those were times when Kings and Queens of powerful nations did whatever they pleased and rarely considered the effect on anyone but themselves. These however, were times when the King did what the people had been hoping for. In times past a King did the greatest good for himself....But in the present, this King did the greatest good for the greatest number. So much had changed.

This was a new age. The world had a new order to it. An era of such unprecedented hope of the masses. The people were citizens no more. They had become Participants. Taking part in making the world better for all. By Sol's example of doing something to help the world become better, Participants adopted the King's philosophy. Most would no longer accept the low standard they had been hypnotized into. Refusing to accept the status quo and just idle in place tolerating the way things are. Gone were the days when a corrupt and egomaniacal leader would speak or behave unethically, and people would presume they had permission to do likewise. This day, this epoch, was a time when permission was found by Participants to be better…kinder…more honorable…and more invested in improving self and society. If something was not right, it didn't have to stay that way. **"*Do something*"**…Became a collective mantra that met people on so many levels as Sol's simple concept of showing he cares was relayed to the entire world. The entire world started to care back. Caring on levels that had long ago eroded in the cultural abyss of passivity and apathy. The world that everyone had been wishing could exist was now breaking forth. A new world in front of a vibrant generation. The generations that followed would forever be indebted to this brave generation, the one that led by example and moved the world forward. Sol may have been the King who brought forth the edicts, but the Participants had come along with him and made this world better.

Today in front of the Delegates once again, Sol instinctively slipped out from behind his Podium with his Folio in hand. It was looking worn and obviously well used. It must have been built to last. This Royal Folio had a few miles on it. Not to mention the day it sailed across Sol's living room when he tried to edict a free transportation program to every person who requests it when they have been out drinking at a pub or bar. When *The King's Scribe* deferred the attempted edict one night it infuriated Sol.

He had tried to force the edict when he received yet another sad story of a young couple killed in a car accident with a drunk driver. The 1A.M. accident left the drunk driver injured, and in the other car, the young man dead and the young woman passenger critically injured, only to die after three days in the hospital.

As Sol read the heart wrenching letter from the young woman's mother, he was deeply grieved and reacted to the situation. The loss was yet another distressing fact of a dystopian society. People driving drunk were already harshly penalized with removal of their Driver Approval Certificate, heavy fines, community service work, and often a period of incarceration. But that still did not prevent irresponsible drunks from making the uninhibited decision to get in the car and drive the few blocks or few miles home.

It was a matter that needed a different solution. And Sol, moving quickly from grief to anger while reading the mother's letter, placed his hand on his folio to lay forth an edict.

With images of the horrific carnage from the 1A.M. accident in his mind. The Fire and Ambulance crews swarmed to dismantle the vehicle from around the victims. Cutting a roof flap and the A and B side posts to flap the passenger door down and out of the way. The driver's side of the vehicle was crumpled in past the steering wheel. The young man had no chance when he was heading straight on the green light and was T-boned at full speed by a drunk driver.

It had happened a million times before…and not just in Seattle…everywhere. The driver sat lifeless and the passenger, the young woman who died three days later, was semi-lucid. Reaching for her husband of just over a year, he wasn't responding to her cry. The fire crews tried to comfort her, to reassure her that everything would be all right…but they wouldn't. They lied. She lost consciousness just as they pulled her free of the wreck…not seeing that her husband's empty body would be left in place until after the drunk who killed him was rescued alive. Her three days of surgeries and attempts at recovery had her fading in and out of consciousness, calling for her husband of a year, that she knew deep down inside, was not able to hear her and she would never see again.

After reading the grieving Mother's letter Sol announced the edict to the King's Scribe. All alone that evening, agitated by the endlessness of deaths from drunk driving, Sol questioned why this young couple's death was not prevented. With no crowd to explain his actions to, the King's Scribe documented the edict just how Sol spoke it as it had many times before in his living room.

Sol dictated, *"From this day forth all drinking establishments in the world will be provided government sponsored transportation for their patrons. Patrons will be transported home for free. Anyone who enters a drinking establishment to imbibe shall be obligated to utilize the government provided transport."*

Sol knew drunk driving was likely never to stop, so he decided to chip away at it and save those he could by sipping from the other side the glass.

Sol was definitely pissed off when he set his hand on the Folio. The sensors in the King's Scribe registered his status. Underneath his hand the red light Sol was waiting for failed to glow. The blue hue pulsed from dim to bright to dim to bright. The edict was not sealed. Sol started to become even angrier.

"Your edict has been deferred, please try again later."

Sol thought there must be some mistake. He was making an edict that was designed to help the people. It would get drunk people home safely and protect innocent drivers. Sealing this edict would benefit everyone. The pubs and bars would draw more patrons in to enjoy meaningful social interaction, spending money in the pubs and connecting with other people. It was a good edict. Sol had thought it through after considering visits to several pubs over the years. He tried to seal the edict again. The letter from a grieving mom would not have come to him if a drunk driver had been kept off the road. The couple that was killed that night had just passed their first year of marriage…a whole life together ahead of them, and without warning, suffering a horrific death in a terrible crash.

Looking at the Folio the edict was clearly documented. It only needed to be sealed. Sol pressed his hand against the warm glass of the Folio. "This time," he thought, "the Scribe will surely seal the edict,"

He was wrong,

"Your edict has been deferred, please try again later."

Maybe it was the intensity he felt at the moment…an intense burning to do something good for the people to try to stop the onslaught of drunk driving that went on, or maybe it was the strain of just being King. It was almost overwhelming at times trying to address the multitude of issues that came before him. And the moment the King's Scribe declined to seal his edict, Sol snapped.

The resources weren't a problem, money wasn't a problem…but what Sol had to draw on within himself was the problem. Sol was feeling the pressure. And he let it fly. In that moment, the smooth tone of the matter-of-fact, British sounding, digital "bitch", talking in the King's Scribe completely triggered him. He grabbed the Folio with the hand he was desperately trying to seal the edict with and rifled it across the room. It bounced off the arm of the chair on the other side of the room and just about landed in the fireplace. Coming to stop on the raised hearth of the fireplace, the blue hue still illuminated the upside down screen of Sol's Folio. Sol felt better. This program was not doing what he wanted and it incensed him…but he just as quickly realised what he was doing. Where his edict was coming from. Passion over reason was a bad place to lead from, as Canadian Prime Minister Pierre Trudeau once intoned. Sol came back to his senses. He got up from his couch and started to head over to the fireplace to retrieve his Folio. As he made a couple of steps to do so he was reminded of Ahmed's words when he was first introduced to the King's Scribe. Ahmed had told Sol;

"Just as with any emotion, when one is compelled to make choices in response to a feeling one is better off taking pause to consider."

And the King's Scribe recognized the feeling-based edict Sol was trying to seal. The system worked perfectly to stop the King from sealing something in haste. Sol embraced the sense of Ahmed's wisdom. He looked at the Folio a few feet away sitting on the hearth. And Sol decided to leave it right where it lay. His edict could wait until morning. As mad as he was tonight it was unlikely he would hear the words that every King wants to hear from his scribe,

"Thank you King Sol, your edict has been sealed."

Standing in front of his Delegates today with the Folio that had been through the last 9 months with him, Sol was ready. He had leaned on "reason" as his inspiration to appoint the Ministers he needed.

Long Live The King

Addressing the patient Delegates who sat before him, Sol glanced down to his Folio and reported, "I don't know where I would be without this thing," he nosed at the Folio in his hand.

"It has brought a lot of information and help to me along the way. It has recorded the past nine months of my reign. Every conversation and interaction as well as every edict and law that has been passed. It has done more than that though. It has connected me to you, our World Counsel Delegates."

The committed group that sat in front of him informed him, guided him, supported him and yes...even challenged him at times. The Face Streams he had over the months had been invaluable. Sol knew, and his Delegates respected the fact he would not have been able to understand a great many situations if it had not been for the updates. Sol spoke of the interactions with marked thankfulness.

"The many FaceStream meetings you have been willing to have with me. No matter what time of day or night, one of you or many of you were there to come to my aid. I am eternally grateful for that."

The women and men of the World Counsel had buoyed him up and made him look good on many occasions. They recognized his sovereign authority and he recognized the cumulative wisdom and information these women and men had to share. They were a vast pool of counsel who had empowered and helped Sol to lead.

Most of the members of the Body of Delegates took comfort in how Sol ran things. The Body found who Sol was and what he represented to be a much-needed salve on the wounds of society. The unanimous decision the Delegates made to appoint a King on that solar eclipse weekend was in no way regretted. Such unity was rare, and it propelled them all to work together pursuing the greatest good for the greatest number in line with Sol's vision. He went on with his opening statements.

"And you have brought many laws forward for me to seal. Some were approved and have been sealed, others, after healthy consult and debate, were not sealed. Still others, such as the *"Old Soldier Program,* revolutionized the way we think about a thing."

Sol had a tiny smirk come across his face as he directed this comment toward the Swedish Delegate area, "We are still developing it. I hope you can be patient Delegate Robinson with the modest beginnings of this Program."

He shot a smile over to where Porter Robinson sat. Dr. Robinson was a mid-40's Swedish research doctor. His anti-aging work had been hailed for its positive effect on the aging process. His procedure slows aging so dramatically that many of his supporters are convinced he has reversed it. Through his protocol, old men and women could be youthful again in so many ways. The Delegates were all familiar with the Old Soldier Program. At a recent Inclusions Session, Dr. Robinson spoke of its success.

There had been concern over the loss of young soldiers engaged in hostilities with terrorists or posted abroad for peacekeeping missions. As well as for those sent to quell an uprising of gangs attempting to leave the Gang City Island. It just seemed senseless to send young men and women into risky territories where armed conflict occurred, and they often would become injured or lose their life. These were often the men and women, who when killed in the line of duty, left a young spouse widowed at home. Or children were left without one parent or the other. Men and women who had a future to live for but saw it either rewritten because of injury or cancelled because of death. The Global Military Unit was powerful enough to go into any dangerous territory and stop insurgents, terrorists, or radical military incursions. But there was often a cost. Troops were injured or killed no matter how potent the force of the GMU was. This compelled Sol and the GMU to find other resources to aid in missions. When he requested his Delegates come up with a solution to the problem, Dr. Porter Robinson led the field by stepping outside the traditional military recruitment box. From that, the *Old Soldier Program* was developed and implemented.

When he first brought forth the *Old Soldier Program* idea it was met with laughter by several of the Delegates. It seemed to be a joke. Old men going into combat...that was just impossible they thought. But it wasn't.

Dr. Porter elaborated on the idea and the Body of Delegates soon realized, taking a phrase out of Bryson Reynolds's playbook, that *It was so crazy it just might work*. Porter's expertise in the anti-aging field was profound and had been underused by culture...until now.

Porter was brief on the day he introduced his concept, so he offered to send a report with projections for the success of his program to the Body of Delegates. At the introduction of the idea, he simply briefed them before tabling the suggestion until the next quarterly meeting.

Sol himself couldn't wait to hear more because he was very intrigued by the idea. If the program was as sound as Porter had been claiming, then the sooner it could be sealed by Sol the better. General Takanaka would have access to all the troops he needed. There were some situations where the GMU needed to deal with terrorist organizations and other para-military groups. Rogue anti-Participant factions that cropped up hoping to make a point or stake a claim at something that was now under the King's authority. Through the Old Soldier Program, the GMU would have all the men and women it needed for the missions...They would just be chronologically much older than the traditional soldier sent off to war.

Porter explained the program. He spoke of how young men and women were compelled to leave their loved ones, their children, and families for tours of duty with the GMU. That is how military life has always been. The military is for the young. Until now.

Porter queried, what if we could make the old young again? Then the military would not have to exploit the strength of youth….it could use the reclaimed youth of the old. Porter offered what seemed to be a hypothetical scenario, but it had an eerie sense of already being proven.

Those over the age of 60 made up 28 percent of the global population. The young were a dying breed in many ways…a noticeably shrinking demographic… and dying in wars and skirmishes was not helping to sustain the only resource that would ensure society continued.

Dr. Porter posed, "In what we call the *Regen-XY Protocol* we use a bio-identical hormone replacement therapy, safely co-administered with other biologically safe substances, substances that would restore the youthfulness of elderly men and women. Restore visual and auditory acuity, rebuild atrophied muscle tissue, enhance digestion and absorption of nutrients, sharpen the nuero-pathways and neuro-chemistry in the brain, aid in developing bone density, and much much more? What if there were a side-effect-free series of substances that would virtually restore the youth of aging men and women? Well there is, we have had fantastic results in our clinical trials."

Dr. Porter's clinic appeared on the screens and Folios in the Chambers. Showing seasoned males, all of them over 60 years of age. The Delegates aimed their attention at the media. It was telling. Older men performing feats that men 30 to 40 years younger would be expected to accomplish. Performing weight bearing exercises like squats, deadlifts, military presses, and pull-ups. Running on the track with the gait of a much more youthful man than they were chronologically. These test subjects were performing at levels they had long left behind. Levels that they, before now, only dreamed of as a once-upon-a-time that they would never see again. Dr. Porter continued.

"With our three month protocol the cell regeneration that takes place restores youthfulness. The only side effect is a psychological one. Basically, ego becomes the only hurdle. The test subjects reported that they had lost their power and relevance in society due to aging. Being in your 60's changes how one is perceived in a society that is run by the 30-year-olds. And the trouble is, we all end up in our 60's, unless life is cut short as so many young soldiers fate has been. But once subjects were about 4 weeks into the program, the subjects of our massive study began regaining it. That sense of power they had years ago. And that triggered certain ego behaviours which proved to be difficult to manage. Quite simply, these men made what one might call, 'A comeback.'

"With this program, men and women over 60 are able to have youthfulness restored. Strength, sleep patterns, vitality, metabolic rates, sexual function, recovery after exercise, vascular health, neurological function, bone density, muscle tone, skin elasticity, digestion…and all the youthful biological and physiological processes that go along with it. The detrimental effects of programmed psychophysiology are introduced to a biological environment of healing that aids in restoration. Through capnometry assessments and Behavioral Breath Analysis, reflexive breathing is restored, which improves CO_2-O_2 chemistry to a range that incites health regeneration.

"So far, the male version of the protocol has been fully tested and proven. We are close to having the same results with elderly women. Reversal of menopause is more complicated than expected and has delayed the progress, but our geneticists are sorting through the complexities of the female reproductive changes. However, for the moment, we are experiencing success with treating men. And it is men, men over 60, who can begin to fill military positions."

The Delegates heard more from Dr. Robinson and from Sol who had seriously considered the Old Soldiers Program. The short presentation spoke of how some of these men may have been in the military at one time or may have wanted to, but both previously experienced candidates and non-experienced candidates 60 years of age and over, have displayed a strong desire to embark on a military tour of duty. They also come with a vast array of foundational knowledge and wisdom that any military operation will benefit from. Delegates were asked by Porter to imagine, the prowess of a 30-year-old coupled with the wisdom of a 60 year old. When given the chance to be part of a military operation for the first time and create a legacy or serve again for a second time, polls revealed that many men in the target age bracket are eager to jump in. These participants are looking for a way to do something important, to give back, and to make a mark in their world. Either in retirement or very near they are ready to do more. Becoming a vibrant healthy, active soldier under the *Old Soldier Program*, gives them that opportunity.

The philosophy underlying the OSP was built off the idea that OSPers are not young men risking their lives and losing everything in the process. Porter continued to enlighten the Delegates.

"If we can tap into the vast resource that is post 60 year olds we can bolster our Global Military Unit troops for any militaristic event. Holding these men in the Reserves benefits all. In all of history the glory of war has been blackened by the horrific loss of youthful men and women. Young individuals with a spouse, children, and a whole life ahead of them. The men, on the *ReGen-XY Protocol*, are very willing to take a one-year to three-year tour of duty in place of a younger woman or man who would otherwise be sent into active duty.

"Participants in the study report they would be willing to join the military. Participants almost unanimously report that if they were to die in service, then they would be leaving a legacy as a war hero. Being just as honest with their feelings about the program, most respondents stated if they returned after a year long enlistment, they would love the opportunity to come back with war stories and experiences that gave them a sense of purpose, renewing their self-esteem and self-worth. This was especially the case we found with the men over 60 who had never been in the military."

As the Delegates listened on, Dr. Porter brought to light some very impacting demography information.

"One extremely salient point I would like to make, is how accurate the 2013 projections of the United Nations were. Seeing the rapid acceleration of the ageing demographic, the reports revealed almost exactly how the pool of young Participants in the world would be outnumbered by the pool of older Participants. A trend that no one has been able to reverse so we are left to work within those boundaries. The prediction that 1 out of every 5 people in the world will be 60 years old by the year 2050 has already been met. We have surpassed that now in the year 2044. We are years ahead of the predicted pace in achieving this imbalance in our global population. Our society, simply cannot afford to lose what is becoming an extinct demographic. Those under the age of thirty have become rare in terms of age distribution across the world. We must find ways to utilize the resource of over 60-year-olds that we possess in this present society."

Porter had elaborated well. And before the proposition was tabled, he answered a brief question about the science of reversing aging. Many of the women and men in the Chambers were starting to consider the value of such an anti-aging protocol for themselves. The question about civilian use was made and Porter suggested that for now, the program would be strictly military. Eventually, there would be inroads made into the public that would offer a scaled down version of the protocol.

"What we do," Porter explained, "Is start them on a protocol of ReGen-XY. A formula injected subcutaneously twice a week. Participants start sleeping better that first night. Recovery and recuperation takes place when one sleeps. The protocol, given in conjunction with a sound nutrition program, and a monitored fitness program, has shown impressive results to say the least."

Dr. Porter had not inflated the value of the research or embellished the results. Old men were becoming young again through his work. He closed his thoughts by stating the clear facts of what was destined to become the *Old Soldier Program* under King Sol.

"We have come to the place where a once deteriorating ageing male or female, can enjoy the quality of life they enjoyed in their youth. That Participant is now ready for the strains military life has to offer."

At that the Delegates tabled the *Old Soldier Program* recommendation. They were an ageing demographic themselves and were excited to Deliberate on it in the coming Inclusions Sessions.

…When Sol had glanced in Porter's direction during his introductory address with his fleeting grin, everyone in the Chambers knew what he was referencing. They also knew that this program would be implemented in the coming weeks and announced to the world at a Great Assembly.

At Sol's playful recognition of him, Delegate Porter Robinson nodded acceptingly and remained attentive to Sol's address. Sol spoke on as he moved closer to the appointment of His Ministers.

"We all know there is wisdom in a multitude of counsellors. And many of you have been that multitude for me. Some of the most meaningful counsel I receive comes from outside these Chambers where the Body of Delegates convenes. The King of the World Meta page is amazingly active and the contributors and posters to the page are amazingly wise. I have learned a great deal from the input and feedback that has come through social media."

On screen came the Meta page Sol was referring to. And the post he was about to share was the main focus. Sol read the delightful correspondence to his Delegates.

'*Dear Sol,*

Thanks for what you have done and for your vision for a better world. Boy did we need it. I hope you are doing well and not taking too much on as King. It must be a huge job. You're doing a great job though. Jetting around the world, hearing everyone's problems, making rules regarding things as small as bicycle path use in urban centers and as large as how to deal with a doctor who abuses his female patients on the exam table. Oh BTW...I just loved your Public Aroma Law. Life is much sweeter out here in my hot Arabian city since you brought that one in. I hope your brother got himself cleaned up LOL.

The broad scope of your judgements is mind boggling. How are you managing it? I sure wouldn't want to be King of the World.

I have a suggestion though. I hope I am not stepping on anyone's toes. Maybe you have already thought of it but how about choosing some people to help you? It might be good to appoint other leaders to deal with some of the things you might get bogged down with or not have time for. Oh...and if you're thinking to ask me, please don't, I am too old and too ready to just relax to get that involved.

Maybe someday we will have the utopia we all want. I hope you don't feel you have to make a utopia that relies completely on "You". I'm sure a "Youtopia" is not what you're looking for. You seem to be a guy who cares about more than just himself. ☺

Anyway...I hope things keep going great for you and Ell. I look forward to seeing what comes next. If you decide to bring others in to lend a hand, I hope you can find the right people for the job.

LLTK (long live the king)
Jether Hobab

NEW! International Inner-Space Program

The Delegates agreed with the advice of the Meta poster Jether Hobab. And Sol agreed with it too. He knew the time had come that it made sense to use the talents of others to continue developing the world that was waiting for them all. Sooner than later was definitely better. So Sol reported.

"I FaceStreamed Mr. Hobab after reading his post. He is a delightful and insightful man. He is a true leader in many ways and another proof to the theory that many women or men could fill the role of a King. I hoped I could convince him to come alongside me as one of my Ministers. But Jether Hobab is certain that at the age of 77, he wants to stay right where he is in his hometown of Qatif, Saudi Arabia. But he is correct, it is good for me to have assistance in the work I do. So now, I will introduce you to those who have agreed to be part of my Team."

Jether wasn't the only one to offer advice to Sol. Streams and streams of comments and ideas came in to the King of the World Meta page. A good number of posts were written by those who thought they could fix things better and faster than Sol. People, whether they were on track or not, were participating. The one main theme that threaded through most of the posts was that things needed to change.

Sol positioned himself to appoint his Minsters. At this time he would introduce them one by one and announce their portfolio. They would seal their commitment by imprinting the Folio next to the Podium. Then they would imprint Sol with their own hand. With the same symbolic Red Ochre Sol had imprinted the Chancellor and Delegates with at his installation, and the Drummer and Chanter at his first address. Each minister would avail themself fully to the King and the world. Sol had imprinted the Delegates 9 months ago and now he himself would be imprinted nine times by people who would be entrusted with great authority to implement edicts that passed from his hand.

The nine were to become The Hands of the King. Sol would elevate the women and men who would lead the world to the next phase with a portion of the authority that flowed from him. All the Delegates were intently participating in the moment. Sol announced the first Minister.

"I would like to introduce you to the **Minister of Equity and Anti-Discrimination**. Please welcome Asha Indrani."

Asha Indrani rolled on stage. Moving toward Sol in her chair, she looked nervous. The Delegates welcomed her with their polite applause. She smiled and accepted their warmth with a head nod and a quick wave. Returning her hands to the wheels of her chair she rolled near to Sol. He had stepped to the side of the Podium and thought to stoop lower to greet her but realized that was not necessary. There was no hesitation or awkwardness from him as he waited for her at the Podium. Sol had been sealed in front of only the few who stood on stage with him at the Speaker's Podium that day 9 months ago, and today, Asha and the 8 Ministers to follow her, would be sealed in front of the entire Body of Delegates. Sol was holding the silver tray that he had pressed his hand to during his Red Ochre ceremony. And somewhat of a sense of excitement at the moment could be found in him.

Asha smoothly stood to meet Sol. Rising out of her wheelchair, the hug offered and received showed no awkwardness. The awkwardness that often accompanies a hug shared with a person sitting in a wheelchair was removed by her ability to stand. Had her chair not sat empty behind her, one would not have perceived Asha had no autonomous use of her legs. Her graceful rise from the chair to greet the King while standing was seamless. The deftly engineered bionic exo-skeleton she wore had sensed her forward lean and intention to stand. It was the saviour of the individual affected with paraplegia. The *Para-ssist* device was almost imperceptible and brilliantly intuitive. She and hundreds of thousands of others would slip into their external muskelo-skeletal system each morning when they woke. Because of the bionics marvel, it was as if with only a thought she rose smoothly and quietly.

The technology Asha benefitted from, allowing a person with paraplegia to stand, had been developed as one of the last tech surges to come out of the International Space Program. Since becoming King, Sol had cancelled the Space Program entirely in order to make better use of the fiscal resources here on Earth. The United States alone had come to spend almost 900 billion dollars on its attempts to go boldly where no man has gone before. In fact, the largest failure in the Space Program's list of blocked attempts at establishing a colony in space fed Sol's decision to dissolve all International Space Programs.

Several years ago, the Mars Colony catastrophe altered everything. The crew had been travelling for 86 days on the way to Mars. They were rotating their third group of Mars colonists through stasis. As they brought group 2 out of stasis it began to be evident that brain damage had occurred for that group. The entire group had not descended to a low enough metabolic rate and failed to receive the oxygen required to feed the cells of their brains. Consequently, their Anterior Cingular Cortex suffered damage resulting in dissonance in the Von Economo Neuron Group. The VEN is the neuron group that coordinates ego and anger responses. Once out of the Stasis Pods, Group 2 began to demand control of the mission. Individually, each of the Group 2 members became more and more forceful and intent on taking control of the mission.

The violence that ensued resulted in several rogue leaders battling for the rights to lead the mission and resulted in physical harm to a number of crew members. The ensuing mid-ship battle ultimately damaged two major components of the

PLSS, *Primary Life Support Systems*. After the damage was done one of the Group 2 brain injured members armed himself and took control of the Space Craft. His immediacy to return to Earth caused the eventual destruction of the entire craft and loss of the entire crew and mission. The forced return to Earth did not use a precalculated safe route that considered objects floating through the flight path. Mars One burned up after striking a small piece of space debris and bending the fins on a crucial ventilation system. The excess heat retention in the craft coupled with the strains of propulsion directed toward a re-entry point, caused the craft to disintegrate when the nuclear power plant that powered the entire craft and all its systems failed to register critical temperatures. The craft rapidly went into meltdown. And Sol, recalling that loss along with tabulating the global cost of space programs from Participant countries, announced at one of the more controversial Inclusions Sessions that the International Space Program would be dissolved.

That left trillions of dollars available for the needs of people right here on earth.

His definitive push to stop the wasteful Space Program and redirect monies from it to exploring technologies to aid humanity here on earth, came after getting a Meta message from a young girl with quadriplegia.

The young girl who sent Sol the letter had been hit by a car while crossing the street and had spent the last 5 years with no ability to move any of her limbs. Now, at 16 years old, she had never truly gotten use to exploring her world from the confines of a powered wheelchair. Her potential for independence gone, she wrote of receiving constant care from her family.

In the message to Sol, she asked the King to do something about her situation. Not so much for her, but for all those after her that might suffer the same debilitation. What brought Sol to his knees compelling him to do something about the scandalous use of the people's money for space exploration, was a passing reference to the Mars Mission made by the girl. In her message she went on about the need to expand research, band together with other tech nations, and find ways to improve the dire situation of those with spinal cord injuries, cognitive disabilities, mental health problems, and nerve disorders. The most impacting statement she made was;

"We can send people to Mars so why can't we make a cripple to walk."

Sol gulped. This young girl was calling herself a 'cripple'. Here she was, lying in her bed or sitting in her wheelchair wasting away and she noticed the harsh disparity of priorities. And she was right. It was a harsh disparity. Her point was powerful even though she was mistaken about people being sent to Mars...the Mars One actually never made it that far before melting down. And Sol took no offense at a disabled girl referring to herself with such harsh terms. Her feelings were strong, and they came through in her brief letter.

The International Space Program had been trying for decades to develop a successful Mars Mission. Sending a group of humans to Mars to begin a colony was a program launched in 2013. The mission came to fruition in the late 2030's when the Mars One group was chosen and travel plans to begin a colony on Mars were set in motion. The more Sol thought about it the more he realized what the value of doing such a thing was. And the value was little...little more than proof of concept. Fulfilling a human desire to conquer the universe and prove humans could do anything that was dreamed of. Space programs did little more to help humanity than add some slick and often beneficial technology. Technology like LED's, infrared thermometers, and the ventricular assist device were among the additions that space programs and associated research gave to society. The myth of microwave ovens and Velcro being part of the Space Program's contributions to society here on Earth were simply propagated in order to engender constituency favour and continue extracting government funds that keep highly paid Space Program staff in a job.

But the reality was, the cost of those over-spent programs was far greater than the value for humans that came out of them. And Sol was not the only one who saw that. In the petition to Sol from the young girl with quadriplegia, her message ended by saying;

"Is it really benefitting us to spend so much time and money on outer space when so many of us have so much wrong with our inner space?"

It was settled. At least for Sol. And after bouncing it off Ell, Ahmed, and Erin, he shut down the Space Program almost overnight. Bryson Reynolds was ecstatic when the news hit his show. Every person on the street whose face he got in was completely in favour of shutting down the ISP.

Once Sol edicted the dissolution and end of the Space Program his administrators quickly responded with a plan to dismantle it. It would be wound down over a two-and-a-half year period. But knowing it was packed with many of the world's most brilliant researchers and scientists, Sol restructured it and renamed it. Like the inmate population of the world's prisons who were *Repurposed* to more necessary work, so too did Sol give Space Program employees the opportunity to be repurposed. The entity that had for decades burned through trillions of dollars like they were throwing it into the sun, transitioned to become the **NEW** International ***Inner-Space*** *Program.* It would have the lion's share of the resources of its predecessor at its disposal.

The focus would now be on human dilemmas that affect millions. The vast and brilliant pool of scientists and researchers who once pursued the mysteries of the universe in space, would now focus their efforts to unravel the mysteries of the human body and disease. The completely Repurposed Space Program would now be part of a synergistic effect on eradicating disease, paralyses, brain disorders, mental health problems, and a great many health issues and conditions that have held humanity at bay for centuries. Their skills would now work toward developing adjuncts to aid paraplegics and to pioneer ways to repair the malfunctioning, diseased, or injured intricate components of the brain and spinal cord. A new program with a new focus. Outer Space would be left to its own and human **Inner Space** would be the bold new world to demystify and conquer.

Things would certainly progress more rapidly in the field of human prosthetic movement devices now that resources were being directed to the place where they could truly make a difference.

It was still true however that society was not completely left without benefits from the largely wasteful Space Program. And the woman standing in front of

Sol, about to press her hand into the cool clay of the Red Ochre tray, was proof of that. Unable to move anything from her rib cage and below since a diving accident at a summer camp as a teen, Asha Indrani was now able to stand up to receive her office.

The technology used by astronauts in zero gravity incorporated almost the same device Asha had affixed to her body. The version used in space provided resistance to the lower limb movement of the astronauts in order to stave off muscle atrophy while in space. Her version worked opposite to the version used in zero gravity environments. It overcame resistance and the exo-skeleton was subtly worn under her clothing. The device mechanically elevated the wearer to a standing erect position. Almost as fast and undetectable as if she had full use of her muscles and nerves. Regardless of its origin, the result was a welcome one. Asha was able to stand elegantly and walk short distances or turn on the spot because of the International Space Program that had run its course and was now defunct. After the momentary welcome and hug by Sol, he directed Asha to press her hand into the dark moist clay saturated with the Red Ochre.

In A Breath She Responded Without Falter

Minister of Equity and Anti-Discrimination.

Sol stood shoulder to shoulder with his Minister now. He spoke Asha's role in front of the Chambers.

"Asha will be the **Minister of Equity and Anti-Discrimination.** This Minister will ensure we move towards being a Diverse, Equitable, and Inclusive Meritocracy. Asha understands that merit isn't confined to traditional measures. Her holistic approach considers the diverse experiences that shape an individual's abilities. For instance, leadership skills developed through community organizing will be valued alongside those gained in corporate settings. Resilience and problem-solving honed by overcoming personal challenges will be seen as equally relevant as those demonstrated in academic projects. This means evaluating not just *what* someone has done, but *how* they've done it, and the transferable skills they've developed along the way.

"Merit manifests in countless ways, reflecting the diverse talents and potential of our population. Asha's meritocracy will recognize the value of skills developed through lived experience, cultural understanding, and diverse educational paths, not just traditional credentials. This means looking beyond the CV to see the full picture of what a candidate brings to the table.

"Imagine two candidates for a leadership position. One has a traditional MBA and years of corporate experience. The other has a background in social work and has led community initiatives. Under the old system, the MBA candidate would likely be favored. Under Asha's meritocracy of DEI, the social worker's experience in building consensus, managing diverse teams, and navigating complex social issues would be given equal weight, if not greater, depending on the specific needs of the role.

"As the Minister of Equity and Anti-Discrimination, Asha will also establish a reliable wage parity process. If you are in any way given a lesser wage than a counterpart of a different race, age, color, or gender, that disparity will be remedied. Under Asha and the Level the Playing Field Act, the value of a person's work will be standardized with consideration for depth and duration of technical training and education required for the role. All who perform the same job will be paid the same.

"In this society, a fundamental shift in economic philosophy has occurred, replacing profit-driven models for essential services like healthcare and education with a focus on public service. Funded by a progressive tax system prioritizing social well-being, a standardized pay scale recognizes the inherent value of all work. While a surgeon might earn slightly more than a nurse due to specialized training, the difference is minimal compared to the old system. Both professions, along with teachers, childcare workers, and skilled tradespeople like master carpenters, are highly valued and fairly compensated, allowing for comfortable and fulfilling lives. Similarly, software engineers, whose skills are vital for technological advancement, will be fairly compensated, but not at inflated levels. The focus is on ensuring all individuals can contribute to society without vast income disparities. Perhaps, for example, value is added through programs where carpenters receive additional benefits like subsidized housing, recognizing the societal need for their skills.

"This system isn't solely driven by monetary compensation. A strong emphasis is placed on the intrinsic rewards of contributing to the community, with social recognition and respect paramount for all professions. Equitable access to education and training removes financial barriers, while doctors might enjoy greater autonomy and engineers find fulfillment in projects benefiting society, like sustainable infrastructure. The system fosters a shift in values, prioritizing personal fulfillment and societal contribution alongside fair compensation, motivating individuals to pursue challenging careers not just for financial gain, but for the inherent satisfaction of making a difference.

"Of paramount importance in Asha's role is to establish that women are paid equal to men. Without question, men have decided the value of women for far too long. Even in the year 2044, the remnants of long-ago patriarchy are yet to be shed completely by society. That females are subject to diminished value at the hands of those men who have set the wheels of our economy in motion is unacceptable. Restitution will be paid in cases where a woman has been underpaid by an employer in comparison to her male counterparts.

"Wherever pay parity or pay equity do not exist, Asha will correct that wrong. Equal pay for equal work will become the only acceptable position along with the parity that says all must be given equal pay regardless of their race, gender, age, level of disability, or ethnicity. The Minister of Equity and Anti-Discrimination will ensure there are no discriminatory practices, no bullying, no multiple standards based on discrimination towards one person or another and the Minister will ensure equity as far as is possible to the best of her abilities."

Sol held out the tray for Asha to place her hand on the clay. She had been eager to feel the cool moist ink flow into the crevices of her palm and creep up the sides of her fingers. Sol looked her straight in the eyes. The screens and folios across the chambers cast the image of the two locked in the moment. Asha set her hand gently on the tray. The tray dipped slightly with the weight of here hand. Sol had not been on this end of the tray before and took a second to adjust to the weight of a hand resting on it. He would remember that for the other Ministers who would come after Asha. Taking a very stolid tone Sol recited.

"Asha Indrani, do you agree to commit to serve the World and the King who bestows this role upon you? And to the best of your abilities uphold the ideals of this position as it befits the King and the Ministry? And through the act of giving your imprint upon my head, you agree to use your hands as extensions of the King's hand?"

Asha emanated the confidence and self-assurance of a woman who was embarking on a fulfilling voyage of sharing her skills and talents. Asha had a history of lifting the human condition to a place that it often had forgotten existed. Asha was a balanced and wise idealist who had always believed the world was far from where it could be. But always within reach of where it should be. Asha was ready to work for Sol and Society, doing everything within her power to fulfill her mandated role. In a breath she responded without falter.

"I do."

She lifted her hand, darkened by the ink from the clay pad. Asha Indrani reached up. And Sol, for the first time, felt the warm inked hand being pressed against his forehead. He now knew what those who stood under his hand had felt while imprinting them. It was an assuring sense, a sense of comfort. A sense that created a unity not often felt by most leaders. All the symbolism of the Red Ochre ceremony and the idea of commitment that it brought was wrapped up in that action. An imprint on the forehead announcing that both were mutually committed. Telling that the one was receiving their power from the other. The first time Sol experienced the ceremony it was he who drew power from those he imprinted. Drawing strength from their power and establishing the commitment of both parties. With the reversal of roles today, the imprint made on Sol's head by the Ministers did much the same. They were now empowered by the King, and they would act as the hands of the King. It was the King who was bestowing strength on them. Their actions in the Red Ochre ceremony told that they would strive with all their talents and resources to do that which would honor and benefit the King and their World. Working together with and for the King to bring about the utopia that all Participants everywhere wanted.

The dark, red handprints of the 9 ministers would soon overlay each other on Sol's forehead. Acknowledging that without the King as the head, the Ministers had no more authority than the average person. He was the head, and they were the hands.

Sol congratulated Asha. The Body of Delegates stood to their feet. The first sealing was done.

The delegates took their seats again…eight more Ministers to go.

Minister of Global Prosperity and Finance

Under the Bankruptcy Recovery Law

"I would like to introduce you to the **Minister of Global Prosperity and Finance.** Please welcome Alika Dangota."

Again, the Body of Delegates responded to the cue with applause. Sol could see the Delegates' question behind their eyes. They had not heard of Asha Indrani. But Alika Dangota, many of them knew.

Many capable leaders and people of insight offered their wisdom to the well-received King. The way Sol chose his Minsters was a very effective method. The perfect candidate, someone who Sol found to be suited for the task, would always find their way before his eyes. But with Alika Dangota the question in the minds of many of the Delegates was, *"Why was the Minister of Global Prosperity and Finance a well-known Nigerian Cement mogul? Why did Sol choose him?"*

Their question was filled with concern. Dangota was a man who actually spoke out against the actions Sol took against his colleague Amyl Rothschild. In the opinion of some, Alika Dangota may have actually been a threat to Sol around the same time Amyl Rothschild was sealed. As somewhat of a surprise to Sol, he learned the portion of Rothschild's money that was redistributed to Alika, was immediately donated to the agriculture industry in Africa. Dangota's generosity was a stark contrast to other colleagues in league with Rothschild. As it turned out, after Rothschild's sealing, Dangota indicated he was not interested in the money of a man like Rothschild. A man who had participated in the African slave trade. And one thing this ultra-rich cement mogul had seen through the years, was that the men *in* power were not always the men **with** power. But here today, the man with the most power in the world was placing one of the richest men in the world in a very powerful position. A Billionaire who ran with the Rule of Nines at times was about to become one of The King's 9?

Seeing Dangota come on stage to stand with Sol was more than just curious for the women and men in the Deliberation Chambers. And Sol was about to answer the Delegates' unspoken question.

"I recently met with Alika to discuss some of his positions on the global economy. Alika Dangota hopes to improve life for as many as he can. Alika has very strong loyalties to Africa. He has recently buried his father who suffered a long debilitating illness. Alika's father was the founder of many great things, including the Concrete Business Alika leads today. While visiting with his father whose declining health was leading to the inevitable, he was reminded of his dad's dream to use his wealth to create a better world. And Alika Dangota hopes to carry on his father's dream. Over 60 years ago Alika Senior, a self-made Billionaire borrowed money from an uncle to start trading in cement, flour, and sugar. The Dangota Group is now valued at over 75 billion dollars. And with Alika ready to pass on the family business to his children, he believes it is time to use his talents to prosper other regions of the world."

Sol was now standing with Alika next to him. He was about to provide the Delegates and Alika with the portfolio.

"I am privileged to have this man of great wisdom and with the acumen to create prosperity for many, as my Minister of Global Prosperity and Finance.

"The Minister will manage the One World currency. He will examine each region that displays lack of prosperity and design industry, manufacturing, or methods specific to the area that will tap into the resources in the region to generate wealth for the country or region. Alika will ensure bank fees are eliminated so the Participants of this world are not forced to pay for a system that uses the Participant's money to make more money for itself. Alika will assess the fiscal responsibility of local and regional governments and of government agencies. Reserving the right to seize any entity that proves to be fiscally irresponsible with the taxpayer's money.

"Alika will be responsible for levying the universal tax and collecting the 10.1% from all income and the 4% consumer tax on all goods and services. Under the *Bankruptcy Recovery Law,* Alika will manage reclaiming the bankruptcy repayments from the estates of the deceased who have claimed bankruptcy and failed to repay while living."

At Sol's gesture of raising the tray in front of Alika, Alika Dangota inked his hand just as Asha had. He was ready to commit to this role in front of the entire Body of Delegates. Sol spoke the oath.

"Alika Dangota, do you agree to commit to serve the World and the King who bestows this role upon you? And to the best of your abilities uphold the ideals of this position as it befits the King and the Ministry? And through the act of giving your imprint upon my head, you agree to use your hands as extensions of the King's hand?"

Alika confidently said. "Yes, I do."

He reached to Sol's brow and Sol tilted his head down just slightly. Alika pressed his imprint on the King's forehead. His imprint now overlaid Asha's from moments before. Alika Dangota received a warm hug from Sol before stepping over to stand with Asha. The Chambers filled with applause once again. Sol continued by greeting the next of his nine ministers.

Minister of Immigration and Acculturation

When in Rome do as the Romans

The stage was slowly filling. Sol's Ministers would soon span the stage with their presence and span the world with their influence and counsel. The Delegates welcomed the **Minister of Immigration and Acculturation** to the stage. As with those before her, Sol stated her role. She would be responsible for all matters pertaining to immigration. Sol outlined her portfolio.

"Sylvie Guillard, The Minster of Immigration and Acculturation will maintain open immigration from all lands, countries, and regions. Her role is to ensure all regions have appropriate processes for welcoming newcomers."

"The Minister of Immigration and Acculturation will ensure all newcomers to a region are provided with acculturation training. Quite simply, if you or I want to go live in a new land or in another country or region, we must make efforts to learn and to practice life there as those inhabiting the area practice. All newcomers will be required to acculturate through the provided two-week acculturation training designed to orientate them to their new land. The provided and mandatory training will inform them of the nuances of the land they are relocating to. Educating the newcomer in the idiosyncrasies, intricacies, and internal workings of their host country. Courtesies, hygiene expectation, public versus private behavior, the expectation to be a contributing Participant in their new homeland, and the vital requirement to treat all persons with equal respect at all times. The Minister will ensure if one chooses to enter a new land, a land that is diverse from that which they originated, the newcomer will strive to do as is done in the land they have come to. Bestowing the respect for the home of another people in ways that one would bestow respect upon being a guest in the house of another family. As it has been said, *When in Rome do as the Romans.*

"One who carries with themselves a set of beliefs, ideals, behaviors, or mores that are not typical of the land they travel to, must respect the beliefs, ideals, behaviors, and mores of their new home. All will be allowed to practice their religion and customs as they wish, but the practices they possess from their previous home or ethnic origins will not be given precedence over the host country that has welcomed that person in. Newcomers must regard the practices and ideals of their new home with respect and esteem. Failure to do so will result in extradition back to the region that newcomer has come from.

The Minister shall also be responsible for the *Newcomer Work Placement Program.* Upon arrival to a new land a newcomer must begin working as a contributing Participant of that society as soon as is feasible. Consideration for the family rearing and parenting needs of a newcomer will inform this requirement for many. Whether you are in your home country or you relocate to a new country, the rules for being a productive Participant are the same. Failure to take on gainful employment after 6 months will result in work being appointed by the Minister of Immigration. Failure to take on that work which is appointed in good faith, will result in deportation of that newcomer and his or her family."

Sol finished reciting the portfolio particulars of the Minister of Immigration and Acculturation. He sobered as he stated the Minister's oath for all to hear.

"Do you, Sylvie Guillard, agree to commit to serve the World and the King who bestows this role upon you? And to the best of your abilities uphold the ideals of this position as it befits the King and the Ministry? And through the act of giving your imprint upon my head, you agree to use your hands as extensions of the King's hand?"

This newest Minister to pass in front of Sol, humbly submitted herself to the task and the King. Saying,

"I do,"

She pressed her imprint on Sol's forehead adding another layer as the third person to commit to the great task of continuing on with creating a better world. She took her place in world leadership in front of the Body of Delegates and alongside Asha and Alika.

Minister of Health, Philosophy, Spirituality, and Religion

All People are Provided With the Right to Choose

Entering next to the Delegates' applause, was the **Minister of Health, Philosophy, Spirituality, and Religion.** Dr. Riechert Strom.

Dr. Strom had cut his teeth on the United Nations international healthcare efforts over two decades ago. He was 21 years old when he brought his brilliance to the United Nations suggesting strategies to embark on a worldwide implementation of his two-part diagnostic and tracking system. Although it was too late to implement during the dissolution of the United Nations, the retinal scan-based system of health care would offer early diagnosis of dozens of potential diseases or chronic conditions in the patient. The process combined the ultra-hi definition imagery of eye scans with some of the principles of the ancient Eastern art of iridology. Dr. Strom pioneered the most effective and most economical diagnostic tool the healthcare world had ever seen. Once diagnosed the patient could be tracked by the captured retinal map which became their health-ID. And due to the unprecedented early detection of disease, interventions could begin and were highly effective during pre-onset conditions.

As a young prodigy, Dr. Strom astonished the medical world. After the UN dissolved, he took his work into the private sector. Since then, Dr. Strom has saved hundreds of thousands of individuals from life altering conditions as a result of his work. And Sol, after meeting Strom, was enamoured with the abilities of this man who was now in his 50's.

"The Minister of Health, Philosophy, Spirituality, and Religion will administrate the free Global Healthcare program. He is responsible to set the consumer value on all legalized recreation drugs. Moneys from those products will be collected by the Ministry of Finance and Prosperity and directed back to The Ministry of Health, Philosophy, Spirituality, and Religion.

"This Minister will uphold the *Abuse of Power Law*. Disciplining or revoking the license to practice of any person in a position of authority, such as a Doctor, Priest, Law Enforcement officer, or Teacher who abuses his or her authority and causes harm or distress to any person in their charge. As a champion of the *Self-Control Act*, where each person is inalienably given the right to have total control over their own health choices, their own life and death choices, and their own moral and religious choices. The Minister shall work to ensure all people are provided with the right to choose that each of us is privileged to have.

"The Minister of Health, Philosophy, Spirituality, and Religion will also ensure each of the following programs and edicts are fulfilled to the level they were intended to be fulfilled when they were sealed. He shall have the full power of the King in his efforts to advance society wellness and culture with the following edicts and programs.

- The *Public Aroma Law*—where an individual must fall within predetermined threshold limits of aroma concentration if he or she interacts in the public.

- The *Free Transport from Drinking Establishments* program for patrons of restaurants and bars. All Participants who enjoy alcoholic beverages at an establishment will be given free transportation home.

- *The Multitude of Counsel Law*—Each of us must consult with at least 3 people over the age of 50 when faced with a potentially life-changing decision.

- *The Voluntary Sterilization Program,* a program that offers $500,000 to those among us who choose to become sterile and therefore not reproduce offspring.

- *The Informed Reproduction and Pregnancy Termination Law*—which guides the rights and freedoms of every person to decide if he or she wants to have a baby, wants not to have a baby, wants to terminate an unborn baby in the approved gestational term, or chooses to adopt a baby or to give their baby up for adoption.

- *The Right to Choose Life or Death Law*—A law that supports the individual right over one's own life. Whether one believes a life is sacred or otherwise, one is given the right to do with his or her life as she or he sees fit...as long as the choice does not harm others.

- And *The Re-Freedom of Religion Law*—A law where all are encouraged to enjoy the freedom to choose and believe whatever religious persuasion they prefer. Its aim is to reduce the religious brainwashing that unwittingly occurs through the uni-lateral teaching and instruction most adherents to religious groups are subject to. The appointed Adversary provided with the Law, is to offer at least one other interpretation or option for understanding the teaching and instruction given the religious adherents at the session. Thereby providing another perspective for the adherent to consider, and therefore they will be less inclined to blindly adopt the statements and instruction or interpretation of the religion they have chosen to be involved in."

Sol spoke the oath, "Riechert Strom, do you agree to commit to serve the World and the King who bestows this role upon you? And to the best of your abilities uphold the ideals of this position as it befits the King and

the Ministry? And through the act of giving your imprint upon my head, you agree to use your hands as extensions of the King's hand?"

Strom imprinted the King, and he affirmed his commitment to serve with integrity, honor, reason, and passion to the best of his abilities. Then he moved to join the three others to the right of Sol.

Hir Word Was Hir Bond

Minister of Social Ethics

Sol took this moment to reassert a necessary point. He spoke momentarily of the distressing state culture had found itself in prior to his appointment as King. A state so dire that he sent a letter to the World Congress. His passion for demanding change was inspired by the unhealthy state of society. Society, Sol saw, which had become an apathetic and thoughtless anthropic system. And in appointing his next minister, a Transgender who had been through a great deal in hir journey, Sol knew that one who has seen the discrimination, hurdles, and ethical dilemmas for hirself, was the perfect candidate for the **Minister of Social Ethics**. Darcy Pomona, fueled for good by empathy for all humans who have or may be suffering socially in some way, was a seasoned advocate for the marginalized. They had advocated for 25 years to have society cast off all judgments of the Transgender individual and by extension, they campaigned against judgments of any person who seems to be different from the norm. Hir thinking was unimpeded by traditional ethical issues that stemmed from religious holdovers buried in bureaucratic policy. And today's appointee was gifted with non-biased acceptance of every person and their place in this world...no matter what.

Seven years ago, Darcy Pomona was awarded the World Congress Social Progress Award for hir work in educating the Thailand public on the progress of Transgender equality and integration in society. They had immigrated to Europe from their home in Thailand in hir thirties. They then returned to Thailand with a mission to reconnect the many disenfranchised Transgender people of Thailand. And now, in hir fifties, this face that represented freedom from hate and judgement, was asked by the King to lead the Ministry of Social Ethics.

Darcy was a tall, slender, 54-year-old Transgender. At the Speaker's Podium with Sol hir pride of self was unmistakable. Wearing a turquoise scarf and a slate gray pant suit that had a coat with long tails and theatrically flared cuffs on both trouser and jacket. They definitely had their own unique style. Darcy had an infectious confidence that could only come with being a person of acceptance who wanted the best for everyone.

Sol delivered the portfolio of his **Minster of Social Ethics**. Informing the Delegates that Darcy Pomona would have zero tolerance for elder abusers, children abusers, LGBTQ2S+IA persecutors, discrimination or harassment, employee abuse, and spousal or partner abuse. Anyone known to participate in these violent and hateful behaviours would be reprimanded on a case-by-case basis. Hir authority to design customized consequences for each case was empowered by Sol. Because each case was moiled with a different set of circumstances. Their Ministry would be a dynamic vehicle to find peace for a great many victims affected by abuse.

Sol went on to explain Darcy would be an advocate for and protector of children. Ensuring all parents were successfully registered in and participated in the *No Parent Left Behind Program*. And ensuring the compensation paid to stay-at-home parents or guardians expressed the value of that work and that choice. Sol recited some of the responsibilities of Minister Pomona.

"Any sign of disregard for social ethics or discrimination towards any Participant in any way will be investigated. The perpetrator of discrimination will be assigned to civil service for a designated amount of time. Those who practice racism or discrimination will be removed from society for re-orientation and sensitivity training.

"The Minister of Social Ethics is commissioned to ensure neither the acceptance and support of LGBTQ2S+IA nor the rejection or opposition of such, is neither militant nor aggressive activism. All parties will be allowed to express their position in a form of civil, mediated debate that is accessible to all participants.

"As well, in an age where the majority of our conversations are recorded by Closed Circuit Drone monitoring systems, and audio capture devices, the Minister of Social Ethics will ensure a person's word is once again their bond, as was the case almost a century ago. One's word bares the same weight as one's signature. The *Your Word is Your Bond Edict* will restore the honor of one's spoken word when making a deal, a promise, or oath.

"As well, the *Personal Humanitarian Day Award* program will be maintained by hir office. Global Participants can take confidence in knowing that each Personal Humanitarian Day awarded to those found to have performed four acts of kindness, will be administrated through Darcy's Ministry."

Sol spoke the oath, "Darcy Pomona, do you agree to commit to serve the World and the King who bestows this role upon you? And to the best of your abilities uphold the ideals of this position as it befits the King and the Ministry? And through the act of giving your imprint upon my head, you agree to use your hands as extensions of the King's hand?"

For Darcy Pomona, the new Minister of Social Ethics, hir word was hir bond as they responded to Sol's recitation of hir oath with,

"I do."

Sealed on the Folio and with the Red Ochre imprint on hir King's forehead they took their place among the other Ministers committed to Sol's cause.

Free Education For All

Minster of Education

The Minster of Education was cued to meet Sol at the Podium next.

Sol had chosen Klara Gird after hearing the amazing developments she had been responsible for in the Scandinavian regions. Finland had been rated as the top place to live in the world, the rating had a lot to do with the high level of education achieved. Not by a few but by every person who had breathe that lived in Finland. The other Scandinavian countries were not far behind. Sweden and Norway sat in the top five on the list and collectively, the Scandinavian world was far and above most regions in the world as far as education.

Sol was in agreement with Klara Gird, the region's iconic schoolmarm. Education of the people made for a better world, less crime, less disease, improved health. Educating a people resulted in better population control. Education has brought peace and freedom in many ways that were elusive without it.

Sol was eager to get the ball rolling with Klara leading the charge on education. In discussions with her she was ready to launch the Worldwide YouTube-U. A university that is totally user driven and offers credit for the learning one participates in through YouTube. Billions of people all over the globe had gained mastery in many areas by watching YouTube videos. And Klara struck a program that gave users University level credit for their YouTube education. Klara had taken education to a whole new strata with YouTube.

The concept of learning through YouTube Videos was not new, but it was definitely an innovative and powerfully re-structured platform for educating people in all areas. The world's most ubiquitous streaming video site contained billions of videos, had billions of users, and millions of those would often turn to the site to learn a skill, a process, a trade, a concept, or knowledge in an area of interest. Klara saw no reason why people shouldn't be able to get credit for this learning, so the YouTube-U was birthed.

Similar to most of the great Web–interactive platforms, YouTube-U was user content driven. Users were the teachers, the students, and the regulators. It was the YouTube-U users that decided who received their diploma and who would have to view and produce more educational content before being granted a pass. A grass-roots ethos of Intellectual Innovation and Integrity drove the platform to ballistic heights.

Users who might be interested in a skill, concept or subject area were to sign up for free. For example, if an unskilled carpenter wanted to get a free education, she or he could enroll in the YouTube-U Carpentry Program. The administrators for that course would send a dozen videos that had to be watched and learned from in the first term. As the learner worked there way through the videos, practicing the skills seen in those basic videos, they would prepare for the term-end project. That project involved producing their own video demonstrating the skills learned in that term. Once their video was posted, they were then subject to peer approval before being allowed to advance to the next level in the program. To advance a YouTube-U student must get 50 video "likes", and 20 positive feedback posts critiquing and offering input about their work. It was truly a peer review model of developing University and Trade level excellence in education. YouTube-U ensured quality learning and skill development had taken place.

Each higher level of a YouTube-U program would then have a series of related videos sent to the person to watch, leading the person to produce their own video on the learned subject, and awaiting peer approval of others who are enrolled in the same course across the world. If the peers who review the skills of their fellow learner find the digital "classmate" to be lacking, the remarks in the posts would identify the deficiency…this kept a person with low merit from advancing. At the end of the full course the final video produced by the advanced student must gain the approval of those who have completed the course in the year before. If the video reviewed is successful, then full accreditation will be granted to the YouTube-U graduate.

Sol absolutely loved this idea. It was a community of learners that he saw as a vital mechanism to bring university accredited education to people all over the world. Conveniently and economically. And Klara Gird would see YouTube-U take flight during her time as Minister of Education.

Sol continued to deliver the particulars of Klara's portfolio.

"The Minister of Education will ensure substandard teachers are repositioned in the education system or encouraged to seek other employment. We will not let poor teachers get in the way of educating the World's students. Our teachers will be measured by evaluations and feedback the students and parents of students provide through the formal evaluation form process.

"The education system will be focused on didactics for 3 hours a day and the remainder of the average school day will be creative activities, conversational learning, and physical activities.

"The minister will ensure all education, including University education, is offered at no cost to the learner. Free education for all will be available worldwide.

"Few can learn without the proper rest. Youth in school will not be required to attend before 10:00AM. This will afford the youth, who physiologically do not release sufficient melatonin to send them off to sleep until well past 1 A.M., to get more sleep. Thus, improving their mental, emotional, intellectual, and physical health. Making the hours they are in school more productive."

Sol completed his statements about Klara's portfolio and recited her oath.

Sol spoke the oath, "Klara Gird, do you agree to commit to serve the World and the King who bestows this role upon you? And to the best of your abilities uphold the ideals of this position as it befits the King and the Ministry? And through the act of giving your imprint upon my head, you agree to use your hands as extensions of the King's hand?"

She eagerly said, "I do".

In fine schoolmarm character Klara was excited to press her hand onto Sol's forehead. She wanted to get to work. Klara Gird, the new Minister of Education was unstoppable in making the world a better place through education. She would have to wait however, at least until the remainder of the Ministers were installed by Sol.

Taking His Vision To The Next Level

Minister of Anti-Corruption

The next Minister to join Sol at the Podium was Jacob Karcher a minster that was intended to be the watchdog. A watchdog for corruption of government, business, institutions, religion, sport and anything else where corruption might creep in.

Seeing the **Minister of Anti-Corruption** take his oath as the others had and imprint the King, gave pause to the Body of Delegates. Many in the Chambers were uncertain how busy this man would be. How much corruption would this Minister find? Seeing Amyl Rothschild's life stripped and his wealth redistributed, gave cause for people in many sectors to step back from some of their more questionable business and leadership activities. The reality was, this Minister still had no shortage of work waiting for him. There were many levels, and many varieties that would be unearthed and consequences meted out.

This Minister, by far the broadest in the reach with his arm empowered by the King, would find and remove anyone in any place who broke the laws and proved to be corrupt. Whether it was a Global multi-national, an insurance fraud of a small business owner, a double dipper on old-age benefits, or an auto dealer or real estate broker that failed to disclose all the information a consumer might want to know. Karcher and his extensive team would find them and deal with them. If a corrupt police officer abuses his power or takes bribes, a politician finds ways to line his pockets with gifts from unsavoury donors, or an international bank scandal occurs, the Minster of Anti-Corruption would come knocking.

Sol spoke the oath, "Jacob Karcher, do you agree to commit to serve the World and the King who bestows this role upon you? And to the best of your abilities uphold the ideals of this position as it befits the King and the Ministry? And through the act of giving your imprint upon my head, you agree to use your hands as extensions of the King's hand?"

With his oath declared, his imprint of commitment on the King's forehead, and standing in his place with the others on stage, Jacob Karcher was eager to begin his role of sniffing out the most corrupt of society.

The Anti-Corruption Minister and the King would be the first to tell us they both had an intense dislike for dishonesty. Corruption was just another accepted facet of a society's failure to advance. And Sol and his new Minister both agreed that humanity does not have to accept corruption any longer.

Inexhaustible Resources of the Entire World

Minister of Military and World Security
Minister of Retribution

L eft to join the group were Tomer Cohen and Togo Takanaka. Tomer had already been appointed and functioning as the Minister of Retribution and The General, orchestrating campaigns against terrorists and rogue cell organizations over the past month, had been kept busy as Sol's **Minister of Military and World Security**.

The two men often worked synergistically. In a world without wars between nations the Military was readily used to fight the wars within regions. The civil uprisings, the terrorism right at home, the organized and gang crime that ripped at society's safety and security. Their work together was effectively dismantling, and consequencing, all those involved in anti-society activities. Tomer and Togo had been dubbed "T-Squared" by Sol when they worked together on certain projects. Projects such as Gang City off the southern coast of Grenada.

In only a few months, several million gang members had been relocated to their glorious new home. A high security island that afforded them all the same comforts as were afforded in their home cities. The island was still under construction in some areas and would eventually house many more millions of gang members and adherents. And it would all be theirs to govern how they saw fit. Even if they destroyed it in the distorted process of creating their own unique society.

The men and women in Gang City had been rounded up by Tomer's Ministry and transported and contained by Takanaka's Ministry. The Gang City was an extremely complicated environment and needed the strength of the Global Military Unit to operate and contain it. It was the biggest self-sustaining prison in the world. More gang members were being relocated there weekly. But not all residents wanted to live there forever.

As it turned out, the enticements of Gang life, even life involved being totally on their own doing whatever they pleased, and being self-sufficient in most every way, was not as good as many in the gangs thought it would be. After a few months, thousands had been killed within the context of their co-habitation environment, and thousands of them were ready for amnesty. They bided their time. Silently existing as if they would be permanent residents of Gang City. Feigning the shared identity with the millions of gang members who were willing to make Gang City their permanent home. Portraying themselves to be content with the whole Gang City scene. But they weren't.

When the General's Aircraft carrier and thousands of troops showed up with armoured personnel carriers to go through the city on Amnesty Day, some Gang City residents were safely escorted out from their Gang Families and placed on the carrier to make their way back to the civilized world. Gang city was certainly no utopia, but those in the civilized world were jubilant to know that millions upon millions of gang members now called it home…whether they liked it or not. It was the reality that gangs would exist, and crimes would be committed. It was the reality that fear of violence by the gangs could spill over into peaceful society and on many occasions violent crime could target an innocent person. So, the new reality was that Tomer and Togo were working to shut it down and seal off the gangs from the rest of the world. Their project had been very effective so far. *Salus populi suprema lex esto,* the greatest good for the greatest number. Or as Tomer, Togo, and Sol applied it, **"Let the welfare of the people be the supreme law."**

An island full of gangs without guns proved to quell the tide of gang crime that had poisoned society for far too long.

As for *The Old Soldiers Program,* it was in a beta phase and gaining in popularity. The ageing demographic it drew from would exponentially grow in the years to come and the OSP under Dr. Strom's anti-aging protocol, was making a huge difference in those who joined the program. This program had changed the lives of many Old Soldiers already and General Takanaka's Global Military Unit was administrating and operating the program with great success.

The General was committed to squash any anti-society group such as a terrorist organization, an organized crime group, internet security threats, threats to national or Global security, organized violence, violent protests, and any threat to King, Country, or Globe. It was powerful and inspiring to see this decorated General receive his authority from the King in front of the Delegates that day. His willingness to serve was unquestioned when he imprinted Sol and received a hug from his King. The Delegates' applause in the Chambers continued for Takanaka until he found his place as the 8th Minister in Sol's group of nine. A group that would itself become the new and improved *Rule of Nines.*

And lastly, Tomer moved next to Sol. This Ministry was potent and the man running it was truly created for this purpose. Calling down fire on the most loathsome men of any society, the child sex abusers among others. Restoring peace and justice finally appeared to be within reach. The man in charge, Tomer Cohen, was a man who was released from prison after killing a school shooter. A man whose depth of experience in high level security complemented the position Sol elevated him to. He was wonderfully committed on every level to fulfilling Sol's mandate as the *Minister of Retribution.* Purposefully meting out those consequences prescribed by Sol. And having a passion for justice and for peace that fueled his difficult work.

Tomer's portfolio as the **Minister of Retribution** would grow over the coming months. At least until the actions he took against wrong proved to chip away at the rock of crime and injustice. A portentous rock that had all but fallen on the people and crushed them. Tomer was indebted to his King for seeing through the clouded veil of a distorted justice system. Seeing past the unchallenged laws of an apathetic world and affirming his actions of curb-side justice. Justice the average person longed to see. Justice that ended the life of a worthless school shooter instead of allowing him to live on and affect the consciousness of the culture he so violently offended.

The portfolio of this Minister was well known across the globe. Tomer was sealed by his word and his hand imprint on Sol's head. Displaying his commitment to lead his Ministry into a peaceful crime-free era. The Minister of Retribution had a magnitudinous portfolio and Sol announced to the Delegates what would be in place under Tomer's hand.

"Tomer Cohen will be responsible for:

- Non-violent punishment of youth who engaged in thievery, vandalism, malicious, or physically harmful acts against another.
- Prescribing essential labour tasks to any who vandalizes or willfully destroys or steals another's property.
- In concert with the Minister of Anti-Corruption, Tomer would aid in stripping away any license or authority an official, Teacher, Priest, Church leader, Coach, Doctor, Law Enforcement officer, or other person with a position of authority would have if found to have abused that authority in some way. Abuses that destroyed the trust given them by the people whom they have betrayed.
- Removal from the society for a blackout period for any person who bullies another. They will be blacked out both digitally and physically, having only isolation until the Minster of Retribution reinstates them in society.
- Sealing of home invaders. Those who presume that they can enter a person's home and proceed to rob it, harm, or torment the occupant in any way, will

be Sealed. A person's home is their castle. An unthreatened sanctuary. If there is any place that must be the absolute repository of peace and security it is one's home. Participants in society should never be vulnerable in their own homes or have the threat of a possible invader terrorizing their safe environment. Any home invasion will not be tolerated. When the sanctity that is the right of a Participant in her or his own home is stolen by a home invader, that invader will be sealed. Home invasion is punished by death because of the fear it imparts to its victim. A fear that persists in the victim long after the home invader has vacated the home they have violated.

- Finding and sealing of pedophiles. It was agreed there is nothing more detestable, loathsome, and destructive as a child sex abuser. If a person is one who has a desire to have sexual contact in any form with children, Tomer will find them. In its plainest terms, if a person is having these unnatural desires and has not yet acted upon them, they are encouraged to get in touch with the Ministry. They are assured grace will be extended and they will be offered a safe place, along with treatment, where one can live out his days and be protected from acting on his impulses. If a person is found to have committed the acts related to pedophilia, the Minster of Retribution assures that the Readers will be most ethical, and professional as they locate and Seal the abuser. Amnesty may be granted in cases where a pedophile turns him or herself in, but the Ministry is compiling an ever-growing list of abusers who will soon be Sealed. And as most know, the reality is that society is better off without some individuals."

Sol hugged his Minsters and handed each a towel with mineral spirits on it. They took a moment and wiped the Red Ochre from their palms as Sol wiped the Red Ochre from his head. The appointments were done. Nine Ministers, all prepared to serve the King and the entire world. Building their forces and their Ministries. And working collaboratively with each other and with the King. The path to the World the way it should be was being taken. Sol recalled the message from the Meta post he shared earlier. A perfect world was within reach, but it could not be all about one person. Working together would prevent the future from being the You-Topia of one man. Working together with his 9 would be the way. Sol now had an official **Rule of Nine**. Women and men committed to pursuing his vision and to consulting within their ranks on ways to get a stagnant apathetic world evolving again and working to keep it moving forward.

The birthing process was complete. The world would become better as The Nine Ministers, Sol, and all the Participants of the world worked together. The world had been teetering on the edge of true greatness before now. A greatness that would be beyond the material progress of establishing a One World Government, one common language, or a universal monetary unity. But this world had been waiting for a man or woman to fearlessly lead it to be better. And it was becoming "better".

The Body of Delegates were proudly surveying what they had started. They had appointed a King to have sovereign authority, and the world was re-forming like it never had before. Many felt a metaphorical new heaven and earth were developing in this new age. As the Delegates looked on like proud parents, Sol and his Nine offered one last oath. It didn't matter where the oath came from or who originally stated it. What mattered is that Sol and his 9 offered it because they meant it. Each one of them was willing to make the commitment and do the work. In a small chorus the 10 on stage proclaimed their oath at the end of the monumental Inclusions Session.

> *"To that oath which I have declared with my voice and with the imprint of my hand, I now add this sacred commitment: I shall consecrate my Office, my energies, and all the wisdom I can summon to the cause of peace among all tribes, tongues, peoples, regions, and nations."*

Sol stepped to the front of the group and with a final word he panned the Chambers.

"Well…" Sol paused, no one knew what was coming next, but he only had one thing to say, "…there's a lot to do so what do you say we get to work?"

The Chambers agreed with their King and his 9 with a closing ovation. The doubts that bubbled up from time to time since Sol first was installed as King of the World were no longer to be seen. He had won the Delegates, and he had won the people. Sol was truly becoming the people's King. The nine months of his reforms were welcome months, and Sol was leading in a way that brought hope and change. Change that mattered. And now, in this Minster appointment session, Sol was taking his vision to the next level.

Sol and his Minsters left the stage and once they retreated to the Fall-Out Room, brief congratulations were exchanged between the Nine. Ahmed entered the room and joined in the congratulations for a moment before he took Sol aside. Like the intuit he was, Sol was right, they did need to get to work. Ahmed informed him of a typhoon that had just ravaged the coast of the Philippines and torn into the inland. Thousands killed and hundreds of thousands left homeless. Sol settled the group and told them the news. The Media screens around the room chimed on and the glow from the embedded folios in the table captured the attention of the group. Celebrations at the appointments would have to wait…

Without missing a beat, The Nine began to systematically design a mission to bring aid, rescue, and recovery operations to the Philippines. Together they possessed all the world's authority and all the world's resources. A mission that would not have been possible had all the world's resources not been at the disposal of one man and those who led under him. There was nothing that would limit their resolution to assist the Philippine nation or any region and people group. With the inexhaustible resources of the entire world at the disposal of the King and his Ministers, regions that were thrust into disaster, unliveable conditions, squalor, and loss for any reason, man-made or natural, would not remain there for long. This King would not let nature, man-made disaster, or calamity hinder him from helping the people. Soon, those affected by this destructive natural disaster would be part of the growing group to have felt the intentions of a truly benevolent King. A King who was committed to do **The Greatest Good for the Greatest Number.**

LONG LIVE THE PEOPLE'S "KING"...OR QUEEN

Scandal Free for
All These Years

The Drones hummed just overhead. Every 15 minutes. You could set a watch by them. They seemed to be in sync with the Shuttles that stopped to drop passengers off at the Cathedral Park station. The park was always active with Moldovan leisure takers. And today, Devorah Tkach was one of them. Another Drone hummed past. They were so small now…about as big as a medium sized bird. When the Drones first arrived in Chișinău Sol had been King for just over two years. The Drones capturing Dev at her bistro table in Cathedral Park were completely integrated into society now. Years ago they were much larger and mostly used to monitor public gatherings or public disturbances. Streaming images back to the Policing Division. Today, in 2058, the 15th anniversary of the appointment of the people's King, the Drones captured and collected all public activity. Indoors, outdoors, the Drones that had become society's watchmen in the air, had little conscious effect on culture. Like a worker bee off in the background everyone accepted their unassuming presence and constant activity. It was well known that either good or bad, the Drones were capturing and logging everything they saw.

The early closed-circuit TV's that had proliferated in the first decade of the century brought cause for concern. Being constantly watched was unsettling for many citizens of that day. Questions arose as to how much of an invasion of privacy and intrusions into public and private life they would be? Would they be used to the detriment of the citizen. The questions that bombarded Sol in the early stages of Drone use were no different. Would these airborne silent watchmen catch and record every negative action and behavior to eventually be used against the individual? Society questioned the Drone use for a few years but by the time the late 2040's rolled around, Drone use and Participant audio and video capture devices were ubiquitous just the same. If something were said or done by a Participant, it was recorded. The more the devices proliferated, the more the devices had proven to be a great success at protecting Participants. Participants accepted their presence and their benefits. The benefit for personal safety and security soon outweighed the concern over "big brother" watching every move. Drone capture devices had become an overseer for culture rather than what was originally thought. The watcher Drone technology was now part of everyday life. A ubiquitous watcher that had become a constant reminder for Participants to be a better version of themselves...in almost every circumstance while in public.

It seemed like everything getting to Moldova was slow. Some regions were always a bit behind the rest of the world. A problem with Amazon's *Sky-Drop* delivery system a few years back triggered delays in the watcher Drone implementation to all regions.

Seven years ago, in 2066, the whole Sky-Drop network fell apart. Hackers re-configured the entire GPS coordinating system in a brilliantly planned hi-tech prank. A massive tech maneuver that cost the industry and consumers billions. There was really nothing to be gained. In true hacker form they did it for no other reason than to prove they could. But their proof-of-concept prank cost billions to recover from.

The hackers spent weeks reprogramming all Drone servers with new delivery coordinates. Instead of delivering their packages to the designated address the Drones and their cargo were rerouted to a remote dessert location in the Arabian Peninsula. Without a trace they just left their flight paths and were lost...off the radar. Six million of them were flown into a pile in the Rub'al Khali dessert.

The largest dessert in the world, encompassing 650,000 square kilometers in the Arabian Peninsula.

It took two days to locate the Drones and all the packages the *Sky-Drop* shipping system had on board. It was treated as an international disaster and the group responsible, were quickly labelled as cyber-terrorists. A group who was seemingly able to do anything they wanted with some of the most secure commercial software systems in the world.

No one knew where these Drones were. That is until a satellite image captured an anomalous mass that had been formed in the Rub'al Khali dessert. It was little wonder that King Sol met with these hackers personally after the Ministry of Anti-Corruption tracked them down. Sol gave them two choices, either be sent off to Gang City with the rest of the world's organized crime rings and gangs or enter the service of the King.

The hackers eagerly chose the latter of the two options. Accepting the chance to use their talents to continue to design and secure the cutting-edge systems Sol's Ministers and body of Delegates needed to successfully run the world. The problem-solving abilities of the new staff in Sol's *Ministry of Technology* was awe inspiring. Give these Hackers a room full of Folios and computing power and they could solve most any problem through the night. Harnessing the power of elite hackers and gamers was one of the most efficient uses of resources Sol could have ever imagined. And quite honestly, as serious as he was about sending the hackers to Gang City, Sol did find it a touch amusing when the satellite images of the Drone pile showed up and he first saw the pictures. The size and scope of that MEGA tech prank was astounding.

Six million Drones made for quite a pile. And the only way to see what the pile spelled was from space. Drones were here to stay but certain subgroups wanted to return to the days when a package was brought to the door by a delivery guy in a nuclear-powered delivery van. In their efforts to make a point, the hacker prank played on the irony and sarcasm of their shipping Drone takeover. It was perfectly clear from the message in the text in the Arabian dessert. Seeing a pile of misguided

Drones that were now rendered lifeless due to the corrupt code, made the larger-than-life statement of the hackers Drone pile all the more intriguing.

"Long live the Dronies" was spelled out in Amazon boxes and packages when seen from space. Their prank was now being called *DroneGate.*

Six million shipping Drones aggregated in their death to declare their long life through a message in Amazon Package Font. The extraordinary skill and coordination the hackers employed was mind boggling.

If Participants with this level of skill were left to act on their anti-social schemes, they clearly could cause a great deal of harm. Therefore, they could not be allowed to continue to enjoy digital freedoms. Their internet privileges would have to be revoked. So, in the true form of a King who intends to do the greatest good for the greatest number, Sol had black-listed the many computer geniuses who conspired to use their skills for anti-social purposes.

To keep track of them, infusions of Qdot-nanocrystals were trans-dermally infused into their blood. These tracers would alert the Ministry of Anti-Corruption to any virtual, digital, or internet prohibited activity. This proved to effectively limit harmful activity by those who were found attempting to cause harm to digital systems. As for those who were yet to be found, well…it was true that the odd internationally crippling prank, like the *Long Live The Drones* episode, might still occur at their hands. Also true was the fact that the Ministry would catch up with them. As for the neophile conglomerate of young and not so young hackers responsible for *DroneGate,* without too much compelling, they quickly made the right choice when faced with a life of Gang City. Sol was quite pleased to have had these minds join his team and use their talents for the betterment of the world. Sol had always been a leader who advocated choice.

However, the damage was vast after the worldwide hijacking of the Drones The yearlong restoration of the Sky-Drop Shipping Drone system was a significant speedbump in progress in many regions. The slowdown had a great deal to do with Moldova being behind larger nations at getting the security Drones that were now used by all countries and regions. Drones had become a major part of Participant security and a major part of tracking the good Participants, and the accumulation of credits in the *Personal Humanitarian Day Award Program.*

With Ukraine to the North and Romania to the west one would think Moldova would have a stream of the latest and greatest of everything these two neighbors had. But ever since the Russia-Ukraine conflict in the 2020's, the tiny country of Moldova was slow to acquire some of the advancements of other regions. When Russia made an attempt to take over parts of the Ukraine after a conflict in that country, a country managing civil discord that ranged from protests over increase in gas prices all the way up to reverting to an older version of the Ukrainian constitution, the advances in trade, tech, and industry simply began moving sluggishly at best into Moldova. Development simply ground to a slow plodding pace. But all was stable now. The few years Moldova had been behind seemed to be in the distant past. Still known for its rich aromatic wines and its brilliant and beautiful women, Moldova had caught up with the pace and was right in stride with the countries and regions surrounding it.

And today, on a beautiful Friday morning, sitting at a coffee shop bistro table, Devorah Tkach was perfectly ok with the frequent passing of Drones overhead. In fact, the reason she was privileged to sit on the edge of the lush Cathedral Park on a Friday morning was because of the Drones.

In his reign as King, Sol had edicted that acts of kindness, valour, or generosity of human spirit, would be rewarded. It was the highly favoured *Personal Humanitarian Day Award Program.* Sure, Drones worked well to capture crime and deviance but Sol advocated kindness amongst humanity and the Drones were just as readily capturing meritorious acts as they were capturing anti-society acts. The program offered a day off work as a reward for four unplanned acts of kindness. Kindness was such a commodity and having every move in society monitored by Drones was much better accepted when these monitoring devices captured Participants doing good in order to provide a reward.

Some Participants were earning their *Personal Humanitarian Day* once a month and others took up to a year to accumulate enough credits to warrant the award.

But earning a day off for doing acts that were good for humanity came to be a sought-after reward for Participants in what some called Sol's YouTopia.

Dev had been captured by the watcher Drones on at least four occasions in the past month. The most recent of those brought her another Personal Humanitarian Day award. Culture had come to love this oft granted day-off. It was so simple, be kind and get rewarded…and the Drones were the witnesses that had now become a well-accepted tech invasion into the lives of everyone.

The recent credit earning situation Dev found herself in was just last Friday. She came across a young woman who had recently made use of the Voluntary Sterilization Program. This young woman had used her VSP payout to get herself good and high. Drugs were readily available through the state regulated *Recreational Drug Use Program*. All drugs were available to users who chose to use them for their pleasure. Sol was consistent in allowing Participants to make their own choices… even if those choices ended up in the person harming or killing themselves. Choice was the most powerful thing a King could give to his people. It was only reasonable for Sol to allow the choice to use drugs under the *Self-Control Act*. And as had been the case since synthetic narcotics came into society, there were always abuses and there were always overdoses and addictions. However, prohibition breeds rebellion and results in more misuse of a narcotic substance than does the liberty to choose to use. When coupled with education about the product, its uses, and its possible effects, outcomes for society were much more favorable than those seen with previous drug classification laws and prohibitions. The elimination of illegal production and sale of drugs and the removal of Drug Cartels was coupled with the move to legalize everything drugs. However, misuse still occurred as with every substance, and what Dev had involved herself in that day was clearly a case of misuse. The young lady Dev encountered had passed out on the steps of the Capriana Monastery, Moldova's most prominent monastery and a well-known tourist attraction.

She had travelled from Soroco, the Romani capital of Moldova, to celebrate her recently completed procedure for sterility with friends. She had pumped a little too much of her favourite recreational drug into her arm in a shooting gallery behind the monastery and stopped breathing when she was walking up the monastery steps. This young recreationalist wanted to enjoy her high in what was believed to be a sacred place.

Devora came across her when another visitor to the Monastery screamed for help. Dev hit the worn stone steps of the monastery running and by the time she got to the unconscious young addict, the girl was vomiting. Dev quickly rolled her over and finger-swept her vomit-filled mouth. The unconscious girl coughed and sputtered but kept breathing until Medics rolled up and carted her off to the ER. Dev was sympathetic towards the beautiful but misguided user. Dev wondered how she might find out if the girl made out ok at the hospital, as she watched the Ambulance drive away. Soon conceding she might never know the outcome, Dev went about her day.

Early the following morning she checked her Humanitarian Day Bank on her G-PAS card and found she had earned 1 full credit. The Drones were making it happen. Catching humanitarian acts and logging them to the account of the subject. And now, on this sunny day at the edges of Cathedral Park, she was cashing in the free day earned from four recent acts of kindness. A day she was excused from work for the good she had done. It was almost too good to be true, but Sol saw how offering a benefit for people to be thoughtful of others, would make people be just that...thoughtful of others. And Dev was happy to fit all the relaxing she could fit into a warm September Friday in the Moldovan capital at Cathedral Park.

Dev sipped her Americano and popped her folio out of her bag. This was a perfect time to catch up on some history. She was usually so busy in her work, editing Moldova's most popular digital newspaper, that she rarely spent time focusing on her passion, world history.

She asked Google to find *"This day in history."* Expecting to see a little farther back in time than what popped up on screen, she was a bit surprised to see pictures of the young King Sol. A Stream from only about 15 years ago. Well at least he looked a little younger than what he looked today.

The Old Soldiers Program had been brought into the public realm. And Sol, Ell and most of the aging demographic had taken advantage of the highly subsidized anti-aging treatment. As for Sol and those of his vintage using the protocol, the late 60's was the new 50. The tagline on the media in front of Dev said,

"15th Anniversary of proposition 9-12.—Scandal free for a decade and a half"

Dev tapped the image. She was curious to see what the story was. The stream started playing and the DBN logo and title on screen advertised the Bryson Reynold's interview of Sol and Ell. She let the stream play.

This King had always intrigued her. His casual and frank style and his accessibility. But most intriguing of all was his lack of corruption. Sol's ability to maintain his integrity while possessing absolute power was one of the most curious aspects of the King of the World. All the power in the world and he continued to be the people's King. Scandal free for all these years.

The Power To Right That Upended Creature

The shadows bounced around the stone patio as the sun filtered through the colored fall leaves above. Dev sat content and peaceful at her bistro table in Cathedral Park coffee shop. The audio in the Stream on her Folio announced the interview. No need to identify this Royal Couple beyond speaking their names. *Ell and Sol*, spoken together, were always understood as referring to the Ell and her husband the King. This couple had captured the imaginations of the world more than any power couple who ever walked a red carpet.

"*A Visit with Sol and Ell*," was all the introduction needed. And Bryson Reynolds, dressed as flamboyantly as if he were still in his 40's, began by welcoming his Ell and his King before listing some of the King's edicts and some of his advances.

"Sol, Ell, thank you for joining me for this visit. We first met fifteen years ago, just weeks after Proposition 9-12 was passed, and you were installed as King."

Bryson's producer cast images from that first Table of Truth visit where Sol joined the panel in the holo-space above the group.

"Oh I remember it well Bryson. I wasn't sure how you'd take me popping into your show that day. I think I had only been King for about a week or two at that point."

"That's right Sol, and I always meant to ask you, what your thinking was about in taking that route. I mean what was your plan by getting right out in front of the whole world the way you did?"

"Bryson, I gotta say, I was terrified at the time. Ell and I just decided that if I was going to do this King thing, if I was going to take the job after the World Congress made me the offer, that I would just meet every moment as myself. Not as King or some untouchable entity. So, when I saw your show after my first address, I just wanted to get out there and be vulnerable and accessible. I thought, if I wasn't the King and had seen you guys on the stream chatting about me, I would jump at the chance to get in front of you and answer some questions. That would be the case if I was just an ordinary guy, so I didn't let being King stop me. I did what an ordinary guy would have done because I knew that's what I really was. I jumped in like anyone would. And I was glad I did."

Ell was waiting to get in on this as well. She had been sitting with Sol that evening and the two of them knew exactly what they were doing.

"Bryson," she began. "At that time this was all so new. It was a new thing for Sol and I, and it was a new thing for the entire world. And we had to know if it was for real. Was this appointment to the position of King of the World more than just a figurehead appointment or some type of social experiment? Would the people accept this, and would the King have support for what he wanted to do. Because Sol meant it when he made his vow to be the people's King. A King looking out for the good of the people. Truly wanting to do the greatest good for the greatest number."

Bryson jumped in…just as he always did throughout his 40-year broadcast career. "And today we see that Ell. We see that the people did accept the King and that he has done the greatest good for the greatest number."

"You're right Bryson, but at the time we were not sure how things would go. So, Sol and I agreed, that very day, if he were to become the King he thought the world needed, then he would have to be accessible. And joining you that day on your show did that. That one decision did more for Sol in the eyes of the people of the world than we could have ever imagined. It was that interview that got the King's social media interaction really moving. People started to ask questions of Sol, they started to send in requests, and streams of suggestions for changes and edicts poured in…and still do to this day.

"So when Sol decided to pop into your show that day, we realized there were no rules. The way the World Congress chose and appointed him as King was rather unorthodox. And the only rules that were in place were basically that Sol could do whatever he wanted to try to better our world. It was a clean slate. Sol could do whatever he thought served him best as he served the world. And things like surprise appearances on your show, or showing up at an appliance factory to go to work for the morning, just to stay connected and to ensure labourers are paid better and treated well, or sitting down at a Coffee shop with a friend for a visit on a Saturday in downtown Seattle, are all things Sol would do to stay connected to the important side of the world. That important side is the Participants that make this world a wonderful place to be. The side that is made up of people that are just like Sol and I were before he became King."

Sol smiled at Ell and looked back to Bryson. "I have a question for you Bryson."

"Well by all means Sol…you know we are all ok with unorthodox here. Fire away."

"Your question, the one you asked me that day I popped into your show, about the tortoise on his back with his belly baking in the sun and me standing over him watching him."

"Ah yes, the Voight-Kamph question I posed to you. I remember"

"Good. And just a little side bar Bryson. I still get people sending me ornamental tortoises as a gift since you asked that question on your show."

"Oh I bet you have quite the collection now Sol."

The three of them were very light sitting together for the conversation. There was nothing tense or uncomfortable. And Dev, the viewer, felt as if she were part of the visit.

"My question to you Bryson is this…what were you trying to get at by asking that question.…" Sol took pause and continued…"That question is based off the classic Harrison Ford movie *Blade Runner*, is that correct?" Sol's tone was inquisitive.

Both Sol and Ell were always curious about that moment. That most odd question from a most odd man during a most odd interview that was streaming across the entire globe had often come to mind. Bryson smiled.

"Wow that was quite a moment Sol. Before I tell you what the intent was, I need to ask you…Has your answer changed? If you saw a creature flipped over baking in the sun today would anyone be able to say you failed to reach out your hand to help?"

Sol looked Bryson straight in the eyes and answered with almost the same words from 30 years previous.

"I did help the creature."

Bryson was excited. Sol had played right into his hands. This was the answer and the Sol that Bryson wanted. He lurched, "That's right Sol, you did help the creature. Even though the creature was moving along his path, and his situation was his own fault. As a result of his own instinct to move forward, he ended up in a place he was incapable of extricating himself from without outside help. The creature needed the help of someone outside of himself. Someone to see his dilemma and step in. One with the power to let him die struggling upside-down baking in the sun, or the power to right that upended creature. And what did you do Sol?

"Every chance you had you reached down and placed your hand on the creature. You extended your sovereign hand in that moment and lifted the creature back to safety. You my friend, have done that for the fifteen years you have been our King. Our world is changed, and it is better for your efforts and it will be sad to see you leave as King when that time comes. I asked you that question Sol because we both knew the answer."

Ell was moved by Bryson's words. She had not seen it in that way. She simply saw Sol fulfilling his pure desire to make the world a better place. And all three of them had some knowing that Sol would soon be ready to step down and appoint a new ruler. Sol and Ell had only talked briefly of it together. But they were almost certain that just as time was the master who chose the moment Sol was called to be the ruler of the entire world, so too would the one to replace Sol be brought into their path at just the right time. And it felt like that time was soon coming.

And of Sol it was true as Bryson said. In his years as the overseer of the entire world, Sol had reached down and righted tortoise after tortoise. The reliable Bryson Reynolds had been watching and dispersing the good that Sol had done year after year. Bryson could see it, and he loved it. Sol had been the people's King. Sol had done the greatest good for the greatest number. The world was better now than it had ever been in all known human history. Better because Sol was the kind of ruler who elevated the people. This was now a world that was filled with Participants not citizens. Citizens inhabit while Participants invest. The world was now filled with Participants who found reason to believe that no situation, crisis, conflict, or event is too dire, hopeless, or devastating for a world working together, under one world ruler, to find a way to turn things around. Yes, the tortoise could be righted. Bryson, Ell, and all the world now had seen, that with grace and empathy, Sol saw a creature struggling in a situation that had gone so wrong and he, like many others would have done, simply did that which would make it right.

A Restored Sense of Fairness

Dev was enthralled by the interview. In this moment everything going on in Cathedral Park and the street around her was just background noise. As she focused in she was mesmerized. Finding Sol and Ell to be absolutely unintimidating and warm, as if she knew them. Her work in the Moldova National Post had her examining a great deal of correspondence and often commenting on the opinions that flooded her desk at times. A good many of those were opinions about this Royal Power-Couple she wished she knew more about. And she was about to know more.

Bryson, after recounting the letter Sol had written into the World Congress before he became king, offered a further list of Sol's reforms and accomplishments. To Dev, this seemed to be a bit of a look back at a great career. A time machine that recounted ones' journey as the journey came to an end. Was Sol coming to the end of his reign?

"Hmm she thought, it all started with that letter."

Dev briefly thought about the letter she had started writing the other day during her lunch break. It was still in draft on her Folio. And she was not sure how to finish it or even if she was to finish it. She began writing because of the many challenging pieces of correspondence that came across her desk. From things as trivial as people wanting to remove speed limit laws and expose the hidden costs of eco-fees on items shipped across the world, to the more grand ideas that extreme sport participants and outdoor enthusiasts who end up trapped in an avalanche or caught on the edge of a mountain, are required to foot the entire bill for their rescue. Or other suggestions from readers quoting the Self-Control Law of Sol's. Saying that adventurers who choose to fly around the world and become lost in the icy Polar waters, are simply on their own. The writers would assert that the adventurer must endure the consequences of their own choice to take on risky adventures. Dev was also one who wanted to see thoughtless choices eradicated from society and those who were killed or injured because of their own "stupidity" were getting exactly what nature says they should.

Dev found herself agreeing with a number of the suggestions that were sent to the Post and disagreeing with just as many. Suggestions like the one recommending parents of teens who engage in bullying or destructive behaviors are allowed to deliver corporal punishment to their child. Suggestions that begged Sol to edict a program teaching the entitled generation that no one is special or entitled. No matter how much moms, dads, and grandmas make a child think they are special and are entitled. The suggestions that passed across Dev's Folio were broad and they were plentiful. As the Editor of the Moldova National Post, Dev saw a big picture of all that society still felt needed to change.

The Moldova National Post was just like digital and paper periodicals all over the world. Participants were ever willing to send along their requests and suggestions that they would implement, if they were King or Queen of the World. That's why Dev just loved the honest answer of Sol to Bryson's next question about 'YouTopia'.

"Sol, when you decided to appoint Ministers to handle your edicts, reforms, and programs, you referenced a Meta message from Jether Hobab. Jether made a reference in jest about 'YouTopia'. What do you say to those who suggest this world has become a YouTopia to some degree? Inferring that some believed you only wanted to make the world better for yourself in overlaying the culture with your view of a better world?"

Sol shocked Bryson with his answer. "I'd tell them they're right."

Bryson had to retool his response. He had thought for certain Sol would have said they're wrong or mistaken. Perhaps pointing out the cynicism of people who were still behaving as citizens a little more than they were Participants. Or perhaps simply pointing to his own accomplishments that have unquestionably helped billions to enjoy a better world. But no, Sol agreed. And then he explained.

"Bryson, if we're honest, everyone wants their YouTopia. Whether in their own apartment, their own family, their own job, their town, country, region, and world. It could be a local or an international government. They may not think that they are really interested in having a perfect world, but don't all governments govern in ways that will bring that about in the world they hope for, and according to their own views? Really, at the base of everyone in leadership everywhere, isn't the idea of their YouTopia always being brought into play? Even the Despots of history, although distorted in their leadership practice and strategies, would have had in mind an improved and possibly YouTopian society as they imagined it."

Bryson was starting to see why Sol agreed with those seeing Sol as a man who created his own YouTopia. He nodded and saw Sol was going to continue answering the question.

"What about a teacher who wants a YouTopia in the classroom. That YouTopia will ensure the classroom runs smoothly according to their views, or the YouTopia of a Mayor or of a town council? Doesn't bringing their ideas to the council table in hopes of passing them, make the world a better place for those affected by their position? Or at least in the belief about the proposition that is brought? Or a CEO of a multi-national business organization? Perhaps she hopes to put plans and processes in place, select managers, administrators, and employees that will work in the best interest of her company to establish the most effective and productive YouTopia-like environment she can.

"This brings prosperity to the business she runs and that benefits everyone involved. Bryson, Consider the Warden who is responsible for running a safe and efficient prison. That warden is interested in implementing his rules and programs that will, in his opinion, make that prison the most effective and safe prison one could hope for. So yes Bryson, I think I have always wanted a YouTopia. But not so I could be the sole beneficiary of new edicts and programs. If in fact my ideas have brought peace, freedom, hope, and inspiration to many people, then I guess my YouTopia is not just mine alone is it?"

Bryson interjected, "I see, so the reality that you have created a YouTopia is not a strike against you. It speaks to the idea that you intended to accomplish the greatest good for the greatest number in much the way any woman or man or other might do. Is that safe to say?"

"Yes, I believe it is Bryson, and the facts are that we all want to have our YouTopia. And that picture does look pretty similar from person to person. It is hard to get everyone to agree completely on what a YouTopia is. It's different for each person. But when we realize that basically we all want the same things, peace, happiness, security, acceptance, and freedom, then we simply have to pick one method to try to get there. And sometimes that means having someone in power who can make that happen. Even though we all may not agree on how that YouTopia comes to be, or the methods and rules that make it happen…we all want it. And if you or I or anyone has the privilege of creating their YouTopia, a utopia that benefits most of us, well, then Bryson…"

Sol had done it again. He had taken Bryson and now Devorah, who was completely withdrawn from her surroundings in Cathedral Park, to the place of being enveloped by reason. As another Drone hummed overhead, Dev gave it a thought. Even the Drones have made the world a better place to live in. Catching the daily acts of kindness by Participants is why Dev is sitting here today…relaxing on a Humanitarian Award Day granted her from the acts she was recorded as doing. She loved the Personal Humanitarian Day Awards Program. She loved King Sol.

And now, sitting at the bistro table, she was in the place that inspires with an epiphany. Dev found herself agreeing with Sol. We all want a world that runs according to his or her plans. Sol had not moved society there in a contrived or despotic way. His YouTopia was clearly designed to make life better for as many people as possible. It took humanity back to one of the simplest rules we all learn as children.…As if to say; *Hey kids, you don't like to be hurt by anyone so don't hurt anyone…you don't like to be stolen from so don't steal from anyone…Hey kids, you don't like to be controlled by anyone so don't control anyone.*

Dev saw that in the way the world had evolved and grown. It was almost as if it had matured in the last 30 years under Sol's rule. Once a child that was slow to advance in social reforms, in so many ways this huge planet has now moved past its childish ways, in Moldova and every region. Participants everywhere had a restored sense of fairness, safety, hope, justice, and security. And the apathy that led to a world of hidden havoc, was whittled away down to a mere twig of its former lumbering self.

If I Were Queen of the World

Sol was unapologetic about his methods. He knew that if any other leader had taken the reigns to the world, she or he would have done much the same thing. Perhaps different tools would have been used but Sol knew that everyone wanted their YouTopia…and he readily admitted he was just like everyone. Sol added one more thought to the discussion.

"It is not selfish if a person wants a YouTopia, a better world for everyone. It is selfish though when that person has the power to make one and she or he neglects to do what it takes to bring us all there together."

Dev agreed. She wanted a YouTopia, she admitted it. And she saw why Sol had ruled in the manner he did. As Bryson Reynolds gave the short list of Sol's reforms, she was able to really see why a YouTopia makes sense. If the right person takes the steps toward their YouTopia, then every Participant gets a little closer to their desired YouTopia.

Bryson offered his viewers the list.

"Well folks, here is a list of some of what Sol has done in the past thirty years to make the world what it is today." The list scrolled on screen as Bryson read.

- Crime is down

- Due to the Voluntary Sterilization Program, it is rare to see children neglected and abused, and our world has fewer drug addicts
- Global population is stable and growing at a controlled rate.
- The removal of pedophiles from society has resulted in child sex abuse becoming almost non-existent, and the lives of thousands have been improved from organ transplants that are harvested from those Sealed
- Free health care has led to a healthier society
- Free education has improved the quality of life for millions worldwide
- Poverty now touches only a very few in society
- The Majority class has less stress, illness, and mental illness because of the lower taxation and higher wages they've been given
- Stay at home parents are paid for that choice in lieu of pursuing a career
- Gay marriage is legal worldwide
- Gender equality and pay equity is a reality. Women and men now have the same earnings and opportunities across vocations and careers
- Spinal cord and neurological repair has improved the lives of thousands since redirecting the Space Program money years ago to the Inner Space Program
- Rape, domestic violence, home invasions, elder abuse, street crime, and pedophilia, are almost completely eradicated
- The religious brainwashing of a generation is being undone because of the Religious Re-Freedom Law
- Participants keep most of their earnings since Taxes were lowered and equalized
- Since Gang City was started our towns and cities are completely free of Gang crime
- The prison system is no longer wasting taxpayer dollars on incarceration since the Inmate Repurposing Program was implemented
- Sporting events are accessible to all because of an adjustment to the salaries athletes are allowed to receive

- People are supported by government and family in transitioning from a life of suffering if they choose to end their life
- There is greater contentment in families and careers because people are getting wise counsel before making major decisions
- Child slavery, the sex-slave trade, and terrorism in all regions of the world has been diminished, almost to nothing and soon will be non-existent
- The Self-Control laws have brought hope to people who are no longer forced to do what the government wants them to do with their own bodies
- The Informed Reproduction and Pregnancy Termination Law protects everyone and gives each of us freedom of choice
- Corruption in government and business is no longer prevalent nor expected thanks to our Anti-Corruption minister

Bryson looked up. "Sol, I could go on, but we are running out of time."

"Yes Bryson, if there is one thing I have learned in the past fifteen years is that time is our master."

"Ah yes, and Sol we were introduced to you at the right time, this is obvious. Our world has never been in a better position. You've alluded to the fact that your time as King will eventually run out. Do you know when that will be Sol?"

Bryson waited for a response. He had asked Sol this question before and the answer was always, "It doesn't look to be any time soon."

Bryson first posed the question after Sol announced he had sealed Amyl Rothschild. That was the first time a threat on Sol's life had been made. At that time the media hype was generating the concern of what the world will do if we lose our King? And now that Sol was approaching his 70's, it was reasonable to think he may be moving on soon. The Checkmate Protocol had sat untouched since it was designed when Sol first became King. Even though Sol had not been assassinated and was in good health thanks to the Hormone replacement protocol people used from the age of fifty into their early 100's, he still needed to consider if time was telling him to step down. Sol was always aware that he may want to resign his position at some point and enjoy normal life again. Just him and Ell doing what they loved to do…be together. And Bryson thought to ask the King once again while recounting his accomplishments in this interview. The whole world waited for Sol's answer.

Just then Dev was distracted from the stream. She hit pause on the Folio to tune in to the scuffle going on a few meters away. There was some shouting from a couple standing in front of a park bench in Cathedral Park. She glanced up and scanned the air above her. Not even noticing the Drones as they had hummed past every 15 minutes, now Dev was annoyed. There were none in the area to catch the scuffle that was mounting. *"Where's a Drone when you need it?"* She snarked to herself as she stuffed her folio in her messenger bag and headed toward the park bench with her coffee in hand. Two or three others in the park were starting to take notice of the angry shouts that rose from the two in a conflict. It was more than just a lover's quarrel. There was some clear aggression going on. The man was pushing in closer and closer to the young woman as she yelled.

"You fu**in bitch…" He accused, "I told you to get your ass home yesterday. And now you fu**in make me come all the way to Chişinău to drag your useless ass home."

"I'm not leaving!" the woman yelled.

As Dev closed in on the couple, she didn't even think she might be in danger. It was easy to trust the Drones would be along soon and soon after that Law Enforcement would be hitting the scene. She quickened her pace when she watched the man roughly grab the woman's arm and holler close in her face.

"You'll go where I tell you to go, you've been here for over a week and you're not making me any money."

Dev was close enough now to see their faces. Was that...? Yes it was. Dev had just seen her last week. She looked better than the last time Dev had seen her on the steps of the museum. Passed out and vomiting never makes a person look good. But this young beautiful woman, Dev recalled, looked surprisingly attractive even while unconscious. Moldovan women had more than their share of looks to begin with. But now this very beautiful girl, at the hand of an aggressive male, looked afraid.

He was a larger man, dressed well, olive skin, dark tightly cut hair, and a thin moustache. Had to be in his mid-twenties. And he was not doing a thing to subdue his anger towards what appeared to be a girlfriend.

Dev quickly realized the young woman being mishandled was not his girlfriend. Even if she were Dev would have done the same thing. It was clear they had a business arrangement, at least according to the yelling man. Dev realized this was a working girl, a young escort or prostitute. And the aggressor was her pimp or handler.

"No, I'm staying in Chişinău. I'm done with you, I'm moving home."

She was trying to be assertive. Trying to make a stand. It was weak though, she was not the one in control of the situation and he was not letting her have her say.

"Listen you little bitch, you're mine and you are coming back to Chişinău right this fu**in minute."

The first of two Drones had now made the scene. Almost overhead of the two arguers to capture the scene and report it back to the Policing Division. The subjects were too engaged to notice. And Dev knew that Law Enforcement would be a minute behind the Drones at least.

"**No!**" she yelled, "I'm staying here!"

More convincing with each protest the conflict escalated. The man raised his hand and brought it down on the side of the girl's head.

SMAACK!!

Dev heard the blow from the few feet she was still away. The girl fell to her knees, and he started dragging her by the arm he had a firm grip on. Dev didn't know if she should stop and demand he let or go or just wait for Law Enforcement to show up. She did neither. Her instincts took over.

A young girl was in trouble and Dev was the only one there to help. She was furious at the man, and she rushed right in. Should she grab him and pull him off?

Her adrenaline was surging...this was an intense moment. The man was much bigger close-up than he seemed from a dozen feet away. The young girl was screaming, *"Oww Oww Oww...Stop...leave me alone."*

Dev was three feet away now, neither of the two in conflict saw her coming. Her coffee in one hand and her messenger bag over her shoulder she yelled,

"HEY!"

As the sound came off her lips she threw her coffee. The cup crumpled against his head and the half cup of coffee left in it shocked the man enough for him to stop dragging the girl away. But he whirled around, and his eyes were fierce. He had the young sex-worker in one hand and Dev saw him reaching inside his jacket with the other. She kept surging toward him and reached into her messenger bag grabbing the only thing she could. Her Folio.

Without hesitation she wheeled the folio out of her bag and smashed it square against the side of his head. His grip on the girl's arm let go and he instantly grabbed at his ear where blood flowed out of a gash Dev made on his head. He fumbled and dropped the gun he was reaching for. A gun that would have been turned on Dev, his attacker. Dev laid another folio clout on him as his head was tilted down. He fell to his knees; she nailed him one more time and the two other Participants who had just stepped into the scene jumped on the man and pinned him to the ground.

The girl was sitting on the ground sobbing a few feet away. Law Enforcement had received the Drone report, and they were screaming up the path to restore the peace. Dev, with her Folio that had a draft letter waiting to be cleaned up and sent to the World Counsel Center still in queue, looked down at the bloodied, coffee-soaked man. He was yelling at his captors to let him go while calling Dev a bitch. Dev was quivering from the adrenaline, and she inhaled deeply paused, and said.

"Things would be different if I were Queen of the World."

THE END

J.R. Brayshaw
www.youtopianow.com
www.kingoftheworld.world

www.ingramcontent.com/pod-product-compliance
Lightning Source LLC
Chambersburg PA
CBHW040502020826
48978CB00027B/1312